John Grisham

John Grisham

The Pelican Brief

A Time to Kill

DEALERFIELD

This edition first published by Cresset Editions in 1994
an imprint of the Random House Group
20 Vauxhall Bridge Road
London SW1V 2SA

This edition specially printed for Dealerfield Ltd 1994

ISBN 1 85927 020 4

Typeset in Baskerville 10/11.5 by
Pure Tech Corporation, Pondicherry, India
Printed and bound in Great Britain by
Mackays of Chatham PLC, Chatham, Kent

CONTENTS

The Pelican Brief

TO MY READING COMMITTEE:
Renée, my wife and unofficial editor; my sisters,
Beth Bryant and Wendy Grisham; my mother-in-law,
Lib Jones; and my friend and co-conspirator,
Bill Ballard

ACKNOWLEDGMENTS

Many thanks to my literary agent, Jay Garon, who discovered my first novel five years ago and peddled it around New York until someone said yes.

Many thanks to David Gernert, my editor, who's also a friend and a fellow baseball purist; and to Steve Rubin and Ellen Archer and the rest of the family at Doubleday; and to Jackie Cantor, my editor at Dell.

Many thanks to those of you who've written. I've tried to answer them all, but if I missed one or two, please forgive.

Special thanks to Raymond Brown, a gentleman and fine lawyer in Pascagoula, Mississippi, who came through in the clutch; and to Chris Charlton, a law school pal who knows the alleys of New Orleans; and to Murray Avent, a friend from Oxford and Ole Miss who now lives in D.C.; and to Greg Block at the *Washington Post*; and, of course, to Richard and the Gang at Square Books.

CHAPTER ONE

He seemed incapable of creating such chaos, but much of what he saw below could be blamed on him. And that was fine. He was ninety-one, paralyzed, strapped in a wheelchair and hooked to oxygen. His second stroke seven years ago had almost finished him off, but Abraham Rosenberg was still alive and even with tubes in his nose his legal stick was bigger than the other eight. He was the only legend remaining on the Court, and the fact that he was still breathing irritated most of the mob below.

He sat in a small wheelchair in an office on the main floor of the Supreme Court Building. His feet touched the edge of the window, and he strained forward as the noise increased. He hated cops, but the sight of them standing in thick, neat lines was somewhat comforting. They stood straight and held ground as the mob of at least fifty thousand screamed for blood.

'Biggest crowd ever!' Rosenberg yelled at the window. He was almost deaf. Jason Kline, his senior law clerk, stood behind him. It was the first Monday in October, the opening day of the new term, and this had become a traditional celebration of the First Amendment. A glorious celebration. Rosenberg was thrilled. To him, freedom of speech meant freedom to riot.

'Are the Indians out there?' he asked loudly.

Jason Kline leaned closer to his right ear. 'Yes!'

'With war paint?'

'Yes! In full battle dress.'

'Are they dancing?'

'Yes!'

The Indians, the blacks, whites, browns, women, gays, tree lovers, Christians, abortion activists, Aryans, Nazis, atheists, hunters, animal lovers, white supremacists, black supremacists, tax protestors, loggers, farmers – it was a massive sea of protest. And the riot police gripped their black sticks.

'The Indians should love me!'

'I'm sure they do.' Kline nodded and smiled at the frail little man with clenched fists. His ideology was simple; government over business, the individual over government, the environment over everything. And the Indians, give them whatever they want.

The heckling, praying, singing, chanting, and screaming grew louder, and the riot police inched closer together. The crowd was larger and rowdier than in recent years. Things were more tense. Violence had become common. Abortion clinics had been bombed. Doctors had been attacked and beaten. One was killed in Pensacola, gagged and bound into the fetal position and burned with acid. Street fights were weekly events. Churches and priests had been abused by militant gays. White supremacists operated from a dozen known, shadowy, paramilitary organizations, and had become bolder in their attacks on blacks, Hispanics, and Asians. Hatred was now America's favorite pastime.

And the Court, of course, was an easy target. Threats, serious ones, against the justices had increased tenfold since 1990. The Supreme Court police had tripled in size. At least two FBI agents were assigned to guard each justice, and another fifty were kept busy investigating threats.

'They hate me, don't they?' he said loudly, staring out the window.

'Yes, some of them do,' Kline answered with amusement.

Rosenberg liked to hear that. He smiled and inhaled deeply. Eighty percent of the death threats were aimed at him.

'See any of those signs?' he asked. He was nearly blind.

'Quite a few.'

'What do they say?'

'The usual. Death to Rosenberg. Retire Rosenberg. Cut Off the Oxygen.'

'They've been waving those same damned signs for years. Why don't they get some new ones?'

The clerk did not answer. Abe should've retired years ago, but they would carry him out one day on a stretcher. His three law clerks did most of the research, but Rosenberg insisted on writing his own opinions. He did so with a heavy felt-tip marker and his words were scrawled across a white legal pad, much like a first-grader learning to write. Slow work, but with a lifetime appointment, who cared about time? The clerks proofed his opinions, and rarely found mistakes.

Rosenberg chuckled. 'We oughta feed Runyan to the Indians.' The Chief Justice was John Runyan, a tough conservative appointed by a Republican and hated by the Indians and most other minorities. Seven of the nine had been appointed by Republican Presidents. For fifteen years Rosenberg had been waiting for a Democrat in the White House. He wanted to quit, needed to quit, but he could not stomach the idea of a right-wing Runyan type taking his beloved seat.

He could wait. He could sit here in his wheelchair and breathe oxygen and protect the Indians, the blacks, the women, the poor, the handicapped, and the environment until he was a hundred and five. And not a single person in the world could do a damned thing about it, unless they killed him. And that wouldn't be such a bad idea either.

The great man's head nodded, then wobbled and rested on his shoulder. He was asleep again. Kline quietly stepped away, and returned to his research in the library. He would return in half an hour to check the oxygen and give Abe his pills.

The office of the Chief Justice is on the main floor, and is larger and more ornate than the other eight. The outer office is used for small receptions and formal gatherings, and the inner office is where the Chief works.

The door to the inner office was closed, and the room was filled with the Chief, his three law clerks, the captain of the Supreme Court police, three FBI agents, and K. O. Lewis, deputy director, FBI. The mood was serious, and a serious effort was under way to ignore the noise from the streets below. It was difficult. The Chief and Lewis discussed the latest series of death threats, and everyone else just listened. The clerks took notes.

In the past sixty days, the Bureau had logged over two hundred threats, a new record. There was the usual assortment of 'Bomb the Court!' threats, but many came with specifics – like names, cases, and issues.

Runyan made no effort to hide his anxiety. Working from a confidential FBI summary, he read the names of individuals and groups suspected of threats. The Klan, the Aryans, the Nazis, the Palestinians, the black separatists, the pro-lifers, the homophobics. Even the IRA. Everyone, it seemed, but the Rotarians and the Boy Scouts. A Middle East group backed by the Iranians had threatened blood on American soil in retaliation for the deaths of two justice ministers in Tehran. There was absolutely no evidence the murders were linked to the U.S. A new domestic terrorist unit of recent fame known as the Underground Army had killed a federal trial judge in Texas with a car bomb. No arrests had been made, but the UA claimed responsibility. It was also the prime suspect in a dozen bombings of ACLU offices, but its work was very clean.

'What about these Puerto Rican terrorists?' Runyan asked without looking up.

'Lightweights. We're not worried,' K. O. Lewis answered casually. 'They've been threatening for twenty years.'

'Well, maybe it's time they did something. The climate is right, don't you think?'

'Forget the Puerto Ricans, Chief.' Runyan liked to be called Chief. Not Chief Justice, nor Mr. Chief Justice. Just Chief. 'They're just threatening because everyone else is.'

'Very funny,' the Chief said without smiling. 'Very funny. I'd hate for some group to be left out.' Runyan threw the summary on his desk and rubbed his temples. 'Let's talk about security.' He closed his eyes.

K. O. Lewis laid his copy of the summary on the Chief's desk. 'Well, the Director thinks we should place four agents with each Justice, at least for the next ninety days. We'll use limousines with escorts to and from work, and the Supreme Court police will provide backup and secure this building.'

'What about travel?'

'It's not a good idea, at least for now. The Director thinks the justices should remain in the D.C. area until the end of the year.'

'Are you crazy? Is he crazy? If I asked my brethren to follow that request they would all leave town tonight and travel for the next month. That's absurd.' Runyan frowned at his law clerks, who shook their heads in disgust. Truly absurd.

Lewis was unmoved. This was expected. 'As you wish. Just a suggestion.'

'A foolish suggestion.'

'The Director did not expect your cooperation on that one. He would, however, expect to be notified in advance of all travel plans so that we can arrange security.'

'You mean, you plan to escort each Justice each time he leaves the city?'

'Yes, Chief. That's our plan.'

'Won't work. These people are not accustomed to being baby-sat.'

'Yes sir. And they're not accustomed to being stalked either. We're just trying to protect you and your honorable brethren, sir. Of course, no one says we have to do anything. I think, sir, that you called us. We can leave, if you wish.'

Runyan rocked forward in his chair and attacked a paper clip, prying the curves out of it and trying to make it perfectly straight. 'What about around here?'

Lewis sighed and almost smiled. 'We're not worried about this building, Chief. It's an easy place to secure. We don't expect trouble here.'

'Then where?'

Lewis nodded at a window. The noise was louder. 'Out there somewhere. The streets are full of idiots and maniacs and zealots.'

'And they all hate us.'

'Evidently. Listen, Chief, we're very concerned about Justice Rosenberg. He still refuses to allow our men inside his home; makes them sit in a car in the street all night. He will allow his favorite Supreme Court officer – what's his name? Ferguson – to sit by the back door, outside, but only from 10 P.M. to 6 A.M. No one gets in the house but Justice Rosenberg and his male nurse. The place is not secure.'

Runyan picked his fingernails with the paper clip and smiled slightly to himself. Rosenberg's death, by any means or method, would be a relief. No, it would be a glorious occasion. The Chief would have to wear black and give a eulogy, but behind locked doors he would chuckle with his law clerks. Runyan liked this thought.

'What do you suggest?' he asked.

'Can you talk to him?'

'I've tried. I've explained to him that he is probably the most hated man in America, that millions of people curse him every day, that most folks would like to see him dead, that he receives four times the hate mail as the rest of us combined, and that he would be a perfect and easy target for assassination.'

Lewis waited. 'And?'

'Told me to kiss his ass, then fell asleep.'

The law clerks giggled properly, then the FBI agents realized humor was permitted and joined in for a quick laugh.

'So what do we do?' asked Lewis, unamused.

'You protect him as best you can, put it in writing, and don't worry about it. He fears nothing, including death, and if he's not sweating it, why should you?'

'The Director is sweating, so I'm sweating, Chief. It's very simple. If one of you guys gets hurt, the Bureau looks bad.'

The Chief rocked quickly in his chair. The racket from outside was unnerving. This meeting had dragged on long enough. 'Forget Rosenberg. Maybe he'll die in his sleep. I'm more concerned over Jensen.'

'Jensen's a problem,' Lewis said, flipping pages.

'I know he's a problem,' Runyan said slowly. 'He's an embarrassment. Now he thinks he's a liberal. Votes like Rosenberg half the time. Next month, he'll be a white supremacist and support segregated schools. Then he'll fall in love with the Indians and want to give them Montana. It's like having a retarded child.'

'He's being treated for depression, you know.'

'I know, I know. He tells me about it. I'm his father figure. What drug?'

'Prozac.'

The Chief dug under his fingernails. 'What about that aerobics instructor he was seeing? She still around?'

'Not really, Chief. I don't think he cares for women.' Lewis was smug. He knew more. He glanced at one of his agents and confirmed this juicy little tidbit.

Runyan ignored it, didn't want to hear it. 'Is he cooperating?'

'Of course not. In many ways he's worse than Rosenberg. He allows us to escort him to his apartment building, then makes us sit in the parking lot all night. He's seven floors up, remember. We can't even sit in the lobby. Might upset his neighbors, he says. So we sit in the car. There are ten ways in and out of the building, and it's impossible to protect him. He likes to play hide-and-seek with us. He sneaks around all the time, so we never know if he's in the building or not. At least with Rosenberg we know where he is all night. Jensen's impossible.'

'Great. If you can't follow him, how could an assassin?'

Lewis hadn't thought of this. He missed the humor. 'The Director is very concerned with Justice Jensen's safety.'

'He doesn't receive that many threats.'

'Number six on the list, just a few less than you, your honor.'

'Oh. So I'm in fifth place.'

'Yes. Just behind Justice Manning. He's cooperating, by the way. Fully.'

'He's afraid of his shadow,' the Chief said, then hesitated. 'I shouldn't have said that. I'm sorry.'

Lewis ignored it. 'In fact, the cooperation has been reasonably good, except for Rosenberg and Jensen. Justice Stone bitches a lot, but he listens to us.'

'He bitches at everyone, so don't take it personally. Where do you suppose Jensen sneaks off to?'

Lewis glanced at one of his agents. 'We have no idea.'

A large section of the mob suddenly came together in one unrestrained chorus, and everyone on the streets seemed to join in. The Chief could not ignore it. The windows vibrated. He stood and called an end to this meeting.

Justice Glenn Jensen's office was on the second floor, away from the streets and the noise. It was a spacious room, yet the smallest of the nine. Jensen was the youngest of the nine, and he was lucky to have an office. When nominated six years earlier at the age of forty-two, he was thought to be a strict constructionist with deep conservative beliefs, much like the man who nominated him. His Senate confirmation had been a slugfest. Before the Judiciary Committee, Jensen performed poorly. On sensitive issues he straddled the fence, and got kicked from both sides. The Republicans were embarrassed. The Democrats smelled blood. The President twisted arms until they broke, and Jensen was confirmed by one very reluctant vote.

But he made it, for life. In his six years, he had pleased no one. Hurt deeply by his confirmation hearings, he vowed to find compassion and rule with it. This had angered Republicans. They felt betrayed, especially when he discovered a latent passion for the rights of criminals. With scarce ideological strain, he quickly left the right, moved to the center, then to the left. Then, with legal scholars scratching their little goatees, Jensen would bolt back to the right and join Justice Sloan in one of his obnoxious antiwomen dissents. Jensen was not fond of women. He was neutral on prayer, skeptical of free speech, sympathetic to tax protestors, indifferent to Indians, afraid of blacks, tough on pornographers, soft on criminals, and fairly consistent in his protection of the environment. And, to the further dismay of the Republicans who shed blood to get him confirmed, Jensen had shown a troubling sympathy for the rights of homosexuals.

At his request, a nasty case called *Dumond* had been assigned to him. Ronald Dumond had lived with his male lover for eight years. They were a happy couple, totally devoted to each other, and quite content to share life's experiences. They wanted to marry, but Ohio laws prohibited such a union. Then the lover caught AIDS, and died a horrible death. Ronald knew exactly how to bury him, but then the lover's family intervened and excluded Ronald from the funeral and burial. Distraught, Ronald sued the family, claiming emotional and psychological damage. The case had bounced around the lower courts for six years, and now had suddenly found itself sitting on Jensen's desk.

At issue was the rights of 'spouses' of gays. *Dumond* had become a battle cry for gay activists. The mere mention of *Dumond* had caused street fights.

And Jensen had the case. The door to his smaller office was closed. Jensen and his three clerks sat around the conference table. They had spent two hours on *Dumond*, and gone nowhere. They were tired of arguing. One clerk, a liberal from Cornell, wanted a broad pronouncement granting sweeping rights to gay partners. Jensen wanted this too, but was not ready to admit it. The other two clerks were skeptical. They knew, as did Jensen, that a majority of five would be impossible.

Talk turned to other matters.

'The Chief's ticked off at you, Glenn,' said the clerk from Duke. They called him by his first name in chambers. 'Justice' was such an awkward title.

Glenn rubbed his eyes. 'What else is new?'

'One of his clerks wanted me to know that the Chief and the FBI are worried about your safety. Says you're not cooperating, and the Chief's rather disturbed. He wanted me to pass it along.' Everything was passed along through the clerks' network. Everything.

'He's supposed to be worried. That's his job.'

'He wants to assign two more Fibbies as bodyguards, and they want access to your apartment. And the FBI wants to drive you to and from work. And they want to restrict your travel.'

'I've already heard this.'

'Yeah, we know. But the Chief's clerk said the Chief wants us to prevail upon you to cooperate with the FBI so that they can save your life.'

'I see.'

'And so we're just prevailing upon you.'

'Thanks. Go back to the network and tell the Chief's clerk that you not only prevailed upon me but you raised all sorts of hell with me and that I appreciated all of your prevailing and hell-raising, but it went in one ear and out the other. Tell them Glenn considers himself a big boy.'

'Sure, Glenn. You're not afraid, are you?'

'Not in the least.'

CHAPTER TWO

Thomas Callahan was one of Tulane's more popular professors, primarily because he refused to schedule classes before 11 A.M. He drank a lot, as did most of his students, and for him the first few hours of each morning were needed for sleep, then resuscitation. Nine and ten o'clock classes were abominations. He was also popular because he was cool – faded jeans, tweed jackets with well-worn elbow patches, no socks, no ties. The liberal-chic-academic look. He was forty-five, but with dark hair and horn-rimmed glasses he could pass for thirty-five, not that he gave a damn how old he looked. He shaved once a week, when it started itching; and when the weather was cool, which was seldom in New Orleans, he would grow a beard. He had a history of closeness with female students.

He was also popular because he taught constitutional law, a most unpopular course but a required one. Due to his sheer brilliance and coolness he actually made con law interesting. No one else at Tulane could do this. No one wanted to, really, so the students fought to sit in con law under Callahan at eleven, three mornings a week.

Eighty of them sat behind six elevated rows and whispered as Callahan stood in front of his desk and cleaned his glasses. It was exactly five after eleven, still too early, he thought.

'Who understands Rosenberg's dissent in *Nash v. New Jersey*?' All heads lowered and the room was silent. Must be a bad hangover. His eyes were red. When he started with Rosenberg it usually meant a rough lecture. No one volunteered. *Nash?* Callahan looked slowly, methodically around the room, and waited. Dead silence.

The doorknob clicked loudly and broke the tension. The door opened quickly and an attractive young female in tight washed jeans and a cotton sweater slid elegantly through it and sort of glided along the wall to the third row, where she deftly maneuvered between the crowded seats until she came to hers and sat down. The guys on the fourth row watched in admiration. The guys on the fifth row strained for a peek. For two brutal years now, one of the few pleasures of law school had been to watch as she graced the halls and rooms with her long legs and baggy sweaters. There was a fabulous body in there somewhere, they could tell. But she was not one to flaunt it. She was just one of the gang, and adhered to the law school dress code of jeans and flannel shirts and old sweaters and oversized khakis. What they wouldn't give for a black leather miniskirt.

She flashed a quick smile at the guy seated next to her, and for a second Callahan and his *Nash* question were forgotten. Her dark red hair fell just to the shoulders. She was that perfect little cheerleader with the perfect teeth and perfect hair that every boy fell in love with at least twice in high school. And maybe at least once in law school.

Callahan was ignoring this entry. Had she been a first-year student, and afraid of him, he might have ripped into her and screamed a few times. 'You're never late for court!' was the old standby law professors had beaten to death.

But Callahan was not in a screaming mood, and Darby Shaw was not afraid of him, and for a split second he wondered if anyone knew he was sleeping with her. Probably not. She had insisted on absolute secrecy.

'Has anyone read Rosenberg's dissent in *Nash v. New Jersey*?' Suddenly, he had the spotlight again, and there was dead silence. A raised hand could mean constant grilling for the next thirty minutes. No volunteers. The smokers on the back row fired up their cigarettes. Most of the eighty scribbled aimlessly on legal pads. All heads were bowed. It would be too obvious and risky to flip through the casebook and find *Nash;* too late for that. Any movement might attract attention. Someone was about to be nailed.

Nash was not in the casebook. It was one of a dozen minor cases Callahan had hurriedly mentioned a week ago, and now he was anxious to see if anyone had read it. He was famous for this. His final exam covered twelve hundred cases, a thousand of which were not in the casebook. The exam was a nightmare, but he was really a sweetheart, a soft grader, and it was a rare dumbass who flunked the course.

He did not appear to be a sweetheart at this moment. He looked around the room. Time for a victim. 'How about it, Mr. Sallinger? Can you explain Rosenberg's dissent?'

Instantly from the fourth row, Sallinger said, 'No sir.'

'I see. Might that be because you haven't read Rosenberg's dissent?'

'It might. Yes sir.'

Callahan glared at him. The red eyes made the arrogant scowl all the more menacing. Only Sallinger saw it though; since everyone else was glued to their legal pads. 'And why not?'

'Because I try not to read dissents. Especially Rosenberg's.'

Stupid. Stupid. Stupid. Sallinger had opted to fight back, but he had no ammo.

'Something against Rosenberg, Mr. Sallinger?'

Callahan revered Rosenberg. Worshiped him. Read books about the man and his opinions. Studied him. Even dined with him once.

Sallinger fidgeted nervously. 'Oh no, sir. I just don't like dissents.'

There was a bit of humor in Sallinger's responses, but not a smile was cracked. Later, over a beer, he and his buddies would roar with laughter when it was told and retold about Sallinger and his distaste for dissents, especially Rosenberg's. But not now.

'I see. Do you read majority opinions?'

Hesitation. Sallinger's feeble attempt at sparring was about to cause humiliation. 'Yes sir. Lots of them.'

'Great. Explain, then, if you will, the majority opinion in *Nash v. New Jersey.*'

Sallinger had never heard of *Nash,* but he would now remember it for the rest of his legal career. 'I don't think I've read that one.'

'So you don't read dissents, Mr. Sallinger, and now we learn that you also neglect majorities. What do you read, Mr. Sallinger, romance novels, tabloids?'

There was some extremely light laughter from behind the fourth row, and it came from students who felt obligated to laugh but at the same time did not wish to call attention to themselves.

Sallinger, red-faced, just stared at Callahan.

'Why haven't you read the case, Mr. Sallinger?' Callahan demanded.

'I don't know. I, uh, just missed it, I guess.'

Callahan took it well. 'I'm not surprised. I mentioned it last week. Last Wednesday, to be exact. It'll be on the final exam. I don't understand why you would ignore a case that you'll see on the final.' Callahan was pacing now, slowly, in front of his desk, staring at the students. 'Did anyone bother to read it?'

Silence. Callahan stared at the floor, and allowed the silence to sink in. All eyes were down, all pens and pencils frozen. Smoke billowed from the back row.

Finally, slowly, from the fourth seat on the third row, Darby Shaw lifted her hand slightly, and the class breathed a collective sigh of relief. She had saved them again. It was sort of expected of her. Number two in their class and within striking distance of number one, she could recite the facts and holdings and concurrences and dissents and majority opinions to virtually every case Callahan could spit at them. She missed nothing. The perfect little cheerleader had graduated magna cum laude with a degree in biology, and planned to graduate magna cum laude with a degree in law, and then make a nice living suing chemical companies for trashing the environment.

Callahan stared at her in mock frustration. She had left his apartment three hours earlier after a long night of wine and law. But he had not mentioned *Nash* to her.

'Well, well, Ms. Shaw. Why is Rosenberg upset?'

'He thinks the New Jersey statute violates the Second Amendment.' She did not look at the professor.

'That's good. And for the benefit of the rest of the class, what does the statute do?'

'Outlaws semiautomatic machine guns, among other things.'

'Wonderful. And just for fun, what did Mr. Nash possess at the time of his arrest?'

'An AK-47 assault rifle.'

'And what happened to him?'

'He was convicted, sentenced to three years, and appealed.' She knew the details.

'What was Mr. Nash's occupation?'

'The opinion wasn't specific, but there was mention of an additional charge of drug trafficking. He had no criminal record at the time of his arrest.'

'So he was a dope pusher with an AK-47. But he has a friend in Rosenberg, doesn't he?'

'Of course.' She was watching him now. The tension had eased. Most eyes followed him as he paced slowly, looking around the room, selecting another victim. More often than not, Darby dominated these lectures, and Callahan wanted a broader participation.

'Why do you suppose Rosenberg is sympathetic?' he asked the class.

'He loves dope pushers.' It was Sallinger, wounded but trying to rally. Callahan placed a premium on class discussion. He smiled at his prey, as if to welcome him back to the bloodletting.

'You think so, Mr. Sallinger?'

'Sure. Dope pushers, child fondlers, gunrunners, terrorists. Rosenberg greatly admires these people. They are his weak and abused children, so he must protect them.' Sallinger was trying to appear righteously indignant.

'And, in your learned opinion, Mr. Sallinger, what should be done with these people?'

'Simple. They should have a fair trial with a good lawyer, then a fair, speedy appeal, then punished if they are guilty.' Sallinger was perilously close to sounding like a law-and-order right-winger, a cardinal sin among Tulane law students.

Callahan folded his arms. 'Please continue.'

Sallinger smelled a trap, but plowed ahead. There was nothing to lose. 'I mean, we've read case after case where Rosenberg has tried to rewrite the Constitution to create a new loophole to exclude evidence to allow an obviously guilty defendant to go free. It's almost sickening. He thinks all prisons are cruel and unusual places, so therefore, under the

Eighth Amendment, all prisoners should go free. Thankfully, he's in the minority now, a shrinking minority.'

'You like the direction of the Court, do you, Mr. Sallinger?' Callahan was at once smiling and frowning.

'Damned right I do.'

'Are you one of those normal, red-blooded, patriotic, middle-of-the-road Americans who wish the old bastard would die in his sleep?'

There were a few chuckles around the room. It was safer to laugh now. Sallinger knew better than to answer truthfully. 'I wouldn't wish that on anyone,' he said, almost embarrassed.

Callahan was pacing again. 'Well, thank you, Mr. Sallinger. I always enjoy your comments. You have, as usual, provided us with the layman's view of the law.'

The laughter was much louder. Sallinger's cheeks flushed and he sank in his seat.

Callahan did not smile. 'I would like to raise the intellectual level of this discussion, okay. Now, Ms. Shaw, why is Rosenberg sympathetic to Nash?'

'The Second Amendment grants the people the right to keep and bear arms. To Justice Rosenberg, it is literal and absolute. Nothing should be banned. If Nash wants to possess an AK-47, or a hand grenade, or a bazooka, the state of New Jersey cannot pass a law prohibiting it.'

'Do you agree with him?'

'No, and I'm not alone. It's an eight-to-one decision. No one followed him.'

'What's the rationale of the other eight?'

'It's obvious, really. The states have compelling reasons to prohibit the sale and possession of certain types of arms. The interests of the state of New Jersey outweigh the Second Amendment rights of Mr. Nash. Society cannot allow individuals to own sophisticated weaponry.'

Callahan watched her carefully. Attractive female law students were rare at Tulane, but when he found one he moved in quickly. Over the past eight years, he had been quite successful. Easy work, for the most part. The women arrived at law school liberated and loose. Darby had been different. He first spotted her in the library during the second semester of her first year, and it took a month to get her to dinner.

'Who wrote the majority opinion?' he asked her.

'Runyan.'

'And you agree with him?'

'Yes. It's an easy case, really.'

'Then what happened to Rosenberg?'

'I think he hates the rest of the Court.'

'So he dissents just for the hell of it.'

'Often, yes. His opinions are becoming more indefensible. Take *Nash.* For a liberal like Rosenberg, the issue of gun control is easy. He should have written the majority opinion, and ten years ago he would have. In *Fordice v. Oregon,* a 1977 case, he took a much narrower interpretation of the Second Amendment. His inconsistencies are almost embarrassing.'

Callahan had forgotten *Fordice.* 'Are you suggesting Justice Rosenberg is senile?'

Much like a punch-drunk fighter, Sallinger waded in for the final round. 'He's crazy as hell, and you know it. You can't defend his opinions.'

'Not always, Mr. Sallinger, but at least he's still there.'

'His body's there, but he's brain-dead.'

'He's breathing, Mr. Sallinger.'

'Yeah, breathing with a machine. They have to pump oxygen up his nose.'

'But it counts, Mr. Sallinger. He's the last of the great judicial activists, and he's still breathing.'

'You'd better call and check,' Sallinger said as his words trailed off. He'd said enough. No, he'd said too much. He lowered his head as the professor glared at him. He hunkered down next to his notebook, and started wondering why he'd said all that.

Callahan stared him down, then began pacing again. It was indeed a bad hangover.

CHAPTER THREE

At least he looked like an old farmer, with straw hat, clean bib overalls, neatly pressed khaki workshirt, boots. He chewed tobacco and spat in the black water beneath the pier. He chewed like a farmer. His pickup, though of recent model, was sufficiently weathered and had a dusty-road look about it. North Carolina plates. It was a hundred yards away, parked in the sand at the other end of the pier.

It was midnight Monday, the first Monday in October, and for the next thirty minutes he was to wait in the dark coolness of the deserted pier, chewing pensively, resting on the railing while staring intently at the sea. He was alone, as he knew he would be. It was planned that way. This pier at this hour was always deserted. The headlights of an occasional car flickered along the shoreline, but the headlights never stopped at this hour.

He watched the red and blue channel lights far from shore. He checked his watch without moving his head. The clouds were low and thick, and it would be difficult to see it until it was almost to the pier. It was planned this way.

The pickup was not from North Carolina, and neither was the farmer. The license plates had been stolen from a wrecked truck at a scrap yard near Durham. The pickup had been stolen in Baton Rouge. The farmer was not from anywhere, and performed none of the thievery. He was a pro, and so someone else did the dirty little deeds.

Twenty minutes into the wait, a dark object floated in the direction of the pier. A quiet, muffled engine hummed and grew louder. The object became a small craft of some sort with a camouflaged silhouette crouching low and working the motor. The farmer moved not an inch in anticipation. The humming stopped and the black rubber raft stalled in the calm water thirty feet from the pier. There were no headlights coming or going along the shore.

The farmer carefully placed a cigarette between his lips, lit it, puffed twice, then thumped it down, halfway to the raft.

'What kind of cigarette?' the man on the water asked upward. He could see the outline of the farmer on the railing, but not the face.

'Lucky Strike,' the farmer answered. These passwords made for such a silly game. How many other black rubber rafts could be expected to drift in from the Atlantic and pinpoint this ancient pier at this precise hour? Silly, but oh so important.

'Luke?' came the voice from the boat.

'Sam,' replied the farmer. The name was Khamel, not Sam, but Sam would do for the next five minutes until Khamel parked his raft.

Khamel did not answer, was not required to, but quickly started the engine and guided the raft along the edge of the pier to the beach. Luke followed from above. They met at the pickup without a handshake. Khamel placed his black Adidas gym bag between them on the seat, and the truck started along the shoreline.

Luke drove and Khamel smoked, and both did a perfect job of ignoring each other. Their eyes did not dare meet. With Khamel's heavy beard, dark glasses, and black turtleneck, his face was ominous but impossible to identify. Luke did not want to see it. Part of his assignment, in addition to receiving this stranger from the sea, was to refrain from looking at him. It was easy, really. The face was wanted in nine countries.

Across the bridge at Manteo, Luke lit another Lucky Strike and determined they had met before. It had been a brief but precisely timed meeting at the airport in Rome, five or six years earlier, as best he could remember. There had been no introductions. It took place in a restroom. Luke, then an impeccably tailored American executive, had placed an eelskin attaché case next to the wall next to the washbasin where he slowly rinsed his hands, and suddenly it was gone. He caught a glimpse of the man – this Khamel, he was now certain – in the mirror. Thirty minutes later, the attaché case exploded between the legs of the British ambassador to Nigeria.

In the guarded whispers of his invisible brotherhood, Luke had often heard of Khamel, a man of many names and faces and languages, an assassin who struck quickly and left no trail, a fastidious killer who roamed the world but could never be found. As they rode north in the darkness, Luke settled low in his seat, the brim of his hat almost on his nose, limp wrist across the wheel, trying to remember the stories he'd heard about his passenger. Amazing feats of terror. There was the British ambassador. The ambush of seventeen Israeli soldiers on the West Bank in 1990 had been credited to Khamel. He was the only suspect in the 1985 car-bomb murders of a wealthy German banker and his family. His fee for that one was rumored to have been three million, cash. Most intelligence experts believed he was the mastermind of the 1981 attempt to kill the Pope. But then, Khamel was blamed for almost every unsolved terrorist attack and assassination. He was easy to blame because no one was certain he existed.

This excited Luke. Khamel was about to perform on American soil. The targets were unknown to Luke, but important blood was about to be shed.

At dawn, the stolen farm truck stopped at the corner of Thirty-first and M streets in Georgetown. Khamel grabbed his gym bag, said nothing, and hit the sidewalk. He walked east a few blocks to the Four Seasons Hotel, bought a *Post* in the lobby, and casually rode the elevator to the seventh floor. At precisely seven-fifteen, he knocked on a door at the end of the hall.

'Yes?' a nervous voice asked from inside.

'Looking for Mr. Sneller,' Khamel said slowly in a perfect generic American tongue as he stuck his thumb over the peephole.

'Mr. Sneller?'

'Yes. Edwin F. Sneller.'

The knob did not turn or click, and the door did not open. A few seconds passed, and a white envelope eased from under the door. Khamel picked it up. 'Okay,' he said loud enough for Sneller or whoever he was to hear.

'It's next door,' Sneller said. 'I'll await your call.' He sounded like an American. Unlike Luke, he'd never seen Khamel, and had no desire to, really. Luke had seen him twice now, and was indeed lucky to be alive.

Khamel's room had two beds and a small table near the window. The shades were drawn tightly; no chance of sunlight. He placed his gym bag on one bed, next to two thick briefcases. He walked to the window and peeked out, then to the phone.

'It's me,' he said to Sneller. 'Tell me about the car.'

'It's parked on the street. Plain white Ford with Connecticut plates. The keys are on the table.' Sneller spoke slowly.

'Stolen?'

'Of course, but sanitized. It's clean.'

'I'll leave it at Dulles shortly after midnight. I want it destroyed, okay?' The English was perfect.

'Those are my instructions. Yes.' Sneller was proper and efficient.

'It's very important, okay? I intend to leave the gun in the car. Guns leave bullets and people see cars, so it's important to completely destroy the car and everything in it. Understand?'

'Those are my instructions,' Sneller repeated. He did not appreciate this lecture. He was no novice at the killing game.

Khamel sat on the edge of the bed. 'The four million was received a week ago, a day late I should add. I'm now in D.C., so I want the next three.'

'It will be wired before noon. That was the agreement.'

'Yes, but I'm worried about the agreement. You were a day late, remember?'

This irritated Sneller, and since the killer was in the next room and not about to come out, he could sound a bit irritated.

'The bank's fault, not ours.'

This irritated Khamel. 'Fine. I want you and your bank to wire the next three million to the account in Zurich as soon as New York opens. That will be about two hours from now. I'll be checking.'

'Okay.'

'Okay, and I want no problem when the job is finished. I'll be in Paris in twenty-four hours, and from there I'll go straight to Zurich. I want all the money waiting for me when I arrive.'

'It will be there, if the job is finished.'

Khamel smiled to himself. 'The job will be finished, Mr. Sneller, by midnight. That is, if your information is correct.'

'As of now it is correct. And no changes are expected today. Our people are in the streets. Everything is in the two briefcases; maps, diagrams, schedules, the tools and articles you requested.'

Khamel glanced at the briefcases behind him. He rubbed his eyes with his right hand. 'I need a nap,' he mumbled into the phone. 'I haven't slept in twenty hours.'

Sneller could think of no response. There was plenty of time, and if Khamel wanted a nap, then Khamel could have a nap. They were paying him ten million.

'Would you like something to eat?' Sneller asked awkwardly.

'No. Call me in three hours, at precisely ten-thirty.' He placed the receiver on the phone, and stretched across the bed.

The streets were clear and quiet for day two of the fall term. The justices spent their day on the bench listening to lawyer after lawyer argue complex and quite dull cases. Rosenberg slept through most of it. He came to life briefly when the attorney general from Texas argued that a certain death-row inmate should be given medication to make him lucid before being lethally injected. If he's mentally ill, how can he be executed? Rosenberg asked incredulously. Easy, said the AG from Texas, his illness can be controlled with medication. So just give him a little shot to make him sane, then give him another shot to kill him. It could all be very nice and constitutional. Rosenberg harangued and bitched for a brief spell, then lost steam. His little wheelchair sat much lower than the massive leather thrones of his brethren. He looked rather pitiful. In years past he was a tiger, a ruthless intimidator who tied even the slickest lawyers in knots. But no more. He began to mumble, and then faded away. The AG sneered at him, and continued.

During the last oral argument of the day, a lifeless desegregation case from Virginia, Rosenberg began snoring. Chief Runyan glared down the bench, and Jason Kline, Rosenberg's senior clerk, took the hint. He slowly pulled the wheelchair backward, away from the bench, and out of the courtroom. He pushed it quickly through the back hallway.

The Justice regained consciousness in his office, took his pills, and informed his clerks he wanted to go home. Kline notified the FBI, and moments later Rosenberg was wheeled into the rear of his van, parked in the basement. Two FBI agents watched. A male nurse, Frederic, strapped the wheelchair in place, and Sergeant Ferguson of the Supreme Court police slid behind the wheel of the van. The Justice allowed no FBI agents near him. They could follow in their car, and they could watch his townhouse from the street, and they were lucky to get that close. He didn't trust cops, and he damned sure didn't trust FBI agents. He didn't need protection.

On Volta Street in Georgetown, the van slowed and backed into a short driveway. Frederic the nurse and Ferguson the cop gently rolled him inside. The agents watched from the street in their black government-issue Dodge Aries. The lawn in front of the townhome was tiny and their car was a few feet from the front door. It was almost 4 P.M.

After a few minutes, Ferguson made his mandatory exit and spoke to the agents. After much debate, Rosenberg had acquiesced a week earlier and allowed Ferguson to quietly inspect each room upstairs and down upon his arrival in the afternoons. Then Ferguson had to leave, but could return at exactly 10 P.M. and sit outside the rear door until exactly 6 A.M. No one but Ferguson could do it, and he was tired of the overtime.

'Everything's fine,' he said to the agents. 'I guess I'll be back at ten.'

'Is he still alive?' one of the agents asked. Standard question.

'Afraid so.' Ferguson looked tired as he walked to the van.

Frederic was chubby and weak, but strength was not needed to handle his patient. After arranging the pillows just so, he lifted him from the wheelchair and placed him carefully on the sofa, where he would remain motionless for the next two hours while dozing and watching CNN. Frederic fixed himself a ham sandwich and a plate of cookies, and scanned a *National Enquirer* at the kitchen table. Rosenberg mumbled something loudly and changed channels with the remote control.

At precisely seven, his dinner of chicken bouillon, boiled potatoes, and stewed onions – stroke food – was placed neatly on the table,and Frederic rolled him up to it. He insisted on feeding himself, and it was not pretty. Frederic watched television. He would clean up the mess later.

By nine, he was bathed, dressed in a gown, and tucked tightly under the covers. The bed was a narrow, reclining, pale green army-hospital job with a hard mattress, push-button controls, and collapsible rails that Rosenberg insisted remain down. It was in a room behind the kitchen that he had used as a small study for thirty years, before the first stroke. The room was now clinical, and smelled of antiseptic and looming death. Next to his bed was a large table with a hospital lamp and at least twenty bottles of pills. Thick, heavy law books were stacked in neat piles around the room. Next to the table, the nurse sat close by in a worn recliner, and began reading from a brief. He would read until he heard snoring – the nightly ritual. He read slowly, yelling the words at Rosenberg, who was stiff, motionless, but listening. The brief was from a case in which he would write the majority opinion. He absorbed every word, for a while.

After an hour of reading and yelling, Frederic was tired and the Justice was drifting away. He raised his hand slightly, then closed his eyes. With a button on the bed, he lowered the lights. The room was almost dark. Frederic jerked backward, and the recliner unfolded. He laid the brief on the floor, and closed his eyes. Rosenberg was snoring.

He would not snore for long.

Shortly after ten, with the house dark and quiet, the door to a bedroom closet upstairs opened slightly, and Khamel eased out. His wristbands, nylon cap, and running shorts were royal blue. His long-sleeved shirt, socks, and Reeboks were white with royal trim. Perfect color coordination. Khamel the jogger. He was clean shaven, and under the cap his very short hair was now blond, almost white.

The bedroom was dark, as was the hall. The stairs creaked slightly under the Reeboks. He was five-ten, and weighed less than a hundred and fifty pounds, with no fat. He kept himself taut and light so the movements would be quick and soundless. The stairs landed in a foyer not far from the front door. He knew there were two agents in a car by the curb, probably not watching the house. He knew Ferguson had arrived seven minutes ago. He could hear the snoring from the back room. While waiting in the closet, he had thought of striking earlier, before Ferguson arrived, so he wouldn't have to kill him. The killing was no problem, but it created another body to worry about. But he guessed, wrongly, that Ferguson probably checked in with the male nurse when he came on duty. If so, then Ferguson would find the carnage and Khamel would lose a few hours. So he waited until now.

He slid through the foyer without a sound. In the kitchen, a small light from the Ventahood illuminated the countertop and made things a bit more dangerous. Khamel cursed himself for not checking the bulb and unscrewing it. Those small mistakes were inexcusable. He dipped under a window looking into the backyard. He could not see Ferguson, although he knew he was seventy-four inches tall, sixty-one years old, had cataracts, and couldn't hit a barn with his .357 magnum.

Both of them were snoring. Khamel smiled to himself as he crouched in the doorway and quickly pulled the .22 automatic and silencer from the Ace bandage wrapped around his waist. He screwed the four-inch tube onto the barrel, and ducked into the room. The nurse was sprawled deep in the recliner, feet in the air, hands dangling, mouth open. Khamel placed the tip of the silencer an inch from his right temple and fired three times. The hands flinched and the feet jerked, but the eyes remained closed. Khamel quickly reached across to the wrinkled and pale head of Justice Abraham Rosenberg, and pumped three bullets into it.

The room had no windows. He watched the bodies and listened for a full minute. The nurse's heels twitched a few times, then stopped. The bodies were still.

He wanted to kill Ferguson inside. It was eleven minutes after ten, a good time for a neighbor to be out with the dog for one last time before bed. He crept through the darkness to the rear door and spotted the cop strolling benignly along the wooden fence twenty feet away. Instinctively, Khamel opened the back door, turned on the patio light, and said 'Ferguson' loudly.

He left the door open and hid in a dark corner next to the refrigerator. Ferguson obediently lumbered across the small patio and into the kitchen. This was not unusual. Frederic often called him in after His Honor was asleep. They would drink instant coffee and play gin rummy.

There was no coffee, and Frederic was not waiting. Khamel fired three bullets into the back of his head, and he fell loudly on the kitchen table.

He turned out the patio light and unscrewed the silencer. He would not need it again. It and the pistol were stuffed into the Ace bandage. Khamel peeked out the front window. The dome light was on and the agents were reading. He stepped over Ferguson, locked the back door, and disappeared into the darkness of the small rear lawn. He jumped two fences without a sound, and found the street. He began trotting. Khamel the jogger.

In the dark balcony of the Montrose Theatre, Glenn Jensen sat by himself and watched the naked and quite active men on the screen below. He ate popcorn from a large box and noticed nothing but the bodies. He was dressed conservatively enough; navy cardigan, chinos, loafers. And wide sunglasses to hide his eyes and a suede fedora to cover his head. He was blessed with a face that was easily forgotten, and once camouflaged it could never be recognized. Especially in a deserted balcony of a near-empty gay porno house at midnight. No earrings, bandannas, gold chains, jewelry, nothing to indicate he was in the market for a companion. He wanted to be ignored.

It had become a challenge, really, this cat-and-mouse game with the FBI and the rest of the world. On this night, they had dutifully stationed themselves in the parking lot outside his building. Another pair parked by the exit near the veranda in the rear, and he allowed them all to sit for four and a half hours before he disguised himself and walked nonchalantly to the garage in the basement and drove away in a friend's car. The building had too many points of egress for the poor Fibbies to monitor him. He was sympathetic to a point, but he had his life to live. If the Fibbies couldn't find him, how could a killer?

The balcony was divided into three small sections with six rows each. It was very dark, the only light being the heavy blue stream from the projector behind. Broken seats and folded tables were piled along the outside aisles. The velvet drapes along the walls were shredded and falling. It was a marvelous place to hide.

He used to worry about getting caught. In the months after his confirmation, he was terrified. He couldn't eat his popcorn, and damned sure couldn't enjoy the movies. He told himself that if he was caught or recognized, or in some awful way exposed, he would simply claim he was doing research for an obscenity case pending. There was always one on the docket, and maybe somehow this might be believed. This excuse could work, he told himself repeatedly, and he grew bolder. But one night in 1990, a theater caught fire, and four people died. Their names were in the paper. Big story. Justice Glenn Jensen happened to be in the rest room when he heard the screams and smelled the smoke. He rushed into the street and disappeared. The dead were all found in the balcony. He knew one of them. He gave up movies for two months, but then started back. He needed more research, he told himself.

And what if he got caught? The appointment was for life. The voters couldn't call him home.

He liked the Montrose because on Tuesdays the movies ran all night, but there was never a crowd. He liked the popcorn, and draft beer cost fifty cents.

Two old men in the center section groped and fondled each other. Jensen glanced at them occasionally, but concentrated on the movie. Sad, he thought, to be seventy years old, staring at death and dodging AIDS, and banished to a dirty balcony to find happiness.

A fourth person soon joined them on the balcony. He glanced at Jensen and the two men locked together, and he walked quietly with his draft beer and popcorn to the top row of the center section. The projector room was directly behind him. To his right and down three rows sat the Justice. In front of him, the gray and mature lovers kissed and whispered and giggled, oblivious to the world.

He was dressed appropriately. Tight jeans, black silk shirt, earring, horn-rimmed shades, and the neatly trimmed hair and mustache of a regular gay. Khamel the homosexual.

He waited a few minutes, then eased to his right and sat by the aisle. No one noticed. Who would care where he sat?

At twelve-twenty, the old men lost steam. They stood, arm in arm, and tiptoed away, still whispering and snickering. Jensen did not look at them. He was engrossed in the movie, a massive orgy on a yacht in the middle of a hurricane. Khamel moved like a cat across the narrow aisle to a seat three rows behind the Justice. He sipped the beer. They were alone. He waited for one minute, and quickly moved down a row. Jensen was eight feet away.

As the hurricane intensified, so did the orgy. The roar of the wind and the screams of the partyers deafened the small theater. Khamel set the beer and popcorn on the floor, and pulled a three-foot strand of yellow nylon ski rope from his waist. He quickly wrapped the ends around both hands, and stepped over the row of chairs in front of him. His prey was breathing heavy. The popcorn box was shaking.

The attack was quick and brutal. Khamel looped the rope just under the larynx, and wrenched it violently. He yanked the rope downward, snapping the head over the back of the seat. The neck broke cleanly. He twisted the rope and tied it behind the neck. He slid a six-inch steel rod through a loop in the knot, and wound the tourniquet until the flesh tore and started to bleed. It was over in ten seconds.

Suddenly the hurricane was over and another orgy began in celebration. Jensen slumped in his seat. His popcorn was scattered around his shoes. Khamel was not one to admire his handiwork. He left the balcony, walked casually through the racks of magazines and devices in the lobby, then disappeared onto the sidewalk.

He drove the generic white Ford with Connecticut plates to Dulles, changed clothes in a rest room, and waited on his flight to Paris.

CHAPTER FOUR

The first lady was on the West Coast attending a series of five-thousand-dollars-a-plate breakfasts where the rich and pretentious gladly shucked out the money for cold eggs and cheap champagne, and the chance to be seen and maybe photographed with the Queen, as she was known. So the President was sleeping alone when the phone rang. In the great tradition of American Presidents, he had in years past thought of keeping a mistress. But now it seemed so non-Republican. Besides, he was old and tired. He often slept alone when the Queen was at the White House.

He was a heavy sleeper. It rang twelve times before he heard it. He grabbed it and stared at the clock. Four-thirty A.M. He listened to the voice, jumped to his feet, and eight minutes later was in the Oval Office. No shower, no tie. He started at Fletcher Coal, his chief of staff, and sat properly behind his desk.

Coal was smiling. His perfect teeth and bald head were shining. Only thirty-seven, he was the boy wonder who four years earlier had rescued a failing campaign and placed his boss in the White House. He was a guileful manipulator and a nasty henchman who had cut and clawed his way through the inner circle until he was now second in command. Many viewed him as the real boss. The mere mention of his name terrified lowly staffers.

'What happened?' the President asked slowly.

Coal paced in front of the President's desk. 'Don't know much. They're both dead. Two FBI agents found Rosenberg around 1 A.M. Dead in bed. His nurse and a Supreme Court policeman were also murdered. All three shot in the head. A very clean job. While the FBI and D.C. police were investigating, they got a call that Jensen had been found dead in some queer club. They found him a couple of hours ago. Voyles called me at four, and I called you. He and Gminski should be here in a minute.'

'Gminski?'

'The CIA should be included, at least for now.'

The President folded his hands behind his head and stretched. 'Rosenberg is dead.'

'Yes. Quite. I suggest you address the nation in a couple of hours. Mabry is working on a rough draft. I'll finish it. Let's wait until daylight, at least seven. If not, it'll be too early and we'll lose much of our audience.'

'The press –'

'Yes. It's out. They filmed the ambulance crew rolling Jensen into the morgue.'

'I didn't know he was gay.'

'Not much doubt about it now. This is the perfect crisis, Mr. President. Think of it. We didn't create it. It's not our fault. No one can blame us. And the nation will be shocked into some degree of solidarity. It's rally around the leader time. It's just great. No downside.'

The President sipped a cup of coffee and stared at the papers on his desk. 'And I'll get to restructure the Court.'

'That's the best part. It'll be your legacy. I've already called Duvall at Justice and instructed him to contact Horton and begin a preliminary list of nominees. Horton gave a speech in Omaha last night, but he's flying in now. I suggest we meet with him later this morning.'

The President nodded with his customary approval of Coal's suggestions. He allowed Coal to sweat the details. He had never been a detail man himself. 'Any suspects?'

'Not yet. I don't know, really. I told Voyles that you would expect a briefing when he arrived.'

'I thought someone said the FBI was protecting the Supreme Court.'

Coal smiled wider and chuckled. 'Exactly. The egg is on Voyles' face. It's quite embarrassing, really.'

'Great. I want Voyles to get his share of the blame. Take care of the press. I want him humiliated. Then maybe we can run his ass off.'

Coal loved this thought. He stopped pacing and scribbled a note on his legal pad. A security guard knocked on the door, then opened it. Directors Voyles and Gminski entered together. The mood was suddenly somber as all four shook hands. The two sat before the President's desk as Coal took his customary position standing near a window, to the side of the President. He hated Voyles and Gminski, and they hated him. Coal thrived on hatred. He had the President's ear, and that was all that mattered. He would become quiet for a few minutes. It was important to allow the President to take charge when others were present.

'I'm very sorry you're here, but thanks for coming,' the President said. They nodded grimly and acknowledged this obvious lie. 'What happened?'

Voyles spoke quickly and to the point. He described the scene at Rosenberg's home when the bodies were found. At 1 A.M. each night, Sergeant Ferguson routinely checked in with the agents sitting in the street. When he didn't show, they investigated. The killings were very clean and professional. He described what he knew about Jensen. Broken neck. Strangulation. Found by another character in the balcony. No one saw anything, evidently. Voyles was not as gruff and blunt as usual. It was a dark day for the Bureau, and he could feel the heat coming. But he'd survived five Presidents, and he could certainly outmaneuver this idiot.

'The two are obviously related,' the President said, staring at Voyles.

'Maybe. Certainly looks that way, but –'

'Come on, Director. In two hundred and twenty years, we've assassinated four Presidents, two or three candidates, a handful of civil rights leaders, couple of governors, but never a Supreme Court Justice. And now, in one night, within two hours, two are assassinated. And you're not convinced they're related?'

'I didn't say that. There must be a link somewhere. It's just that the methods were so different. And so professional. You must remember, we've had thousands of threats against the Court.'

'Fine. Then who are your suspects?'

No one cross-examined F. Denton Voyles. He glared at the President. 'It's too early for suspects. We're still gathering evidence.'

'How'd the killer get into Rosenberg's place?'

'No one knows. We didn't watch him go in, you understand? Evidently, he was there for some time, hiding in a closet or an attic, maybe. Again, we weren't invited. Rosenberg refused to allow us into his home. Ferguson routinely inspected the place each afternoon when the Justice arrived from work. It's still too early, but we've found no evidence of the murderer. None, except three bodies. We'll have ballistics and autopsies by late this afternoon.'

'I want to see them here as soon as you have them.'

'Yes, Mr. President.'

'I also want a short list of suspects by 5 P.M. today. Is that clear?'

'Certainly, Mr. President.'

'And I would like a report on your security and where it broke down.'

'You're assuming it broke down.'

'We have two dead judges, both of whom were being protected by the FBI. I think the American people deserve to know what went wrong, Director. Yes, it broke down.'

'Do I report to you, or the American people?'

'You report to me.'

'And then you call a press conference and report to the American people, right?'

'Are you afraid of the scrutiny, Director?'

'Not one bit. Rosenberg and Jensen are dead because they refused to cooperate with us. They were very much aware of the danger, yet they couldn't be bothered. The other seven are cooperating, and they're still alive.'

'For the moment. We'd better check. They're dropping like flies.'

The President smiled at Coal, who snickered and almost sneered at Voyles. Coal decided it was time to speak. 'Director, did you know Jensen was hanging around such places?'

'He was a grown man with a lifetime appointment. If he chose to dance naked on tables we couldn't stop him.'

'Yes sir,' Coal said politely. 'But you didn't answer my question.'

Voyles breathed deeply and looked away. 'Yes. We suspected he was a homosexual, and we knew he liked certain movie houses. We have neither the authority nor the desire, Mr. Coal, to divulge such information.'

'I want those reports by this afternoon,' the President said. Voyles was watching a window, listening but not responding. The President looked at Robert Gminski, director of the CIA.

'Bob, I want a straight answer.'

Gminski tightened and frowned. 'Yes sir. What is it?'

'I want to know if these killings are in any way linked to any agency, operation, group, whatever, of the United States Government.'

'Come on! Are you serious, Mr. President! That's absurd.'

Gminski appeared to be shocked, but the President, Coal, even Voyles, knew anything was possible these days at the CIA.

'Dead serious, Bob.'

'I'm serious too. And I assure you we had nothing to do with it. I'm shocked you would even think it. Ridiculous!'

'Check it out, Bob. I want to be damned certain. Rosenberg did not believe in national security. He made thousands of enemies in intelligence. Just check it out, okay.'

'Okay, okay.'

'And I want a report by five today.'

'Sure. Okay. But it's a waste of time.'

Fletcher Coal moved to the desk next to the President. 'I suggest we meet here at five this afternoon, gentlemen. Is that agreeable?'

They both nodded and stood. Coal escorted them to the door without a word. He closed it.

'You handled it real well,' he said to the President. 'Voyles knows he's vulnerable. I smell blood. We'll go to work on him with the press.'

'Rosenberg is dead,' the President repeated to himself. 'I just can't believe it.'

'I've got an idea for television.' Coal was pacing again, very much in charge. 'We need to cash in on the shock of it all. You need to appear tired, as if you were up all night handling the crisis. Right? The entire nation will be watching, waiting for you to give details and to reassure. I think you should wear something warm and comforting. A coat and tie at 7 A.M. may seem a bit rehearsed. Let's relax a little.'

The President was listening intently. 'A bathrobe?'

'Not quite. But how about a cardigan and slacks? No tie. White button-down. Sort of the grandfather image.'

'You want me to address the nation in this hour of crisis in a sweater?'

'Yes. I like it. A brown cardigan with a white shirt.'

'I don't know.'

'The image is good. Look, Chief, the election is a year from next month. This is our first crisis in ninety days, and what a wonderful crisis it is. The people need to see you in something different, especially at seven in the morning. You need to look casual, down-home, but in control. It'll be worth five, maybe ten points in the ratings. Trust me, Chief.'

'I don't like sweaters.'

'Just trust me.'

'I don't know.'

CHAPTER FIVE

Darby Shaw awoke in the early darkness with a touch of a hangover. After fifteen months of law school, her mind refused to rest for more than six hours. She was often up before daybreak, and for this reason she did not sleep well with Callahan. The sex was great, but sleep was often a tug-of-war with pillows and sheets pulled back and forth.

She watched the ceiling and listened to him snore occasionally in his Scotch-induced coma. The sheets were wrapped like ropes around his knees. She had no cover, but she was not cold. October in New Orleans is still muggy and warm. The heavy air rose from Dauphine Street below, across the small balcony outside the bedroom and through the open french doors. It brought with it the first stream of morning light. She stood in the doors and covered herself with his terry-cloth robe. The sun was rising, but Dauphine was dark. Daybreaks went unnoticed in the French Quarter. Her mouth was dry.

Downstairs in the kitchen, Darby brewed a pot of thick French Market chicory. The blue numbers on the microwave said it was now ten minutes before six. For a light drinker, life with Callahan was a constant struggle. Her limit was three glasses of wine. She had neither a law license nor a job, and she could not afford to get drunk every night and sleep late. And she weighed a hundred and twelve pounds and was determined to keep it there. He had no limit.

She drank three glasses of ice water, then poured a tall mug full of chicory. She flipped on lights as she climbed the stairs, and eased back into the bed. She flicked the remote controls, and suddenly, there was the President sitting behind his desk looking somehow rather odd in a brown cardigan with no tie. It was an NBC News special report.

'Thomas!' She slapped him on his shoulder. No movement. 'Thomas! Wake up!' She pressed a button and the volume roared. The President said good morning.

'Thomas!' She leaned toward the television. Callahan kicked at the sheets and sat up, rubbing his eyes and trying to focus. She handed him the coffee.

The President had tragic news. His eyes were tired and he looked sad, but the rich baritone exuded confidence. He had notes but didn't use them. He looked deep into the camera, and explained to the American people the shocking events of last night.

'What the hell,' Callahan mumbled. After announcing the deaths, the President launched into a flowery obituary for Abraham Rosenberg. A towering legend, he called him. It was a strain, but the President kept a straight face while lauding the distinguished career of one of the most hated men in America.

Callahan gaped at the television. Darby stared at it. 'That's very touching,' she said. She was frozen on the end of the bed. He had been briefed by the FBI and CIA, he explained, and they were assuming the killings were related. He had ordered an immediate, thorough investigation, and those responsible would be brought to justice.

Callahan sat upright and covered himself with the sheets. He blinked his eyes and combed his wild hair with his fingers. 'Rosenberg? Murdered?' he mumbled, glaring at the screen. His foggy head had cleared immediately, and the pain was there but he couldn't feel it.

'Check out the sweater,' Darby said, sipping the coffee, staring at the orange face with heavy makeup and the brilliant silver hair plastered carefully in place. He was a wonderfully handsome man with a soothing voice; thus he had succeeded greatly in politics. The wrinkles in his forehead squeezed together, and he was even sadder now as he talked of his close friend Justice Glenn Jensen.

'The Montrose Theatre, at midnight,' Callahan repeated.

'Where is it?' she asked. Callahan had finished law school at Georgetown.

'Not sure. But I think it's in the gay section.'

'Was he gay?'

'I've heard rumors. Evidently.' They were both sitting on the end of the bed with the sheets over their legs. The President was ordering a week of national mourning. Flags at half-staff. Federal offices closed tomorrow. Funeral arrangements were incomplete. He rambled for a few more minutes, still deeply saddened, even shocked, very human, but nonetheless the President and clearly in charge. He signed off with his patented grandfather's smile of complete trust and wisdom and reassurance.

An NBC reporter on the White House lawn appeared and filled in the gaps. The police were mute, but there appeared to be no suspects at the moment, and no leads. Yes, both justices had been under the protection of the FBI, which had no comment. Yes, the Montrose was a place frequented by homosexuals. Yes, there had been many threats against both men, especially Rosenberg. And there could be many suspects before it was all over.

Callahan turned off the set and walked to the french doors, where the early air was growing thicker. 'No suspects,' he mumbled.

'I can think of at least twenty,' Darby said.

'Yeah, but why the combination? Rosenberg is easy, but why Jensen? Why not McDowell or Yount, both of whom are consistently more liberal than Jensen? It doesn't make sense.' Callahan sat in a wicker chair by the doors and fluffed his hair.

'I'll get you some more coffee,' Darby said.

'No, no. I'm awake.'

'How's your head?'

'Fine, if I could've slept for three more hours. I think I'll cancel class. I'm not in the mood.'

'Great.'

'Damn, I can't believe this. That fool has two nominations. That means eight of the nine will be Republican choices.'

'They have to be confirmed first.'

'We won't recognize the Constitution in ten years. This is sick.'

'That's why they were killed, Thomas. Someone or some group wants a different Court, one with an absolute conservative majority. The election is next year. Rosenberg is, or was, ninety-one. Manning is eighty-four. Yount is early eighties. They could die soon, or live ten more years. A Democrat may be elected President. Why take a chance? Kill them now, a year before the election. Makes perfect sense, if one was so inclined.'

'But why Jensen?'

'He was an embarrassment. And, obviously, he was an easier target.'

'Yes, but he was basically a moderate with an occasional leftward impulse. And he was nominated by a Republican.'

'You want a Bloody Mary?'

'Good idea. In a minute. I'm trying to think.'

Darby reclined on the bed, sipped the coffee, and watched the sunlight filter across the balcony. 'Think of it, Thomas. The timing is beautiful. Reelection, nominations, politics, all that. But think of the violence and the radicals, the zealots, the pro-lifers and gay haters, the Aryans and Nazis, think of all the groups capable of killing, and all the threats against the Court, and the timing is perfect for an unknown, inconspicuous group to knock them off. It's morbid, but the timing is great.'

'And who is such a group?'

'Who knows?'

'The Underground Army?'

'They're not exactly inconspicuous. They killed Judge Fernandez in Texas.'

'Don't they use bombs?'

'Yeah, experts with plastic explosives.'

'Scratch them.'

'I'm not scratching anybody right now.' Darby stood and retied the robe. 'Come on. I'll fix you a Bloody Mary.'

'Only if you drink with me.'

'Thomas, you're a professor. You can cancel your classes if you want to. I am a student and –'

'I understand the relationship.'

'I cannot cut any more classes.'

'I'll flunk you in con law if you don't cut classes and get drunk with me. I've got a book of Rosenberg opinions. Let's read them, sip Bloody Marys, then wine, then whatever. I miss him already.'

'I have Federal Procedure at nine, and I can't miss it.'

'I intend to call the dean and have all classes canceled. Then will you drink with me?'

'No. Come on, Thomas.' He followed her down the stairs to the kitchen and the coffee and the liquor.

CHAPTER SIX

Without removing the receiver from his shoulder, Fletcher Coal punched another button on the phone on the desk in the Oval Office. Three lines were blinking, holding. He paced slowly in front of the desk and listened while scanning a two-page report from Horton at Justice. He ignored the President, who was crouched in front of the windows, gripping his putter with gloved hands, staring fiercely first at the yellow ball, then slowly across the blue carpet to the brass putting cup ten feet away. Coal growled something into the receiver. His words were unheard by the President, who lightly tapped the ball and watched it roll precisely into the cup. The cup clicked, cleared itself, and the ball rolled three feet to the side. The President inched forward in his socks to the next ball, and breathed downward at it. It was an orange one. He tapped it just so, and it rolled straight into the cup. Eight in a row. Twenty-seven out of thirty.

'That was Chief Runyan,' Coal said, slamming the receiver down. 'He's quite upset. He wanted to meet with you this afternoon.'

'Tell him to take a number.'

'I told him to be here at ten tomorrow morning. You have the Cabinet at ten-thirty, and National Security at eleven-thirty.'

Without looking up, the President gripped the putter and studied the next ball. 'I can't wait. What about the polls?' He swung carefully and followed the ball.

'I just talked to Nellson. He ran two, beginning at noon. The computer is digesting it now, but he thinks the approval rating will be somewhere around fifty-two or fifty-three.'

The golfer looked up briefly and smiled, then returned to his game. 'What was it last week?'

'Forty-four. It was the cardigan without the tie. Just like I said.'

'I thought it was forty-five,' he said as he tapped a yellow one and watched it roll perfectly into the cup.

'You're right. Forty-five.'

'That's the highest in –'

'Eleven months. We haven't been above fifty since Flight 402 in November of last year. This is a wonderful crisis, Chief. The people are shocked, yet many of them are happy Rosenberg is gone. And you're the man in the middle. Just wonderful.' Coal punched a blinking button and picked up the receiver. He slammed it down without a word. He straightened his tie and buttoned his jacket.

'It's five-thirty, Chief. Voyles and Gminski are waiting.'

He putted and watched the ball. It was an inch to the right, and he grimaced. 'Let them wait. Let's do a press conference at nine in the morning. I'll take Voyles with me, but I'll keep his mouth shut. Make him stand behind me. I'll give some more details and answer a few questions. Networks'll carry it live, don't you think?'

'Of course. Good idea. I'll get it started.'

He picked off his gloves and threw them in a corner. 'Show them in.' He carefully leaned his putter against the wall and slid into his Bally loafers. As usual, he had changed clothes six times since breakfast, and now wore a glen plaid double-breasted suit with a red and navy polka-dot tie. Office attire. The jacket hung on a rack by the door. He sat at his desk and scowled at some papers. He nodded at Voyles and Gminski, but neither stood nor offered to shake hands. They sat across the desk, and Coal took his usual standing position like a sentry who couldn't wait to fire. The President pinched the bridge of his nose as if the stress of the day had delivered a migraine.

'It's been a long day, Mr. President,' Bob Gminski said to break the ice. Voyles looked at the windows.

Coal nodded, and the President said, 'Yes, Bob. A very long day. And I have a bunch of Ethiopians invited for dinner tonight, so let's be brief. Let's start with you, Bob. Who killed them?'

'I do not know, Mr. President. But I assure you we had nothing to do with it.'

'Do you promise me, Bob?' He was almost prayerful.

Gminski raised his right hand with the palm facing the desk.

'I swear. On my mother's grave, I swear.'

Coal nodded smugly as if he believed him, and as if his approval meant everything.

The President glared at Voyles, whose stocky figure filled the chair and was still draped with a bulky trench coat. The Director chewed his gum slowly and sneered at the President.

'Ballistics? Autopsies?'

'Got 'em,' Voyles said as he opened his briefcase.

'Just tell me. I'll read it later.'

'The gun was small-caliber, Probably a .22. Point-blank range for Rosenberg and his nurse, powder burns indicate. Hard to tell for Ferguson, but the shots were fired from no farther than twelve inches away. We didn't see the shooting, you understand? Three bullets into each head. They picked two out of Rosenberg; found another in his pillow. Looks like he and the nurse were asleep. Same type slugs, same gun, same gunman, evidently. Complete autopsy summaries are being prepared, but there were no surprises. Causes of deaths are quite obvious.'

'Fingerprints?'

'None. We're still looking, but it was a very clean job. Appears as if he left nothing but the slugs and the bodies.'

'How'd he get into the house?'

'No apparent signs of entry. Ferguson searched the place when Rosenberg arrived around four. Routine procedure. He filed his written report two hours later, and it says he inspected two bedrooms, a bath, and three closets upstairs, and each room downstairs, and of course found nothing. Says he checked all windows and doors. Pursuant to Rosenberg's instructions, our agents were outside, and they estimate Ferguson's four o'clock inspection took from three to four minutes. I suspect the killer was waiting and hiding when the Justice returned and Ferguson walked through.'

'Why?' Coal insisted.

Voyles' red eyes watched the President and ignored his hatchet man. 'This man is obviously very talented. He killed a Supreme Court Justice – maybe two – and left virtually no trail. A professional assassin, I would guess. Entry would not be a problem for him. Eluding a cursory inspection by Ferguson would be no problem for him. He's probably very patient. He wouldn't risk an entry when the house was occupied and cops around. I think he entered sometime in the afternoon and simply waited, probably in a closet upstairs, or perhaps in the attic. We found two small pieces of attic insulation on the floor under the retractable stairs; suggests they had recently been used.'

'Really doesn't matter where he was hiding,' the President said. 'He wasn't discovered.'

'That's correct. We were not allowed to inspect the house, you understand?'

'I understand he's dead. What about Jensen?'

'He's dead too. Broken neck, strangled with a piece of yellow nylon rope that can be found in any hardware store. The medical examiners doubt the broken neck killed him. They're reasonably confident the rope did. No fingerprints. No witnesses. This is not the sort of place where witnesses come rushing forward, so I don't expect to find any. Time of death was around twelve-thirty this morning. The killings were two hours apart.'

The President scribbled notes. 'When did Jensen leave his apartment?'

'Don't know. We're relegated to the parking lot, remember. We followed him home around 6 P.M., then watched the building for seven hours until we found out he'd been strangled in a queer joint. We were following his demands, of course. He sneaked out of the building in a friend's car. Found it two blocks from the joint.'

Coal took two steps forward with his hands clasped rigidly behind him. 'Director, do you think one assassin did both jobs?'

'Who in hell knows. The bodies are still warm. Give us a break. There's precious little evidence right now. With no witnesses, no prints, no screwups, it'll take time to piece this thing together. Could be the same man, I don't know. It's too early.'

'Surely you have a gut feeling,' the President said.

Voyles paused and glanced at the windows. 'Could be the same guy, but he must be superman. Probably two or three, but regardless, they had to have a lot of help. Someone fed them a lot of information.'

'Such as?'

'Such as how often Jensen goes to the movies, where does he sit, what time does he get there, does he go by himself, does he meet a friend. Information we didn't have, obviously. Take Rosenberg. Someone had to know his little house had no security system, that our boys were kept outside, that Ferguson arrived at ten and left at six and had to sit in the backyard, that –'

'You knew all this,' the President interrupted.

'Of course we did. But I assure you we didn't share it with anyone.' The President shot a quick conspiratorial glance at Coal, who was scratching his chin, deep in thought.

Voyles shifted his rather wide rear and gave Gminski a smile, as if to say, 'Let's play along with them.'

'You're suggesting a conspiracy,' Coal said intelligently with deep eyebrows.

'I'm not suggesting a damned thing. I am proclaiming to you, Mr. Coal, and to you, Mr. President, that, yes, in fact, a large number of people conspired to kill them. There may be only one or two killers, but they had a lot of help. It was too quick and clean and well organized.'

Coal seemed satisfied. He stood straight and again clasped his hands behind him.

'Then who are the conspirators?' the President asked. 'Who are your suspects?'

Voyles breathed deeply and seemed to settle in his chair. He closed the briefcase and laid it at his feet. 'We don't have a prime suspect, at the moment, just a few good possibilities. And this must be kept very quiet.'

Coal sprang a step closer. 'Of course it's confidential,' he snapped. 'You're in the Oval Office.'

'And I've been here many times before. In fact, I was here when you were running around in dirty diapers, Mr. Coal. Things have a way of leaking out.'

'I think you've had leaks yourself,' Coal said.

The President raised his hand. 'It's confidential, Denton. You have my word.' Coal retreated a step.

Voyles watched the President. 'Court opened Monday, as you know, and the maniacs have been in town for a few days. For the past two weeks, we've been monitoring various movements. We know of at least eleven members of the Underground Army who've been in the D.C. area for a week. We questioned a couple today, and released them. We know the group has the capability, and the desire. It's our strongest possibility, for now. Could change tomorrow.'

Coal was not impressed. The Underground Army was on everyone's list.

'I've heard of them,' the President said stupidly.

'Oh yes. They're becoming quite popular. We believe they killed a trial judge in Texas. Can't prove it, though. They're very proficient with explosives. We suspect them in at least a hundred bombings of abortion clinics, ACLU offices, porno houses, gay clubs, all over the country. They're just the people who would hate Rosenberg and Jensen.'

'Other suspects?' Coal asked.

'There's an Aryan group called White Resistance that we've been watching for two years. It operates out of Idaho and Oregon. The leader gave a speech in West Virginia last week, and has been in the area for a few days. He was spotted Monday in the demonstration outside the Supreme Court. We'll try to talk to him tomorrow.'

'But are these people professional assassins?' Coal asked.

'They don't advertise, you understand. I doubt if any group performed the actual killings. They just hired the assassins and provided the legwork.'

'So who're the assassins?' the President asked.

'We may never know, frankly.'

The President stood and stretched his legs. Another hard day at the office. He smiled down at Voyles across the desk. 'You have a difficult task.' It was the grandfather's voice, filled with warmth and understanding. 'I don't envy you. If possible, I would like a two-page typewritten double-spaced report by 5 p.m. each day, seven days a week, on the progress of the investigation. If something breaks, I expect you to call me immediately.'

Voyles nodded but did not speak.

'I'm having a press conference in the morning at nine. I would like for you to be here.'

Voyles nodded but did not speak. Seconds passed and no one spoke. Voyles stood noisily and tied the strap around the trench coat. 'Oh well, we'll be going. You've got the Ethiopians and all.' He handed the ballistics and autopsy reports to Coal, knowing the President would never read them.

'Thanks for coming, gentlemen,' the President said warmly. Coal closed the door behind them, and the President grabbed the putter. 'I'm not eating with the Ethiopians,' he said, staring at the carpet and a yellow ball.

'I know it. I've already sent your apologies. This is a great hour of crisis, Mr. President, and you are expected to be here in this office surrounded by your advisers, hard at work.'

He putted, and the ball rolled perfectly into the cup. 'I want to talk to Horton. These nominations must be perfect.'

'He's sent a short list of ten. Looks pretty good.'

'I want young conservative white men opposed to abortion, pornography, queers, gun control, racial quotas, all that crap.' He missed a putt, and kicked off his loafers. 'I want judges who hate dope and criminals and are enthusiastic about the death penalty. Understand?'

Coal was on the phone, punching numbers and nodding at his boss. He would select the nominees, then convince the President.

K. O. Lewis sat with the Director in the back of the quiet limousine as it left the White House and crawled through rush-hour traffic. Voyles had nothing to say. So far, in the early hours of the tragedy, the press had been brutal. The buzzards were circling. No less than three congressional subcommittees had already announced hearings and investigations into the deaths. And the bodies were still warm. The politicians were giddy and wrestling for the spotlight. One outrageous statement fueled another. Senator Larkin from Ohio hated Voyles, and Voyles hated Senator Larkin from Ohio, and the senator had called a press conference three hours earlier and announced his subcommittee would immediately begin investigating the FBI's protection of the two dead justices. But Larkin had a girlfriend, a rather young one, and the FBI had some photographs, and Voyles was confident the investigation could be delayed.

'How's the President?' Lewis finally asked.

'Which one?'

'Not Coal. The other one.'

'Swell. Just swell. He's awfully tore up about Rosenberg, though.'

'I bet.'

They rode in silence in the direction of the Hoover Building. It would be a long night.

'We've got a new suspect,' Lewis finally said.

'Do tell.'

'A man named Nelson Muncie.'

Voyles slowly shook his head. 'Never heard of him.'

'Neither have I. It's a long story.'

'Gimme the short version.'

'Muncie is a very wealthy industrialist from Florida. Sixteen years ago his niece was raped and murdered by an Afro-American named Buck Tyrone. The little girl was twelve. Very, very brutal rape and murder. I'll spare you the details. Muncie has no children, and idolized his niece. Tyrone was tried in Orlando, and given the death penalty. He was guarded heavily because there were a bunch of threats. Some Jewish lawyers in a big New York firm filed all sorts of appeals, and in 1984 the case arrives at the Supreme Court. You guessed it; Rosenberg falls in love with Tyrone and concocts this ridiculous Fifth Amendment self-incrimination argument to exclude a confession the punk gave a week after he was arrested. An eight-page confession that he, Tyrone, wrote himself. No confession, no case. Rosenberg writes a convoluted five-to-four opinion overturning the conviction. An extremely controversial decision. Tyrone goes free. Then, two years later he disappears and has not been seen since. Rumor has it Muncie paid to have Tyrone castrated, mutilated, and fed to the sharks. Just a rumor, say the Florida authorities. Then in 1989, Tyrone's main lawyer on the case, man named Kaplan, is gunned down by an apparent mugger outside his apartment in Manhattan. What a coincidence.'

'Who tipped you?'

'Florida called two hours ago. They're convinced Muncie paid a bunch of money to eliminate both Tyrone and his lawyer. They just can't prove it. They've got a reluctant, unidentified informant who says he knows Muncie and feeds them a little info. He says Muncie has been talking for years about eliminating Rosenberg. They think he went a little over the edge when his niece was murdered.'

'How much money has he got?'

'Enough. Millions. No one is sure. He's very secretive. Florida is convinced he's capable.'

'Let's check it out. Sounds interesting.'

'I'll get on it tonight. Are you sure you want three hundred agents on this case?'

Voyles lit a cigar and cracked his window. 'Yeah, maybe four hundred. We need to crack this baby before the press eats us alive.'

'It won't be easy. Except for the slugs and the rope, these guys left nothing.'

Voyles blew smoke out the window. 'I know. It's almost too clean.'

CHAPTER SEVEN

The chief slouched behind his desk with a loosened tie and a haggard look. Around the room, three of his brethren and a half-dozen clerks sat and talked in subdued tones. The shock and fatigue were evident. Jason Kline, Rosenberg's senior clerk, looked especially hard-hit. He sat on a small sofa and stared blankly at the floor while Justice Archibald Manning, now the senior Justice, talked of protocol and funerals. Jensen's mother wanted a small, private Episcopal service Friday in Providence. Rosenberg's son, a lawyer, had delivered to Runyan a list of instructions the Justice had prepared after his second stroke in which he wanted to be cremated after a non-military ceremony and his ashes dropped over the Sioux Indian Reservation in South Dakota. Though Rosenberg was Jewish, he had abandoned the religion and claimed to be agnostic. He wanted to be buried with the Indians. Runyan thought that was appropriate, but did not say so. In the outer office, six FBI agents sipped coffee and whispered nervously. There had been more threats during the day, several coming within hours of the President's early morning address. It was dark now, almost time to escort the remaining justices home. Each had four agents as bodyguards.

Justice Andrew McDowell, at sixty-one now the youngest member of the Court, stood in the window, smoking his pipe and watching traffic. If Jensen had a friend on the Court, it was McDowell. Fletcher Coal had informed Runyan that the President would not only attend Jensen's service but wanted to deliver a eulogy. No one in the inner office wanted the President to say a word. The Chief had asked McDowell to prepare a few words. A shy man who avoided speeches, McDowell twirled his bow tie and tried to picture his friend in the balcony with a rope around his neck. It was too awful to think about. A Justice of the Supreme Court, one of his distinguished brethren, one of the nine, hiding in such a place watching those movies and being exposed in such a ghastly manner. What a tragic embarrassment. He thought of himself standing before the crowd in the church and looking at Jensen's mother and family, and knowing that every thought would be on the Montrose Theatre. They would ask each other in whispered voice, 'Did you know he was gay?' McDowell, for one, did not know, nor did he suspect. Nor did he want to say anything at the funeral.

Justice Ben Thurow, age sixty-eight, was not as concerned about burying the dead as he was about catching the killers. He had been a federal prosecutor in Minnesota, and his theory grouped the suspects into two classes; those acting out of hatred and revenge, and those seeking to affect future decisions. He had instructed his clerks to begin the research.

Thurow was pacing around the room. 'We have twenty-seven clerks and seven justices,' he said to the group but to no one in particular. 'It's obvious we won't get much work done for the next couple of weeks, and all close decisions must wait until we have a full bench. That could take months. I suggest we put our clerks to work trying to solve the killings.'

'We're not police,' Manning said patiently.

'Can we at least wait until after the burials before we start playing Dick Tracy?' McDowell said without turning from the window.

Thurow ignored them, as usual. 'I'll direct the research. Loan me your clerks for two weeks, and I think we can put together a short list of solid suspects.'

'The FBI is very capable, Ben,' the Chief said. 'They haven't asked for our help.'

'I'd rather not discuss the FBI,' Thurow said. 'We can mope around here in official mourning for two weeks, or we can go to work and find these bastards.'

'What makes you so sure you can solve this?' Manning asked.

'I'm not sure I can, but I think it's worth a try. Our brethren were murdered for a reason and that reason is directly related to a case or an issue already decided or now pending before this Court. If it's retribution, then our task is almost impossible. Hell, everybody hates us for one reason or another. But if it's not revenge or hatred, then perhaps someone wanted a different Court for a future decision. That's what's intriguing. Who would kill Abe and Glenn because of how they might vote on a case this year, next year, or five years from now? I want the clerks to pull up every case now pending in the eleven circuits below.'

Justice McDowell shook his head. 'Come on, Ben. That's over five thousand cases, a small fraction of which will eventually end up here. It's a wild-goose chase.'

Manning was equally unimpressed. 'Listen, fellas. I served with Abe Rosenberg for thirty-one years, and I often thought of shooting him myself. But I loved him like a brother. His liberal ideas were accepted in the sixties and seventies, but grew old in the eighties, and are now resented in the nineties. He became a symbol for everything that's wrong in this country. He has been killed, I believe, by one of these radical right-wing hate groups, and we can research cases till hell freezes over and not find anything. It's retribution, Ben. Pure and simple.'

'And Glenn?' Thurow asked.

'Evidently our friend had some strange proclivities. Word must have spread, and he was an easy target for such groups. They hate homosexuals, Ben.'

Ben was still pacing, still ignoring. 'They hate all of us, and if they killed out of hatred the cops'll catch them. Maybe. But what if they killed to manipulate this Court? What if some group seized this moment of unrest and violence to eliminate two of us, and thus realign the Court? I think it's very possible.'

The Chief cleared his throat. 'And I think we'll do nothing until after they are buried, or scattered. I'm not saying no, Ben, just wait a few days. Let the dust settle. The rest of us are still in shock.'

Thurow excused himself and left the room. His bodyguards followed him down the hall.

Justice Manning stood with his cane and addressed the Chief. 'I will not make it to Providence. I hate flying, and I hate funerals. I'll be having one myself before long, and I do not enjoy the reminder. I'll send my sympathies to the family. When you see them, please apologize for me. I'm a very old man.' He left with a clerk.

'I think Justice Thurow has a point,' said Jason Kline. 'We at least need to review the pending cases and those likely to arrive here from the lower circuits. It's a long shot, but we may stumble across something.'

'I agree,' said the Chief. 'It's just a bit premature, don't you think?'

'Yes, but I'd like to get started anyway.'

'No. Wait till Monday, and I'll assign you to Thurow.'

Kline shrugged and excused himself. Two clerks followed him to Rosenberg's office, where they sat in the darkness and sipped the last of Abe's brandy.

In a cluttered study carrel on the fifth level of the law library, between the racks of thick, seldom-used law books, Darby Shaw scanned a printout of the Supreme Court's docket. She had been through it twice, and though it was loaded with controversy, she found nothing that interested her. *Dumond* was causing riots. There was a child pornography case from New Jersey, a sodomy case from Kentucky, a dozen death penalty appeals, a dozen assorted civil rights cases, and the usual array of tax, zoning, Indian, and antitrust cases. From the computer she had pulled summaries of each, then reviewed them twice. She compiled a neat list of possible suspects, but they would be obvious to everyone. The list was now in the garbage.

Callahan was certain it was the Aryans or the Nazis or the Klan; some easily identifiable collection of domestic terrorists; some radical band of vigilantes. It had to be right-wingers; that much was obvious, he felt. Darby was not so sure. The hate groups were too obvious. They had made too many threats, thrown too many rocks, held too many parades, made too many speeches. They needed Rosenberg alive because he was such an irresistible target for their hatred. Rosenberg kept them in business. She thought it was somebody much more sinister.

He was sitting in a bar on Canal Street, drunk by now, waiting on her though she had not promised to join him. She had checked on him at lunch, and found him on the balcony upstairs, drunk and reading his book of Rosenberg opinions. He had decided to cancel con law for a week; said he might not be able to teach it anymore now that his hero was dead. She told him to sober up, and she left.

A few minutes after ten, she walked to the computer room on the fourth level of the library and sat before a monitor. The room was empty. She pecked away at the keyboard, found what she wanted, and soon the printer was spewing forth page after page of appeals pending in the eleven federal appellate courts around the country. An hour later, the printer stopped, and she now possessed a six-inch-thick summary of the eleven dockets. She hauled it back to her study carrel and placed it in the center of the cluttered desk. It was after eleven, and the fifith level was deserted. A narrow window gave an uninspiring view of a parking lot and trees below.

She kicked off her shoes again and inspected the red paint on the toes. She sipped a warm Fresca and stared blankly at the parking lot. The first assumption was easy – the killings were done by the same group for the same reasons. If not, then the search was hopeless. The second assumption was difficult – the motive was not hatred or revenge, but rather manipulation. There was a case or an issue out there on its way to the Supreme Court, and someone wanted different justices. The third assumption was a bit easier – the case or issue involved a great deal of money.

The answer would not be found in the printout sitting before her. She flipped through it until midnight, and left when the library closed.

CHAPTER EIGHT

At noon Thursday a secretary carried a large sack decorated with grease spots and filled with deli sandwiches and onion rings into a humid conference room on the fifith floor of the Hoover Building. In the center of the square room, a mahogany table with twenty chairs along each side was surrounded with the top FBI people from across the country. All ties were loosened and sleeves rolled up. A thin cloud of blue smoke hung around the cheap government chandelier five feet above the table.

Director Voyles was talking. Tired and angry, he puffed on his fourth cigar of the morning and walked slowly in front of the screen at his end of the table. Half the men were listening. The other half had pulled reports from the pile in the center of the table and read about the autopsies, the lab report on the nylon rope, Nelson Muncie, and a few other quickly researched subjects. The reports were quite thin.

Listening carefully and reading intently was Special Agent Eric East, only a ten-year man but a brilliant investigator. Six hours earlier Voyles had picked him to lead the investigation. The rest of the team had been selected throughout the morning, and this was the organizational meeting.

East was listening and hearing what he already knew. The investigation could take weeks, probably months. Other than the slugs, nine of them, the rope, and the steel rod used in the tourniquet, there was no evidence. The neighbors in Georgetown had seen nothing; no exceptionally suspicious characters at the Montrose. No prints. No fibers. Nothing. It takes remarkable talent to kill so cleanly, and it takes a lot of money to hire such talent. Voyles was pessimistic about finding the gunmen. They must concentrate on whoever hired them.

Voyles was talking and puffing. 'There's a memo on the table regarding one Nelson Muncie, a millionaire from Jacksonville, Florida, who's allegedly made threats against Rosenberg. The Florida authorities are convinced Muncie paid a bunch of money to have the rapist and his lawyer killed. The memo covers it. Two of our men talked with Muncie's lawyer this morning, and were met with great hostility. Muncie is out of the country, according to his lawyer, and of course he has no idea when he will return. I've assigned twenty men to investigate him.'

Voyles relit his cigar and looked at a sheet of paper on the table. 'Number four is a group called White Resistance, a small group of middle-aged commandos we've been watching for about three years. You've got a memo. Pretty weak suspect, really. They'd rather throw firebombs and burn crosses. Not a lot of finesse. And, most importantly, not much money. I doubt seriously if they could hire guns as slick as these. But I've assigned twenty men anyway.'

East unwrapped a heavy sandwich, sniffed it, but decided to leave it alone. The onion rings were cold. His appetite had vanished. He listened and made notes. Number six on the list was a bit unusual. A psycho named Clinton Lane had declared war on homosexuals. His only son had moved from their family farm in Iowa to San Francisco to enjoy the gay life, but had quickly died of AIDS. Lane cracked up, and burned the Gay Coalition office in Des Moines. Caught and sentenced to four years, he escaped in 1989 and had not been found. According to the memo, he had set up an extensive coke-smuggling operation and made millions. And he used the money in his own little private war against gays and lesbians. The FBI had been trying to catch him for five years, but it was believed he operated out of Mexico. For years he had written hate mail to the Congress, the Supreme Court, the President. Voyles was not impressed with Lane as a suspect. He was a nut who was way out in left field, but no stone would go unturned. He assigned only six agents.

The list had ten names. Between six and twenty of the best special agents were assigned to each suspect. A leader was chosen for each unit. They were to report twice daily to East, who would meet each morning and each afternoon with the Director. A hundred or so more agents would scour the streets and countryside for clues.

Voyles talked of secrecy. The press would follow like bloodhounds, so the investigation must be extremely confidential. Only he, the Director, would speak to the press, and he would have precious little to say.

He sat down, and K. O. Lewis delivered a rambling monologue about the funerals, and security, and a request from Chief Runyan to assist in the investigation.

Eric East sipped cold coffee, and stared at the list.

In thirty-four years, Abraham Rosenberg wrote no fewer than twelve hundred opinions. His production was a constant source of amazement to constitutional scholars. He occasionally ignored the dull antitrust cases and tax appeals, but if the issue showed the barest hint of real controversy, he waded in with both fists. He wrote majority opinions, concurrences to majorities, concurrences to dissents, and many, many dissents. Often he dissented alone. Every hot issue in thirty-four years had received an opinion of some sort from Rosenberg. The scholars and critics loved him. They published books and essays and critiques about him and his work. Darby found five separate hardback compilations of his opinions, with editorial notes and annotations. One book contained nothing but his great dissents.

She skipped class Thursday and secluded herself in the study carrel on the fifth level of the library. The computer printouts were scattered neatly on the floor. The Rosenberg books were open and marked and stacked on top of each other.

There was a reason for the killings. Revenge and hatred would be acceptable for Rosenberg alone. But add Jensen to the equation, and revenge and hatred made less sense. Sure he was hateable, but he had not aroused passions like Yount or even Manning.

She found no books of critical thought on the writings of Justice Glenn Jensen. In six years, he had authored only twenty-eight majority opinions, the lowest production on the Court. He had written a few dissents, and joined a few concurrences, but he was a painfully slow worker. At times his writing was clear and lucid, at times disjointed and pathetic.

She studied Jensen's opinions. His ideology swung radically from year to year. He was generally consistent in his protection of the rights of criminal defendants, but there were enough exceptions to astound any scholar. In seven attempts, he had voted with the Indians five times. He had written three majority opinions strongly protective of the environment. He was near perfect in support of tax protestors.

But there were no clues. Jensen was too erratic to take seriously. Compared to the other eight, he was harmless.

She finished another warm Fresca, and put away for the moment her notes on Jensen. Her watch was hidden in a drawer. She had no idea what time it was. Callahan had sobered up and wanted a late dinner at Mr. B's in the Quarter. She needed to call him.

Dick Mabry, the current speechwriter and word wizard, sat in a chair beside the President's desk and watched as Fletcher Coal and the President read the third draft of a proposed eulogy for Justice Jensen. Coal had rejected the first two, and Mabry was still uncertain about what they wanted. Coal would suggest one thing. The President wanted something else. Earlier in the day, Coal had called and said to forget the eulogy because the President would not attend the funeral. Then the President had called, and asked him to prepare a few words because Jensen was a friend and even though he was a queer he was still a friend.

Mabry knew Jensen was not a friend, but he was a freshly assassinated justice who would enjoy a highly visible funeral.

Then Coal had called and said they weren't sure if the President was going but work up something just in case. Mabry's office was in the Old Executive Office Building next door to the White House, and during the day small bets had been placed on whether the President would attend the funeral of a known homosexual. The office odds were three to one that he would not.

'Much better, Dick,' Coal said, folding the paper.

'I like it too,' the President said. Mabry had noticed that the President usually waited for Coal to express approval or displeasure over his words.

'I can try again,' Mabry said, standing.

'No, no,' Coal insisted. 'This has the right touch. Very poignant. I like it.'

He walked Mabry to the door and closed it behind him.

'What do you think?' the President asked.

'Let's call it off. I'm getting bad vibes. Publicity would be great, but you'd be speaking these beautiful words over a body found in a gay porno house. Too risky.'

'Yeah. I think you're –'

'This is our crisis, Chief. The ratings continue to improve, and I just don't want to take a chance.'

'Should we send someone?'

'Of course. What about the Vice President?'

'Where is he?'

'Flying in from Guatemala. He'll be in tonight.' Coal suddenly smiled to himself. 'This is great VP stuff, you know. A gay funeral.'

The President chuckled. 'Perfect.'

Coal stopped smiling and began pacing in front of the desk. 'Slight problem. Rosenberg's service is Saturday, only eight blocks from here.'

'I'd rather go to hell for a day.'

'I know. But your absence would be very conspicuous.'

'I could check into Walter Reed with back spasms. It worked before.'

'No, Chief. Reelection is next year. You must stay away from hospitals.'

The President slapped both hands on his desk and stood. 'Dammit, Fletcher! I can't go to his service because I can't keep from smiling. He was hated by ninety percent of the American people. They'll love me if I don't go.'

'Protocol, Chief. Good taste. You'll be burned by the press if you don't go. Look, it won't hurt, okay. You don't have to say a word. Just ease in and out, look real sad, and allow the cameras to get a good look. Won't take an hour.'

The President was gripping his putter and crouching over an orange ball. 'Then I'll have to go to Jensen's.'

'Exactly. But forget the eulogy.'

He putted. 'I met him only twice, you know.'

'I know. Let's quietly attend both services, say nothing, then disappear.'

He putted again. 'I think you're right.'

CHAPTER NINE

Thomas Callahan slept late and alone. He had gone to bed early, and sober, and alone. For the third day in a row he had canceled classes. It was Friday, and Rosenberg's service was tomorrow, and out of respect for his idol, he would not teach con law until the man was properly put to rest.

He fixed coffee and sat on the balcony in his robe. The temperature was in the sixties, the first cold snap of the fall, and Dauphine Street below bustled with brisk energy. He nodded to the old woman without a name on the balcony across the street. Bourbon was a block away and the tourists were already out with their little maps and cameras. Dawn went unnoticed in the Quarter, but by ten the narrow streets were busy with delivery trucks and cabs.

On these late mornings, and they were many in number, Callahan cherished his freedom. He was twenty years out of law school, and most of his contemporaries were strapped into seventy-hour weeks in pressurized law factories. He had lasted two years in private practice. A behemoth in D.C. with two hundred lawyers hired him fresh out of Georgetown and stuck him in a cubbyhole office writing briefs for the first six months. Then he was placed on an assembly line answering interrogatories about IUDs twelve hours a day, and expected to bill sixteen. He was told that if he could cram the next twenty years into the next ten, he just might make partner at the weary age of thirty-five.

Callahan wanted to live past fifty, so he retired from the boredom of private law. He earned a master's in law, and became a professor. He slept late, worked five hours a day, wrote an occasional article, and for the most part enjoyed himself immensely. With no family to support, his salary of seventy thousand a year was more than sufficient to pay for his two-story bungalow, his Porsche, and his liquor. If death came early, it would be from whiskey and not work.

He had sacrificed. Many of his pals from law school were partners in the big firms with fancy letterheads and half-million-dollar earnings. They rubbed shoulders with CEOs from IBM and Texaco and State Farm. They power-schmoozed with senators. They had offices in Tokyo and London. But he did not envy them.

One of his best friends from law school was Gavin Verheek, another dropout from private practice who had gone to work for the government. He first worked in the civil rights division at Justice, then transferred to the FBI. He was now special counsel to the Director. Callahan was due in Washington Monday for a conference of con law professors. He and Verheek planned to eat and get drunk Monday night.

He needed to call and confirm their eating and drinking, and to pick his brain. He dialed the number from memory. The call was routed then rerouted, and after five minutes of asking for Gavin Verheek, the man was on the phone.

'Make it quick,' Verheek said.

'So nice to hear your voice,' Callahan said.

'How are you, Thomas?'

'It's ten-thirty. I'm not dressed. I'm sitting here in the French Quarter sipping coffee and watching pedestrians on Dauphine. What're you doing?'

'What a life. Here it's eleven-thirty, and I haven't left the office since they found the bodies Wednesday morning.'

'I'm just sick, Gavin. He'll nominate two Nazis.'

'Well, of course, in my position, I cannot comment on such matters. But I suspect you're correct.'

'Suspect my ass. You've already seen his short list of nominees, haven't you, Gavin? You guys are already doing background checks, aren't you? Come on, Gavin, you can tell me. Who's on the list? I'll never tell.'

'Neither will I, Thomas. But I promise this – your name is not among the few.'

'I'm wounded.'

'How's the girl?'

'Which one?'

'Come on, Thomas. The girl?'

'She's beautiful and brilliant and soft and gentle –'

'Keep going.'

'Who killed them, Gavin? I have a right to know. I'm a taxpayer and I have a right to know who killed them.'

'What's her name again?'

'Darby. Who killed them, and why?'

'You could always pick names, Thomas. I remember women you turned down because you didn't like the names. Gorgeous, hot women, but with flat names. Darby. Has a nice erotic touch to it. What a name. When do I meet her?'

'I don't know.'

'Has she moved in?'

'None of your damned business. Gavin, listen to me. Who did it?'

'Don't you read the papers? We have no suspects. None. *Nada.*'

'Surely you have a motive.'

'Mucho motives. Lots of hatred out there, Thomas. Weird combination, wouldn't you say? Jensen's hard to figure. The Director has ordered us to research pending cases and recent decisions and voting patterns and all that crap.'

'That's great, Gavin. Every con law scholar in the country is now playing detective and trying to solve the murders.'

'And you're not?'

'No. I threw a binge when I heard the news, but I'm sober now. The girl, however, has buried herself in the same research you're doing. She's ignoring me.'

'Darby. What a name. Where's she from?'

'Denver. Are we on for Monday?'

'Maybe. Voyles wants us to work around the clock until the computers tell us who did it. I plan to work you in, though.'

'Thanks. I'll expect a full report, Gavin. Not just the gossip.'

'Thomas, Thomas. Always fishing for information. And I, as usual, have none to give you.'

'You'll get drunk and tell all, Gavin. You always do.'

'Why don't you bring Darby? How old is she? Nineteen?'

'Twenty-four, and she's not invited. Maybe later.'

'Maybe. Gotta run, pal. I meet with the Director in thirty minutes. The tension is so thick around here you can smell it.'

Callahan punched the number for the law school library and asked if Darby Shaw had been seen. She had not.

Darby parked in the near-empty lot of the federal building in Lafayette, and entered the clerk's office on the first floor. It was noon Friday, court was not in session, and the hallways were deserted. She stopped at the counter and looked through an open window, and waited. A deputy clerk, late for lunch and with an attitude, walked to the window. 'Can I help you?' she asked in the tone of a lowly civil servant who wanted to do anything but help.

Darby slid a strip of paper through the window. 'I would like to see this file.' The clerk took a quick glance at the name of the case, and looked at Darby. 'Why?' she asked.

'I don't have to explain. It's public record, isn't it?'

'Semipublic.'

Darby took the strip of paper and folded it. 'Are you familiar with the Freedom of Information Act?'

'Are you a lawyer?'

'I don't have to be a lawyer to look at this file.'

The clerk opened a drawer in the counter, and took out a key ring. She nodded, pointing with her forehead. 'Follow me.'

The sign on the door said JURY ROOM, but inside there were no tables or chairs, only file cabinets and boxes lining the walls. Darby looked around the room.

The clerk pointed to a wall. 'That's it, on this wall. The rest of the room is other junk. This first file cabinet has all the pleadings and correspondence. The rest is discovery, exhibits, and the trial.'

'When was the trial?'

'Last summer. It went on for two months.'

'Where's the appeal?'

'Not perfected yet. I think the deadline is November 1. Are you a reporter or something?'

'No.'

'Good. As you obviously know, these are indeed public records. But the trial judge has placed certain restrictions. First, I must have your name and the precise hours you visited this room. Second, nothing can be taken from this room. Third, nothing in this file can be copied unitl the appeal is perfected. Fourth, anything you touch in here must be put back exactly where you found it. Judge's orders.'

Darby stared at the wall of file cabinets. 'Why can't I make copies?'

'Ask His Honor, okay? Now, what's your name?'

'Darby Shaw.'

The clerk scribbled the information on a clipboard hanging near the door. 'How long will you be?'

'I don't know. Three or four hours.'

'We close at five. Find me at the office when you leave.' She closed the door with a smirk. Darby opened a drawer full of pleadings, and began flipping through files and taking notes. The lawsuit was seven years old, with one plaintiff and thirty-eight wealthy corporate defendants who had collectively hired and fired no less than fifteen law firms from all over the country. Big firms, many with hundreds of lawyers in dozens of offices.

Seven years of expensive legal warfare, and the outcome was far from certain. Bitter litigation. The trial verdict was only a temporary victory for the defendants. The verdict had been purchased or in some other way illegally obtained, claimed the plaintiff in its motions for a new trial. Boxes of motions. Accusations and counteraccusations. Requests for sanctions and fines flowing rapidly to and from both sides. Pages and pages of affidavits detailing lies and abuses by the lawyers and their clients. One lawyer was dead.

Another had tried suicide, according to a classmate of Darby's who had worked on the fringes of the case during the trial. Her friend had been employed in a summer clerkship with a big firm in Houston, and was kept in the dark but heard a little.

Darby unfolded a chair and stared at the file cabinets. It would take five hours just to find everything.

The publicity had not been good for the Montrose. Most of its customers wore dark sunglasses after dark, and tended to enter and exit rather quickly. And now that a U.S. Supreme Court Justice had been found in the balcony, the place was famous and the curious drove by at all hours pointing and taking pictures. Most of the regulars went elsewhere. The bravest darted in when the traffic was light.

He looked just like a regular when he darted in and paid his money inside the door without looking at the cashier. Baseball cap, black sunglasses, jeans, neat hair, leather jacket. He was well disguised, but not because he was a homosexual and ashamed to be hanging around such places.

It was midnight. He climbed the stairs to the balcony, smiling at the thought of Jensen wearing the tourniquet. The door was locked. He took a seat in the center section on the floor, away from anyone else.

He had never watched queer movies before, and after this night he had no plans to watch another one. This was his third such smut house in the past ninety minutes. He kept the sunglasses on and tried to avoid the screen. But it was difficult, and this irritated him.

There were five other people in the theater. Four rows up and to his right were two lovebirds, kissing and playing. Oh, for a baseball bat and he could put them out of their misery. Or a nice little piece of yellow ski rope.

He suffered for twenty minutes, and was about to reach in his pocket when a hand touched his shoulder. A gentle hand. He played it cool.

'Could I sit by you?' came the rather deep and manly voice from just over his shoulder.

'No, and you can remove your hand.'

The hand moved. Seconds passed, and it was obvious there would be no more requests. Then he was gone.

This was torture for a man violently opposed to pornography. He wanted to vomit. He glanced behind him, then reached carefully into the leather jacket and removed a black box, six inches by five and three inches thick. He laid it on the floor between his legs. With a scalpel, he made a careful incision in the cushion of the seat next to him, then, while glancing around, inserted the black box into the cushion. There were springs in this one, a real antique, and he delicately twisted the box from one side to the other until it was in place with the switch and the tube barely visible through the incision.

He took a deep breath. Although the device had been built by a true professional, a legendary genius at miniature explosives, it was not pleasant carrying the damned thing around in a coat pocket, just centimeters from his heart and most other vital organs. And he wasn't particularly comfortable sitting next to it now.

This was his third plant of the night, and he had one more, at another movie house where they showed old-fashioned heterosexual pornography. He was almost looking forward to it, and this irritated him.

He looked at the two lovers, who were oblivious to the movie and growing more excited by the minute, and wished they could be sitting right there when the little black box began silently spewing forth its gas, and then thirty seconds later when the fireball would flash-fry every object between the screen and the popcorn machine. He would like that.

But his was a nonviolent group, opposed to the indiscriminate killing of innocent and/or insignificant people. They had killed a few necessary victims. Their specialty, however, was the demolition of structures used by the enemy. They picked easy targets: unarmed abortion clinics, unprotected ACLU offices, unsuspecting smut houses. They were having a field day. Not one single arrest in eighteen months.

It was twelve-forty, time to leave and hurry four blocks to his car for another black box, then six blocks over to the Pussycat Cinema, which closed at one-thirty. The Pussycat was either eighteen or nineteen on the list, he couldn't remember which, but he was certain that in exactly three hours and twenty minutes the dirty movie business in D.C. would take a helluva blow. Twenty-two of these little joints were supposed to receive black boxes tonight, and at 4 A.M. they were all supposed to be closed and deserted, and demolished. Three all-nighters were scratched from the list, because his was a nonviolent group.

He adjusted his sunglasses and took one last look at the cushion next to him. Judging from the cups and popcorn on the floor, the place got swept once a week. No one would notice the switch and tube barely visible between the ragged threads. He cautiously flipped the switch, and left the Montrose.

CHAPTER TEN

Eric East had never met the President, nor been in the White House. And he'd never met Fletcher Coal, but he knew he wouldn't like him.

He followed Director Voyles and K. O. Lewis into the Oval Office at seven Saturday morning. There were no smiles or handshakes. East was introduced by Voyles. The President nodded from behind the desk but did not stand. Coal was reading something.

Twenty porno houses had been torched in the D.C. area, and many were still smoldering. They had seen the smoke above the city from the back of the limo. At a dump called Angels a janitor had been badly burned and was not expected to live.

An hour ago they had received word that an anonymous caller to a radio station had claimed responsibility for the Underground Army, and he promised more of the same in celebration of the death of Rosenberg.

The President spoke first. He looked tired, East thought. It was such an early hour for him. 'How many places got bombed?'

'Twenty here,' Voyles answered. 'Seventeen in Baltimore and around fifteen in Atlanta. It appears as though the assault was carefully coordinated because all the explosions happened at precisely 4 A.M.'

Coal looked up from his memo. 'Director, do you believe it's the Underground Army?'

'As of now they're the only ones claiming responsibility. It looks like some of their work. Could be.' Voyles did not look at Coal when he spoke to him.

'So when do you start making arrests?' the President asked.

'At the precise moment we obtain probable cause, Mr. President. That's the law, you understand.'

'I understand this outfit is your top suspect in the killings of Rosenberg and Jensen, and that you're certain it killed a federal trial judge in Texas, and it most likely bombed at least fifty-two smut houses last night. I don't understand why they're bombing and killing with immunity. Hell, Director, we're under siege.'

Voyles' neck turned red, but he said nothing. He just looked away while the President glared at him. K. O. Lewis cleared his throat. 'Mr. President, if I may, we are not convinced the Underground Army was involved with the deaths of Rosenberg and Jensen. In fact, we have no evidence linking them. They are only one of a dozen suspects. As I've said before, the killings were remarkably clean, well organized, and very professional. Extremely professional.'

Coal stepped forward. 'What you're trying to say, Mr. Lewis, is that you have no idea who killed them, and you may never know.'

'No, that's not what I'm saying. We'll find them, but it will take time.'

'How much time?' asked the President. It was an obvious, sophomoric question with no good answer. East immediately disliked the President for asking it.

'Months,' Lewis said.

'How many months?'

'Many months.'

The President rolled his eyes and shook his head, then with great disgust stood and walked to the window. He spoke to the window. 'I can't believe there's no relation between what happened last night and the dead judges. I don't know. Maybe I'm just paranoid.'

Voyles shot a quick smirk at Lewis. Paranoid, insecure, clueless, dumb, out of touch. Voyles could think of many others.

The President continued, still pondering the window. 'I just get nervous when assassins are loose around here and bombs are going off. Who can blame me? We haven't killed a President in over thirty years.'

'Oh, I think you're safe, Mr. President,' Voyles said with a trace of amusement. 'The Secret Service has things under control.'

'Great. Then why do I feel as though I'm in Beirut?' He was almost mumbling into the window.

Coal sensed the awkwardness and picked up a thick memo from the desk. He held it and spoke to Voyles, much like a professor lecturing to his class.

'This is the short list of potential nominees to the Supreme Court. There are eight names, each with a biography. It was prepared by Justice. We started with twenty names, then the President, Attorney General Horton, and myself cut it to eight, none of whom have any idea they are being considered.'

Voyles still looked away. The President slowly returned to his desk, and picked up his copy of the memo. Coal continued.

'Some of these people are controversial, and if they are ultimately nominated we'll have a small war getting them approved by the Senate. We'd prefer not to start fighting now. This must be kept confidential.'

Voyles suddenly turned and glared at Coal. 'You're an idiot, Coal! We've done this before, and I can assure you when we start checking on these people the cat's out of the bag. You want a thorough background investigation, and yet you expect everyone contacted to keep quiet. It doesn't work that way, son.'

Coal stepped closer to Voyles. His eyes were glowing. 'You bust your ass to make sure these names are kept out of the papers until they're nominated. You make it work, Director. You plug the leaks and keep it out of the papers, understand.'

Voyles was on his feet, pointing at Coal. 'Listen, asshole, you want them checked out, you do it yourself. Don't start giving me a bunch of boy scout orders.'

Lewis stood between them, and the President stood behind his desk, and for a second or two nothing was said. Coal placed his memo on the desk and retreated a few steps, looking away. The president was now the peacemaker. 'Sit down, Denton. Sit down.'

Voyles returned to his seat while staring at Coal. The President smiled at Lewis and everyone took a seat. 'We're all under a lot of pressure,' the President said warmly.

Lewis spoke calmly. 'We'll perform the routine investigations on your names, Mr. President, and it will be done in the strictest of confidence. You know, however, that we cannot control every person we talk to.'

'Yes, Mr. Lewis, I know that. But I extra caution. These men are young and will shape and reshape the Constitution long after I'm dead. They're staunchly conservative, and the press will eat them alive. They must be free from warts and skeletons in the closet. No dope smokers, or illegitimate children, or DUIs, or radical student activity, or divorces. Understand? No surprises.'

'Yes, Mr. President. But we cannot guarantee total secrecy in our investigations.'

'Just try, okay.'

'Yes, sir.' Lewis handed the memo to Eric East.

'Is that all?' Voyles asked.

The President glanced at Coal, who was ignoring them all and standing before the window. 'Yes, Denton, that's all. I'd like to have these names checked out in ten days. I want to move fast on this.'

Voyles was standing. 'You'll have it in ten days.'

Callahan was irritated when he knocked on the door to Darby's apartment. He was quite perturbed and had a lot on his mind, a lot that he wanted to say, but he knew better than to start a fight because there was something he wanted much worse than to blow off a little steam. She had avoided him for four days now while she played detective and barricaded herself in the law library. She had skipped classes and failed to return his calls, and in general neglected him during his hour of crisis. But he knew when she opened the door he would smile and forget about being neglected.

He held a liter of wine and a real pizza from Mama Rosa's. It was after ten, Saturday nigh. He knocked again, and looked up and down the street at the neat duplexes and bungalows. The chain rattled from inside, and he instantly smiled. The neglect vanished.

'Who is it?' she asked through the chain.

'Thomas Callahan, remember? I'm at your door begging you to let me in so we can play and be friends again.'

The door opened and Callahan stepped in. She took the wine and pecked him on the cheek. 'Are we still buddies?' he asked.

'Yes, Thomas. I've been busy.' He followed her through the cluttered den to the kitchen. A computer and an assortment of thick books covered the table.

'I called. Why didn't you call me back?'

'I've been out,' she said, opening a drawer and removing a corkscrew.

'You've got a machine. I've been talking to it.'

'Are you trying to fight, Thomas?'

He looked at her bare legs. 'No! I swear I'm not mad. I promise. Please forgive me if I appear to be upset.'

'Stop it.'

'When can we go to bed?'

'Are you sleepy?'

'Anything but. Come on, Darby, it's been three nights.'

'Five. What kind of pizza?' She removed the cork and poured two glasses. Callahan watched every move.

'Oh, it's one of those Saturday night specials where they throw on everything headed for the garbage. Shrimp tails, eggs, crawfish heads. Cheap wine too. I'm a little low on cash, and I'm leaving town tomorow so I have to watch what I spend, and since I'm leaving I though I'd just come on over and get laid tonight so I wouldn't be tempted by some contagious woman in D.C. What do you think?'

Darby was opening the pizza box. 'Looks like sausage and peppers.'

'Can I still get laid?'

'Maybe later. Drink your wine and let's chat. We haven't had a long talk in a while.'

'I have. I've been talking to your machine all week.'

He took his wineglass and the bottle and followed her closely to the den, where she turned on the stereo. They relaxed on the sofa.

'Let's get drunk,' he said.

'You're so romantic.'

I've got some romance for you.'

'You've been drunk for a week.'

'No I haven't. Eighty percent of a week. It's your fault for avoiding me.'

'What's wrong with you, Thomas?'

'I've got the shakes. I'm all keyed up and I need companionship to knock the edge off. Whatta you say?'

'Let's get half drunk.' She sipped her wine and draped her legs across his lap. He held his breath as if in pain.

'What time is your flight?' she asked.

He was gulping now. 'One-Thirty. Nonstop to National. I'm supposed to register at five, and there's a dinner at eight. After that I may be forced to roam the streets looking for love.'

She smiled. 'Okay, okay. We'll do it in a minute. But let's talk first.'

Callahan breathed a sigh of relief. 'I can talk for ten minutes, the I'll just collapse.'

'What's up for Monday?'

'The usual eight hours of airhead debate on the future of the Fifth Amendment, then a committee will draft a proposed conference report that no one will approve. More debate Tuesday, another report, perhaps an altercation or two, then we adjourn with nothing accomplished and go home. I'll be in late Tuesday evening, and I'd like a date at a very nice restaurant, after which we can go back to my place for an intellectual discussion and animal sex. Where's the pizza?'

'In there. I'll get it.'

He was stroking her legs. 'Don't move. I'm not the least bit hungry.'

'Why do you go to these conferences?'

'I'm a member, and I'm a professor, and we're just sort of expected to roam the country attending meetings with other educated idiots and adopting reports nobody reads. If I didn't go, the dean would think I was not contributing to the academic environment.'

She refilled the wineglasses. 'You're uptight, Thomas.'

'I know. It's been a rough week. I hate the thought of a bunch of Neanderthals rewriting the Constitution. We'll live in a police state in ten years. I can't do anything about it, so I'll probably resort to alcohol.'

Darby sipped slowly and watched him. The music was soft and the lights low. 'I'm getting a buzz,' she said.

'That's about right for you. A glass and a half and you're history. If you were Irish you could drink all night.'

'My father was half Scottish.'

'Not good enough.' Callahan crossed his feet on the coffee table and relaxed. He gently rubbed her ankles. 'Can I paint your toes?'

She said nothing. He had a fetish for her toes, and insisted on doing the nails with bright red polish at least twice a month. They'd seen it in *Bull Durham*, and though he wasn't as neat and sober as Kevin Costner, she had grown to enjoy the intimacy of it.

'No toes tonight?' he asked.

'Maybe later. You look tired.'

'I'm relaxing, but I'm filled with virile male electricity, and you will not put me off by telling me I look tired.'

'Have some more wine.'

Callahan had more wine, and sank deeper in the sofa. 'So, Ms. Shaw, who done it?'

'Profesionals. Haven't you read the papers?'

'Of course. But who's behind the profesionals?'

'I don't know. After last night, the unanimous choice seems to be the Underground Army.'

'But you're not convinced.'

'No. There have been no arrests. I'm not convinced.'

'And you've got some obscure suspect unknown to the rest of the country.'

'I had one, but now I'm not so sure. I spent three days tracking it down, even summarized it all real nice and neat in my little computer, and printed out a thin rough draft of a brief which I have now discarded.'

Callahan stared at her. 'You're telling me you skipped classes for three days, ignored me, worked around the clock playing Sherlock Holmes, and now you're throwing it away.'

'It's over there on the table.'

'I can't believe this. While I sulked around in loneliness all week, I knew it was for a worthy cause. I knew my suffering was for the good of the country because you would peel away the onion and tell me tonight or perhaps tomorrow who done it.'

'It can't be done, at least not with legal research. There's no pattern, no common thread in the murders. I almost burned up the computers at the law school.'

'Ha! I told you so. You forget, dear, that I am a genius at constitutional law, and I knew immediately that Rosenberg and Jensen had nothing in common but black robes and death threats. The Nazis or Aryans or Kluxers or Mafia or some other group killed them because Rosenberg was Rosenberg, and because Jensen was the easiest target and somewhat of an embarrassment.'

'Well, why don't you call the FBI and share your insights with them? I'm sure they're sitting by the phone.'

'Don't be angry. I'm sorry. Please forgive me.'

'You're an ass, Thomas.'

'Yes, but you love me, don't you?'

'I don't know.'

'Can we still go to bed? you promised.'

'We'll see.'

Callahan placed his glass on the table, and attacked her. 'Look, baby. I'll read your brief, okay. And then we'll talk about it, okay. But I'm not thinking clearly right now, and I won't be able to continue until you take my weak and trembling hand and lead me to your bed.'

'Forget my little brief.'

'Please, dammit, Darby, please.'

She grabbed his neck and pulled him to her. They kissed long and hard, a wet, almost violent kiss.

CHAPTER ELEVEN

The cop stuck his thumb on the button next to the name of Gray Grantham, and held it down for twenty seconds. Then a brief pause. Then another twenty seconds. Pause. Twenty seconds. Pause. Twenty seconds. He thought this was funny because Grantham was a night owl and had probably slept less than three or four hours, and now all this incessant buzzing echoing throughout his hallway. He pushed again and looked at his patrol car parked illegally on the curb under the streetlight. It was almost dawn, Sunday, and the street was empty. Twenty seconds. Pause. Twenty seconds.

Maybe Grantham was dead. Or maybe he was comatose from booze and a late night on the town. Maybe he had someone's woman up there and had no plans to answer the door. Pause. Twenty seconds.

The mike crackled. 'Who is it!'

'Police!' answered the cop, who was black and emphasized the *po* in *police* just for the fun of it.

'What do you want?' Grantham demanded.

'Maybe I gotta warrant.' The cop was near laughter.

Grantham's voice softened, and he sounded wounded. 'Is this Cleve?'

'It is.'

'What time is it, Cleve?'

'Almost five-thirty.'

'It must be good.'

'Don't know. Sarge didn't say, you know. He just said to wake you up 'cause he wanted to talk.'

'Why does he always want to talk before the sun comes up?'

'Stupid question, Grantham.'

A slight pause. 'Yeah, I guess so. I presume he wants to talk right now.'

'No. You got thirty minutes. He said be there at six.'

'Where?'

'There's a little coffee shop on Fourteenth near the Trinidad Playground. It's dark and safe, and Sarge likes it.'

'Where does he find these places?'

'You know, for a reporter you can ask the dumbest questions. The name of the place is Glenda's, and I suggest you get going or you'll be late.'

'Will you be there?'

'I'll drop in, just to make sure you're okay.'

'I thought you said it was safe.'

'It is safe, for that part of town. Can you find it?'

'Yeah, I'll be there as soon as I can.

'Have a nice day, Grantham.'

Sarge was old, very black, with a head full of brilliant white hair that sprang out in all directions. He wore thick sunglasses whenever he was awake, and most of his coworkers in the West Wing of the White House thought he was half blind. He held his head sideways and smiled like Ray Charles. He sometimes bumped into door facings and desks as he unloaded trash cans and dusted furniture. He walked slowly and gingerly as if counting his steps. He worked patiently, always with a smile, always with a kind word for anyone willing to give him one. For the most part he was ignored and dismissed as just another friendly, old, partially disabled black janitor.

Sarge could see around corners. His territory was the West Wing, where he had been cleaning for thirty years now. Cleaning and listening. Cleaning and seeing. He picked up after some terribly important people who were often too busy to watch their words, especially in the presence of poor old Sarge.

He knew which doors stayed open, and which walls were thin, and which air vents carried sound. He could disappear in an instant, then reappear in a shadow where the terribly important people could not see him.

He kept most of it to himself. But from time to time, he fell heir to a juicy bit of information that could be pieced together with another one, and Sarge would make the judgement call that it should be repeated. He was very careful. He had three years until retirement, and he took no chances.

No one ever suspected Sarge of leaking stories to the press. There were usually enough big mouths within any White House to lay blame on each other. It was hilarious, really. Sarge would talk to Grantham at the *Post,* then wait excitedly for the story, then listen to the wailing in the basement when the heads rolled.

He was an impeccable source, and he talked only to Grantham. His son Cleve, the cop, arranged the meetings, always at odd hours at dark and inconspicuous places. Sarge wore his sunglasses. Grantham wore the same with a hat or cap of some sort. Cleve usually sat with them and watched the crowed.

Grantham arrived at Glenda's a few minutes after six, and walked to a booth in the rear. There were three other customers. Glenda herself was frying eggs on a grill near the register. Cleve sat on a stool watching her.

They shook hands. A cup of coffee had been poured for Grantham.

'Sorry I'm late,' he said.

'No problem, my friend. Good to see you.' Sarge had a raspy voice that was difficult to suppress with a whisper. No one was listening.

Grantham gulped coffee. 'Busy week at the White House.'

'You could say that. Lot of excitement. Lot of happiness.'

'You don't say.' Grantham could not take notes at these meetings. It would be too obvious, Sarge said when he laid the ground rules.

'Yes. The President and his boys were elated with the news of Justice Rosenberg. This made them very happy.'

'What about Justice Jensen?'

'Well, as you noticed, the President attended the memorial service, but did not speak. He had planned to give a eulogy, but backed out because he would have been saying nice things about a gay fella.'

'Who wrote the eulogy?'

'The speechwriters. Mainly Mabry. Worked on it all day Thursday, then he backed out.

'He also went to Rosenberg's service.'

'Yes, he did. But he didn't want to. Said he'd rather go to hell for a day. But in the end, he chickened out and went anyway. He's quite happy Rosenberg was murdered. There was almost a festive mood around the place Wednesday. Fate has dealt him a wonderful hand. He now gets to restructure the Court, and he's very excited about this.'

Grantham listened hard. Sarge continued.

'There's a short list of nominees. The original had twenty or so names, then it was cut to eight.'

'Who did the cutting?'

'Who do you think? The President and Fletcher Coal. They're terrified of leaks at this point. Evidently the list is nothing but young conservative judges, most of whom are obscure.'

'Any names?'

'Just two. A certain man named Pryce from Idaho, and one named MacLawrence from Vermont. That's all I know about names. I think they are both federal judges. Nothing more on this.'

'What about the investigation?'

'I haven't heard much, but as usual I'll keep my ears open. There doesn't appear to be much going on.'

'Anything else?'

'No. When will you run it?'

'In the morning.'

'It'll be fun.'

'Thanks, Sarge.'

The sun was up now and the café was noisier. Cleve strolled over and sat next to his father. 'You guys about finished?'

'We are,' Sarge said.

Cleve glanced around. 'I think we need to leave. Grantham goes first, I'll follow, then Pop here can stay as long as he wants.'

'Mighty nice of you,' Sarge said.

'Thanks, fellas,' Grantham said as he headed for the door.

CHAPTER TWELVE

Verheek was late as usual. In the twenty-three-year history of their friendship, he had never been on time, and it was never a matter of being only a few minutes late. He had no concept of time and wasn't bothered with it. He wore a watch but never looked at it. Late for Verheek meant at least an hour, sometimes two, especially when the person kept waiting was a friend who expected him to be late and would forgive him

So Callahan sat for an hour in the bar, which suited him just fine. After eight hours of scholarly debate, he despised the Constitution and those who taught it. He needed Chivas in his veins, and after two doubles on the rocks he was feeling better. He watched himself in the mirror behind the rows of liquor, and in the distance over his shoulder he watched and waited for Gavin Verheek. Small wonder his friend couldn't cut it in private practice, where life depended upon the clock.

When the third double was served, an hour and eleven minutes after 7 P.M., Verheek strolled to the bar and ordered a Moosehead.

'Sorry I'm late,' he said as they shook hands. 'I knew you'd appreciate the extra time alone with your Chivas.'

'You look tired,' Callahan said as he inspected him. Old and tired. Verheek was aging badly and gaining weight. His forehead had grown an inch since their last visit, and his pale skin highlighted the heavy circles under his eyes. 'How much do you weigh?'

'None of your business,' he said, gulping the beer. 'Where's our table?'

'It's reserved for eight-thirty. I figured you would be at least ninety minutes late.'

'Then I'm early.'

'You could say that. Did you come from work?'

'I live at work now. The Director wants no less than a hundred hours a week until something breaks. I told my wife I'd be home for Christmas.'

'How is she?'

'Fine. A very patient lady. We get along much better when I live at the office.' She was wife number three in seventeen years.

'I'd like to meet her.'

'No, you wouldn't. I married the first two for sex and they enjoyed it so much they shared it with others. I married this one for money and she's not much to look at. You wouldn't be impressed.' He emptied the bottle. 'I doubt if I can hang on until she dies.'

'How old is she?'

'Don't ask. I really love her, you know. Honest. But after two years I now realize we have nothing in common but an acute awareness of the stock market.' He looked at the bartender. 'Another beer, please.'

Callahan chuckled and sipped his drink. 'How much is she worth?'

'Not nearly as much as I thought. I'm not sure really. Somewhere around five million, I think. She cleaned out husbands one and two, and I think she was attracted to me for the challenge of marrying just an average joe. That, and the sex is great, she said. They all say that, you know.'

'You always picked losers, Gavin, even in law school. You're attracted to neurotic and depressed women.'

'And they're attracted to me.' He turned the bottle up and drained half of it. 'Why do we always eat in this place?'

'I don't know. It's sort of traditional. It brings back fond memories of law school.'

'We hated law school, Thomas. Everyone hates law school. Everyone hates lawyers.'

'You're in a fine mood.'

'Sorry. I've slept six hours since they found the bodies. The Director screams at me at least five times a day. I scream at everybody under me. It's one big brawl over there.'

'Drink up, big boy. Our table's ready. Let's drink and eat and talk, and try to enjoy these few hours together.'

'I love you more than my wife, Thomas. Do you know that?'

'That's not saying much.'

'You're right.'

They followed the maître d' to a small table in the corner, the same table they always requested. Callahan ordered another round, and explained they would be in no hurry to eat.

'Did you see that damned thing in the *Post*?' Verheek asked.

'I saw it. Who leaked it?'

'Who knows. The Director got the short list Saturday morning, hand-delivered by the President himself, with rather explicit demands about secrecy. He showed the list to no one over the weekend, then this morning the story hit with the names of Pryce and MacLawrence. Voyles went berserk when he saw it, and a few minutes later the President called. He rushed to the White House and they had a huge cuss fight. Voyles tried to attack Fletcher Coal, and had to be restrained by K. O. Lewis. Very nasty.'

Callahan hung on every word. 'This is pretty good.'

'Yeah. I'm telling you this part because later, after a few more drinks, you'll expect me to tell you who else is on the list and I won't do it. I'm trying to be a friend, Thomas.'

'Keep going.'

'Anyway, there's no way the leak came from us. Impossible. It had to come from the White House. The place is full of people who hate Coal, and it's leaking like rusty pipes.'

'Coal probably leaked it.'

'Maybe so. He's a sleazy bastard, and one theory has him leaking Pryce and MacLawrence to scare everyone, then later announcing two nominees who appear more moderate. It sounds like something he would do.'

'I've never heard of Pryce and MacLawrence.'

'Join the club. They're both very young, early forties, with precious little experience on the bench. We haven't checked them out, but they appear to be radically conservative.'

'And the rest of the list?'

'That was quick. Two beers down, and you've already popped the question.'

The drinks arrived. 'I want some of those mushrooms stuffed with crabmeat,' Verheek told the waiter. 'Just to munch on. I'm starving.'

Callahan handed over his empty glass. 'Bring me an order too.'

'Don't ask again, Thomas. You may have to carry me out of here in three hours, but I'll never tell. You know that. Let's say that Pryce and MacLawrence to be reflective of the entire list.'

'All unknowns?'

'Basically, yes.'

Callahan sipped the Scotch slowly and shook his head. Verheek removed his jacket and loosened his tie. 'Let's talk about women.'

'No.'

'How old is she?'

'Twenty-four, but very mature.'

'You could be her father.'

'I may be. Who knows.'

'Where's she from?'

'Denver. I told you that.'

'I love Western girls. They're so independent and unpretentious and they tend to wear Levis and have long legs. I may marry one. Does she have money?'

'No. Her father was killed in a plane crash four years ago and her mother got a nice settlement.'

'Then she has money.'

'She's comfortable.'

'I'll bet she is. Do you have a photo?'

'No. She's not a grandchild or a poodle.'

'Why didn't you bring a picture?'

'I'll get her to send you one. Why is this so amusing to you?'

'It's hilarious. The great Thomas Callahan, he of the disposable women, has fallen hard.'

'I have not.'

'It must be a record. What, nine, ten months now?' You've actually maintained a steady relationship for almost a year, haven't you?'

'Eight months and three weeks, but don't tell anyone, Gavin. It's not easy for me.'

'Your secret's safe. Just give me all the details. How tall is she?'

'Five-eight, hundred and twelve pounds, long legs, tight Levis, independent, unpretentious, your typical Western girl.'

'I must find one for myself. Are you gonna marry her?'

'Of course not! Finish your drink.'

'Are you, like, monogamous now?'

'Are you?'

'Hell no. Never have been. But we're not talking about me, Thomas, we're talking about Peter Pan here, Cool Hand Callahan, the man with the monthly version of the world's most gorgeous woman. Tell me, Thomas, and don't lie to your best friend, just look me in the eyes and tell me if you have succumbed to a state of monogamy.'

Verheek was leaning halfway across the table, watching and grinning stupidly.

'Not so loud,' Callahan said, looking around.

'Answer me.'

'Give me the other names on the list, and I'll tell you.'

Verheek withdrew. 'Nice try. I think the answer is yes. I think you're in love with this gal, but too cowardly to admit it. I think she's got your number, pal.'

'Okay, she does. Do you feel better?'

'Yeah, much better. When can I meet her?'

'When can I meet your wife?'

'You're confused, Thomas. There's a basic difference here.

'You don't want to meet my wife, but I do want to meet Darby.

You see. I assure you they are very dissimilar.'

Callahan smiled and sipped. Verheek relaxed and crossed his legs in the aisle. He tilted the green bottle to his lips.

'You're wired, buddy,' Callahan said.

'I'm sorry. I'm drinking as fast as I can.'

The mushrooms were served in simmering skillets. Verheek stuffed two in his mouth and chewed furiously. Callahan watched. The Chivas had knocked off the hunger pains, and he would wait a few minutes. He preferred alcohol over food anyway.

Four arabs noisily filled a table next to them, yakking and jabbering in their language. All four ordered Jack Daniel's.

'Who killed them, Gavin?'

He chewed for a minute, then swallowed hard. 'If knew, I wouldn't tell. But I swear I do not know. It's baffling. The killers vanished without a trace. It was meticulously planned and perfectly executed. Not a clue.'

'Why the combination?'

He stuffed another in his mouth. 'Quite simple. It's so simple, it's easy to overlook. They were such natural targets. Rosenberg had no security system in his townhouse. Any decent cat burglar could come and go. And poor Jensen was hanging around those places at midnight. They were exposed. At the exact moment each died, the other seven Supremes had FBI agents in their homes. That's why they were selected. They were stupid.'

'Then who selected them?'

'Someone with a lot of money. The killers were professionals, and they were probably out of the country within hours. We figure there were three, maybe more. The mess at Rosenberg's could have been done by just one. We figure there were at least two working on Jensen. One or more looking out while the guy with the rope did his thing. Even though it was a dirty little place, it was open to the public, and quite risky. But they were good, very good.'

'I've read a lone assassin theory.'

'Forget it. It's impossible for one man to kill both of them. Impossible.'

'How much would these killers charge?'

'Millions. And it took a bunch of money to plan it all.'

'And you have no idea?'

'Look, Thomas, I'm not involved in the investigation, so you'll have to ask those guys. I'm sure they know a helluva lot more than I do. I'm just a lowly government lawyer.'

'Yeah, who just happens to be on a first-name basis with the Chief Justice.'

'He calls occasionally. This is boring. Let's get back to women. I hate lawyer talk.'

'Have you talked to him lately?'

'Picking, Thomas, always picking. Yes, we chatted briefly this morning. He's got all twenty-seven law clerks scouring the federal dockets high and low looking for clues. It's fruitless, and I told him so. Every case that reaches the Supreme Court has at least two parties, and each party involved would certainly benefit if one or two or three justices would disappear and be replaced by one or two or three more sympathetic to its cause. There are thousands of appeals that could eventually end up here, and you can't just pick one and say "This is it! This is the one that got 'em killed." It's silly.'

'What did he say?'

'Of course he agreed with my brilliant analysis. I think he called after he read the *Post* story to see if he could squeeze something out of me. Can you believe the nerve?'

The waiter hovered over them with a hurried look.

Verheek glanced at the menu, closed it, and handed it to him.

'Grilled swordfish, blue cheese, no vegetable.'

'I'll eat the mushrooms,' Callahan said. The waiter disappeared.

Callahan reached into his coat pocket and removed a thick envelope. He laid it on the table next to the empty Moosehead.

'Take a look at this when you get a chance.'

'What is it?'

'It's sort of a brief.'

'I hate briefs, Thomas. In fact, I hate the law, and the lawyers, and with the exception of you, I hate law professors.'

'Darby wrote it.'

'I'll read it tonight. What's it about?'

'I think I told you. She is very bright and intelligent, and a very aggressive student. She writes better than most. Her passion, other than me of course, is constitutional law.'

'Poor thing.'

'She took off four days last week, totally ignored me and the rest of the world, and came up with her own theory, which she has now discarded. But read it anyway. It's fascinating.'

'Who's the suspect?'

The Arabs erupted in screaming laughter, slapping each other and spilling whiskey. They watched them for a minute until they died down.

'Don't you hate a bunch of drunks?' Verheek said.

'It's sickening.'

Verheek stuffed the envelope into his coat on the back of his chair. 'What's her theory?'

'It's a bit unusual. But read it. I mean, it can't hurt, can it? You guys need the help.'

'I'll read it only because she wrote it. How is she in bed?'

'How's your wife in bed?'

'Rich. In the shower, in the kitchen, at the grocery. She's rich in everything she does.'

'It can't last.'

'She'll file by the end of the year. Maybe I'll get the townhouse and some change.'

'No prenuptial agreement?'

'Yes there is, but I'm a lawyer, remember. It's got more loopholes than a tax reform act. A buddy of mine prepared it. Don't you love the law?'

'Let's talk about something else.'

'Women?'

'I've got an idea. You want to meet the girl, right?'

'We're talking about Darby?'

'Yes. Darby.'

'I'd love to meet her.'

'We're going to St. Thomas during Thanksgiving. Why don't you meet us there?'

'Do I have to bring my wife?'

'No. She's not invited.'

'Will she run around in a little string job on the beach? Sort of put on a show for us?'

'Probably.'

'Wow. I can't believe this.'

'You can get a condo next to us, and we'll have a ball.'

'Beautiful, beautiful. Just beautiful.'

CHAPTER THIRTEEN

The phone rang four times, the answering machine clicked on, the recorded voice echoed through the apartment, the beep, then no message. It rang again four times, same routine, and no message. A minute later it rang again, and Gray Grantham grabbed it from bed. He sat on a pillow, trying to focus.

'Who is it?' he asked in pain. There was no light coming through the window.

The voice on the other end was low and timid. 'Is this Gray Grantham with the *Washington Post*?'

'It is. Who's calling?'

Slowly, 'I can't give you my name.'

The fog lifted and he focused on the clock. It was five-forty.

'Okay, forget the name. Why are you calling?'

'I saw your story yesterday about the White House and the nominees.

'That's good.' You and a million others. 'Why are you calling me at this obscene hour?'

'I'm sorry. I'm on my way to work and stopped at a pay phone. I can't call from home or the office.'

The voice was clear, articulate, and appeared to be intelligent. 'What kind of office?'

'I'm an attorney.'

Great. Washington was home for half a million lawyers. 'Private or government?'

A slight hesitation. 'Uh, I'd rather not say.'

'Okay. Look, I'd rather be sleeping. Why, exactly, did you call?'

'I may know something about Rosenberg and Jensen.'

Grantham sat on the edge of the bed. 'Such as –'

A much longer pause. 'Are you recording this?'

'No. Should I?'

'I don't know. I'm really very scared and confused, Mr. Grantham. I prefer not to record this. Maybe the next call, okay?'

'Whatever you want. I'm listening.'

'Can this call be traced?'

'Possibly, I guess. But you're at a pay phone, right? What difference does it make?'

'I don't know. I'm just scared.'

'It's okay. I swear I'm not recording and I swear I won't trace it. Now, what's on your mind?'

'Well, I think I may know who killed them.'

Grantham was standing. 'That's some pretty valuable knowledge.'

'It could get me killed. Do you think they're following me?'

'Who? Who would be following you?'

'I don't know.' The voice trailed off, as if he was looking over his shoulder.

Grantham was pacing by the bed. 'Relax. Why don't you tell me your name, okay. I swear it's confidential.'

'Garcia.'

'That's not a real name, is it?'

'Of course not, but it's the best I can do.'

'Okay, Garcia. Talk to me.'

'I'm not certain, okay. But I think I stumbled across something at the office that I was not supposed to see.'

'Do you have a copy of it?'

'Maybe.'

'Look, Garcia. You called me, right. Do you want to talk or not?'

'I'm not sure. What will you do if I tell you something?'

'Check it out thoroughly. If we're gonna accuse someone of the assassinations of two Supreme Court Justices, believe me, the story will be handled delicately.'

There was a very long silence. Grantham froze by the rocker and waited. 'Garcia. Are you there?'

'Yeah. Can we talk later?'

'Of course. We can talk now.'

'I need to think about this. I haven't eaten or slept in a week, and I'm not thinking rationally. I might call you later.'

'Okay, okay. That's fine. You can call me at work at –'

'No. I won't call you at work. Sorry I woke you.'

He hung up. Grantham looked at the row of numbers on his phone and punched seven digits, waited, then six more, then four more. He scribbled a number on a pad by the phone, and hung up. The pay phone was on Fifteenth Street in Pentagon City.

Gavin Verheek slept four hours and woke up drunk. When he arrived at the Hoover Building an hour later, the alcohol was fading and the pain was settling in. He cursed himself and he cursed Callahan, who no doubt would sleep until noon and wake up fresh and alive and ready for the flight to New Orleans. They had left the restaurant when it closed at midnight, then hit a few bars and joked about catching a skin flick or two, but since their favorite movie house had been bombed they couldn't. So they just drank until three or four.

He had a meeting with Director Voyles at eleven, and it was imperative to appear sober and alert. It would be impossible. He told his secretary to close the door, and explained to her that he had caught a nasty virus, maybe the flu, and he was to be left alone at his desk unless it was awfully damned important. She studied his eyes and seemed to sniff more than usual. The smell of beer does not always evaporate with sleep.

She left and closed the door behind her. He locked it. To make things equal, he called Callahan's room, but no one answered.

What a life. His best friend earned almost as much as he did, but worked thirty hours in a busy week, and had his pick of pliant young things twenty years his junior. Then he remembered their grand plans for the week in St. Thomas, and the thought of Darby strolling along the beach. He would go, even if it caused a divorce.

A wave of nausea rippled through his chest and up his esophagus, and he quickly lay still on the floor. Cheap government carpet. He breathed deeply, and the pounding started at the top of his head. The plaster ceiling was not spinning, and this was encouraging. After three minutes, it was evident he would not vomit, at least not now.

His briefcase was within reach, and he carefully slid it next to him. He found the envelope inside with the morning paper. He opened it, unfolded the brief, and held it with both hands six inches above his face.

It was thirteen letter-sized pages of computer paper, all double-spaced with wide margins. He could handle it. Notes were scribbled in the margins by hand and whole sections were marked through. The words FIRST DRAFT were handwritten with a felt pen across the top. Her name, address, and phone number were typed on the cover sheet.

He would skim it for a few minutes while he was on the floor, then hopefully he would feel like sitting at the desk and going through the motions of being an important government lawyer. He thought of Voyles, and the pounding intensified.

She wrote well, in the standard, scholarly legal fashion of long sentences filled with large words. But she was clear. She avoided the double-talk and legal lingo most students strive so desperately for. She would never make it as an attorney employed by the United States Government.

Gavin had never heard of her suspect, and was certain it was not on anyone's list. Technically, it was not a brief, but more of a story about a lawsuit in Louisiana. She told the facts succinctly, and made them interesting. Fascinating, really. He was not skimmimg.

The facts took four pages, then she filled the next three with brief histories of the parties. It dragged a bit here, but he kept reading. He was hooked. On page eight, the brief or whatever it was summarized the trial.

On nine, it mentioned the appeal, and the final three pages laid an implausible trail to the removal of Rosenberg and Jensen from the Court. Callahan said she had already discarded this theory, and she appeared to lose steam at the end.

But it was highly readable. For a moment he had forgotten his current state of pain, and read thirteen pages of a law student's brief while lying on the floor on dirty carpet with a million thing to do.

There was a soft knock at the door. He slowly sat up, gingerly stood, and walked to the door. 'Yes'.

It was the secretary. 'I hate to bother. But the Director wants you in his office in ten minutes.'

Verheek opened the door. 'What?'

'Yes sir. Ten minutes.'

He rubbed his eyes and breathed rapidly. 'What for?'

'I get demoted for asking those questions, sir.'

'Do you have any mouthwash?'

'Well, yes, I believe so. Do you want it?'

'I wouldn't have asked if I didn't want it. Bring it to me. Do you have any gum?'

'Gum?'

'Chewing gum.'

'Yes sir. Do you want it too?'

'Just bring me the mouthwash and gum, and some aspirin if you have it.' He walked to his desk and sat down, holding his head in his hands and rubbing his temples. He heard her banging drawers, and then she was before him with the goods.

'Thanks. I'm sorry I snapped.' He pointed at the brief in a chair by the door. 'Send that brief to Eric East, he's on the fourth floor. Write a note from me. Tell him to look it over when he has a minute.'

She left with the brief.

Fletcher Coal opened the door to the Oval Office, and spoke gravely to K. O. Lewis and Eric East. The President was in Puerto Rico viewing hurricane damage, and Director Voyles now refused to meet with Coal alone. He sent his underlings.

Coal waved them to a sofa, and he sat across the coffee table. His coat was buttoned and his tie was perfect. He never relaxed. East had heard tales about his habits. He worked twenty hours a day, seven days a week, drank nothing but water, and ate most meals from a vending machine in the basement. He could read like a computer, and spent hours each day reviewing memos, reports, correspondence, and mountains of pending legislation. He had perfect recall. For a week now they had brought daily reports of their investigation to this office, and handed them to Coal, who devoured the material and memorized it for the next metting. If they misstated something, he would terrorize them. He was hated, but it was impossible not to respect him. He was smarter than them, and he worked harder. And he knew it.

He was smug in the emptiness of the Oval Office. His boss was away performing for the cameras, but the real power had stayed behind to run the country.

K. O. Lewis placed a four-inch stack of the latest on the table.

'Anything new?' Coal asked.

'Maybe. The French authorities were routinely reviewing footage taken by the security cameras at the Paris airport, and they thought they recognized a face. The checked it against two other cameras in the concourse, different angles, then reported to Interpol. The face is disguised, but Interpol believes it is Khamel, the terrorist. I'm sure you've heard of –'

'I have.'

'They've studied the footage at length, and are almost certain he exited a plane that arrived nonstop from Dulles last Wednesday, about ten hours after Jensen was found.'

'The Concorde?'

'No, United. Based on the time and the locations of the cameras, they have ways of determining the gates and flights.'

'And Interpol contacted the CIA?'

'Yes. They talked to Gminski around one this afternoon.'

Coal's face registered nothing. 'How certain are they?'

'Eighty percent. He's a master of disguise, and it would be a bit unusual for him to travel in such a manner. So there's room for doubt. We've got photos and a summary for the President's review. Frankly, I've studied the pictures, and I can't tell anything. But Interpol knows him.'

'He hasn't been willingly photographed in years, has he?'

'Not that we know of. And rumor has it he goes under the knife and gets a new face every two or three years.'

Coal pondered this for a second. 'Okay. What if it's Khamel, and what if he was involved in the killings? What does it mean?'

'It means we'll never find him. There are at least nine countries, including Israel, actively stalking him right now. It means he was paid a bunch of money by someone to use his talents here. We've said all along the killer or killers were professionals who were gone before the bodies were cold.'

'So it means little.'

'You could say that.'

'Fine. What else do you have?'

Lewis glanced at Eric East. 'Well, we have the usual daily summary.'

'They've been rather dry as of late.'

'Yes, they have. We have three hundred and eighty agents working twelve hours a day. Yesterday they interviewed one hundred and sixty people in thirty states. We have –'

Coal held up his hand. 'Save it. I'll read the summary. It seems safe to say there is nothing new.'

'Maybe a small new wrinkle.' Lewis looked at Eric East, who was holding a copy of the brief.

'What is it?' Coal asked.

East shifted uncomfortably. The brief had been passed upward all day until Voyles read it and liked it. He viewed it as a long shot, unworthy of serious attention, but the brief mentioned the President, and he loved the idea of making Coal and his boss sweat. He instructed Lewis and East to deliver the brief to Coal, and to treat it as an important theory the Bureau was taking seriously. For the first time in a week, Voyles had smiled when he talked of the idiots in the Oval Office reading this little brief and running for cover. Play it up, Voyles said. Tell them we intend to pursue with twenty agents.

'It's a theory that has surfaced in the last twenty-four hours, and Director Voyles is quite intrigued by it. He's afraid it could be damaging to the President.'

Coal was stone-faced, never flinching. 'How's that?'

East placed the brief on the table. 'It's all here in this report.'

Coal glanced at it, then studied East. 'Fine. I'll read it later. Is that all?'

Lewis stood and buttoned his jacket. 'Yes, we'll be going.'

Coal followed them to the door.

THERE WAS NO FANFARE when Air Force One landed at Andrews a few minutes after ten. The Queen was off raising money, and no friends or family greeted the President as he bounced off the plane and darted into his limousine. Coal was waiting. The President sunk low in the seat. 'I didn't expect you,' he said.

'I'm sorry. We need to talk.' The limo sped away toward the White House.

'It's late and I'm tired.'

'How was the hurricane?'

'Impressive. It blew away a million shacks and cardboard huts, and now we'll rush down with a couple of billion and build new homes and power plants. They need a good hurricane every five years.'

'I've got the disaster declaration ready.'

'Okay. What's so important?'

Coal handed over a copy of what was now known as the pelican brief.

'I don't want to read,' said the President. 'Just tell me about it.'

'Voyles and his motley crew have stumbled across a suspect that no one has mentioned until now. A most obscure, unlikely suspect. An eager-beaver law student at Tulane wrote this damned thing, and it somehow made its way to Voyles, who read it and decided it had merit. Keep in mind, they are desperate for suspects. The theory is so farfetched it's incredible, and on its face it doesn't worry me. But Voyles worries me. He's decided he must pursue with enthusiasm, and the press is watching every move he makes. There could be leaks.'

'We can't control his investigation.'

'We can manipulate it. Gminski is waiting at the White House, and –'

'Gminski!'

'Relax, Chief. I personally handed him a copy of this three hours ago, and swore him to secrecy. He may be incompetent, but he can keep a secret. I trust him much more than Voyles.'

'I don't trust either one of them.'

Coal liked to hear this. He wanted the President to trust no one but him. 'I think you should ask the CIA to immediately investigate this. I would like to know everything before Voyles starts digging. Neither will find anything, but if we know more than Voyles, you can convince him to back off. It makes sense, Chief.'

The President was frustrated. 'It's domestic. CIA has no business snooping around. It's probably illegal.'

'It is illegal, technically. But Gminski will do it for you, and he can do it quickly, secretly, and more thoroughly than the FBI.'

'It's illegal.'

'It's been done before, Chief, many times.'

The President watched the traffic. His eyes were puffy and red, but not from fatigue. He had slept three hourse on the plane. But he'd spent the day looking sad and concerned for the cameras, and it was hard to snap out of it.

He took the brief and tossed it on the empty seat next to him. 'Is it someone we know?'

'Yes.'

CHAPTER FOURTEEN

Because it is a city of the night, New Orleans wakes slowly. It's quiet until well after dawn, then shakes the cobwebs and eases into the morning. There's no early rush except on the corridors to and from the suburbs, and the busy streets downtown. This is the same for all cities. But in the French Quarter, the soul of New Orleans, the smell of last night's whiskey and jambalaya and blackened redfish lingers not far above the empty streets until the sun can be seen. An hour or two later, it is replaced with the aroma of French Market coffee and beignets, and around this time the sidewalks reluctantly show signs of life.

Darby curled herself in a chair on the small balcony, sipping coffee and waiting on the sun. Callahan was a few feet away, through the open french doors, still wrapped in sheets and dead to the world. There was a trace of a breeze, but the humidity would return by noon. She pulled his robe closer around her neck, and inhaled the richness of his cologne. She thought of her father, and his baggy cotton button-downs he allowed her to wear when she was a teenager. She would roll the sleeves tightly to her elbows and let the tails hang to her knees, then walk the malls with her friends, secure in her belief that no one was cooler. Her father was her friend. By the time she finished high school, she had the run of his closet, as long as things were washed and neatly pressed and put back on the hangers. She could still smell the Grey Flannel he splashed on his face every day.

If he was living, he would be four years older than Thomas Callahan. Her mother had remarried and moved to Boise. Darby had a brother in Germany. The three seldom talked. Her father had been the glue in a fractious family, and his death had scattered them.

Twenty other people died in the plane crash, and before the funeral arrangements were complete the lawyers were calling. It was her first real exposure to the legal world, and it was not pleasant. The family attorney was a real estate type who knew nothing about litigation. A slick ambulance chaser got next to her brother, and he persuaded the family to sue quickly. His name was Herschel, and for two years the family suffered as Herschel stalled and lied and bungled the case. They settled a week before trial for half a million, after Herschel's cut, and Darby got a hundred thousand.

She decided to be a lawyer. If a clown like Herschel could do it and make big bucks while wreaking havoc on society, then she certainly could do it for a nobler purpose. She thought of Herschel often. When she passed the bar exam, her first lawsuit would be filed against him for malpractice. She wanted to work for an environmental firm. Finding a job, she knew, would not be a problem.

The hundred thousand was intact. Her mother's new husband was a paper company executive who was a little older and a lot wealthier, and shortly after their marriage she divided her portion of the settlement between Darby and her brother. She said the money reminded her of her deceased husband, and the gesture was symbolic. Though she still loved their father, she had a new life in a new city with a new husband who would retire in five years with money to burn. Darby had been confused by the symbolic gesture, but appreciated it and took the money.

The hundred thousand had doubled. She placed most of it in mutual funds, but only in those without holdings in chemical and petroleum companies. She drove an Accord and lived modestly. Her wardrobe was basic law school, purchased from factory outlet stores. She and Callahan enjoyed the better restaurants in town, and never ate at the same place twice. It was always Dutch treat.

He cared little for money, and never pressed her for information. She had more than the typical law student, but Tulane had its share of rich kids.

They dated for a month before they went to bed. She laid the ground rules, and he anxiously agreed to them. There would be no other women. They would be very discreet. And he had to stop drinking so much.

He stuck to the first two, but the drinking continued. His father, grandfather, and brothers were heavy drinkers, and it was sort of expected of him. But for the first time in his life, Thomas Callahan was in love, madly in love, and he knew the point at which the Scotch was interfering with his woman. He was careful. With the exception of last week and the personal trauma of losing Rosenberg, he never drank before 5 P.M. When they were together, he abandoned the Chivas when he'd had enough and thought it might affect his performance.

It was amusing to watch a forty-five-year-old man fall for the first time. He struggled to maintain a level of coolness, but in their private little moments he was as silly as a sophomore.

She kissed him on the cheek, and covered him with a quilt. Her clothes were placed neatly on a chair. She locked the front door quietly behind her. The sun was up now, peeking through the buildings across Dauphine. The sidewalk was empty.

She had a class in three hours, then Callahan and con law at eleven. There was a mock court appellate brief due in a week. Her casenote for law review was gathering dust. She was behind in classwork for two courses. It was time to be a student again. She had wasted four days playing detective, and she cursed herself for it.

The Accord was around the corner and down a half a block.

They watched her, and it was enjoyable. Tight jeans, baggy sweater, long legs, sunglasses to hide the eyes with no makeup. They watched her close the door and walk quickly along Royale, then disappear around the corner. The hair was shoulder-length and appeared to be dark red.

It was her.

He carried his lunch in a little brown paper bag, and found an empty park bench with his back to New Hampshire. He hated Dupont Circle, with its bums, druggies, perverts, aging hippies, and black-leather punks with red spiked hair and vicious tongues. Across the fountain, a well-dressed man with a loudspeaker was assembling his group of animal rights activists for a march to the White House. The leather people jeered and cursed them, but four mounted policemen were close enough to prevent trouble.

He looked at his watch and peeled a banana. Noon, and he preferred to eat elsewhere. The meeting would be brief. He watched the cursing and jeering, and saw his contact emerge through the crowd. Their eyes met, a nod, and he was sitting on the bench next to him. His name was Booker, from Langley. They met here occasionally, when the lines of communication became tangled or blurred and their bosses needed to hear real words that no one else would hear.

Booker had no lunch. He began shelling roasted peanuts and throwing the hulls under the circular bench. 'How's Mr. Voyles?'

'Mean as hell. The usual.'

He threw peanuts in his mouth. 'Gminski was in the White House until midnight las night,' Booker said.

There was no response to this. Voyles knew it.

Booker continued. 'They've panicked over there. This little pelican thing has scared them. We've read it too, you know, and we're almost certain you guys are not impressed, but for some reason Coal is terrified of it and he's got the President upset. We sort of figure you guys are just having a little fun with Coal and his boss, and since the brief mentions the President and has that photo in it, we figure it's sort of fun for you guys. Know what I mean?'

He took an inch off the banana, and said nothing.

The animal lovers moved away in ragged formation as the leather lovers hissed at them.

'Anyway, it's none of our business, and should be none of our business except the President now wants us to secretly investigate the pelican brief before you guys can get to it. He's convinced we'll find nothing, and he wants to know there's nothing to it so he can convince Voyles to back off.'

'There's nothing to it.'

Booker watched a drunk urinate in the fountain. The cops were riding off into the sun. 'Then Voyles is having a little fun, right?'

'We are pursuing all leads.'

'No real suspects, though?'

'No.' The banana was history. 'Why are they so worried about us investigating this little thing?'

Booker crunched on a small peanut still in the hull. 'Well, to them it's quite simple. They are livid over the revelation of Pryce and MacLawrence as nominees, and of course it's all your fault. They distrust Voyles immensely. And if you guys start digging into the pelican brief, they're terrified the press will find out and the President will take a beating. Reelection is next year, blah, blah, blah.'

'What did Gminski tell the President?'

'That he had no desire to interfere with an FBI investigation, that we had better things to do, and that it would be illegal as hell. But since the President was begging so hard and Coal was threatening so much, we'd do it anyway. And here I am talking to you.'

'Voyles appreciates it.'

'We're gonna start digging today, but the whole thing is absurd. We'll go through the motions, stay out of the way, and in a week or so tell the president the whole theory is a shot in the dark.'

He folded down the top of his brown bag, and stood. 'Good. I'll report to Voyles. Thanks.' He walked toward Connecticut, away from the leather punks, and was gone.

The monitor was on a cluttered table in the center of the newsroom, and Gray Grantham glared at it amid the hum and roar of the gathering and reporting. The words were not coming, and he sat and glared. The phone rang. He punched his button, and grabbed the receiver without leaving the monitor.

'Gray Grantham.'

'It's Garcia.'

He forgot the monitor. 'Yeah, so what's up?'

'I have two questions. First, do you record these calls, and second, can you trace them?'

'No and yes. We don't record until we ask permission, and we can trace but we don't. I thought you said you would not call me at work.'

'Do you want me to hang up?'

'No. It's fine. I'd rather talk at 3 P.M. at the office than 6 A.M. in bed.'

'Sorry. I'm just scared, that's all. I'll talk to you as long as I can trust you, but if you ever lie to me, Mr. Grantham, I'll quit talking.'

'It's a deal. When do you start talking?'

'I can't talk now. I'm at a pay phone downtown, and I'm in a hurry.'

'You said you had a copy of something.'

'No, I said I might have a copy of something. We'll see.'

'Okay. So when might you call again?'

'Do I have to make an appointment?'

'No. But I'm in and out a lot.'

'I'll call during lunch tomorrow.'

'I'll be waiting right here.'

Garcia was gone. Grantham punched seven digits, then six, then four. He wrote the number, then flipped through the yellow pages until he found Pay Phones Inc. The Vendor Location listed the number on Pennsylvania Avenue near the Justice Department.

CHAPTER FIFTEEN

The argument started with dessert, a portion of the meal Callahan preferred to drink. She was nice enough when she clicked off the drinks he'd already consumed with dinner: two double Scotches while they waited on a table, one more before they ordered, and with the fish two bottles of wine, of which she'd had two glasses. He was drinking too fast and getting sloppy, and by the time she finished rattling off this accounting he was angry. He ordered Drambuie for desssert, because it was his favorite, and because it was suddenly a matter of principle. He gulped it and she was furious.

Darby spooned her coffee and ignored him. Mouton's was packed, and she just wanted to leave without a scene and get to her apartment alone.

The argument turned nasty on the sidewalk as they walked away from the restaurant. He pulled they keys to the Porsche from his pocket, and she said he was too drunk to drive. Give her the keys. He gripped them and staggered on in the direction of the parking lot, three blocks away. She said she would walk. Have a nice one, he said. She followed a few steps behind, embarrassed at the stumbling figure in front of her. She pleaded with him. His blood level was at least point-two-zero. He was a law professor, dammit. He would kill someone. He staggered faster, coming perilously close to the curb, then weaving away. He yelled over his shoulder, something about driving better drunk than she could sober. She fell behind. She'd taken a ride before when he was like this, and she knew what a drunk could do in a Porsche.

He crossed the street blindly, hands stuck deep in his pockets as if out for a casual stroll in the late night. He misjudged the curb, hit it with the toes instead of the sole, and went sprawling and bouncing and cursing along the sidewalk. He scrambled up quickly before she could reach him. Leave me alone, dammit, he told her. Just give me the keys, she begged, or I'm walking. He shoved her away. Have a nice one, he said with a laugh. She'd never seen him this drunk. He'd never touched her in anger, drunk or not.

Next to the parking lot was a greasy little dive with neon beer signs covering the windows. She looked inside the open door for help, but thought, how stupid. It was filled with drunks.

She yelled at him as he approached the Porsche. 'Thomas! Please! Let me drive!' She was on the sidewalk and would go no farther.

He stumbled on, waving her off, mumbling to himself. He unlocked the door, squeezed downward, and disappeared between the other cars. The engine started and roared as he gunned it.

Darby leaned on the side of the building a few feet from the parking lot's exit. She looked at the street, and almost hoped for a cop. She would rather have him arrested than dead.

It was too far to walk. She would watch him drive away, then call a cab, then ignore him for a week. At least a week. Have a nice one, she repeated to herself. He gunned it again and squealed tires.

The explosion knocked her to the sidewalk. She landed on all fours, face down, stunned for a second, then immediately aware of the heat and the tiny pieces of fiery debris falling in the street. She gaped in horror at the parking lot. The Porsche flipped in a perfect violent somersault and landed upside down. The tires and wheels and doors and fenders slung free. The car was a brilliant fireball, roaring away with flames instantly devouring it.

Darby started toward it, screaming for him. Debris fell around her and the heat slowed her. She stopped thirty feet away, screaming with hands over her mouth.

Then a second explosion flipped it again and drove her away. She tripped, and her head fell hard on the bumper of another car. The pavement was hot to her face, and that was the last she remembered for a moment.

The dive emptied and the drunks were everywhere. They stood along the sidewalk and stared. A couple tried to advance, but the heat reddened their faces and kept them away. Thick, heavy smoke billowed from the fireball, and within seconds two other cars were on fire. There were shouts and voices in panic.

'Whose car is it!'

'Call 911!'

'Is anybody in it!'

'Call 911!'

They dragged her by the elbows back to the sidewalk, to the center of the crowd. She was repeating the name Thomas. A cold cloth came from the dive and was placed on her forehead.

The crowd thickened and the street was busy. Sirens, she heard sirens as she came around. There was a knot on the back of her head, and a coldness on her face. Her mouth was dry. 'Thomas. Thomas,' she repeated.

'It's okay, it's okay,' said a black face just above her. He was carefully holding her head and patting her arm. Other faces stared downward. They all nodded in agreement. 'It's okay.'

The sirens were screaming now. She gently removed the cloth, and her eyes focused. There were red and blue lights flashing from the street.

The sirens were deafening. She sat up. They leaned her against the building beneath the neon beer signs. They eased away, watching her carefully.

'You all right, miss?' asked the black man.

She couldn't answer. Didn't try to. Her head was broken. 'Where is Thomas?' she asked, looking at the crack in the sidewalk.

They looked at each other. The first fire truck screamed to a halt twenty feet away, and the crowd parted. Firemen jumped and scrambled in all directions.

'Where is Thomas?' she repeated.

'Miss, who is Thomas?' asked the black man.

'Thomas Callahan,' she said softly, as if everyone knew him.

'Was he in that car?'

She nodded, then closed her eyes. The sirens wailed and died, and in between she heard the shouts of anxious men, and the popping of the fire. She could smell the burning.

The second and third fire trucks came blaring in from different directions. A cop shoved his way through the crowd. 'Police. Outta the way. Police.' He pushed and shoved until he found her. He fell to his knees and waved a badge under her nose. 'Ma'am, Sergeant Rupert, NOPD.'

Darby heard this but thought nothing of it. He was in her face, this Rupert with bushy hair, a baseball cap, black and gold Saints jacket. She stared blankly at him.

'Is that your car, ma'am? Someone said it was your car.'

She shook her head. No.

Rupert was grabbing her elbows and pulling up. He was talking to her, asking if she was all right, and at the same time pulling her up and it hurt like hell. The head was fractured, split, busted, and she was in shock but what did this moron care. She was on her feet. The knees wouldn't lock, and she was limp. He kept asking if she was all right. The black man looked at Rupert as if he was crazy.

There, the legs worked now, and she and Rupert were walking through the crowd, behind a fire truck, around another one to an unmarked cop car. She lowered her head and refused to look at the parking lot. Rupert chatted incessantly. Something about an ambulance. He opened the front door and gingerly placed her in the passenger's seat.

Another cop squatted in the door and started asking questions. He wore jeans and cowboy boots with pointed toes. Darby leaned forward and placed her head in her hands. 'I think I need help,' she said.

'Sure, lady. Help's on the way. Just a coupla questions. What's your name?'

'Darby Shaw. I think I'm in shock. I'm very dizzy, and I think I need to throw up.'

'The ambulance is on the way. Is that your car over there?'

'No.'

Another cop car, one with decals and words and lights, squealed to a stop in front of Rupert's. Rupert disappeared for a moment. The cowboy cop suddenly closed her door, and she was all alone in the car. She leaned forward and vomited between her legs. She started crying. She was cold. She slowly laid her head on the driver's seat, and curled into a knot. Silence. Then darkness.

Someone was knocking on the window above her. She opened her eyes, and the man wore a uniform and a hat with a badge on it. The door was locked.

'Open the door, lady!' he yelled.

She sat up and opened the door. 'Are you drunk, lady?'

The head was pounding. 'No,' she said desperately.

He opened the door wider. 'Is this your car?'

She rubbed her eyes. She had to think.

'Lady, is this your car?'

'No!' She glared at him. 'No. It's Rupert's.'

'Okay. Who the hell is Rupert?'

There was one fire truck left and most of the crowd was gone. This man in the door was obviously a cop. 'Sergeant Rupert. One of you guys,' she said.

This made him mad. 'Get outta the car, lady.'

Gladly. Darby crawled out on the passenger's side, and stood on the sidewalk. In the distance, a solitary fireman hosed down the burnt frame of the Porsche.

Another cop in a uniform joined him and they met her on the sidewalk.

The first cop asked, 'What's your name?'

'Darby Shaw.'

'Why were you passed out in the car?'

She looked at the car. 'I don't know. I got hurt and Rupert put me in the car. Where's Rupert?'

The cops looked at each other. 'Who the hell's Rupert?' the first cop asked.

This made her mad and the anger cleared away the cobwebs.

'Rupert said he was a cop.'

The second cop asked, 'How'd you get hurt?'

Darby glared at him. She pointed to the parking lot across the street.

'I was supposed to be in that car over there. But I wasn't, so I'm here, listening to your stupid questions. Where's Rupert?'

They looked blankly at each other. The first cop said, 'Stay here,' and he walked across the street to another cop car where a man in a suit was talking to a small group. They whispered, then the first cop and the man in the suit walked back to the sidewalk where Darby waited. The man in the suit said, 'I'm Lieutenant Olson, New Orleans PD. Did you know the man in the car?' He pointed to the parking lot.

The knees went weak, and she bit her lip. She nodded.

'What's his name?'

'Thomas Callahan.'

Olson looked at the first cop. 'That's what the computer said. Now, who's this Rupert?'

Darby screamed. 'He said he was a cop!'

Olson looked sympathetic. 'I'm sorry. There's no cop named Rupert.'

She was sobbing loudly. Olson helped her to the hood of Rupert's car, and held her shoulders while the crying subsided and she fought to regain control.

'Check the plates,' Olson told the second cop, who quickly scribbled down the tag number from Rupert's car and called it in.

Olson gently held both her shoulders with his hands and looked at her eyes. 'Were you with Callahan?'

She nodded, still crying but much quieter. Olson glanced at the first cop.

'How did you get in this car?' Olson asked slowly and softly.

She wiped her eyes with her finger and stared at Olson. 'This guy Rupert, who said he was a cop, came and got me from over there, and brought me over here. He put me in the car, and this other cop with cowboy boots starting asking questions. Another cop car pulled up, and they left. Then I guess I passed out. I don't know. I would like to see a doctor.'

'Get my car,' Olson said to the first cop.

The second cop was back with a puzzled look. 'The computer has no record of this tag number. Must be fake tags.'

Olson took her arm and led her to his car. He spoke quickly to the two cops. 'I'm taking her to Charity. Wrap this up and meet me there. Impound the car. We'll check it later.'

She sat in Olson's car listening to the radio squawk and staring at the parking lot. Four cars had burned. The Porsche was upside down in the center, nothing but a crumpled frame. A handful of firemen and other emergency types milled about. A cop was stringing yellow crime-scene tape around the lot.

She touched the knot on the back of her head. No blood. Tears dripped off her chin.

Olson slammed his door, and they eased through the parked cars and headed for St. Charles. He had the blue lights on, but no sirens.

'Do you feel like talking?' he asked.

They were on St. Charles. 'I guess,' she said. 'He's dead, isn't he?'

'Yes, Darby. I'm sorry. I take it he was the only one in the car.'

'Yes.'

'How'd you get hurt?'

He gave her a handkerchief, and she wiped her eyes. 'I fell or something. There were two explosions, and I think the second one knocked me down. I don't remember everything. Please, tell me who Rupert is.'

'I have no idea. I don't know a cop named Rupert, and there was no cop here with cowboy boots.'

She thought about this for a block and a half.

'What did Callahan do for a living?'

'A law professor at Tulane. I'm a student there.'

'Who would want to kill him?'

She stared at the traffic lights and shook her head. 'You're certain it was intentional?'

'No doubt about it. It was a very powerful explosive. We found a piece of a foot stuck in a chain-link fence eighty feet away. I'm sorry, okay. He was murdered.'

'Maybe someone got the wrong car.'

'That's always possible. We'll check out everything. I take it you were supposed to be in the car with him.'

She tried to speak, but could not hold the tears. She buried her face in the handkerchief.

He parked between two ambulances near the emergency entrance at Charity, and left the blue lights on. He helped her quickly inside to a dirty room where fifty people sat in various degrees of pain and discomfort. She found a seat by the water fountain. Olson talked to the lady behind the window, and he raised his voice but Darby couldn't understand him. A small boy with a bloody towel around his foot cried in his mother's lap. A young black girl was about to give birth. There was not a doctor or nurse in sight. No one was in a hurry.

Olson crouched in front of her. 'It'll be a few minutes. Sit tight. I'm gonna move the car, and I'll be back in a minute. Do you feel like talking?'

'Yeah, sure.'

He was gone. She checked again for blood, and found none. The double doors opened wide, and two angry nurses came after the girl in labor. They sort of dragged her away, back through the doors and down the hall.

Darby waited, then followed. With the red eyes and handkerchief, she looked like some child's mother. The hall was a zoo with nurses and orderlies and the wounded yelling and moving about. She turned a corner and saw an EXIT sign. Through the door, into another hall, much quieter, another door, and she was on a loading dock. There were lights in the alley. Don't run. Be strong. It's okay. No one's watching. She was on the street, walking briskly. The cool air cleared her eyes. She refused to cry.

Olson would take his time, and when he returned he would figure they had called her name and she was back there getting worked on. He would wait. And wait.

She turned corners, and saw Rampart. The Quarter was just ahead. She could get lost there. There were people on Royal, tourist types strolling along. She felt safer. She entered the Holiday Inn, paid with plastic, and got a room on the fifth floor. After the door was bolted and chained, she curled up on the bed with all the lights on.

Mrs. Verheek rolled her plump but rich ass away from the center of the bed, and grabbed the phone. 'It's for you, Gavin!' she yelled into the bathroom. Gavin emerged with shaving cream on half his face, and took the receiver from his wife, who burrowed deep into the bed. Like a hog rutting in mud, he thought.

'Hello,' he snapped.

It was a female voice he'd never heard before. 'This is Darby Shaw. Do you know who I am?'

He smiled instantly, and for a second thought of the string bikini on St. Thomas. 'Well, yes. I believe we have a mutual friend.'

'Did you read the little theory I wrote?'

'Ah, yes. The pelican brief, as we refer to it.'

'And who is we?'

Verheek sat in a chair by the night table. This was no social call. 'Why are you calling, Darby?'

'I need some answers, Mr. Verheek. I'm scared to death.'

'It's Gavin, okay?'

'Gavin. Where is the brief now?'

'Here and there. What's wrong?'

'I'll tell you in a minute. Just tell me what you did with the brief.'

'Well, I read it, then sent it to another division, and it was seen by some folks within the Bureau, then shown to Director Voyles, who sort of liked it.'

'Has it been seen outside the FBI?'

'I can't answer that, Darby.'

'Then I won't tell you what's happened to Thomas.'

Verheek pondered this for a long minute. She waited patiently. 'Okay. Yes, it's been seen outside the FBI. By whom and by how many, I don't know.'

'He's dead, Gavin. He was murdered around ten last night. Someone planted a car bomb for both of us. I got lucky, but now they're after me.'

Verheek was hovering over the phone, scribbling notes. 'Are you hurt?'

'Physically, I'm okay.'

'Where are you?'

'New Orleans.'

'Are you certain, Darby? I mean, I know you're certain, but, dammit, who would want to kill him?'

'I met a couple of them.'

'How'd you –'

'It's a long story. Who saw the brief, Gavin? Thomas gave it to you Monday night. It's been passed around, and forty-eight hours later he's dead. And I'm supposed to be dead with him. It fell into the wrong hands, wouldn't you say?'

'Are you safe?'

'Who the hell knows?'

'Where are you staying? What's your phone number?'

'Not so fast, Gavin. I'm moving real slow right now. I'm at a pay phone, so no cute stuff.'

'Come on, Darby! Give me a break! Thomas Callahan was my best friend. You've got to come in.'

'And what might that mean?'

'Look, Darby, give me fifteen minutes, and we'll have a dozen agents pick you up. I'll catch a flight and be there before noon. You can't stay on the streets.'

'Why, Gavin? Who's after me? Talk to me, Gavin.'

'I'll talk to you when I get there.'

'I don't know. Thomas is dead because he talked to you. I'm not that anxious to meet you right now.'

'Darby, look, I don't know who or why, but I assure you you're in a very dangerous situation. We can protect you.'

'Maybe later.'

He breathed deeply and sat on the edge of the bed. 'You can trust me, Darby.'

'Okay, I trust you. But what about those other people? This is heavy, Gavin. My little brief has someone awfully upset, wouldn't you say?'

'Did he suffer?'

She hesitated. 'I don't think so.' The voice was cracking.

'Will you call me in two hours? At the office. I'll give you an inside number.'

'Give me the number, and I'll think about it.'

'Please, Darby. I'll go straight to the Director when I get there. Call me at eight, your time.'

'Give me the number.'

The bomb exploded too late to make the Thursday morning edition of the *Times-Picayune*. Darby flipped through it hurriedly in the hotel room. Nothing. She watched the television, and there it was. A live shot of the burned-out Porsche, still sitting amid the debris in the parking lot, secluded nicely with yellow tape running everywhere. The police were treating it as a homicide. No suspects. No comment. Then the name of Thomas Callahan, age forty-five, a prominent professor of law at Tulane. The dean was suddenly there with a microphone in his face, talking about Professor Callahan and the shock of it all.

The shock of it all, the fatigue, the fear, the pain, and Darby buried her head in the pillow. She hated crying, and this would be the last of it for a while. Mourning would only get her killed.

CHAPTER SIXTEEN

Even though it was a wonderful crisis, with the ratings up and Rosenberg dead, with his image clean and polished and America feeling good about itself because he was in command, with the Democrats running for cover and reelection next year in the bag, he was sick of this crisis and its relentless predawn meetings. He was sick of F. Denton Voyles and his smugness and arrogance, and his squatty little figure sitting on the other side of his desk in a wrinkled trench coat looking out a window while he addressed the President of the United States. He would be here in a minute for another meeting before breakfast, another tense encounter in which Voyles would tell only a portion of what he knew.

He was sick of being in the dark, and fed only what bits and crumbs Voyles chose to throw his way. Gminski would throw him a few, and somehow in the midst of all this crumb scattering and gathering he was supposed to get enough and be satisfied. He knew nothing compared to them. At least he had Coal to plow through their paper and memorize it all, and keep them honest.

He was sick of Coal, too. Sick of his perfectness and sleeplessness. Sick of his brilliance. Sick of his penchant for beginning each day when the sun was somewhere over the Atlantic, and planning every damned minute of every damned hour until it was over the Pacific. Then he, Coal, would load up a box of the day's junk, take it home, read it, decipher it, store it, then come in a few hours later blazing away with all the painfully boring mishmash he had just devoured. When Coal was tired, he slept five hours a night, but normal was three or four. He left his office in the West Wing at eleven each night, read all the way home in the back of his limo, then about the time the limo cooled off Coal was waiting on it for the return ride to the White House. He considered it a sin to arrive at his desk after 5 A.M. And if he could work a hundred and twenty hours a week, then everyone else should be able to do at least eighty. He demanded eighty. After three years, no one in this Administration could remember all the people fired by Fletcher Coal for not working eighty hours a week. Happened at least three times a month.

Coal was happiest on mornings when the tension was thick and a nasty meeting was planned. In the past week this thing with Voyles had kept him smiling. He was standing beside the desk, going through the mail while the President scanned the *Post* and two secretaries scurried about.

The President glanced at him. Perfect black suit, white shirt, red silk tie, a bit too much grease on the hair above the ears. He was sick of him, but he'd get over it when the crisis passed and he could get back to golf and Coal could sweat the details. He told himself he had that kind of energy and stamina when he was only thirty-seven, but he knew better.

Coal snapped his fingers, glared at the secretaries, and they happily ran from the Oval Office.

'And he said he wouldn't come if I was here. That's hilarious.' Coal was clearly amused.

'I don't think he likes you,' the President said.

'He loves people he can run over.'

'I guess I need to be sweet to him.'

'Lay it on thick, Chief. He has to back off. This theory is so weak it's comical, but in his hands it could be dangerous.'

'What about the law student?'

'We're checking. She appears harmless.'

The President stood and stretched. Coal shuffled papers. A secretary on the intercom announced the arrival of Voyles.

'I'll be going,' Coal said. He would listen and watch from around the corner. At his insistence, three closed-circuit cameras were installed in the Oval Office. The monitors were in a small, locked room in the West Wing. He had the only key. Sarge knew of the room, but had not bothered to enter. Yet. The cameras were invisible and supposedly a big secret.

The President felt better knowing Coal would at least be watching. He met Voyles at the door with a warm handshake and guided him to the sofa for a warm, friendly little chat. Voyles was not impressed. He knew Coal would be listening. And watching.

But in the spirit of the moment, Voyles removed his trench coat and laid it properly on a chair. He did not want coffee.

The President crossed his legs. He was wearing the brown cardigan. The grandfather.

'Denton,' he said gravely. 'I want to apologize for Fletcher Coal. He doesn't have much finesse.'

Voyles nodded slightly. You stupid bastard. There are enough wires in this office to electrocute half the bureaucrats in D.C. Coal was somewhere in the basement hearing about his lack of finesse. 'He can be an ass, can't he?' Voyles grunted.

'Yes, he can. I have to really watch him. He's very bright and drives hard, but he tends to overdo it at times.'

'He's a son of a bitch, and I'll say it to his face.' Voyles glanced at an air vent above the portrait of Thomas Jefferson where a camera watched it all below.

'Yes, well, I'll keep him out of your way until this thing is over.'

'You do that.'

The President slowly sipped from his coffee and pondered what to say next. Voyles was not known for his conversation.

'I need a favor.'

Voyles stared with rigid and unblinking eyes. 'Yes, sir.'

'I need the scoop on this pelican thing. It's a wild idea, but, hell, it mentions me, sort of. How serious are you taking it?'

Oh, this was funny. Voyles fought off a smile. It was working. Mr. President and Mr. Coal were sweating the pelican brief. They had received it late Tuesday, worried with it all day Wednesday, and now in the waking hours of Thursday were on their knees begging about something one notch above a practical joke.

'We're investigating, Mr. President.' It was a lie, but how could he know? 'We are pursuing all leads, all suspects. I wouldn't have sent it over if I wasn't serious.' The wrinkles squeezed together on the tanned forehead, and Voyles wanted to laugh.

'What have you learned?'

'Not much, but we just started. We got it less than forty-eight hours ago, and I assigned fourteen agents in New Orleans to start digging. It's all routine.' The lies sounded so good he could almost hear Coal choking.

Fourteen! It hit him in the gut so hard he sat up straight and placed the coffee on a table. Fourteen Fibbies out there flashing badges, asking questions, and it was just a matter of time before this thing got out. 'Fourteen, you say. Sounds like it's pretty serious.'

Voyles was unyielding. 'We're very serious, Mr. President. They've been dead a week, and the trail's growing colder. We're tracking leads as fast as we can. My men are working around the clock.'

'I understand all that, but how serious is this pelican theory?'

Damn, this was fun. The brief had yet to be sent to New Orleans. In fact, New Orleans had not been contacted. He had instructed Eric East to mail a copy to that office with orders to quietly ask a few questions. It was a dead end, just like a hundred others they were chasing.

'I doubt if there's anything to it, Mr. President, but we've got to check it out.'

The wrinkles relaxed and there was a touch of a smile. 'I don't have to tell you, Denton, how much this nonsense could hurt if the press found out.'

'We don't consult the press when we investigate.'

'I know. Let's not get into that. I just wish you would back off this thing. I mean, what the hell, it's absurd, and I could really get burned. Know what I'm saying?'

Voyles was brutal. 'Are you asking me to ignore a suspect, Mr. President?'

Coal leaned toward the screen. No, I'm telling you to forget this pelican brief! He almost said it out loud. He could make it real plain for Voyles. He could spell it out, then slap the dumpy little wretch if he got smart. But he was hiding in a locked room, away from the action. And, for the moment, he knew he was where he belonged.

The President shifted and recrossed his legs at the knees. 'Come on, Denton, you know what I'm saying. There are bigger fish in the pond. The press is watching this investigation, just dying to find out who's a suspect. You know how they are. I don't have to tell you that I have no friends with the press. Even my own press secretary dislikes me. Ha, ha, ha. Forget about it for a while. Back off and chase the real suspects. This thing is a joke, but it could embarrass the hell out of me.'

Denton looked hard at him. Relentless.

The President shifted again. 'What about this Khamel thing? Sounds pretty good, huh?'

'Could be.'

'Yeah. Since we're talking numbers, how many men have you assigned to Khamel?'

Voyles said, 'Fifteen,' and almost laughed. The President's mouth fell open. The hottest suspect in the game gets fifteen, and this damned pelican thing gets fourteen.

Coal smiled and shook his head. Voyles had been caught in his own lies. On the bottom of page four of the Wednesday report, Eric East and K. O. Lewis gave the number at thirty, not fifteen. Relax, Chief, Coal whispered to the screen. He's playing with you.

The President was anything but relaxed. 'Good god, Denton. Why only fifteen? I thought this was a significant break.'

'Maybe a few more than that. I'm running this investigation, Mr. President.'

'I know. And you're doing a fine job. I'm not meddling. I just wish you'd consider spending your time elsewhere. That's all. When I read the pelican brief I almost vomited. If the press saw it and started digging, I'd be crucified.'

'So you're asking me to back off?'

The President leaned forward and stared fiercely at Voyles. 'I'm not asking, Denton. I'm telling you to leave it alone. Ignore it for a couple of weeks. Spend your time elsewhere. If it flares up again, take another look. I'm still the boss around here, remember?'

Voyles relented and managed a tiny smile. 'I'll make you a deal. Your hatchet man Coal has done a number on me with the press. They've eaten my lunch over the security we provided to Rosenberg and Jensen.'

The President nodded solemnly.

'You get that pit bull off my ass, keep him away from me, and I'll forget the pelican theory.'

'I don't make deals.'

Voyles sneered but kept his cool. 'Good. I'll send fifty agents to New Orleans tomorrow. And fifty the next day. We'll be flashing badges all over town and doing our damnedest to attract attention.'

The President jumped to his feet and walked to the windows overlooking the Rose Garden. Voyles sat motionless and waited.

'All right, all right. It's a deal. I can control Fletcher Coal.'

Voyles stood and walked slowly to the desk. 'I don't trust him, and if I smell him one more time during this investigation, the deal's off and we investigate the pelican brief with all the weight I can muster.'

The President held up his hands and smiled warmly. 'It's a deal.'

Voyles was smiling and the President was smiling, and in the closet near the Cabinet Room Fletcher Coal was smiling at a screen. Hatchet man, pit bull. He loved it. Those were the words that created legends.

He turned off the screens and locked the door behind him. They would talk another ten minutes about the background checks on the short list, and he would listen in his office where he had audio but no video. He had a staff meeting at nine. A firing at ten. And he had some typing to do. With most memos, he simply dictated into the machine and handed the tape to a secretary. But occasionally, Coal found it necessary to resort to the phantom memo. These were always widely circulated in the West Wing, and always controversial as hell, and usually dripped to the press. Becuase they came from no one, they could be found lying on almost every desk. Coal would scream and accuse. He had fired people for phantom memos, all of which came from his typewriter.

It was four single-spaced paragraphs on one page, and it summarized what he knew about Khamel and his recent flight out of Washington. And there were vague links to the Libyans and Palestinians. Coal admired it. How long before it would be in the *Post* or the *Times*? He made little bets with himself about which paper would get it first.

The director was at the White House, and from there would fly to New York and return tomorrow. Gavin camped outside the office of K. O. Lewis until there was a small opening. He was in.

Lewis was irritated, but always the gentleman. 'You look scared.'

'I've just lost my best friend.'

Lewis waited for more.

'His name was Thomas Callahan. He's the guy from Tulane who brought me the pelican brief, and it got passed around, then sent to the White House and who knows where else, and now he's dead. Blown to bits by a car bomb last night in New Orleans. Murdered, K. O.'

'I'm sorry.'

'It's not a matter of being sorry. Evidently the bomb was intended for Callahan and the student who wrote it, a girl by the name of Darby Shaw.'

'I saw her name on the brief.'

'That's right. They've been dating, and were supposed to be in the car together when it exploded. But she survived, and I get this call this morning at five, and it's her. Scared to death.'

Lewis listened, but was already dismissing it. 'You're not certain it was a bomb.'

'She said it was a bomb, okay. It went BOOM! and blew the hell out of everything, okay. I'm certain he's dead.'

'And you think there's a connection between his death and the brief?'

Gavin was a lawyer, untrained in the art of investigation, and he did not wish to appear gullible. 'There could be. I think so, yes. Don't you?'

'Doesn't matter, Gavin. I just got off the phone with the Director. Pelican's off our list. I'm not sure it was ever on, but we're spending no more time on it.'

'But my friend's been killed with a car bomb.'

'I'm sorry. I'm sure the authorities down there are investigating.'

'Listen to me, K.O. I'm asking for a favor.'

'Listen to me, Gavin. I don't have any favors. We're chasing enough rabbits right now, and if the Director says stop, then we stop. You're free to talk to him. I wouldn't advise it.'

'Maybe I'm not handling this right. I thought you would listen to me, and at least act interested.'

Lewis was walking around the desk. 'Gavin, you look bad. Take the day off.'

'No. I'll go to my office, wait an hour, and come back in here and do this again. Can we try it again in an hour?'

'No. Voyles was explicit.'

'So was the girl, K.O. He was murdered, and now she's hiding somewhere in New Orleans afraid of her shadow, calling us for help, and we're too busy.'

'I'm sorry.'

'No, you're not. It's my fault. I should've thrown the damned thing in the garbage.'

'It served a valuable purpose, Gavin.' Lewis placed his hand on his shoulder as if his time was up and he was tired of this drivel. Gavin jerked away and headed for the door.

'Yeah, it gave you guys something to play with. I should've burned it.'

'It's too good to burn, Gavin.'

'I'm not giving up. I'll be back in an hour, and we'll do this again. This didn't go right.' Verheek slammed the door behind him.

She entered Rubinstein Brothers from Canal Street, and got lost between the racks of men's shirts. No one followed her in. She quickly picked out a navy parka, men's small, a genderless pair of aviator sunglasses, and a British driving cap that was also a men's small but fit. She paid for it with plastic. As the clerk ran the card through, she picked the tags off, and put the parka on. It was baggy, like something she would wear to class. She stuffed her hair under the hooded collar. The clerk watched discreetly. She exited on Magazine Street, and got lost in the crowd.

Back on Canal. A busload of tourists swarmed into the Sheraton, and she joined them. She went to the wall of phones, found the number, and called Mrs. Chen, her neighbor in the duplex next door. Had she seen or heard anyone? Very early, there was a knock on the door. It was still dark, and woke them. She didn't see anyone, just heard the knock. Her car was still on the street. Everything okay? Yes, all's fine. Thanks.

She watched the tourists and punched the inside number for Gavin Verheek. Inside meant a minor hassle only, and after three minutes of refusing to give her name and repeating his, she had him.

'Where are you?' he asked.

'Let me explain something. For the moment, I will not tell you or anyone else where I am. So don't ask.'

'All right. I guess you're making the rules.'

'Thank you. What did Mr. Voyles say?'

'Mr. Voyles was at the White House and unavailable. I'll try to talk to him later today.'

'That's pretty weak, Gavin. You've been at the office for almost four hours, and you have nothing. I expected more.'

'Be patient, Darby.'

'Patience will get me killed. They're after me, aren't they, Gavin?'

'I don't know.'

'What would you do if you knew you were supposed to be dead, and the people trying to kill you have had assassinated two Supreme Court Justices, and knocked off a simple law professor, and they have billions of dollars which they obviously don't mind using to kill with? What would you do, Gavin?'

'Go to the FBI.'

'Thomas went to the FBI, and he's dead.'

'Thanks, Darby. That's not fair.'

'I'm not worried about fairness or feelings. I'm more concerned with staying alive until noon.'

'Don't go to your apartment.'

'I'm not stupid. They've already been there. And I'm sure they're watching his apartment.'

'Where's his family?'

'His parents live in Naples, Florida. I guess the university will contact them. I don't know. He has a brother in Mobile, and I thought of calling him and trying to explain all this.'

She saw a face. He walked among the tourists at the registration desk. He held a folded newspaper and tried to appear at home, just another guest, but his walk was a bit hesitant and his eyes were searching. The face was long and thin with round glasses and a shiny forehead.

'Gavin, listen to me. Write this down. I see a man I've seen before, not long ago. An hour maybe. Six feet two or three, thin, thirty years old, glasses, receding hair, dark in color. He's gone. He's gone.'

'Who the hell is it?'

'We haven't met, dammit!'

'Did he see you? Where the hell are you?'

'In a hotel lobby. I don't know if he saw me. I'm gone.'

'Darby! Listen to me. Whatever you do, keep in touch with me, okay?'

'I'll try.'

The rest room was around the corner. She went to the last stall, locked the door behind her, and stayed there for an hour.

CHAPTER SEVENTEEN

The photographer's name was Croft, and he'd worked for the *Post* for seven years until his third drug conviction sent him away for nine months. Upon parole, he declared himself to be a free-lance artist, and advertised as such in the yellow pages. The phone seldom rang. He did a little of this work; this slithering around shooting people who did not know they were targets. Many of his clients were divorce lawyers who needed dirt for trial. After two years of free-lancing, he had picked up a few tricks and now considered himself a halfass private investigator. He charged forty bucks an hour when he could get it.

Another client was Gray Grantham, an old friend from his newspaper days who called when he needed dirt. Grantham was a serious, ethical reporter with just a touch of sleaze, and when he needed a dirty trick, he called. He liked Grantham becuase he was honest about his sleaziness. The rest were so pious.

He was in Grantham's Volvo becuase it had a phone. It was noon, and he was smoking his lunch, wondering if the smell would linger with all the windows down. He did his best work half-stoned. When you stare at motels for a living, you need to be stoned.

There was a nice breeze coming in from the passenger's side, blowing the smell onto Pennsylvania. He was parked illegally, smoking dope, and not really concerned. He had less than an ounce on him, and his probation officer smoked it too, so what the hell.

The phone booth was a block and a half ahead, on the sidewalk but away from the street. With his telephoto lens, he could almost read the phone book hanging from the rack. Piece of cake. A large woman was inside, filling the booth and talking with her hands. Croft took a drag and watched the mirror for cops. This was a tow-away zone. Traffic was heavy on Pennsylvania.

At twenty after twelve, the woman fought her way out of the booth, and from nowhere a young man with a nice suit appeared and closed the door. Croft got his Nikon and rested the lens on the steering wheel. It was cool and sunny, and the sidewalk bustled with lunch traffic. The shoulders and heads moved quickly by. A gap. Click. A gap. Click. The subject was punching numbers and glancing around. This was their man.

He talked for thirty seconds, and the car phone rang three times and stopped. It was the signal from Grantham at the *Post.* This was their man, and he was talking. Croft fired away. Get all you can get, Grantham had said. A gap. Click. Click. Heads and shoulders. A gap. Click. Click. His eyes darted around as he talked, but he kept his back to the street. Full face. Click. Croft burned a roll of thirty-six in two minutes, then grabbed another Nikon. He screwed on the lens, and waited for a mob to pass.

He took the last drag and thumped it into the street. This was so easy. Oh sure, it took talent to capture the image in a studio, but this street work was much more fun. There was something felonious about stealing a face with a hidden camera.

The subject was a man of few words. He hung up, looked around, opened the door, looked around, and started toward Croft. Click, click, click. Full face, full figure, walking faster, getting closer, beautiful, beautiful. Croft worked feverishly, then at the last moment laid the Nikon in the seat and looked at Pennsylvania as their man walked by and disappeared in a group of secretaries.

What a fool. When you're on the run, never use the same pay phone twice.

Garcia was shadow boxing. He had a wife and child, he said, and he was scared. There was a career ahead with plenty of money, and if he paid his dues and kept his mouth shut he would be a wealthy man. But he wanted to talk. He rambled on about how he wanted to talk, had something to say and all, but just couldn't make the decision. He didn't trust anyone.

Grantham didn't push. He let him ramble long enough for Croft to do his number. Garcia would eventually spill his guts. He wanted to so badly. He had called three times now, and was growing comfortable with his new friend Grantham, who'd played this game many times and knew how it worked. The first step was to relax and build trust, to treat them with warmth and respect, to talk about right and wrong and moralities. Then they would talk.

The pictures were beautiful. Croft was not his first choice. He was usually so bombed you could tell it in the photography. But Croft was sleazy and discreet, with a working knowledge of journalism, and he happened to be available on short notice. He had picked twelve and blown them to five by seven, and they were outstanding. Right profile. Left profile. Full face into the phone. Full face looking at the camera. Full figure less than twenty feet away. Piece of cake, Croft said.

Garcia was under thirty, a very nice-looking, clean-cut lawyer. Dark, short hair. Dark eyes. Maybe Hispanic, but the skin was not dark. The clothes were expensive. Navy suit, probably wool. No stripes or patterns. Basic white spread collar with a silk tie. Basic black or burgundy wing tips with a sparkling shine. The absence of a briefcase was puzzling. But then, it was lunch, and he probably ran from the office to make the call, then back to the office. The Justice Department was a block away.

Grantham studied the pictures and kept an eye on the door. Sarge was never late. It was dark and the club was filling up. Grantham's was the only white face within three blocks.

Of the tens of thousands of government lawyers in D.C., he had seen a few who knew how to dress, but not many. Especially the younger ones. They started at forty a year and clothes were not important. Clothes were important to Garcia, and he was too young and well dressed to be a government lawyer.

So he was a private one, in a firm for about three or four years now and hitting somewhere around eighty grand. Great. That narrowed it down to fifty thousand lawyers and no doubt expanding by the moment.

The door opened and a cop walked in. Through the smoke and haze, he could tell it was Cleve. This was a respectable joint with no dice or whores, so the presence of a cop was not alarming. He sat in the booth across from Grantham.

'Did you pick this place?' Grantham asked.

'Yeah. You like it?'

'Let's put it like this. We're trying to be inconspicuous, right? I'm here picking up secrets from a White House employee. Pretty heavy stuff. Now tell me, Cleve, do I look inconspicuous sitting here in all my whiteness?'

'I hate to tell you this, Grantham, but you're not nearly as famous as you think. You see those dudes at the bar.' They looked at the bar lined with construction workers. 'I'd give you my paycheck if any dude there has ever read the *Washington Post*, heard of Gray Grantham, or gives a damn what happens at the White House.'

'Okay, okay. Where's Sarge?'

'Sarge is not feeling well. He gave me a message for you.'

Wouldn't work. He could use Sarge as an unnamed source, but not Sarge's son or anyone else Sarge talked to. 'What's wrong with him?'

'Old age. He didn't want to talk tonight, but it's urgent, he says.'

Grantham listened and waited.

'I've got an envelope in my car, all licked and sealed real tight. Sarge got real blunt when he gave it to me, and told me not to open it. Just take it to Mr. Grantham. I think it's important.'

'Let's go.'

They made their way through the crowd to the door. The patrol car was parked illegally at the curb. Cleve opened the passenger door, and pulled the envelope from the glove box. 'He got this in the West Wing.'

Grantham stuffed it in his pocket. Sarge was not one to lift things, and in the course of their relationship he had never produced a document.

'Thanks, Cleve.'

'He wouldn't tell me what it is – told me I'll just have to wait and read it in the paper.'

'Tell Sarge I love him.'

'I'm sure that'll give him a thrill.'

The patrol car drove away, and Grantham hurried to his Volvo, now filled with the stench of burnt grass. He locked the door, turned on the dome light, and ripped open the envelope. It was clearly an internal White House memo, and it was about an assassin named Khamel.

He was flying across town. Out of Brightwood, onto Sixteenth and south toward central Washington. It was almost seven-thirty, and if he could put it together in an hour, it would make the Late City edition, the largest of half a dozen editions that began rolling off the presses at ten-thirty. Thank god for the little yuppie car phone he had been embarrassed to buy. He called Smith Keen, the assistant managing editor/investigations, who was still in the newsroom on the fifth floor. He called a friend at the foreign desk, and asked him to pull everything on Khamel.

He was suspicious of the memo. The words were too sensitive to put on paper, then sling around the office like the latest policy on coffee or bottled water or vacations. Someone, probably Fletcher Coal, wanted the world to know that Khamel had emerged as a suspect, and that he was an Arab of all things, and had close ties to Libya and Iran and Iraq, countries led by fiery idiots who hated America. Someone in the White House of Fools wanted the story on the front page.

But it was a helluva story and it was front-page news. He and Smith Keen had it finished by nine. They found two old pictures of a man widely believed to be Khamel, but so dissimilar they appeared to be of different people. Keen said run both of them. The file on Khamel was thin. Much rumor and legend, but little meat. Grantham mentioned the Pope, the British diplomat, the German banker, and the ambush of the Israeli soldiers. And now, according to a confidential source at the White House, a most reliable and trusted source, Khamel was a suspect in the killings of Justices Rosenberg and Jensen.

Twenty-four hours after hitting the street, she was still alive. If she could make it to morning, she could start another day with new ideas about what to do and where to go. For now, she was tired. She was in a room on the fifteenth floor of the Marriott, with the door bolted, lights on, and the mighty can of Mace lying on the bedspread. Her thick, dark red hair was now in a paper sack in the closet. The last time she cut her hair she was three years old, and her mother whipped her tail.

It took two painful hours with dull scissors to cut it off yet leave some semblance of style. She would keep it under a cap or hat until who knows when. It took another two hours to color it black. She could've bleached it and gone blonde, but that would be obvious. She assumed she was dealing with professionals, and for some unfathomable reason she determined at the drugstore that they might expect her to do this and become a blonde. And what the hell. The stuff came in a bottle, and if she woke up tomorrow with a wild hair she could go blonde. The chameleon strategy. Change colors every day and drive 'em crazy. Clairol had at least eighty-five shades.

She was dead tired but afraid of sleep. She had not seen her friend from the Sheraton during the day, but the more she moved around the more the faces looked the same. He was out there, she knew. And he had friends. If they could assassinate Rosenberg and Jensen, and knock off Thomas Callahan, she would be easy.

She couldn't go near her car, and she didn't want to rent one. Rentals leave records. And they were probably watching. She could fly, but they were stalking the airports. Take a bus, but she'd never bought a ticket or seen the inside of a Greyhound.

And after they realized she had disappeared, they would expect her to run. She was just an amateur, a little college girl brokenhearted after watching her man blown to bits and fried. She would make a mad dash somewhere, get out of the city, and they would pick her off.

She rather liked the city at this moment. It had a million hotel rooms, almost as many alleys and dives and bars, and it always had crowds of people strolling along Bourbon, Chartres, Dauphine, and Royal. She knew it well, especially the Quarter, where life was within walking distance. She would move from hotel to hotel for a few days, until when? She didn't know when. She didn't know why. Moving just seemed intelligent under the circumstances. She would stay off the streets in the mornings, and try to sleep then. She would change clothes and hats and sunglasses. She would start smoking, and keep one in her face. She would move until she got tired of moving, then she might leave. It was okay to be scared. She had to keep thinking. She would survive.

She thought of calling the cops, but not now. They took names and kept records, and they could be dangerous. She thought of calling Thomas' brother in Mobile, but there wasn't a single thing the poor man could do to help her at this moment. She thought of calling the dean, but how could she explain the brief, Gavin Verheek, the FBI, the car bomb, Rosenberg and Jensen, and her on the run and make it sound believable.

Forget the dean. She didn't like him anyway. She thought of calling a couple of friends from law school, but people talk, and people listen, and they could be out there listening to the people talking about poor Callahan. She wanted to talk to Alice Stark, her best friend. Alice was worried, and Alice would go to the cops and tell them her friend Darby Shaw was missing. She would call Alice tomorrow.

She dialed room service, and ordered a Mexican salad and a bottle of red wine. She would drink all of it, then sit in a chair with the Mace and watch the door until she fell asleep.

CHAPTER EIGHTEEN

Gminski's limo made a wild U-turn on Canal as if it owned the street, and came to a sudden stop in front of the Sheraton. Both rear doors flew open. Gminski was out first, followed quickly by three aides who scurried after him with bags and briefcases.

It was almost 2 A.M., and the Director was obviously in a hurry. He did not stop at the front desk, but went straight for the elevators. The aides ran behind him and held the elevator door for him, and no one spoke as they rode up six floors.

Three of his agents were waiting in a corner room. One of them opened the door, and Gminski barged through it without any sort of greeting. The aides threw the bags on one bed. The Director yanked off his jacket and threw it in a chair.

'Where is she?' he snapped at an agent by the name of Hooten. The one named Swank opened the curtains, and Gminski walked to the window.

Swank was pointing to the Marriott, across the street and down a block. 'She's on the fifteenth floor, third room from the street, lights are still on.'

Gminski stared at the Marriott. 'You're certain?'

'Yes. We saw her go in, and she paid with a credit card.'

'Poor kid,' Gminski said as he walked away from the window. 'Where was she last night?'

'Holiday Inn on Royal. Paid with a credit card.'

'Have you seen anyone following her?' the Director asked.

'No.'

'I need some water,' he said to an aide, who jumped toward the ice bucket and rattled cubes.

Gminski sat on the edge of the bed, laced his fingers together, and cracked every possible knuckle. 'What do you think?' he asked Hooten, the oldest of the three agents.

'They're chasing her. They're looking under rocks. She's using credit cards. She'll be dead in forty-eight hours.'

'She's not completely stupid,' Swank inserted. 'She cut her hair and colored it black. She's moving around. It's apparent she has no plans to leave the city any time soon. I'll give her seventy-two hours before they find her.'

Gminski sipped his water. 'This means her little brief is directly on point. And it means our friend is now a very desperate man. Where is he?'

Hooten answered quickly. 'We have no idea.'

'We have to find him.'

'He hasn't been seen in three weeks.'

Gminski set the glass on the desk, and picked up a room key. 'So what do you think?' he asked Hooten.

'Do we bring her in?' Hooten asked.

'It won't be easy,' Swank said. 'She may have a gun. Someone could get hurt.'

'She's a scared kid,' Gminski said. 'She's also a civilian, not a member. We can't go around snatching civilians off the sidewalk.'

'Then she won't last long,' Swank said.

'How do you take her?' Gminski asked.

'There are ways,' Hooten answered. 'Catch her on the street. Go to her room. I could be inside her room in less than ten minutes if I left right now. It's not that difficult. She's not a pro.'

Gminski paced slowly around the room and everyone watched him. He glanced at his watch. 'I'm not inclined to take her. Let's sleep four hours, and meet here at six-thirty. Sleep on it. If you can convince me to snatch her, then I'll say do it. Okay?'

They nodded obediently.

The wine worked. She dozed in the chair, then made it to the bed and slept hard. The phone was ringing. The bedspread was hanging to the floor, and her feet were on the pillows. The phone was ringing. The eyelids were glued together. The mind was numb and lost in dreams, but somewhere in the deep recesses something worked and told her the phone was ringing.

The eyes opened but saw little. The sun was up, the lights were on, and she stared at the phone. No, she did not ask for a wake-up call. She thought about this for a second, then she was certain. No wake-up call. She sat on the edge of the bed and listened to it ring. Five times, ten, fifteen, twenty. It would not stop. Could be a wrong number, but they would stop after twenty rings.

It was not a wrong number. The cobwebs began to clear, and she moved closer to the phone. With the exception of the registration clerk and may be his boss, and perhaps room service, not a single living soul knew she was in this room. She had ordered food, but made no other calls.

It stopped ringing. Good, wrong number. She walked to the bathroom, and it was ringing again. She counted. After the fourteenth ring, she lifted the receiver. 'Hello.'

'Darby, it's Gavin Verheek. Are you okay?'

She sat on the bed. 'How'd you get the number?'

'We have ways. Listen, have –'

'Wait, Gavin. Wait a minute. Let me think. The credit card, right?'

'Yes. The credit card. The paper trail. It's the FBI, Darby. We have ways. It's not that difficult.'

'Then they could do it too.'

'I suppose. Stay in the small joints and pay with cash.'

There was a thick knot in her stomach, and she stretched on the bed. Just like that. Not difficult. The paper trail. She could be dead. Killed along the paper trail.

'Darby, are you there?'

'Yes.' She looked at the door to make sure it was chained. 'Yes, I'm here.'

'Are you safe?'

'I thought so.'

'We've got some information. There will be a memorial service tomorrow at three on campus, with burial afterward in the city. I've talked to his brother, and the family wants me to serve as a pallbearer. I'll be there tonight. I think we should meet.'

'Why should we meet?'

'You've got to trust me, Darby. Your life is in danger right now, and you need to listen to me.'

'What're you guys up to?'

There was a pause. 'What do you mean?'

'What did Director Voyles say?'

'I haven't talked to him.'

'I thought you were his attorney, so to speak. What's the matter, Gavin?'

'We're taking no action at this time.'

'And what might that mean, Gavin? Talk to me.'

'That's why we need to meet. I don't want to do this over the phone.'

'The phone is working fine, and it's all you're going to get right now. So let's have it, Gavin.'

'Why won't you trust me?' He was wounded.

'I'm hanging up, okay. I don't like this. If you guys know where I am, then someone could be out there in the hallway waiting.'

'Nonsense, Darby. You've got to use your head. I've had your room number for an hour, and done nothing but call. We're on your side, I swear.'

She thought about this. It made sense, but they had found her so easily. 'I'm listening. You haven't talked to the Director, but the FBI's taking no action. Why not?'

'I'm not sure. He made the decision yesterday to back off the pelican brief, and gave instructions to leave it alone. That's all I can tell you.'

'That's not very much. Does he know about Thomas? Does he know that I'm supposed to be dead because I wrote it and forty-eight hours after Thomas gave it to you, his old buddy from law school, they, whoever in hell they are, tried to kill both of us? Does he know all this, Gavin?'

'I don't think so.'

'That means no, doesn't it?'

'Yes. It means no.'

'Okay, listen to me. Do you think he was killed because of the brief?'

'Probably.'

'That means yes, doesn't it?'

'Yes.'

'Thanks. If Thomas was murdered because of the brief, then we know who killed him. And if we know who killed Thomas, then we know who killed Rosenberg and Jensen. Right?'

Verheek hesitated.

'Just say yes, dammit!' Darby snapped.

'I'll say probably.'

'Fine. *Probably* means yes for a lawyer. I know it's the best you can do. It's a very strong *probably*, yet you're telling me the FBI is backing off my little suspect.'

'Settle down, Darby. Let's meet tonight and talk about it. I could save your life.'

She carefully laid the receiver under a pillow, and walked to the bathroom. She brushed her teeth and what was left of her hair, then threw the toiletries and change of clothes into a new canvas bag. She put on the parka, cap, and sunglasses, and quietly closed the door behind her. The hall was empty. She walked up two flights to the seventeenth, then took the elevator to the tenth, then casually walked down ten flights to the lobby. The door from the stairway opened near the rest rooms, and she was quickly inside the women's. The lobby appeared to be deserted. She went to a stall, locked the door, and waited for a while.

Friday morning in the Quarter. The air was cool and clean without the lingering smell of food and sin. Eight A.M. – too early for people. She walked a few blocks to clear her head and plan the day. On Dumaine near Jackson Square she found a coffee shop she'd seen before. It was nearly empty and had a pay phone in the back. She poured her own thick coffee, and set it on a table near the phone. She could talk here.

Verheek was on the phone in less than a minute. 'I'm listening,' he said.

'Where will you stay tonight?' she asked, watching the front door.

'Hilton, by the river.'

'I know where it is. I'll call late tonight or early in the morning. Don't track me again. I'm into cash now. No plastic.'

'That's smart, Darby. Keep moving.'

'I may be dead by the time you get here.'

'No, you won't. Can you find a *Washington Post* down there?'

'Maybe. Why?'

'Get one quick. This morning's. Nice little story about Rosenberg and Jensen and perhaps who done it.'

'I can't wait. I'll call later.'

The first newsstand did not have the *Post.* She zigzagged toward Canal, covering her tracks, watching her rear, down St. Ann, along the antique shops on Royal, through the seedy bars on both sides of Bienville, and finally to the French Market along Decatur and North Peters. She was quick but nonchalant. She walked with an air of business, her eyes darting in all directions behind the shades. If they were back there somewhere in the shadows watching and keeping up, they were good.

She bought a *Post* and a *Times-Picayune* from a sidewalk vendor, and found a table in a deserted corner of Café du Monde.

Front page. Citing a confidential source, the story dwelt on the legend of Khamel and his sudden involvement in the killings. In his younger days, it said, he had killed for his beliefs, but now he just did it for money. Lots of money, speculated a retired intelligence expert who allowed himself to be quoted but certainly not identified. The photos were blurred and indistinct, but ominous beside each other. They could not be of the same person. But then, said the expert, he was unidentifiable and had not been photographed in over a decade.

A waiter finally made it by, and she ordered coffee and a plain bagel. The expert said many thought he was dead. Interpol believed he had killed as recently as six months ago. The expert doubted he would travel by commercial air. The FBI had him at the top of their list.

She opened the New Orleans paper slowly. Thomas did not make page one, but his picture was on page two with a long story. The cops were treating it as a homicide, but there wasn't much to go on. A white female had been seen in the area shortly before the explosion. The law school was in shock, according to the dean. The cops said little. Services were tomorrow on campus. A horrible mistake had been made, the dean said. If it was murder, then someone had obviously killed the wrong person.

Her eyes were wet, and suddenly she was afraid again. Maybe it was simply a mistake. It was a violent city with crazy people, and maybe someone got their wires crossed and the wrong car was chosen. Maybe there was no one out there stalking her.

She put the sunglasses on and looked at his photo. They had pulled it from the law school annual, and there was that smirk he habitually wore when he was the professor. He was clean shaven, and so handsome.

Grantham's Khamel story electrified Washington Friday morning. It mentioned neither the memo nor the White House, so the hottest game in town was speculating about the source.

The game was especially hot in the Hoover Building. In the office of the Director, Eric East and K. O. Lewis paced nervously about while Voyles talked to the President for the third time in two hours. Voyles was cussing, not directly at the President, but all around him. He cussed Coal, and when the President cussed back, Voyles suggested they set up the polygraph, strap in everyone on his staff, beginning with Coal, and just see where the damned leaks were coming from. Yes, hell yes, he, Voyles, would take the test, and so would everyone who worked in the Hoover Building. And they cussed back and forth. Voyles was red and sweating, and the fact that he was yelling into the telephone and the President was on the other end receiving all this mattered not a bit. He knew Coal was listening somewhere.

Evidently, the President gained control of the conversation and launched into a long-winded sermon of some sort. Voyles wiped his forehead with a handkerchief, sat in his ancient leather swivel, and began controlled breathing to lower the pressure and pulse. He had survived one heart attack and was due for another, and had told K. O. Lewis many times that Fletcher Coal and his idiot boss would eventually kill him. But he'd said that about the last three Presidents. He pinched the fat wrinkles on his forehead and sunk lower into the chair. 'We can do that, Mr. President.' He was almost pleasant now. He was a man of swift and radical mood swings, and suddenly before their eyes he was courteous. A real charmer. 'Thank you, Mr. President. I'll be there tomorrow.'

He hung up gently, and spoke with his eyes closed. 'He wants us to place that *Post* reporter under surveillance. Says we've done it before, so will we do it again? I told him we would.'

'What type of surveillance?' asked K.O.

'Let's just follow him in the city. Around the clock with two men. See where he goes at night, who he sleeps with. He's single, isn't he?'

'Divorced seven years ago,' Lewis answered.

'Make damned sure we don't get caught. Do it with plain-clothes, and switch 'em up every three days.'

'Does he really believe the leaks are coming from us?'

'No, I don't think so. If we were leaking, why would he want us to trail the reporter? I think he knows it's his own people. And he wants to catch them.'

'It's a small favor,' Lewis added helpfully.

'Yeah. Just don't get caught, okay?'

The office of L. Matthew Barr was tucked away on the third floor of a tacky and decaying office building on M Street in Georgetown. There were no signs on the doors. An armed guard in a coat and tie turned people away at the elevator. The carpet was worn and the furniture was old. Dust covered it, and it was apparent the Unit spent no money on housekeeping.

Barr ran the Unit, which was an unofficial, hidden, little division of the Committee to Reelect the President. CRP had a vast suite of plush offices across the river in Rosslyn. It had windows that opened and secretaries who smiled and maids that cleaned every night. But not this dump.

Fletcher Coal stepped off the elevator and nodded at the security guard, who nodded back without making another move. They were old acquaintances. He made his way through the small maze of dingy offices in the direction of Barr's. Coal took pride in being honest with himself, and he honestly did not fear any man in Washington, maybe with the possible exception of Matthew Barr. Sometimes he feared him, sometimes not, but he always admired him.

Barr was an ex-Marine, ex-CIA, ex-spy with two felony convictions for security scams from which he earned millions and buried the money. He had served a few months in one of the country clubs, but no real time. Coal had personally recruited Barr to head the Unit, which officially did not exist. It had an annual budget of four million, all cash from various slush funds, and Barr supervised a small band of highly trained thugs who quietly did the work of the Unit.

Barr's door was always locked. He opened it and Coal entered. The meeting would be brief, as usual.

'Let me guess,' Barr started. 'You want to find the leak.'

'In a way, yes. I want you to follow this reporter, Grantham, around the clock and see who he's talking to. He's getting some awfully good stuff, and I'm afraid it's coming from us.'

'You're leaking like cardboard.'

'We've got some problems, but the Khamel story was a plant. Did it myself.'

Barr smiled at this. 'I thought so. It seemed too clean and pat.'

'Did you ever run across Khamel?'

'No. Ten years ago we were sure he was dead. He likes it that way. He has no ego, so he'll never get caught. He can live in a paper shack in São Paulo for six months, eating roots and rats, then fly off to Rome to murder a diplomat, then off to Singapore for a few months. He doesn't read his press clippings.'

'How old is he?'

'Why are you interested?'

'I'm fascinated. I think I know who hired him to kill Rosenberg and Jensen.'

'Oh, really. Can you share this bit of gossip?'

'No. Not yet.'

'He's between forty and forty-five, which is not that old, but he killed a Lebanese general when he was fifteen. So he's had a long career. This is all legend, you understand. He can kill with either hand, either foot, a car key, a pencil, whatever. He's an expert marksman with all weapons. Speaks twelve languages. You've heard all this, haven't you?'

'Yeah, but it's fun.'

'Okay. He's believed to be the most proficient and expensive assassin in the world. In his early years he was just another terrorist, but he was much too talented for simple bomb throwing. So he became an assassin for hire. He's a bit older now, and kills just for money.'

'How much money?'

'Good question. He's probably in the ten-to-twenty-million-a-job range, and there's not but one other guy I know of in that league. One theory believes he shares it with other terrorist groups. No one knows, really. Let me guess, you want me to find Khamel and bring him back alive.'

'You leave Khamel alone. I sort of like the work he did here.'

'He's very talented.'

'I want you to follow Gray Grantham and find out who he's talking to.'

'Any ideas?'

'A couple. There's a man by the name of Milton Hardy who works as a janitor in the West Wing.' Coal threw an envelope on the desk. 'He's been around for a long time, appears to be half blind, but I think he sees and hears a lot. Follow him for a week or two. Everyone calls him Sarge. Make plans to take him out.'

'This is great, Coal. We're spending all this money to track blind Negroes.'

'Just do as I say. Make it three weeks.' Coal stood and headed for the door.

'So you know who hired the killer?' Barr said.

'We're getting close.'

'The Unit is more than anxious to help.'

'I'm sure.'

CHAPTER NINETEEN

Mrs. Chen owned the duplex, and had been renting the other half to female law students for fifteen years. She was picky but private, and lived and let live as long as all was quiet. It was six blocks from campus.

It was dark when she answered the door. The person on the porch was an attractive young lady with short dark hair and a nervous smile. Very nervous.

Mrs. Chen frowned at her until she spoke.

'I'm Alice Stark, a friend of Darby's. May I come in?' She glanced over her shoulder. The street was quiet and still. Mrs. Chen lived alone with the doors and windows locked tightly, but she was a pretty girl with an innocent smile, and if she was a friend of Darby's, then she could be trusted. She opened the door, and Alice was inside.

'Something's wrong,' Mrs. Chen said.

'Yes. Darby is in a bit of trouble, but we can't talk about it. Did she call this afternoon?'

'Yes. She said a young woman would look through her apartment.'

Alice breathed deeply and tried to appear calm. 'It'll just take a minute. She said there was a door through a wall somewhere. I prefer not to use the front or rear doors.' Mrs. Chen frowned and her eyes asked, Why not? but she said nothing.

'Has anyone been in the apartment in the last two days?' Alice asked. She followed Mrs. Chen down a narrow hallway.

'I've seen no one. There was a knock early yesterday before the sun, but I didn't look.' She moved a table away from a door, pushed a key around, and opened it.

Alice stepped in front of her. 'She wanted me to go in alone, okay?' Mrs. Chen wanted to check it out, but she nodded and closed the door behind Alice. It opened into a tiny hallway that was suddenly dark. To the left was the den, and a light switch that couldn't be used. Alice froze in the darkness. The apartment was black and hot with a thick smell of old garbage. She'd expected to be alone, but she was a second-year law student, dammit!, not some hotshot private detective.

Get a grip. She fumbled through a large purse and found a pencil-thin flashlight. There were three of them in there. Just in case. In case of what? She didn't know. Darby had been quite specific. No lights could be seen through the windows. They could be watching.

Who in hell are they? Alice wanted to know. Darby didn't know, said she would explain it later but first the apartment had to be examined.

Alice had been in the apartment a dozen times in the past year, but she'd been allowed to enter through the front door with a full array of lights and other conveniences. She had been in all the rooms, and felt confident she could feel around in the darkness. The confidence was gone. Vanished. Replaced with trembling fear.

Get a grip. You're all alone. They wouldn't camp out here with a nosy woman next door. If they had indeed been here, it was only for a brief visit.

After staring at the end of it, she determined that the flashlight worked. It glowed with all the energy of a fading match. She pointed it at the floor, and saw a faint round circle the size of a small orange. The circle was shaking.

She tiptoed around a corner in the direction of the den. Darby said there was a small lamp on the bookshelves next to the television, and that the light was always on. She used it as a nightlight, and it was supposed to cast a faint glow across the den to the kitchen. Either Darby lied, or the bulb was gone, or someone had unscrewed it. It didn't matter, really, at this point, because the den and kitchen were pitch-black.

She was on the rug in the center of the den, inching toward the kitchen table where there was supposed to be a computer. She kicked the edge of the coffee table, and the flashlight quit. She shook it. Nothing. She found number two in the purse.

The odor was heavier in the kitchen. The computer was on the table along with an assortment of empty files and casebooks. She examined the mainframe with her dinky little light. The power switch was on the front. She pushed it, and the monochrome screen slowly warmed up. It emitted a greenish light that covered the table but did not escape the kitchen.

Alice sat down in front of the keyboard and began pecking. She found Menu, then List, then Files. The Directory covered the screen. She studied it closely. There were supposed to be somewhere around forty entries, but she saw no more than ten. Most of the hard-drive memory was gone. She turned on the laser printer, and within seconds the Directory was on paper. She tore it off and stuffed it in the purse.

She stood with her flashlight and inspected the clutter around the computer. Darby estimated the number of floppy disks at twenty, but they were all gone. Not a single floppy. The casebooks were for con law and civil procedure, and so dull and generic no one would want them. The red expandable files were stacked neatly together, but empty.

It was a clean, patient job. He or they had spent a couple of hours erasing and gathering, then left with no more than one briefcase or bag of goods.

In the den by the television, Alice peeked out the side window. The red Accord was still there, not four feet from the window. It looked fine.

She twisted the bulb in the nightlight, and quickly flicked the switch on, then off. Worked perfectly. She unscrewed it just as he or they had left it.

Her eyes had focused; she could see the outlines of doors and furniture. She turned the computer off, and eased through the den to the hall.

Mrs. Chen was waiting exactly where she'd left her. 'Okay?' she asked.

'Everything's fine,' Alice said. 'Just watch it real close. I'll call you in a day or two to see if anyone has been by. And please, don't tell anyone I was here.'

Mrs. Chen listened intently as she moved the table in front of the door. 'What about her car?'

'It'll be fine. Just watch it.'

'Is she all right?'

They were in the den, almost to the front door. 'She's gonna be fine. I think she'll be back in a few days. Thank you, Mrs. Chen.'

Mrs. Chen closed the door, bolted it, and watched from the small window. The lady was on the sidewalk, then gone in the darkness.

Alice walked three blocks to her car.

Friday night in the Quarter! Tulane played in the Dome tomorrow, then the Saints on Sunday, and the rowdies were out by the thousands, parking everywhere, blocking streets, roaming in noisy mobs, drinking from go cups, crowding bars, just having a delightful time raising hell and enjoying themselves. The Inner Quarter was gridlocked by nine.

Alice parked on Poydras, far away from where she wanted to park, and was an hour late when she arrived at the crowded oyster bar on St. Peter, deep in the Quarter. There were no tables. They were packed three deep at the bar. She retreated to a corner with a cigarette machine, and surveyed the people. Most were students in town for the game.

A waiter walked directly to her. 'Are you looking for another female?' he asked.

She hesitated. 'Well, yes.'

He pointed beyond the bar. 'Around the corner, first room on the right, there's some small tables. I think your friend is there.'

Darby was in a tiny booth, crouched over a beer bottle, with sunglasses and a hat. Alice squeezed her hand. 'It's good to see you.' She studied the hairdo, and was amused by it. Darby removed the sunglasses. The eyes were red and tired.

'I didn't know who else to call.'

Alice listened with a blank face, unable to think of something appropriate and unable to take her eyes off the hair. 'Who did the hair?' she asked.

'Nice, huh. It's sort of the punk look, which I think is making a comeback and will certainly impress folks when I start interviewing for a job.'

'Why?'

'Someone tried to kill me, Alice. My name's on a list that some very nasty people are holding. I think they're following me.'

'Kill? Did you say "kill"? Who would want to kill you, Darby?'

'I'm not sure. What about my apartment?'

Alice stopped looking at the hair, and handed her the printout of the Directory. Darby studied it. It was real. This was not a dream or a mistake. The bomb had found the right car. Rupert and the cowboy had had their hands on her. The face she had seen was looking for her. They had gone to her apartment and erased what they wanted to erase. They were out there.

'What about floppies?'

'None. Not a single one. The expandable files on the kitchen table were placed together real neat and are real empty. Everything else appears to be in order. They unscrewed the bulb in the nightlight, so there's total darkness. I checked it. Works fine. These are very patient people.'

'What about Mrs. Chen?'

'She's seen nothing.'

Darby stuffed the printout into a pocket. 'Look, Alice, suddenly I'm very scared. You don't need to be seen with me. Maybe this was not a good idea.'

'Who are these people?'

'I don't know. They killed Thomas, and they tried to kill me. I got lucky, and now they're after me.'

'But why, Darby?'

'You don't want to know, and I'm not going to tell. The more you know, the more danger you're in. Trust me, Alice. I can't tell you what I know.'

'But I won't tell. I swear.'

'What if they make you tell?'

Alice glanced around as if all was fine. She studied her friend. They had been close since freshman orientation. They had studied hours together, shared notes, sweated exams, teamed up for mock trials, gossiped about men. Alice was hopefully the only student who knew about Darby and Callahan. 'I want to help, Darby. I'm not afraid.'

Darby had not touched the beer. She slowly spun the bottle. 'Well, I'm terrified. I was there when he died, Alice. The ground shook. He was blown to pieces and I was supposed to be with him. It was intended for me.'

'Then go to the cops.'

'Not yet. Maybe later. I'm afraid to. Thomas went to the FBI, and two days later we were supposed to be dead.'

'So the FBI is after you?'

'I don't think so. They started talking, and someone was listening very closely, and it found the wrong ears.'

'Talked about what! Come on, Darby. It's me. Your best friend. Stop playing games.'

Darby took the first tiny swallow from the bottle. Eye contact was avoided. She stared at the table. 'Please, Alice. Allow me to wait. There's no sense telling you something that could get you killed.' A long pause. 'If you want to help, go to the memorial service tomorrow. Watch everything. Spread the word that I called you from Denver where I'm staying with an aunt with a name you don't know, and that I've dropped out this semester but I'll be back in the spring. Make sure that rumor gets started. I think some people will be listening carefully.'

'Okay. The paper mentioned a white female near the scene when he was killed, as if she might be a suspect or something.'

'Or something. I was there and I was supposed to be a victim. I'm reading the papers with a magnifying glass. The cops are clueless.'

'Okay, Darby. You're smarter than I am. You're smarter than every person I've ever met. So what now?'

'First, go out the back door. There's a white door at the end of the hall where the rest rooms are. It goes into a storage room, then to the kitchen, then out the back door. Don't stop. The alley leads to Royal. Catch a cab and ride back to your car. Watch your rear.'

'Are you serious?'

'Look at this hair, Alice. Would I mutilate myself like this if I was playing games?'

'Okay, okay. Then what?'

'Go to the service tomorrow, start the rumor, and I'll call you within two days.'

'Where are you staying?'

'Here and there. I move around a lot.'

Alice stood and pecked her on the cheek. Then she was gone.

For two hours, Verheek stomped the floor, picking up magazines, tossing them around, ordering room service, unpacking, stomping. Then for the next two hours, he sat on the bed, sipping a hot beer and staring at the phone. He would do this until midnight, he told himself, and then, well, then what?

She said she would call.

He could save her life if she would only call.

At midnight, he threw another magazine and left the room. An agent in the New Orleans office had helped a little, and given him a couple of law school hangouts close to campus. He would go there and mix and mingle, drink a beer, and listen. The students were in town for the game. She wouldn't be there, and it wouldn't matter because he'd never seen her. But maybe he would hear something, and he could drop a name, leave a card, make a friend who knew her or maybe knew someone who knew her. A long shot, but a helluva lot more productive than staring at the phone.

He found a seat at the bar in a joint called Barrister's, three blocks from campus. It had a nice little varsity look to it with football schedules and pinups on the walls. The crowd was rowdy and under thirty.

The bartender looked like a student. After two beers, the crowd thinned and the bar was half empty. There would be another wave in a moment.

Verheek ordered number three. It was one-thirty. 'Are you a law student?' he asked the bartender.

'Afraid so.'

'It's not that bad, is it?'

He was wiping around the peanuts. 'I've had more fun.'

Verheek longed for the bartenders who served his beer in law school. Those guys knew the art of conversation. Never met a stranger. Talk about anything.

'I'm a lawyer,' Verheek said in desperation.

Oh, hey, wow, this guy's a lawyer. How rare. Someone special. The kid walked off.

Little son of a bitch. I hope you flunk out. Verheek grabbed his bottle and turned to face the tables. He felt like a grandfather amid the children. Though he hated law school and the memories of it, there had been some long Friday nights in the bars of Georgetown with his pal Callahan. Those were good memories.

'So what kind of law?' The bartender was back. Gavin turned to the bar, and smiled.

'Special counsel, FBI.'

He was still wiping. 'So you're in Washington?'

'Yeah, in town for the game Sunday. I'm a Redskins freak.' He hated the Redskins and every other organized football team. Don't get the kid started on football. 'Where do you go to school?'

'Here. Tulane. I'll finish in May.'

'Then where?'

'Probably Cincinnati for a clerkship for a year or two.'

'You must be a good student.'

He shrugged it off. 'You need a beer?'

'No. Did you have Thomas Callahan?'

'Sure. You know him?'

'I was in law school with him at Georgetown.' Verheek pulled a card from his pocket and handed it to the kid. 'I'm Gavin Verheek.' The kid looked at it, then politely laid it next to the ice. The bar was quiet and the kid was tired of chitchat.

'Do you know a student by the name of Darby Shaw?'

The kid glanced at the tables. 'No. I haven't met her, but I know who she is. I think she's second year.' A long, rather suspicious pause. 'Why?'

'We need to talk to her.' We, as in FBI. Not simply he, as in Gavin Verheek. The 'we' part sounded much graver. 'Does she hang out in here?'

'I've seen her a few times. She's hard to miss.'

'I've heard.' Gavin looked at the tables. 'Do you think these guys might know her?'

'Doubt it. They're all first year. Can't you tell? They're over there arguing property rights and search and seizure.'

Yeah, those were the days. Gavin pulled a dozen cards from his pocket and laid them on the bar. 'I'll be at the Hilton for a few days. If you see her, or hear anything, drop one of these.'

'Sure. There was a cop in last night asking questions. You don't think she was involved in his death?'

'No, not at all. We just need to talk to her.'

'I'll keep my eyes open.'

Verheek paid for the beer, thanked the kid again, and was on the sidewalk. He walked three blocks to the Half Shell. It was almost two. He was dead tired, half drunk, and a band cranked up the second he walked through the door. The place was dark, packed, and fifty fraternity joes with their sorority sues were immediately dancing on tables. He weaved through the uprising and found safety in the back near the bar. They were three deep, shoulder to shoulder, and no one moved. He clawed his way forward, got a beer to be cool, and realized again he was by far the oldest one there. He retreated to a dark but crowded corner. It was hopeless. He couldn't hear himself think, let alone carry on a conversation.

He watched the bartenders: all young, all students. The oldest looked late twenties, and he rang up check after check as if he was closing out. His moves were hurried, as if it was time to go. Gavin studied every move.

He quickly untied his apron, flung it in a corner, ducked under the bar, and was gone. Gavin elbowed through the mob, and caught him as he stepped through the kitchen door. He had an FBI business card ready. 'I'm sorry. I'm with the FBI.' He stuck the card in his face. 'Your name is?'

The kid froze, and looked wildly at Verheek. 'Uh, Fountain. Jeff Fountain.'

'Fine, Jeff. Look, nothing's wrong, okay? Just a couple of questions.' The kitchen had shut down hours ago,and they were alone. 'Just take a second.'

'Well, okay. What's up?'

'You're a law student, right?' Please say yes. His friend said most of the bartenders here were law students.

'Yes. At Loyola.'

Loyola! Where the hell! 'Yeah, well, that's what I thought. You've heard about Professor Callahan at Tulane. Funeral's tomorrow.'

'Sure. It's all over the papers. Most of my friends go to Tulane.'

'Do you know a second-year student there by the name of Darby Shaw? Very attractive female.'

Fountain smiled. 'Yeah, she dated a friend of mine last year. She's in here occasionally.'

'How long ago?'

'It's been a month or two. What's wrong?'

'We need to talk to her.' He handed Fountain a stack of cards. 'Hang on to these. I'll be at the Hilton for a few days. If you see her around, or if you hear anything, drop one of these.'

'What might I hear?'

'Something about Callahan. We need to see her real bad, okay?'

'Sure.' He stuck the cards in a pocket.

Verheek thanked him and returned to the revelry. He inched through the mob, listening to the attempts at conversation. A fresh mob was entering, and he wrestled his way out the door. He was too old for this.

Six blocks away, he parked illegally in front of a fraternity house next to the campus. His last stop for the night would be a dark little pool hall, which, at the moment, was not crowded. He paid for beer at the bar, and surveyed the place. There were four pool tables and the action was light. A young man in a T-shirt walked to the bar and ordered another beer. The shirt was green and gray with the words TULANE LAW SCHOOL stamped across the front with what appeared to be an inmate identification number under the words.

Verheek spoke without hesitating. 'You a law student?'

The young man glanced at him while pulling money from his jeans. 'Afraid so.'

'Did you know Thomas Callahan?'

'Who are you?'

'FBI. Callahan was a friend of mine.'

The student sipped the beer and was suspicious. 'I was in his con law class.'

Bingo! So was Darby. Verheek tried to appear uninterested. 'Do you know Darby Shaw?'

'Why do you want to know?'

'We need to talk to her. That's all.'

'Who is we?' The student was even more suspicious. He took a step closer to Gavin as if he wanted some hard answers.

'FBI,' Verheek said nonchalantly.

'You got a badge or something?'

'Sure,' he said as he pulled a card from his pocket. The student read it carefully, then handed it back. 'You're a lawyer, not an agent.'

This was a very valid point, and the lawyer knew he would lose his job if his boss knew he was asking questions and in general impersonating an agent. 'Yes, I'm a lawyer. Callahan and I were in law school together.'

'Then why do you want to see Darby Shaw?'

The bartender had eased closer and was eavesdropping.

'Do you know her?'

'I don't know,' the student said, and it was obvious he did in fact know her but was not about to talk. 'Is she in trouble?'

'No. You know her, don't you?'

'Maybe. Maybe not.'

'Look, what's your name?'

'Show me a badge, and I'll tell you my name.'

Gavin took a long drink from the bottle and smiled at the bartender. 'I need to see her, okay. It's very important. I'll be at the Hilton for a few days. If you see her, ask her to call.' He offered the card to the student, who looked at it and walked away.

At three, he unlocked the door to his room, and checked the phone. No messages. Wherever Darby was, she still had not called. Assuming, of course, she was still alive.

CHAPTER TWENTY

Garcia called for the last time. Grantham took the call before dawn Saturday, less than two hours before they were to meet for the first time. He was backing out, he said. The time was not right. If the story broke, then some very powerful lawyers and their very rich clients would fall hard, and these people were not accustomed to falling, and they would take people with them. And Garcia might get hurt. He had a wife and little daughter. He had a job that he could endure because the money was great. Why take chances? He had done nothing wrong. His conscience was clear.

'Then why do you keep calling me?' Grantham asked.

'I think I know why they were killed. I'm not certain, but I've got a good idea. I saw something, okay.'

'We've had this conversation for a week now, Garcia. You saw something, or you have something. And it's all useless unless you show it to me.' Grantham opened a file and took out the five by sevens of the man on the phone. 'You're driven by a sense of morality, Garcia. That's why you want to talk.'

'Yeah, but there's a chance they know that I know. They've been treating me funny, as if they want to ask if I saw it. But they can't ask because they're not sure.'

'These are the guys in your firm?'

'Yeah. No. Wait. How'd you know I was in a firm? I haven't told you that.'

'It's easy. You go to work too early to be a government lawyer. You're in one of those two-hundred-lawyer firms where they expect the associates and junior partners to work a hundred hours a week. The first time you called me you said you were on the way to the office, and it was something like 5 A.M.'

'Well, well, what else do you know?'

'Not much. We're playing games, Garcia. If you're not willing to talk, then hang up and leave me alone. I'm losing sleep.'

'Sweet dreams.' Garcia hung up. Grantham stared at the receiver.

Three times in the past eight years he had unlisted his phone number. He lived by the phone, and his biggest stories came out of nowhere over the phone. But after or during each big one, there had been a thousand insignificant ones from sources who felt compelled to call at all hours of the night with their hot little morsels. He was known as a reporter who would face a firing squad before revealing a source, so they called and called and called. He'd get sick of it, and get a new, unlisted number. Then hit a dry spell. Then rush to get back in the D.C. directory.

He was there now. Gray S. Grantham. The only one in the book. They could get him at work twelve hours a day, but it was so much more secretive and private to call him at home, especially at odd hours when he was trying to sleep.

He fumed over Garcia for thirty minutes, then fell asleep. He was in a rhythm and dead to the world when it rang again. He found it in the darkness. 'Hello.'

It was not Garcia. It was a female. 'Is this Gray Grantham with the *Washington Post*?'

'It is. And who are you?'

'Are you still on the story about Rosenberg and Jensen?'

He sat in the darkness and stared at the clock. Five-thirty. 'It's a big story. We've got a lot of people on it, but, yes, I'm investigating.'

'Have you heard of the pelican brief?'

He breathed deeply and tried to think. 'The pelican brief. No. What is it?'

'It's a harmless little theory about who killed them. It was taken to Washington last Sunday by a man named Thomas Callahan, a professor of law at Tulane. He gave it to a friend with the FBI, and it was passed around. Things snowballed, and Callahan was killed in a car bombing Wednesday night in New Orleans.'

The lamp was on and he was scribbling. 'Where are you calling from?'

'New Orleans. A pay phone, so don't bother.'

'How do you know all this?'

'I wrote the brief.'

He was wide awake now, wild-eyed and breathing rapidly. 'Okay. If you wrote it, tell me about it.'

'I don't want to do it that way, because even if you had a copy you couldn't run the story.'

'Try me.'

'You couldn't. It'll take some thorough verification.'

'Okay. We've got the Klan, the terrorist Khamel, the Underground Army, the Aryans, the –'

'Nope. None of the above. They're a bit obvious. The brief is about an obscure suspect.'

He was pacing at the foot of the bed, holding the phone. 'Why can't you tell me who it is?'

'Maybe later. You seem to have these magical sources. Let's see what you find.'

'Callahan will be easy to check out. That's one phone call. Give me twenty-four hours.'

'I'll try to call Monday morning. If we're gonna do business, Mr. Grantham, you must show me something. The next time I call, tell me something I don't know.'

She was at a pay phone in the dark. 'Are you in danger?' he asked.

'I think so. But I'm okay for now.'

She sounded young, mid-twenties, maybe. She wrote a brief. She knew the law professor. 'Are you a lawyer?'

'No, and don't spend your time digging after me. You've got work to do, Mr. Grantham, or I'll go elsewhere.'

'Fine. You need a name.'

'I've got one.'

'I mean a code name.'

'You mean like spies and all. Gee, this could be fun.'

'Either that or give me your real name.'

'Nice try. Just call me Pelican.'

His parents were good Irish Catholics, but he had sort of quit many years ago. They were a handsome couple, dignified in mourning, well tanned and dressed. He had seldom mentioned them. They walked hand-in-hand with the rest of the family into Rogers Chapel. His brother from Mobile was shorter and looked much older. Thomas said he had a drinking problem.

For half an hour, students and faculty had streamed into the small chapel. The game was tonight and there was a nice crowd on campus. A television van was parked in the street. A cameraman kept a respectable distance and shot the front of the chapel. A campus policeman watched him carefully and kept him in place.

It was odd seeing these law students with dresses and heels and coats and ties. In a dark room on the third floor of Newcomb Hall, the Pelican sat with her face to the window and watched the students mill about and speak softly and finish their cigarettes. Under her chair were four newspapers, already read and discarded. She'd been there for two hours, reading by sunlight and waiting on the service. There was no other place to be. She was certain the bad guys were lurking in the bushes around the chapel, but she was learning patience. She had come early, would stay late, and move in the shadows. If they found her, maybe they would do it quick and it would be over.

She gripped a wadded paper towel and dried her eyes. It was okay to cry now, but this was the last one. The people were all inside, and the television van left. The paper said it was a memorial service with private burial later. There was no casket inside.

She had selected this moment to run, to rent a car and drive to Baton Rouge, then jump on the first plane headed to any place except New Orleans. She would get out of the country, perhaps Montreal or Calgary. She would hide there for a year and hope the crime would be solved and the bad guys put away.

But it was a dream. The quickest route to justice ran smack through her. She knew more than anyone. The Fibbies had circled close, then backed off, and were now chasing who knows who. Verheek had gotten nowhere, and he was close to the Director. She would have to piece it together. Her little brief had killed Thomas, and now they were after her. She knew the identity of the man behind the murders of Rosenberg and Jensen and Callahan, and this knowledge made her rather unique.

Suddenly, she leaned forward. The tears dried on her cheeks. There he was! The thin man with the narrow face! He was wearing a coat and tie and looked properly mournful as he walked quickly to the chapel. It was him! The man she'd last seen in the lobby of the Sheraton on, when was it, Thursday morning. She'd been talking to Verheek when he strolled suspiciously through.

He stopped at the door, jerked his head nervously around – he was a klutz, really, a giveaway. He stared for a second at three cars parked innocently on the street, less than fifty yards away. He opened the door, and was in the chapel. Beautiful. The bastards killed him, and now they joined his family and friends for last respects.

Her nose touched the window. The cars were too far away, but she was certain there was a man in one watching for her. Surely they knew she was not so dumb and so heartbroken as to show up and mourn her lover. They knew that. She had eluded them for two and a half days. The tears were gone.

Ten minutes later, the thin man came out by himself, lit a cigarette, and strolled with hands stuck deep in his pockets towards the three cars. He was sad. What a guy.

He walked in front of the cars but did not stop. When he was out of sight, a door opened and a man in a green Tulane sweatshirt emerged from the middle car. He walked down the street after the thin one. He was not thin. He was short, thick, and powerful. A regular stump.

He disappeared down the sidewalk behind the thin man, behind the chapel. Darby poised on the edge of the folding chair. Within a minute, they emerged on the sidewalk from behind the building. They were together now, whispering, but for only a moment because the thin man peeled off and disappeared down the street. Stump walked quickly to his car and got in. He just sat there, waiting for the service to break up and get one last look at the crowd on the off chance that she was in fact stupid enough to show up.

It had taken less than ten minutes for the thin man to sneak inside, scan the crowd of, say, two hundred people, and determine she was not there. Perhaps he was looking for the red hair. Or bleached blond. No, it made more sense for them to have people already in there, sitting around prayerfully and looking sad, looking for her or anyone who might resemble her. They could nod or shake or wink at the thin man.

This place was crawling with them.

Havana was a perfect sanctuary. It mattered not if ten or a hundred countries had bounties on his throat. Fidel was an admirer and occasional client. They drank together, shared women, and smoked cigars. He had the run of the place: a nice little apartment on Calle de Torre in the old section, a car with a driver, a banker who was a wizard at blitzing money around the world, any size boat he wanted, a military plane if needed, and plenty of young women. He spoke the language and his skin was not pale. He loved the place.

He had once agreed to kill Fidel, but couldn't do it. He was in place and two hours away from the murder, but just wouldn't pull it off. There was too much admiration. It was back in the days when he did not always kill for money. He pulled a double cross, and confessed to Fidel. They faked an ambush, and word spread that the great Khamel had been gunned down in the streets of Havana.

Never again would he travel by commercial air. The photographs in Paris were embarrassing for such a professional. He was losing his touch; getting careless in the twilight of his career. Got his picture on the front pages in America. How shameful. His client was not pleased.

The boat was a forty-foot schooner with two crew members and a young woman, all Cubans. She was below in the cabin. He had finished with her a few minutes before they saw the lights of Biloxi. He was all business now, inspecting his raft, packing his bag, saying nothing. The crew members crouched on the deck and stayed away from him.

At exactly nine, they lowered the raft onto the water. He dropped his bag into it, and was gone. They heard the trolling motor as he disappeared into the blackness of the Sound. They were to remain anchored until dawn, then haul it back to Havana. They held perfect papers declaring them to be Americans, in the event they were discovered and someone began asking questions.

He eased patiently through the still water, dodging buoy lights and the sight of an occasional small craft. He held perfect papers too, and three weapons in the bag.

It had been years since he struck twice in one month. After he was allegedly gunned down in Cuba, there had been a five-year drought. Patience was his forte. He averaged one a year.

And this little victim would go unnoticed. No one would suspect him. It was such a small job, but his client was adamant and he happened to be in the neighborhood, and the money was right, so here he was in another six-foot rubber raft cruising toward a beach, hoping like hell his pal Luke would be there dressed not as a farmer, but a fisherman this time.

This would be the last for a long time, maybe forever. He had more money than he could ever spend or give away. And he had started making small mistakes.

He saw the pier in the distance, and moved away from it. He had thirty minutes to waste. He followed the shoreline for a quarter of a mile, then headed for it. Two hundred yards out, he turned off the trolling motor, unhitched it, and dropped it into the water. He lay low in the raft, worked a plastic oar when necessary, and gently guided himself to a dark spot behind a row of cheap brick buildings thirty feet ashore. He stood in two feet of water and ripped holes in the raft with a small pocketknife. It sank and disappeared. The beach was deserted.

Luke was alone at the end of the pier. It was exactly eleven, and he was in place with a rod and reel. He wore a white cap, and the bill moved slowly back and forth as he scanned the water in seach of the raft. He checked his watch.

Suddenly a man was beside him, appearing from nowhere like an angel. 'Luke?' the man said.

This was not the code. Luke was startled. He had a gun in the tackle box at his feet, but there was no way. 'Sam?' he asked. Maybe he had missed something. Maybe Khamel couldn't find the pier from the raft.

'Yes, Luke, it's me. Sorry about the deviation. Trouble with the raft.'

Luke's heart settled and he breathed relief.

'Where's the vehicle?' Khamel asked.

Luke glanced at him ever so quickly. Yes, it was Khamel, and he was staring at the ocean behind dark glasses.

Luke nodded at a building. 'Red Pontiac next to the liquor store.'

'How far to New Orleans?'

'Half an hour,' Luke said as he reeled in nothing.

Khamel stepped back, and hit him twice at the base of the neck. Once with each hand. The vertebrae burst and snapped the spinal cord. Luke fell hard and moaned once. Khamel watched him die, then found the keys in a pocket. He kicked the corpse off into the water.

***

Edwin Sneller or whatever his name was did not open the door, but quietly slid the key under it. Khamel picked it up, and opened the door to the next room. He walked in, and moved quickly to the bed where he placed his bag, then to the window where the curtains were open and the river was in the distance. He pulled the curtains together, and studied the lights of the French Quarter below.

He walked to the phone and punched Sneller's number.

'Tell me about her,' Khamel said softly to the floor.

'There are two photos in the briefcase.'

Khamel opened it and removed the photos. 'I've got them.'

'They're numbered, one and two. One we got from the law school yearbook. It's about a year old, and the most current we have. It's a blowup from a tiny picture, so we lost a lot of detail. The other photo is two years old. We lifted it from a yearbook at Arizona State.'

Khamel held both pictures. 'A beautiful woman.'

'Yes. Quite beautiful. All that lovely hair is gone, though. Thursday night she paid for a hotel room with a credit card. We barely missed her Friday morning. We found long strands of hair on the floor and a small sample of something we now know to be black hair color. Very black.'

'What a shame.'

'We haven't seen her since Wednesday night. She's proven to be elusive: credit card for a room Wednesday, credit card at another hotel Thursday, then nothing from last night. She withdrew five thousand in cash from her checking account Friday afternoon, so the trail has become cold.'

'Maybe she's gone.'

'Could be, but I don't think so. Someone was in her apartment last night. We've got the place wired, and we were late by two minutes.'

'Moving sort of slow, aren't you?'

'It's a big town. We've camped out at the airport and train station. We're watching her mother's house in Idaho. No sign. I think she's still here.'

'Where would she be?'

'Moving around, changing hotels, using pay phones, staying away from the usual places. The New Orleans police are looking for her. They talked to her after the bomb Wednesday, then lost her. We're looking, they're looking, she'll turn up.'

'What happened with the bomb?'

'Very simple. She didn't get in the car.'

'Who made the bomb?'

Sneller hesitated. 'Can't say.'

Khamel smiled slightly as he took some street maps from the briefcase. 'Tell me about the maps.'

'Oh, just a few points of interest around town. Her place, his place, the law school, the hotels she's been to, the bomb site, a few little bars she enjoys as a student.'

'She's stayed in the Quarter so far.'

'She's smart. There are a million places to hide.'

Khamel picked up the most recent photo, and sat on the other bed. He liked this face. Even with short dark hair, it would be an intriguing face. He could kill it, but it would not be pleasant.

'It's a shame, isn't it?' he said, almost to himself.

'Yes. It's a shame.'

CHAPTER TWENTY-ONE

Gavin Verheek had been a tired old man when he arrived in New Orleans, and after two nights of barhopping he was drained and weakened. He had hit the first bar not long after the burial, and for seven hours had sipped beer with the young and restless while talking of torts and contracts and Wall Street firms and other things he despised. He knew he shouldn't tell strangers he was FBI. He wasn't FBI. There was no badge.

He prowled five or six bars Saturday night. Tulane lost again, and after the game the bars filled with rowdies. Things got hopeless, and he quit at midnight.

He was sleeping hard with his shoes on when the phone rang. He lunged for it. 'Hello! Hello!'

'Gavin?' she asked.

'Darby! Is this you?'

'Who else?'

'Why haven't you called before now?'

'Please, don't start asking a bunch of stupid questions. I'm at a pay phone, so no funny stuff.'

'Come on, Darby. I swear you can trust me.'

'Okay, I trust you. Now what?'

He looked at his watch, and began untying his shoelaces.

'Well, you tell me. What's next? How long do you plan to hide in New Orleans?'

'How do you know I'm in New Orleans?'

He paused for a second.

'I'm in New Orleans,' she said. 'And I assume you want me to meet with you, and become close friends, then come in, as you say, and trust you guys to protect me forever.'

'That's correct. You'll be dead in a matter of days if you don't.'

'Get right to the point, don't you?'

'Yes. You're playing games and you don't know what you're doing.'

'Who's after me, Gavin?'

'Could be a number of people.'

'Who are they?'

'I don't know.'

'Now you're playing games, Gavin. How can I trust you if you won't talk to me?'

'Okay. I think it's safe to say your little brief hit someone in the gut.

You guessed right, the wrong people learned of the brief, and now Thomas is dead. And they'll kill you the instant they find you.'

'We know who killed Rosenberg and Jensen, don't we, Gavin?'

'I think we do.'

'Then why doesn't the FBI do something?'

'We may be in the midst of a cover-up.'

'Bless you for saying that. Bless you.'

'I could lose my job.'

'Who would I tell, Gavin? Who's covering up what?'

'I'm not sure. We were very interested in the brief until the White House pressed hard, now we've dismissed it.'

'I can understand that. Why do they think they can kill me and it will be kept quiet?'

'I can't answer that. Maybe they think you know more.'

'Can I tell you something? Moments after the bomb, while Thomas was in the car burning and I was semiconscious, a cop named Rupert took me to his car and put me inside. Another cop with cowboy boots and jeans started asking me questions. I was sick and in shock. They disappeared, Rupert and his cowboy, and they never returned. They were not cops, Gavin. They watched the bomb, and went to plan B when I wasn't in the car. I didn't know it, but I was probably a minute or two away from a bullet in the head.'

Verheek listened with his eyes closed. 'What happened to them?'

'Not sure. I think they got scared when the real cops swarmed on the scene. They vanished. I was in their car, Gavin. They had me.'

'You have to come in, Darby. Listen to me.'

'Do you remember our phone chat Thursday morning when I suddenly saw a face that looked familiar and I described it to you?'

'Of course.'

'That face was at the memorial service yesterday, along with some friends.'

'Where were you?'

'Watching. He walked in a few minutes late, stayed ten minutes, then sneaked out and met with Stump.'

'Stump?'

'Yes, he's one of the gang. Stump, Rupert, Cowboy, and the Thin Man. Great characters. I'm sure there are others, but I haven't met them yet.'

'The next meeting will be the last, Darby. You have about forty-eight hours to live.'

'We'll see. How long will you be in town?'

'A few days. I'd planned to stay until I found you.'

'Here I am. I may call you tomorrow.'

Verheek breathed deeply. 'Okay, Darby. Whatever you say. Just be careful.'

She hung up. He threw the phone across the room, and cursed it.

Two blocks away and fifteen floors up, Khamel stared at the television and mumbled rapidly to himself. It was a movie about people in a big city. They spoke English, his third language, and he repeated every word in his best generic American tongue. He did this for hours. He had absorbed the language while hiding in Belfast, and in the past twenty years had watched thousands of American movies. His favorite was *Three Days of the Condor.* He watched it four times before he figured out who was killing whom and why. He could have killed Redford.

He repeated every word out loud. He had been told his English could pass for that of an American, but one slip, one tiny mistake, and she would be gone.

The volvo was parked in a lot a block and a half from its owner, who paid one hundred dollars a month for the space and for what he thought was security. They eased through the gate that was supposed to be locked.

It was a 1986 GL without a security system, and within seconds the driver's door was open. One sat on the trunk and lit a cigarette. It was almost 4 A.M. Sunday.

The other one opened a small tool case he kept in his pocket, and went to work on the yuppie car phone that Grantham had been embarrassed to buy. The dome light was enough, and he worked quickly. Easy work. With the receiver open, he installed a tiny transmitter and glued it in place. A minute later, he eased out of the car and squatted at the rear bumper. The one with the cigarette handed him a small black cube, which he stuck under the car to a grille and behind the gas tank. It was a magnetized transmitter, and it would send signals for six days before it died and needed replacing.

They were gone in less than seven minutes. Monday, as soon as he was spotted entering the *Post* building on Fifteenth, they would enter his apartment and fix his phones.

CHAPTER TWENTY-TWO

Her second night in the bed and breakfast was better than the first. She slept until mid-morning. Maybe she was used to it now. She stared at the curtains over the tiny window and determined that there had been no nightmares, no movements in the dark with guns and knives emerging and attacking. It was a thick, heavy sleep, and she studied the curtains for a long time while the brain woke up.

She tried to be disciplined about her thinking. This was her fourth day as the Pelican, and to see number five she would have to think like a fastidious killer. It was day number four of the rest of her life. She was supposed to be dead.

But after the eyes opened, and she realized she was indeed alive and safe, and the door wasn't squeaking and the floor wasn't cracking, and there was no gunman lurking in the closet, her first thought was always of Thomas. The shock of his death was fading, and she found it easier to put aside the sound of the explosion and the roar of the fire. She knew he had been blown to pieces and killed instantly. She knew he did not suffer.

So she thought of other things, like the feel of him next to her, and his whispering and snickering when they were in bed and the sex was over and he wanted to cuddle. He was a cuddler, and he wanted to play and kiss and caress after the lovemaking. And giggle. He loved her madly, had fallen hard, and for the first time in his life could be silly with a woman. Many times in the middle of his lectures, she had thought of his cooing and snickering, and bit her lip to keep from smiling.

She loved him too. And it hurt so badly. She wanted to stay in bed and cry for a week. The day after her father's funeral, a psychiatrist had explained that the soul needs a brief, very intense period of grieving, then it moves to the next phase. But it must have the pain; it must suffer without restraint before it can properly move on. She took his advice, and grieved without courage for two weeks, then got tried of it and moved to the next stage. It worked.

But it wasn't working with Thomas. She couldn't scream and throw things the way she wanted. Rupert and Thin Man and the rest of the boys were denying her a healthy mourning.

After a few minutes of Thomas, she thought of them next. Where would they be today? Where could she go without being seen? After two nights in this place, should she find another room? Yes, she would do that. After dark. She would call and reserve a room at another tiny guest house. Where were they staying? Were they patrolling the streets hoping to simply bump into her? Did they know where she was at this moment? No. She would be dead. Did they know she was now a blonde?

The hair got her out of bed. She walked to the mirror over the desk, and looked at herself. It was even shorter now, and very white. Not a bad job. She had worked on it for three hours last night. If she lived another two days, she would cut some more and go back to black. If she lived another week, she might be bald.

A hunger pain hit, and for a second she thought about food. She was not eating, and this would have to change. It was almost ten. Oddly, this bed and breakfast didn't cook on Sunday mornings. She would venture out to find food and a Sunday *Post*, and to see if they could catch her now that she was a butch blonde.

She showered quickly, and the hair took less than a minute. No makeup. She put on a new pair of Army fatigues and a new flight jacket, and she was ready for battle. The eyes were covered with aviator shades.

Although she had made a few entrances, she had not exited a building through the front door in four days. She crept through the dark kitchen, unlocked the rear door, and stepped onto the alley behind the little inn. It was cool enough to wear the flight jacket without being suspicious. Silly, she thought. In the French Quarter, she could wear the hide and head of a polar bear and not appear suspicious. She walked briskly through the alley with her hands deep in the fatigues and her eyes darting behind the shades.

He saw her when she stepped onto the sidewalk next to Burgundy Street. The hair under the cap was different, but she was still five-eight and she couldn't change that. The legs were still long and she walked a certain way, and after four days he could pick her out of a crowd regardless of the face and hair. The cowboy boots – snakeskin with pointed toes – hit the sidewalk and started following.

She was a smart girl, turning every corner, changing streets every block, walking quickly but not too fast. He figured she was headed for Jackson Square, where there was a crowd on Sundays and she thought she could disappear. She could stroll about with the tourists and the locals, maybe eat a bite, enjoy the sun, pick up a paper.

Darby casually lit a cigarette and puffed as she walked. She could not inhale. She tried three days ago, and got dizzy. Such a nasty habit. How ironic it would be if she lived through all this only to die from lung cancer. Please, let her die of cancer.

He was sitting at a table in a crowded sidewalk café at the corner of St. Peter and Chartres, and he was less than ten feet away when she saw him. A split second later, he saw her, and she probably would have made it if she hadn't hesitated for a step and swallowed hard when she saw him. He saw her, and probably would have been only suspicious, but the slight hesitation and the curious look gave her away. She kept walking, but faster now.

It was Stump. He was on his feet and weaving through the tables when she lost sight of him. At ground level, he was anything but chubby. He seemed quick and muscular. She lost him for a second on Chartres as she ducked between the arches of St. Louis Cathedral. The church was open, and she thought maybe she should get inside, as if it would be a sanctuary and he would not kill her there. Yes, he would kill her there, or on the street, or in a crowd. Anywhere he caught her. He was back there, and Darby wanted to know how fast he was coming. Was he just walking real fast and trying to play it cool? Was he sort of jogging? Or was he barreling down the sidewalk preparing to make a flying tackle as soon as he caught sight of her? She kept moving.

She hung a left on St. Ann, crossed the street, and was almost to Royal when she took a quick glance behind her. He was coming. He was on the other side of the street, but very much in pursuit.

The nervous look over the shoulder nailed her. It was a dead giveaway, and he was into a jog now.

Get to Bourbon Street, she decided. Kickoff was four hours away, and the Saints fans were out in force celebrating before the game because there would be little to celebrate afterward. She turned on Royal and ran hard for a few steps, then slowed to a fast walk. He turned on Royal and was trotting. He was poised to break and run hard at any second. Darby moved to the center of the street where a group of football rowdies were moving around, killing time. She turned left on Dumaine, and started running. Bourbon was ahead and there were people everywhere.

She could hear him now. No sense looking anymore. He was back there, running and gaining. When she turned onto Bourbon, Mr. Stump was fifty feet behind her, and the race was over. She saw her angels as they made a noisy exit from a bar. Three large, overweight young men dressed in a wild assortment of black and gold Saints garb stepped into the middle of the street just as Darby ran to them.

'Help!' she screamed wildly and pointed at Stump. 'Help me! That man is after me! He's trying to rape me!'

Well, hell, now, sex in the streets of New Orleans is not at all uncommon, but they'd be damned if this girl was going to be abused.

'Please help me!' she screamed pitifully. Suddenly, the street was silent. Everyone froze, including Stump, who stopped for a step or two, then rushed forward. The three Saints stepped in front of him with folded arms and glowing eyes. It was over in seconds. Stump used both hands at once: a right to the throat of the first one, and a vicious blow to the mouth of the second. They squealed and fell hard. Number three was not about to run. His two buddies were hurt and this upset him. He would have been a piece of cake for Stump, but number one fell on Stump's right foot and this threw him off. As he yanked his foot away, Mr. Benjamin Chop of Thibodaux, Louisiana, number three, kicked him squarely in the crotch, and Stump was history. As Darby eased back into the crowd, she heard him cry in pain.

While he was falling, Mr. Chop kicked him in the ribs. Number two, with blood all over his face, charged wild-eyed into Stump, and the massacre was on. He curled around his hands, which were curled around his severely damaged testicles, and they kicked him and cursed him without mercy until someone yelled, 'Cops,' and this saved his life. Mr. Chop and number two helped number one to his feet, and the Saints were last seen darting into a bar. Stump made it to his feet, and crawled away like a dog hit by a Mack truck but still alive and determined to die at home.

She hid in a dark corner of a pub on Decatur, drinking coffee then a beer, coffee then a beer. Her hands shook and her stomach flipped. The po'boys smelled delicious, but she could not eat. After three beers in three hours, she ordered a plate of boiled shrimp and switched to spring water.

The alcohol had calmed her, and the shrimp settled her. She was safe in here, she thought, so why not watch the game and just sit here, maybe, until it closed.

The pub was packed at kickoff. They watched the wide screen above the bar, and got drunk. She was a Saints fan now. She hoped her three buddies were okay and enjoying the game. The crowd yelled and cursed the Redskins.

Darby stayed in her little corner until the game was long over, then slid into the darkness.

At some point in the fourth quarter, with the Saints down by four field goals, Edwin Sneller hung up the phone and turned off the television. He stretched his legs, then returned to the phone and called Khamel next door.

'Listen to my English,' the assassin said. 'Tell me if you hear a trace of an accent.'

'Okay. She's here,' Sneller said. 'One of our men saw her this morning at Jackson Square. He followed her for three blocks, then lost her.'

'How did he lose her?'

'Doesn't matter, does it? She got away, but she's here. Her hair is very short and almost white.'

'White?'

Sneller hated to repeat himself, especially to this mongrel.

'He said it was not blond but white, and she was wearing green Army pants and a brown bomber jacket. Somehow she recognized him, and took off.'

'How would she recognize him? Has she seen him before?'

These idiot questions. It was hard to believe he was considered Superman. 'I can't answer that.'

'How's my English?'

'Perfect. There's small card under your door. You need to see it.'

Khamel laid the phone on a pillow and walked to the door. In a second he was back on the phone. 'Who is this?'

'The name is Verheek. Dutch, but he's an American. Works for the FBI in Washington. Evidently, he and Callahan were friends. They finished law school together at Georgetown, and Verheek was an honorary pallbearer at the memorial service yesterday. Last night he was hanging out in a bar not far from the campus, and was asking questions about the girl. Two hours ago, one of our men was in the same bar posing as an FBI agent, and he struck up a conversation with the bartender, who turns out to be a law student who knows the girl. They watched football and talked for a while, then the kid produced the card. Look on the back. He's in room 1909 at the Hilton.'

'That's a five-minute walk.' The street maps were scattered on one bed.

'Yes. We've made a few phone calls to Washington. He's not an agent, just a lawyer. He knew Callahan, and he might know the girl. It's obvious he's trying to find her.'

'She would talk to him, wouldn't she?'

'Probably.'

'How's my English?'

'Perfect.'

Khamel waited an hour and left the hotel. With the coat and tie, he was just an average joe strolling along Canal at dusk headed for the river. He carried a large gym bag and smoked a cigarette, and five minutes later entered the lobby of the Hilton. He worked his way through the crowd of fans returning from the Dome. The elevator stopped on the twentieth floor, and he walked one flight down to the nineteenth.

There was no answer at 1909. If the door had opened with the chain locked, he would have apologized and explained he had the wrong room. If the door had opened without the chain and with a face in the crack, he would have kicked it sharply and been inside. But it did not open.

His new pal Verheek was probably hanging around a bar, passing out cards, begging kids to talk to him about Darby Shaw. What a nut.

He knocked again, and while he waited he slid a six-inch plastic ruler between the door and the facing, and worked it gently until the bolt clicked. Locks were minor nuisances for Khamel. Without a key, he could open a locked car and start the engine in less than thirty seconds.

Inside, he locked the door behind him, and placed his bag on the bed. Like a surgeon, he picked the gloves from a pocket and pulled them tightly over his fingers. He laid a .22 and silencer on the table.

The phone was quick work. He plugged the recorder into the jack under the bed, where it could sit for weeks before it was noticed. He called the weather station twice to test the recorder. Perfect.

His new pal Verheek was a slob. Most of the clothes in the room were dirty and simply thrown in the direction of the suitcase sitting on a table. He had not unpacked. A cheap garment bag hung in the closet with one solitary shirt.

Khamel covered his tracks and settled low in the closet. He was a patient man, and he could wait for hours. He held the .22 just in case this clown happened to barge into the closet and he had to kill him with bullets. If not, he would just listen.

CHAPTER TWENTY-THREE

Gavin quit the bars Sunday. He was getting nowhere. She had called him, and she was not hanging around those places, so what the hell. He was drinking too much and eating too much, and he was tired of New Orleans. He already had a flight booked for late Monday afternoon, and if she didn't call again he was finished playing detective.

He couldn't find her, and it wasn't his fault. Cabdrivers got lost in this city. Voyles would be screaming by noon. He had done his best.

He was stretched on the bed in nothing but boxer shorts, flipping through a magazine and ignoring the television. It was almost eleven. He would wait on her until twelve, then try to sleep.

It rang at exactly eleven. He pushed a button and remotely killed the television. 'Hello.'

It was her. 'It's me, Gavin.'

'So you're alive.'

'Barely.'

He sat on the edge of the bed. 'What's happened?'

'They saw me today, and one of their goons, my friend Stump, chased me through the Quarter. You haven't met Stump, but he's the one who watched you and everyone else walk into the chapel.'

'But you got away.'

'Yeah. A small miracle, but I got away.'

'What happened to Stump?'

'He was mortally wounded. He's probably lying in a bed somewhere wearing an ice pack in his shorts. He was just a few steps from me when he picked a fight with the wrong guys. I'm scared, Gavin.'

'Did he follow you from somewhere?'

'No. We just sort of met on the street.'

Verheek paused a second. Her voice was shaking, but under control. She was losing her cool. 'Look, Darby. I've got a flight out of here tomorrow afternoon. I have this little job and my boss expects me to be at the office. So I can't hang around New Orleans for the next month hoping you don't get killed and hoping you come to your senses and trust me. I'm leaving tomorrow, and I think you need to go with me.'

'Go where?'

'To Washington. To my house. To someplace other than where you are.'

'What happens then?'

'Well, you get to live, for one thing. I'll plead with the Director, and

I promise you'll be safe. We'll do something, dammit. Anything beats this.'

'What makes you think we can just fly out of here?'

'Because we'll have three FBI agents surrounding you. Because I'm not a complete dumbass. Look, Darby, tell me where you want to meet right now, and within fifteen minutes I'll come get you with three agents. These guys have guns, and they're not afraid of your little Stump and his pals. We'll get you out of the city tonight, and take you to Washington tomorrow. I promise you'll personally meet my boss, the Honorable F. Denton Voyles, tomorrow, and we'll go from there.'

'I thought the FBI was not involved.'

'It's not involved, but it may be.'

'Then where do the three agents come from?'

'I've got friends.'

She thought for a moment, and her voice was suddenly stronger. 'Behind your hotel is a place called Riverwalk. It's a shopping area with restaurants and –'

'I spent two hours there this afternoon.'

'Good. On the second level is a clothing store called Frenchmen's Bend.'

'I saw it.'

'At precisely noon tomorrow, I want you to stand by the entrance, and wait for five minutes.'

'Come on, Darby. You won't be alive at noon tomorrow. Enough of this cat and mouse.'

'Just do as I say, Gavin. We've never met, so I have no idea what you look like. Wear a black shirt of some type and a red baseball cap.'

'Where might I find such articles?'

'Just get them.'

'Okay, okay, I'll have them. I guess you want me to pick my nose with a shovel or something. This is silly.'

'I'm not in a silly mood, and if you don't shut up we'll call it off.'

'It's your neck.'

'Please, Gavin.'

'I'm sorry. I'll do whatever you say. That's a very busy spot to be.'

'Yes, it is. I just feel safer in a crowd. Stand by the door for five minutes or so, and hold a folded newspaper. I'll be watching. After five minutes, walk inside the store, and go to the right rear corner where there's a rack of safari jackets. Browse around a bit, and I'll find you.'

'And what might you be wearing?'

'Don't worry about me.'

'Fine. Then what do we do?'

'You and I, and only you and I, will leave the city. I don't want anyone else to know of this. Do you understand?'

'No, I don't understand. I can arrange security.'

'No. Gavin. I'm the boss, okay. No one else. Forget your three agent friends. Agreed?'

'Agreed. How do you propose we leave the city?'

'I've got a plan for that too.'

'I don't like any of your plans, Darby. These thugs are breathing down your neck, and now you're getting me in the middle of it. This is not what I wanted. It's much safer to do it my way. Safer for you, safer for me.'

'But you'll be there at noon, won't you?'

He stood by the bed and spoke with his eyes closed. 'Yes. I'll be there. I just hope you make it.'

'How tall are you?'

'Five-ten.'

'How much do you weigh?'

'I was afraid of this. I usually lie, you know. Two hundred, but I plan to lose it. I swear.'

'I'll see you tomorrow, Gavin.'

'I hope I see you, dear.'

She was gone. He hung up. 'Son of a bitch!' he yelled to the walls. 'Son of a bitch!' He walked along the end of the bed a few times, then to the bathroom, where he closed the door and turned on the shower.

He cussed her in the shower for ten minutes, then stepped out, and dried himself. It was more like two hundred and fifteen pounds, and all of it was situated badly on the five-nine frame. It was painful to look at. Here he was, about to meet this gorgeous woman who suddenly trusted him with her life, and what a slob he was.

He opened the door. The room was dark. Dark? He had left on the lights. What the hell? He headed for the switch next to the dresser.

The first blow crushed his larynx. It was a perfect blow that came from the side, somewhere near the wall. He grunted painfully and fell to one knee, which made the second blow so easy, like an ax on a fat log. It hit like a rock at the base of the skull, and Gavin was dead.

Khamel flipped on a light, and looked at the pitiful nude figure frozen on the floor. He was not one to admire his work. He didn't want carpet burns, so he lifted the pudgy corpse onto his shoulders and laid it across the bed. Working quickly without any wasted motion, Khamel turned on the television and raised it to full volume, unzipped his bag, removed a cheap .25 caliber automatic, and placed it precisely on the right temple of the late Gavin Verheek. He covered the gun and the head with two pillows, and pulled the trigger. Now the critical part: he took one pillow and placed it under the head, threw the other one on the floor, and carefully curled the fingers of the right hand around the pistol, leaving it twelve inches from the head.

He took the recorder from under the bed, and ran the telephone wire directly into the wall. He punched a button, listened, and there she was. He turned off the television.

Every job was different. He had once stalked his prey for three weeks in Mexico City, then caught him in bed with two prostitutes. It was a dumb mistake, and during his career he had been assisted by numerous dumb mistakes by the opposition. This guy was a dumb mistake, a stupid lawyer pilfering around running his mouth, passing out cards with his room number on the back. He had stuck his nose into the world of big-league killing, and look at him now.

With a little luck, the cops would look around the room for a few minutes and declare it to be another suicide. They would go through the motions and ask themselves a couple of questions they could not answer, but there were always some of those. Because he was an important FBI lawyer, an autopsy would be done in a day or so, and probably by Tuesday an examiner would suddenly discover it was not a suicide.

By Tuesday, the girl would be dead and he would be in Managua.

CHAPTER TWENTY-FOUR

His usual, official sources at the White House denied any knowledge of the pelican brief. Sarge had never heard of it. Long-shot phone calls to the FBI produced nothing. A friend at Justice denied ever hearing about it. He dug all weekend, and had nothing to show for it. The story about Callahan was verified when he found a copy of the New Orleans paper. When her call came in at the newsroom Monday, he had nothing fresh to tell her. But at least she called.

The Pelican said she was at a pay phone, so don't bother.

'I'm still digging,' he said. 'If there's such a brief in town, it's being closely protected.'

'I assure you it's there, and I understand why it's being protected.'

'I'm sure you can tell me more.'

'Lots more. The brief almost got me killed yesterday, so I may be ready to talk sooner than I thought. I need to spill my guts while I'm still alive.'

'Who's trying to kill you?'

'Same people who killed Rosenberg and Jensen, and Thomas Callahan.'

'Do you know their names?'

'No, but I've seen at least four of them since Wednesday. They're here in New Orleans, snooping around, hoping I'll do something stupid and they can kill me.'

'How many people know about the pelican brief?'

'Good question. Callahan took it to the FBI, and I think from there it went to the White House where it evidently caused quite a fuss, and from there who knows. Two days after he handed it to the FBI, Callahan was dead. I, of course, was supposed to have been killed with him.'

'Were you with him?'

'I was close, but not close enough.'

'So you're the unidentified female on the scene?'

'That's how the paper described me.'

'Then the police have your name?'

'My name is Darby Shaw. I am a second-year law student at Tulane. Thomas Callahan was my professor and lover. I wrote the brief, gave it to him, and you know the rest. Are you getting all this?'

Grantham scribbled furiously. 'Yes. I'm listening.'

'I'm rather tired of the French Quarter, and I plan to leave today. I'll call you from somewhere tomorrow. Do you have access to presidential campaign disclosure forms?'

'It's public record.'

'I know that. But how quickly can you get the information?'

'What information?'

'A list of all major contributors to the President's last election.'

'That's not difficult. I can have it by this afternoon.'

'Do that, and I'll call you in the morning.'

'Okay. Do you have a copy of the brief?'

She hesitated. 'No, but it's memorized.'

'And you know who's doing the killing?'

'Yes, and as soon as I tell you, they'll put your name on the hit list.'

'Tell me now.'

'Let's take it slow. I'll call you tomorrow.'

Grantham listened hard, then hung up. He took his notepad and zigzagged through the maze of desks and people to the glass office of his editor, Smith Keen. Keen was a hale and hearty type with an open-door policy that ensured chaos in his office. He was finishing a phone chat when Grantham barged in and closed the door.

'That door stays open,' Keen said sharply.

'We have to talk, Smith.'

'We'll talk with the door open. Open the damned door.'

'I'll open it in just a second.' Grantham spoke with both palms facing the editor. Yes, it was serious. 'Let's talk.'

'Okay. What is it?'

'It's big, Smith.'

'I know it's big. You shut the damned door, so I know it's big.'

'I just finished my second phone conversation with a young lady by the name of Darby Shaw, and she knows who killed Rosenberg and Jensen.'

Keen sat slowly and glared at Grantham. 'Yes, son, that's big. But how do you know? How does she know? What can you prove?'

'I don't have a story yet, Smith, but she's talking to me. Read this.' Grantham handed over a copy of the newspaper account of Callahan's death. Keen read it slowly.

'Okay. Who's Callahan?'

'One week ago today, he handed a little paper known as the pelican brief to the FBI here in town. Evidently, the brief implicates an obscure person in the killings. The brief gets passed around, then sent to the White House, then beyond that no one knows. Two days later, Callahan cranks his Porsche for the last time. Darby Shaw claims to be the unidentified female mentioned there. She was with Callahan, and was supposed to die with him.'

'Why was she supposed to die?'

'She wrote the brief, Smith. Or she claims she did.'

Keen sank deeper into his seat and placed his feet on the desk. He studied the photo of Callahan. 'Where's the brief?'

'I don't know.'

'What's in it?'

'Don't know that either.'

'Then we don't have anything, do we?'

'Not yet. But what if she tells me everything that's in it?'

'And when will she do this?'

Grantham hesitated. 'Soon, I think. Real soon.'

Keen shook his head and threw the copy on the desk. 'If we had the brief, we'd have a helluva story, Gray, but we couldn't run it. There's gotta be some heavy, painful, flawless, and accurate verification before we can run it.'

'But I've got the green light?'

'Yeah, but you keep me posted every hour. Don't write a word until we talk.'

Grantham smiled and opened the door.

This was not forty-bucks-an-hour work. Not even thirty, or twenty. Croft knew he'd be lucky to squeeze fifteen out of Grantham for this needle-in-the-haystack Mickey Mouse crap. If he'd had other work, he'd have told Grantham to find someone else, or better yet, do it himself.

But things had been slow, and he could do a lot worse than fifteen bucks an hour. He finished a joint in the last stall, flushed it, and opened the door. He stuck the dark sunglasses over his ears, and entered the hallway that led to the atrium where four escalators carried a thousand lawyers up to their little rooms, where they would spend the day bitching and threatening by the hour. He had Garcia's face memorized. He was even dreaming of this kid with the bright face and good looks, the slim physique draped with an expensive suit. He would know him if he saw him.

He stood by a pillar, holding a newspaper and trying to watch everyone from behind the dark shades. Lawyers everywhere, scurrying upward with their smug little faces and carrying their smug little attaché cases. Man, how he hated lawyers. Why did they all dress alike? Dark suits. Dark shoes. Dark faces. An occasional nonconformist with a daring little bow tie. Where did they all come from? Shortly after his arrest with the drugs, the first lawyers had been a group of angry mouthpieces hired by the *Post.* Then he hired his own, an overpriced moron who couldn't find the courtroom. Then, the prosecutor was of course a lawyer. Lawyers, lawyers.

Two hours in the morning, two hours at lunch, two hours during the evening, and then Grantham would have another building for him to patrol. Ninety bucks a day was cheap, and he would give this up as soon as he got a better deal. He told Grantham this was hopeless, just shooting in the dark. Grantham agreed, but said to keep shooting. It's all they could do. He said Garcia was scared and wouldn't call anymore. They had to find him.

In his pocket he had two photos just in case, and from the directory he had made a list of the firms in the building. It was a long list. The building had twelve floors filled mainly with firms filled with nothing but these fancy little esquires. He was in a den of snakes.

By nine-thirty the rush was over, and some of the faces looked familiar coming back down the escalators, headed no doubt for the courtrooms and agencies and commissions. Croft eased through the revolving doors, and wiped his feet on the sidewalk.

Four blocks away, Fletcher Coal paced in front of the President's desk and listened intently to the phone in his ear. He frowned, then closed his eyes, then glared at the President as if to say, 'Bad news, Chief. Really bad news.' The President held a letter and peered at Coal over his reading glasses. Coal's pacing back and forth like Der Führer really irritated him, and he made a mental note to say something about it.

Coal slammed the phone down.

'Don't slam the damned phones!' the President said.

Coal was unfazed. 'Sorry. That was Zikman. Gray Grantham called thirty minutes ago, and asked if he had any knowledge of the pelican brief.'

'Wonderful. Fabulous. How'd he get a copy of it?'

Coal was still pacing. 'Zikman knows nothing about it, so his ignorance was genuine.'

'His ignorance is always genuine. He's the dumbest ass on my staff, Fletcher, and I want him gone.'

'Whatever.' Coal sat in a chair across the desk and folded his hands in a little steeple in front of his chin. He was very deep in thought, and the President tried to ignore him. They thought for a moment.

'Voyles leaked it?' the President finally said.

'Maybe, if it was leaked. Grantham is known for bluffing. We can't be certain he's seen the brief. Maybe he heard about it, and he's fishing.'

'Maybe, my ass. What if they run some crazy story about that damned thing? What then?' The President slapped his desk and bolted to his feet. 'What then, Fletcher? That paper hates me!' He moped to the windows.

'They can't run it without another source, and there can't be another source because there's no truth to it. It's a wild idea that's gone much further than it deserves.'

The President sulked for a while and stared through the glass. 'How did Grantham find out about it?'

Coal stood and began pacing, but much slower now. He was still painfully in thought. 'Who knows. No one here knows about it but you and I. They brought one copy, and it's locked away in my office. I personally Xeroxed it once, and gave it to Gminski. I swore him to secrecy.'

The President sneered at the windows.

Coal continued. 'Okay, you're right. There could be a thousand copies out there by now. But it's harmless, unless of course our friend actually did these dirty deeds, then –'

'Then my ass is cooked.'

'Yes, I would say our asses are cooked.'

'How much money did we take?'

'Millions, directly and indirectly.' And legally and illegally, but the President knew little of these transactions and Coal chose to stay quiet.

The President walked slowly to the sofa. 'Why don't you call Grantham? Pick his brain. See what he knows. If he's bluffing, it'll be obvious. What do you think?'

'I don't know.'

'You've talked to him before, haven't you? Everyone knows Grantham.'

Coal was now pacing behind the sofa. 'Yeah, I've talked to him. But if I suddenly call out of nowhere, he'll be suspicious.'

'Yeah, I guess you're right.' The President paced on one end of the sofa, and Coal on the other.

'What's the downside?' the President finally asked.

'Our friend could be involved. You asked Voyles to back off our friend. Our friend could be exposed by the press. Voyles covers his tail and says you told him to chase other suspects and ignore our friend. The *Post* goes berserk with another cover-up smear. And we can forget reelection.'

'Anything else?'

Coal thought for a second. 'Yeah, this is all completely off the wall. The brief is fantasy. Grantham will find nothing, and I'm late for a staff meeting.' He walked to the door. 'I've got a squash game for lunch. Be back at one.'

The President watched the door close, and breathed easier. He had eighteen holes planned for the afternoon, so forget the pelican thing. If Coal wasn't worried, neither was he.

He punched numbers on his phone, waited patiently, and finally had Bob Gminski on the line. The director of the CIA was a terrible golfer, one of the few the President could humiliate, and he invited him to play this afternoon. Certainly, said Gminski, a man with a thousand things to do but, well, it was the President so he would be delighted to join him.

'By the way, Bob, what about this pelican thing in New Orleans?'

Gminski cleared his throat and tried to sound relaxed. 'Well, Chief, I told Fletcher Coal Friday that it was very imaginative and a fine work of fiction. I think its author should forget about law school and pursue a career as a novelist. Ha, ha, ha.'

'Great, Bob. Nothing to it then.'

'We're digging.'

'See you at three.' The President hung up, and went straight for his putter.

CHAPTER TWENTY-FIVE

Riverwalk runs for a quarter of a mile along the water, and is always crowded. It is packed with two hundred shops and cafés and restaurants on several levels, most under the same roof, and several with doors leading onto a boardwalk next to the river. It's at the foot of Poydras Street, a stone's throw from the Quarter.

She arrived at eleven, and sipped espresso in the rear of a tiny bistro while trying to read the paper and appear calm. Frenchmen's Bend was one level down and around a corner. She was nervous, and the espresso didn't help.

She had a list in her pocket of things to do, specific steps at specific moments, even words and sentences she had memorized in the event things went terribly wrong and Verheek got out of control. She had slept two hours, and spent the rest of the time with a legal pad diagraming and charting. If she died, it would not be from a lack of preparation.

She could not trust Gavin Verheek. He was employed by a law enforcement agency that at times operated by its own rules. He took orders from a man with a history of paranoia and dirty tricks. His boss reported to a President in charge of an administration run by fools. The President had rich, sleazy friends who gave him lots of money.

But at this moment, dear, there was no one else to trust. After five days and two near misses, she was throwing in the towel. New Orleans had lost its allure. She needed help, and if she had to trust cops, the Fibbies were as clean as any.

Eleven forty-five. She paid for the espresso, waited for a crowd of shoppers, and fell in behind them. There were a dozen people browsing in Frenchmen's Bend as she walked past the entrance where her friend should be in about ten minutes. She eased into a bookstore two doors down. There were at least three stores in the vicinity from which she could shop and hide and watch the front door of Frenchmen's Bend. She chose the bookstore because the clerks weren't pushy and killing time was expected of the customers. She looked at the magazines first, then with three minutes to go she stepped between two rows of cookbooks and watched for Gavin.

Thomas said he was never on time. An hour late was early for him, but she would give him fifteen minutes and she'd be gone.

She expected him at precisely noon, and there he was. Black sweatshirt, red baseball cap, folded newspaper. He was a bit thinner than she expected, but he could lose a few pounds. Her heart pounded away. Be cool, she said. Just be cool, dammit.

She held a cookbook to her eyes and peered over it. He had gray hair and dark skin. The eyes were hidden behind sunglasses. He fidgeted and looked irritated, the way he sounded on the phone. He passed the newspaper from hand to hand, shifted his weight from foot to foot, and glanced around nervously.

He was okay. She liked the way he looked. He had a vulnerable, nonprofessional manner about him that said he was scared too.

After five minutes, he walked through the door as he was told, and went to the right rear of the store.

Khamel had been trained to welcome death. He had been close to it many times, but never afraid of it. And after thirty years of expecting it, nothing, absolutely nothing, made him tense. He got somewhat excited about sex, but that was it. The fidgeting was an act. The jittery little movements were contrived. He'd survived face-offs with men almost as talented as he, and he could certainly handle this little rendezvous with a desperate child. He picked through the safari jackets and tried to appear nervous.

He had a handkerchief in his pocket, because he suddenly had caught a cold so his voice was a bit thick and scratchy. He had listened to the recording a hundred times, and he was confident he had the inflection and rhythm and slight upper Midwest accent. But Verheek was a bit more nasal; thus, the handkerchief for the cold.

It was difficult to allow anyone to approach from the rear, but he knew he must. He did not see her. She was behind him but very close when she said, 'Gavin.'

He jerked quickly around. She was holding a white Panama hat and speaking to it. 'Darby,' he said, pulling the handkerchief out for a fake sneeze. Her hair was a gold color and shorter than his. He sneezed and coughed. 'Let's get out of here,' he said. 'I don't like this idea.'

Darby didn't like it either. It was Monday and her classmates were going about their business of clawing through law school, and here she was camouflaged to the max and playing cloak and dagger with this man who could get her killed. 'Just do as I say, okay. Where'd you get the cold?'

He sneezed into the handkerchief and talked as low as possible. It sounded painful. 'Last night. I left the air on too low. Let's get out of here.'

'Follow me.' They left the store. Darby took his hand, and they walked quickly down a flight of stairs leading to the boardwalk.

'Have you seen them?' he asked.

'No. Not yet. But I'm sure they're around.'

'Where the hell are we going?' The voice was scratchy.

They were on the boardwalk, almost jogging, talking without looking at each other. 'Just come with me.'

'You're going too fast, Darby. We look suspicious. Slow down. Look, this is crazy. Let me make a phone call, and we'll be safe and secure. I can have three agents here in ten minutes.' He was sounding good. This was working. They were holding hands, running for their lives.

'Nope.' She slowed. The boardwalk was crowded, and a line had formed beside the *Bayou Queen,* a paddle wheeler. They stopped at the end of the line.

'What the hell is this?' he asked.

'Do you bitch about everything?' she almost whispered.

'Yes. Especially stupid things, and this is very stupid. Are we getting on this boat?'

'Yes.'

'Why?' he sneezed again, then coughed out of control. He could take her out now with one hand, but there were people everywhere. People in front, people behind. He took great pride in his cleanliness, and this would be a dirty place to do it. Get on the boat, play along for a few more minutes, see what happens. He would get her on the upper deck, kill her, dump her in the river, then start yelling. Another terrible drowning accident. That might work. If not, he'd be patient. She'd be dead in an hour. Gavin was a bitch, so keep bitching.

'Because I've got a car a mile upriver at a park where we'll stop in thirty minutes,' she explained in a low voice. 'We get off the boat, into the car, and we haul ass.'

The line was moving now. 'I don't like boats. They make me seasick. This is dangerous, Darby.' He coughed and looked around like a man pursued.

'Relax, Gavin. It's gonna work.'

Khamel tugged at his pants. They were thirty-six inches in the waist and covered eight layers of briefs and gym shorts. The sweatshirt was extra large, and instead of weighing one-fifty, he could pass for one-ninety. Whatever. It seemed to be working.

They were almost to the steps of the *Bayou Queen*. 'I don't like this,' he mumbled loud enough for her to hear.

'Just shut up,' she said.

The man with the gun ran to the end of the line and elbowed his way through the people with their bags and cameras. The tourists were packed tightly together as if a ride on the riverboat was the greatest trip in the world. He had killed before, but never in such a public place as this. The back of her head was visible through the crowd. He shoved his way desperately through the line. A few cursed him, but he couldn't care less. The gun was in a pocket, but as he neared the girl he yanked it out and kept it by his right leg. She was almost to the steps, almost on the boat. He shoved harder and knocked people out of the way. They protested angrily until they saw the gun, then they began yelling. She was holding hands with the man, who was talking nonstop. She was about to step up onto the boat when he knocked the last person out of the way and quickly stuck the gun into the base of the skull just below the red baseball cap. He fired once, and people screamed and fell to the ground.

Gavin fell hard into the steps. Darby screamed and backed away in horror. Her ears were ringing from the shot, and voices were yelling and people were pointing. The man with the gun was running hard toward a row of shops and a crowd of people. A heavy man with a camera was yelling at him, and Darby watched for a second as he disappeared. Maybe she'd seen him before, but she couldn't think now. She was yelling and couldn't stop.

'He's got a gun!' a woman near the boat yelled, and the crowd backed away from Gavin, who was on all fours with a small pistol in his right hand. He rocked pitifully back and forth like an infant trying to crawl. Blood streamed from his chin and puddled under his face. His head hung almost to the boards. His eyes were closed. He moved forward just a few inches, his knees now in the dark red puddle.

The crowd backed farther away, horrified at the sight of this wounded man fighting death. He teetered and wobbled forward again, headed nowhere but wanting to move, to live. He started yelling; loud painful moans in a language Darby did not recognize.

The blood was pouring, gushing from the nose and chin. He was wailing in that unknown tongue. Two crew members from the boat hovered on the steps, watching but afraid to move. The pistol concerned them.

A woman was crying, then another. Darby inched farther back. 'He's Egyptian,' a small, dark woman said. That news meant nothing to the crowd, now mesmerized.

He rocked forward and lunged to the edge of the boardwalk. The gun dropped into the water. He collapsed on his stomach with his head hanging over and dripping into the river. Shouts came from the rear, and two policemen rushed to him.

A hundred people now inched forward to see the dead man. Darby shuffled backward, then left the scene. The cops would have questions, and since she had no answers, she preferred not to talk. She was weak and needed to sit for a while, and think. There was an oyster bar inside Riverwalk. It was crowded for lunch, and she found the rest rooms in the back. She locked the door and sat on a toilet.

Shortly after dark, she left Riverwalk. The Westin Hotel is two blocks away, and she hoped maybe she could make it there without being gunned down on the sidewalk. Her clothes were different and hidden under a new black trench coat. The sunglasses and hat were also new. She was tired of spending good money on disposable clothes. She was tired of a lot of things.

She made it to the Westin in one piece. There were no rooms, and she sat in the well-lit lounge for an hour drinking coffee. It was time to run, but she couldn't get careless. She had to think.

Maybe she was thinking too damned much. Maybe they now thought of her as a thinker, and planned accordingly.

She left the Westin, and walked to Poydras, where she flagged a cab. An elderly black man sat low behind the wheel.

'I need to go to Baton Rouge,' she said.

'Lord, honey, that's a heckuva ride.'

'How much?' she asked quickly.

He thought a second. 'A hundred and fifty.'

She crawled in the backseat and threw two bills over the seat. 'There's two hundred. Get there as fast as you can, and watch your rear. We may be followed.'

He turned off the meter and stuffed the money in his shirt pocket. Darby lay down in the backseat and closed her eyes. This was not an intelligent move, but playing the percentages was getting nowhere. The old man was a fast driver, and within minutes they were on the expressway.

The ringing in her ears had stopped, but she still heard the gunshot and saw him on all fours, rocking back and forth, trying to live just a moment longer. Thomas had once referred to him as Dutch Verheek, but said the nickname was dropped after law school when they became serious about their careers. Dutch Verheek was not an Egyptian.

She had caught just a glimpse of his killer as he was running away. There was something familiar about him. He had glanced to his right just once as he was running, and something clicked. But she was screaming and hysterical, and it was a blur.

Everything blurred. Halfway to Baton Rouge, she fell into a deep sleep.

CHAPTER TWENTY-SIX

Director Voyles stood behind his executive swivel chair. His jacket was off, and most of the buttons on his tired and wrinkled shirt were unfastened. It was 9 P.M., and judging from the shirt he had been at the office at least fifteen hours. And he hadn't thought of leaving.

He listened to the receiver, mumbled a few instructions, and hung it up. K. O. Lewis sat across the desk. The door was open; the lights were on; no one had left. The mood was somber with small huddles of soft whispers.

'That was Eric East,' Voyles said, sitting gently into the chair. 'He's been there about two hours, and they just finished the autopsy. He watched it, his first. Single bullet to the right temple, but death came sooner from a single blow at C-2 and C-3. The vertebrae were shattered into tiny chips and pieces. No powder burns on his hand. Another blow severely bruised his larynx, but did not cause death. He was nude. Estimate of between ten and eleven last night.'

'Who found him?' Lewis asked.

'Maids checked in around eleven this morning. Will you deliver the news to his wife?'

'Yea, sure,' K. O. said. 'When's the body coming back?'

'East said they'll release it in a couple of hours, and it should be here by 2 A.M. Tell her we'll do whatever she wants. Tell her I'm sending a hundred agents in tomorrow to blanket the city. Tell her we'll find the killer, etc., etc.'

'Any evidence?'

'Probably not. East said they've had the hotel room since 3 P.M., and it appears to be a clean job. No forced entry. No signs of resistance. Nothing that would be of any help, but it's a bit early.' Voyles rubbed his red eyes, and thought for a while.

'How could he go down for a simple funeral, and end up dead?' Lewis asked.

'He was snooping around on this pelican thing. One of our agents, guy named Carlton, told East that Gavin was trying to find the girl, and that the girl had called him, and that he might need some help bringing her in. Carlton talked to him a few times, and gave him the names of a few student hangouts in the city. That was all, so he says. Carlton says that he, Carlton, was a bit worried about Gavin throwing his FBI weight around. Said he thought he was sort of a klutz.'

'Has anyone seen the girl?'

'She's probably dead. I've instructed New Orleans to find her, if possible.'

'Her little brief is getting folks killed right and left. When do we take it seriously?'

Voyles nodded at the door, and Lewis got up and closed it. The Director was standing again, cracking his knuckles and thinking aloud. 'We have to cover our asses. I think we should assign at least two hundred agents to pelican, but try like hell to keep it quiet. There's something there, K.O., something really nasty. But at the same time, I promised the President we would back off. He personally asked me to back off the pelican brief, remember, and I said we would, in part because we thought it was a joke.' Voyles managed a tight smile. 'Well, I taped our little conversation when he asked me to back off. I figure he and Coal tape everything within a half mile of the White House, so why can't I? I had my best body mike, and I've listened to the tape. Clear as a bell.'

'I'm not following.'

'Simple. We go in and investigate like mad. If this is it, we crack the case, get the indictments, and everyone's happy. But it'll be a bitch to do in a hurry. Meanwhile, idiot and Coal over there know nothing about the investigation. If the press gets wind of it, and if the pelican brief is on target, then I'll make damned sure the country knows the President asked us to back off because it's one of his pals.'

Lewis was smiling. 'It'll kill him.'

'Yes! Coal will hemorrhage, and the President will never recover. The election is next year, K.O.'

'I like it, Denton, but we have to solve this thing.'

Denton walked slowly behind his chair, and slid out of his shoes. He was even shorter now. 'We'll look under every stone, K.O., but it won't be easy. If it's Mattiece, then we've got a very wealthy man in a very elaborate plot to use very talented killers to take out two justices. These people don't talk, and they don't leave trails. Look at our friend Gavin. We'll spend two thousand hours digging around that hotel, and I'll bet you there won't be a shred of useful evidence. Just like Rosenberg and Jensen.'

'And Callahan.'

'And Callahan. And probably the girl, if we ever find her body.'

'I'm somewhat responsible, Denton. Gavin came to me Thursday morning after he learned of Callahan, and I didn't listen. I knew he was going down there, but I just didn't listen.'

'Look, I'm sorry he's dead. He was a fine lawyer and he was loyal to me. I value that. I trusted Gavin. But he got himself killed because he stepped out of bounds. He had no business playing cop and trying to find the girl.'

Lewis stood and stretched. 'I'd better go see Mrs. Verheek. How much do I tell her?

'Let's say it looks like a burglary, cops ain't sure down there, still investigating, we'll know more tomorrow, etc. Tell her I'm devastated, and we'll do whatever she wants.'

Coal's limo stopped abruptly at the curb so an ambulance could scream by. The limo was wandering aimlessly through the city, a ritual not unusual when Coal and Matthew Barr met to talk about really dirty business. They sat deep in the back of it, sipping drinks. Coal was indulging in a spring water. Barr had a sixteen-ounce Bud purchased from a convenience store.

They ignored the ambulance.

'I must know what Grantham knows,' Coal was saying. 'Today he called Zikman, Zikman's aide Trandell, Nelson DeVan, one of my many former assistants who's now with the Committee to Reelect. And these are just the ones I know of. All in one day. He's hot on this pelican brief.'

'You think he's seen it?' The limo was moving again.

'No. Not at all. If he knew what was in it, he wouldn't be fishing for it. But dammit, he knows about it.'

'He's good. I've watched him for years. He seems to move in the shadows and keeps in touch with an odd network of sources. He's written some crazy stuff, but it's usually accurate as hell.'

'That's what worries me. He's tenacious, and he smells blood with this story.'

Barr sipped from the can. 'Of course, it would be asking too much if I wanted to know what was in the brief.'

'Don't ask. It's so damned confidential it's frightening.'

'Then how does Grantham know about it?'

'Perfect question. And that's what I want to know. How'd he find out, and how much does he know? Where are his sources?'

'We got his car phone, but we haven't been inside the apartment yet.'

'Why not?'

'We almost got caught this morning by his cleaning lady. We'll try again tomorrow.'

'Don't get caught, Barr. Remember Watergate.'

'They were morons, Fletcher. We, on the other hand, are quite talented.'

'That's right. So tell me, can you and your quite talented associates bug Grantham's phone at the *Post*?'

Barr turned and frowned at Coal. 'Have you lost your mind? Impossible. That place is busy at all hours. They have security guards. The works.'

'It could be done.'

'Then do it, Coal. If you know so damned much, you do it.'

'Start thinking about ways to do it, okay. Just give it some thought.'

'Okay. I've thought about it. It's impossible.'

Coal was amused by this thought, and his amusement irritated Barr. The limo eased into downtown.

'Tap his apartment,' Coal instructed. 'I want a report twice a day on all his calls.' The limo stopped, and Barr climbed out.

CHAPTER TWENTY-SEVEN

Breakfast at Dupont Circle. It was quite chilly, but at least the addicts and transvestites were still unconscious somewhere in their sick little worlds. A few winos lay about like driftwood. But the sun was up and he felt safe, and anyway he was still an FBI agent with a shoulder harness and a piece under his arm. Who was he to fear? He hadn't used it in fifteen years, and he seldom left the office, but he'd love to yank it out and blast away.

His name was Trope, a very special assistant to Mr. Voyles. He was so special that no one except he and Mr. Voyles knew about these secret little chats with Booker from Langley. He sat on a circular bench with his back to New Hampshire, and unpacked a store-bought breakfast of banana and muffin. He checked his watch. Booker was never late. Trope always arrived first, then Booker five minutes later, and they always talked quickly and Trope left first, then Booker. They were both office boys now, far into their twilights but very close to their bosses, who from time to time grew weary of trying to figure out what the hell the other was doing, or perhaps just needed to know something quick.

His real name was Trope, and he wondered if Booker was a real name. Probably not. Booker was from Langley, and they were so paranoid even the pencil pushers probably had fakes. He took an inch off the banana. Hell, the secretaries over there probably had three or four names.

Booker strolled near the fountain with a tall white cup of coffee. He glanced around, then sat down next to his friend. Voyles wanted this meeting, so Trope would speak first.

'We lost a man in New Orleans,' he said.

Booker cuddled the hot cup and sipped. 'He got himself killed.'

'Yeah, but he's still dead. Were you there?'

'Yes, but we didn't know he was there. We were close, but watching others. What was he doing?'

Trope unwrapped the cold muffin. 'We don't know. Went down for the funeral, tried to find the girl, found someone else, and here we are.' He took a long bite and the banana was finished. Now to the muffin. 'It was a clean job, wasn't it?'

Booker shrugged. What did the FBI know about killing people? 'It was okay. Pretty weak effort at suicide, from what we hear.' He sipped the hot coffee.

'Where's the girl?' Trope asked.

'We lost her at O'Hare. Maybe she's in Manhattan, but we're not certain. We're looking.'

'And they're looking.' Trope sipped cold coffee.

'I'm sure they are.'

They watched a wino stagger from his bench and fall. His head hit first with a thud, but he probably felt nothing. He rolled over and his forehead was bleeding.

Booker checked his watch. These meetings were extremely brief. 'What are Mr. Voyles' plans?'

'Oh, he's going in. He sent fifty troops last night, with more today. He doesn't like losing people, especially someone he knows.'

'What about the White House?'

'Not going to tell them, and maybe they won't find out. What do they know?'

'They know Mattiece.'

Trope managed a slight smile at this thought. 'Where is Mr. Mattiece?'

'Who knows. In the past three years, he's been seen little in this country. He owns at least a half-dozen homes in as many countries, and he's got jets and boats, so who knows.'

Trope finished the muffin and stuffed the wrapper in the sack. 'The brief nailed him, didn't it?'

'It's beautiful. And if he'd played it cool, the brief would have been ignored. But he goes berserk, starts killing people, and the more he kills the more credibility the brief has.'

Trope glanced at his watch. Too long already, but this was good stuff. 'Voyles says we may need your help.'

Booker nodded. 'Done. But this will be a very difficult matter. First, the probable gunman is dead. Second, the probable bagman is very elusive. There was an elaborate conspiracy, but the conspirators are gone. We'll try to find Mattiece.'

'And the girl?'

'Yes. We'll try.'

'What's she thinking?'

'How to stay alive.'

'Can't you bring her in?' Trope asked.

'No. We don't know where she is, and we can't just snatch innocent civilians off the streets. She doesn't trust anyone right now.'

Trope stood with his coffee and sack. 'I can't blame her.' He was gone.

Grantham held a cloudy fax photo sent to him from Phoenix. She was a junior at Arizona State, a very attractive twenty-year-old coed. She was listed as a biology major from Denver. He had called twenty Shaws in

Denver before he stopped. The second fax was sent by AP stringer in New Orleans. It was a copy of her freshman photo at Tulane. The hair was longer. Somewhere in the middle of the yearbook, the stringer had found a photo of Darby Shaw drinking a Diet Coke at a law school picnic. She wore a baggy sweater with faded jeans that fit just right, and it was obvious the photo was placed in the year book by a great admirer of Darby's. It looked like something out of *Vogue*. She was laughing at something or someone at the picnic. The teeth were perfect and the face was warm. He had tacked this one onto the small corkboard beside his news desk.

There was a fourth fax, a photo of Thomas Callahan, just for the record.

He placed his feet on the desk. It was almost nine-thirty, Tuesday. The newsroom hummed and rocked like a well-organized riot. He'd made eighty phone calls in the last twenty-four hours, and had nothing to show but the four photos and a stack of campaign finance forms. He was getting nowhere, and, really, why bother? She was about to tell all.

He skimmed the *Post*, and saw the strange story about one Gavin Verheek and his demise. The phone rang. It was Darby.

'Seen the *Post*?' she asked.

'I write the *Post*, remember.'

She was not in the mood for small talk. 'The story about the FBI lawyer murdered in New Orleans, have you seen it?'

'I'm just reading it. Does it mean something to you?'

'You could say that. Listen carefully, Grantham. Callahan gave the brief to Verheek, who was his best friend. Friday, Verheek came to New Orleans for the funeral. I talked to him by phone over the weekend. He wanted to help me, but I was scared. We agreed to meet yesterday at noon. Verheek was murdered in his room around eleven Sunday night. Got all that?'

'Yeah, I got it.'

'Verheek didn't show for our meeting. He was, of course, dead by then. I got scared, and left the city. I'm in New York.'

'Okay.' Grantham wrote furiously. 'Who killed Verheek?'

'I do not know. There's a lot more to the story. I've read the *Post* and the *New York Times* from front to back, and I've seen nothing about another killing in New Orleans. It happened to a man I was talking to and I thought was Verheek. It's a long story.'

'Sounds like it. When do I get this long story?'

'When can you come to New York?'

'I can be there by noon.'

'That's a little quick. Let's plan on tomorrow. I'll call you at this time tomorrow with instructions. You must be careful, Grantham.'

He admired the jeans and the smile on the corkboard. 'It's Gray, okay? Not Grantham.'

'Whatever. There are some powerful people afraid of what I know. If I tell you, it could kill you. I've seen the bodies, okay, Gray? I've heard bombs and gunshots. I saw a man's brains yesterday, and I have no idea who he was or why he was killed, except that he knew about the pelican brief. I thought he was my friend. I trusted him with my life, and he was shot in the head in front of fifty people. As I watched him die, it occurred to me that perhaps he was not my friend. I read the paper this morning, and I realize he was definitely not my friend.'

'Who killed him?'

'We'll talk about it when you get here.'

'Okay, Darby.'

'There's one small point to cover. I'll tell you everything I know, but you can never use my name. I've already written enough to get at least three people killed, and I'm quite confident I'll be next. But I don't want to ask for more trouble. I shall always be unidentified, okay, Gray?'

'It's a deal.'

'I'm putting a lot of trust in you, and I'm not sure why. If I ever doubt you, I'll disappear.'

'You have my word, Darby. I swear.'

'I think you're making a mistake. This is not your average investigative job. This one could get you killed.'

'By the same people who killed Rosenberg and Jensen?'

'Yes.'

'Do you know who killed Rosenberg and Jensen?'

'I know who paid for the killings. I know his name. I know his business. I know his politics.'

'And you'll tell me tomorrow?'

'If I'm still alive.' There was a long pause as both thought of something appropriate.

'Perhaps we should talk immediately,' he said.

'Perhaps. But I'll call you in the morning.'

Grantham hung up, and for a moment admired the slightly blurred photo of this very beautiful law student who was convinced she was about to die. For a second he succumbed to thoughts of chivalry and gallantry and rescue. She was in her early twenties, liked older men, according to the photo of Callahan, and suddenly she trusted him to the exclusion of all others. He would make it work. And he would protect her.

The motorcade moved quietly out of downtown. He was due for a speech at College Park in an hour, and he relaxed in his limo with his jacket off, reading the words Mabry had put together. He shook his head and wrote in the margins. On a normal day, this would be a pleasant drive out of the city to a beautiful campus for a light little speech, but it wasn't working out. Coal was seated next to him in the limo.

The Chief of Staff routinely avoided these trips. He treasured the moments the President was out of the White House and he had the run of the place. But they needed to talk.

'I'm tired of Mabry's speeches,' the President said in frustration. 'They're all sounding the same. I swear I gave this one last week at the Rotary convention.'

'He's the best we've got, but I'm exploring,' Coal said without looking up from his memo. He'd read the speech, and it wasn't that bad. But Mabry had been writing for six months, and the ideas were stale and Coal wanted to fire him anyway.'

The President glanced at Coal's memo. 'What's that?'

'The short list.'

'Who's left?'

'Siler-Spence, Watson, and Calderon.' Coal flipped a page.

'That's just great, Fletcher. A woman, a black, and a Cuban. Whatever happened to white men? I thought I said I wanted young white men. Young, tough, conservative judges with impeccable credentials and years to live. Didn't I say that?'

Coal kept reading. 'They have to be confirmed, Chief.'

'We'll get 'em confirmed. I'll twist arms until they break, but they'll be confirmed. Do you realize that nine of every ten white men in this country voted for me?'

'Eighty-four percent.'

'Right. So what's wrong with white men?'

'This is not exactly patronage.'

'The hell it's not. It's patronage pure and simple. I reward my friends, and I punish my enemies. That's how you survive in politics. You dance with the ones that brought you. I can't believe you want a female and a black. You're getting soft, Fletcher.'

Coal flipped another page. He'd heard this before. 'I'm more concerned with reelection,' he said quietly.

'And I'm not? I've appointed so many Asians and Hispanics and women and blacks you'd think I was a Democrat. Hell, Fletcher, what's wrong with white people? Look, there must be a hundred good, qualified, conservative judges out there, right? Why can't you find just two, only two, who look and think like I do?'

'You got ninety percent of the Cuban vote.'

The President tossed the speech in a seat and picked up the morning's *Post*. 'Okay, let's go with Calderon. How old is he?'

'Fifty-one. Married, eight kids, Catholic, poor background, worked his way through Yale, very solid. Very conservative. No warts or skeletons, except he was treated for alcoholism twenty years ago. He's been sober since. A teetotaler.'

'Has he ever smoked dope?'

'He denies it.'

'I like him.' The President was reading the front page.

'So do I. Justice and FBI have checked his underwear, and he's very clean. Now, do you want Siler-Spence or Watson?'

'What kind of name is Siler-Spence? I mean, what's wrong with these women who use hyphens? What if her name was Skowinski, and she married a guy named Levondowski? Would her little liberated soul insist she go through life as F. Gwendolyn Skowinski-Levondowski? Give me a break. I'll never appoint a woman with a hyphen.'

'You already have.'

'Who?'

'Kay Jones-Roddy, ambassador to Brazil.'

'Then call her home and fire her.'

Coal managed a slight grin and placed the memo on the seat. He watched the traffic through his window. They would decide on number two later. Calderon was in the bag, and he wanted Linda Siler-Spence, so he would keep pushing the black and force the President to the woman. Basic manipulation.

'I think we should wait another two weeks before announcing them,' he said.

'Whatever,' the President mumbled as he read a story on page one. He would announce them when he got ready, regardless of Coal's timetable. He was not yet convinced they should be announced together.

'Judge Watson is a very conservative black judge with a reputation for toughness. He would be ideal.'

'I don't know,' the President mumbled as he read about Gavin Verheek.

Coal had seen the story on page two. Verheek was found dead in a room at the Hilton in New Orleans under strange circumstances. According to the story, official FBI was in the dark and had nothing to say about why Verheek was in New Orleans. Voyles was deeply saddened. Fine, loyal employee, etc.

The President flipped through the paper. 'Our friend Grantham has been quiet.'

'He's digging. I think he's heard of the brief, but just can't get a handle on it. He's called everyone in town, but doesn't know what to ask. He's chasing rabbits.'

'Well, I played golf with Gminski yesterday,' the President said smugly. 'And he assures me everything's under control. We had a real heart-to-heart talk over eighteen holes. He's a horrible golfer, couldn't stay out of the sand and water. It was funny, really.'

Coal had never touched a golf club, and hated the idle chatter about handicaps and such. 'Do you think Voyles is investigating down there?'

'No. He gave me his word he would not. Not that I trust him, but Gminski didn't mention Voyles.'

'How much do you trust Gminski?' Coal asked with a quick glance and frown at the President.

'None. But if he knew something about the pelican brief, I think he would tell me. . . .' The President's words trailed off, and he knew he sounded naive.

Coal grunted his disbelief.

They crossed the Anacostia River and were in Prince Georges County. The President picked up the speech and looked out his window. Two weeks after the killings, and the ratings were still above fifty percent. The Democrats had no visible candidate out there making noise. He was strong and getting stronger. Americans were tired of dope and crime, and noisy minorities getting all the attention, and liberal idiots interpreting the Constitution in favor of criminals and radicals. This was his moment. Two nominations to the Supreme Court at the same time. It would be his legacy.

He smiled to himself. What a wonderful tragedy.

CHAPTER TWENTY-EIGHT

The taxi stopped abruptly at the corner of Fifth and Fifty-second, and Gray, doing exactly what he was told, paid quickly and jumped out with his bag. The car behind was honking and flipping birds, and he thought how nice it was to be back in New York City.

It was almost 5 P.M., and the pedestrians were thick on Fifth, and he figured that was precisely what she wanted. She had been specific. Take this flight from National to La Guardia. Take a cab to the Vista Hotel in the World Trade Center. Go to the bar, have a drink, maybe two, watch your rear, then after an hour catch a cab to the corner of Fifth and Fifty-second. Move quickly, wear sunglasses, and watch for everything because if he was being followed he could get them killed.

She made him write it all down. It was a bit silly, a bit of overkill, but she had a voice he couldn't argue with. Didn't want to, really. She was lucky to be alive, she said, and she would take no more chances. And if he wanted to talk to her, then he would do exactly as he was told.

He wrote it down. He fought the crowd and walked as fast as possible up Fifth to Fifty-ninth to the Plaza, up the steps and through its lobby, then out onto Central Park South. No one could follow him. And if she was this cautious, no one could follow her.

The sidewalk was packed along Central Park South, and as he neared Sixth Avenue he walked even faster. He was keyed up, and regardless of how restrained he tried to be, he was terribly excited about meeting her. On the phone she had been cool and methodical, but with a trace of fear and uncertainty. She was just a law student, she said, and she didn't know what she was doing, and she would probably be dead in a week if not sooner, but anyway this was the way the game would be played. Always assume you're being followed, she said. She had survived seven days of being chased by bloodhounds, so please do as she said.

She said to duck into the St. Moritz at the corner of Sixth, and he did. She had reserved a room for him under the name of Warren Clark. He paid cash for the room, and rode the elevator to the ninth floor. He was to wait. Just sit and wait, she'd said.

He stood in the window for an hour and watched Central Park grow dark. The phone rang.

'Mr. Clark?' a female asked.

'Uh, yes.'

'It's me. Did you arrive alone?'

'Yes. Where are you?'

'Six floors up. Take the elevator to the eighteenth, then walk down to the fifteenth. Room 1520.'

'Okay. Now?'

'Yes. I'm waiting.'

He brushed his teeth again, checked his hair, and ten minutes later was standing before room 1520. He felt like a sophomore on his first date. He hadn't had butterflies this bad since high school football.

But he was Gray Grantham of the *Washington Post,* and this was just another story and she was just another woman, so grab the reins, buddy.

He knocked, and waited. 'Who is it?'

'Grantham,' he said to the door.

The bolt clicked, and she opened the door slowly. The hair was gone, but she smiled, and there was the cover girl. She shook his hand firmly. 'Come in.'

She closed and bolted the door behind him. 'Would you care for a drink?' she asked.

'Sure, what do you have?'

'Water, with ice.'

'Sounds great.'

She walked into a small sitting room where the television was on with no sound. 'In here,' she said. He set his bag on the table, and took a seat on the sofa. She was standing at the bar, and for a quick second he admired the jeans. No shoes. Extra-large sweatshirt with the collar to one side where a bra strap peeked through.

She handed him the water, and sat in a chair by the door.

'Thanks,' he said.

'Have you eaten?' she asked.

'You didn't tell me to.'

She chuckled at this. 'Forgive me. I've been through a lot. Let's order room service.'

He nodded and smiled at her. 'Sure. Anything you want is fine with me.'

'I'd love a greasy cheeseburger with fries and a cold beer.'

'Perfect.'

She picked up the phone and ordered the food. Grantham walked to the window and watched the lights crawling along Fifth Avenue.

'I'm twenty-four. How old are you?' She was on the sofa now, sipping ice water.

He took the chair nearest to her. 'Thirty-eight. Married once. Divorced seven years and three months ago. No children. Live alone with a cat. Why'd you pick the St. Moritz?'

'Rooms were available, and I convinced them it was important to pay with cash and present no identification. Do you like it?'

'It's fine. Sort of past its prime.'

'This is not exactly a vacation.'

'It's fine. How long do you think we might be here?'

She watched him carefully. He'd published a book six years earlier on HUD scandals, and though it didn't sell she'd found a copy in a public library in New Orleans. He looked six years older than the photo on the dust jacket, but he was aging nicely with a touch of gray over the ears.

'I don't know how long you'll stay,' she said. 'My plans are subject to change by the minute. I may see a face on the street and fly to New Zealand.'

'When did you leave New Orleans?'

'Monday night. I took a cab to Baton Rouge, and that would have been easy to follow. I flew to Chicago, where I bought four tickets to four different cities, including Boise, where my mother lives. I jumped on the plane to La Guardia at the last moment. I don't think anyone followed.'

'You're safe.'

'Maybe for the moment. We'll both be hunted when this story is published. Assuming it's published.'

Gray rattled his ice and studied her. 'Depends on what you tell me. And it depends on how much can be verified from other sources.'

'The verification is up to you. I'll tell you what I know, and from there you're on your own.'

'Okay. When do we start talking?'

'After dinner. I'd rather do it on a full stomach. You're in no hurry, are you?'

'Of course not. I've got all night, and all day tomorrow, and the next day and the next. I mean, you're talking about the biggest story in twenty years, so I'll hang around as long as you'll talk to me.'

Darby smiled and looked away. Exactly a week ago, she and Thomas were waiting for dinner in the bar at Mouton's. He was wearing a black silk blazer, denim shirt, red paisley tie and heavily starched khakis. Shoes, but no socks. The shirt was unbuttoned and the tie was loose. They had talked about the Virgin Islands and Thanksgiving and Gavin Verheek while they waited on a table. He was drinking fast, and that was not unusual. He got drunk later, and it saved her life.

She had lived a year in the past seven days, and she was having a real conversation with a live person who did not wish her dead. She crossed her feet on the coffee table. It was not uncomfortable having him here in her room. She relaxed. His face said, 'Trust me.' And why not? Whom else could she trust?

'What are you thinking about?' he asked.

'It's been a long week. Seven days ago I was just another law student busting my tail to get to the top. Now look at me.'

He was looking at her. Trying to be cool, not like a gawking sophomore, but he was looking. The hair was dark and very short, and quite stylish, but he liked the long version in yesterday's fax.

'Tell me about Thomas Callahan,' he said.

'Why?'

'I don't know. He's part of the story, isn't he?'

'Yeah. I'll get to it later.'

'Fine. Your mother lives in Boise?'

'Yes, but she knows nothing. Where's your mother?'

'Short Hills, New Jersey,' he answered with a smile. He crunched on an ice cube and waited for her. She was thinking.

'What do you like about New York?' she asked.

'The airport. It's the quickest way out.'

'Thomas and I were here in the summer. It's hotter than New Orleans.'

Suddenly, Grantham realized she was not just a hot little coed, but a widow in mourning. The poor lady was suffering. She had not been checking out his hair or his clothes or his eyes. She was in pain. Dammit!

'I'm very sorry about Thomas,' he said. 'I won't ask about him again.'

She smiled but said nothing.

There was a loud knock. Darby jerked her feet off the table, and glared at the door. Then she breathed deeply. It was the food.

'I'll get it,' Gray said. 'Just relax.'

CHAPTER TWENTY-NINE

For centuries, a quiet but mammoth battle of nature raged without interference along the coastline of what would become Louisiana. It was a battle for territory. No humans were involved until recent years. From the south, the ocean pushed inland with its tides and winds and floods. From the north, the Mississippi River hauled down an inexhaustible supply of freshwater and sediment, and fed the marshes with the soil they needed to vegetate and thrive. The saltwater from the Gulf eroded the coastline and burned the freshwater marshes by killing the grasses that held them together. The river responded by draining half the continent and depositing its soil in lower Louisiana. It slowly built a long succession of sedimentary deltas, each of which in turn eventually blocked the river's path and forced it to change course yet again. The lush wetlands were built by the deltas.

It was an epic struggle of give-and-take, with the forces of nature firmly in control. With the constant replenishment from the mighty river, the deltas not only held their own against the Gulf, but expanded.

The marshlands were a marvel of natural evolution. Using the rich sediment as food, they grew into a green paradise of cypress and oak and dense patches of pickerelweed and bulrush and cattails. The water was filled with crawfish, shrimp, oysters, red snappers, flounder, pompano, bream, crabs, and alligators. The coastal plain was a sanctuary for wildlife. Hundreds of species of migratory birds came to roost.

The wetlands were vast and limitless, rich and abundant.

Then oil was discovered there in 1930, and the rape was on. The oil companies dredged ten thousand miles of canals to get to the riches. They crisscrossed the fragile delta with a slashing array of neat little ditches. They sliced the marshes to ribbons.

They drilled, found oil, then dredged like maniacs to get to it. Their canals were perfect conduits for the Gulf and its saltwater, which ate away at the marshes.

Since oil was found, tens of thousands of acres of wetlands have been devoured by the ocean. Sixty square miles of Louisiana vanishes every year. Every fourteen minutes, another acre disappears under water.

In 1979, an oil company punched a hole deep in Terrebonne Parish and hit oil. It was a routine day on just another rig, but it was not a routine hit. There was a lot of oil. They drilled again an eighth of a mile away, and hit another big one. They backed off a mile, drilled, and hit an even bigger one. Three miles away, they struck gold again.

The oil company capped the wells and pondered the situation, which had all the markings of a major new field.

The oil company was owned by Victor Mattiece, a Cajun from Lafayette who'd made and lost several fortunes drilling for oil in south Louisiana. In 1979, he happened to be wealthy, and more importantly, he had access to other people's money. He was quickly convinced he had just tapped a major reserve. He began buying land around the capped wells.

Secrets are crucial but hard to keep in the oilfields. And Mattiece knew if he threw around too much money, there would soon be a mad rush of drilling around his new gold mine. A man of infinite patience and planning, he looked at the big picture and said no to the quick buck. He decided he would have it all. He huddled with his lawyers and other advisers, and devised a plan to methodically buy the surrounding land under a myriad of corporate names. They formed new companies, used some of his old ones, purchased all or portions of struggling firms, and went about the business of acquiring acreage.

Those in the business knew Mattiece, and knew he had money and could get more. Mattiece knew they knew, so he quietly unleashed two dozen faceless entities upon the landowners of Terrebonne Parish. It worked without a major hitch.

The plan was to consolidate territory, then dredge yet another channel through the hapless and beleaguered marshlands so that the men and their equipment could get to the rigs and the oil could be brought out with haste. The canal would be thirty-five miles long and twice as wide as the others. There would be a lot of traffic.

Because Mattiece had money, he was a popular man with the politicians and bureaucrats. He played their game skillfully. He sprinkled money around where needed. He loved politics, but hated publicity. He was paranoid and reclusive.

As the land acquisition sailed smoothly along, Mattiece suddenly found himself short of cash. The industry turned downward in the early eighties, and his other rigs stopped pumping. He needed big money, and he wanted partners adept at putting it up and remaining silent about it. So he stayed away from Texas. He went overseas and found some Arabs who studied his maps and believed his estimate of a mammoth reserve of crude and natural gas. They bought a piece of the action, and Mattiece had plenty of cash again.

He did the sprinkling act, and obtained official permission to gouge his way through the delicate marshes and cypress swamps. The pieces were falling majestically into place, and Victor Mattiece could smell a billion dollars. Maybe two or three.

Then an odd thing happened. A lawsuit was filed to stop the dredging and drilling. The plaintiff was an obscure environmental outfit known simply as Green Fund.

The lawsuit was unexpected because for fifty years Louisiana had allowed itself to be devoured and polluted by oil companies and people like Victor Mattiece. It had been a trade-off. The oil business employed many and paid well. The oil and gas taxes collected in Baton Rouge paid the salaries of state employees. The small bayou villages had been turned into boomtowns. The politicians from the governors down took the oil money and played along. All was well, and so what if some of the marshlands suffered.

Green Fund filed the lawsuit in the U.S. District Court in Lafayette. A federal judge halted the project pending a trial on all issues.

Mattiece went over the edge. He spent weeks with his lawyers plotting and scheming. He would spare no expense to win. Do whatever it took, he instructed them. Break any rule, violate any ethic, hire any expert, commission any study, cut any throat, spend any amount of money. Just win the damned lawsuit.

Never one to be seen, he assumed an even lower profile. He moved to the Bahamas and operated from an armed fortress at Lyford Cay. He flew to New Orleans once a week to meet with the lawyers, then returned to the island.

Though invisible now, he made certain his political contributions increased. His jackpot was still safe beneath Terrebonne Parish, and he would one day extract it, but one never knows when one will be forced to call in favors.

By the time the Green Fund lawyers, both of them, had waded in ankle deep, they had identified over thiry separate defendants. Some owned land. Some did exploring. Others laid pipe. Others drilled. The joint ventures and limited partnerships and corporate associations were an impenetrable maze.

The defendants and their legions of high-priced lawyers answered with a vengeance. They filed a thick motion asking the judge to dismiss the lawsuit as frivolous. Denied. They asked him to allow the drilling to continue while they waited on a trial. Denied. They squealed with pain and explained in another heavy motion how much money was already tied up in exploration, drilling, etc. Denied again. They filed motions by the truckload, and when they were all denied and it was evident there would one day be a trial by jury, the oil lawyers dug in and played dirty.

Luckily for Green Fund's lawsuit, the heart of the new oil reserve was near a ring of marshes that had been for years a natural refuge for waterfowl. Ospreys, egrets, pelicans, ducks, cranes, geese, and many others migrated to it. Though Louisiana has not always been kind to its land, it has shown a bit more sympathy for its animals. Since the verdict would one day be rendered by a jury of average and hopefully ordinary people, the Green Fund lawyers played heavy on the birds.

The pelican became the hero. After thirty years of insidious contamination by DDT and other pesticides, the Louisiana brown pelican perched on the brink of extinction. Almost too late, it was classified as an endangered species, and afforded a higher class of protection. Green Fund seized the majestic bird, and enlisted a half-dozen experts from around the country to testfy on its behalf.

With a hundred lawyers involved, the lawsuit moved slowly. At times it went nowhere, which suited Green Fund just fine. The rigs were idle.

Seven years after Mattiece first buzzed over Terrebonne Bay in his jet helicopter and followed the swamplands along the route his precious canal would take, the pelican suit went to trial in Lake Charles. It was a bitter trial that lasted ten weeks. Green Fund sought money damages for the havoc already inflicted, and it wanted a permanent injunction against further drilling.

The oil companies brought in a fancy litigator from Houston to talk to the jury. He wore elephant-skin boots and a Stetson, and could talk like a Cajun when necessary. He was stout medicine, especially when compared to the Green Fund lawyers, both of whom had beards and very intense faces.

Green Fund lost the trial, and it was not altogether unexpected. The oil companies spent millions, and it's difficult to whip a bear with a switch. David pulled it off, but the best bet is always on Goliath. The jurors were not impressed with the dire warnings about pollution and the frailness of wetland ecology. Oil meant money, and folks needed jobs.

The judge kept the injunction in place for two reasons. First, he thought Green Fund had proven its point about the pelican, a federally protected species. And it was apparent to all that Green Fund would appeal, so the matter was far from over.

The dust settled for a while, and Mattiece had a small victory. But he knew there would be other days in other courtrooms. He was a man of infinite patience and planning.

CHAPTER THIRTY

The tape recorder was in the center of the small table with four empty beer bottles around.

He made notes as he talked. 'Who told you about the lawsuit?'

'A guy named John Del Greco. He's a law student at Tulane, a year ahead of me. He clerked last summer for a big firm in Houston, and the firm was on the periphery of the hostilities. He was not close to the trial, but the rumors and gossip were heavy.'

'And all the firms were from New Orleans and Houston?'

'Yes, the principal litigation firms. But these companies are from a dozen different cities, so of course they brought their local counsel with them. There were lawyers from Dallas, Chicago, and several other cities. It was a circus.'

'What's the status of the lawsuit?'

'From the trial level, it will be appealed to the Fifth Circuit Court of Appeals. That appeal has not been perfected, but should be in a month or so.'

'Where's the Fifth Circuit?'

'New Orleans. About twenty-four months after it arrives there, a three-judge panel will hear and decide. The losing party will undoubtedly request a rehearing by the full panel, and this will take another three or four months. There are enough defects in the verdict to insure either a reversal or a remand.'

'What's a remand?'

'The appellate court can do any of three things. Affirm the verdict, reverse the verdict, or find enough error to send the whole thing back for a new trial. If it goes back, it's been remanded. They can also affirm part, reverse part, remand part, sort of scramble things up.'

Gray shook his head in frustration as he scribbled away. 'Why would anyone want to be a lawyer?'

'I've asked myself that a few times in the past week.'

'Any idea what the Fifth Circuit might do?'

'None. They haven't even seen it yet. The plaintiffs are alleging a multitude of procedural sins by the defendants, and given the nature of the conspiracy, a lot of it's probably true. It could be reversed.'

'Then what happens?'

'The fun starts. If either side is unhappy with the Fifth Circuit, they can appeal to the Supreme Court.'

'Surprise, surprise.'

'Each year the Supreme Court receives thousands of appeals, but is very selective about what it takes. Because of the money and pressure and issues involved, this one has a decent chance of being heard.'

'From today, how long would it take for the case to be decided by the Supreme Court?'

'Anywhere from three to five years.'

'Rosenberg would have died from natural causes.'

'Yes, but there could be a Democrat in the White House when he died from natural causes. So take him out now when you can sort of predict his replacement.'

'Makes sense.'

'Oh, it's beautiful. If you're Victor Mattiece, and you've only got fifty million or so, and you want to be a billionaire, and you don't mind killing a couple of Supremes, then now is the time.'

'But what if the Supreme Court refused to hear the case?'

'He's in good shape if the Fifth Circuit affirms the trial verdict. But if it reverses, and the Supreme Court denies cert, he's got problems. My guess is that he would go back to square one, stir up some new litigation, and try it all again. There's too much money involved to lick his wounds and go home. When he took care of Rosenberg and Jensen, one has to assume he committed himself to a cause.'

'Where was he during the trial?'

'Completely invisible. Keep in mind, it is not public knowledge that he's the ringleader of the litigation. By the time the trial started, there were thirty-eight corporate defendants. No individuals were named, just corporations. Of the thirty-eight, seven are traded publicly, and he owns no more than twenty percent of any one. These are just small firms traded over the counter. The other thirty-one are privately held, and I couldn't get much information. But I did learn that many of these private companies are owned by each other, and some are even owned by the public corporations. It's almost impenetrable.'

'But he's in control.'

'Yes. I suspect he owns or controls eighty percent of the project. I checked out four of the private companies, and three are chartered offshore. Two in the Bahamas, and one in the Caymans. Del Greco heard that Mattiece operates from behind offshore banks and companies.'

'Do you remember the seven public companies?'

'Most of them. They, of course, were footnoted in the brief, a copy of which I do not have. But I've rewritten most of it in longhand.'

'Can I see it?'

'You can have it. But it's lethal.'

'I'll read it later. Tell me about the photograph.'

'Mattiece is from a small town near Lafayette, and in his younger years was a big money man for politicians in south Louisiana. He was a shadowy type back then, always in the background giving money. He spent big bucks on Democrats locally and Republicans nationally, and over the years he was wined and dined by big shots from Washington. He has never sought publicity, but his kind of money is hard to hide, especially when it's being handed out to politicians. Seven years ago, when the president was the Vice President, he was in New Orleans for a Republican fundraiser. All the heavy hitters were there, including Mattiece. It was ten thousand dollars a plate, so the press tried to get in. Somehow a photographer snapped a picture of Mattiece shaking hands with the VP. The New Orleans paper ran it the next day. It's a wonderful picture. They're grinning at each other like best friends.'

'It'll be easy to get.'

'I stuck it on the last page of the brief, just for the fun of it. This is fun, isn't it?'

'I'm having a ball.'

'Mattiece dropped out of sight a few years ago, and is now believed to live in several places. He's very eccentric. Del Greco said most people believe he's demented.'

The recorder beeped, and Gray changed tapes. Darby stood and stretched her long legs. He watched her as he fumbled with the recorder. Two other tapes were already used and marked.

'Are you tired?' he asked.

'I haven't been sleeping well. How many more questions?'

'How much more do you know?'

'We've covered the basics. There are some gaps we can fill in the morning.'

Gray turned off the recorder and stood. She was at the window, stretching and yawning. He relaxed on the sofa.

'What happened to the hair?' he asked.

Darby sat in a chair and pulled her feet under her. Red toenails. Her chin rested on her kness. 'I left it in a hotel in New Orleans. How did you know about it?'

'I saw a photograph.'

'From where?'

'Three photos, actually. Two from the Tulane yearbook, and one from Arizona State.'

'Who sent them to you?'

'I have contacts. They were faxed to me, so they weren't that good. But there was this gorgeous hair.'

'I wish you hadn't done that.'

'Why?'

'Every phone call leaves a trail.'

'Come on, Darby. Give me a little credit.'

'You were snooping around on me.'

'Just a little background. That's all.'

'No more, okay? If you want something from me, just ask. If I say no, then leave it alone.'

Grantham shrugged and agreed. Forget the hair. On to less sensitive matters. 'So who selected Rosenberg and Jensen? Mattiece is not a lawyer.'

'Rosenberg is easy. Jensen wrote little on environmental issues, but he was consistent in voting against all types of development. If they shared common ground with any consistency, it was protecting the environment.'

'And you think Mattiece figured this out by himself?'

'Of course not. A pretty wicked legal mind presented him with the two names. He has a thousand lawyers.'

'And none in D.C.?'

Darby raised her chin and frowned at him. 'What did you say?'

'None of his lawyers are in D.C.'

'I didn't say that.'

'I thought you said the law firms were primarily from New Orleans and Houston and other cities. You didn't mention D.C.'

Darby shook her head. 'You're assuming too much. I can think of at least two D.C. firms that I ran across. One is White and Blazevich, a very old, powerful, rich Republican firm with four hundred lawyers.'

Gray moved to the edge of the sofa.

'What's the matter?' she asked. He was suddenly wired. He was on his feet walking to the door, then back to the sofa.

'This may fit. This may be it, Darby.'

'I'm listening.'

'Are you listening?'

'I swear I'm listening.'

He was at the window. 'Okay, last week I got three phone calls from a lawyer in D.C. named Garcia, but that's not his name. He said he knew something and saw something about Rosenberg and Jensen, and he wanted so badly to tell me what he knew. But he got scared and disappeared.'

'There are a million lawyers in D.C.'

'Two million. But I know he works in a private firm. He sort of admitted it. He was sincere and very frightened, thought they were following. I asked who they were, and he of course wouldn't say.'

'What happened to him?'

'We had a meeting planned for last Saturday morning, and he called early and said forget it. Said he was married and had a good job, and why risk it. He never admitted it, but I think he has a copy of something that he was about to show me.'

'He could be your verification.'

'What if he works for White and Blazevich? We've suddenly narrowed it to four hundred lawyers.'

'The haystack is much smaller.'

Grantham darted to his bag, flipped through some papers, and presto! pulled out a five-by-seven black and white. He dropped it in her lap. 'This is Mr. Garcia.'

Darby studied the picture. It was a man on a busy sidewalk. The face was clear. 'I take it he didn't pose for this.'

'Not exactly.' Grantham was pacing.

'Then how'd you get it?'

'I cannot reveal my sources.'

She slid it onto the coffee table, and rubbed her eyes. 'You're scaring me, Grantham. This has a sleazy feel to it. Tell me it's not sleazy.'

'It's just a little sleazy, okay. The kid was using the same pay phone, and that's a mistake.'

'Yes, I know. That's a mistake.'

'And I wanted to know what he looked like.'

'Did you ask if you could take his photograph?'

'No.'

'Then it's sleazy as hell.'

'Okay. It's sleazy as hell. But I did it, and there it is, and it could be our link to Mattiece.'

'Our link?'

'Yes, our link. I thought you wanted to nail Mattiece.'

'Did I say that? I want him to pay, but I'd rather leave him alone. He's made a believer out of me, Gray. I've seen enough blood to last me a long time. You take this ball and run with it.'

He didn't hear this. He walked behind her to the window, then back to the bar. 'You mentioned two firms. What's the other?'

'Brim, Stearns, and somebody. I didn't get a chance to check them out. It's sort of odd because neither firm is listed as counsel of record for any of the defendants, but both firms, especially White and Blazevich, kept popping up as I went through the file.'

'How big is Brim, Stearns, and somebody?'

'I can find out tomorrow.'

'As big as White and Blazevich?'

'I doubt it.'

'Just guess. How big?'

'Two hundred lawyers.'

'Okay. Now we're up to six hundred lawyers in two firms. You're the lawyer, Darby. How can we find Garcia?'

'I'm not a lawyer, and I'm not a private detective. You're the investigative reporter.' She didn't like this 'we' business.

'Yeah, but I've never been in a law office, except for the divorce.'

'Then you're very fortunate.'

'How can we find him?'

She was yawning again. They had been talking for almost three hours, and she was exhausted. This could resume in the morning. 'I don't know how to find him, and I really haven't given it much thought. I'll sleep on it, and explain it to you in the morning.'

Grantham was suddenly calm. She stood and walked to the bar for a glass of water.

'I'll get my things,' he said, picking up the tapes.

'Would you do me a favor?' she asked.

'Maybe.'

She paused and looked at the sofa. 'Would you mind sleeping on the sofa tonight? I mean, I haven't slept well in a long time, and I need the rest. It would, well, it would be nice if I knew you were in here.'

He swallowed hard, and looked at the sofa. They both looked at the sofa. It was a five-footer at most, and did not appear to be the least bit comfortable.

'Sure,' he said, smiling at her. 'I understand.'

'I'm spooked, okay?'

'I understand.'

'It's nice to have someone like you around.' She smiled demurely, and Gray melted.

'I don't mind,' he said. 'No problem.'

'Thanks.'

'Lock the door, get in the bed, and sleep well. I'll be right here, and everything's all right.'

'Thanks.' She nodded and smiled again, then closed the door to her bedroom. He listened, and she did not lock it.

He sat on the sofa in the darkness, watching her door. Some time after midnight, he dozed and slept with his knees not far from his chin.

CHAPTER THIRTY-ONE

Her boss was Jackson Feldman, and he was the executive editor, and this was her turf, and she didn't take any crap off anyone but Mr. Feldman. Especially an insolent brat like Gray Grantham, who was standing in front of Mr. Feldman's door, guarding it like a Doberman. She glared at him, and he sneered at her, and this had been going on for ten minutes, ever since they huddled in there and closed the door. Why Grantham was waiting outside, she did not know. But this was her turf.

Her phone rang, and Grantham yelled at her. 'No calls!'

Her face was instantly red, and her mouth flew open. She picked up the receiver, listened for a second, then said, 'I'm sorry, but Mr. Feldman is in a meeting.' She glared at Grantham, who was shaking his head as if to dare her. 'Yes, I'll have him call you back as soon as possible.' She hung up.

'Thanks!' Grantham said, and this threw her off guard. She was about to say something nasty, but with the 'Thanks' her mind went blank. He smiled at her. And it made her even madder.

It was five-thirty, time for her to leave, but Mr. Feldman asked her to stay. He was still smirking at her over there by the door, not ten feet away. She had never liked Gray Grantham. But then, there weren't too many people at the *Post* she did like. A news aide approached and appeared headed for the door when the Doberman stepped in front of him. 'Sorry, you can't go in right now,' Grantham said.

'And why not?'

'They're in a meeting. Leave it with her.' He pointed at the secretary, who despised being pointed at and despised being referred to simply as 'her.' She had been here for twenty-one years.

The news aide was not easily intimidated. 'That's fine. But Mr. Feldman instructed me to have these papers here at precisely five-thirty. It's precisely five-thirty, here I am, and here are the papers.'

'Look, we're real proud of you. But you can't go in, understand? Now just leave the papers with that nice lady over there, and the sun will come up tomorrow.' Grantham moved squarely in front of the door, and appeared ready for combat if the kid insisted.

'I'll take those,' the secretary said. She took them, and the news aide left.

'Thanks!' Grantham said loudly again.

'I find you to be very rude,' she snapped.

'I said "Thanks." ' He tried to look hurt.

'You're a real smartass.'

'Thanks!'

The door suddenly opened, and a voice called out, 'Grantham.'

He smiled at her, and stepped inside. Jackson Feldman was standing behind his desk. The tie was down to the second button and the sleeves were rolled to the elbows. He was six-six, with no fat. At fifty-eight, he ran two marathons a year and worked fifteen hours a day.

Smith Keen was also standing, and holding the four-page outline of a story along with a copy of Darby's handwritten reproduction of the pelican brief. Feldman's copy was lying on the desk. They appeared dazed.

'Close the door,' Feldman said to Grantham.

Gray closed the door and sat on the edge of a table. No one spoke.

Feldman rubbed his eyes roughly, then looked at Keen. 'Wow,' he finally said.

Gray smiled. 'You mean that's it. I hand you the biggest story in twenty years, and you are so moved you say "Wow."'

'Where's Darby Shaw?' Keen asked.

'I can't tell you. It's part of the deal.'

'What deal?' Keen asked.

'I can't tell you that either.'

'When did you talk to her?'

'Last night, and again this morning.'

'And this was in New York?' Keen asked.

'What difference does it make where we talked? We talked, okay. She talked. I listened. I flew home. I wrote the outline. So what do you think?'

Feldman slowly folded his thin frame and sat deep in his chair. 'How much does the White House know?'

'Not sure. Verheek told Darby that it was delivered to the White House one day last week, and at the time the FBI thought it should be pursued. Then for some reason, after the White House had it, the FBI backed off. That's all I know.'

'How much did Mattiece give the President three years ago?'

'Millions. Virtually all of it through a myriad of PACs that he controls. This guy is very smart. He's got all kinds of lawyers, and they figure out ways to funnel money here and there. It's probably legal.'

The editors were thinking slowly. They were stunned, as if they'd just survived a bomb blast. Grantham was quite proud, and swung his feet under the table like a kid on a pier.

Feldman slowly picked up the papers clipped together and flipped through until he found the photograph of Mattiece and the President. He shook his head.

'It's dynamite, Gray,' Keen said. 'We just can't run without a bunch of corroboration. Hell, you're talking about the world's greatest job of verifying. This is powerful stuff, son.'

'How can you do it?' Feldman asked.

'I've got some ideas.'

'I'd like to hear them. You could get yourself killed with this.'

Grantham jumped to his feet, and stuck his hands in his pockets. 'First, we'll try to find Garcia.'

'We? Who's we?' Keen asked.

'Me, okay. Me. I'll try to find Garcia.'

'Is the girl in on this?' Keen asked.

'I can't answer that. It's part of the deal.'

'Answer the question,' Feldman said. 'Look at where we are if she gets killed helping you with the story. It's much too risky. Now where is she and what have you guys got planned?'

'I'm not telling where she is. She's a source, and I always protect my sources. No, she's not helping with the investigation. She's just a source, okay?'

They stared at him in disbelief. They looked at each other, and finally Keen shrugged.

'Do you want some help?' Feldman asked.

'No. She insists on me doing it alone. She's very scared, and you can't blame her.'

'I got scared just reading the damned thing,' Keen said.

Feldman kicked back in his chair and crossed his feet on the desk. Size fourteens. He smiled for the first time. 'You've got to start with Garcia. If he can't be found, then you could dig for months on Mattiece and not put it together. And before you start digging on Mattiece, let's have a long talk. I sort of like you, Grantham, and this is not worth getting killed over.'

'I see every word you write, okay?' Keen said.

'And I want a daily report, okay?' Feldman said.

'No problem.'

Keen walked to the glass wall and watched the madness in the newsroom. In the course of each day, the chaos came and went a half a dozen times. Things got crazy at five-thirty. The news was being written, and the second story conference was at six-thirty.

Feldman watched from his desk. 'This could be the end of the slump,' he said to Gray without looking at him. 'What's it been, five, six years?'

'Try seven,' Keen said.

'I've written some good stories,' Gray said defensively.

'Sure,' Feldman said, still watching the newsroom. 'But you've been hitting doubles and triples. The last grand slam was a long time ago.'

'There have been a lot of strikeouts too,' Keen added helpfully.

'Happens to all of us,' Gray said. 'But this grand slam will be in the seventh game of the World Series.' He opened the door.

Feldman glared at him. 'Don't get hurt, and don't allow her to get hurt. Understand?'

Gray smiled and left the office.

He was almost to Thomas Circle when he saw the blue lights behind him. The cop did not pass, but stayed on his bumper. He was oblivious to both the speed limit and his speedometer. It would be his third ticket in sixteen months.

He parked in a small lot next to an apartment house. It was dark, and the blue lights flashed in his mirrors. He rubbed his temples.

'Step out,' the cop demanded from the bumper.

Gray opened the door and did what he was told. The cop was black, and was suddenly smiling. It was Cleve. He pointed to the patrol car. 'Get in.'

They sat in the car under the blue lights and stared at the Volvo. 'Why do you do this to me?' Gray asked.

'We have quotas, Grantham. We have to stop so many white people and harass them. Chief wants to even things out. The white cops pick on innocent poor black folks, so us black cops have to pick on innocent rich white folks.'

'I suppose you're gonna handcuff me and beat the hell out of me.'

'Only if you ask me to. Sarge can't talk anymore.'

'I'm listening.'

'He smells something around the place. He's caught a few strange looks, and he's heard a thing or two.'

'Such as?'

'Such as they're talking about you, and how much they need to know what you know. He thinks they might be listening.'

'Come on, Cleve. Is he serious?'

'He's heard them talk about you and how you're asking questions about the pelican something or other. You've got 'em shook up.'

'What has he heard about this pelican thing?'

'Just that you're hot on it, and they're serious about it. These are mean and paranoid people, Gray. Sarge says to be careful where you go and who you talk to.'

'And we can't meet anymore?'

'Not for a while. He wants to lay low, and run things through me.'

'We'll do that. I need his help, but tell him to be careful. This is very touchy.'

'What is this pelican business?'

'I can't say. But tell Sarge it could get him killed.'

'Not Sarge. He's smarter than all of them over there.'

Gray opened the door and got out. 'Thanks, Cleve.'

He turned off the blue lights. 'I'll be around. I'm working nights for the next six months, so I'll try and keep an eye on you.'

'Thanks.'

Rupert paid for his cinnamon roll and sat on a bar stool overlooking the sidewalk. It was midnight, exactly midnight, and Georgetown was winding down. A few cars sped along M Street, and the remaining pedestrians headed for home. The coffee shop was busy, but not crowded. He sipped black coffee.

He recognized the face on the sidewalk, and moments later the man was sitting on the next bar stool. He was a flunkie of some sort. They had met a few days ago in New Orleans.

'So what's the score?' Rupert asked.

'We can't find her. And that worries us because we got some bad news today.'

'And?'

'Well, we heard voices, unconfirmed, that the bad guys have freaked out, and that the number one bad guy wants to start killing everybody. Money is no object, and these voices tell us he'll spend whatever it takes to snuff this thing out. He's sending in big boys with big guns. Of course, they say he's deranged, but he's mean as hell and money can kill a lot of people.'

This killing talk did not faze Rupert. 'Who's on the list?'

'The girl. And I guess anyone else on the outside who happens to know about that little paper.'

'So what's my plan?'

'Hang around. We'll meet here tomorrow night, same time. If we find the girl, it'll be your show.'

'How do you plan to find her?'

'We think she's in New York. We have ways.'

Rupert pulled off a piece of cinnamon roll and stuffed it in his mouth. 'Where would you be?'

The messenger thought of a dozen places he might go, but, dammit, they were like Paris and Rome and Monte Carlo, places he'd seen and places everyone went to. He couldn't think of that one exotic spot where he would go and hide for the rest of his life. 'I don't know. Where would you be?'

'New York City. You can live there for years and never be seen. You speak the language and know the rules. It's the perfect hiding place for an American.'

'Yeah, I guess you're right. You think she's there?'

'I don't know. At times she's clever. Then she has bad moments.'

The messenger was on his feet. 'Tomorrow night,' he said.

Rupert waved him off. What a goofy little twerp, he thought. Running around whispering important messages in coffee shops and beer joints. Then running back to his boss and reliving it all in vivid detail.

He threw the coffee cup in the trash and was on the sidewalk.

CHAPTER THIRTY-TWO

Brim, Stearns, and Kidlow had a hundred and ninety lawyers, according to the latest edition of the Martindale-Hubbell Legal Directory. And White and Blazevich had four hundred and twelve, so hopefully Garcia was only one of a possible six hundred and two. But if Mattiece used other D.C. firms, the number would be higher and they didn't have a chance.

As expected, White and Blazevich had no one named Garcia. Darby searched for another Hispanic name, but found none. It was one of those lily-white silk-stocking outfits filled with Ivy Leaguers with long names that ended in numerals. There were a few female names sprinkled about, but only two were partners. Most of the women had joined after 1980. If she lived long enough to finish law school, she would not consider working for a factory like White and Blazevich.

Grantham had suggested she check for Hispanics because Garcia was a bit unusual for an alias. Maybe the guy was Hispanic, and since Garcia is common for them, then maybe he just said it real quick. It didn't work. There were no Hispanics in this firm.

According to the directory, their clients were big and rich. Banks, Fortune 500s, and lots of oil companies. They listed four of the defendants in the lawsuit as clients, but not Mr. Mattiece. There were chemical companies and shipping lines, and White and Blazevich also represented the governments of South Korea, Libya, and Syria. Silly, she thought. Some of our enemies hire our lawyers to lobby our government. But then, you can hire lawyers to do anything.

Brim, Stearns, and Kidlow was a smaller version of White and Blazevich, but, gosh, there were four Hispanic names listed. She wrote them down. Two men and two women. She figured this firm must have been sued for race and sex discrimination. In the past ten years they had hired all kinds of people. The client list was predictable: oil and gas, insurance, banks, government relations. Pretty dull stuff.

She sat in a corner of the Fordham law library for an hour. It was Friday morning, ten in New York and nine in New Orleans, and instead of hiding in a library she'd never seen before, she was supposed to be sitting in Federal Procedure under Alleck, a professor she never liked but now missed sorely. Alice Stark would be sitting next to her. One of her favorite law nerds, D. Ronald Petrie, would be sitting behind her asking for a date and making lewd comments. She missed him too. She missed the quiet mornings on Thomas' balcony, sipping coffee and waiting for the French Quarter to shake its cobwebs and come to life. She missed the smell of cologne on his bathrobe.

She thanked the librarian, and left the building. On Sixty-second, she headed east toward the park. It was a brilliant October morning with a perfect sky and cool wind. A pleasant change from New Orleans, but difficult to appreciate under the circumstances. She wore new Ray-Bans and a muffler up to her chin. The hair was still dark, but she would cut no more. She was determined to walk without looking over her shoulder. They probably weren't back there, but she knew it would be years before she could stroll along a street without a doubt.

The trees in the park were a magnificent display of yellow and orange and red. The leaves fell gently in the breeze. She turned south on Central Park West. She would leave tomorrow, and spend a few days in Washington. If she survived, she would then leave the country, go maybe to the Caribbean. She'd been there twice, and there were a thousand little islands where most people spoke some form of English.

Now was the time to leave the country. They'd lost her trail, and she'd already checked on flights to Nassau and Jamaica. She could be there by dark.

She found a pay phone in the rear of a bagel shop on Sixth, and punched Gray's number at the *Post*. 'It's me,' she said.

'Well, well. I was afraid you had skipped the country.'

'Thinking about it.'

'Can you wait a week?'

'Probably. I'll be there tomorrow. What do you know?'

'I'm just gathering junk. I've got copies of the annual statements for the seven public corporations involved in the suit.'

'It's lawsuit, not suit. A suit is something you wear.'

'How can you ever forgive me? Mattiece is neither an officer nor director of any.'

'What else?'

'Just the thousand phone calls routine. I spent three hours yesterday hanging around courthouses looking for Garcia.'

'You won't find him at a courthouse, Gray. He's not that kind of lawyer. He's in a corporate firm.'

'I take it you have a better idea.'

'I've got several ideas.'

'Well, then, I'm just sitting here waiting on you.'

'I'll call you when I get there.'

'Don't call me at home.'

She paused for a second. 'May I ask why not?'

'There's a chance someone is listening, and maybe following. One of my best sources thinks I've ruffled enough feathers to get myself placed under surveillance.'

'Fabulous. And you want me to rush down there and team up with you?'

'We'll be safe, Darby. We just have to be careful.'

She gripped the phone and clenched her teeth. 'How dare you talk to me about being careful! I've been dodging bombs and bullets for ten days now, and you're smug enough to tell me to be careful. Kiss my ass, Grantham! Maybe I should stay away from you.'

There was a pause as she looked around the tiny café. Two men at the nearest table looked at her. She was much too loud. She turned away and breathed deeply.

Grantham spoke slowly. 'I'm sorry. I –'

'Forget it. Just forget it.'

He waited a moment. 'Are you okay?'

'I'm terrific. Never felt better.'

'Are you coming to D.C.?'

'I don't know. I'm safe here, and I'll be much safer when I get on a plane and leave the country.'

'Sure, but I thought you had this wonderful idea about finding Garcia, then hopefully nailing Mattiece. I thought you were outraged and morally indignant and motivated by revenge. What's happened to you?'

'Well, for one, I have this burning desire to see my twenty-fifth birthday. I'm not selfish, but perhaps I'd like to see my thirtieth too. That would be nice.'

'I understand.'

'I'm not sure you understand. I think you're more concerned with Pulitzers and glory than my pretty little neck.'

'I assure you that's not true. Trust me, Darby. You'll be safe. You've told me the story of your life. You must trust me.'

'I'll think about it.'

'That's not definite.'

'No, it's not. Give me some time.'

'Okay.'

She hung up, and ordered a bagel. A dozen languages rattled around her as the café was suddenly packed. Run, baby, run, her good sense told her. Take a cab to the airport. Pay cash for a ticket to Miami. Find the nearest flight south, and get on the plane. Let Grantham dig and wish him the best. He was very good, and he'd find a way to break the story. And she would read about it one day while lying on a sun-drenched beach sipping a piña colada and watching the windsurfers.

Stump limped by on the sidewalk. She caught a glimpse of him through the crowd and through the window. Her mouth was suddenly dry and she was dizzy. He didn't look inside. He just ambled by, looking rather lost. She ran through the tables and watched him through the door. He limped slightly to the corner of Sixth and Fifty-eighth and waited for the light. He started to cross Sixth, then changed his mind and crossed Fifty-eighth. A taxi almost smeared him.

He was going nowhere, just strolling along with a slight limp.

Croft saw the kid as he stepped from an elevator into the atrium. He was with another young lawyer, and they didn't have their briefcases so it was obvious they were headed for a late lunch. After five days of watching lawyers, Croft had learned their habits.

The building was on Pennsylvania, and Brim, Stearns, and Kidlow covered floors three through eleven. Garcia left the building with his buddy, and they laughed their way down the sidewalk. Something was very funny. Croft followed as closely as possible. They walked and laughed for five blocks, then, just as he figured, they ducked into a yuppie corporate fern bar for a quick bite.

Croft called Grantham three times before he got him. It was almost two, and the lunch was winding down by now, and if Grantham wanted to catch the guy, then stay close to the damned phone. Gray slammed it down. They would meet back at the building.

Garcia and his friend walked a bit slower on the return. It was a beautiful day, and it was Friday, and they enjoyed this brief respite from the grind of suing people or whatever they did for two hundred bucks an hour. Croft hid behind his sunshades and kept his distance.

Gray was waiting in the lobby near the elevators. Croft was close behind them as they spun through the revolving door. He pointed quickly to their man. Gray caught the signal and punched the elevator button. It opened and he stepped in just before Garcia and his friend. Croft stayed behind.

Garcia punched number six a split second before Gray punched it too. Gray read the paper and listened as the two lawyers talked football. The kid was no more than twenty-seven or twenty-eight. The voice maybe had a vague familiarity to it, but it had been on the phone and there was nothing distinctive about it. The face was close, but he couldn't study it. The odds said go for it. He looked very similar to the man in the photograph, and he worked for Brim, Stearns, and Kidlow, and one of its countless clients was Mr. Mattiece. He would give it a shot, but be cautious. He was a reporter. It was his job to go barging in with questions.

They left the elevator on six still yakking about the Redskins, and Gray loitered behind them, casually reading the paper. The firm's lobby was rich and opulent, with chandeliers and Oriental rugs, and on one wall thick gold letters with the firm's name. The lawyers stopped at the front desk and picked up their phone messages. Gray strolled purposefully in front of the receptionist, who eyed him carefully.

'May I help you, sir?' she asked in the tone that meant, 'What the hell do you want?'

Gray did not miss a step. 'I'm in a meeting with Roger Martin.' He'd found the name in the phone book, and he'd called from the lobby a minute earlier to make sure lawyer Martin was in today. The building directory listed the firm on floors three through eleven, but did not list all one hundred and ninety lawyers. Using the yellow pages listing, he made a dozen quick calls to find a lawyer on each floor. Roger Martin was the man on the sixth floor.

He frowned at the receptionist. 'I've been meeting with him for two hours.'

This puzzled her, and she could think of nothing to say. Gray was around the corner and into a hallway. He caught a glimpse of Garcia entering his office four doors down.

The name beside the door was David M. Underwood. Gray did not knock on it. He wanted to strike quickly, and perhaps exit quickly. Mr. Underwood was hanging his jacket on a rack.

'Hi. I'm Gray Grantham with the *Washington Post.* I'm looking for a man named Garcia.'

Underwood froze and looked puzzled. 'How'd you get in here?' he asked.

The voice was suddenly familiar. 'I walked. You are Garcia, aren't you?'

He pointed to a desk plate with his name in gold letters. 'David M. Underwood. There's no one on this floor named Garcia. I don't know of a Garcia in this firm.'

Gray smiled as if to play along. Underwood was scared. Or irritated.

'How's your daughter?' Gray asked.

Underwood was coming around the desk, staring and getting very perturbed. 'Which one?'

This didn't fit. Garcia had been quite concerned about his daughter, a baby, and if there had been more than one, he would have mentioned it.

'The youngest. And your wife?'

Underwood was now within striking distance, and inching closer. It was obvious he was a man unafraid of physical contact.

'I don't have a wife. I'm divorced.' He held up his left first, and for a split second Gray thought he'd gone wild. Then he saw the four ringless fingers. No wife. No ring. Garcia adored his wife, and there would be a ring. It was now time to leave.

'What do you want?' Underwood demanded.

'I thought Garcia was on this floor,' he said, easing away.

'Is your pal Garcia a lawyer?'

'Yes.'

Underwood relaxed a bit. 'Not in this firm. We have a Perez and a Hernandez, and maybe one other. But I don't know a Garcia.'

'Well, it's a big firm,' Gray said by the door. 'Sorry to bother.'

Underwood was following. 'Look, Mr. Grantham, we're not accustomed to reporters barging in around here. I'll call security, and maybe they can help you.'

'Won't be necessary. Thanks.' Grantham was in the hall and gone. Underwood reported to security.

Grantham cursed himself in the elevator. It was empty except for him, and he cursed out loud. Then he thought of Croft, and was cursing him when the elevator landed and opened, and there was Croft in the lobby near the pay phones. Cool it, he told himself.

They left the building together. 'Didn't work,' Gray said.

'Did you talk to him?'

'Yep. Wrong man.'

'Dammit. I knew it was him. It was the kid in the photos, wasn't it?'

'No. Close but no cigar. Keep trying.'

'I'm really tired of this, Grantham. I've –'

'You're getting paid, aren't you? Do it for one more week, okay? I can think of harder work.'

Croft stopped on the sidewalk, and Gray kept walking. 'One more week, and I'm through,' Croft yelled to him. Grantham waved him off.

He unlocked the illegally parked Volvo and sped back to the *Post.* It was not a smart move. It was quite stupid, and he was much too experienced for such a mistake. He would omit it from his daily chat with Jackson Feldman and Smith Keen.

Feldman was looking for him, another reporter said, and he walked quickly to his office. He smiled sweetly to the secretary, who was poised to attack. Keen and Howard Krauthammer, the managing editor, were waiting with Feldman. Keen closed the door and handed Gray a newspaper. 'Have you seen this?'

It was the New Orleans paper, the *Times-Picayune,* and the front-page story was about the deaths of Verheek and Callahan, along with big photos. He read it quickly while they watched him. It talked about their friendship, and their strange deaths just six days apart. And it mentioned Darby Shaw, who had disappeared. But no link to the brief.

'I guess the cat's out of the bag,' Feldman said.

'It's nothing but the basics,' Gray said. 'We could've run this three days ago.'

'Why didn't we?' asked Krauthammer.

'There's nothing here. It's two dead bodies, the name of the girl, and a thousand questions, none of which they answered. They've found a cop who'll talk, but he knows nothing beyond the blood and gore.'

'But they're digging, Gray,' Keen said.

'You want me to stop them?'

'The *Times* has picked it up,' Feldman said. 'They're running something tomorrow or Sunday. How much can they know?'

'Why ask me? Look, it's possible they have a copy of the brief. Very unlikely, but possible. But they haven't talked to the girl. We've got the girl, okay. She's ours.'

'We hope,' said Krauthammer.

Feldman rubbed his eyes and stared at the ceiling. 'Let's say they have a copy of the brief, and that they know she wrote it, and now she's vanished. They can't verify it right now, but they're not afraid to mention the brief without naming Mattiece. Let's say they know Callahan was her professor, among other things, and that he brought the brief here and gave it to his good friend Verheek. And now they're dead and she's on the run. That's a pretty damned good story, wouldn't you say, Gray?'

'It's a big story,' Krauthammer said.

'It's peanuts compared to what's coming,' Gray said. 'I don't want to run it because it's the tip of the iceberg, and it'll attract every paper in the country. We don't need a thousand reporters bumping into each other.'

'I say we run it,' Krauthammer said. 'If not, the *Times* will beat our ass with it.'

'We can't run the story,' Gray said.

'Why not?' asked Krauthammer.

'Because I'm not going to write it, and if it's written by someone else here, then we lose the girl. It's that simple. She's debating right now about whether to jump on a plane and leave the country, and one mistake by us and she's gone.'

'But she's already spilled her guts,' Keen said.

'I gave her my word, okay. I will not write the story until it's pieced together and Mattiece can be named. It's very simple.'

'You're using her, aren't you?' Keen asked.

'She's a source. But she's not in the city.'

'If the *Times* has the brief, then they know about Mattiece,' Feldman said. 'And if they know about Mattiece, you can bet they're digging like hell to verify it. What if they beat us?'

Krauthammer grunted in disgust. 'We're going to sit on our asses and lose the biggest story I've seen in twenty years. I say we run what we've got. It's just the surface, but it's a helluva story right now.'

'No,' Gray said. 'I won't write it until I have all of it.'

'And how long might that take?' Feldman asked.

'A week, maybe.'

'We don't have a week,' Krauthammer said.

Gray was desperate. 'I can find out how much the *Times* knows. Give me forty-eight hours.'

'They're running something tomorrow or Sunday,' Feldman said again.

'Let 'em run it. I'll bet money it'll be the same story with probably the same mug shots. You guys are assuming a hell of a lot. You're assuming they've got a copy of the brief, but its author doesn't have a copy of it. We don't have a copy of it. Let's wait, and read their little story, then go from there.'

The editors studied each other. Krauthammer was frustrated. Keen was anxious. But the boss was Feldman, and he said, 'Okay. If they run something in the morning, we'll meet here at noon and look at it.'

'Fine,' Gray said quickly and reached for the door.

'You'd better move fast, Grantham,' Feldman said. 'We can't sit on this much longer.'

Grantham was gone.

CHAPTER THIRTY-THREE

The Limousine moved patiently in the Beltway rush hour. It was dark, and Matthew Barr read with the aid of a reading light in the ceiling. Coal sipped Perrier and watched the traffic. He had the brief memorized, and could have simply explained it to Barr, but he wanted to watch his reaction.

Barr had no reaction until he got to the photograph, then slowly shook his head. He laid it on the seat, and thought about it for a moment. 'Very nasty,' he said.

Coal grunted.

'How true is it?' Barr asked.

'I'd love to know.'

'When did you first see it?'

'Tuesday of last week. It came over from the FBI in one of their daily reports.'

'What'd the President say?'

'He was not that happy with it, but there was no cause for alarm. It's just another wild shot in the dark, we thought. He talked to Voyles about it, and Voyles agreed to leave it alone for a while. Now I'm not so sure.'

'Did the President ask Voyles to back off?' Barr asked the question slowly.

'Yes.'

'That's awfully close to obstruction of justice, assuming of course the brief turns out to be true.'

'And what if it's true?'

'Then the President has problems. I've got one conviction for obstruction, so I've been there. It's like mail fraud. It's broad and wide and fairly easy to prove. Were you in on it?'

'What do you think?'

'Then I think you've got problems too.'

They rode in silence and watched the traffic. Coal had thought through the obstruction angle, but he wanted Barr's opinion. He wasn't worried about criminal charges. The President had one brief little chat with Voyles, asked him to look elsewhere for the time being, and that was it. Hardly the work of felons. But Coal was terribly concerned with re-election, and a scandal involving a major contributor like Mattiece would be devastating. The thought was sickening – a man the President knew and took millions from paid money to have two Supreme Court Justices knocked off so his pal the President could appoint more reasonable men to the bench so that the oil could be harvested. The Democrats would fall in the streets howling with glee. Every subcommittee in Congress would hold hearings. Every newspaper would run it every day for a year. The Justice Department would be forced to investigate. Coal would be forced to take the blame and resign. Hell, everyone in the White House, except the President, would have to go.

It was a nightmare of horrific proportions.

'We've got to find out if the brief is true,' Coal said to the window.

'If people are dying, then it's true. Give me a better reason for killing Callahan and Verheek.'

There was no other reason, and Coal knew it. 'I want you to do something.'

'Find the girl.'

'No. She's either dead or hiding in a cave somewhere. I want you to talk to Mattiece.'

'I'm sure he's in the yellow pages.'

'You can find him. We need to establish a link that the President knows nothing about. We need to first determine how much of this is true.'

'And you think Victor will take me into his confidence and tell me his secrets.'

'Yes, eventually. You're not a cop, remember. Assume it's true, and he thinks he's about to be exposed. He's desperate and he's killing people. What if you told him the press had the story and the end was near, and if he is inclined to disappear, then now's the time? You're coming to him from Washington, remember? From the inside. From the President, or so he thinks. He'll listen to you.'

'Okay. What if he tells me it's true? What's in it for us?'

'I've got some ideas, all in the category of damage control. The first thing we'll do is immediately appoint two nature lovers to the Court. I mean, wild-eyed radical bird watchers. It would show that down deep we're good little environmentalists. And it would kill Mattiece and his oil field, etc. We could do this in a matter of hours. Almost simultaneously, the President will call in Voyles and the Attorney General and Justice and demand an immediate investigation into Mattiece. We'll leak copies of the brief to every reporter in town, then hunker down and ride out the storm.'

Barr was smiling with admiration.

Coal continued. 'It won't be pretty, but it's far better than sitting back and hoping the brief is a work of fiction.'

'How do you explain that photograph?'

'You can't. It'll hurt for a while, but it was seven years ago, and people go crazy. We'll portray Mattiece as a good citizen back then, but now he's a madman.'

'He is a madman.'

'Yes, he is. And right now he's like a wounded dog backed in a corner. You must convince him to throw in the towel, and haul ass. I think he'll listen to you. And I think we'll find out from him if it's true.'

'So how do I find him?'

'I've got a man working on that. I'll pull some strings, and make a contact. Be ready to go on Sunday.'

Barr smiled to the window. He would like to meet Mattiece.

The traffic slowed. Coal slowly sipped his water. 'Anything on Grantham?'

'Not really. We're listening and watching, but nothing exciting. He talks to his mother and a couple of gals, but nothing worth reporting. He works a lot. He left town Wednesday and returned Thursday.'

'Where did he go?'

'New York. Probably working on some story.'

Cleve was supposed to be at the corner of Rhode Island and Sixth at exactly 10 P.M., but he wasn't. Gray was supposed to race down Rhode Island until Cleve caught him, so that if anyone was indeed following him they would think he was simply a dangerous driver. He raced down Rhode Island, through Sixth at fifty miles per hour, and watched for blue lights. There were none. He looped around, and fifteen minutes later barreled down Rhode Island again. There! He saw blue lights and pulled to the curb.

It was not Cleve. It was a white cop who was very agitated. He jerked Gray's license, examined it, and asked if he'd been drinking. No sir, he said. The cop wrote the ticket, and proudly handed it to Gray, who sat behind the wheel staring at the ticket until he heard voices coming from the rear bumper.

Another cop was on the scene, and they were arguing. It was Cleve, and he wanted the white cop to forget the ticket, but the white cop explained it had already been written and besides the idiot was doing fifty-six miles an hour through the intersection. He's a friend, Cleve said. Then teach him how to drive before he kills somebody, the white cop said as he got in his patrol car and drove away.

Cleve was snickering as he looked in Gray's window. 'Sorry about that,' he said with a smile.

'It's all your fault.'

'Slow it down next time.'

Gray threw the ticket on the floorboard. 'Let's talk quick. You said Sarge said the boys in the West Wing are talking about me. Right?'

'Right.'

'Okay, I need to know from Sarge if they're talking about any other reporters, especially from the *New York Times*. I need to know if they think anybody else is hot on the story.'

'Is that all?'

'Yes. I need it quick.'

'Slow it down,' Cleve said loudly and walked to his car.

Darby paid for the room for the next seven days, in part because she wanted a familiar place to return to if necessary, and in part because she wanted to leave some new clothes she had purchased. It was sinful, this running and leaving everything behind. The clothes were nothing fancy, sort of upscale safari law school, but they cost even more in New York, and it would be nice to keep them. She would not take risks over clothes, but she liked the room and she liked the city and she wanted the clothes.

It was time to run again, and she would travel light. She carried a small canvas bag when she darted from the St. Moritz into a waiting cab. It was almost 11 P.M., Friday, and Central Park South was busy. Across the street, a line of horses and carriages waited for customers and brief excursions through the park.

The cab took ten minutes to get to Seventy-second and Broadway, which was the wrong direction, but this entire journey should be hard to follow. She walked thirty feet, and disappeared into the subway. She had studied a map and a book of the system, and she hoped it would be easy. The subway was not appealing because she'd never used it and she'd heard the stories. But this was the Broadway line, the most commonly used train in Manhattan, and it was rumored to be safe, at times. And things weren't so swell above the ground. The subway could hardly be worse.

She waited in the correct spot with a group of drunk but well-dressed teenagers, and the train arrived in a couple of minutes. It wasn't crowded, and she took a seat near the center doors. Stare at the floor and hold the bag, she kept telling herself. She looked at the floor, but from behind the dark shades, she studied the people. It was her lucky night. No street punks with knives. No beggars. No perverts, at least none she could spot. But for a novice, it was nerve-racking anyway.

The drunk kids exited at Times Square, and she got off quickly at the next stop. She had never seen Penn Station, but this was not the time to sightsee. Maybe one day she could return and spend a month and admire the city without watching for Stump and Thin Man and who knows who else who was out there. But not now.

She had five minutes, and found her train as it was boarding. Again, she sat in the rear and watched every passenger. There were no familiar faces. Surely, please, surely, they had not stuck to her on this jagged escape. Once again, her mistake had been credit cards. She had bought four tickets at O'Hare with American Express, and somehow they knew she was in New York. She was certain Stump had not seen her, but he was in the city, and of course he had friends. There could be twenty of them. But then, she was not certain of anything.

The train left six minutes late. It was half empty. She pulled a paperback from the bag and pretended to read it.

Fifteen minutes later, they stopped in Newark, and she got off. She was a lucky girl. There were cabs lined up outside the station, and ten minutes later she was at the airport.

CHAPTER THIRTY-FOUR

It was Saturday morning, and the Queen was in Florida taking money from the rich, and it was clear and cool outside. He wanted to sleep late, then play golf whenever he woke up. But it was seven, and he was sitting at his desk wearing a tie, listening to Fletcher Coal suggest what they ought to do about this and about that. Richard Horton, the Attorney General, had talked to Coal, and now Coal was alarmed.

Someone opened the door and Horton entered alone. They shook hands and Horton sat across the desk. Coal stood nearby, and this really irritated the President.

Horton was dull but sincere. He was not dumb or slow, he just thought carefully about everything before he acted. He thought about each word before he said it. He was loyal to the President, and could be trusted for sound judgment.

'We are seriously considering a formal grand jury investigation into the deaths of Rosenberg and Jensen,' he announced gravely. 'In light of what's happened in New Orleans, we think this should be pursued immediately.'

'The FBI is investigating,' the President said. 'They've got three hundred agents on the case. Why should we get involved?'

'Are they investigating the pelican brief?' Horton asked. He knew the answer. He knew Voyles was in New Orleans at this moment with hundreds of agents. He knew they had talked to hundreds of people, collected a pile of useless evidence. He knew the President had asked Voyles to back off, and he knew Voyles was not telling the President everything.

Horton had never mentioned the pelican brief to the President, and the fact that he even knew about the damned thing was exasperating. How many more knew about it? Probably thousands.

'They are pursuing all leads,' Coal said. 'They gave us a copy of it almost two weeks ago, so we assume they're pursuing it.'

Exactly what Horton expected out of Coal. 'I feel strongly that the Administration should investigate this matter at once.' He spoke as though this was all memorized, and this irritated the President.

'Why?' asked the President.

'What if the brief is on target? If we do nothing, and the truth eventually surfaces, the damage will be irreparable.'

'Do you honestly believe there's any truth to it?' the President asked.

'It's awfully suspicious. The first two men who saw it are dead, and the person who wrote it has disappeared. It is perfectly logical, if one is so inclined to kill Supreme Court Justices. There are no other compelling suspects. From what I hear, the FBI is baffled. Yes, it needs to be pursued.'

Horton's investigations leaked worse than the White House basement, and Coal was terrified of this clown impaneling a grand jury and calling witnesses. Horton was an honorable man, but the Justice Department was filled with lawyers who talked too much.

'Don't you think it's a bit premature?' Coal asked.

'I don't think so.'

'Have you seen the papers this morning?' Coal asked.

Horton had glanced at the front page of the *Post*, and read the sports section. It was Saturday, after all. He had heard that Coal read eight newspapers before dawn, so he didn't like this question.

'I've read a couple of them,' he said.

'I've looked at several,' Coal said modestly. 'And there's not a word anywhere about those two dead lawyers or the girl or Mattiece or anything related to the brief. If you start a formal investigation at this point, it'll be front-page news for a month.'

'Do you think it will simply go away?' Horton asked Coal.

'It might. For obvious reasons, we hope so.'

'I think you're optimistic, Mr. Coal. We don't normally sit back and wait for the press to do our investigating.'

Coal grinned and almost laughed at this one. He smiled at the President, who shot him a quick look, and Horton started a slow burn.

'What's wrong with waiting a week?' asked the President.

'Nothing,' shot Coal.

Just that quick the decision was made to wait a week, and Horton knew it. 'Things could blow up in a week,' he said without conviction.

'Wait a week,' the President ordered. 'We'll meet here next Friday, and go from there. I'm not saying no, Richard, just wait seven days.'

Horton shrugged. This was more than he expected. He'd covered his rear. He would go straight to his office and dictate a lengthy memo detailing everything he could remember about this meeting, and his neck would be protected.

Coal stepped forward and handed him a sheet of paper.

'What's this?'

'More names. Do you know them?'

It was the bird-watcher list: four judges who were much too liberal for comfort, but Plan B called for radical environmentalists on the Court.

Horton blinked several times and studied it hard. 'You must be kidding.'

'Check 'em out,' said the President.

'These guys are off-the-wall liberals,' Horton mumbled.

'Yes, but they worship the sun and moon, and trees and birds,' Coal explained helpfully.

Horton caught on, and suddenly smiled. 'I see. Pelican lovers.'

'They're almost extinct, you know,' the President said.

Coal headed for the door. 'I wish they'd been wiped out ten years ago.'

She hadn't called by nine when Gray arrived at his desk in the newsroom. He'd read the *Times* and there was nothing in it. He spread the New Orleans paper over the clutter and skimmed it. Nothing. They had reported all they knew. Callahan, Verheek, Darby, and a thousand unanswered questions. He had to assume the *Times* and maybe the *Times-Picayune* in New Orleans had seen the brief or heard about it, and thus knew of Mattiece. And he had to assume they were clawing like cats to verify it. But he had Darby, and they would find Garcia, and if Mattiece could be verified, they would do it.

At the moment, there was no alternative plan. If Garcia was gone or refused to help, they would be forced to explore the dark and murky world of Victor Mattiece. Darby would not last long at that, and he didn't blame her. He was uncertain how long he would last.

Smith Keen appeared with a cup of coffee and sat on the desk. 'If the *Times* had it, would they hold off until tomorrow?'

Gray shook his head. 'No. If they had more than the *Times-Picayune,* it would've run today.'

'Krauthammer wants to run what we've got. He thinks we can name Mattiece.'

'I don't follow.'

'He's leaning on Feldman. His angle is that we can run the whole story about Callahan and Verheek getting killed over this brief, which happens to name Mattiece who happens to be a friend of the President's, without directly accusing Mattiece. He says we can be extremely cautious and make sure the story says Mattiece is named in the brief, but not named by us. And since the brief is causing all this death, then it has been verified to some extent.'

'He wants to hide behind the brief.'

'Exactly.'

'But it's all speculation until it's confirmed. Krauthammer's losing it. Assume for a second that Mr. Mattiece is in no way involved with this. Completely innocent. We run the story with his name in it, and then what? We look like fools, and we get sued for the next ten years. I'm not writing the story.'

'He wants someone else to write it.'

'If this paper runs a pelican story not written by me, the girl is gone, okay. I thought I explained that yesterday.'

'You did. And Feldman heard you. He's on your side, Gray, and I am too. But if this thing's true, it'll blow up in a matter of days. We all believe that. You know how Krauthammer hates the *Times,* and he's afraid those bastards'll run it.'

'They can't run it, Smith. They may have a few more facts than the *Times-Picayune,* but they can't name Mattiece. Look, we'll verify before anyone. And when it's nailed down, I'll write the story with everyone's name along with that cute little picture of Mattiece and his friend in the White House, and the fat lady will sing.'

'We? You said it again. You said, "We'll verify it." '

'My source and I, okay.' Gray opened a drawer and found the photo of Darby and the Diet Coke. He handed it to Keen, who admired it.

'Where is she?' he asked.

'I'm not sure. I think she's on her way here from New York.'

'Don't get her killed.'

'We're being very cautious.' Gray looked over both shoulders and leaned closer. 'In fact, Smith, I think I'm being followed. I just wanted you to know.'

'Who might they be?'

'It came from a source at the White House. I'm not using my phones.'

'I'd better tell Feldman.'

'Okay. I don't think it's dangerous, yet.'

'He needs to know.' Keen jumped to his feet and disappeared.

She called within minutes. 'I'm here,' she said. 'I don't know how many I've brought with me, but I'm here, and alive, for the moment.'

'Where are you?'

'Tabard Inn on N Street. I saw an old friend on Sixth Avenue yesterday. Remember Stump, who was grievously wounded on Bourbon Street? Did I tell you that story?'

'Yes.'

'Well, he's walking again. A slight limp, but he was wandering around Manhattan yesterday. I don't think he saw me.'

'Are you serious! That's scary, Darby.'

'It's worse than scary. I left six trails when I left last night, and if I see him in this city, limping along a sidewalk somewhere, I intend to surrender. I'll walk up to him and turn myself in.'

'I don't know what to say.'

'Say as little as possible, because these people have radar. I'll play private eye for three days, and I'm out of here. If I live to see Wednesday morning, I'm on a plane to Aruba or Trinidad or some place with a beach. When I die, I want to be on a beach.'

'When do we meet?'

'I'm thinking about that. I want you to do two things.'

'I'm listening.'

'Where do you park your car?'

'Close to my apartment.'

'Leave it there, and go rent another one. Nothing fancy, just a generic Ford or something. Pretend someone's watching you through a rifle scope. Go to the Marbury Hotel in Georgetown and get a room for three nights. They'll take cash – I've already checked. Do it under another name.'

Grantham took notes and shook his head.

'Can you sneak out of your apartment after dark?' she asked.

'I think so.'

'Do it, and take a cab to the Marbury. Have them deliver the rental car to you there. Take two cabs to the Tabard Inn, and walk into the restaurant at exactly nine tonight.'

'Okay. Anything else?'

'Bring clothes. Plan to be away from your apartment for at least three days. And plan to stay away from the office.'

'Really, Darby, I think the office is safe.'

'I'm not in the mood to argue. If you're going to be difficult, Gray, I'll simply disappear. I'm convinced I'll live longer the sooner I get out of the country.'

'Yes, ma'am.'

'That's a good boy.'

'I assume there's a master plan rattling around somewhere in your brain.'

'Maybe. We'll talk about it over dinner.'

'Is this sort of like a date?'

'Let's eat a bite and call it business.'

'Yes, ma'am.'

'I'm hanging up now. Be cautious, Gray. They're watching.' She was gone.

She was sitting at table thirty-seven, in a dark corner of the tiny restaurant when he found her at exactly nine. The first thing he noticed was the dress, and as he walked to the table he knew the legs were under it but he couldn't see them. Maybe later when she stood. He wore a coat and tie, and they were an attractive couple.

He sat close to her in the darkness so they could both watch the small crowd. The Tabard Inn appeared old enough to have served food to Thomas Jefferson. A rowdy crowd of Germans laughed and talked on the patio outside the restaurant. The windows were open and the air was cool, and for one brief moment it was easy to forget why they were hiding.

'Where'd you get the dress?'

'You like it?'

'It's very nice.'

'I shopped a little this afternoon. Like most of my recent wardrobe, it's disposable. I'll probably leave it in the room the next time I flee for my life.'

The waiter was before them with menus. They ordered drinks. The restaurant was quiet and harmless.

'How'd you get here?' he asked.

'Around the world.'

'I'd like to know.'

'I took a train to Newark, a plane to Boston, a plane to Detroit, and a plane to Dulles. I was up all night, and twice I forgot where I was.'

'How could they follow that?'

'They couldn't. I paid with cash, something I'm running out of.'

'How much do you need?'

'I'd like to wire some from my bank in New Orleans.'

'We'll do it Monday. I think you're safe, Darby.'

'I've thought that before. In fact, I felt very safe when I was getting on the boat with Verheek, except it wasn't Verheek. And I felt very safe in New York. Then Stump waddled down the sidewalk, and I haven't eaten since.'

'You look thin.'

'Thanks. I guess. Have you eaten here?' She looked at her menu.

He looked at his. 'No, but I hear the food is great. You changed your hair again.' It was light brown, and there was a trace of mascara and blush. And lipstick.

'It's going to fall out if I keep seeing these people.'

The drinks arrived, and they ordered.

'We expect something in the *Times* in the morning.' He would not mention the New Orleans paper because it had pictures of Callahan and Verheek. He assumed she'd seen it.

This didn't seem to interest her. 'Such as?' she asked, looking around.

'We're not sure. We hate to get beat by the *Times*. It's an old rivalry.'

'I'm not interested in that. I know nothing about journalism, and don't care to learn. I'm here because I have one, and only one, idea about finding Garcia. And if it doesn't work, and quickly, I'm out of here.'

'Forgive me. What would you like to talk about?'

'Europe. What's your favorite place in Europe?'

'I hate Europe, and I hate Europeans. I go to Canada and Australia, and New Zealand occasionally. Why do you like Europe?'

'My grandfather was a Scottish immigrant, and I've got a bunch of cousins over there. I've visited twice.'

Gray squeezed the lime in his gin and tonic. A party of six entered from the bar and she watched them carefully. When she talked her eyes darted quickly around the room.

'I think you need a couple of drinks to relax,' Gray said.

She nodded but said nothing. The six were seated at a nearby table and began speaking in French. It was pleasant to hear.

'Have you ever heard Cajun French?' she asked.

'No.'

'It's a dialect that's rapidly disappearing, just like the wetlands. They say it cannot be understood by Frenchmen.'

'That's fair. I'm sure the Cajuns can't understand the French.'

She took a long drink of white wine. 'Did I tell you about Chad Brunet?'

'I don't think so.'

'He was a poor Cajun boy from Eunice. His family survived by trapping and fishing in the marshes. He was a very bright kid who attended LSU on a full academic scholarship, then was admitted to law school at Stanford, where he finished with the highest grade point average in the school's history. He was twenty-one when he was admitted to the California bar. He could have worked for any law firm in the country, but he took a job with an environmental defense outfit in San Francisco. He was brilliant, a real legal genius who worked very hard and was soon winning huge lawsuits against oil and chemical companies. At the age of twenty-eight, he was a highly polished courtroom lawyer. He was feared by big oil and other corporate polluters.' She took a sip of wine. 'He made a lot of money, and established a group to preserve the Louisiana wetlands. He wanted to participate in the pelican case, as it was known, but had too many other trial commitments. He gave Green Fund a lot of money for litigation expenses. Shortly before the trial started in Lafayette, he announced he was coming home to assist the Green Fund lawyers. There were a couple of stories about him in the New Orleans paper.'

'What happened to him?'

'He committed suicide.'

'What?'

'A week before the trial, they found him in a car with the engine running. A garden hose ran from the exhaust pipe into the front seat. Just another simple suicide from carbon monoxide poisoning.'

'Where was the car?'

'In a wooded area along Bayou Lafourche near the town of Galliano. He knew the area well. Some camping gear and fishing equipment were in the trunk. No suicide note. The police investigated, but found nothing suspicious. The case was closed.'

'This is incredible.'

'He had had some problems with alcohol, and had been treated by an analyst in San Francisco. But the suicide was a surprise.'

'Do you think he was murdered?'

'A lot of people do. His death was a big blow to Green Fund. His passion for the wetlands would've been potent in the courtroom.'

Gray finished his drink and rattled the ice. She inched closer to him. The waiter appeared, and they ordered.

CHAPTER THIRTY-FIVE

The lobby of the Marbury Hotel was empty at 6 A.M. Sunday when Gray found a copy of the *Times*. It was six inches deep and weighed twelve pounds, and he wondered how much thicker they planned to make it. He raced back to his room on the eighth floor, spread the paper on the bed, and hovered over it as he skimmed intensely. The front page was empty, and this was crucial. If they had the big story, it would of course be there. He feared large photographs of Rosenberg, Jensen, Callahan, Verheek, maybe Darby and Khamel, who knows, maybe they had a nice picture of Mattiece, and all of these would be lined up on the front page like a cast of characters, and the *Times* had beat them again. He had dreamed of this while he had slept, which had not been for long.

But there was nothing. And the less he found, the faster he skimmed until he was down to sports and classifieds, and he stopped and sort of danced to the phone. He called Smith Keen, who was awake. 'Have you seen it?' he asked.

'Ain't it beautiful,' Keen said. 'I wonder what happened.'

'They don't have it, Smith. They're digging like hell, but they don't have it yet. Who did Feldman talk to?'

'He never says. But it was supposed to be reliable.'

Keen was divorced and lived alone in an apartment not far from the Marbury.

'Are you busy?' Gray asked.

'Well, not exactly. It's almost six-thirty on Sunday morning.'

'We need to talk. Pick me up outside the Marbury Hotel in fifteen minutes.'

'The Marbury Hotel?'

'It's a long story. I'll explain.'

'Ah, the girl. You lucky stiff.'

'I wish. She's in another hotel.'

'Here? In Washington?'

'Yes. Fifteen minutes.'

'I'll be there.'

Gray nervously sipped coffee from a paper cup and waited in the lobby. She'd made him paranoid, and he half expected thugs to be hiding on the sidewalk with automatic weapons. This frustrated him. He saw Keen's Toyota ease by on M Street, and he walked quickly to it.

'What would you like to see?' Keen said as he drove away from the curb.

'Oh, I don't know. It's a beautiful day. How about Virginia?'

'As you wish. Did you get kicked out of your apartment?'

'Not exactly. I'm following orders from the girl. She thinks like a field marshal, and I'm here because I was told to be here. I must stay until Tuesday, or until she gets jumpy and moves me again. I'm in room eight-thirty-three if you need me, but don't tell anyone.'

'I assume you want the *Post* to pay for this,' Keen said with a smile.

'I'm not thinking about money right now. The same people who tried to kill her in New Orleans turned up in New York on Friday, or so she thinks. They have amazing talent in pursuit, and she's being painfully cautious.'

'Well, if you're being followed by someone, and she's being followed by someone, then perhaps she knows what she's doing.'

'Oh, listen, Smith, she knows exactly what she's doing. She's so good it's scary, and she's leaving here Wednesday morning for good. So we've got two days to find Garcia.'

'What if Garcia's overrated? What if you find him and he won't talk, or what if he knows nothing? Have you thought about that?'

'I've had nightmares about that. I think he knows something big. There's a document or a piece of paper, something tangible, and he's got it. He referred to it a time or two, and when I pressed him he wouldn't admit it. But the day we were supposed to meet, he planned to show it to me. I'm convinced of that. He's got something, Smith.'

'And if he won't show it to you?'

'I'll break his neck.'

They crossed the Potomac and cruised by Arlington Cemetery. Keen lit his pipe and cracked a window. 'What if you can't find Garcia?'

'Plan B. She's gone and the deal's off. Once she leaves the country, I have permission to do anything with the brief except use her name as a source. The poor girl is convinced she's dead regardless of whether we get the story, but she wants as much protection as possible. I can never use her name, not even as the author of the brief.'

'Does she talk much about the brief?'

'Not the actual writing of it. It was a wild idea, she pursued it, and had almost dismissed it when bombs stared going off. She's sorry she wrote the damned thing. She and Callahan were really in love, and she's loaded down with a lot of pain and guilt.'

'So what's Plan B?'

'We attack the lawyers. Mattiece is too devious and slippery to penetrate without subpoenas and warrants and things we can't dispense, but we know his lawyers. He's represented by two big firms here in town, and we go after them. A lawyer or a group of them carefully analyzed the

Supreme Court, and suggested the names of Rosenberg and Jensen. Mattiece wouldn't know who to kill. So his lawyers told him. It's a conspiracy angle.'

'But you can't make them talk.'

'Not about a client. But if the lawyers are guilty, and we start asking questions, something'll break. We'll need a dozen reporters making a million phone calls to lawyers, paralegals, law clerks, secretaries, copy room clerks, everybody. We assault these bastards.'

Keen puffed his pipe and was noncommittal. 'Who are the firms?'

'White and Blazevich, and Brim, Stearns, and Kidlow. Check our library on them.'

'I've heard of White and Blazevich. It's a big Republican outfit.'

Gray nodded and sipped the last of his coffee.

'What if it's another firm?' Keen asked. 'What if the firm is not in Washington? What if the conspirators don't break? What if there's only one legal mind at work here and it belongs to a part-time paralegal in Shreveport? What if one of Mattiece's inhouse lawyers devised the scheme?'

'Sometimes you irritate the hell out of me. Do you know that?'

'These are valid questions. What if?'

'Then we go to Plan C.'

'And what's that?'

'I don't know yet. She hasn't gotten that far.'

She had instructed him to stay off the streets and to eat in his room. He had a sandwich and fries in a bag, and was obediently walking to his room on the eighth floor of the Marbury. An Asian maid was pushing her cart near his room. He stopped at his door and pulled the key from his pocket.

'You forget something, sir?' the maid asked.

Gray looked at her. 'I beg your pardon.'

'You forget something?'

'Well, no. Why?'

The maid took a step closer to him. 'You just left, sir, and now you are back.'

'I left four hours ago.'

She shook her head and took another step for a closer look.

'No sir. A man left your room ten minutes ago.' She hesitated and studied his face intently. 'But, sir, now I think it was another man.'

Gray glanced at the room number on the door. 833. He started at the woman. 'Are you certain another man was in this room?'

'Yes, sir. Just minutes ago.'

He panicked. He walked quickly to the stairs, and ran down eight flights. What was in the room? Nothing but clothes. Nothing about Darby. He stopped and reached into a pocket. The note with the Tabard Inn address and her phone number was in the pocket. He caught his breath, and eased into the lobby.

He had to find her, and quick.

Darby found an empty table in the reading room on the second floor of the Edward Bennett Williams Law Library at Georgetown. In her new hobby as a traveling critic of law school libraries, she found Georgetown's to be the nicest so far. It was a separate five-story building across a small courtyard from McDonough Hall, the law school. The library was new, sleek, and modern, but still a law library and quickly filling with Sunday students now thinking of final exams.

She opened volume five of Martindale-Hubbell, and found the section for D.C. firms. White and Blazevich ran for twenty-eight pages. Names, birth dates, birthplaces, schools, professional organizations, distinctions, awards, committees, and publications of four hundred and twelve lawyers, the partners first, then the associates. She took notes on a legal pad.

The firm had eighty-one partners, and the rest were associates. She grouped them by alphabet, and wrote every name on the legal pad. She was just another law student checking out law firms in the relentless chase of employment.

The work was boring and her mind wandered. Thomas had studied here twenty years ago. He'd been a top student and claimed to have spent many hours in the library. He'd written for the law journal, a chore she would be enduring under normal circumstances.

Death was a subject she'd analyzed from different angles in the past ten days. Except for going quietly in one's sleep, she was undecided as to the best approach. A slow, agonizing demise from a disease was a nightmare for the victim and the loved ones, but at least there was time for preparation and farewells. A violent, unexpected death was over in a second and probably best for the deceased. But the shock was numbing for those left behind. There were so many painful questions. Did he suffer? What was his last thought? Why did it happen? And watching the quick death of a loved one was beyond description.

She loved him more because she watched him die, and she told herself to stop hearing the explosion, and stop smelling the smoke, and stop watching him die. If she survived three more days, she would be in a place where she could lock the door and cry and throw things until the grieving was over. She was determined to make it to that place. She was determined to grieve, and to heal. It was the least she deserved.

She memorized names until she knew more about White and Blazevich than anyone outside the firm. She eased into the darkness and caught a cab to the hotel.

Matthew Barr went to New Orleans, where he met with a lawyer who instructed him to fly to a certain hotel in Fort Lauderdale. The lawyer was vague about what would happen at the hotel, but Barr checked in Sunday night and found a room waiting for him. A note at the desk said he would receive a call in the early a.m.

He called Fletcher Coal at home at ten, and briefed him on the journey so far.

Coal had other things on his mind. 'Grantham's gone crazy. He and a guy named Rifkin with the *Times* are making calls everywhere. They could be deadly.'

'Have they seen the brief?'

'I don't know if they've seen it, but they've heard of it. Rifkin called one of my aides at home yesterday and asked what he knew about the pelican brief. The aide knew nothing, and got the impression Rifkin knew even less. I don't think he's seen it, but we can't be certain.'

'Damn, Fletcher. We can't keep up with a bunch of reporters. Those guys make a hundred phone calls a minute.'

'Just two. Grantham and Rifkin. You've already got Grantham wired. Do the same for Rifkin.'

'Grantham's wired, but he's using neither the phone in his apartment nor the one in his car. I called Bailey from the airport in New Orleans. Grantham hasn't been home in twenty-four hours, but his car's still there. They called and knocked on his door. He's either dead in the apartment, or he sneaked out last night.'

'Maybe he's dead.'

'I don't think so. We were following, and so were the Fibbies. I think he got wind of it.'

'You must find him.'

'He'll turn up. He can't get too far away from the newsroom on the fifth floor.'

'I want Rifkin wired too. Call Bailey tonight and get it started, okay?'

'Yes sir,' Barr said.

'What do you think Mattiece would do if he thought Grantham had the story and was about to spread it across the front page of the *Washington Post*?' Coal asked.

Barr stretched on the hotel bed and closed his eyes. Months ago he had made the decision never to cross Fletcher Coal. He was an animal.

'He's not afraid of killing people, is he?' Barr said.

'Do you think you'll see Mattiece tomorrow?'

'I don't know. These guys are very secretive. They speak in hushed tones behind closed doors. They've told me little.'

'Why do they want you in Fort Lauderdale?'

'I do not know, but it's much closer to the Bahamas. I think I'm going there tomorrow, or perhaps he's coming here. I just don't know.'

'Perhaps you should exaggerate the Grantham angle. Mattiece will snuff out the story.'

'I'll think about it.'

'Call me in the morning.'

She stepped on the note when she opened her door. It said: *Darby, I'm on the patio. It's urgent, Gray.* She took a deep breath and crammed the note in her pocket. She locked the door, and followed the narrow, winding hallways to the lobby, then through the dark sitting room, by the bar, through the restaurant, and onto the patio. He was at a small table, partially hidden by a brick wall.

'Why are you here?' she demanded in a whisper as she sat close to him. He looked tired and worried.

'Where have you been?' he asked.

'That's not as important as why you're here. You're not supposed to come here unless I say so. What's going on?'

He gave her a quick summary of his morning, from the first phone call to Smith Keen to the maid in the hotel. He'd spent the rest of the day darting all over the city in various cabs, almost eighty bucks' worth of cabs, and he waited until dark to sneak into the Tabard Inn. He was certain he had not been followed.

She listened. She watched the restaurant and the entrance to the patio, and heard every word.

'I have no idea how anyone could find my room,' he said.

'Did you tell anyone your room number?'

He thought for a second. 'Only Smith Keen. But he'd never repeat it.'

She was not looking at him. 'Where were you when you told him your room number?'

'In his car.'

She shook her head slowly. 'I distinctly told you not to tell anyone. Didn't I?'

He would not answer.

'It's all fun and games, isn't it, Gray? Just another day at the beach. You're a big stud reporter who's had death threats before, but you're fearless. The bullets will bounce off, won't they? You and I can spend a few days here frolicking around town playing detective so you can win a Pulitzer and get rich and famous, and the bad guys aren't really so bad because, hey, you're Gray Grantham of the *Washington Post* and that makes you a mean son of a bitch.'

'Come on, Darby.'

'I've tried to impress upon you how dangerous these people are. I've seen what they can do. I know what they'll do to me if they find me. But no, Gray, it's all a game to you. Cops and robbers. Hide-and-seek.'

'I'm convinced, okay?'

'Listen, hotshot, you'd better be convinced. One more screwup and we're dead. I'm out of lucky breaks. Do you understand?'

'Yes! I swear I understand.'

'Get a room here. Tomorrow night, if we're alive, I'll find you another small hotel.'

'What if this place is full?'

'Then you can sleep in my bathroom with the door closed.'

She was dead serious. He felt like a first-grader who'd just received his first spanking. They didn't speak for five minutes.

'So how'd they find me?' he finally asked.

'I would assume the phones in your apartment are tapped, and your car is bugged. And I would assume Smith Keen's car is also wired. These people are not amateurs.'

CHAPTER THIRTY-SIX

He spent the night in room 14 upstairs, but slept little. The restaurant opened at six, and he sneaked down for coffee, then sneaked back to his room. The inn was quaint and ancient, and had somehow been formed when three old townhouses were connected. Small doors and narrow hallways ran in all directions. The atmosphere was timeless.

It would be a long, tiresome day, but it would all be spent with her, and he looked forward to it. He'd made a mistake, a bad one, but she'd forgiven him. At precisely eight-thirty, he knocked on the door to room 1. She quickly opened it, then closed it behind him.

She was a law student again, with jeans and a flannel shirt. She poured him coffee, and sat at the small table where the phone was surrounded by notes from a legal pad.

'Did you sleep well?' she asked, but only out of courtesy.

'No.' He threw a copy of the *Times* on the bed. He'd already scanned it, and it was empty again.

Darby took the phone and punched the number of the Georgetown law school. She looked at him, and listened, then said, 'Placement office, please.' There was a long pause. 'Yes, this is Sandra Jernigan. I'm a partner with White and Blazevich here in town, and we're having a problem with our computers. We're trying to reconstruct some payroll records, and the accountants have asked me to ask you for the names of your students who clerked here last summer. I think there were four of them.' She listened for a second. 'Jernigan. Sandra Jernigan,' she repeated. 'I see. How long will it take?' A pause. 'And your name is, Joan. Thank you, Joan.' Darby covered the receiver and breathed deeply. Gray watched intently, but with an admiring grin.

'Yes, Joan. Seven of them. Our records are a mess. Do you have their addresses and social security numbers? We need it for tax purposes. Sure. How long will it take? Fine. We have an office boy in the area. His name is Snowden, and he'll be there in thirty minutes. Thank you, Joan.' Darby hung up and closed her eyes.

'Sandra Jernigan?' he said.

'I'm not good at lying,' she said.

'You're wonderful. I guess I'm the office boy.'

'You could pass for an office boy. You have an aging law school dropout look about you.' And you're sort of cute, she thought to herself.

'I like the flannel shirt.'

She took a long drink of cold coffee. 'This could be a long day.'

'So far, so good. I get the list, and meet you in the library. Right?'

'Yes. The placement office is on the fifth floor of the law school. I'll be in room 336. It's a small conference room on the third floor. You take a cab first. I'll meet you there in fifteen minutes.'

'Yes, ma'am.' Grantham was out the door. Darby waited five minutes, then left with her canvas bag.

The cab ride was short but slow in the morning traffic. Life on the lam was bad enough, but running and playing detective at the same time was too much. She'd been in the cab five minutes before she thought about being followed. And maybe that was good. Maybe a hard day as an investigative reporter would take her mind off Stump and the other tormentors. She would work today, and tomorrow, and by late Wednesday she would be on a beach.

They would start with the law school at Georgetown. If it was a dead end, they would try the one at George Washington. If there was time, they would try American University. Three strikes, and she was gone.

The cab stopped at McDonough Hall, at the grungy base of Capitol Hill. With her bag and flannel shirt, she was just one of many law students milling about before class. She took the stairs to the third level, and closed the door to the conference room behind her. The room was used for an occasional class and on campus job interviews. She spread her notes on the table, and was just another law student preparing for class.

Within minutes, Gray eased through the door. 'Joan's a sweet lady,' he said as he placed the list on the table. 'Names, addresses, and social security numbers. Ain't that nice.'

Darby looked at the list and pulled a phone book from her bag. They found five of the names in the book. She looked at her watch. 'It's five minutes after nine. I'll bet no more than half of these are in class at this moment. Some will have later classes. I'll call these five, and see who's at home. You take the two with no phone number, and get their class schedules from the registrar.'

Gray looked at his watch. 'Let's meet back here in fifteen minutes.' He left first, then Darby. She went to the pay phones on the first level outside the classrooms, and dialed the number of James Maylor.

A male voice answered, 'Hello.'

'Is this Dennis Maylor?' she asked.

'No. I'm James Maylor.'

'Sorry.' She hung up. His address was ten minutes away. He didn't have a nine o'clock class, and if he had one at ten he would be home for another forty minutes. Maybe.

She called the other four. Two answered and she confirmed, and there was no answer at the other two.

Gray waited impatiently in the registrar's office on the third floor. A part-time student clerk was trying to find the registrar, who was somewhere in the back. The student informed him that she wasn't sure if they could give out class schedules. Gray said he was certain they could if they wanted to.

The registrar walked suspiciously around a corner. 'May I help you?'

'Yes, I'm Gray Grantham with the *Washington Post,* and I'm trying to find two of your students, Laura Kaas and Michael Akers.'

'Is there a problem?' she asked nervously.

'Not at all. Just a few questions. Are they in class this morning?' He was smiling, and it was a warm, trusting smile that he flashed usually at older women. It seldom failed him.

'Do you have an ID or something?'

'Certainly.' He opened his wallet and slowly waved it at her, much like a cop who knows he's a cop and doesn't care to spell it out.

'Well, I really should talk to the dean, but –'

'Fine. Where's his office?'

'But he's not here. He's out of town.'

'I just need their class schedules so I can find them. I'm not asking for home addresses or grades or transcripts. Nothing confidential or personal.'

She glanced at the part-time student clerk, who sort of shrugged, like 'What's the big deal?' 'Just a minute,' she said, and disappeared around the corner.

Darby was waiting in the small room when he laid the computer printouts on the table. 'According to these, Akers and Kaas should be in class right now,' he said.

Darby looked at the schedules. 'Akers has criminal procedure. Kaas has administrative law; both from nine to ten. I'll try to find them.' She showed Gray her notes. 'Maylor, Reinhart, and Wilson were at home. I couldn't get Ratliff and Linney.'

'Maylor's the closest. I can be there in a few minutes.'

'What about a car?' Darby asked.

'I called Hertz. It's supposed to be delivered to the *Post* parking lot in fifteen minutes.'

Maylor's apartment was on the third floor of a warehouse converted for students and others on very low budgets. He answered the door shortly after the first knock. He spoke through the chain.

'Looking for James Maylor,' Gray said like an old pal.

'That's me.'

'I'm Gray Grantham with the *Washington Post.* I'd like to ask you a couple of very quick questions.'

The door was unchained and opened. Gray stepped inside the two-room apartment. A bicycle was parked in the center, and took up most of the space.

'What's up?' Maylor asked. He was intrigued by this, and appeared eager to answer questions.

'I understand you clerked for White and Blazevich last summer.'

'That's correct. For three months.'

Gray scribbled on his notepad. 'What section were you in?'

'International. Mostly grunt work. Nothing glamorous. A lot of research and rough drafting of agreements.'

'Who was your supervisor?'

'No single person. There were three associates who kept me busy. The partner above them was Stanley Coopman.'

Gray pulled a photograph from his coat pocket. It was Garcia on the sidewalk. 'Do you recognize this face?'

Maylor held the picture and studied it. He shook his head. 'I don't think so. Who is he?'

'He's a lawyer, I think with White and Blazevich.'

'It's a big firm. I was stuck in the corner of one section. It's over four hundred lawyers, you know.'

'Yeah, so I've heard. You're sure you haven't seen him?'

'Positive. They cover twelve floors, most of which I never went on.'

Gray placed the photo in his pocket. 'Did you meet any other clerks?'

'Oh. Sure. A couple from Georgetown that I already knew, Laura Kaas and JoAnne Ratliff. Two guys from George Washington, Patrick Franks and a guy named Vanlandingham; a girl from Harvard named Elizabeth Larson; a girl from Michigan named Amy MacGregor; and a guy from Emory named Moke, but I think they fired him. There are always a lot of clerks in the summer.'

'You plan to work there when you finish?'

'I don't know. I'm not sure I'm cut out for the big firms.'

Gray smiled and stuck the notepad in his rear pocket. 'Look, you've been in the firm. How would I find this guy?'

Maylor pondered this for a second. 'I assume you can't go there and start asking around.'

'Good assumption.'

'And all you've got is the picture?'

'Yep.'

'Then I guess you're doing the right thing. One of the clerks will recognize him.'

'Thanks.'

'Is the guy in trouble?'

'Oh no. He may have witnessed something. It's probably a long shot.' Gray opened the door. 'Thanks again.'

Darby studied the fall listing of classes on the bulletin board across the lobby from the phones. She wasn't exactly sure what she'd do when the nine o'clock classes were over, but she was trying like hell to think of something. The bulletin board was exactly like the one at Tulane: class listings tacked neatly in a row; notices for assignments; ads for books, bikes, rooms, roommates, and a hundred other necessities stuck haphazardly about; announcements of parties, intramural games, and club meetings. A young woman with a backpack and hiking books stopped nearby and looked at the board. She was undoubtedly a student.

Darby smiled at her. 'Excuse me. Would you happen to know Laura Kaas?'

'Sure.'

'I need to give her a message. Could you point her out?'

'Is she in class?'

'Yeah, she's in administrative law under Ship, room 207.'

They walked and chatted in the direction of Ship's admin law. The lobby was suddenly busy as four classrooms emptied. The hiker pointed to a tall, heavyset girl walking toward them. Darby thanked her, and followed Laura Kaas until the crowd thinned and scattered.

'Excuse me, Laura. Are you Laura Kaas?' The big girl stopped and stared. 'Yes.'

This was the part she didn't like; the lying. 'I'm Sara Jacobs, and I'm working on a story for the *Washington Post*. Can I ask you a few questions?' She selected Laura Kaas first because she did not have a class at ten. Michael Akers did. She would try him at eleven.

'What about?'

'It'll just take a minute. Could we step in here?' Darby was nodding and walking to an empty classroom. Laura followed slowly.

'You clerked for White and Blazevich last summer.'

'I did.' She spoke slowly, suspiciously.

Sara Jacobs fought to control her nerves. This was awful. What section?'

'Tax.'

'You like tax, huh?' It was a weak effort at small talk.

'I did. Now I hate it.'

Darby smiled like this was the funniest thing she'd heard in years. She pulled a photo from her pocket, and handed it to Laura Kaas.

'Do you recognize this man?'

'No.'

'I think he's a lawyer with White and Blazevich.'

'There are plenty of them.'

'Are you certain?'

She handed it back. 'Yep. I never left the fifth floor. It would take years to meet everyone, and they come and go so fast. You know how lawyers are.'

Laura glanced around, and the conversation was over. 'I really appreciate this,' Darby said.

'No problem,' Laura said on her way out the door.

At exactly ten-thirty, they met again in room 336. Gray had caught Ellen Reinhart in the driveway as she was leaving for class. She had worked in the litigation section under a partner by the name of Daniel O'Malley, and spent most of the summer in a class action trial in Miami. She was gone for two months, and spent little time in the Washington office. White and Blazevich had offices in four cities, including Tampa. She did not recognize Garcia, and she was in a hurry.

Judith Wilson was not at her apartment, but her roommate said she would return around one.

They scratched off Maylor, Kaas, and Reinhart. They whispered their plans, and split again. Gray left to find Edward Linney, who according to the list had clerked the past two summers at White and Blazevich. He was not in the phone book, but his address was in Wesley Heights, north of Georgetown's main campus.

At ten forty-five, Darby found herself loitering again in front of the bulletin board, hoping for another miracle. Akers was a male, and there were different ways to approach him. She hoped he was where he was supposed to be – in room 201 studying criminal procedure. She eased that way and waited a moment or two until the door opened and fifty law students emptied into the hall. She could never be a reporter. She could never walk up to strangers and start asking a bunch of questions. It was awkward and uncomfortable. But she walked up to a shy-looking young man with sad eyes and thick glasses, and said, 'Excuse me. Do you happen to know Michael Akers? I think he's in this class.'

The guy smiled. It was nice to be noticed. He pointed at a group of men walking toward the front entrance. 'That's him, in the gray sweater.'

'Thanks.' She left him standing there. The group disassembled as it left the building, and Akers and a friend were on the sidewalk.

'Mr. Akers,' she called after him.

They both stopped and turned around, then smiled as she nervously approached them. 'Are you Michael Akers?' she asked.

'That's me. Who are you?'

'My name is Sara Jacobs, and I'm working on a story for the *Washington Post*. Can I speak to you alone?'

'Sure.' The friend took the hint and left.

'What about?' Akers asked.

'Did you clerk for White and Blazevich last summer?'

'Yes.' Akers was friendly and enjoying this.

'What section?'

'Real estate. Boring as hell, but it was a job. Why do you want to know?'

She handed him the photo. 'Do you recognize this man? He works for White and Blazevich.'

Akers wanted to recognize him. He wanted to be helpful and have a long conversation with her, but the face did not register.

'Kind of a suspicious picture, isn't it?' he said.

'I guess. Do you know him?'

'No. I've never seen him. It's an awfully big firm. The partners wear name badges to their meetings. Can you believe it? The guys who own the firm don't know each other. There must be a hundred partners.'

Eighty-one, to be exact. 'Did you have a supervisor?'

'Yeah, a partner named Walter Welch. A real snot. I didn't like the firm, really.'

'Do you remember any other clerks?'

'Sure. The place was crawling with summer clerks.'

'If I needed their names, could I get back with you?'

'Anytime. This guy in trouble?'

'I don't think so. He may know something.'

'I hope they all get disbarred. A bunch of thugs, really. It's a rotten place to work. Everything's political.'

'Thanks.' She smiled, and turned away. He admired the rear view, and said, 'Call me anytime.'

'Thanks.'

Darby, the investigative reporter, walked next door to the library building, and climbed the stairs to the fifth floor where the *Georgetown Law Journal* had a suite of crowded offices. She'd found the most recent edition of the *Journal* in the library, and noticed that JoAnne Ratliff was an assistant editor. She suspected most law reviews and law journals were much the same. The top students hung out there and prepared their scholarly articles and comments. They were superior to the rest of the students, and were a clannish bunch who appreciated their brilliant minds. They hung out in the law journal suite. It was their second home.

She stepped inside and asked the first person where she might find JoAnne Ratliff. He pointed around a corner. Second door on the right.

The second door opened into a cluttered workroom lined with rows of books. Two females were hard at work.

'JoAnne Ratliff,' Darby said.

'That's me,' an older woman of maybe forty responded.

'Hi. My name is Sara Jacobs, and I'm working on a story for the *Washington Post.* Can I ask you a few quick questions?'

She slowly laid her pen on the table, and frowned at the other woman. Whatever they were doing was terribly important, and this interruption was a real pain in the ass. They were significant law students.

Darby wanted to smirk and say something smart. She was number two in her class, dammit!, so don't act so high and mighty.

'What's the story about?' Ratliff asked.

'Could we speak in private?'

They frowned at each other again.

'I'm very busy,' Ratliff said.

So am I, thought Darby. You're checking citations for some meaningless article, and I'm trying to nail the man who killed two Supreme Court Justices.

'I'm sorry,' Darby said. 'I promise I'll just take a minute.'

They stepped into the hall. 'I'm very sorry to disturb you, but I'm in sort of a rush.'

'And you're a reporter with the *Post*?' It was more of a challenge than a question, and she was forced to lie some more. She told herself she could lie and cheat and steal for two days, then it was off to the Caribbean and Grantham could have it.

'Yes. Did you work for White and Blazevich last summer?'

'I did. Why?'

Quickly, the photo. Ratliff took it and analyzed it.

'Do you recognize him?'

She shook her head slowly. 'I don't think so. Who is he?'

This bitch'll make a fine lawyer. So many questions. If she knew who he was, she wouldn't be standing in this tiny hallway acting like a reporter and putting up with this haughty legal eagle.

'He's a lawyer with White and Blazevich,' Darby said as sincerely as possible. 'I thought you might recognize him.'

'Nope.' She handed the photo back.

Enough of this. 'Well, thanks. Again, sorry to bother.'

'No problem,' Ratliff said as she disappeared through the door.

She jumped into the new Hertz Pontiac as it stopped at the corner, and they were off in traffic. She had seen enough of the Georgetown Law School.

'I struck out,' Gray said. 'Linney wasn't home.'

'I talked to Akers and Ratliff, and both said no. That's five of seven who don't recognize Garcia.'

'I'm hungry. You want some lunch?'

'That's fine.'

'Is it possible to have five clerks work three months in a law firm and not one of them recognize a young associate?'

'Yeah, it's not only possible, it's very probable. This is a long shot, remember. Four hundred lawyers means a thousand people when you add secretaries, paralegals, law clerks, office clerks, copy room clerks, mail room clerks, all kinds of clerks and support people. The lawyers tend to keep to themselves in their own little sections.'

'Physically, are the sections on separate territory?'

'Yes. It's possible for a lawyer in banking on the third floor to go weeks without seeing an acquaintance in litigation on the tenth floor. These are very busy people, remember.'

'Do you think we've got the wrong firm?'

'Maybe the wrong firm, maybe the wrong law school.'

'The first guy, Maylor, gave me two names of George Washington students who clerked there last summer. Let's get them after lunch.' He slowed and parked illegally behind a row of small buildings.

'Where are we?' she asked.

'A block off Mount Vernon Square, downtown. The *Post* is six blocks that way. My bank is four blocks that way. And this little deli is just around the corner.'

They walked to the deli, which was filling fast with lunch traffic. She waited at a table by the window as he stood in line and ordered club sandwiches. Half the day had flown by, and though she didn't enjoy this line of work, it was nice to stay busy and forget about the shadows. She wouldn't be a reporter, and at the moment a career in law looked doubtful. Not long ago, she'd thought of being a judge after a few years in practice. Forget it. It was much too dangerous.

Gray brought a tray of food and iced tea, and they began eating.

'Is this a typical day for you?' she asked.

'This is what I do for a living. I snoop all day, write the stories late in the afternoon, then dig until late at night.'

'How many stories a week?'

'Sometimes three or four, sometimes none. I pick and choose, and there's little supervision. This is a bit different. I haven't run one in ten days.'

'What if you can't link Mattiece? What'll you write about the story?'

'Depends on how far I get. We could've run that story about Verheek and Callahan, but why bother. It was a big story, but they had nothing to go with it. It scratched thc surface and stopped.'

'And you're going for the big bang.'

'Hopefully. If we can verify your little brief, then we'll run one helluva story.'

'You can see the headlines, can't you?'

'I can. The adrenaline is pumping. This will be the biggest story since –'

'Watergate?'

'No. Watergate was a series of stories that started small and kept getting bigger. Those guys chased leads for months and kept pecking away until the pieces came together. A lot of people knew different parts of the story. This, my dear, is very different. This is a much bigger story, and the truth is known only by a very small group. Watergate was a stupid burglary and a bungled cover-up. These are masterfully planned crimes by very rich and smart people.'

'And the cover-up?'

'That comes next. After we link Mattiece to the killings, we run the big story. The cat's out of the bag, and a half a dozen investigations will crank up overnight. This place will be shell-shocked, especially at the news that the President and Mattiece are old friends. As the dust is settling, we go after the Administration and try to determine who knew what and when.'

'But first, Garcia.'

'Ah, yes. I know he's out there. He's a lawyer in this city, and he knows something very important.'

'What if we stumble across him, and he won't talk?'

'We have ways.'

'Such as?'

'Torture, kidnapping, extortion, threats of all types.'

A burly man with a contorted face was suddenly beside the table. 'Hurry up!' he yelled. 'You're talkin' too much!'

'Thanks, Pete,' Gray said without looking up. Pete was lost in the crowd, but could be heard yelling at another table. Darby dropped her sandwich.

'He owns the place,' Gray explained. 'It's part of the ambience.'

'How charming. Does it cost extra?'

'Oh no. The food's cheap, so he depends on volume. He refuses to serve coffee because he doesn't want socializing. He expects us to eat like refugees and get out.'

'I'm finished.'

Gray looked at his watch. 'It's twelve-fifteen. We need to be at Judith Wilson's apartment at one. Do you want to wire the money now?'

'How long will it take?'

'We can start the wire now, and pick the money up later.'

'Let's go.'

'How much do you want to wire?'

'Fifteen thousand.'

Judith Wilson lived on the second floor of a decaying old house filled with two-room student apartments. She was not there at one, and they drove around for an hour. Gray became a tour guide. He drove slowly by the Montrose Theatre, still boarded and burned out. He showed her the daily circus at Dupont Circle.

They were parked on the street at two-fifteen when a red Mazda stopped in the narrow driveway. 'There she is,' Gray said, and got out. Darby stayed in the car.

He caught Judith near the front steps. She was friendly enough. They chatted, he showed her the photo, she looked at it for a few seconds and began shaking her head. Moments later he was in the car.

'Zero for six,' he said.

'That leaves Edward Linney, who probably is our best shot because he clerked there two summers.'

They found a pay phone at a convenience store three blocks away, and Gray called Linney's number. No answer. He slammed the phone down and got in the car. 'He wasn't at home at ten this morning, and he's not at home now.'

'Could be in class,' Darby said. 'We need his schedule. You should've picked it up with the others.'

'You didn't suggest it then.'

'Who's the detective here? Who's the big-shot investigative reporter with the *Washington Post*? I'm just a lowly ex-law student who's thrilled to be sitting here in the front seat watching you operate.'

What about the backseat? he almost said. 'Whatever. Where to?'

'Back to the law school,' she said. 'I'll wait in the car while you march in there and get Linney's class schedule.'

'Yes, ma'am.'

A different student was behind the desk in the registrar's office. Gray asked for the class schedule for Edward Linney, and the student went to look for the registrar. Five minutes later, the registrar walked slowly around the corner and glared at him.

He flashed the smile. 'Hi, remember me? Gray Grantham with the *Post*. I need another class schedule.'

'The dean says no.'

'I thought the dean was out of town.'

'He is. The assistant dean says no. No more class schedules. You've already gotten me in a lot of trouble.'

'I don't understand. I'm not asking for personal records.'

'The assistant dean says no.'

'Where is the assistant dean?'

'He's busy.'

'I'll wait. Where's his office?'

'He'll be busy for a long time.'

'I'll wait for a long time.'

She dug in and folded her arms. 'He will not allow you to have any more class schedules. Our students are entitled to privacy.'

'Sure they are. What kind of trouble have I caused?'

'Well, I'll just tell you.'

'Please do.'

The student clerk eased around the corner and disappeared.

'One of the students you talked to this morning called White and Blazevich, and they called the assistant dean, and the assistant dean called me and said no more class schedules will be given to reporters.'

'Why should they care?'

'They care, okay? We've had a long relationship with White and Blazevich. They hire a lot of our students.'

Gray tried to look pitiful and helpless. 'I'm just trying to find Edward Linney. I swear he's not in trouble. I just need to ask him a few questions.'

She smelled victory. She had backed down a reporter from the *Post,* and she was quite proud. So offer him a crumb. 'Mr. Linney is no longer enrolled here. That's all I can say.'

He backed toward the door, and mumbled, 'Thanks.'

He was almost to the car when someone called his name. It was the student from the registrar's office.

'Mr. Grantham,' he said as he ran to him. 'I know Edward. He's sort of dropped out of school for a while. Personal problems.'

'Where is he?'

'His parents put him in a private hospital. He's being detoxified.'

'Where is it?'

'Silver Spring. A place called Parklane Hospital.'

'How long's he been there?'

'About a month.'

Grantham shook his hand. 'Thanks. I won't tell anyone you told me.'

'He's not in trouble, is he?'

'No. I promise.'

They stopped at the bank, and Darby left with fifteen thousand in cash. Carrying the money scared her. Linney scared her. White and Blazevich suddenly scared her.

Parklane was a detox center for the rich, or for those with expensive insurance. It was a small building, surrounded by trees and sitting alone a half mile off the highway. This might be difficult, they decided.

Gray entered the lobby first, and asked the receptionist for Edward Linney.

'He is a patient here,' she said rather officially.

He used his best smile. 'Yes. I know he is a patient. They told me at the law school that he was a patient. What room is he in?'

Darby entered the lobby and strolled to the water fountain for a very long drink.

'He's in room 22, but you can't see him.'

'They told me at the law school I could see him.'

'And who might you be?'

He was so friendly. 'Gray Grantham, with the *Washington Post.* They told me at the law school I could ask him a couple of questions.'

'I'm sorry they told you that. You see, Mr. Grantham, we run this hospital, and they run their law school.'

Darby picked up a magazine and sat on a sofa.

His smile faded considerably, but was still there. 'I understand that,' he said, still courteous. 'Could I see the administrator?'

'Why?'

'Because this is a very important matter, and I must see Mr. Linney this afternoon. If you won't allow it, then I have to talk to your boss. I will not leave here until I speak to the administrator.'

She gave him her best go-to-hell look, and backed away from the counter. 'Just a moment. You may have a seat.'

'Thank you.'

She left and Gray turned to Darby. He pointed to a set of double doors that appeared to lead to the only hallway. She took a deep breath, and walked quickly through them. They opened into a large junction from which three sterile corridors branched out. A brass plate pointed to rooms 18 through 30. It was the center wing of the hospital, and the hall was dark and quiet with thick, industrial carpet and floral wallpaper.

This would get her arrested. She would be tackled by a large security guard or a heavy nurse and taken to a locked room where the cops would rough her up when they arrived, and her sidekick out there would stand and watch helplessly as they led her away in shackles. Her name would be in the paper, the *Post,* and Stump, if he was literate, would see it, and they'd get her.

As she crept along by these closed doors, the beaches and piña coladas seemed unreachable. The door to number 22 was closed and had the names Edward L. Linney and Dr. Wayne McLatchee tacked on it. She knocked.

The administrator was more of an ass than the receptionist. But then, he was paid well for it. He explained they had strict policies about visitation. These were very sick and delicate people, his patients, and they had to protect them. And their doctors, who were the finest in their field, were very strict about who could see the patients. Visitation was allowed only on Saturdays and Sundays, and even then only a carefully selected group of people, usually just family and friends, could sit with the patients, and then only for thirty minutes. They had to be very strict.

These were fragile people, and they certainly could not withstand interrogation by a reporter, regardless of how grave the circumstances.

Mr. Grantham asked when Mr. Linney might be discharged. Absolutely confidential, the administrator exclaimed. Probably when the insurance expired, suggested Mr. Grantham, who was talking and stalling and halfway expecting to hear loud and angry voices coming from behind the double doors.

This mention of insurance really agitated the administrator. Mr. Grantham asked if he, the administrator, would ask Mr. Linney if he would answer two questions from Mr. Grantham, and the whole thing would take less than thirty seconds.

Out of the question, snapped the administrator. They had strict policies.

A voice answered softly, and she stepped into the room. The carpet was thicker and the furniture was made from wood. He sat on the bed in a pair of jeans, no shirt, reading a thick novel. She was struck by his good looks.

'Excuse me,' she said warmly as she closed the door behind her.

'Come in,' he said with a soft smile. It was the first nonmedical face he'd seen in two days. What a beautiful face. He closed the book.

She walked to the end of the bed. 'I'm Sara Jacobs, and I'm working on a story for the *Washington Post.*'

'How'd you get in?' he asked, obviously glad she was in.

'Just walked. Did you clerk last summer for White and Blazevich?'

'Yes, and the summer before. They offered me a job when I graduate. If I graduate.'

She handed him the photo. 'Do you recognize this man?'

He took it and smiled. 'Yeah. His name is, uh, wait a minute. He works in the oil and gas section on the ninth floor. What's his name?'

Darby held her breath.

Linney closed his eyes hard and tried to think. He looked at the photo, and said, 'Morgan. I think his name is Morgan. Yep.'

'His last name is Morgan?'

'That's him. I can't remember his first name. It's something like Charles, but that's not it. I think it starts with a *C*.'

'And you're certain he's in oil and gas?' Though she couldn't remember the exact number, she was certain there was more than one Morgan at White and Blazevich.

'Yeah.'

'On the ninth floor?'

'Yeah. I worked in the bankruptcy section on the eighth floor, and oil and gas covers half of eight and all of nine.'

He handed the photo back.

'When are you getting out?' she asked. It would be rude to run from the room.

'Next week, I hope. What's this guy done?'

'Nothing. We just need to talk to him.' She was backing away from the bed. 'I have to run. Thanks. And good luck.'

'Yeah. No problem.'

She quietly closed the door behind her, and scooted toward the lobby. The voice came from behind her.

'Hey! You! What're you doing?'

Darby turned and faced a tall, black security guard with a gun on his hip. She looked completely guilty.

'What're you doing?' he demanded again as he backed her into the wall.

'Visiting my brother,' she said. 'And don't yell at me again.'

'Who's your brother?'

She nodded at his door. 'Room 22.'

'You can't visit right now. This is off limits.'

'It was important. I'm leaving, okay?'

The door to 22 opened, and Linney looked at them.

'This your sister?' the guard demanded.

Darby pleaded with her eyes.

'Yeah, leave her alone,' Linney said. 'She's leaving.'

She exhaled and smiled at Linney. 'Mom will be up this weekend.'

'Good,' Linney said softly.

The guard backed off, and Darby almost ran to the double doors. Grantham was preaching to the administrator about the cost of health care. She walked quickly through the doors, into the lobby, and was almost to the front door when the administrator spoke to her.

'Miss! Oh, miss! Can I have your name?'

Darby was out the front door, headed for the car. Grantham shrugged at the administrator, and casually left the building. They jumped in, and sped away.

'Garcia's last name is Morgan. Linney recognized him immediately, but he had trouble with the name. First name starts with a *C*.' She was digging through her notes from Martindale-Hubbell. 'Said he works in oil and gas on the ninth floor.'

Grantham was speeding away from Parklane. 'Oil and gas!'

'That's what he said.' She found it. 'Curtis D. Morgan, oil and gas section, age twenty-nine. There's another Morgan in litigation, but he's a partner and, let's see, he's fifty-one.'

'Garcia is Curtis Morgan,' Gray said with relief. He looked at his watch. 'It's a quarter till four. We'll have to hurry.'

'I can't wait.'

Rupert picked them up as they turned out of Parklane's driveway. The rented Pontiac was flying all over the street. He drove like an idiot just to keep up, then radioed ahead.

CHAPTER THIRTY-SEVEN

Matthew Barr had never experienced a speedboat before, and after five hours of a bone-jarring voyage through the ocean he was soaked and in pain. His body was numb, and when he saw land he said a prayer, the first in decades. Then he resumed his nonstop cursing of Fletcher Coal.

They docked at a small marina near a city that he believed to be Freeport. The captain had said something about Freeport to the man known as Larry when they left Florida. No other word was spoken during the ordeal. Larry's role in the journey was uncertain. He was at least six-six, with a neck as thick as a utility pole, and he did nothing but watch Barr, which was okay at first but after five hours became quite a nuisance.

They stood awkwardly when the boat stopped. Larry was the first one out, and he motioned for Barr to join him. Another large man was approaching on the pier, and together they escorted Barr to a waiting van. The van was suspiciously short of windows.

At this point, Barr preferred to say good-bye to his new pals, and simply disappear in the direction of Freeport. He'd catch a plane to D.C., and slap Coal the moment he saw his shining forehead. But he had to be cool. They wouldn't dare hurt him.

The van stopped moments later at a small airstrip, and Barr was escorted to a black Lear. He admired it briefly before following Larry up the steps. He was cool and relaxed; just another job. After all, he was at one time one of the best CIA agents in Europe. He was an ex-Marine. He could take care of himself.

He sat by himself in the cabin. The windows were covered, and this annoyed him. But he understood. Mr. Mattiece treasured his privacy, and Barr could certainly respect that. Larry and the other heavyweight were at the front of the cabin, flipping through magazines and completely ignoring him.

Thirty minutes after takeoff, the Lear began its descent, and Larry lumbered toward him.

'Put this on,' he demanded as he handed over a thick, cloth blindfold. At this point, a rookie would panic. An amateur would start asking questions. But Barr had been blindfolded before, and while he was having serious doubts about this mission, he calmly took the blindfold and covered his eyes.

The man who removed the blindfold introduced himself as Emil, an assistant to Mr. Mattiece. He was a small, wiry type with dark hair and a thin mustache winding around the lip. He sat in a chair four feet away and lit a cigarette.

'Our people tell us you are legitimate, sort of,' he said with a friendly smile. Barr looked around the room. There were no walls, only windows in small panes. The sun was bright and pierced his eyes. A plush garden surrounded a series of fountains and pools outside the room. They were in the rear of a very large house.

'I'm here on behalf of the President,' Barr said.

'We believe you.' Emil nodded. He was undoubtedly a Cajun.

'May I ask who you are?' Barr said.

'I'm Emil, and that's enough. Mr. Mattiece is not feeling well. Perhaps you should leave your message with me.'

'I have orders to speak directly to him.'

'Orders from Mr. Coal, I believe.' Emil never stopped smiling.

'That's correct.'

'I see. Mr. Mattiece prefers not to meet you. He wants you to talk to me.'

Barr shook his head. Now, if push came to shove, if things got out of hand, then he would gladly talk to Emil if it was necessary. But for now, he would hold firm.

'I am not authorized to talk to anyone but Mr. Mattiece,' Barr said properly.

The smile almost disappeared. Emil pointed beyond the pools and fountains to a large gazebo-shaped building with tall windows from floor to ceiling. Rows of perfectly manicured shrubs and flowers surrounded it. 'Mr. Mattiece is in his gazebo. Follow me.'

They left the sun room and walked slowly around a wading pool. Barr had a thick knot in his stomach, but he followed his little friend as if this was simply another day at the office. The sound of falling water echoed through the garden. A narrow boardwalk led to the gazebo. They stopped at the door.

'I'm afraid you must remove your shoes,' Emil said with a smile. Emil was barefoot. Barr untied his shoes and placed them next to the door.

'Do not step on the towels,' Emil said gravely.

The towels?

Emil opened the door for Barr, who stepped in alone. The room was perfectly round, about fifty feet in diameter. There were three chairs and a sofa, all covered with white sheets. Thick cotton towels were on the floor in perfect little trails around the room. The sun shone brightly through skylights. A door opened, and Victor Mattiece emerged from a small room.

Barr froze and gawked at the man. He was thin and gaunt, with long gray hair and a dirty beard. He wore only a pair of white gym shorts, and walked carefully on the towels without looking at Barr.

'Sit over there,' he said, pointing at a chair. 'Don't step on the towels.'

Barr avoided the towels and took his seat. Mattiece turned his back and faced the windows. His skin was leathery and dark bronze. His bare feet were lined with ugly veins. His toenails were long and yellow. He was crazy as hell.

'What do you want?' he asked quietly to the windows.

'The President sent me.'

'He did not. Fletcher Coal sent you. I doubt if the President knows you're here.'

Maybe he wasn't crazy. He spoke without moving a muscle in his body.

'Fletcher Coal is the President's chief of staff. He sent me.'

'I know about Coal. And I know about you. And I know about your little Unit. Now, what do you want?'

'Information.'

'Don't play games with me. What do you want?'

'Have you read the pelican brief?' Barr asked.

The frail body did not flinch. 'Have you read it?'

'Yes,' Barr answered quickly.

'Do you believe it to be true?'

'Perhaps. That's why I'm here.'

'Why is Mr. Coal so concerned about the pelican brief?'

'Because a couple of reporters have wind of it. And if it's true, then we need to know immediately.'

'Who are these reporters?'

'Gray Grantham with the *Washington Post*. He picked it up first, and he knows more than anyone. He's digging hard. Coal thinks he's about to run something.'

'We can take care of him, can't we?' Mattiece said to the windows. 'Who's the other one?'

'Rifkin with the *Times*.'

Mattiece still had not moved an inch. Barr glanced around at the sheets and towels. Yes, he had to be crazy. The place was sanitized and smelled of rubbing alcohol. Maybe he was ill.

'Does Mr. Coal believe it to be true?'

'I don't know. He's very concerned about it. That's why I'm here, Mr. Mattiece. We have to know.'

'What if it's true?'

'Then we have problems.'

Mattiece finally moved. He shifted his weight to the right leg, and folded his arms across his narrow chest. But his eyes never moved. Sand dunes and sea oats were in the distance, but not the ocean.

'Do you know what I think?' he said quietly.

'What?'

'I think Coal is the problem. He gave the brief to too many people. He handed it to the CIA. He allowed you to see it. This really disturbs me.'

Barr could think of no response. It was ludicrous to imply that Coal wanted to distribute the brief. The problem is you, Mattiece. You killed the justices. You panicked and killed Callahan. You're the greedy bastard who was not content with a mere fifty million.

Mattiece turned slowly and looked at Barr. The eyes were dark and red. He looked nothing like the photo with the Vice President, but that was seven years ago. He'd aged twenty years in the last seven, and perhaps gone off the deep end along the way.

'You clowns in Washington are to blame for this,' he said, somewhat louder.

Barr could not look at him. 'Is it true, Mr. Mattiece? That's all I want to know.'

Behind Barr, a door opened without a sound. Larry, in his socks and avoiding the towels, eased forward two steps and stopped.

Mattiece walked on the towels to a glass door, and opened it. He looked outside and spoke softly. 'Of course it's true.' He walked through the door, and closed it slowly behind him. Barr watched as the idiot shuffled along a sidewalk toward the sand dunes.

What now? he thought. Perhaps Emil would come get him. Perhaps.

Larry inched forward with a rope, and Barr did not hear or feel anything until it was too late. Mattiece did not want blood in his gazebo, so Larry simply broke the neck and choked him until it was over.

CHAPTER THIRTY-EIGHT

The game plan called for her to be on this elevator at this point in the search, but she thought enough unexpected events had occurred to warrant a change in the game plan. He thought not. They had engaged in a healthy debate over this elevator ride, and here she was. He was right; this was the quickest route to Curtis Morgan. And she was right; it was a dangerous route to Curtis Morgan. But the other routes could be just as dangerous. The entire game plan was deadly.

She wore her only dress and her only pair of heels. Gray said she looked really nice, but that was to be expected. The elevator stopped on the ninth floor, and when she walked off it there was a pain in her stomach and she could barely breathe.

The receptionist was across a plush lobby. The name WHITE AND BLAZEVICH covered the wall behind her in thick, brass lettering. Her knees were weak, but she made it to the receptionist, who smiled properly. It was ten minutes before five.

'May I help you?' she asked. The nameplate proclaimed her to be Peggy Young.

'Yes,' Darby managed, clearing her throat. 'I have a five o'clock appointment with Curtis Morgan. My name is Dorothy Blythe.'

The receptionist was stunned. Her mouth fell open, and she stared blankly at Darby, now Dorothy. She couldn't speak.

Darby's heart stopped. 'Is something the matter?'

'Well, no. I'm sorry. Just a moment.' Peggy Young stood quickly, and disappeared in a rush.

Run! Her heart pounded like a drum. Run! She tried to control her breathing, but she was battling hyperventilation. Her legs were rubbery. Run!

She looked around, trying to be nonchalant as if she was just another client waiting on her lawyer. Surely they wouldn't gun her down here in the lobby of a law office.

He came first, followed by the receptionist. He was about fifty with bushy gray hair and a terrible scowl. 'Hi,' he said, but only because he had to. 'I'm Jarreld Schwabe, a partner here. You say you have an appointment with Curtis Morgan.'

Keep it up. 'Yes. At five. Is there a problem?'

'And your name is Dorothy Blythe?'

Yeah, but you can call me Dot. 'That's what I said. Yes. What's the matter?' She sounded genuinely irritated.

He was inching closer. 'When did you make the appointment?'

'I don't know. About two weeks ago. I met Curtis at a party in Georgetown. He told me he was an oil and gas lawyer, and I happen to need one. I called the office here, and made an appointment. Now, will you please tell me what's going on?' She was amazed at how well these words were coming from her dry mouth.

'Why do you need an oil and gas lawyer?'

'I don't think I have to explain myself to you,' she said, real bitch-like.

The elevator opened, and a man in a cheap suit approached quickly to join the conversation. Darby scowled at him. Her legs would give way just any second.

Schwabe was really bearing down. 'We don't have any record of such an appointment.'

'Then fire the appointment secretary. Do you welcome all new clients this way?' Oh, she was indignant, but Schwabe did not let up.

'You can't see Curtis Morgan,' he said.

'And why not?' she demanded.

'He's dead.'

The knees were jelly and about to go. A sharp pain rippled through the stomach. But, she thought quickly, it was okay to looked shocked. He was, after all, supposed to be her new lawyer.

'I'm sorry. Why didn't anyone call me?'

Schwabe was still suspicious. 'As I said, we have no record of a Dorothy Blythe.'

'What happened to him?' she asked, stunned.

'He was mugged a week ago. Shot by street punks, we believe.'

The guy in the cheap suit took a step closer. 'Do you have any identification?'

'Who in the hell are you?' she snapped loudly.

'He's security,' said Schwabe.

'Security for what?' she demanded, even louder. 'Is this a law firm or a prison?'

The partner looked at the man in the cheap suit, and it was obvious neither knew exactly what to do at this point. She was very attractive, and they had upset her, and her story was somewhat believable. They relaxed a little.

'Why don't you leave, Ms. Blythe?' Schwabe said.

'I can't wait!'

The security man reached to assist her. 'Here,' he said.

She slapped his hand. 'Touch me and I'll sue your ass first thing tomorrow morning. Get away from me!'

This shook them a bit. She was mad and lashing out. Perhaps they were being a bit hard.

'I'll see you down,' the security man said.

'I know how to leave. I'm amazed you clowns have any clients.' She was stepping backward. Her face was red, but not from anger. It was fear. 'I've got lawyers in four states, and I've never been treated like this,' she yelled at them. She was in the center of the lobby. 'I paid a half a million last year in legal fees, and I've got a million to pay next year, but you idiots won't get any of it.' The closer she got to the elevator, the louder she yelled. She was a crazy woman. They watched her until the elevator door opened and she was gone.

Gray paced along the end of the bed, holding the phone and waiting for Smith Keen. Darby was stretched out on the bed with her eyes closed.

Gray stopped. 'Hello, Smith. I need you to check something quick.'

'Where are you?' Keen asked.

'A hotel. Look back six or seven days. I need the obituary for Curtis D. Morgan.'

'Who's he?'

'Garcia.'

'Garcia! What happened to Garcia?'

'He died, obviously. Shot by muggers.'

'I remember that. We ran a story last week about a young lawyer who was robbed and shot.'

'Probably him. Can you check it for me? I need his wife's name and address if we have it.'

'How'd you find him?'

'It's a long story. We'll try to talk to his widow tonight.'

'Garcia's dead. This is weird, baby.'

'It's more than weird. The kid knew something, and they knocked him off.'

'Do you think you're safe?'

'Who knows?'

'Where's the girl?'

'She's with me.'

'What if they're watching his house?'

Gray hadn't thought about it. 'We'll have to take that chance. I'll call you back in fifteen minutes.'

He placed the phone on the floor and sat in an antique rocker. There was a warm beer on the table, and he took a long drink. He watched her. A forearm covered both eyes. She was in jeans and a sweatshirt. The dress was thrown in a corner. The heels had been kicked across the room.

'You okay?' he asked softly.

'Wonderful.'

She was a real smartass, and he liked that in a woman. Of course, she was almost a lawyer, and they must teach smartassness in law school. He sipped the beer and admired the jeans. He enjoyed this brief moment of uninterrupted staring without getting caught.

'Are you staring at me?' she asked.

'Yes.'

'Sex is the last thing on my mind.'

'Then why'd you mention it?'

'Because I can feel you lusting after my red toenails.'

'True.'

'I've got a headache. A real, genuine, pounding headache.'

'You've worked for it. Can I get you something?'

'Yes. A one-way ticket to Jamaica.'

'You can leave tonight. I'll take you to the airport right now.'

She removed the forearm from her eyes and gently massaged both temples. 'I'm sorry I cried.'

He finished the beer with a long drink. 'You earned the right.' She was in tears when she stepped off the elevator. He was waiting like an expectant father, except he had a .38 in his coat pocket – a .38 she knew nothing about.

'So what do you think of investigative reporting?' he asked.

'I'd rather butcher hogs.'

'Well, in all honesty, not every day is this eventful. Some days I simply sit at my desk and make hundreds of phone calls to bureaucrats who have no comment.'

'Sounds great. Let's do that tomorrow.'

He kicked his shoes off and placed his feet on the bed. She closed her eyes and breathed deeply. Minutes passed without a word.

'Do you know that Louisiana is known as the Pelican State?' she asked with her eyes closed.

'No. I didn't know that.'

'It's a shame really, because the brown pelicans were virtually wiped out in the early 1960s.'

'What happened to them?'

'Pesticides. They eat nothing but fish, and the fish live in river water filled with chlorinated hydrocarbons from pesticides. The rains wash the pesticides from the soil into small streams which eventually empty into rivers which eventually empty into the Mississippi. By the time the pelicans in Louisiana eat the fish, they are loaded with DDT and other chemicals which accumulate in the fatty tissues of the birds. Death is seldom immediate, but in times of stress such as hunger or bad weather, the pelicans and eagles and cormorants are forced to draw upon their reserves, and can literally be poisoned by their own fat. If they don't die, they are usually unable to reproduce. Their eggs are so thin and fragile they crack during incubation. Did you know that?'

'Why would I know that?'

'In the late sixties, Louisiana began transplanting brown pelicans from southern Florida, and over the years the population has slowly increased. But the birds are still very much in danger. Forty years ago there were thousands of them. The cypress swamp that Mattiece wants to destroy is home to only a few dozen pelicans.'

Gray pondered these things. She was silent for a long time.

'What day is it?' she asked without opening her eyes.

'Monday.'

'I left New Orleans a week ago today. Thomas and Verheek had dinner two weeks ago today. That, of course, was the fateful moment when the pelican brief changed hands.'

'Three weeks ago tomorrow, Rosenberg and Jensen were murdered.'

'I was an innocent little law student minding my own business and having a wonderful love affair with my professor. I guess those days are gone.'

Law school and the professor might be gone, he thought. 'What're your plans?'

'I have none. I'm just trying to get out of this damned mess and stay alive. I'll run off somewhere and hide for a few months, maybe a few years. I've got enough money to live for a long time. If and when I reach the point when I'm not looking over my shoulder, I might come back.'

'To law school?'

'I don't think so. The law has lost its allure.'

'Why'd you want to be a lawyer?'

'Idealism, and money. I thought I could change the world and get paid for it.'

'But there are so damned many lawyers already. Why do all these bright students keep flocking to law school?'

'Simple. It's greed. They want BMWs and gold credit cards. If you go to a good law school, finish in the top ten percent, and get a job with a big firm, you'll be earning six figures in a few short years, and it only goes up. It's guaranteed. At the age of thirty-five, you'll be a partner raking in at least two hundred thousand a year. Some earn much more.'

'What about the other ninety percent?'

'It's not such a good deal for them. They get the leftovers.'

'Most lawyers I know hate it. They'd rather be doing something else.'

'But they can't leave it because of the money. Even a lousy lawyer in a small office can earn a hundred thousand a year after ten years of practice, and he may hate it, but where can he go and match the money?'

'I detest lawyers.'

'And I guess you think reporters are adored.'

Good point. Gray looked at his watch, then picked up the phone. He dialed Keen's number. Keen read him the obit, and the *Post* story about the senseless street killing of this young lawyer. Gray took notes.

'A couple of other things,' Keen said. 'Feldman is very concerned about your safety. He expected a briefing in his office today, and he was pissed when he didn't get one. Make sure you report to him before noon tomorrow. Understand?'

'I'll try.'

'Do more than try, Gray. We're very nervous over here.'

'The *Times* is sucking wind, isn't it?'

'I'm not worried about the *Times* right now. I'm much more concerned about you and the girl.'

'We're fine. Everything's lovely. What else have you got?'

'You have three messages in the past two hours from a man named Cleve. Says he's a cop. Do you know him?'

'Yes.'

'Well, he wants to talk tonight. Says it's urgent.'

'I'll call him later.'

'Okay. You guys be careful. We'll be here till late, so check in.'

Gray hung up and looked at his notes. It was almost seven. 'I'm going to see Mrs. Morgan. I want you to stay here.'

She sat between the pillows and crossed her arms on her knees. 'I'd rather go.'

'What if they're watching the house?' he asked.

'Why would they watch the house? He's dead.'

'Maybe they're suspicious now, because a mysterious client appeared today looking for him. Even though he's dead, he's attracting attention.'

She thought about this for a minute. 'No. I'm going.'

'It's too risky, Darby.'

'Don't talk to me about risks. I've survived in the minefields for twelve days. This is easy.'

He waited on her by the door. 'By the way, where am I staying tonight?'

'Jefferson Hotel.'

'Do you have the phone number?'

'What do you think?'

'Dumb question.'

The private jet with Edwin Sneller aboard landed at National in Washington a few minutes after seven. He was delighted to leave New York. He'd spent six days there bouncing off the walls in his suite at the Plaza. For almost a week, his men had checked hotels and watched airports and walked streets, and they knew damned well they were wasting their time, but orders were orders. They were told to stay there until something broke and they could move on. It was silly trying to find the girl in Manhattan, but they had to stay close in case she made a mistake like a phone call or a plastic transaction that could be traced, and suddenly they were needed.

She made no mistakes until two-thirty this afternoon when she needed money and went to the account. They knew this would happen, especially if she planned to leave the country and was afraid to use plastic. At some point, she would need cash, and she'd have to wire it since the bank was in New Orleans and she wasn't. Sneller's client owned eight percent of the bank; not a lot, but a nice little twelve-million-dollar holding that could make things happen. A few minutes after three, he'd received a call from Freeport.

They did not suspect her to be in Washington. She was a smart girl who was running away from trouble, not to it. And they certainly didn't expect her to link up with the reporter. They had no idea, but now it seemed so logical. And it was worse than critical.

Fifteen thousand went from her account to his, and suddenly Sneller was back in business. He had two men with him. Another private jet was en route from Miami. He had asked for a dozen men immediately. It would be a quick job, or no job at all. There was not a second to spare.

Sneller was not hopeful. With Khamel on the team, everything seemed possible. He had killed Rosenberg and Jensen so cleanly, then disappeared without a trace. Now he was dead, shot in the head because of one little innocent female law student.

The Morgan house was in a neat suburb in Alexandria. The neighborhood was young and affluent, with bikes and tricycles in every yard.

Three cars were parked in the drive. One had Ohio plates. Gray rang the doorbell and watched the street. Nothing suspicious.

An older man opened the door slightly. 'Yes,' he said softly.

'I'm Gray Grantham with the *Washington Post,* and this is my assistant, Sara Jacobs.' Darby forced a smile. 'We would like to speak with Mrs. Morgan.'

'I don't think so.'

'Please. It's very important.'

He looked at them carefully. 'Wait a minute.' He closed the door and disappeared.

The house had a narrow wooden porch with a small veranda over it. They were in the darkness and could not be seen from the street. A car passed slowly.

He opened the door again. 'I'm Tom Kupcheck, her father, and she doesn't want to talk.'

Gray nodded as if this was understandable. 'We won't be five minutes. I promise.'

He walked onto the porch and closed the door behind him. 'I guess you're hard of hearing. I said she doesn't want to talk.'

'I heard you, Mr. Kupcheck. And I respect her privacy, and I know what she's been through.'

'Since when do you guys respect anyone's privacy?'

Evidently, Mr. Kupcheck had a short fuse. It was about to blow.

Gray kept calm. Darby backed away. She'd been involved in enough altercations for one day.

'Her husband called me three times before he died. I talked to him on the phone, and I don't believe his death was a random killing by street punks.'

'He's dead. My daughter is upset. She doesn't want to talk. Now get the hell out of here.'

'Mr. Kupcheck,' Darby said warmly. 'We have reason to believe your son-in-law was a witness to some highly organized criminal activity.'

This calmed him a bit, and he glared at Darby. 'Is that so? Well, you can't ask him about it, can you? My daughter knows nothing. She's had a bad day and she's on medication. Now leave.'

'Can we see her tomorrow?' Darby asked.

'I doubt it. Call first.'

Gray handed him a business card. 'If she wants to talk, use the number on the back. I'm staying at a hotel. I'll call around noon tomorrow.'

'You do that. For now, just leave. You've already upset her.'

'We're sorry,' Gray said, as they walked off the porch. Mr. Kupcheck opened the door but watched them as they left. Gray stopped, and turned to him. 'Has any other reporter called or stopped by?'

'A bunch of them called the day after he was killed. They wanted all sorts of stuff. Rude people.'

'But none in the past few days?'

'No. Now leave.'

'Any from the *New York Times*?'

'No.' He stepped inside and slammed the door.

They hurried to the car parked four doors down. There was no traffic on the street. Gray zigzagged through the short suburban streets, and crisscrossed his way out of the neighborhood. He watched the mirror until he was convinced they were not being followed.

'End of Garcia,' Darby said as they entered 395 and headed for the city.

'Not yet. We'll make one final, dying gasp tomorrow, and maybe she'll talk to us.'

'If she knew something, her father would know. And if her father knew, why wouldn't he cooperate? There's nothing there, Gray.'

This made perfect sense. They rode in silence for a few minutes. Fatigue was setting in.

'We can be at the airport in fifteen minutes,' he said. 'I'll drop you off, and you can be out of here in thirty minutes. Take a plane anywhere, just vanish.'

'I'll leave tomorrow. I need some rest, and I want to think about where to go. Thanks.'

'Do you feel safe?'

'At this moment, yes. But it's subject to change in seconds.'

'I'll be glad to sleep in your room tonight. Just like in New York.'

'You didn't sleep in my room in New York. You slept on a sofa in the sitting room.' She was smiling, and this was a good sign.

He was smiling too. 'Okay. I'll sleep in the sitting room tonight.'

'I don't have a sitting room.'

'Well, well. Then where can I sleep?'

Suddenly, she was not smiling. She bit her lip and her eyes watered. He had pushed too far. It was Callahan again.

'I'm just not ready,' she said.

'When might you be ready?'

'Gray, please. Just leave it alone.'

She watched the traffic ahead and said nothing. 'I'm sorry,' he said.

Slowly, she lay down in the seat and placed her head in his lap. He gently rubbed her shoulder, and she clutched his hand. 'I'm scared to death,' she said quietly.

CHAPTER THIRTY-NINE

He had left her room around ten, after a bottle of wine and egg rolls. He had called Mason Paypur, the night police reporter for the *Post,* and asked him to check with his sources about the Morgan street killing. It had happened downtown in an area not noted for killings; just a few muggings and beatings.

He was tired and discouraged. And he was unhappy because she would leave tomorrow. The *Post* owed him six weeks of vacation, and he was tempted to leave with her. Mattiece could have his oil. But he was afraid he'd never come back, which wouldn't be the end of his world except for the troublesome fact that she had money and he didn't. They could skip along the beaches and frolic in the sun for about two months on his money, then it would be up to her. And, more importantly, she hadn't invited him to join in her getaway. She was grieving. When she mentioned Thomas Callahan, he could feel the pain.

He was now at the Jefferson Hotel on Sixteenth, pursuant, of course, to her instructions. He called Cleve at home.

'Where are you?' Cleve asked, irritated.

'A hotel. It's a long story. What's up?'

'They put Sarge on medical leave for ninety days.'

'What's wrong with him?'

'Nothing. He says they want him out of the place for a while. It's like a bunker over there. Everybody's been told to shut up and speak to no one. They're scared to death. They made Sarge leave at noon today. He thinks you could be in serious danger. He's heard your name a thousand times in the past week. They're obsessed with you and how much you know.'

'Who's they?'

'Coal, of course, and his aide Birchfield. They run the West Wing like the Gestapo. Sometimes they include, what's his name, the little squirrel with the bow tie? Domestic affairs?'

'Emmitt Waycross.'

'That's him. It's mainly Coal and Birchfield making the threats and plotting strategy.'

'What kind of threats?'

'No one in the White House, except for the President, can talk to the press on the record or off without Coal's approval. This includes the press secretary. Coal clears everything.'

'That's incredible.'

'They're terrified. And Sarge thinks they're dangerous.'

'Okay. I'm hiding.'

'I stopped by your apartment late last night. I wish you'd tell me when you disappear.'

'I'll check in tomorrow night.'

'What're you driving?'

'A rented Pontiac with four doors. Very sporty.'

'I checked the Volvo this afternoon. It's fine.'

'Thanks, Cleve.'

'You okay?'

'I think so. Tell Sarge I'm fine.'

'Call me tomorrow. I'm worried.'

He slept four hours and was awake when the phone rang. It was dark outside, and would remain that way for at least two hours. He stared at the phone, and picked it up on the fifth ring.

'Hello,' he said suspiciously.

'Is this Gray Grantham?' It was a very timid female.

'Yes. Who is this?'

'Beverly Morgan. You stopped by last night.'

Gray was on his feet, listening hard, wide awake. 'Yes. I'm sorry if we upset you.'

'No. My father is very protective. And angry. The reporters were awful after Curtis was killed. They called from everywhere. They wanted old pictures of him and new photos of me and the child. They called at all hours. It was terrible, and my father got tired of it. He pushed two of them off the porch.'

'I guess we were lucky.'

'I hope he didn't offend you.' The voice was hollow and detached, yet trying to be strong.

'Not at all.'

'He's asleep now, downstairs on the sofa. So we can talk.'

'Why aren't you asleep?' he asked.

'I'm taking some pills to make me sleep, and I'm all out of sync. I've been sleeping days and rambling nights.' It was obvious she was awake and wanted to talk.

Gray sat on the bed and tried to relax. 'I can't imagine the shock of something like this.'

'It takes several days for it to become real. At first, the pain is horrible. Just horrible. I couldn't move my body without hurting. I couldn't think because of the shock and disbelief. I went through the motions to get through the funeral, which now seems like a bad dream. Is this boring?'

'Not at all.'

'I've got to get off these pills. I sleep so much I don't get to talk to adults. Plus, my father tends to run people off. Are you taping this?'

'No. I'm just listening.'

'He was killed a week ago tonight. I thought he was working very late, which was not unusual. They shot him and took his wallet, so the cops couldn't identify him. I saw on the late news where a young lawyer had been murdered downtown, and I knew it was Curtis. Don't ask me how they knew he was a lawyer without knowing his name. It's strange, all the little weird things that go with a murder.'

'Why was he working late?'

'He worked eighty hours a week, sometimes more. White and Blazevich is a sweatshop. They try to kill the associates for seven years, and if they can't kill them they make them partners. Curtis hated the place. He was tired of being a lawyer.'

'How long was he there?'

'Five years. He was making ninety thousand a year, so he put up with the hassle.'

'Did you know he called me?'

'No. My father told me you said that, and I've thought about it all night. What did he say?'

'He never identified himself. He used the code name of Garcia. Don't ask how I learned his identity – it'll take hours. He said he possibly knew something about the assassinations of Justices Rosenberg and Jensen, and he wanted to tell me what he knew.'

'Randy Garcia was his best friend in elementary school.'

'I got the impression he had seen something at the office, and perhaps someone at the office knew he had seen it. He was very nervous, and always called from pay phones. He thought he was being followed. We had planned to meet early Saturday before last, but he called that morning and said no. He was scared, and said he had to protect his family. Did you know any of this?'

'No. I knew he was under a great deal of stress, but he'd been that way for five years. He never brought the office home with him. He hated the place, really.'

'Why'd he hate the place?'

'He worked for a bunch of cutthroats, a bunch of thugs who'd watch you bleed for a buck. They spend tons of money on this marvelous facade of respectability, but they are scum. Curtis was a top student and had his pick of jobs. They were such a great bunch of guys when they recruited him, and complete monsters to work with. Very unethical.'

'Why did he stay with the firm?'

'The money kept getting better. He almost left a year ago, but the job offer fell through. He was very unhappy, but he tried to keep it to himself. I think he felt guilty for making such a big mistake. We had a little routine around here. When he came home, I would ask him how his day went. Sometimes this was at ten at night, so I knew it was a bad day. But he always said the day had been profitable; that was the word, profitable. And then we talked about our baby. He didn't want to talk about the office, and I didn't want to hear it.'

Well, so much for Garcia. He's dead, and he told his wife nothing. 'Who cleaned out his desk?'

'Someone at the office. They brought his stuff Friday, all neatly packaged and taped in three cardboard boxes. You're welcome to go through it.'

'No, thanks. I'm sure it's been sanitized. How much life insurance did he have?'

She paused for a second. 'You're a smart man, Mr. Grantham. Two weeks ago, he bought a million-dollar term policy with double indemnity for accidental death.'

'That's two million dollars.'

'Yes sir. I guess you're right. I guess he was suspicious.'

'I don't think he was killed by muggers, Mrs. Morgan.'

'I can't believe this.' She choked a little, but fought it off.

'Have the cops asked you a lot of questions?'

'No. It's just another D.C. mugging that went one step further. No big deal. Happens every day.'

The insurance bit was interesting, but useless. Gray was getting tired of Mrs. Morgan and her unhurried monotone. He was sorry for her, but if she knew nothing, it was time to say good-bye.

'What do you think he knew?' she asked.

This could take hours. 'I don't know,' Gray answered, glancing at his watch. 'He said he knew something about the killings, but that's as far as he would go. I was convinced we would meet somewhere and he would spill his guts and show me something. I was wrong.'

'How would he know anything about those dead judges?'

'I don't know. He just called me out of the blue.'

'If he had something to show you, what would it be?' she asked.

He was the reporter. He was supposed to ask the questions. 'I have no idea. He never hinted.'

'Where would he hide such a thing?' The question was sincere, but irritating. Then it hit him. She was going somewhere with this.

'I don't know. Where did he keep his valuable papers?'

'We have a lockbox at the bank for deeds and wills and stuff. I've always known about the lockbox. He handled all the legal business, Mr. Grantham. I looked at the lockbox last Thursday with my father, and there was nothing unusual in it.'

'You didn't expect anything unusual, did you?'

'No. Then Saturday morning, early, it was still dark, I was going through his papers in his desk in the bedroom. We have this antique rolltop desk that he used for his personal correspondence and papers, and I found something a bit unusual.'

Gray was on his feet, holding the phone, and staring wildly at the floor. She had called at four in the morning. She had chitchatted for twenty minutes. And she waited until he was ready to hang up to drop the bomb.

'What is it?' he asked as coolly as possible.

'It's a key.'

He had a lump in his throat. 'A key to what?'

'Another lockbox.'

'Which bank?'

'First Columbia. We've never banked there.'

'I see. And you knew nothing about this other lockbox?'

'Oh no. Not until Saturday morning. I was puzzled by it, still am, but I found all of our legal papers in the old lockbox, so I had no reason to check this one. I figured I'd run by when I felt like it.'

'Would you like me to check it for you?'

'I thought you would say that. What if you find what you're looking for?'

'I don't know what I'm looking for. But what if I find something he left behind, and this something proves to be very, let's say, newsworthy?'

'Use it.'

'No conditions?'

'One. If it disparages my husband in any way, you can't use it.'

'It's a deal. I swear.'

'When do you want the key?'

'Do you have it in your hand?'

'Yes.'

'If you'll stand on the front porch, I'll be there in about three seconds.'

The private jet from Miami had brought only five men, so Edwin Sneller had only seven to plan with. Seven men, no time, and precious little equipment. He had not slept Monday night. His hotel suite was a mini-command center as they stared at maps through the night, and tried to plan the next twenty-four hours. A few things were certain. Grantham had an apartment, but he was not there. He had a car he was not using. He worked at the *Post,* and it was on Fifteenth Street. White and Blazevich was in a building on Tenth near New York, but she would not return there. Morgan's widow lived in Alexandria. Beyond that, they were searching for two people out of three million.

These were not the type of men you could rustle out of the bunkhouse and send in to fight. They had to be found and hired, and he'd been promised as many as possible by the end of the day.

Sneller was no novice at the killing game, and this was hopeless. This was desperation. The sky was falling. He would do his best under the circumstances, but Edwin Sneller had one foot out the back door.

She was on his mind. She had met Khamel on his terms, and walked away from it. She had dodged bullets and bombs, and evaded the best in the business. He would love to see her, not to kill her, but to congratulate her. A rookie running loose and living to tell about it.

They would concentrate on the *Post* building. It was the one spot he had to come back to.

CHAPTER FORTY

The downtown traffic was bumper to bumper, and that suited Darby just fine. She was in no hurry. The bank lobby opened at nine-thirty, and some time around seven, over coffee and untouched bagels in her room, he had convinced her that she should be the one to visit the vault. She was not really convinced, but a woman should do it, and there weren't many available. Beverly Morgan told Gray that her bank, First Hamilton, froze their box as soon as they learned of Curtis's death, and that she was allowed only to view the contents and make an inventory. She was also allowed to copy the will, but the original was placed back in the box and secured in the vault. The box would be released only after the tax auditors finished their work.

So the immediate question was whether or not First Columbia knew he was dead. The Morgans had never banked there. Beverly had no idea why he chose it. It was a huge bank with a million customers, and they decided that the odds were against it.

Darby was tired of playing the odds. She'd blown a wonderful opportunity last night to get on a plane, and now here she was about to be Beverly Morgan matching wits with First Columbia so she could steal from a dead man. And what was her sidekick going to do? He was going to protect her. He had this gun, which scared her to death and had the same effect on him though he wouldn't admit it, and he planned to play bodyguard by the front door while she pilfered the lockbox.

'What if they know he's dead,' she asked, 'and I tell them he isn't?'

'Then slap the bitch in the face and run like hell. I'll catch you at the front door. I've got a gun, and we'll blast our way down the sidewalk.'

'Come on, Gray. I don't know if I can do this.'

'You can do it, okay? Play it cool. Be assertive. Be a smartass. It should come natural.'

'Thanks so much. What if they call security on me? I have this sudden phobia of security guards.'

'I'll rescue you. I'll come blazing through the lobby like a SWAT team.'

'We'll all be killed.'

'Relax, Darby. It'll work.'

'Why are you so chipper?'

'I smell it. Something's in that lockbox, Darby. And you have to bring it out, kid. It's all riding on you.'

'Thanks for easing the pressure.'

They were on E Street near Ninth. Gray slowed the car, then parked illegally in a loading zone forty feet from the front entrance of First Columbia. He jumped out. Darby's exit was slower. Together, they walked quickly to the door. It was almost ten. 'I'll wait here,' he said, pointing to a marble column. 'Go do it.'

'Go do it,' she mumbled as she disappeared inside the revolving door. She was always the one being fed to the lions. The lobby was as big as a football field, with columns and chandeliers and fake Persian rugs.

'Safe deposit boxes?' she asked a young woman behind the information desk. The girl pointed to a corner in the far right.

'Thanks,' she said, and strolled toward it. The lines in front of the tellers were four deep to her left, and to her right a hundred busy vice presidents talked on their phones. It was the largest bank in the city, and no one noticed her.

The vault was behind a set of massive bronze doors that were polished enough to appear almost golden, no doubt to give the appearance of infinite safety and invulnerability. The doors were opened slightly to allow a select few in and out. To the left, an important-looking lady of sixty sat behind a desk with the words SAFE DEPOSIT BOXES across its front. Her name was Virginia Baskin.

Virginia Baskin stared at Darby as she approached the desk. There was no smile.

'I need access to a box,' Darby said without breathing. She hadn't breathed in the last two and a half minutes.

'The number, please,' Ms. Baskin said as she hit the keyboard and turned to the monitor.

'F566.'

She punched the number and waited for the words to flash on the screen. She frowned, and moved her face to within inches of it. Run! Darby thought. She frowned harder and scratched her chin. Run, before she picks up the phone and calls the guards. Run, before the alarms go off and my idiot cohort comes blazing through the lobby.

Ms. Baskin withdrew her head from the monitor. 'That was rented just two weeks ago,' she said almost to herself.

'Yes,' Darby said as if she had rented it.

'I assume you're Mrs. Morgan,' she said, pecking on the keyboard.

Keep assuming, baby. 'Yes, Beverly Anne Morgan.'

'And your address?'

'891 Pembroke, Alexandria.'

She nodded at the screen as if it could see her and give its approval. She pecked again. 'Phone number?'

'703-664-5980.'

Ms. Baskin liked this too. So did the computer. 'Who rented this box?'

'My husband, Curtis D. Morgan.'

'And his social security number?'

Darby casually opened her new, rather large leather shoulder bag, and pulled out her wallet. How many wives memorized their husband's social security number? She opened the wallet.

'510-96-8686.'

'Very well,' Ms. Baskin said properly as she left the keyboard and reached into her desk. 'How long will this take?'

'Just a minute.'

She placed a wide card on a small clipboard on the desk, and pointed at it. 'Sign here, Mrs. Morgan.'

Darby nervously signed on the second slot. Mr. Morgan had made the first entry the day he rented the box.

Ms. Baskin glanced at the signature while Darby held her breath.

'Do you have your key?' she asked.

'Of course,' Darby said with a warm smile.

Ms. Baskin took a small box from the drawer, and walked around the desk. 'Follow me.' They went through the bronze doors. The vault was as big as a branch bank in the suburbs. Designed along the lines of a mausoleum, it was a maze of hallways and small chambers. Two men in uniform walked by. They passed four identical rooms with walls lined with rows of lockboxes. The fifth room held F566, evidently, because Ms. Baskin stepped into it and opened her little black box. Darby looked nervously around and behind her.

Virginia was all business. She walked to F566, which was shoulder-high, and stuck in the key. She rolled her eyes at Darby as if to say, 'Your turn, dumbass.' Darby yanked the key from a pocket, and inserted it next to the other one. Virginia then turned both keys, and slid the box two inches from its slot. She removed the bank's key.

She pointed to a small booth with a folding wooden door. 'Take it in there. When you finish, lock it back in place and come to my desk.' She was leaving the room as she spoke.

'Thanks,' Darby said. She waited until Virginia was out of sight, then slid the box from the wall. It was not heavy. The front was six inches by twelve, and it was a foot and a half long. The top was open, and inside were two items: a thin, brown, legal-sized envelope, and an unmarked videotape.

She didn't need the booth. She stuffed the envelope and videotape in her shoulder bag, and slid the box back into its slot. She left the room.

Virginia had rounded the corner of her desk when Darby walked behind her. 'I'm finished,' she said.

'My, that was quick.'

Damned right. Things happen fast when your nerves are popping through your skin. 'I found what I needed,' she said.

'Very well.' Ms. Baskin was suddenly a warm person. 'You know, that awful story in the paper last week about that lawyer. You know, the one killed by muggers not far from here. Wasn't his name Curtis Morgan? Seems like it was Curtis Morgan. What a shame.'

Oh, you dumb woman. 'I didn't see that,' Darby said. 'I've been out of the country. Thanks.'

Her step was a bit quicker the second time through the lobby. The bank was crowded, and there were no security guards in sight. Piece of cake. It was about time she pulled a job without being grabbed.

The gunman was guarding the marble column. The revolving door spun her onto the sidewalk, and she was almost to the car before he caught her. 'Get in the car!' She demanded.

'What'd you find?' he demanded.

'Just get outta here.' She yanked the door open, and jumped in. He started the car and sped away.

'Talk to me,' he said.

'I cleaned out the box,' she said. 'Is anyone behind us?'

He glanced in the mirror. 'How the hell do I know? What is it?'

She opened her purse and pulled out the envelope. She opened it. Gray slammed on the brakes and almost smashed a car in front.

'Watch where you're going!' she yelled.

'Okay! Okay. What's in the envelope!'

'I don't know! I haven't read it yet, and if you get me killed, I'll never read it.'

The car was moving again. Gray breathed deeply. 'Look, let's stop yelling, okay. Let's be cool.'

'Yes. You drive, and I'll be cool.'

'Okay. Now. Are we cool?'

'Yes. Just relax. And watch where you're going. Where are you going?'

'I don't know. What's in the envelope?'

She pulled out a document of some sort. She glanced at him, and he was staring at the document. 'Watch where we're going.'

'Just read the damned thing.'

'It makes me carsick. I can't read in the car.'

'Dammit! Dammit! Dammit!'

'You're yelling again.'

He yanked the wheel to the right and pulled into another tow-away zone on E Street. Horns honked as he slammed his brakes. He glared at her.

'Thanks,' she said, and started reading it aloud.

It was a four-page affidavit, typed real neat and sworn to under oath before a notary public. It was dated Friday, the day before the last phone call to Grantham. Under oath, Curtis Morgan said he worked in the oil and gas section of White and Blazevich, and had since he joined the firm five years earlier. His clients were privately owned oil exploration firms from many countries, but primarily Americans. Since he joined the firm he had worked for a client who was engaged in a huge lawsuit in south Louisiana. The client was a man named Victor Mattiece, and Mr. Mattiece, whom he'd never met but was well known to the senior partners of White and Blazevich, wanted desperately to win the lawsuit and eventually harvest millions of barrels of oil from the swamplands of Terrebonne Parish, Louisiana. There were also hundreds of millions of cubic yards of natural gas. The partner supervising the case for White and Blazevich was F. Sims Wakefield, who was very close to Victor Mattiece and often visited him in the Bahamas.

They sat in the tow-away zone with the bumper of the Pontiac protruding perilously into the right lane, and were oblivious to the cars swerving around it. She read slowly, and he sat with his eyes closed.

Continuing, the lawsuit was very important to White and Blazevich. The firm was not directly involved in the trial and appeal, but everything crossed Wakefield's desk. He worked on nothing but the pelican case, as it was known. He spent most of his time on the phone with either Mattiece or one of a hundred lawyers working on the case. Morgan averaged ten hours a week on the case, but always on the periphery. His billings were handed directly to Wakefield, and this was unusual because all other billings went to the oil and gas billing clerk, who turned them in to accounting. He'd heard rumors over the years, and firmly believed Mattiece was not paying White and Blazevich its standard hourly rate. He believed the firm had taken the case for a percentage of the harvest. He'd heard the figure of ten percent of the net profits from the wells. This was unheard of in the industry.

Brakes squealed loudly, and they braced for the impact. It barely missed. 'We're about to be killed,' Darby snapped.

Gray yanked the gearshift into Drive, and pulled the right front wheel over the curb and onto the sidewalk. Now they were out of traffic. The car was angled across a forbidden space with its front bumper on the sidewalk and its rear bumper barely out of traffic. 'Keep reading,' he snapped back.

Continuing, on or about September 28, Morgan was in Wakefield's office. He walked in with two files and a stack of documents unrelated to the pelican case. Wakefield was on the phone. As usual, secretaries were in and out. The office was always in a state of disruption. He stood around for a few minutes waiting for Wakefield to get off the phone, but the conversation dragged on. Finally, after waiting fifteen minutes, Morgan picked up his files and documents from Wakefield's cluttered desk, and left. He went to his office at the other end of the building, and started working at his desk. It was about two in the afternoon. As he reached for a file, he found a handwritten memo on the bottom of the stack of documents he had just brought to his office. He had inadvertently taken it from Wakefield's desk. He immediately stood, with the intention of returning to Wakefield. Then he read it. And he read it again. He glanced at the telephone. Wakefield's line was still busy. A copy of the memo was attached to the affidavit.

'Read the memo,' Gray snapped.

'I'm not through with the affidavit,' she snapped back. It would do no good to argue with her. She was the legal mind, and this was a legal document, and she would read it exactly as she pleased.

Continuing, he was stunned by the memo. And he was immediately terrified of it. He walked out of his office and down the hall to the nearest Xerox, and copied it. He returned to his office, and placed the original memo in the same position under the files on his desk. He would swear he'd never seen it.

The memo was two paragraphs handwritten on White and Blazevich internal stationery. It was from M. Velmano, who is Marty Velmano, a senior partner. It was dated September 28, directed to Wakefield, and read:

Sims:

Advise client, research is complete – and the bench will sit much softer if Rosenberg is retired. The second retirement is a bit unusual. Einstein found a link to Jensen, of all people. The boy, of course, has those other problems.

Advise further that the pelican should arrive here in four years, assuming other factors.

There was no signature.

Gray was chuckling and frowning at the same time. His mouth was open. She was reading faster.

Continuing, Marty Velmano was a ruthless shark who worked eighteen hours a day, and felt useless unless someone near him was bleeding. He was the heart and soul of White and Blazevich. To the power people of Washington, he was a tough operator with plenty of money. He lunched with congressmen, and played golf with cabinet members. He did his throat cutting behind his office door.

Einstein was the nickname for Nathaniel Jones, a demented legal genius the firm kept locked away in his own little library on the sixth floor. He read every case decided by the Supreme Court, the eleven federal appellate courts, and the supreme courts of the fifty states. Morgan had never met Einstein. Sightings were rare around the firm.

After he copied it, he folded his copy of the memo and placed it in a desk drawer. Ten minutes later, Wakefield stormed into his office, very disturbed and pale. They scratched around Morgan's desk, and found the memo. Wakefield was angry as hell, which was not unusual. He asked if Morgan had read this. No, he insisted. Evidently he mistakenly picked it up when he left his office, he explained. What's the big deal? Wakefield was furious. He lectured Morgan about the sanctity of one's desk. He was a blithering idiot, rebuking and expounding around Morgan's office. He finally realized he was overreacting. He tried to settle down, but the impression had been made. He left with the memo.

Morgan hid the copy in a law book in the library on the ninth floor. He was shocked at Wakefield's paranoia and hysterics. Before he left that afternoon, he precisely arranged the articles and papers in his desk and on his shelves. The next morning, he checked them. Someone had gone through his desk during the night.

Morgan became very careful. Two days later, he found a tiny screwdriver behind a book on his credenza. Then he found a small piece of black tape wadded up and dropped in his trash can. He assumed his office was wired and his phones were bugged. He caught suspicious looks from Wakefield. He saw Velmano in Wakefield's office more than usual.

Then Justices Rosenberg and Jensen were killed. There was no doubt in his mind it was the work of Mattiece and his associates. The memo did not mention Mattiece, but it referred to a 'client.' Wakefield had no other clients. And no one client had as much to gain from a new Court as Mattiece.

The last paragraph of the affidavit was frightening. On two occasions after the assassinations, Morgan knew he was being followed. He was taken off the pelican case. He was given more work, more hours, more demands. He was afraid of being killed. If they would kill two justices, they would kill a lowly associate.

He signed it under oath before Emily Stanford, a notary public. Her address was typed under her name.

'Sit tight. I'll be right back,' Gray said as he opened his door and jumped out. He dodged cars and dashed across E Street. There was a pay phone outside a bakery. He punched Smith Keen's number and looked at his rented car parked haphazardly across the street.

'Smith, it's Gray. Listen carefully and do as I say. I've got another source on the pelican brief. It's big, Smith, and I need you and Krauthammer in Feldman's office in fifteen minutes.'

'What is it?'

'Garcia left a farewell message. We have one more stop, and we're coming in.'

'We? The girl's coming in?'

'Yes. Get a TV with a VCR in the conference room. I think Garcia wants to talk to us.'

'He left a tape?'

'Yes. Fifteen minutes.'

'Are you safe?'

'I think so. I'm just nervous as hell, Smith.' He hung up and ran back to the car.

Ms. Stanford owned a court reporting service on Vermont. She was dusting the bookshelves when Gray and Darby walked in. They were in a hurry.

'Are you Emily Stanford?' he asked.

'Yes. Why?'

He showed her the last page of the affidavit. 'Did you notarize this?'

'Who are you?'

'Gray Grantham with the *Washington Post.* Is this your signature?'

'Yes. I notarized it.'

Darby handed her the photograph of Garcia, now Morgan, on the sidewalk. 'Is this the man who signed the affidavit?' she asked.

'This is Curtis Morgan. Yes. That's him.'

'Thank you,' Gray said.

'He's dead, isn't he?' Ms. Stanford asked. 'I saw it in the paper.'

'Yes, he's dead,' Gray said. 'Did you by chance read this affidavit?'

'Oh no. I just witnessed his signature. But I knew something was wrong.'

'Thank you, Ms. Stanford.' They left as fast as they'd come.

The thin man hid his shiny forehead under a ragged fedora. His pants were rags and his shoes were torn, and he sat in his ancient wheelchair in front of the *Post* and held a sign proclaiming him to be HUNGRY AND HOMELESS. He rolled his head from shoulder to shoulder as if the muscles in his neck had collapsed from hunger. A paper bowl with a few dollars and coins was in his lap, but it was his money. Maybe he could do better if he was blind.

He looked pitiful, sitting there like a vegetable, rolling his head, wearing green Kermit the Frog sunglasses. He watched every move on the street.

He saw the car fly around the corner and park illegally. The man and the woman jumped out, and ran toward him. He had a gun under the ragged quilt, but they were moving too fast. And there were too many people on the sidewalk. They entered the *Post* building.

He waited a minute, then rolled himself away.

CHAPTER FORTY-ONE

Smith Keen was pacing and fidgeting in front of Feldman's office door as the secretary looked on. He saw them weaving hurriedly down the aisle between the rows of desks. Gray was leading and holding her hand. She was definitely attractive, but he would appreciate it later. They were breathless.

'Smith Keen, this is Darby Shaw,' Gray said between breaths.

They shook hands. 'Hello,' she said, looking around at the sprawling newsroom.

'My pleasure, Darby. From what I hear, you are a remarkable woman.'

'Right,' Grantham said. 'We can chitchat later.'

'Follow me,' Keen said, and they were off again. 'Feldman wanted to use the conference room.' They cut across the cluttered newsroom, and walked into a plush room with a long table in the center of it. It was full of men who were talking but immediately shut up when she walked in. Feldman closed the door.

He reached for her hand. 'I'm Jackson Feldman, executive editor. You must be Darby.'

'Who else?' Gray said, still breathing hard.

Feldman ignored him and looked around the table. He pointed. 'This is Howard Krauthammer, managing editor; Ernie DeBasio, assistant managing editor/foreign; Elliot Cohen, assistant managing editor/national; and Vince Litsky, our attorney.'

She nodded politely and forgot each name as she heard it. They were all at least fifty, all in shirtsleeves, all deeply concerned. She could feel the tension.

'Give me the tape,' Gray said.

She took it from her bag and handed it to him. The television and VCR were at the end of the room on a portable stand. He pushed the tape into the VCR. 'We got this twenty minutes ago, so we haven't seen it.'

Darby sat in a chair against the wall. The men inched toward the screen and waited for an image.

On a black screen was the date – October 12. Then Curtis Morgan was sitting at a table in a kitchen. He held a switch that evidently worked the camera.

'My name is Curtis Morgan, and since you're watching this, I'm probably dead.' It was a helluva first sentence. The men grimaced and inched closer.

'Today is October 12, and I'm doing this at my house. I'm alone. My wife is at the doctor. I should be at work, but I called in sick. My wife knows nothing about any of this. I've told no one. Since you're watching this, you've also seen this. [*He holds up the affidavit.*] This is an affidavit I've signed, and I plan to leave it with this video, probably in a safe deposit box in a bank downtown. I'll read the affidavit, and discuss other things.'

'We've got the affidavit,' Gray said quickly. He was standing against the wall next to Darby. No one looked at him. They were glued to the screen. Morgan slowly read the affidavit. His eyes darted from the pages to the camera, back and forth, back and forth.

It took him ten minutes. Each time Darby heard the word *Pelican*, she closed her eyes and slowly shook her head. It had all come down to this. It was a bad dream. She tried to listen.

When Morgan finished the affidavit, he laid it on the table, and looked at some notes on a legal pad. He was comfortable and relaxed. He was a handsome kid who looked younger than twenty-nine. He was at home, so there was no tie. Just a starched white button-down. White and Blazevich was not an ideal place to work, he said, but most of the four hundred lawyers were honest and probably knew nothing about Mattiece. In fact, he doubted if many besides Wakefield, Velmano, and Einstein were involved in the conspiracy. There was a partner named Jarreld Schwabe who was sinister enough to be involved, but Morgan had no proof. (Darby remembered him well.) There was an ex-secretary who'd quit abruptly a few days after the assassinations. Her name was Miriam LaRue, and she'd worked in the oil and gas section for eighteen years. She might know something. She lives in Falls Church. Another secretary whom he would not name had told him she overheard a conversation between Wakefield and Velmano, and the topic was whether he, Morgan, could be trusted. But she just heard bits and pieces. They treated him differently after the memo was found on his desk. Especially Schwabe and Wakefield. It was as if they wanted to throw him up against the wall and threaten his life if he told of the memo, but they couldn't do it because they weren't sure he'd seen it. And they were afraid to make a big deal out of it. But he'd seen it, and they were almost certain he'd seen it. And if they conspired to kill Rosenberg and Jensen, well, hell, he was just an associate. He could be replaced in seconds.

Litsky the lawyer shook his head in disbelief. The numbness was wearing off, and they moved a bit in their seats.

Morgan commuted by car, and twice he was trailed. Once during lunch, he saw a man watching him. He talked about his family for a while, and started to ramble. It was apparent he'd run out of hard news.

Gray handed the affidavit and the memo to Feldman, who read it and passed it to Krauthammer, who passed it on.

Morgan finished with a chilling farewell: 'I don't know who will see this tape. I'll be dead, so it won't really matter, I guess. I hope you use this to nail Mattiece and his sleazy lawyers. But if the sleazy lawyers are watching this tape, then you can all go straight to hell.'

Gray ejected the tape. He rubbed his hands together and smiled at the group. 'Well, gentlemen, did we bring you enough verification, or do you want more?'

'I know those guys.' Litsky said, dazed. 'Wakefield and I played tennis a year ago.'

Feldman was up and walking. 'How'd you find Morgan?'

'It's a long story,' Gray said.

Give me a real short version.'

'We found a law student at Georgetown who clerked for White and Blazevich last summer. He identified a photograph of Morgan.'

'How'd you get the photograph?' Litsky asked.

'Don't ask. It doesn't go with the story.'

'I say run the story,' Krauthammer said loudly.

'Run it,' said Elliot Cohen.

'How'd you learn he was dead?' Feldman asked.

'Darby went to White and Blazevich yesterday. They broke the news.'

'Where was the video and affidavit?'

'In a lockbox at First Columbia. Morgan's wife gave me the key at five this morning. I've done nothing wrong. The pelican brief has been verified fully by an independent source.'

'Run it,' said Ernie DeBasio. 'Run it with the biggest headline since NIXON RESIGNS.'

Feldman stopped near Smith Keen. The two friends eyed each other carefully. 'Run it,' said Keen.

He turned to the lawyer. 'Vince?'

'There's no question, legally. But I'd like to see the story after it's written.'

'How long will it take to write it?' the editor asked Gray.

'The brief portion is already outlined. I can finish it up in an hour or so. Give me two hours on Morgan. Three at the most.'

Feldman hadn't smiled since he shook hands with Darby. He paced to the other side of the room, and stood in Gray's face. 'What if this tape's a hoax?'

'Hoax? We're talking dead bodies, Jackson. I've seen the widow. She's a real, live widow. This paper ran the story of his murder. He's dead.

Even his law firm says he's dead. And that's him on the tape, talking about dying. I know that's him. And we talked to the notary public who witnessed his signature on the affidavit. She identified him.' Gray was getting louder and looking around the room. 'Everything he said verifies the pelican brief. Everything. Mattiece, the lawsuit, the assassinations. Then we've got Darby, the author of the brief. And more dead bodies, and they've chased her all over the country. There are no holes, Jackson. It's a story.'

He finally smiled. 'It's more than a story. Have it written by two. It's eleven now. Use this conference room and close the door.' Feldman was pacing again. 'We'll meet here at exactly two and read the draft. Not a word.'

The men stood and filed from the room, but not before each shook hands with Darby Shaw. They were uncertain whether to say congratulations or thanks or whatever, so they just smiled and shook her hands. She kept her seat.

When they were alone, Gray sat beside her and they held hands. The clean conference table was before them. The chairs were placed perfectly around it. The walls were white, and the room was lit by fluorescent lights and two narrow windows.

'How do you feel?' he asked.

'I don't know. This is the end of the road, I guess. We made it.'

'You don't sound too happy.'

'I've had better months. I'm happy for you.'

He looked at her. 'Why are you happy for me?'

'You put the pieces together and it hits tomorrow. It's got Pulitzer written all over it.'

'I hadn't thought about that.'

'Liar.'

'Okay, maybe once. But when you got off the elevator yesterday and told me Garcia was dead, I quit thinking about Pulitzers.'

'It's not fair. I do all the work. We used my brains and looks and legs, and you get all the glory.'

'I'll be glad to use your name. I'll credit you as the author of the brief. We'll put your picture on the front page, along with Rosenberg, Jensen, Mattiece, the President, Verheek, and –'

'Thomas? Will his picture run with the story?'

'It's up to Feldman. He'll edit this one.'

She thought about this, and said nothing.

'Well, Ms. Shaw, I've got three hours to write the biggest story of my career. A story that will shock the world. A story that could bring down a presidency. A story that will solve the assassinations. A story that will make me rich and famous.'

'You'd better let me write it.'

'Would you? I'm tired.'

'Go get your notes. And some coffee.'

They closed the door and cleared the table. A news aide rolled in a PC with a printer. They sent him after a pot of coffee. Then some fruit. They outlined the story in sections, beginning with the assassinations, then the pelican case in south Louisiana, then Mattiece and his link to the President, then the pelican brief and all the havoc it created, Callahan, Verheek, then Curtis Morgan and his muggers, then White and Blazevich and Wakefield, Velmano, and Einstein. Darby preferred to write in longhand. She scaled down the litigation and the brief, and what was known of Mattiece. Gray took the rest, and typed out rough notes on the machine.

Darby was a model of organization, with notes neatly arranged on the table, and words carefully written on paper. He was a whirlwind of chaos – papers on the floor, talking to the computer, printing random paragraphs that were discarded by the time they were on paper. She kept telling him to be quiet. This is not a law school library, he explained. This is a newspaper. You work with a phone in each ear and someone yelling at you.

At twelve-thirty, Smith Keen sent in food. Darby ate a cold sandwich and watched the traffic below. Gray was digging through campaign reports.

She saw him. He was leaning on the side of a building across Fifteenth Street, and he would not have been suspicious except he had been leaning on the side of the Madison Hotel an hour earlier. He was sipping something from a tall Styrofoam cup, and watching the front entrance to the *Post*. He wore a black cap, denim jacket, and jeans. He was under thirty. And he just stood there staring across the street. She nibbled on her sandwich, and watched him for ten minutes. He sipped from his cup and never moved.

'Gray, come here, please.'

'What is it?' He walked over. She pointed to the man with the black cap.

'Watch him carefully,' she said. 'Tell me what he's doing.'

'He's drinking something, probably coffee. He's leaning on the side of that building, and he's watching this building.'

'What's he wearing?'

'Denim from head to toe, and a black cap. Looks like boots. What about it?'

'I saw him an hour ago standing over there by the hotel. He was sort of hidden by that telephone van, but I know it was him. Now he's over there.'

'So?'

'So for the past hour, at least, he's been moving around doing nothing but watching this building.'

Gray nodded. This was no time for a smart comment. The guy looked suspicious, and she was concerned. She'd been tracked for two weeks now, from New Orleans to New York, and now maybe to Washington, and she knew more about being followed than he did.

'What're you saying, Darby?'

'Give me one good reason why this man, who obviously is not a street bum, would be doing this.'

The man looked at his watch, and walked slowly along the sidewalk until he was gone. Darby looked at her watch.

'It's exactly one,' she said. 'Let's check every fifteen minutes, okay?'

'Okay. I doubt if it's anything,' he said, trying to be comforting. It didn't work. She sat at the table, and looked at the notes.

He watched her and slowly returned to the computer.

Gray typed furiously for fifteen minutes, then walked back to the window. Darby watched him carefully. 'I don't see him,' he said.

He did see him at one-thirty. 'Darby,' he said, pointing to the spot where she'd first seen him. She looked out the window, and slowly focused on the man with the black cap. Now he had a dark green windbreaker, and he was not facing the *Post*. He watched his boots, and every ten seconds or so glanced at the front entrance. This made him all the more suspicious, but he was partially hidden behind a delivery truck. The Styrofoam cup was gone. He lit a cigarette. He glanced at the *Post*, then watched the sidewalk in front of it.

'Why do I have this knot in my stomach?' Darby said.

'How could they follow you? It's impossible.'

'They knew I was in New York. That seemed impossible at the time.'

'Maybe they're following me. I've been told they were watching. That's what the guy's doing. Why should he know you're here? The dude's following me.'

'Maybe,' she said slowly.

'Have you seen him before?'

'They don't introduce themselves.'

'Look. We've got thirty minutes, and they're back in here with knives to carve up our story. Let's finish it, then we can watch dude out there.'

They returned to their work. At one forty-five, she stood in the window again, and the man was gone. The printer was rattling the first draft, and she began proofing.

The editors read with their pencils. Litsky the lawyer read for sheer pleasure. He seemed to enjoy it more than the others.

It was a long story, and Feldman was busy cutting like a surgeon. Smith Keen scribbled in the margins. Krauthammer liked what he saw.

They read slowly in silence. Gray proofed it again. Darby was at the window. Dude was back again, now wearing a navy blazer with the jeans. It was cloudy and in the sixties, and he was sipping from the cup. He huddled over it to stay warm. He took a drink, looked at the *Post*, looked at the street, and back to the cup. He was in front of a different building, and at exactly two-fifteen he began looking north along Fifteenth.

A car stopped on his side of the street. The rear door opened, and there he was. The car sped away, and he looked around. Limping ever so slightly, Stump walked casually to the man with the black cap. They spoke for seconds, then Stump walked south to the intersection of Fifteenth and L. Dude stayed in place.

She glanced around the room. They were immersed in the story. Stump was out of sight, so she couldn't show him to Gray, who was reading and smiling. No, they were not watching the reporter. They were waiting on the girl.

And they had to be desperate. They were standing on the street hoping somehow a miracle would happen and the girl would emerge from the building, and they could take her out. They were scared. She was inside spilling her guts and waving copies of that damned brief. Tomorrow morning the game would be over. Somehow they had to stop her. They had their orders.

She was in a room full of men, and suddenly she was not safe.

Feldman finished last. He slid his copy to Gray. 'Minor stuff. Should take about an hour. Let's talk phone calls.'

'Just three, I think,' Gray said. 'The White House, FBI, and White and Blazevich.'

'You only named Sims Wakefield at the firm. Why?' asked Krauthammer.

'Morgan fingered him the most.'

'But the memo is from Velmano. I think he should be named.'

'I agree,' said Smith Keen.

'Me too,' said DeBasio.

'I wrote his name in,' Feldman said. 'We'll get Einstein later. Wait until four-thirty or five before you call the White House and White and Blazevich. If you do it sooner, they may go nuts and run to court.'

'I agree,' said Litsky the lawyer. 'They can't stop it, but they can try. I'd wait until five before I called them.'

'Okay,' Gray said. 'I'll have it reworked by three-thirty. Then I'll call the FBI for their comment. Then the White House, then White and Blazevich.'

Feldman was almost out the door. 'We'll meet again here at three-thirty. Stay close to your phones.'

When the room was empty again, Darby locked the door and pointed to the window. 'You've heard me mention Stump?'

'Don't tell me.'

They scanned the street below.

'Afraid so. He met with our little friend, then disappeared. I know it was him.'

'I guess I'm off the hook.'

'I guess you are. I really want to get out of here.'

'We'll think of something. I'll alert our security. You want me to tell Feldman?'

'No. Not yet.'

'I know some cops.'

'Great. And they can just walk up and beat the hell out of him.'

'These cops'll do it.'

'They can't bother these people. What are they doing wrong?'

'Just planning murder.'

'How safe are we in this building?'

Gray thought a moment. 'Let me tell Feldman. We'll get two security guards posted by this door.'

'Okay.'

Feldman approved the second draft at three-thirty, and Gray was given the green light to call the FBI. Four phones were brought to the conference room, and the recorder was plugged in. Feldman, Smith Keen, and Krauthammer listened on extensions.

Gray called Phil Norvell, a good acquaintance and sometime source, if there was such a thing within the Bureau. Norvell answered his own line.

'Phil, Gray Grantham with the *Post*.'

'I think I know who you're with, Gray.'

'I've got the recorder on.'

'Must be serious. What's up?'

'We're running a story in the morning detailing a conspiracy in the assassinations of Rosenberg and Jensen. We're naming Victor Mattiece, an oil speculator, and two of his lawyers here in town. We also mention Verheek, not in the conspiracy, of course. We believe the FBI knew about Mattiece early on, but refused to investigate at the urging of the White House. We wanted to give you guys a chance to comment.'

There was no response on the other end.

'Phil, are you there?'

'Yes. I think so.'

'Any comment?'

'I'm sure we will have a comment, but I'll have to call you back.'

'We're going to press soon, so you need to hurry.'

'Well, Gray, this is a shot in the ass. Could you hold it a day?'

'No way.'

Norvell paused. 'Okay. Let me see Mr. Voyles, and I'll call you back.'

'Thanks.'

'No, thank you, Gray. This is wonderful. Mr. Voyles will be thrilled.'

'We're waiting.' Gray punched a button and cleared the line. Keen turned off the recorder.

They waited eight minutes, and Voyles himself was on the line. He insisted on speaking to Jackson Feldman. The recorder was back on.

'Mr. Voyles?' Feldman said warmly. The two had met many times, so the 'mister' was unnecessary.

'Call me Denton, dammit. Look, Jackson, what's your boy got? This is crazy. You guys are jumping off a cliff. We've investigated Mattiece, still investigating him, and it's too early to move on him. Now, what's your boy got?'

'Does the name Darby Shaw mean anything?' Feldman grinned at her when he asked the question. She was standing against the wall.

Voyles was slow to respond. 'Yes,' he said simply.

'My boy has the pelican brief, Denton, and I'm sitting here looking at Darby Shaw.'

'I was afraid she was dead.'

'No. She's very much alive. She and Gray Grantham have confirmed from another source the facts set forth in the brief. It's a large story, Denton.'

Voyles sighed deeply, and threw in the towel. 'We are pursuing Mattiece as a suspect,' he said.

'The recorder's on, Denton, be careful.'

'Well, we need to talk. I mean, man to man. I may have some deep background for you.'

'You're welcome to come here.'

'I'll do that. I'll be there in twenty minutes.'

The editors were terribly amused at the idea of the great F. Denton Voyles hopping in his limo and rushing to the *Post*. They had watched him for years, and knew he was a master at cutting his losses. He hated the press, and this willingness to talk on their turf and under their gun meant only one thing – he would point the finger at someone else. And the likely target was the White House.

Darby had no desire to meet the man. Her thoughts were on escape. She could point at the man in the black cap, but he'd been gone for thirty minutes now. And what could the FBI do? They had to catch him first, then what? Charge him with loitering and planning an ambush? Torture him and make him tell all? They probably wouldn't believe her.

She had no desire to deal with the FBI. She didn't want their protection. She was about to take a trip, and no one would know where to. Maybe Gray. Maybe not.

He punched the number for the White House, and they picked up the extensions. Keen turned on the recorder.

'Fletcher Coal, please. This is Gray Grantham with the *Washington Post*, and it's very urgent.'

He waited. 'Why Coal?' Keen asked.

'Everything has to be cleared through him,' Gray said with his hand over the receiver.

'Says who?'

'Says a source.'

The secretary returned with the message that Mr. Coal was on his way. Please hold. Gray was smiling. The adrenaline was pumping.

Finally, 'Fletcher Coal.'

'Yes, Mr. Coal. Gray Grantham at the *Post*. I am recording the conversation. Do you understand that?'

'Yes.'

'Is it true you have issued a directive to all White House personnel, except the President, to the effect that all communications with the press must first be cleared by you?'

'Absolutely untrue. The press secretary handles those matters.'

'I see. We're running a story in the morning which, in summary, verifies the facts set forth in the pelican brief. Are you familiar with the pelican brief?'

Slowly, 'I am.'

'We have confirmed that Mr. Mattiece contributed in excess of four million dollars to the President's campaign three years ago.'

'Four million, two hundred thousand, all through legal channels.'

'We also believe the White House intervened and attempted to obstruct the FBI investigation into Mr. Mattiece, and we wanted your comment, if any.'

'Is this something you believe, or is it something you intend to print?'

'We are trying to confirm it now.'

'And who do you think will confirm it for you?'

'We have sources, Mr. Coal.'

'Indeed you do. The White House emphatically denies any involvement with this investigation. The President asked to be apprised as to the status of the entire investigation after the tragic deaths of Justices Rosenberg and Jensen, but there has been no direct or indirect involvement from the White House into any aspect of the investigation. You have received some bad information.'

'Does the President consider Victor Mattiece a friend?'

'No. They met on one occasion, and as I stated, Mr. Mattiece was a significant contributor, but he is not a friend of the President.'

'He was the largest contributor, though, wasn't he?'

'I cannot confirm that.'

'Any other comment?'

'No. I'm sure the press secretary will address this in the morning.'

They hung up and Keen turned off the recorder. Feldman was on his feet rubbing his hands together. 'I'd give a year's pay to be in the White House right now,' he said.

'He's cool, isn't he?' Gray said with admiration.

'Yeah, but his cool ass is now sitting deep in boiling water.'

CHAPTER FORTY-TWO

For a man accustomed to throwing his weight around and watching everyone flinch, it was difficult to come humbly forward with hat in hand and ask for a break. He swaggered as humbly as he could through the newsroom with K. O. Lewis and two agents in tow. He wore his customary wrinkled trench coat with the belt tied tightly around the center of his short and dumpy physique. He was not striking, but his manner and walk left no doubt he was a man accustomed to getting his way. All dressed in dark coats, they resembled a Mafia don with bodyguards. The busy newsroom grew silent as they walked quickly through it. Though not striking, F. Denton Voyles was a presence, humble or not.

A small, tense group of editors huddled in the short hallway outside Feldman's office. Howard Krauthammer knew Voyles, and met him as he approached. They shook hands and whispered. Feldman was on the phone to Mr. Ludwig, the publisher, who was in China. Smith Keen joined the conversation and shook hands with Voyles and Lewis. The two agents kept to themselves a few feet away.

Feldman opened his door, looked toward the newsroom, and saw Denton Voyles. He motioned for him to come in. K. O. Lewis followed. They exchanged routine pleasantries until Smith Keen closed the door and they took a seat.

'I take it you have solid confirmation of the pelican brief,' Voyles said.

'We do,' Feldman answered. 'Why don't you and Mr. Lewis read a draft of the story? I think it will explain things. We're going to press in about an hour, and the reporter, Mr. Grantham, wants you to have the opportunity to comment.'

'I appreciate that.'

Feldman picked up a copy of the draft and handed it to Voyles, who took it gingerly. Lewis leaned over, and they immediately started reading. 'We'll step outside,' Feldman said. 'Take your time.' He and Keen left the office, and closed the door. The agents moved closer.

Feldman and Keen walked across the newsroom to the conference door. Two large security guards stood in the hall. Gray and Darby were alone inside when they entered.

'You need to call White and Blazevich,' Feldman said.

'Waiting on you.'

They picked up the extensions. Krauthammer was gone for the moment, and Keen handed his phone to Darby. Gray punched the numbers.

'Marty Velmano, please,' Gray said. 'Yes, this is Gray Grantham with the *Washington Post*, and I need to speak to him. It's very urgent.'

'One moment, please,' the secretary said.

A moment, passed, and another secretary was on the phone. 'Mr. Velmano's office.'

Gray identified himself again, and asked for her boss.

'He's in a meeting,' she said.

'So am I,' Gray said. 'Go to the meeting, tell him who I am, and tell him his picture will be on the front page of the *Post* at midnight tonight.'

'Well, yes sir.'

Within seconds, Velmano said, 'Yes, what's going on?'

Gray identified himself for the third time, and explained about the recorder.

'I understand,' Velmano snapped.

'We're running a story in the morning about your client, Victor Mattiece, and his involvement in the assassinations of Justices Rosenberg and Jensen.'

'Great! We'll sue your ass for the next twenty years. You're out in left field, buddy. We'll own the *Post*.'

'Yes sir. Remember, I'm recording this.'

'Record all you want! You'll be named as a defendant. This will be great! Victor Mattiece will own the *Washington Post*! This is fabulous!'

Gray shook his head in disbelief at Darby. The editors smiled at the floor. This was about to be very funny.

'Yes sir. Have you heard of the pelican brief? We have a copy.'

Dead silence. Then a distant grunt, like the last gasp of a dying dog. Then more silence.

'Mr. Velmano. Are you there?'

'Yes.'

'We also have a copy of a memo you sent to Sims Wakefield, dated September 28, in which you suggest your client's position will be greatly improved if Rosenberg and Jensen are removed from the Court. We have a source that tells us this idea was researched by one called Einstein, who sits in a library on the sixth floor, I believe.'

Silence.

Gray continued. 'We have the story ready to run, but I wanted to give you the chance to comment. Would you care to comment, Mr. Velmano?'

'I have a headache.'

'Okay. Anything else?'

'Will you run the memo word for word?'

'Yes.'

'Will you run my picture?'

'Yes, It's an old one from a Senate hearing.'

'You son of a bitch.'

'Thank you. Anything else?'

'I notice you've waited until five o'clock. An hour earlier, and we could've run to court and stopped this damned thing.'

'Yes sir. It was planned that way.'

'You son of a bitch.'

'Okay.'

'You don't mind ruining people, do you?' His voice trailed off, and he was almost pitiful. What a marvelous quote. Gray had mentioned the recorder twice, but Velmano was too shocked to remember it.

'No sir. Anything else?'

'Tell Jackson Feldman the lawsuit will be filed at nine in the morning, just as soon as the courthouse opens.'

'I'll do that. Do you deny you wrote the memo?'

'Of course.'

'Do you deny the existence of the memo?'

'It's a fabrication.'

'There's no lawsuit, Mr. Velmano, and I think you know it.' Silence, then, 'You son of a bitch.'

The phones clicked, and they were listening to the dial tone. They smiled at each other in disbelief.

'Don't you want to be a journalist, Darby?' Smith Keen asked.

'Oh, this is fun,' she said. 'But I was almost mugged twice yesterday. No, thanks.'

Feldman stood and pointed to the recorder. 'I wouldn't use any of that.'

'But I sort of liked the part about ruining lives. And what about the lawsuit threats?' Gray asked.

'You don't need it, Gray. The story takes up the entire front page now. Maybe later.'

There was a knock at the door. It was Krauthammer. 'Voyles wants to see you,' he said to Feldman.

'Bring him in here.'

Gray stood quickly and Darby walked to the window. The sun was fading and the shadows were falling. Traffic inched along the street. There was no sign of Stump and his band of confederates, but they were there, no doubt waiting on darkness, no doubt plotting one last effort to kill her, either for prevention or revenge. Gray said he had a plan to exit the building without gunfire after the deadline. He wasn't specific.

Voyles entered with K. O. Lewis. Feldman introduced them to Gray Grantham, and to Darby Shaw. Voyles walked to her, smiling and looking up. 'So you're the one who started all this,' he said in an attempt at admiration. It didn't work.

She instantly despised him. 'I think it was Mattiece,' she said coolly. He turned away and took off the trench coat.

'Can we sit?' he asked in general.

They sat around the table – Voyles, Lewis, Feldman, Keen, Grantham, and Krauthammer. Darby stood by the window.

'I have some comments for the record,' Voyles announced, taking a sheet of paper from Lewis. Gray began taking notes.

'First, we received a copy of the pelican brief two weeks ago today, and submitted it to the White House on the same day. It was personally delivered by the deputy director, K. O. Lewis, to Mr. Fletcher Coal, who received it with our daily summary to the White House. Special agent Eric East was present during the meeting. We thought it raised enough questions to be pursued, but it was not pursued for six days, until Mr. Gavin Verheek, special counsel to the director, was found murdered in New Orleans. At that time, the FBI immediately began a full-scale investigation of Victor Mattiece. Over four hundred agents from twenty-seven offices have taken part in the investigation, logging over eleven thousand hours, interviewing over six hundred people, and going to five foreign countries. The investigation is continuing in full force at this time. We believe Victor Mattiece to be the prime suspect in the assassinations of Justices Rosenberg and Jensen, and at this time we are attempting to locate him.'

Voyles folded the paper and handed it back to Lewis.

'What will you do if you find Mattiece?' Grantham asked.

'Arrest him.'

'Do you have a warrant?'

'We'll have one soon.'

'Do you have any idea where he is?'

'Frankly, no. We've been trying to locate him for a week, with no success.'

'Did the White House interfere with your investigation of Mattiece?'

'I'll discuss it off the record. Agreed?'

Gray looked at the executive editor. 'Agreed,' Feldman said.

Voyles stared at Feldman, then Keen, then Krauthammer, then Grantham. 'We're off the record, right? You cannot use this under any circumstances. Do we understand this?'

They nodded and watched him carefully. Darby was watching too.

Voyles looked suspiciously at Lewis. 'Twelve days ago, in the Oval Office, the President of the United States asked me to ignore Victor Mattiece as a suspect. In his words, he asked me to back off.'

'Did he give a reason?' asked Grantham.

'The obvious. He said it would be very embarrassing and seriously damage his reelection efforts. He felt there was little merit to the pelican brief, and if it was investigated, then the press would learn of it, and he would suffer politically.'

Krauthammer listened with his mouth open. Keen stared at the table. Feldman hung on every word.

'Are you certain?' Gray asked.

'I recorded the conversation. I have a tape, which I will not allow anyone to hear unless the President first denies this.'

There was a long silence as they admired this mean little bastard and his tape recorder. A tape!

Feldman cleared his throat. 'You just saw the story. There was a delay by the FBI from the time it had the brief until it began its investigation. This must be explained in the story.'

'You have my statement. Nothing more.'

'Who killed Gavin Verheek?' Gray asked.

'I will not talk about the specifics of the investigation.'

'But do you know?'

'We have an idea. But that's all I'll say.'

Gray glanced around the table. It was obvious Voyles had nothing else to say now, and everyone relaxed at the same time. The editors savored the moment.

Voyles loosened his tie, and almost smiled. 'This is off the record, of course, but how did you guys find out about Morgan, the dead lawyer?'

'I will not discuss the specifics of the investigation,' Gray said with a wicked grin. They all laughed.

'What do you do now?' Krauthammer asked Voyles.

'There'll be a grand jury by noon tomorrow. Quick indictments. We'll try to find Mattiece, but it'll be difficult. We have no idea where he is. He's spent most of the past five years in the Bahamas, but owns homes in Mexico, Panama, and Paraguay.'

Voyles glanced at Darby for the second time. She was leaning against the wall by the window, hearing it all.

'What time does the first edition come off the press?' Voyles asked.

'They roll off all night, starting at ten-thirty,' said Keen.

'Which edition will this story run in?'

'Late City, a few minutes before midnight. It's the largest edition.'

'Will it have Coal's picture on the front?'

Keen looked at Krauthammer, who looked at Feldman. 'I guess it should. We'll quote you as saying the brief was personally delivered to Fletcher Coal, who we'll also quote as saying Mattiece gave the President four point two million. Yes, I think Mr. Coal should have his face on the front, along with everyone else.'

'I think so too,' Voyles said. 'If I have a man here at midnight, can I pick up a few copies of it?'

'Certainly,' Feldman said. 'Why?'

'Because I want to personally deliver it to Coal. I want to knock on his door at midnight, see him in his pajamas, and flash the paper in his face. Then I want to tell him I'll be back with a grand jury subpoena, and shortly after that I'll be back with an indictment. And shortly after that, I'll be back with the handcuffs.'

He said this with such pleasure it was frightening.

'I'm glad you don't carry a grudge,' Gray said. Only Smith Keen thought it was funny.

'Do you think he'll be indicted?' Krauthammer asked innocently.

Voyles glanced at Darby again. 'He'll take the fall for the President. He'd volunteer for a firing squad to save his boss.'

Feldman checked his watch and pushed away from the table.

'Could I ask a favor?' Voyles asked.

'Certainly. What?'

'I'd like to spend a few minutes alone with Ms. Shaw. That is, if she doesn't mind.'

Everyone looked at Darby, who shrugged her approval. The editors and K. O. Lewis stood in unison and filed out of the room. Darby took Gray's hand and asked him to stay. They sat opposite Voyles at the table.

'I wanted to talk in private,' Voyles said, looking at Gray.

'He stays,' she said. 'It's off the record.'

'Very well.'

She beat him to the punch. 'If you plan to interrogate me, I won't talk without an attorney present.'

He was shaking his head. 'Nothing like that. I was just wondering what's next for you.'

'Why should I tell you?'

'Because we can help.'

'Who killed Gavin?'

'Voyles hesitated. 'Off the record.'

'Off the record,' said Gray.

'I'll tell you who we think killed him, but first tell me how much you talked to him before he died.'

'We talked several times over the weekend. We were supposed to meet last Monday, and leave New Orleans.'

'When did you last talk to him?'

'Sunday night.'

'And where was he?'

'In his room at the Hilton.'

Voyles breathed deeply, and looked at the ceiling. 'And you discussed with him the meeting on Monday?'

'Yes.'

'Had you met him before?'

'No.'

'The man who killed him was the same man you were holding hands with when he lost his brains.'

She was afraid to ask. Gray did it for her. 'Who was that?'

'The great Khamel.'

She choked and covered her eyes, and tried to say something. But it wouldn't work.

'This is rather confusing,' Gray said, straining to be rational.

'Rather, yes. The man who killed Khamel is a contract operative hired independently by the CIA. He was on the scene when Callahan was killed, and I think he made contact with Darby.'

'Rupert,' she said quietly.

'That's not his real name, of course, but Rupert'll do. He's probably got twenty names. If it's who I think it is, he's a British chap who's very reliable.'

'Do you have any idea how confusing this is?' She asked.

'I can imagine.'

'Why was Rupert in New Orleans? Why was he following her?' Gray asked.

'It's a very long story, and I don't know all of it. I try to keep my distance from the CIA, believe me. I have enough to worry about. It goes back to Mattiece. A few years ago, he needed some money to move along his grand scheme. So he sold a piece of it to the Libyan government. I'm not sure if it was legal, but enter the CIA. Evidently they watched Mattiece and the Libyans with a great deal of interest, and when the litigation sprang up, the CIA monitored it. I don't think they suspected Mattiece in the Supreme Court killings, but Bob Gminski was handed a copy of your little brief just a few hours after we delivered a copy to the White House. Fletcher Coal gave it to him. I have no idea who Gminski told of the brief, but the wrong words hit the wrong ears, and twenty-four hours later, Mr. Callahan is dead. And you, my dear, were very lucky.'

'Then why don't I feel lucky?' she said.

'That doesn't explain Rupert,' Gray said.

'I don't know this for a fact, but I suspect Gminski immediately sent Rupert to follow Darby. I think the brief initially scared Gminski more than the rest of us. He probably sent Rupert to trail her, in part to watch, and in part to protect. Then the car exploded, and suddenly Mr. Mattiece just confirmed the brief. Why else would you kill Callahan and Darby? I have reason to believe there were dozens of CIA people in New Orleans hours after the car exploded.'

'But why?' Gray asked.

'The brief had been legitimized, and Mattiece was killing people. Most of his business is in New Orleans. And I think the CIA was very concerned about Darby. Lucky for her. They came through when it counted.'

'If the CIA moved so fast, why didn't you?' she asked.

'Fair question. We didn't think that much of the brief, and we didn't know half as much as the CIA. I swear, it seemed like such a long shot, and we had a dozen other suspects. We underestimated it. Plain and simple. Plus, the President asked us to back off, and it was easy to do because I'd never heard of Mattiece. Had no reason to. Then my friend Gavin got himself killed, and I sent in the troops.'

'Why would Coal give the brief to Gminski?' Gray asked.

'It scared him. And, truthfully, that's one reason we sent it over. Gminski is, well, he's Gminski, and he sometimes does things his way without regard for little obstacles like laws and such. Coal wanted the brief checked out, and he figured Gminski would do it quickly and quietly.'

'So Gminski didn't level with Coal.'

'He hates Coal, which is perfectly understandable. Gminski dealt with the President, and, no, he didn't level with him. It all happened so fast. Remember, Gminski, Coal, the President, and I first saw the brief just two weeks ago today. Gminski was probably waiting to tell the President some of the story, but just hadn't got the chance.'

Darby pushed her chair away, and walked back to the window. It was dark now, and the traffic was still slow and heavy. It was nice to have these mysteries revealed to her, but they created more mysteries. She just wanted to leave. She was tired of running and being chased; tired of playing reporter with Gray; tired of wondering who did what and why; tired of the guilt for writing the damned thing; tired of buying a new toothbrush every three days. She longed for a small house on a deserted stretch of beach with no phones and no people, especially ones hiding behind vehicles and buildings. She wanted to sleep for three days without nightmares and without seeing shadows. It was time to go.

Gray watched her carefully. 'She was followed to New York, then here,' he said to Voyles. 'Who is it?'

'Are you positive?' Voyles asked.

'They were on the street all day watching the building,' Darby said, nodding to the window.

'We've watched them,' Gray said. 'They're out there.'

Voyles seemed skeptical. 'Have you seen them before?' he asked Darby.

'One of them. He watched Thomas' memorial service in New Orleans. He chased me through the French Quarter. He almost found me in Manhattan, and I saw him chatting with another fella about five hours ago. I know it's him.'

'Who is it?' Gray asked Voyles again.

'I don't think CIA would chase you.'

'Oh, he chased me.'

'Do you see them now?'

'No. They disappeared two hours ago. But they're out there.'

Voyles stood and stretched his thick arms. He walked slowly around the table, unwrapping a cigar. 'Mind if I smoke?'

'Yes, I mind,' she said without looking at him. He laid it on the table.

'We can help,' he said.

'I don't want your help,' she said to the window.

'What do you want?'

'I want to leave the country, but when I do, I want to make damned sure no one follows. Not you, not them, not Rupert nor any of his pals.'

'You'll have to come back and testify before the grand jury.'

'Only if they can find me. I'm going to a place where subpoenas are frowned upon.'

'What about the trial? You'll be needed at trial.'

'That's at least a year from now. I'll think about it then.'

Voyles placed the cigar in his mouth, but did not light it. He paced and analyzed better with one between his teeth. 'I'll make you a deal.'

'I'm not in the mood for deals.' She was leaning against the wall now, looking at him and looking at Gray.

'It's a good one. I've got planes and helicopters and plenty of men who carry guns and are not the least bit afraid of those boys out there playing hide-and-seek. First, we'll get you out of the building, and no one will know it. Second, we'll put you on my plane and fly you anywhere you want. Third, you can disappear from there. You have my word we will not follow. But, and fourth, you allow me to contact you through Mr. Grantham here if, and only if, it becomes urgently necessary.'

She was looking at Gray as the offer was made, and it was obvious he liked the deal. She kept a poker face, but, damn, it sounded good. If she had trusted Gavin after the first phone call, he would be alive and she would never have held hands with Khamel. If she'd simply left New Orleans with him when he suggested, he would not have been murdered. She'd thought about this every five minutes for the past seven days.

This thing was bigger than she was. There comes a time when you give up and start trusting people. She didn't like this man, but for the past ten minutes he had been remarkably honest with her.

'Is it your plane and your pilots?'

'Yes.'

'Where is it?'

'Andrews.'

'Let's do it like this. I get on the plane, and it's headed for Denver. And no one is on it but me, Gray, and the pilots. And thirty minutes after we take off, I instruct the pilot to go to, let's say, Chicago. Can he do that?'

'He has to file a flight plan before he leaves.'

'I know. But you're the director of the FBI, and you can pull some strings.'

'Okay. What happens when you get to Chicago?'

'I get off the plane alone, and it returns to Andrews with Gray.'

'And what do you do in Chicago?'

'I get lost in a busy airport, and catch the first flight out.'

'That'll work, but you have my word we won't follow.'

'I know. Forgive me for being so cautious.'

'It's a deal. When do you wish to leave?'

She looked at Gray. 'When?'

'It'll take me an hour to revise it again, and add Mr. Voyles' comments.'

'An hour,' she said to Voyles.

'I'll wait.'

'Could we talk in private?' she said to Voyles while nodding at Gray.

'Certainly.' He grabbed his trench coat, and stopped at the door. He smiled at her. 'You're a helluva lady, Ms. Shaw. Your brains and guts are bringing down one of the sickest men in this country. I admire you. And I promise I'll always level with you.'

He stuck the cigar in the middle of his chubby smile and left the room.

They watched the door close. 'Do you think I'll be safe?' she asked.

'Yes. I think he's sincere. Plus, he has men with guns who can get you out of here. It's okay, Darby.'

'You can leave with me, can't you?'

'Sure.'

She walked to him and put her arms around his waist. He held her tightly, and closed his eyes.

At seven, the editors gathered around the table for the last time Tuesday night. They quickly read the section Gray added to include Voyles' comments. Feldman walked in late with an enormous smile.

'You will not believe this,' he said. 'I've had two phone calls. Ludwig called from China. The President found him there and begged him to hold the story for twenty-four hours. Ludwig said the man was near tears. Ludwig, being the gentleman, listened respectfully, and politely declined. The second call was from Judge Roland, an old friend of mine. Seems as though the boys at White and Blazevich called him away from the dinner table and requested permission to file an injunction tonight with an immediate hearing. Judge Roland listened quite disrespectfully, and impolitely declined.'

'Let's run this baby!' Krauthammer yelled.

CHAPTER FORTY-THREE

The takeoff was smooth and the jet was headed due west, supposedly for Denver. It was adequate but not luxurious, but then it was owned by the taxpayers and held by a man who cared nothing for the finer things. No good whiskey, Gray determined as he opened the cabinets. Voyles was an abstainer, and at the moment this really irritated Gray since he was a guest and dying of thirst. He found two semichilled Sprites in the refrigerator, and handed one to Darby. She popped the top of the can.

The jet appeared to be level. The copilot appeared in the door of their cabin. He was polite and introduced himself.

'We were told that we would have a new destination shortly after takeoff.'

'That's correct,' Darby said.

'Fine. Uh, we'll need to know something in about ten minutes.'

'Okay.'

'Is there any liquor on this thing?' Gray asked.

'Sorry.' The copilot smiled, and returned to the cockpit.

Darby and her long legs consumed most of the small sofa, but he was determined to join her. He lifted her feet and sat at the end of it. They were in his lap. Red toenails. He rubbed her ankles and thought only of this first major event – the holding of the feet. It was terribly intimate for him, but didn't seem to faze her. She was smiling a little now, unwinding. It was over.

'Were you scared?' he asked.

'Yes. And you?'

'Yes, but I felt safe. I mean, it's hard to feel vulnerable with six armed buddies using their bodies as shields. It's hard to feel watched in the rear of a van with no windows.'

'Voyles loved it, didn't he?'

'He was like Napoleon, making plans and directing troops. It's a big moment for him. He'll take a shot in the morning, but it'll bounce off. The only person who can fire him is the President, and I'd say Voyles has control of him at the moment.'

'And the murders are solved. He has to feel good about that.'

'I think we've added ten years to his career. What have we done!'

'I think he's cute,' Darby said. 'I didn't like him at first, but he sort of grows on you. And he's human. When he mentioned Verheek, I saw a trace of water in his eyes.'

'A real sweetheart. I'm sure Fletcher Coal will be delighted to see this cute little man in a few hours.'

Her feet were long and thin. Perfect, really. He rubbed along the top of them, and felt like a sophomore moving up from the knee on the second date. They were pale, and needed sun, and he knew that in a few short days they would be brown with sand permanently stuck between the toes. He had not been invited to visit later, and this was disturbing. He had no idea where she was going, and this was intentional. He was not certain she knew her destination.

The foot play reminded her of Thomas. He'd get half drunk and smear polish around the nails. With the jet humming and shaking softly, he was suddenly many miles removed from her. He'd been dead for two weeks, but it seemed much longer. There'd been so many changes. It was better this way. If she was at Tulane, walking by his office, seeing his classroom, talking to the other professors, staring at his apartment from the street, it would be awfully painful. The little reminders are nice for the long run, but during the mourning they get in the way.

She was a different person now, with a different life in a different place.

And a different man was rubbing her feet. He was an ass at first, cocky and abrasive, a typical reporter. But he was thawing rapidly, and under the jaded layer she was finding a warm man who obviously liked her very much.

'Tomorrow's a big day for you,' she said.

He took a sip of straight Sprite. He would pay an outrageous sum of money for a ice-cold imported beer in a green bottle. 'Big day,' he said, admiring the toes. It would be more than a big day, but he felt the need to understate it. At this moment, she had his attention, not the chaos of tomorrow.

'What'll happen?' she asked.

'I'll probably go back to the office and wait for it to hit. Smith Keen said he would be there all night. A lot of people will be in early. We'll gather in the conference room, and they'll bring more televisions. We'll spend the morning watching it break. It'll be great fun listening to the official White House response. White and Blazevich will say something. Who knows about Mattiece. Chief Runyan will have a comment. Voyles will be very visible. The lawyers will assemble grand juries. And the politicians will be delirious. They'll hold press conferences all day on Capitol Hill. It will be a rather significant news day. I hate you'll miss it.'

She gave a little sarcastic snort. 'What's your next story?'

'Probably Voyles and his tape. You have to anticipate a White House denial of any interference, and if the ink gets too hot for Voyles, he'll attack with a vengeance. I'd like to have the tape.'

'And after that?'

'Depends on a lot of unknowns. After six o'clock in the morning, the competition gets much stiffer. There'll be a million rumors and a thousand stories, but every paper in the country will be wedging in.'

'But you'll be the star,' she said with admiration, not sarcasm.

'Yeah, I'll get my fifteen minutes.'

The copilot knocked on the door and opened it. He looked at Darby.

'Atlanta,' she said, and he closed the door.

'Why Atlanta?' Gray asked.

'You ever changed planes at Atlanta?'

'Sure.'

'You ever got lost changing planes at Atlanta?'

'I think so.'

'I rest my case. It's huge and wonderfully busy.'

He emptied the can and set it on the floor. 'Where to from there?' He knew he shouldn't ask because she hadn't volunteered. But he wanted to know.

'I'll catch a quick flight somewhere. I'll do my four-airports-in-one-night routine. It's probably unnecessary, but I'll feel safer. I'll eventually land somewhere in the Caribbean.'

Somewhere in the Caribbean. That narrowed it to a thousand islands. Why was she so vague? Did she not trust him? He was sitting here playing with her feet and she wouldn't tell him where she was going.

'What do I tell Voyles?' he asked.

'I'll call you when I get there. Or I might drop you a line.'

Great! They could be pen pals. He could send her his stories and she could send postcards from the beach.

'Will you hide from me?' he asked, looking at her.

'I don't know where I'm going, Gray. I won't know until I get there.'

'But you'll call?'

'Eventually, yes. I promise.'

By 11 P.M., only five lawyers remained in the offices of White and Blazevich, and they were in Marty Velmano's on the tenth floor. Velmano, Sims Wakefield, Jarreld Schwabe, Nathaniel (Einstein) Jones, and a retired partner named Frank Cortz. Two bottles of Scotch sat on the edge of Velmano's desk. One was empty, the other almost there. Einstein sat alone in one corner, mumbling to himself. He had wild, curly gray hair and a pointed nose, and indeed looked crazy. Especially now. Sims Wakefield and Jarreld Schwabe sat in front of the desk with ties off and sleeves rolled up.

Cortz finished a phone chat with an aide to Victor Mattiece. He handed the phone to Velmano, who placed it on the desk.

'That was Strider,' Cortz reported. 'They're in Cairo in the penthouse suite of some hotel. Mattiece will not talk to us. Strider says he's over the edge, acting very bizarre. He's locked himself in a room, and, needless to say, he ain't coming to this side of the ocean. Strider says they've told the boys with the guns to get out of town immediately. The chase is off. The fat lady is singing.'

'So what're we supposed to do?' asked Wakefield.

'We're on our own,' said Cortz. 'Mattiece has washed his hands of us.'

They spoke quietly and deliberately. The screaming ended hours ago. Wakefield blamed Velmano for the memo. Velmano blamed Cortz for bringing in a sleazy client like Mattiece in the first place. That was twelve years ago, Cortz screamed back, and we've enjoyed his fees ever since. Schwabe blamed Velmano and Wakefield for being so careless with the memo. They dragged Morgan through the mud again and again. It had to be him. Einstein sat in the corner and watched them. But that was all behind them now.

'Grantham mentioned only me and Sims,' Velmano said. 'The rest of you guys may be safe.'

'Why don't you and Sims skip the country?' Schwabe said.

'I'll be in New York at 6 A.M.' Velmano said. 'Then to Europe for a month on the trains.'

'I can't run,' Wakefield said. 'I've got a wife and six kids.'

They'd heard him whine about his six kids for five hours now. As if they didn't have families. Velmano was divorced, and his two children were grown. They could handle it. And he could handle it. It was time to retire anyway. He had plenty of money stashed away, and he loved Europe, especially Spain, and so it was adios for him. He sort of pitied Wakefield, who was only forty-two and didn't have a lot of money. He earned well, but his wife was a spendthrift who had a penchant for babies. Wakefield was unbalanced at the moment.

'I don't know what I'll do,' Wakefield said for the thirtieth time. 'I just don't know.'

Schwabe tried to be a bit helpful. 'I think you should go home and tell your wife. I don't have one, but if I did I'd try to brace her for it.'

'I can't do that,' Wakefield said pitifully.

'Sure you can. You can tell her now, or wait six hours and she'll see your picture on the front page. You have to go tell her, Sims.'

'I can't do that.' He was almost in tears again.

Schwabe looked at Velmano and Cortz.

'What about my children?' he asked again. 'My oldest son is thirteen.' He rubbed his eyes.

'Come on, Sims. Get a grip,' Cortz said.

Einstein stood and walked to the door. 'I'll be at my place in Florida. Don't call unless it's urgent.' He opened the door and slammed it behind him.

Wakefield stood weakly and started for the door.

'Where are you going, Sims?' asked Schwabe.

'To my office.'

'What for?'

'I need to lie down. I'm okay.'

'Let me drive you home,' Schwabe said. They watched him carefully. He was opening the door.

'I'm fine,' he said, and he sounded stronger. He closed it when he left.

'You think he's okay?' Schwabe asked Velmano. 'He worries me.'

'I wouldn't say he's okay,' Velmano said. 'We've all had better days. Why don't you go check on him in a few minutes?'

'I'll do that,' Schwabe said.

Wakefield walked deliberately to the stairway and down one flight to the ninth floor. He picked up speed as he approached his office. He was crying when he locked the door behind him.

Do it quick! Forget the note. If you write it, you'll talk yourself out of it. There's a million in life insurance. He opened a desk drawer. Don't think about the kids. It would be the same if he died in a plane crash. He pulled the .38 from under a file. Do it quick! Don't look at their pictures on the wall.

Maybe they'll understand one day. He stuck it deep in his mouth, and pulled the trigger.

The limo stopped abruptly in front of the two-story home in Dumbarton Oaks, in upper Georgetown. It blocked the street and that was fine because it was twenty minutes after midnight, and there was no traffic. Voyles and two agents jumped from the rear of the car, and walked quickly to the front door. Voyles held a newspaper. He banged the door with his fist.

Coal was not asleep. He was sitting in the dark in the den in his pajamas and bathrobe, so Voyles was quite pleased when he opened his door.

'Nice pajamas,' Voyles said, admiring his pants.

Coal stepped onto the tiny concrete porch. The two agents were watching from the narrow sidewalk. 'What the hell do you want?' he asked slowly.

'Just brought you this,' Voyles said, sticking the paper in his face.

'Gotta a nice picture of you right next to the President hugging Mattiece. I know how much you like newspapers, so I thought I'd bring you one.'

'Your face'll be in it tomorrow,' Coal said as if he'd already written the story.

Voyles threw the paper at his feet, and started walking off. 'I got some tapes, Coal. You start lying, and I'll jerk your pants off in public.'

Coal stared at him, but said nothing.

Voyles was near the street. 'I'll be back in two days with a grand jury subpoena,' he yelled. 'I'll come about two in the morning and serve it myself.' He was at the car. 'Next I'll bring an indictment. Of course, by then your ass'll be history and the President'll have a new bunch of idiots telling him what to do.' He disappeared into the limo, and it sped away.

Coal picked up the paper, and went inside.

CHAPTER FORTY-FOUR

Gray and Smith Keen sat alone in the conference room, reading the words in print. He was many years beyond the excitement of seeing his stories on the front page, but this one brought a rush with it. There had been none bigger. The faces were lined neatly across the top: Mattiece hugging the President, Coal talking importantly on the phone in an offical White House photo, Velmano sitting before a Senate subcommittee, Wakefield cropped from a bar convention picture, Verheek smiling at the camera in an FBI release, Callahan from the yearbook, and Morgan in a photo taken from the video. Mrs. Morgan had consented. Paypur, the night police reporter, had told them about Wakefield an hour earlier. Gray was depressed about it. But he wouldn't blame himself.

They began drifting in around 3 A.M. Krauthammer brought a dozen doughnuts, and promptly ate four of them while he admired the front page. Ernie DeBasio was next. Said he hadn't slept any. Feldman arrived fresh and hyper. By four-thirty, the room was full and four televisions were going. CNN got it first, and within minutes the networks were live from the White House, which had no comment at the moment but Zikman would say something at seven.

With the exception of Wakefield's death, there was nothing new initially. The networks bounced back and forth between the White House, the Supreme Court, and the news desks. They waited at the Hoover Building, which was very quiet at the moment. They flashed the photos from the papers. They couldn't find Velmano. They speculated about Mattiece. CNN showed live footage of the Morgan house in Alexandria, but Morgan's father-in-law kept the cameras off the property. NBC had a reporter standing in front of the building where White and Blazevich had offices, but he had nothing new. And though she wasn't quoted in the story, there was no secret about the identity of the author of the brief. There was much speculation about Darby Shaw.

At seven, the room was packed and silent. The four screens were identical as Zikman walked nervously to the podium in the White House press room. He was tired and haggard. He read a short statement in which the White House admitted receiving the campaign money from a number of channels controlled by Victor Mattiece, but he emphatically denied any of the money was dirty. The President had met Mr. Mattiece only once, and that was when he was the Vice President. He had not spoken to the man since being elected President, and certainly did not consider him a friend, in spite of the money. The campaign had received over fifty million, and the President handled none of it. He had a committee for that. No one in the White House had attempted to interfere with the investigation of Victor Mattiece as a suspect, and any allegations to the contrary were flat wrong. Based on their limited knowledge, Mr. Mattiece no longer lived in this country. The President welcomes a full investigation into the allegations contained in the *Post* story, and if Mr. Mattiece was the perpetrator of these heinous crimes, then he must be brought to justice. This was simply a statement for the time being. A full press conference would follow. Zikman darted from the podium.

It was a weak performance by a troubled press secretary, and Gray was relieved. He suddenly found himself crowded, and needed fresh air. He found Smith Keen outside the door.

'Let's go eat breakfast,' he whispered.

'Sure.'

'I need to run by my apartment too, if you don't mind. I haven't seen it in four days.'

They flagged a cab on Fifteenth, and enjoyed the crisp autumn air rushing in the open windows.

'Where's the girl?' Keen asked.

'I have no idea. I last saw her in Atlanta, about nine hours ago. She said she was headed for the Caribbean.'

Keen was grinning. 'I assume you'll want a long vacation soon.'

'How'd you guess?'

'There's a lot of work to be done, Gray. Right now we're in the middle of the explosion, and the pieces start falling to earth very soon. You're the man of the hour, but you must keep pushing. You must pick up the pieces.'

'I know my job, Smith.'

'Yeah, but you've got this faraway look in your eyes. It worries me.'

'You're an editor. You get paid for worrying.'

They stopped at the intersection at Pennsylvania Avenue. The White House sat majestically before them. It was almost November, and the wind blew leaves across the lawn.

CHAPTER FORTY-FIVE

After eight days in the sun, the skin was brown enough and the hair was returning to its natural color. Maybe she hadn't ruined it. She walked miles up and down the beaches and ate nothing but broiled fish and island fruit. She slept a lot the first few days, then got tired of it.

She had spent the first night in San Juan, where she found a travel agent who claimed to be an expert on the Virgin Islands. The lady found a small room in a guest house in downtown Charlotte Amalie, on the island of St. Thomas. Darby wanted crowds and lots of traffic on narrow streets, at least for a couple of days. Charlotte Amalie was perfect. The guest house was on a hillside, four blocks away from the harbor, and her tiny room was on the third floor. There were no shutters or curtains on the cracked window, and the sun woke her the first morning, a sensuous wake-up call that summoned her to the window and displayed for her the majesty of the harbor. It was breathtaking. A dozen cruise ships of all sizes sat perfectly still in the shimmering water. They stretched in a careless formation almost to the horizon. In the foreground, near the pier, a hundred sailboats dotted the harbor and seemed to keep the bulky tourist ships at bay. The water under the sailboats was a clear, soft blue, and as smooth as glass. It gently curled around Hassel Island, and grew darker until it was indigo and then violet as it touched the horizon. A perfect row of cumulus clouds marked the line where the water met the sky.

Her watch was in a bag, and she had no plans to wear it for at least six months. But she glanced at her wrist anyway. The window opened with a strain, and the sounds of the shopping district echoed through the streets. The warmth filtered in like a sauna.

She stood in the small window for an hour that first morning on the island, and watched the harbor come to life. There was no hurry. It woke gently as the big ships inched through the water, and soft voices came from the decks of the sailboats. The first person she saw on a boat jumped into the water for a morning swim.

She could grow accustomed to this. Her room was small but clean. There was no air conditioner, but the fan worked fine and it was not unpleasant. The water ran most of the time. She decided to stay here a couple of days, maybe a week. The building was one of dozens packed tightly together along streets that ran down to the harbor. For the moment, she liked the safety of crowds and streets. She could walk and find whatever she needed. St. Thomas was known for its shopping, and she cherished the idea of buying clothes she could keep.

There were fancier rooms, but this would do for now. When she left San Juan, she vowed to stop looking over her shoulder. She'd seen the paper in Miami, and she'd watched the frenzy on a television in the airport, and she knew Mattiece had disappeared. If they were stalking now, it was simply revenge. And if they found her after the crisscrossing journey she had taken, then they were not human, and she would never lose them.

They weren't back there, and she believed this. She stayed close to the small room for two days, never venturing far. The shopping district was a short walk away. Only four blocks long and two blocks deep, it was a maze of hundreds of small and unique stores selling everything. The sidewalks and alleys were crammed with Americans from the big ships. She was just another tourist with a wide straw hat and colorful shorts.

She bought her first novel in a year and a half, and read it in two days while lying on the small bed under the gentle rush from the ceiling fan. She vowed to read nothing about the law until she was fifty. At least once an hour, she walked to the open window and studied the harbor. Once she counted twenty cruise ships waiting to dock.

The room served its purpose. She spent time with Thomas, and cried, and was determined to do it for the last time. She wanted to leave the guilt and pain in this tiny corner of Charlotte Amalie, and exit with the good memories and a clean conscience. It was not as difficult as she tried to make it, and by the third day there were no more tears. She'd thrown the paperback only once.

On the fourth morning, she packed her new bags and took a ferry to Cruz Bay, twenty minutes away on the island of St. John. She took a taxi along the North Shore Road. The windows were down and the wind blew across the backseat. The music was a rhythmic mixture of blues and reggae. The cabdriver tapped the wheel and sang along. She tapped her foot and closed her eyes to the breeze. It was intoxicating.

He left the road at Maho Bay, and drove slowly toward the water. She'd picked this spot from a hundred islands because it was undeveloped. Only a handful of beach houses and cottages were permitted in this bay. The driver stopped on a narrow, tree-lined road, and she paid him.

The house was almost at the point where the mountain met the sea. The architecture was pure Caribbean – white wood frame under a red tile roof – and built barely on the incline to provide for the view. She walked down a short trail from the road, and up the steps to the house. It was a single story with two bedrooms and a porch facing the water. It cost two thousand a week, and she had it for a month.

She placed her bags on the floor of the den, and walked to her porch.

The beach started thirty feet below her. The waves rolled silently to the shore. Two sailboats sat motionless in the bay, which was secluded by mountains on three sides. A rubber raft full of kids splashing moved aimlessly between the boats.

The nearest dwelling was down the beach. She could barely see its roof above the trees. A few bodies relaxed in the sand. She quickly changed into a tiny bikini, and walked to the water.

It was almost dark when the taxi finally stopped at the trail. He got out, paid the driver, and looked at the lights as the cab drove in front of him and disappeared. He had one bag, and he eased along the trail to the house, which was unlocked. The lights were on. He found her on the porch, sipping a frozen drink and looking like a native with bronze skin.

She was waiting on him, and this was so damned important. He didn't want to be treated like a houseguest. Her face smiled instantly, and she set her drink on the table.

They kissed on the porch for a long minute.

'You're late,' she said as they held each other.

'This was not the easiest place to find,' Gray said. He was rubbing her back, which was bare down to the waist where a long skirt began and covered most of the legs. He would see them later.

'Isn't it beautiful?' she said, looking at the bay.

'It's magnificent,' he said. He stood behind her as they watched a sailboat drift toward the sea. He held her shoulders. 'You're gorgeous.'

'Let's go for a walk.'

He changed quickly into a pair of shorts, and found her waiting by the water. They held hands and walked slowly.

'Those legs need work,' she said.

'Rather pale, aren't they?' he said.

Yes, she thought, they were pale, but they weren't bad. Not bad at all. The stomach was flat. A week on the beach with her, and he'd look like a lifeguard. They splashed water with their feet.

'You left early,' she said.

'I got tired of it. I've written a story a day since the big one, yet they want more. Keen wanted this, and Feldman wanted that, and I was working eighteen hours a day. Yesterday I said good-bye.'

'I haven't seen a paper in a week,' she said.

'Coal quit. They've set him up to take the fall, but indictments look doubtful. I don't think the President did much, really. He's just dumb and can't help it. You read about Wakefield?'

'Yes.'

'Velmano, Schwabe, and Einstein have been indicted, but they can't find Velmano. Mattiece, of course, has been indicted, along with four of his people. There'll be more indictments later. It dawned on me a few days ago that there was no big cover-up at the White House, so I lost steam. I think it killed his reelection, but he's not a felon. The city's a circus.'

They walked in silence as it grew darker. She'd heard enough of this, and he was sick of it too. There was half a moon, and it reflected on the still water. She put her arm around his waist, and he pulled her closer. They were in the sand, away from the water. The house was a half a mile behind them.

'I've missed you,' she said softly.

He breathed deeply but said nothing.

'How long will you stay?' she asked.

'I don't know. A couple of weeks. Maybe a year. It's up to you.'

'How about a month?'

'I can do a month.'

She smiled at him, and his knees were weak. She looked at the bay, at the moon's reflection in the center of it as the sail-boat crawled by. 'Let's take it a month at a time, okay Gray?'

'Perfect.'

A Time to Kill

To Renée,
A woman of uncommon beauty,
A fiercely loyal friend,
A compassionate critic,
A doting mother,
A perfect wife.

AUTHOR'S NOTE

Since I am prone to start projects that never quite get finished, my goal when I began writing this book was simply to complete it. I could envision a neat pile of typed pages over in the corner of my office, and one day I would be able to point to it with some measure of pride and explain to clients and friends that it was a novel I had written. Surely, somewhere in the deep recesses of my mind, I dreamed of getting it published, but I honestly can't remember such thoughts, at least not when I started writing. It would become my first prolonged effort at fiction.

I began in the fall of 1984, just three years out of law school and still very wet behind the ears. In those early days of my legal career I spent many hours in courtrooms, watching good lawyers try their cases. I have always been fascinated by courtrooms – still am. People discuss things in open court that they wouldn't dare mention outside their homes. The greatest dramas occur not on screens or stages, but in countless courtrooms across this country.

One day I stumbled upon a horrible trial in which a young girl testified against the man who brutally raped her. It was a gut-wrenching experience for me, and I was only a spectator. One moment she was courageous, the next pitifully frail. I was mesmerized. I could not imagine the nightmare she and her family had been through. I wondered what I would do if she were my daughter. As I watched her suffer before the jury, I wanted personally to shoot the rapist. For one brief yet interminable moment, I wanted to be her father. I wanted justice. There was a story there.

I became obsessed with the idea of a father's retribution. What would a jury of average and ordinary people do to such a father? Naturally there would be a great deal of sympathy, but would there be enough for an acquittal? The idea for this novel emerged over a three-month period in which I thought of little else.

I wrote the first chapter in longhand on a legal pad, and asked Renée, my wife, to read it. She was impressed, and said she would like to read the second chapter. A month later I gave her chapters two and three, and she said she was hooked. Renée reads five or six novels a week – mysteries, suspense, thrillers, espionage, all sorts of fiction – and she has little patience with a story that doesn't work.

I approached the writing of this book much like a hobby, an hour here and an hour there, with a somewhat disciplined effort to write at least a page a day. I never abandoned it. I remember a four-week period in which nothing was written. I occasionally skipped a day, but for the most part I plowed ahead with blind diligence. I thought the story was wonderful, but I wasn't sure about the writing. Renée liked it, so I kept going.

After a year, I was amazed at how quickly the pages had piled up, and I realized that the book was half finished. My original goal was forgotten, and I caught myself thinking of publishing contracts and royalty statements and fancy lunches with agents and editors – the dreams of every unpublished novelist.

Three years after I started, Renée read the last chapter and we shipped it off to New York. The working title was *Deathknell,* a bad idea that was scrapped as soon as the manuscript landed in the office of my new agent, Jay Garon. Jay had seen the first three chapters, and immediately sent me a contract of representation. Sixteen other agents had passed, as well as a dozen publishers. Jay took the manuscript, and told me to start writing another book. I followed his advice.

A year passed and nothing happened. I was deep into the writing of *The Firm* when Jay called in April 1988 with the wonderful news that this book would indeed be published. Bill Thompson at Wynwood Press had read the manuscript and immediately bought it. Under his guidance, I worked through countless revisions and found a new title, *A Time to Kill.* I think it was the sixth or seventh one I decided on. I'm not good with titles.

Wynwood printed 5,000 copies and published the book in June 1989. It sold well within a hundred miles of home, but was neglected by the rest of the world. There was no paperback deal, no foreign rights. But it was a first novel, and most of them are ignored. Better things were just around the corner.

I finished *The Firm* in 1989, and sent it to Jay. Doubleday/Dell bought it, and when it was published in hardcover in March 1991, my writing career took a dramatic turn. The success of *The Firm* has aroused new interest in *A Time to Kill.*

There's a lot of autobiography in this book. I no longer practice law, but for ten years I did so in a manner very similar to Jake Brigance. I represented people, never banks or insurance companies or big corporations. I was a street lawyer. Jake and I are the same age. I played quarterback in high school, though not very well. Much of what he says and does is what I think I would say and do under the circumstances. We both drive Saabs. We've both felt the unbearable pressure of murder trials, which is something I tried to capture in the story. We've both lost sleep over clients and vomited in courthouse rest rooms.

This one came from the heart. It's a first novel, and at times it rambles, but I wouldn't change a word if given the chance.

Oxford, Mississippi
January 30, 1992

CHAPTER ONE

Billy Ray Cobb was the younger and smaller of the two rednecks. At twenty-three he was already a three-year veteran of the state penitentiary at Parchman. Possession, with intent to sell. He was a lean, tough little punk who had survived prison by somehow maintaining a ready supply of drugs that he sold and sometimes gave to the blacks and the guards for protection. In the year since his release he had continued to prosper, and his small-time narcotics business had elevated him to the position of one of the more affluent rednecks in Ford County. He was a businessman, with employees, obligations, deals, everything but taxes. Down at the Ford place in Clanton he was known as the last man in recent history to pay cash for a new pickup truck. Sixteen thousand cash, for a custom-built, four-wheel drive, canary yellow, luxury Ford pickup. The fancy chrome wheels and mudgrip racing tires had been received in a business deal. The rebel flag hanging across the rear window had been stolen by Cobb from a drunken fraternity boy at an Ole Miss football game. The pickup was Billy Ray's most prized possession. He sat on the tailgate drinking a beer, smoking a joint, watching his friend Willard take his turn with the black girl.

Willard was four years older and a dozen years slower. He was generally a harmless sort who had never been in serious trouble and had never been seriously employed. Maybe an occasional fight with a night in jail, but nothing that would distinguish him. He called himself a pulpwood cutter, but a bad back customarily kept him out of the woods. He had hurt his back working on an offshore rig somewhere in the Gulf, and the oil company paid him a nice settlement, which he lost when his ex-wife cleaned him out. His primary vocation was that of a part-time employee of Billy Ray Cobb, who didn't pay much but was liberal with his dope. For the first time in years Willard could always get his hands on something. And he always needed something. He'd been that way since he hurt his back.

She was ten, and small for her age. She lay on her elbows, which were stuck and bound together with yellow nylon rope. Her legs were spread grotesquely with the right foot tied tight to an oak sapling and the left to a rotting, leaning post of a long-neglected fence. The ski rope had cut into her ankles and the blood ran down her legs. Her face was bloody and swollen, with one eye bulging and closed and the other eye half open so she could see the other white man sitting on the truck. She did not look at the man on top of her. He was breathing hard and sweating and cursing. He was hurting her.

When he finished, he slapped her and laughed, and the other man laughed in return, then they laughed harder and rolled around the grass by the truck like two crazy men, screaming and laughing. She turned away from them and cried softly, careful to keep herself quiet. She had been slapped earlier for crying and screaming. They promised to kill her if she didn't keep quiet.

They grew tired of laughing and pulled themselves onto the tailgate, where Willard cleaned himself with the little nigger's shirt, which by now was soaked with blood and sweat. Cobb handed him a cold beer from the cooler and commented on the humidity. They watched her as she sobbed and made strange, quiet sounds, then became still. Cobb's beer was half empty, and it was not cold anymore. He threw it at the girl. It hit her in the stomach, splashing white foam, and it rolled off in the dirt near some other cans, all of which had originated from the same cooler. For two six-packs now they had thrown their half-empty cans at her and laughed. Willard had trouble with the target, but Cobb was fairly accurate. They were not ones to waste beer, but the heavier cans could be felt better and it was great fun to watch the foam shoot everywhere.

The warm beer mixed with the dark blood and ran down her face and neck into a puddle behind her head. She did not move.

Willard asked Cobb if he thought she was dead. Cobb opened another beer and explained that she was not dead because niggers generally could not be killed by kicking and beating and raping. It took much more, something like a knife or a gun or a rope to dispose of a nigger. Although he had never taken part in such a killing, he had lived with a bunch of niggers in prison and knew all about them. They were always killing each other, and they always used a weapon of some sort. Those who were just beaten and raped never died. Some of the whites were beaten and raped, and some of them died. But none of the niggers. Their heads were harder. Willard seemed satisfied.

Willard asked what he planned to do now that they were through with her. Cobb sucked on his joint, chased it with beer, and said he wasn't through. He bounced from the tailgate and staggered across the small clearing to where she was tied. He cursed her and screamed at her to wake up, then he poured cold beer in her face, laughing like a crazy man.

She watched him as he walked around the tree on her right side, and she stared at him as he stared between her legs. When he lowered his pants she turned to the left and closed her eyes. He was hurting her again.

She looked out through the woods and saw something – a man running wildly through the vines and underbrush. It was her daddy, yelling and pointing at her and coming desperately to save her. She cried out for him, and he disappeared. She fell asleep.

When she awoke one of the men was lying under the tailgate, the other under a tree. They were asleep. Her arms and legs were numb. The blood and beer and urine had mixed with the dirt underneath her to form a sticky paste that glued her small body to the ground and crackled when she moved and wiggled. Escape, she thought, but her mightiest efforts moved her only a few inches to the right. Her feet were tied so high her buttocks barely touched the ground. Her legs and arms were so deadened they refused to move.

She searched the woods for her daddy and quietly called his name. She waited, then slept again.

When she awoke the second time they were up and moving around. The tall one staggered to her with a small knife. He grabbed her left ankle and sawed furiously on the rope until it gave way. Then he freed the right leg, and she curled into a fetal position with her back to them.

Cobb strung a length of quarter-inch ski rope over a limb and tied a loop in one end with a slip knot. He grabbed her and put the noose around her head, then walked across the clearing with the other end of the rope and sat on the tailgate, where Willard was smoking a fresh joint and grinning at Cobb for what he was about to do. Cobb pulled the rope tight, then gave a vicious yank, bouncing the little nude body along the ground and stopping it directly under the limb. She gagged and coughed, so he kindly loosened the rope to spare her a few more minutes. He tied the rope to the bumper and opened another beer.

They sat on the tailgate drinking, smoking, and staring at her. They had been at the lake most of the day, where Cobb had a friend with a boat and some extra girls who were supposed to be easy but turned out to be untouchable. Cobb had been generous with his drugs and beer, but the girls did not reciprocate. Frustrated, they left the lake and were driving to no place in particular when they happened across the girl. She was walking along a gravel road with a sack of groceries when Willard nailed her in the back of the head with a beer can.

'You gonna do it?' asked Willard, his eyes red and glazed.

Cobb hesitated. 'Naw, I'll let you do it. It was your idea.'

Willard took a drag on his joint, then spit and said, 'Wasn't my idea. You're the expert on killin' niggers. Do it.'

Cobb untied the rope from the bumper and pulled it tight. It peeled bark from the limb and sprinkled fine bits of elm around the girl, who was watching them carefully now. She coughed.

Suddenly, she heard something – like a car with loud pipes. The two men turned quickly and looked down the dirt road to the highway in the distance. They cursed and scrambled around, one slamming the tailgate and the other running toward her. He tripped and landed near her. They cursed each other while they grabbed her, removed the rope from her neck, dragged her to the pickup and threw her over the tailgate into the bed of the truck. Cobb slapped her and threatened to kill her if she did not lie still and keep quiet. He said he would take her home if she stayed down and did as told; otherwise, they would kill her. They slammed the doors and sped onto the dirt road. She was going home. She passed out.

Cobb and Willard waved at the Firebird with the loud pipes as it passed them on the narrow dirt road. Willard checked the back to make sure the little nigger was lying down. Cobb turned onto the highway and raced away.

'What now?' Willard asked nervously.

'Don't know,' Cobb answered nervously. 'But we gotta do something fast before she gets blood all over my truck. Look at her back there, she's bleedin' all over the place.'

Willard thought for a minute while he finished a beer. 'Let's throw her off a bridge,' he said proudly.

'Good idea. Damned good idea.' Cobb slammed on the brakes. 'Gimme a beer,' he ordered Willard, who stumbled out of the truck and fetched two beers from the back.

'She's even got blood on the cooler,' he reported as they raced off again.

Gwen Hailey sensed something horrible. Normally she would have sent one of the three boys to the store, but they were being punished by their father and had been sentenced to weed-pulling in the garden. Tonya had been to the store before by herself – it was only a mile away – and had proven reliable. But after two hours Gwen sent the boys to look for their little sister. They figured she was down at the Pounders' house playing with the many Pounders kids, or maybe she had ventured past the store to visit her best friend, Bessie Pierson.

Mr. Bates at the store said she had come and gone an hour earlier. Jarvis, the middle boy, found a sack of groceries beside the road.

Gwen called her husband at the paper mill, then loaded Carl Lee, Jr., into the car and began driving the gravel roads around the store. They drove to a settlement of ancient shotgun houses on Graham Plantation to check with an aunt. They stopped at Broadway's store a mile from Bates Grocery and were told by a group of old black men that she had not been seen. They crisscrossed the gravel roads and dusty field roads for three square miles around their house.

Cobb could not find a bridge unoccupied by niggers with fishing poles. Every bridge they approached had four or five niggers hanging off the sides with large straw hats and cane poles, and under every bridge on the banks there would be another group sitting on buckets with the same straw hats and cane poles, motionless except for an occasional swat at a fly or a slap at a mosquito.

He was scared now. Willard had passed out and was of no help, and he was left alone to dispose of the girl in such a way that she could never tell. Willard snored as he frantically drove the gravel roads and county roads in search of a bridge or ramp on some river where he could stop and toss her without being seen by half a dozen niggers with straw hats. He looked in the mirror and saw her trying to stand. He slammed his brakes, and she crashed into the front of the bed, just under the window. Willard ricocheted off the dash into the floorboard, where he continued to snore. Cobb cursed them both equally.

Lake Chatulla was nothing more than a huge, shallow, man-made mudhole with a grass-covered dam running exactly one mile along one end. It sat in the far southwest corner of Ford County, with a few acres in Van Buren County. In the spring it would hold the distinction of being the largest body of water in Mississippi. But by late summer the rains were long gone, and the sun would cook the shallow water until the lake would dehydrate. Its once ambitious shorelines would retreat and move much closer together, creating a depthless basin of reddish brown water. It was fed from all directions by innumerable streams, creeks, sloughs, and a couple of currents large enough to be named rivers. The existence of all these tributaries necessarily gave rise to a good number of bridges near the lake.

It was over these bridges the yellow pickup flew in an all-out effort to find a suitable place to unload an unwanted passenger. Cobb was desperate. He knew of one other bridge, a narrow wooden one over Foggy Creek. As he approached, he saw niggers with cane poles, so he turned off a side road and stopped the truck. He lowered the tailgate, dragged her out, and threw her in a small ravine lined with kudzu.

Carl Lee Hailey did not hurry home. Gwen was easily excited, and she had called the mill numerous times when she thought the children had been kidnapped. He punched out at quitting time, and made the thirty-minute drive home in thirty minutes. Anxiety hit him when he turned onto his gravel drive and saw the patrol car parked next to the front porch. Other cars belonging to Gwen's family were scattered along the long drive and in the yard, and there was one car he didn't recognize. It had cane poles sticking out the side windows, and there were at least seven straw hats sitting in it.

Where were Tonya and the boys?

As he opened the front door he heard Gwen crying. To his right in the small living room he found a crowd huddled above a small figure lying on the couch. The child was covered with wet towels and surrounded by crying relatives. As he moved to the couch the crying stopped and the crowd backed away. Only Gwen stayed by the girl. She softly stroked her hair. He knelt beside the couch and touched the girl's shoulder. He spoke to his daughter, and she tried to smile. Her face was bloody pulp covered with knots and lacerations. Both eyes were swollen shut and bleeding. His eyes watered as he looked at her tiny body, completely wrapped in towels and bleeding from ankles to forehead.

Carl Lee asked Gwen what happened. She began shaking and wailing, and was led to the kitchen by her brother. Carl Lee stood and turned to the crowd and demanded to know what happened.

Silence.

He asked for the third time. The deputy, Willie Hastings, one of Gwen's cousins, stepped forward and told Carl Lee that some people were fishing down by Foggy Creek when they saw Tonya lying in the middle of the road. She told them her daddy's name, and they brought her home.

Hastings shut up and stared at his feet.

Carl Lee stared at him and waited. Everyone else stopped breathing and watched the floor.

'What happened, Willie?' Carl Lee yelled as he stared at the deputy.

Hastings spoke slowly, and while staring out the window repeated what Tonya had told her mother about the white men and their pickup, and the rope and the trees, and being hurt when they got on her. Hastings stopped when he heard the siren from the ambulance.

The crowd filed solemnly through the front door and waited on the porch, where they watched the crew unload a stretcher and head for the house.

The paramedics stopped in the yard when the front door opened and Carl Lee walked out with his daughter in his arms. He whispered gently to her as huge tears dripped from his chin. He walked to the rear of the ambulance and stepped inside. The paramedics closed the door and carefully removed her from his embrace.

CHAPTER TWO

Ozzie Walls was the only black sheriff in Mississippi. There had been a few others in recent history, but for the moment he was the only one. He took great pride in that fact, since Ford County was seventy-four percent white and the other black sheriffs had been from much blacker counties. Not since Reconstruction had a black sheriff been elected in a white county in Mississippi.

He was raised in Ford County, and he was kin to most of the blacks and a few of the whites. After desegregation in the late sixties, he was a member of the first mixed graduating class at Clanton High School. He wanted to play football nearby at Ole Miss, but there were already two blacks on the team. He starred instead at Alcorn State, and was a defensive tackle for the Rams when a knee injury sent him back to Clanton. He missed football, but enjoyed being the high sheriff, especially at election time when he received more white votes than his white opponents. The white kids loved him because he was a hero, a football star who had played on TV and had his picture in magazines. Their parents respected him and voted for him because he was a tough cop who did not discriminate between black punks and white punks. The white politicians supported him because, since he became the sheriff, the Justice Department stayed out of Ford County. The blacks adored him because he was Ozzie, one of their own.

He skipped supper and waited in his office at the jail for Hastings to report from the Hailey house. He had a suspect. Billy Ray Cobb was no stranger to the sheriff's office. Ozzie knew he sold drugs – he just couldn't catch him. He also knew Cobb had a mean streak.

The dispatcher called in the deputies, and as they reported to the jail Ozzie gave them instructions to locate, but not arrest, Billy Ray Cobb. There were twelve deputies in all – nine white and three black. They fanned out across the county in search of a fancy yellow Ford pickup with a rebel flag in the rear window.

When Hastings arrived he and the sheriff left for the Ford County hospital. As usual, Hastings drove and Ozzie gave orders on the radio. In the waiting room on the second floor they found the Hailey clan. Aunts, uncles, grandparents, friends, and strangers crowded into the small room and some waited in the narrow hallway. There were whispers and quiet tears. Tonya was in surgery.

Carl Lee sat on a cheap plastic couch in a dark corner with Gwen next to him and the boys next to her. He stared at the floor and did not notice the crowd. Gwen laid her head on his shoulder and cried softly.

The boys sat rigidly with their hands on knees, occasionally glancing at their father as if waiting on words of reassurance.

Ozzie worked his way through the crowd, quietly shaking hands and patting backs and whispering that he would catch them. He knelt before Carl Lee and Gwen. 'How is she?' he asked. Carl Lee did not see him. Gwen cried louder and the boys sniffed and wiped tears. He patted Gwen on the knee and stood. One of her brothers led Ozzie and Hastings out of the room into the hall, away from the family. He shook Ozzie's hand and thanked him for coming.

'How is she?' Ozzie asked.

'Not too good. She's in surgery and most likely will be there for a while. She's got broken bones and a bad concussion. She's beat up real bad. There's rope burns on her neck like they tried to hang her.'

'Was she raped?' he asked, certain of the answer.

'Yeah. She told her momma they took turns on her and hurt her real bad. Doctors confirmed it.'

'How's Carl Lee and Gwen?'

'They're tore up pretty bad. I think they're in shock. Carl Lee ain't said a word since he got here.'

Ozzie assured him they would find the two men, and it wouldn't take long, and when they found them they would be locked up someplace safe. The brother suggested he should hide them in another jail, for their own safety.

Three miles out of Clanton, Ozzie pointed to a gravel driveway. 'Pull in there,' he told Hastings, who turned off the highway and drove into the front yard of a dilapidated house trailer. It was almost dark.

Ozzie took his night stick and banged violently on the front door. 'Open up, Bumpous!'

The trailer shook and Bumpous scrambled to the bathroom to flush a fresh joint.

'Open up, Bumpous!' Ozzie banged. 'I know you're in there. Open up or I'll kick in the door.'

Bumpous yanked the door open and Ozzie walked in. 'You know, Bumpous, evertime I visit you I smell somethin' funny and the commode's flushin'. Get some clothes on. I gotta job for you.'

'W-what?'

'I'll explain it outside where I can breathe. Just get some clothes on and hurry.'

'What if I don't want to?'

'Fine. I'll see your parole officer tomorrow.'

'I'll be out in a minute.'

Ozzie smiled and walked to his car. Bobby Bumpous was one of his favorites. Since his parole two years earlier, he had led a reasonably clean life, occasionally succumbing to the lure of an easy drug sale for a quick buck. Ozzie watched him like a hawk and knew of such transactions, and Bumpous knew Ozzie knew; therefore, Bumpous was usually most eager to help his friend, Sheriff Walls. The plan was to eventually use Bumpous to nail Billy Ray Cobb for dealing, but that would be postponed for now.

After a few minutes he marched outside, still tucking his shirttail and zipping his pants. 'Who you lookin' for?' he demanded.

'Billy Ray Cobb.'

'That's no problem. You can find him without me.'

'Shut up and listen. We think Cobb was involved in a rape this afternoon. A black girl was raped by two white men, and I think Cobb was there.'

'Cobb ain't into rape, Sheriff. He's into drugs, remember?'

'Shut up and listen. You find Cobb and spend some time with him. Five minutes ago his truck was spotted at Huey's. Buy him a beer. Shoot some pool, roll dice, whatever. Find out what he did today. Who was he with? Where'd he go? You know how he likes to talk, right?'

'Right.'

'Call the dispatcher when you find him. They'll call me. I'll be somewhere close. You understand?'

'Sure, Sheriff. No problem.'

'Any questions?'

'Yeah. I'm broke. Who's gonna pay for this?'

Ozzie handed him a twenty and left. Hastings drove in the direction of Huey's, down by the lake.

'You sure you can trust him?' Hastings asked.

'Who?'

'That Bumpous kid.'

'Sure I trust him. He's proved very reliable since he was paroled. He's a good kid tryin' to go straight, for the most part. He supports his local sheriff and would do anything I ask.'

'Why?'

'Because I caught him with ten ounces of pot a year ago. He'd been outta jail about a year when I caught his brother with an ounce, and I told him he was lookin' at thirty years. He started cryin' and carryin' on, cried all night in his cell. By mornin' he was ready to talk. Told me his supplier was his brother, Bobby. So I let him go and went to see Bobby. I knocked on his door and I could hear the commode flushin'. He wouldn't come to the door, so I kicked it in. I found him in his underwear in the bathroom tryin' to unstop the commode. There was dope all over the place. Don't know how much he flushed, but most of it was comin' back out in the overflow. Scared him so bad he wet his drawers.'

'You kiddin'?'

'Nope. The kid pissed all over himself. He was a sight standin' there with wet drawers, a plunger in one hand, dope in the other, and the room fillin' up with commode water.'

'What'd you do?'

'Threatened to kill him.'

'What'd he do?'

'Started cryin'. Cried like a baby. Cried 'bout his momma and prison and all this and that. Promised he'd never screw up again.'

'You arrest him?'

'Naw, I just couldn't. I talked real ugly to him and threatened him some more. I put him on probation right there in his bathroom. He's been fun to work with ever since.'

They drove by Huey's and saw Cobb's truck in the gravel parking lot with a dozen other pickups and four-wheel drives. They parked behind a black church on a hill up the highway from Huey's, where they had a good view of the honky tonk, or tonk as it was affectionately called by the patrons. Another patrol car hid behind some trees at the other end of the highway. Moments later Bumpous flew by and wheeled into the parking lot. He locked his brakes, spraying gravel and dust, then backed next to Cobb's truck. He looked around and casually entered Huey's. Thirty minutes later the dispatcher advised Ozzie that the informant had found the subject, a male white, at Huey's, an establishment on Highway 305 near the lake. Within minutes two more patrol cars were hidden close by. They waited.

'What makes you so sure it's Cobb?' Hastings asked.

'I ain't sure. I just got a hunch. The little girl said it was a truck with shiny wheels and big tires.'

'That narrows it down to two thousand.'

'She also said it was yellow, looked new, and had a big flag hangin' in the rear window.'

'That brings it down to two hundred.'

'Maybe less than that. How many of those are as mean as Billy Ray Cobb?'

'What if it ain't him?'

'It is.'

'If it ain't?'

'We'll know shortly. He's got a big mouth, 'specially when he's drinkin'.'

For two hours they waited and watched pickups come and go. Truck drivers, pulpwood cutters, factory workers, and farmhands parked their pickups and jeeps in the gravel and strutted inside to drink, shoot pool, listen to the band, but mainly to look for stray women. Some would leave and walk next door to Ann's Lounge, where they would stay for a few minutes and return to Huey's. Ann's Lounge was darker both inside and out, and it lacked the colorful beer signs and live music that made Huey's such a hit with the locals. Ann's was known for its drug traffic, whereas Huey's had it all – music, women, happy hours, poker machines, dice, dancing, and plenty of fights. One brawl spilled through the door into the parking lot, where a group of wild rednecks kicked and clawed each other at random until they grew winded and returned to the dice table.

'Hope that wasn't Bumpous,' observed the sheriff.

The restrooms inside were small and nasty, and most of the patrons found it necessary to relieve themselves between the pickups in the parking lot. This was especially true on Mondays when ten-cent beer night drew rednecks from four counties and every truck in the parking lot received at least three sprayings. About once a week an innocent passing motorist would get shocked by something he or she saw in the parking lot, and Ozzie would be forced to make an arrest. Otherwise, he left the places alone.

Both tonks were in violation of numerous laws. There was gambling, drugs, illegal whiskey, minors, they refused to close on time, etc. Shortly after he was elected the first time Ozzie made the mistake, due in part to a hasty campaign promise, of closing all the honky tonks in the county. It was a horrible mistake. The crime rate soared. The jail was packed. The court dockets multiplied. The rednecks united and drove in caravans to Clanton, where they parked around the courthouse on the square. Hundreds of them. Every night they invaded the square, drinking, fighting, playing loud music, and shouting obscenities at the horrified town folk. Each morning the square resembled a landfill with cans and bottles thrown everywhere. He closed the black tonks too, and break-ins, burglaries, and stabbings tripled in one month. There were two murders in one week.

Finally, with the city under siege, a group of local ministers met secretly with Ozzie and begged him to ease up on the tonks. He politely reminded them that during the campaign they had insisted on the closings. They admitted they were wrong and pleaded for relief. Yes, they would support him in the next election. Ozzie relented, and life returned to normal in Ford County.

Ozzie was not pleased that the establishments thrived in his county, but he was convinced beyond any doubt that his law-abiding constituents were much safer when the tonks were open.

At ten-thirty the dispatcher radioed that the informant was on the phone and wanted to see the sheriff. Ozzie gave his location, and a minute later they watched Bumpous emerge and stagger to his truck. He spun tires, slung gravel, and raced toward the church.

'He's drunk,' said Hastings.

He wheeled through the church parking lot and came to a screeching stop a few feet from the patrol car. 'Howdy, Sheriff!' he yelled.

Ozzie walked to the pickup. 'What took so long?'

'You told me to take all night.'

'You found him two hours ago.'

'That's true, Sheriff, but have you ever tried to spend twenty dollars on beer when it's fifty cents a can?'

'You drunk?'

'Naw, just havin' a good time. Could I have another twenty?'

'What'd you find out?'

' 'Bout what?'

'Cobb!'

'Oh, he's in there all right.'

'I know he's in there! What else?'

Bumpous quit smiling and looked at the tonk in the distance. 'He's laughin' about it, Sheriff. It's a big joke. Said he finally found a nigger who was a virgin. Somebody asked how old she was, and Cobb said eight or nine. Everybody laughed.'

Hastings closed his eyes and dropped his head. Ozzie gritted his teeth and looked away. 'What else did he say?'

'He's bad drunk. He won't remember any of it in the mornin'. Said she was a cute little nigger.'

'Who was with him?'

'Pete Willard.'

'Is he in there?'

'Yep, they're both laughin' about it.'

'Where are they?'

'Left-hand side, next to the pinball machines.'

Ozzie smiled. 'Okay, Bumpous. You did good. Get lost.'

Hastings called the dispatcher with the two names. The dispatcher relayed the message to Deputy Looney, who was parked in the street in front of the home of County Judge Percy Bullard. Looney rang the doorbell and handed the judge two affidavits and two arrest warrants. Bullard scribbled on the warrants and returned them to Looney, who thanked His Honor and left. Twenty minutes later Looney handed the warrants to Ozzie behind the church.

At exactly eleven, the band quit in mid-song, the dice disappeared, the dancers froze, the cue balls stopped rolling, and someone turned on the lights. All eyes followed the big sheriff as he and his men swaggered slowly across the dance floor to a table by the pinball machines. Cobb, Willard, and two others sat in a booth, the table littered with empty beer cans. Ozzie walked to the table and grinned at Cobb.

'I'm sorry, sir, but we don't allow niggers in here,' Cobb blurted out, and the four burst into laughter. Ozzie kept grinning.

When the laughing stopped, Ozzie said, 'You boys havin' a good time, Billy Ray?'

'We was.'

'Looks like it. I hate to break things up, but you and Mr. Willard need to come with me.'

'Where we goin'?' Willard asked.

'For a ride.'

'I ain't movin',' Cobb vowed. With that, the other two scooted from the booth and joined the spectators.

'I'm placin' you both under arrest,' Ozzie said.

'You got warrants?' Cobb asked.

Hastings produced the warrants, and Ozzie threw them among the beer cans. 'Yeah, we got warrants. Now get up.'

Willard stared desperately at Cobb, who sipped a beer and said, 'I ain't goin' to jail.'

Looney handed Ozzie the longest, blackest nightstick ever used in Ford County. Willard was panic-stricken. Ozzie cocked it and struck the centre of the table, sending beer and cans and foam in all directions. Willard bolted upright, slapped his wrists together and thrust them at Looney, who was waiting with the handcuffs. He was dragged outside and thrown into a patrol car.

Ozzie tapped his left palm with the stick and grinned at Cobb. 'You have the right to remain silent. Anything you say will be used against you in court. You have the right to a lawyer. If you can't afford one, the state'll furnish one. Any questions?'

'Yeah, what time is it?'

'Time to go to jail, big man.'

'Go to hell, nigger.'

Ozzie grabbed his hair and lifted him from the booth, then drove his face into the floor. He jammed a knee into his spine and slid his nightstick under his throat, and pulled upward while driving the knee deeper into his back. Cobb squealed until the stick began crushing his larynx.

The handcuffs were slapped into place, and Ozzie dragged him by his hair across the dance floor, out the door, across the gravel and threw him into the back seat with Willard.

News of the rape spread quickly. More friends and relatives crowded into the waiting room and the halls around it. Tonya was out of surgery and listed as critical. Ozzie talked to Gwen's brother in the hall and told of the arrests. Yes, they were the ones, he was sure.

CHAPTER THREE

Jake Brigance rolled across his wife and staggered to the small bathroom a few feet from his bed, where he searched and groped in the dark for the screaming alarm clock. He found it where he had left it, and killed it with a quick and violent slap. It was 5:30 A.M., Wednesday, May 15.

He stood in the dark for a moment, breathless, terrified, his heart pounding rapidly, staring at the fluorescent numbers glowing at him from the face of the clock, a clock he hated. Its piercing scream could be heard down the street. He flirted with cardiac arrest every morning at this time when the thing erupted. On occasion, about twice a year, he was successful in shoving Carla onto the floor, and she would maybe turn it off before returning to bed. Most of the time, however, she was not sympathetic. She thought he was crazy for getting up at such an hour.

The clock sat on the windowsill so that Jake was required to move around a bit before it was silenced. Once up, Jake would not permit himself to crawl back under the covers. It was one of his rules. At one time the alarm was on the nightstand, and the volume was reduced. Carla would reach and turn it off before Jake heard anything. Then he would sleep until seven or eight and ruin his entire day. He would miss being in the office by seven, which was another rule. The alarm stayed in the bathroom and served its purpose.

Jake stepped to the sink and splashed cold water on his face and hair. He switched on the light and gasped in horror at the sight in the mirror. His straight brown hair shot in all directions, and the hairline had receded at least two inches during the night. Either that or his forehead had grown. His eyes were matted and swollen with the white stuff packed in the corners. A seam in a blanket left a bright red scar along the left side of his face. He touched, then rubbed it and wondered if it would go away. With his right hand he pushed his hair back and inspected the hairline. At thirty-two, he had no gray hair. Gray hair was not the problem. The problem was pattern baldness, which Jake had richly inherited from both sides of his family. He longed for a full, thick hairline beginning an inch above his eyebrows. He still had plenty of hair, Carla told him. But it wouldn't last long at the rate it was disappearing. She also assured him he was as handsome as ever, and he believed her. She had explained that a receding hairline gave him a look of maturity that was essential for a young attorney. He believed that too.

But what about old, bald attorneys, or even mature, middle-aged bald attorneys? Why couldn't the hair return after he grew wrinkles and gray sideburns and looked very mature?

Jake pondered these things in the shower. He took quick showers, and he shaved and dressed quickly. He had to be at the Coffee Shop at 6:00 A.M. – another rule. He turned on lights and slammed and banged drawers and closet doors in an effort to arouse Carla. This was the morning ritual during the summer when she was not teaching school. He had explained to her numerous times that she had all day to catch up on any lost sleep, and that these early moments should be spent together. She moaned and tunneled deeper under the covers. Once dressed, Jake jumped on the bed with all fours and kissed her in the ear, down the neck, and all over the face until she finally swung at him. The he yanked the covers off the bed and laughed as she curled up and shivered and begged for the blankets. He held them and admired her dark, tanned, thin, almost perfect legs. The bulky nightshirt covered nothing below the waist, and a hundred lewd thoughts danced before him.

About once a month this ritual would get out of hand. She would not protest, and the blankets would be jointly removed. On those mornings Jake undressed even quicker and broke at least three of his rules. That's how Hanna was conceived.

But not this morning. He covered his wife, kissed her gently, and turned out the lights. She breathed easier, and fell asleep.

Down the hall he quietly opened Hanna's door and knelt beside her. She was four, the only child, and there would be no others. She lay in her bed surrounded by dolls and stuffed animals. He kissed her lightly on the cheek. She was as beautiful as her mother, and the two were identical in looks and manners. They had large bluish-gray eyes that could cry instantly, if necessary. They wore their dark hair the same way – had it cut by the same person at the same time. They even dressed alike.

Jake adored the two women in his life. He kissed the second one goodbye and went to the kitchen to make coffee for Carla. On his way out he released Max, the mutt, into the backyard, where she simultaneously relieved herself and barked at Mrs. Pickle's cat next door.

Few people attacked the morning like Jake Brigance. He walked briskly to the end of the driveway and got the morning papers for Carla. It was dark, clear, and cool with the promise of summer rapidly approaching.

He studied the darkness up and down Adams Street, then turned and admired his house. Two homes in Ford County were on the National Register of Historic Places, and Jake Brigance owned one of them. Although it was heavily mortgaged, he was proud of it nonetheless. It was a nineteenth-century Victorian built by a retired railroad man who died on the first Christmas Eve he spent in his new home. The facade was a huge, centered gable with hipped roof over a wide, inset front porch. Under the gable a small portico covered with bargeboard hung gently over the porch. The five supporting pillars were round and painted white and slate blue. Each column bore a handmade floral carving, each with a different flower – daffodils, irises, and sunflowers. The railing between the pillars was filled with lavish lacework. Upstairs, three bay windows opened onto a small balcony, and to the left of the balcony an octagonal tower with stained-glass windows protruded and rose above the gable until it peaked with an iron-crested finial. Below the tower and to the left of the porch, a wide, graceful veranda with ornamental railing extended from the house and served as a carport. The front panels were a collage of gingerbread, cedar shingles, scallops, fish scales, tiny intricate gables, and miniature spindles.

Carla had located a paint consultant in New Orleans, and the fairy chose six original colors – mostly shades of blue, teal, peach, and white. The paint job took two months and cost Jake five thousand dollars, and that did not include the countless hours he and Carla had spent dangling from ladders and scraping cornices. And although he was not wild about some of the colors, he had never dared suggest repainting.

As with every Victorian, the house was gloriously unique. It had a piquant, provocative, engaging quality derived from an ingenuous, joyous, almost childlike bearing. Carla had wanted it since before they married, and when the owner in Memphis finally died and the estate was closed, they bought it for a song because no one else would have it. It had been abandoned for twenty years. They borrowed heavily from two of the three banks in Clanton, and spent the next three years sweating and doting over their landmark. Now people drove by and took pictures of it.

The third local bank held the mortgage on Jake's car, the only Saab in Ford County. And a red Saab at that. He wiped the dew from the windshield and unlocked the door. Max was still barking and had awakened the army of bluejays that lived in Mrs. Pickle's maple tree. They sang to him and called farewell as he smiled and whistled in return. He backed into Adams Street. Two blocks east he turned south on Jefferson, which two blocks later ran dead end into Washington Street. Jake had often wondered why every small Southern town had an Adams, a Jefferson, and a Washington, but no Lincoln or Grant. Washington Street ran east and west on the north side of the Clanton square.

Because Clanton was the county seat it had a square, and the square quite naturally had a courthouse in the center of it. General Clanton had laid out the town with much thought, and the square was long and wide and the courthouse lawn was covered with massive oak trees, all lined neatly and spaced equally apart. The Ford County courthouse was well into its second century, built after the Yankees burned the first one. It defiantly faced south, as if telling those from the North to politely and eternally kiss its ass. It was old and stately, with white columns along the front and black shutters around the dozens of windows. The original red brick had long since been painted white, and every four years the Boy Scouts added a thick layer of shiny enamel for their traditional summer project. Several bond issues over the years had allowed additions and renovations. The lawn around it was clean and neatly trimmed. A crew from the jail manicured it twice a week.

Clanton had three coffee shops – two for the whites and one for the blacks, and all three were on the square. It was not illegal or uncommon for whites to eat at Claude's, the black cafe on the west side. And it was safe for the blacks to eat at the Tea Shoppe, on the south side, or the Coffee Shop on Washington Street. They didn't, however, since they were told they could back in the seventies. Jake ate barbecue every Friday at Claude's, as did most of the white liberals in Clanton. But six mornings a week he was a regular at the Coffee Shop.

He parked the Saab in front of his office on Washington Street and walked three doors to the Coffee Shop. It had opened an hour earlier and by now was bustling with action. Waitresses scurried about serving coffee and breakfast and chatting incessantly with the farmers and mechanics and deputies who were the regulars. This was no white-collar cafe. The white collars gathered across the square at the Tea Shoppe later in the morning and discussed national politics, tennis, golf, and the stock market. At the Coffee Shop they talked about local politics, football, and bass fishing. Jake was one of the few white collars allowed to frequent the Coffee Shop. He was well liked and accepted by the blue collars, most of whom at one time or another had found their way to his office for a will, a deed, a divorce, a defense, or any one of a thousand other problems. They picked at him and told crooked lawyer jokes, but he had a thick skin. They asked him to explain Supreme Court rulings and other legal oddities during breakfast, and he gave a lot of free legal advice at the Coffee Shop. Jake had a way of cutting through the excess and discussing the meat of any issue. They appreciated that. They didn't always agree with him, but they always got honest answers. They argued at times, but there were never hard feelings.

He made his entrance at six, and it took five minutes to greet everyone, shake hands, slap backs, and say smart things to the waitresses. By the time he sat at his table his favorite girl, Dell, had his coffee and regular breakfast of toast, jelly, and grits. She patted him on the hand and called him honey and sweetheart and generally made a fuss over him. She griped and snapped at the others, but had a different routine for Jake.

He ate with Tim Nunley, a mechanic down at the Chevrolet place, and two brothers, Bill and Bert West, who worked at the shoe factory north of town. He splashed three drops of Tabasco on his grits and stirred them artfully with a slice of butter. He covered the toast with a half inch of homemade strawberry jelly. Once his food was properly prepared, he tasted the coffee and started eating. They ate quietly and discussed how the crappie were biting.

In a booth by the window a few feet from Jake's table, three deputies talked among themselves. The big one, Marshall Prather, turned to Jake and asked loudly, 'Say, Jake, didn't you defend Billy Ray Cobb a few years ago?'

The cafe was instantly silent as everyone looked at the lawyer. Startled not by the question but by its response, Jake swallowed his grits and searched for the name.

'Billy Ray Cobb,' he repeated aloud. 'What kind of case was it?'

'Dope,' Prather said. 'Caught him sellin' dope about four years ago. Spent time in Parchman and got out last year.'

Jake remembered. 'Naw, I didn't represent him. I think he had a Memphis lawyer.'

Prather seemed satisfied and returned to his pancakes. Jake waited.

Finally he asked, 'Why? What's he done now?'

'We picked him up last night for rape.'

'Rape!'

'Yeah, him and Pete Willard.'

'Who'd they rape?'

'You remember that Hailey nigger you got off in that murder trial a few years ago?'

'Lester Hailey. Of course I remember.'

'You know his brother Carl Lee?'

'Sure. Know him well. I know all the Haileys. Represented most of them.'

'Well, it was his little girl.'

'You're kidding?'

'Nope.'

'How old is she?'

'Ten.'

Jake's appetite disappeared as the cafe returned to normal. He played with his coffee and listened to the conversation change from fishing to Japanese cars and back to fishing. When the West brothers left, he slid into the booth with the deputies.

'How is she?' he asked.

'Who?'

'The Hailey girl.'

'Pretty bad,' said Prather. 'She's in the hospital.'

'What happened?'

'We don't know everything. She ain't been able to talk much. Her momma sent her to the store. They live on Craft Road behind Bates Grocery.'

'I know where they live.'

'Somehow they got her in Cobb's pickup and took her out in the woods somewhere and raped her.'

'Both of them?'

'Yeah, several times. And they kicked her and beat her real bad. Some of her kinfolks didn't know her, she was beat so bad.'

Jake shook his head. 'That's sick.'

'Sure is. Worst I've ever seen. They tried to kill her. Left her for dead.'

'Who found her?'

'Buncha niggers fishin' down by Foggy Creek. Saw her floppin' out in the middle of the road. Had her hands tied behind her. She was talkin' a little – told them who her daddy was and they took her home.'

'How'd you know it was Billy Ray Cobb?'

'She told her momma it was a yellow pickup truck with a rebel flag hangin' in the rear window. That's about all Ozzie needed. He had it figured out by the time she got to the hospital.'

Prather was careful not to say too much. He liked Jake, but he was a lawyer and he handled a lot of criminal cases.

'Who is Pete Willard?'

'Some friend of Cobb's.'

'Where'd y'all find them?'

'Huey's.'

'That figures.' Jake drank his coffee and thought of Hanna.

'Sick, sick, sick,' Looney mumbled.

'How's Carl Lee?'

Prather wiped syrup from his mustache. 'Personally, I don't know him, but I ain't ever heard anything bad about him. They're still at the hospital. I think Ozzie was with them all night. He knows them real well, of course, he knows all those folks real well. Hastings is kin to the girl somehow.'

'When's the preliminary hearing?'

'Bullard set it for one P.M. today. Ain't that right, Looney?'

Looney nodded.

'Any bond?'

'Ain't been set yet. Bullard's gonna wait till the hearing. If she dies, they'll be lookin' at capital murder, won't they?'

Jake nodded.

'They can't have a bond for capital murder, can they, Jake?' Looney asked.

'They can but I've never seen one. I know Bullard won't set a bond for capital murder, and if he did, they couldn't make it.'

'If she don't die, how much time can they get?' asked Nesbit, the third deputy.

Others listened as Jake explained. 'They can get life sentences for the rape. I assume they will also be charged with kidnapping and aggravated assault.'

'They already have.'

'Then they can get twenty years for the kidnapping and twenty years for the aggravated assault.'

'Yeah, but how much time will they serve?' asked Looney.

Jake thought a second. 'They could conceivably be paroled in thirteen years. Seven for the rape, three for the kidnapping, and three for the aggravated assault. That's assuming they're convicted on all charges and sentenced to the maximum.'

'What about Cobb? He's got a record.'

'Yeah, but he's not habitual unless he's got two prior convictions.'

'Thirteen years,' Looney repeated, shaking his head.

Jake stared through the window. The square was coming to life as pickups full of fruits and vegetables parked next to the sidewalk around the courthouse lawn, and the old farmers in faded overalls neatly arranged the small baskets of tomatoes and cucumbers and squash on the tailgates and hoods. Watermelons from Florida were placed next to the dusty slick tires, and the farmers left for an early-morning meeting under the Vietnam monument, where they sat on benches and chewed Red Man and whittled while they caught up on the gossip. They're probably talking about the rape, Jake thought. It was daylight now, and time for the office. The deputies were finished with their food, and Jake excused himself. He hugged Dell, paid his check, and for a second thought of driving home to check on Hanna.

At three minutes before seven, he unlocked his office and turned on the lights.

Carl Lee had difficulty sleeping on the couch in the waiting room. Tonya was serious but stable. They had seen her at midnight, after the doctor warned that she looked bad. She did. Gwen had kissed the little bandaged face while Carl Lee stood at the foot of the bed, subdued, motionless, unable to do anything but stare blankly at the small figure surrounded by machines, tubes, and nurses. Gwen was later sedated and taken to her mother's house in Clanton. The boys went home with Gwen's brother.

The crowd had dispersed around one, leaving Carl Lee alone on the couch. Ozzie brought coffee and doughnuts at two, and told Carl Lee all he knew about Cobb and Willard.

Jake's office was a two-story building in a row of two-story buildings overlooking the courthouse on the north side of the square, just down from the Coffee Shop. The building was built by the Wilbanks family back in the 1890s, back when they owned Ford County. And there had been a Wilbanks practicing law in the building from the day it was built until 1979, the year of the disbarment. Next door to the east was an insurance agent Jake had sued for botching a claim for Tim Nunley, the mechanic down at the Chevrolet place. To the west was the bank with the mortgage on the Saab. All the buildings around the square were two-story brick except the banks. The one next door had also been built by the Wilbankses and had just two floors, but the one on the southeast corner of the square had three floors, and the newest one, on the southwest corner, had four floors.

Jake practiced alone, and had since 1979, the year of the disbarment. He liked it that way, especially since there was no other lawyer in Clanton competent enough to practice with him. There were several good lawyers in town, but most were with the Sullivan firm over in the bank building with four floors. Jake detested the Sullivan firm. Every lawyer detested the Sullivan firm except those in it. There were eight in all, eight of the most pompous and arrogant jerks Jake had ever met. Two had Harvard degrees. They had the big farmers, the banks, the insurance companies, the railroads, everybody with money. The other fourteen lawyers in the county picked up the scraps and represented people – living, breathing human souls, most of whom had very little money. These were the 'street lawyers' – those in the trenches helping people in trouble. Jake was proud to be a street lawyer.

His offices were huge. He used only five of the ten rooms in the building. Downstairs there was a reception room, a large conference room, a kitchen, and a smaller storage and junk room. Upstairs, Jake had his vast office and another smaller office he referred to as the war room. It had no windows, no telephones, no distractions. Three offices sat empty upstairs and two downstairs. In years past these had been occupied by the prestigious Wilbanks firm, long before the disbarment. Jake's office upstairs, *the* office, was immense; thirty by thirty with a ten-foot hardwood ceiling, hardwood floors, huge fireplace, and three desks – his work desk, a small conference desk in one corner, and a rolltop desk in another corner under the portrait of William Faulkner. The antique oak furniture had been there for almost a century, as had the books and shelves that covered one wall. The view of the square and courthouse was impressive, and could be enhanced by opening the French doors and walking onto a small balcony overhanging the sidewalk next to Washington Street. Jake had, without a doubt, the finest office in Clanton. Even his bitter enemies in the Sullivan firm would concede that much.

For all the opulence and square footage, Jake paid the sum of four hundred dollars a month to his landlord and former boss, Lucien Wilbanks, who had been disbarred in 1979.

For decades the Wilbanks family ruled Ford County. They were proud, wealthy people, prominent in farming, banking, politics, and especially law. All the Wilbanks men were lawyers, and were educated at Ivy League schools. They founded banks, churches, schools, and several served in public office. The firm of Wilbanks & Wilbanks had been the most powerful and prestigious in north Mississippi for many years.

Then came Lucien. He was the only male Wilbanks of his generation. There was a sister and some nieces, but they were expected only to marry well. Great things were expected of Lucien as a child, but by the third grade it was evident he would be a different Wilbanks. He inherited the law firm in 1965 when his father and uncle were killed in a plane crash. Although he was forty, he had just recently, several months prior to their deaths, completed his study of the law by correspondence courses. Somehow he passed the bar exam. He took control of the firm and clients began disappearing. Big clients, like insurance companies, banks, and farmers, all left and went to the newly established Sullivan firm. Sullivan had been a junior partner in the Wilbanks firm until Lucien fired him and evicted him, after which he left with the other junior partners and most of the clients. Then Lucien fired everyone else – associates, secretaries, clerks – everyone but Ethel Twitty, his late father's favorite secretary.

Ethel and John Wilbanks had been very close through the years. In fact she had a younger son who greatly resembled Lucien. The poor fellow spent most of his time in and out of various nut houses. Lucien jokingly referred to him as his retarded brother. After the plane crash, the retarded brother appeared in Clanton and started telling folks he was the illegitimate son of John Wilbanks. Ethel was humiliated, but couldn't control him. Clanton seethed with scandal. A lawsuit was filed by the Sullivan firm as counsel for the retarded brother seeking a portion of the estate. Lucien was furious. A trial ensued, and Lucien vigorously defended his honor and pride and family name. He also vigorously defended his father's estate, all of which had been left to Lucien and his sister. At trial the jury noted the striking resemblance between Lucien and Ethel's son, who was several years younger. The retarded brother was strategically seated as close as possible to Lucien. The Sullivan lawyers instructed him to walk, talk, sit, and do everything just like Lucien. They even dressed him like Lucien. Ethel and her husband denied the boy was any kin to the Wilbanks, but the jury felt otherwise. He was found to be an heir of John Wilbanks, and was awarded one third of the estate. Lucien cursed the jury, slapped the poor boy, and was carried screaming from the courtroom and taken to jail. The jury's decision was reversed and dismissed on appeal, but Lucien feared more litigation if Ethel ever changed her story. Thus, Ethel Twitty remained with the Wilbanks firm.

Lucien was satisfied when the firm disintegrated. He never intended to practice law like his ancestors. He wanted to be a criminal lawyer, and the old firm's clientele had become strictly corporate. He wanted the rapes, the murders, the child abuses, the ugly cases no one else wanted. He wanted to be a civil rights lawyer and litigate civil liberties. But most of all, Lucien wanted to be a radical, a flaming radical of a lawyer with unpopular cases and causes, and lots of attention.

He grew a beard, divorced his wife, renounced his church, sold his share of the country club, joined the NAACP and ACLU, resigned from the bank board, and in general became the scourge of Clanton. He sued the schools because of segregation, the governor because of the prison, the city because it refused to pave streets in the black section, the bank because there were no black tellers, the state because of capital punishment, and the factories because they would not recognize organized labor. He fought and won many criminal cases, and not just in Ford County. His reputation spread, and a large following developed among blacks, poor whites, and the few unions in north Mississippi. He stumbled into some lucrative personal injury and wrongful death cases. There were some nice settlements. The firm, he and Ethel, was more profitable than ever. Lucien did not need the money. He had been born with it and never thought about it. Ethel did the counting.

The law became his life. With no family, he became a workaholic. Fifteen hours a day, seven days a week, Lucien practiced law with a passion. He had no other interests, except alcohol. In the late sixties he noticed an affinity for Jack Daniel's. By the early seventies he was a drunk, and when he hired Jake in 1978 he was a full-fledged alcoholic. But he never let booze interfere with his work; he learned to drink and work at the same time. Lucien was always half drunk, and he was a dangerous lawyer in that condition. Bold and abrasive by nature, he was downright frightening when he was drinking. At trial he would embarrass the opposing attorneys, insult the judge, abuse the witnesses, then apologize to the jury. He respected no one and could not be intimidated. He was feared because he would say and do anything. People walked lightly around Lucien. He knew it and loved it. He became more and more eccentric. The more he drank, the crazier he acted, then people talked about him even more, so he drank even more.

Between 1966 and 1978 Lucien hired and disposed of eleven associates. He hired blacks, Jews, Hispanics, women, and not one kept the pace he demanded. He was a tyrant around the office, constantly cursing and berating the young lawyers. Some quit the first month. One lasted two years. It was difficult to accept Lucien's craziness. He had the money to be eccentric – his associates did not.

He hired Jake in 1978 fresh from law school. Jake was from Karaway, a small town of twenty-five hundred, eighteen miles west of Clanton. He was clean-cut, conservative, a devout Presbyterian with a pretty wife who wanted babies. Lucien hired him to see if he could corrupt him. Jake took the job with strong reservations because he had no other offers close to home.

A year later Lucien was disbarred. It was a tragedy for those very few who liked him. The small union at the shoe factory north of town had called a strike. It was a union Lucien had organized and represented. The factory began hiring new workers to replace the strikers, and violence followed. Lucien appeared on the picket line to rally his people. He was drunker than normal. A group of scabs attempted to cross the line and a brawl erupted. Lucien led the charge, was arrested and jailed. He was convicted in city court of assault and battery and disorderly conduct. He appealed and lost, appealed and lost.

The State Bar Association had grown weary of Lucien over the years. No other attorney in the state had received as many complaints as had Lucien Wilbanks. Private reprimands, public reprimands, and suspensions had all been used, all to no avail. The Complaints Tribunal and Disciplinary Committee moved swiftly. He was disbarred for outrageous conduct unbecoming a member of the bar. He appealed and lost, appealed and lost.

He was devastated. Jake was in Lucien's office, the big office upstairs, when word came from Jackson that the Supreme Court had upheld the disbarment. Lucien hung up the phone and walked to the doors overlooking the square. Jake watched him closely, waiting for the tirade. But Lucien said nothing. He walked slowly down the stairs, stopped and stared at Ethel, who was crying, and then looked at Jake. He opened the door and said, 'Take care of this place. I'll see you later.'

They ran to the front window and watched him speed away from the square in his ragged old Porsche. For several months there was no word from him. Jake labored diligently on Lucien's cases while Ethel kept the office from chaos. Some of the cases were settled, some left for other lawyers, some went to trial.

Six months later Jake returned to his office after a long day in court and found Lucien asleep on the Persian rug in the big office. 'Lucien! Are you all right?' he asked.

Lucien jumped up and sat in the big leather chair behind the desk. He was sober, tanned, relaxed.

'Jake, my boy, how are you?' he asked warmly.

'Fine, just fine. Where have you been?'

'Cayman Islands.'

'Doing what?'

'Drinking rum, lying on the beach, chasing little native girls.'

'Sounds like fun. Why did you leave?'

'It got boring.'

Jake sat across the desk. 'It's good to see you, Lucien.'

'Good to see you, Jake. How are things around here?'

'Hectic. But okay, I guess.'

'Did you settle Medley?'

'Yeah. They paid eighty thousand.'

'That's very good. Was he happy?'

'Yes, seemed to be.'

'Did Cruger go to trial?'

Jake looked at the floor. 'No, he hired Fredrix. I think it's set for trial next month.'

'I should've talked to him before I left.'

'He's guilty, isn't he?'

'Yes, very. It doesn't matter who represents him. Most defendants are guilty. Remember that.' Lucien walked to the French doors and gazed at the courthouse. 'What are your plans, Jake?'

'I'd like to stay here. What are your plans?'

'You're a good man, Jake, and I want you to stay. Me, I don't know. I thought about moving to the Caribbean, but I won't. It's a nice place to visit, but it gets old. I have no plans really. I may travel. Spend some money. I'm worth a ton, you know.'

Jake agreed. Lucien turned and waved his arms around the room. 'I want you to have all this, Jake. I want you to stay here and keep some semblance of a firm going. Move into this office; use this desk that my grandfather brought from Virginia after the Civil War. Keep the files, cases, clients, books, everything.'

'That's very generous, Lucien.'

'Most of the clients will disappear. No reflection on you – you'll be a great lawyer someday. But most of my clients have followed me for years.'

Jake didn't want most of his clients. 'How about rent?'

'Pay me what you can afford. Money will be tight at first, but you'll make it. I don't need money, but you do.'

'You're being very kind.'

'I'm really a nice guy.' They both laughed awkwardly. Jake quit smiling. 'What about Ethel?'

'It's up to you. She's a good secretary who's forgotten more law than you'll ever know. I know you don't like her, but she would be hard to replace. Fire her if you want to. I don't care.'

Lucien headed for the door. 'Call me if you need me. I'll be around. I want you to move into this office. It was my father's and grandfather's. Put my junk in some boxes, and I'll pick it up later.'

Cobb and Willard awoke with throbbing heads and red, swollen eyes. Ozzie was yelling at them. They were in a small cell by themselves. Through the bars to the right was a cell where the state prisoners were held awaiting the trip to Parchman. A dozen blacks leaned through the bars and glared at the two white boys as they struggled to clear their eyes. To the left was a smaller cell, also full of blacks. Wake up, Ozzie yelled, and stay quiet, or he would integrate his jail.

Jake's quiet time was from seven until Ethel arrived at eight-thirty. He was jealous with this time. He locked the front door, ignored the phone, and refused to make appointments. He meticulously planned his day. By eight-thirty he would have enough work dictated to keep Ethel busy and quiet until noon. By nine he was either in court or seeing clients. He would not take calls until eleven, when he methodically returned the morning's messages – all of them. He never delayed returning a phone call – another rule. Jake worked systematically and efficiently with little wasted time. These habits he had not learned from Lucien.

At eight-thirty Ethel made her usual noisy entrance downstairs. She made fresh coffee and opened the mail as she had every day for the past forty-one years. She was sixty-four and looked fifty. She was plump, but not fat, well kept, but not attractive. She chomped on a greasy sausage and biscuit brought from home and read Jake's mail.

Jake heard voices. Ethel was talking to another woman. He checked his appointment book – none until ten.

'Good morning, Mr. Brigance,' Ethel announced through the intercom.

'Morning, Ethel.' She preferred to be called Mrs. Twitty. Lucien and everyone else called her that. But Jake had called her Ethel since he had fired her shortly after the disbarment.

'There's a lady here to see you.'

'She doesn't have an appointment.'

'Yes, sir, I know.'

'Make one for tomorrow morning after ten-thirty. I'm busy now.'

'Yes, sir. But she says it's urgent.'

'Who is it?' he snapped. It was always urgent when they dropped in unannounced, like dropping by a funeral home or a Laundromat. Probably some urgent question about Uncle Luke's will or the case set for trial in three months.

'A Mrs. Willard,' Ethel replied.

'First name?'

'Earnestine Willard. You don't know her, but her son's in jail.'

Jake saw his appointments on time, but drop-ins were another matter. Ethel either ran them off or made appointments for the next day or so. Mr. Brigance was very busy, she would explain, but he could work you in day after tomorrow. This impressed people.

'Tell her I'm not interested.'

'But she says she must find a lawyer. Her son has to be in court at one this afternoon.'

'Tell her to see Drew Jack Tyndale, the public defender. He's good and he's free.'

Ethel relayed the message. 'But, Mr. Brigance, she wants to hire you. Someone told her you're the best criminal lawyer in the county.' The amusement was obvious in Ethel's voice.

'Tell her that's true, but I'm not interested.'

Ozzie handcuffed Willard and led him down the hall to his office in the front section of the Ford County jail. He removed the handcuffs and seated him in a wooden chair in the center of the cramped room. Ozzie sat in the big chair across the desk and looked down at the defendant.

'Mr. Willard, this here is Lieutenant Griffin with the Mississippi Highway Patrol. Over here is Investigator Rady with my office, and this here is Deputy Looney and Deputy Prather, whom you met last night but I doubt if you remember it. I'm Sheriff Walls.'

Willard jerked his head fearfully to look at each one. He was surrounded. The door was shut. Two tape recorders sat side by side near the edge of the sheriff's desk.

'We'd like to ask you some questions, okay?'

'I don't know.'

'Before I start, I wanna make sure you understand your rights. First of all, you have the right to remain silent. Understand?'

'Uh huh.'

'You don't have to talk if you don't want to, but if you do, anything you say can and will be used against you in court. Understand?'

'Uh huh.'

'Can you read and write?'

'Yeah.'

'Good, then read this and sign it. It says you've been advised of your rights.'

Willard signed. Ozzie pushed the red button on one of the tape recorders.

'You understand this tape recorder is on?'

'Uh huh.'

'And it's Wednesday, May 15, at eight forty-three in the mornin'.'

'If you say so.'

'What's your full name?'

'James Louis Willard.'

'Nickname?'

'Pete. Pete Willard.'

'Address?'

'Route 6, Box 14, Lake Village, Mississippi.'

'What road?'

'Bethel Road.'

'Who do you live with?'

'My momma, Earnestine Willard. I'm divorced.'

'You know Billy Ray Cobb?'

Willard hesitated and noticed his feet. His boots were back in the cell. His white socks were dirty and did not hide his two big toes. Safe question, he thought.

'Yeah, I know him.'

'Was you with him yesterday?'

'Uh huh.'

'Where were y'all?'

'Down at the lake.'

'What time did you leave?'

' 'Bout three.'

'What were you drivin'?'

'I wasn't.'

'What were you ridin' in?'

Hesitation. He studied his toes. 'I don't think I wanna talk no more.'

Ozzie pushed another button and the recorder stopped. He breathed deeply at Willard. 'You ever been to Parchman?'

Willard shook his head.

'You know how many niggers at Parchman?'

Willard shook his head.

' 'Bout five thousand. You know how many white boys are there?'

'No.'

' 'Bout a thousand.'

Willard dropped his chin to his chest. Ozzie let him think for a minute, then winked at Lieutenant Griffin.

'You got any idea what those niggers will do to a white boy who raped a little black girl?'

No response.

'Lieutenant Griffin, tell Mr. Willard how white boys are treated at Parchman.'

Griffin walked to Ozzie's desk and sat on the edge. He looked down at Willard. 'About five years ago a young white man in Helena County, over in the delta, raped a black girl. She was twelve. They were waiting on him when he got to Parchman. Knew he was coming. First night about thirty blacks tied him over a fifty-five-gallon drum and climbed on. The guards watched and laughed. There's no sympathy for rapists. They got him every night for three months, and then killed him. They found him castrated, stuffed in the drum.'

Willard cringed, then threw his head back and breathed heavily toward the ceiling.

'Look, Pete,' Ozzie said, 'we're not after you. We want Cobb. I've been after that boy since he left Parchman. I want him real bad. You help us get Cobb and I'll help you as much as I can. I ain't promisin' nothin', but me and the D.A. work close together. You help me get Cobb, and I'll help you with the D.A. Just tell us what happened.'

'I wanna lawyer,' Willard said.

Ozzie dropped his head and groaned. 'What's a lawyer gonna do, Pete? Get the niggers off of you? I'm tryin' to help you and you're bein' a wiseass.'

'You need to listen to the sheriff, son. He's trying to save your life,' Griffin said helpfully.

'There's a good chance you could get off with just a few years here in this jail,' Rady said.

'It's much safer than Parchman,' Prather said.

'Choice is yours, Pete,' Ozzie said. 'You can die at Parchman or stay here. I'll even consider makin' you a trusty if you behave.'

Willard dropped his head and rubbed his temples. 'Okay, okay.'

Ozzie punched the red button.

'Where'd you find the girl?'

'Some gravel road.'

'Which road?'

'I don't know. I's drunk.'

'Where'd you take her?'

'I don't know.'

'Just you and Cobb?'

'Yeah.'

'Who raped her?'

'We both did. Billy Ray went first.'

'How many times?'

'I don't remember. I's smokin' weed and drinkin'.'

'Both of you raped her?'

'Yeah.'

'Where'd you dump her?'

'Don't remember. I swear I don't remember.'

Ozzie pushed another button. 'We'll type this up and get you to sign it.'

Willard shook his head. 'Just don't tell Billy Ray.'

'We won't,' promised the sheriff.

CHAPTER FOUR

Percy Bullard fidgeted nervously in the leather chair behind the huge, battered oak desk in the judge's chambers behind the courtroom, where a crowd had gathered to see about the rape. In the small room next door the lawyers gathered around the coffee machine and gossiped about the rape.

Bullard's small black robe hung in a corner by the window that looked north over Washington Street. His size-six feet were wearing jogging shoes that barely touched the floor. He was a small, nervous type who worried about preliminary hearings and every other routine hearing. After thirteen years on the bench he had never learned to relax. Fortunately, he was not required to hear big cases; those were for the Circuit Court judge. Bullard was just a County Court judge, and he had reached his pinnacle.

Mr. Pate, the ancient courtroom deputy, knocked on the door.

'Come in!' Bullard demanded.

'Afternoon, Judge.'

'How many blacks out there?' Bullard asked abruptly.

'Half the courtroom.'

'That's a hundred people! They don't draw that much for a good murder trial. Whatta they want?'

Mr. Pate shook his head.

'They must think we're trying these boys today.'

'I guess they're just concerned,' Mr. Pate said softly.

'Concerned about what? I'm not turning them loose. It's just a preliminary hearing.' He quieted and stared at the window. 'Is the family out there?'

'I think so. I recognize a few of them, but I don't know her parents.'

'How about security?'

'Sheriff's got ever deputy and ever reserve close to the courtroom. We checked everbody at the door.'

'Find anything?'

'No, sir.'

'Where are the boys?'

'Sheriff's got them. They'll be here in a minute.'

The judge seemed satisfied. Mr. Pate laid a handwritten note on the desk.

'What is it?'

Mr. Pate inhaled deeply. 'It's a request from a TV crew from Memphis to film the hearing.'

'What!' Bullard's face turned red and he rocked furiously in the swivel chair. 'Cameras,' he yelled. 'In my courtroom!' He ripped the note and threw the pieces in the direction of the trash can. 'Where are they?'

'In the rotunda.'

'Order them out of the courthouse.'

Mr. Pate left quickly.

Carl Lee Hailey sat on the row next to the back. Dozens of relatives and friends surrounded him in the rows of padded benches on the right side of the courtroom. The benches on the left side were empty. Deputies milled about, armed, apprehensive, keeping a nervous watch on the group of blacks, and especially on Carl Lee, who sat bent over, elbows on knees, staring blankly at the floor.

Jake looked out his window across the square to the rear of the courthouse, which faced south. It was 1:00 P.M. He had skipped lunch, as usual, and had no business across the street, but he did need some fresh air. He hadn't left the building all day, and although he had no desire to hear the details of the rape, he hated to miss the hearing. There had to be a crowd in the courtroom because there were no empty parking spaces around the square. A handful of reporters and photographers waited anxiously near the rear of the courthouse by the wooden doors where Cobb and Willard would enter.

The jail was two blocks off the square on the south side, down the highway. Ozzie drove the car with Cobb and Willard in the back seat. With a squad car in front and one behind, the procession turned off Washington Street into the short driveway leading under the veranda of the courthouse. Six deputies escorted the defendants past the reporters, through the doors, and up the back stairs to the small room just outside the courtroom.

Jake grabbed his coat, ignored Ethel, and raced across the street. He ran up the back stairs, through a small hall outside the jury room, and entered the courtroom from a side door just as Mr. Pate led His Honor to the bench.

'All rise for the court,' Mr. Pate shouted. Everyone stood. Bullard stepped to the bench and sat down.

'Be seated,' he yelled. 'Where are the defendants? Where? Bring them in then.'

Cobb and Willard were led, handcuffed, into the courtroom from the small holding room. They were unshaven, wrinkled, dirty, and looked confused. Willard stared at the large group of blacks while Cobb turned his back. Looney removed the handcuffs and seated them next to Drew Jack Tyndale, the public defender, at the long table where the defense sat. Next to it was a long table where the county prosecutor, Rocky Childers, sat taking notes and looking important.

Willard glanced over his shoulder and again checked on the blacks. On the front row just behind him sat his mother and Cobb's mother, each with a deputy for protection. Willard felt safe with all the deputies. Cobb refused to turn around.

From the back row, eighty feet away, Carl Lee raised his head and looked at the backs of the two men who raped his daughter. They were mangy, bearded, dirty-looking strangers. He covered his face and bent over. The deputies stood behind him, backs against the wall, watching every move.

'Now listen,' Bullard began loudly. 'This is just a preliminary hearing, not a trial. The purpose of a preliminary hearing is to determine if there is enough evidence that a crime has been committed to bind these defendants over to the grand jury. The defendants can even waive this hearing if they want to.'

Tyndale stood. 'No sir, Your Honor, we wish to proceed with the hearing.'

'Very well. I have copies of affidavits sworn to by Sheriff Walls charging both defendants with rape of a female under the age of twelve, kidnapping, and aggravated assault. Mr. Childers, you may call your first witness.'

'Your Honor, the State calls Sheriff Ozzie Walls.'

Jake sat in the jury box, along with several other attorneys, all of whom pretended to be busy reading important materials. Ozzie was sworn and sat in the witness chair to the left of Bullard, a few feet from the jury box.

'Would you state your name?'

'Sheriff Ozzie Walls.'

'You're the sheriff of Ford County?'

'Yes.'

'I know who he is,' Bullard mumbled as he flipped through the file.

'Sheriff, yesterday afternoon, did your office receive a call about a missing child?'

'Yes, around four-thirty.'

'What did your office do?'

'Deputy Willie Hastings was dispatched to the residence of Gwen and Carl Lee Hailey, the parents of the girl.'

'Where was that?'

'Down on Craft Road, back behind Bates Grocery.'

'What did he find?'

'He found the girl's mother, who made the call. Then drove around searchin' for the girl.'

'Did he find her?'

'No. When he returned to the house, the girl was there. She'd been found by some folks fishin', and they took her home.'

'What shape was the girl in?'

'She'd been raped and beaten.'

'Was she conscious?'

'Yeah. She could talk, or mumble, a little.'

'What did she say?'

Tyndale jumped to his feet. 'Your Honor, please, I know hearsay is admissible in a hearing like this, but this is triple hearsay.'

'Overruled. Shut up. Sit down. Continue, Mr. Childers.'

'What did she say?'

'Told her momma it was two white men in a yellow pickup truck with a rebel flag in the window. That's about all. She couldn't say much. Had both jaws broken and her face kicked in.'

'What happened then?'

'The deputy called an ambulance and she was taken to the hospital.'

'How is she?'

'They say she's critical.'

'What happened then?'

'Based on what I knew at the time I had a suspect in mind.'

'So what'd you do?'

'I located an informant, a reliable informant, and placed him in a beer joint down by the lake.'

Childers was not one to dwell on details, especially in front of Bullard. Jake knew it, as did Tyndale. Bullard sent every case to the grand jury, so every preliminary was a formality. Regardless of the case, the facts, the proof, regardless of anything, Bullard would bind the defendant over to the grand jury. If there was insufficient proof, let the grand jury turn them loose, not Bullard. He had to be reelected, the grand jury did not. Voters got upset when criminals were cut loose. Most defense lawyers in the county waived the preliminary hearings before Bullard. Not Jake. He viewed such hearings as the best and quickest way to look at the prosecution's case. Tyndale seldom waived a preliminary hearing.

'Which beer joint?'

'Huey's.'

'What'd he find out?'

'Said he heard Cobb and Willard, the two defendants over there, braggin' 'bout rapin' a little black girl.'

Cobb and Willard exchanged stares. Who was the informant? They remembered little from Huey's.

'What'd you find at Huey's?'

'We arrested Cobb and Willard, then we searched a pickup titled in the name of Billy Ray Cobb.'

'What'd you find?'

'We towed it in and examined it this mornin'. Lot of blood stains.'

'What else?'

'We found a small T-shirt covered with blood.'

'Whose T-shirt?'

'It belonged to Tonya Hailey, the little girl who was raped. Her daddy, Carl Lee Hailey, identified it this mornin'.'

Carl Lee heard his name and sat upright. Ozzie stared straight at him. Jake turned and saw Carl Lee for the first time.

'Describe the truck.'

'New yellow Ford half-ton pickup. Big chrome wheels and mud tires. Rebel flag in the rear window.'

'Owned by who?'

Ozzie pointed at the defendants. 'Billy Ray Cobb.'

'Does it match the description given by the girl?'

'Yes.'

Childers paused and reviewed his notes. 'Now, sheriff, what other evidence do you have against these defendants?'

'We talked to Pete Willard this mornin' at the jail. He signed a confession.'

'You did what!' Cobb blurted. Willard cowered and looked for help.

'Order! Order!' shouted Bullard as he banged his gavel. Tyndale separated his clients.

'Did you advise Mr. Willard of his rights?'

'Yes.'

'Did he understand them?'

'Yes.'

'Did he sign a statement to that effect?'

'Yes.'

'Who was present when Mr. Willard made his statement?'

'Me, two deputies, my investigator, Rady, and Lieutenant Griffin with the Highway Patrol.'

'Do you have the confession?'

'Yes.'

'Please read it.'

The courtroom was still and silent as Ozzie read the short statement. Carl Lee stared blankly at the two defendants. Cobb glared at Willard, who picked dirt off his boots.

'Thank you, Sheriff,' Childers said when Ozzie finished. 'Did Mr. Willard sign the confession?'

'Yes, in front of three witnesses.'

'The State has nothing further, Your Honor.'

Bullard shouted, 'You may cross-examine, Mr. Tyndale.'

'I have nothing at this time, Your Honor.'

Good move, thought Jake. Strategically, for the defense, it was best to stay quiet at preliminary hearings. Just listen, take notes, let the court reporter record the testimony, and stay quiet. The grand jury would see the case anyway, so why bother? And never allow the defendants to testify. Their testimony would serve no purpose and haunt them at trial. Jake knew they would not testify because he knew Tyndale.

'Call your next witness,' demanded the Judge.

'We have nothing further, Your Honor.'

'Good. Sit down. Mr. Tyndale, do you have any witnesses?'

'No, Your Honor.'

'Good. The court finds there is sufficient evidence that numerous crimes have been committed by these defendants, and the court orders Mr. Cobb and Mr. Willard to be held to await action by the Ford County grand jury, which is scheduled to meet on Monday, May 27. Any questions?'

Tyndale rose slowly. 'Yes, Your Honor, we would request the court to set a reasonable bond for these de –'

'Forget it,' snapped Bullard. 'Bail will be denied as of now. It's my understanding that the girl is in critical condition. If she dies, there will of course be other charges.'

'Well, Your Honor, in that case, I would like to request a bail hearing a few days from now, in the hopes that her condition improves.'

Bullard studied Tyndale carefully. Good idea, he thought. 'Granted. A bail hearing is set for next Monday, May 20, in this courtroom. Until then the defendants will remain in the custody of the Ford County sheriff. Court's adjourned.'

Bullard rapped the gavel and disappeared. The deputies swarmed around the defendants, handcuffed them, and they too disappeared from the courtroom, into the holding room, down the back stairs, past the reporters, and into the squad car.

The hearing was typical for Bullard – less than twenty minutes. Justice could be very swift in his courtroom.

Jake talked to the other lawyers and watched the crowd file silently through the enormous wooden doors at the rear of the courtroom. Carl Lee was in no hurry to leave, and motioned for Jake to follow him. They met in the rotunda. Carl Lee wanted to talk, and he excused himself from the crowd and promised to meet them at the hospital. He and Jake walked down the winding staircase to the first floor.

'I'm truly sorry, Carl Lee,' Jake said.

'Yeah, me too.'

'How is she?'

'She'll make it.'

'How's Gwen?'

'Okay, I guess.'

'How about you?'

They walked slowly down the hall toward the rear of the courthouse. 'It ain't sunk in yet. I mean, twenty-four hours ago everthing was fine. Now look at us. My little girl's layin' up in the hospital with tubes all over her body. My wife's crazy and my boys are scared to death, and all I think about is gettin' my hands on those bastards.'

'I wish I could do something, Carl Lee.'

'All you can do is pray for her, pray for us.'

'I know it hurts.'

'You gotta little girl, don't you, Jake?'

'Yeah.'

Carl Lee said nothing as they walked in silence. Jake changed the subject. 'Where's Lester?'

'Chicago.'

'What's he doing?'

'Workin' for a steel company. Good job. Got married.'

'You're kidding? Lester, married?'

'Yeah, married a white girl.'

'White girl! What's he want with a white girl?'

'Aw, you know Lester. Always an uppity nigger. He's on his way home now. Be in late tonight.'

'What for?'

They stopped at the rear door. Jake asked again: 'What's Lester coming in for?'

'Family business.'

'Y'all planning something?'

'Nope. He just wants to see his niece.'

'Y'all don't get excited.'

'That's easy for you to say, Jake.'

'I know.'

'What would you plan, Jake?'

'What do you mean?'

'You gotta little girl. Suppose she's layin' up in the hospital, beat and raped. What would you do?'

Jake looked through the window of the door and could not answer. Carl Lee waited.

'Don't do anything stupid, Carl Lee.'

'Answer my question. What would you do?'

'I don't know. I don't know what I'd do.'

'Lemme ask you this. If it was your little girl, and if it was two niggers, and you could get your hands on them, what would you do?'

'Kill them.'

Carl Lee smiled, then laughed. 'Sure you would, Jake, sure you would. Then you'd hire some big-shot lawyer to say you's crazy, just like you did in Lester's trial.'

'We didn't say Lester was crazy. We just said Bowie needed killing.'

'You got him off, didn't you?'

'Sure.'

Carl Lee walked to the stairs and looked up. 'This how they get to the courtroom?' he asked without looking at Jake.

'Who?'

'Those boys.'

'Yeah. Most of the time they take them up those stairs. It's quicker and safer. They can park right outside the door here, and run them up the stairs.'

Carl Lee walked to the rear door and looked through the window at the veranda. 'How many murder trials you had, Jake?'

'Three. Lester's and two more.'

'How many were black?'

'All three.'

'How many you win?'

'All three.'

'You pretty good on nigger shootin's, ain't you?'

'I guess.'

'You ready for another one?'

'Don't do it, Carl Lee. It's not worth it. What if you're convicted and get the gas chamber? What about the kids? Who'll raise them? Those punks aren't worth it.'

'You just told me you'd do it.'

Jake walked to the door next to Carl Lee. 'It's different with me. I could probably get off.'

'How?'

'I'm white, and this is a white county. With a little luck I could get an all-white jury, which will naturally be sympathetic. This is not New York or California. A man's supposed to protect his family. A jury would eat it up.'

'And me?'

'Like I said, this ain't New York or California. Some whites would admire you, but most would want to see you hang. It would be much harder to win an acquittal.'

'But you could do it, couldn't you, Jake?'

'Don't do it, Carl Lee.'

'I have no choice, Jake. I'll never sleep till those bastards are dead. I owe it to my little girl, I owe it to myself, and I owe it to my people. It'll be done.'

They opened the doors, walked under the veranda and down the driveway to Washington Street, across from Jake's office. They shook hands. Jake promised to stop by the hospital tomorrow to see Gwen and the family.

'One more thing, Jake. Will you meet me at the jail when they arrest me?'

Jake nodded before he thought. Carl Lee smiled and walked down the sidewalk to his truck.

CHAPTER FIVE

Lester Hailey married a Swedish girl from Wisconsin, and although she still professed love for him, Lester suspected the novelty of his skin was beginning to fade. She was terrified of Mississippi, and flatly refused to travel south with Lester even though he assured her she would be safe. She had never met his family. Not that his people were anxious to meet her – they were not. It was not uncommon for Southern blacks to move north and marry white girls, but no Hailey had ever mixed. There were many Haileys in Chicago; most were kin, and all married black. The family was not impressed with Lester's blonde wife. He drove to Clanton in his new Cadillac, by himself.

It was late Wednesday night when he arrived at the hospital and found some cousins reading magazines in the second-floor waiting room. He embraced Carl Lee. They had not seen each other since the Christmas holidays, when half the blacks in Chicago trooped home to Mississippi and Alabama.

They stepped into the hall, away from the relatives. 'How is she?' Lester asked.

'Better. Much better. Might go home this weekend.'

Lester was relieved. When he left Chicago eleven hours earlier she had been near death, according to the cousin who had called and scared him from bed. He lit a Kool under the NO SMOKING sign and stared at his big brother. 'You okay?'

Carl Lee nodded and glanced down the hall.

'How's Gwen?'

'Crazier than normal. She's at her momma's. You come by yourself?'

'Yeah,' Lester answered defensively.

'Good.'

'Don't get smart. I didn't drive all day to hear crap about my wife.'

'Okay, okay. You still got gas?'

Lester smiled and chuckled. He had been plagued by stomach gas since the day he married the Swede. She prepared dishes he couldn't pronounce, and his system behaved violently. He longed for collards, peas, okra, fried chicken, barbecue pork, and fatback.

They found a small waiting room on the third floor with folding chairs and a card table. Lester bought two cups of stale, thick coffee from a machine and stirred the powdered cream with his finger. He listened intently as Carl Lee detailed the rape, the arrests, and the hearing. Lester found some napkins and diagrammed the courthouse and the jail. It had been four years since his murder trial, and he had trouble with the drawings. He had spent only a week in jail, prior to posting bond, and had not visited the place since his acquittal. In fact, he had left for Chicago shortly after his trial. The victim had relatives.

They made plans and discarded them, plotting well past midnight.

At noon Thursday Tonya was removed from intensive care and placed in a private room. She was listed as stable. The doctors relaxed, and her family brought candy, toys, and flowers. With two broken jaws and a mouthful of wire, she could only stare at the candy. Her brothers ate most of it. They clung to her bed and held her hand, as if to protect and reassure. The room stayed full of friends and strangers, all patting her gently and saying how sweet she was, all treating her as someone special, someone who had been through this horrible thing. The crowd moved in shifts, from the hall into her room, and back into the hall, where the nurses watched carefully.

The wounds hurt, and at times she cried. Every hour the nurses cleared a path through the visitors and found the patient for a dose of painkiller.

That night in her room, the crowd hushed as the Memphis station talked about the rape. The television showed pictures of the two white men, but she couldn't see very well.

The Ford County Courthouse opened at 8:00 A.M. and closed at 5:00 P.M. every day except Friday, when it closed at four-thirty. At four-thirty on Friday Carl Lee was hiding in a first-floor restroom when they locked the courthouse. He sat on a toilet and listened quietly for an hour. No janitors. No one. Silence. He walked through the wide, semidark hall to the rear doors, and peeked through the window. No one in sight. He listened for a while. The courthouse was deserted. He turned and looked down the long hall, through the rotunda and through the front doors, two hundred feet away.

He studied the building. The two sets of rear doors opened to the inside into a large, rectangular entrance area. To the far right was a set of stairs, and to the left was an identical stairway. The open area narrowed and led into the hall. Carl Lee pretended to be on trial. He grabbed his hands behind him, and touched his back to the rear door. He walked to his right thirty feet to the stairs; up the stairs, ten steps, then a small landing, then a ninety-degree turn to the left, just like Lester said; then, ten more steps to the holding room. It was a small room, fifteen by fifteen, with nothing but a window and two doors. One door he opened, and walked into the huge courtroom in front of the rows of padded pews.

He walked to the aisle and sat in the front row. Surveying the room, he noticed in front of him the railing, or bar, as Lester called it, which separated the general public from the area where the judge, jury, witnesses, lawyers, defendants, and clerks sat and worked.

He walked down the aisle to the rear doors and examined the courtroom in detail. It looked much different from Wednesday. Back down the aisle, he returned to the holding room and tried the other door, which led to the area behind the bar where the trial took place. He sat at the long table where Lester and Cobb and Willard had sat. To the right was another long table where the prosecutors sat. Behind the tables was a row of wooden chairs, then the bar with swinging gates on both ends. The judge sat high and lordly behind the elevated bench, his back to the wall under the faded portrait of Jefferson Davis, frowning down on everyone in the room. The jury box was against the wall to Carl Lee's right, to the judge's left, under the yellow portraits of other forgotten Confederate heroes. The witness stand was next to the bench, but lower, of course, and in front of the jury. To Carl Lee's left, opposite the jury box, was a long, enclosed workbench covered with large red docket books. Clerks and lawyers usually milled around behind it during a trial. Behind the workbench, through the wall, was the holding room.

Carl Lee stood, still as though handcuffed, and walked slowly through the small swinging gate in the bar, and was led through the first door into the holding room; then down the steps, ten of them, through the narrow, shadowy stairway; then he stopped. From the landing halfway down the steps, he could see the rear doors of the courthouse and most of the entrance area between the doors and the hall. At the foot of the stairs, to the right, was a door that he opened and found a crowded, junky janitor's closet. He closed the door and explored the small room. It turned and ran under the stairway. It was dark, dusty, crowded with brooms and buckets and seldom used. He opened the door slightly and looked up the stairs.

For another hour he roamed the courthouse. The other rear stairway led to another holding room just behind the jury box. One door went to the courtroom, the other to the jury room. The stairs continued to the third floor, where he found the county law library and two witness rooms, just as Lester said.

Up and down, up and down, he traced and retraced the movements to be made by the men who raped his daughter.

He sat in the judge's chair and surveyed his domain. He sat in the jury box and rocked in one of the comfortable chairs. He sat in the witness chair and blew into the microphone. It was finally dark at seven when Carl Lee raised a window in the restroom next to the janitor's closet, and slid quietly through the bushes and into the darkness.

'Who would you report it to?' Carla asked as she closed the fourteen-inch pizza box and poured some more lemonade.

Jake rocked slightly in the wicker swing on the front porch and watched Hanna skip rope on the sidewalk next to the street.

'Are you there?' she asked.

'No.'

'Who would you report it to?'

'I don't plan to report it,' he said.

'I think you should.'

'I think I shouldn't.'

'Why not?'

His rocking gained speed and he sipped the lemonade. He spoke slowly. 'First of all, I don't know for sure that a crime is being planned. He said some things any father would say, and I'm sure he's having thoughts any father would have. But as far as actually planning a crime, I don't think so. Secondly, what he said to me was said in confidence, just as if he was a client. In fact, he probably thinks of me as his lawyer.'

'But even if you're his lawyer, and you know he's planning a crime, you have to report it, don't you?'

'Yes. If I'm certain of his plans. But I'm not.'

She was not satisfied. 'I think you should report it.'

Jake did not respond. It wouldn't matter. He ate his last bite of crust and tried to ignore her.

'You want Carl Lee to do it, don't you?'

'Do what?'

'Kill those boys.'

'No, I don't.' He was not convincing. 'But if he did, I wouldn't blame him because I'd do the same thing.'

'Don't start that again.'

'I'm serious and you know it. I'd do it.'

'Jake, you couldn't kill a man.'

'Okay. Whatever. I'm not going to argue. We've been through it before.'

Carla yelled at Hanna to move away from the street. She sat next to him in the swing and rattled her ice cubes. 'Would you represent him?'

'I hope so.'

'Would the jury convict him?'

'Would you?'

'I don't know.'

'Well, think of Hanna. Just look at that sweet little innocent child out there skipping rope. You're a mother. Now think of the little Hailey girl, lying there, beaten, bloody, begging for her momma and daddy –'

'Shut up, Jake!'

He smiled. 'Answer the question. You're on the jury. Would you vote to convict the father?'

She placed her glass on the windowsill and suddenly became interested in her cuticles. Jake smelled victory.

'Come on. You're on the jury. Conviction or acquittal?'

'I'm always on the jury around here. Either that or I'm being cross-examined.'

'Convict or acquit?'

She glared at him. 'It would be hard to convict.'

He grinned and rested his case.

'But I don't see how he could kill them if they're in jail.'

'Easy. They're not always in jail. They go to court and they're transported to and from. Remember Oswald and Jack Ruby. Plus, they get out if they can make bail.'

'When can they do that?'

'Bonds will be set Monday. If they bond out, they're loose.'

'And if they can't?'

'They remain in jail until trial.'

'When is the trial?'

'Probably late summer.'

'I think you should report it.'

Jake bolted from the swing and went to play with Hanna.

CHAPTER SIX

K. T. Bruster, or Cat Bruster, as he was known, was, to his knowledge, the only one-eyed black millionaire in Memphis. He owned a string of black topless joints in town, all of which he operated legally. He owned blocks of rental property, which he operated legally, and he owned two churches in south Memphis, which were also operated legally. He was a benefactor for numerous black causes, a friend of the politicians, and a hero to his people.

It was important for Cat to be popular in the community because he would be indicted again and tried again, and in all likelihood acquitted again by his peers, half of whom were black. The authorities had found it impossible to convict Cat of killing people and of selling such things as women, cocaine, stolen goods, credit cards, food stamps, untaxed liquor, guns, and light artillery.

He had one eye with him. The other one was somewhere in a rice paddy in Vietnam. He lost it the same day in 1971 that his buddy Carl Lee Hailey was hit in the leg. Carl Lee carried him for two hours before they found help. After the war he returned to Memphis and brought with him two pounds of hashish. The proceeds went to buy a small saloon on South Main, and he almost starved before he won a whore in a poker game with a pimp. He promised her she could quit whoring if she would take off her clothes and dance on his tables. Overnight he had more business than he could seat, so he bought another bar, and brought in more dancers. He found his niche in the market, and within two years he was a very wealthy man.

His office was above one of his clubs just off South Main between Vance and Beale, in the roughest part of Memphis. The sign above the sidewalk advertised Bud and breasts, but much more was for sale behind the black windows.

Carl Lee and Lester found the lounge – Brown Sugar – around noon, Saturday. They sat at the bar, ordered Bud, and watched the breasts.

'Is Cat in?' Carl Lee asked the bartender when he walked behind them. He grunted and returned to the sink, where he continued his beer mug washing. Carl Lee glanced at him between sips and dance routines.

'Another beer!' Lester said loudly without taking his eyes off the dancers.

'Cat Bruster here?' Carl Lee asked firmly when the bartender brought the beer.

'Who wants to know?'

'I do.'

'So.'

'So me and Cat are good friends. Fought together in 'Nam.'

'Name?'

'Hailey. Carl Lee Hailey. From Mississippi.'

The bartender disappeared, and a minute later emerged from between two mirrors behind the liquor. He motioned for the Haileys, who followed him through a small door, past the restrooms and through a locked door up the stairs. The office was dark and gaudy. The carpet on the floor was gold, on the walls, red, on the ceiling, green. A green shag ceiling. Thin steel bars covered the two blackened windows, and for good measure a set of heavy, dusty, burgundy drapes hung from ceiling to floor to catch and smother any sunlight robust enough to penetrate the painted glass. A small, ineffective chrome chandelier with mirror panes rotated slowly in the center of the room, barely above their heads.

Two mammoth bodyguards in matching three-piece black suits dismissed the bartender and seated Lester and Carl Lee, and stood behind them.

The brothers admired the furnishings. 'Nice, ain't it?' Lester said. B.B. King mourned softly on a hidden stereo.

Suddenly, Cat entered from a hidden door behind the marble and glass desk. He lunged at Carl Lee. 'My man! My man! Carl Lee Hailey!' He shouted and grabbed Carl Lee. 'So good to see you, Carl Lee! So good to see you!'

Carl Lee stood and they bearhugged. 'How are you, my man!' Cat demanded.

'Doin' fine, Cat, just fine. And you?'

'Great! Great! Who's this?' He turned to Lester and threw a hand in his chest. Lester shook it violently.

'This here's my brother, Lester,' Carl Lee said. 'He's from Chicago.'

'Glad to know you, Lester. Me and the big man here are mighty tight. Mighty tight.'

'He's told me all about you,' Lester said. Cat admired Carl Lee. 'My, my, Carl Lee. You lookin' good. How's the leg?'

'It's fine, Cat. Tightens up sometimes when it rains, but it's fine.'

'We mighty tight, ain't we?'

Carl Lee nodded and smiled. Cat released him. 'You fellas want a drink?'

'No thanks,' said Carl Lee.

'I'll take a beer,' said Lester. Cat snapped his fingers and a bodyguard disappeared. Carl Lee fell into his chair and Cat sat on the edge of his desk, his feet dangling and swinging like a kid on a pier. He grinned at Carl Lee, who squirmed under all the admiration.

'Why don't you move to Memphis and go to work for me?' Cat said. Carl Lee knew it was coming. Cat had been offering him jobs for ten years.

'No thanks, Cat. I'm happy.'

'And I'm happy for you. What's on your mind?'

Carl Lee opened his mouth, hesitated, crossed his legs and frowned. He nodded, and said, 'Need a favor, Cat. Just a small favor.'

Cat spread his arms. 'Anything, big man, anything you want.'

'You remember them M-16's we used in 'Nam? I need one of them. As quick as possible.'

Cat recoiled his arms and folded them across his chest. He studied his friend. 'That's a bad gun. What kinda squirrels you huntin' down there?'

'It ain't for squirrels.'

Cat analyzed them both. He knew better than to ask why. It was serious, or Carl Lee wouldn't be there. 'Semi?'

'Nope. The real thing.'

'You talkin' some cash.'

'How much?'

'It's illegal as hell, you know?'

'If I could buy it at Sears I wouldn't be here.'

Cat grinned again. 'When do you need it?'

'Today.'

The beer arrived and was served to Lester. Cat moved behind his desk, to his orange vinyl captain's chair. 'Thousand bucks.'

'I got it.'

Cat was mildly surprised, but didn't show it. Where did this simple small-town Mississippi nigger find a thousand dollars? Must have borrowed it from his brother.

'Thousand for anyone else, but not for you, big man.'

'How much?'

'Nothin', Carl Lee, nothin'. I owe you somethin' worth much more than money.'

'I'll be glad to pay for it.'

'Nope. I won't hear it. The gun's yours.'

'That's mighty kind, Cat.'

'I'd give you fifty of them.'

'Just need one. When can I get it?'

'Lemme check.' Cat phoned someone and mumbled a few sentences into the receiver. The orders given, he hung up and explained it would take about an hour.

'We can wait,' Carl Lee said.

Cat removed the patch from his left eye and wiped the empty socket with a handkerchief. 'I gotta better idea.' He snapped at the bodyguards. 'Get my car. We'll drive over and pick it up.'

They followed Cat through a secret door and down a hall. 'I live here, you know.' He pointed. 'Through that door is my pad. Usually keep some naked women around.'

'I'd like to see it,' Lester volunteered.

'That's okay,' said Carl Lee.

Farther down the hall Cat pointed to a thick, black, shiny iron door at the end of a short hallway. He stopped as if to admire it. 'That's where I keep my cash. Post a guard in there around the clock.'

'How much?' Lester asked with a sip of beer.

Cat glared at him and continued down the hall. Carl Lee frowned at his brother and shook his head. Where the hall ended they climbed a narrow stairway to the fourth floor. It was darker, and somewhere in the darkness Cat found a button on a wall. They waited silently for a few seconds until the wall opened and revealed a bright elevator with red carpet and a NO SMOKING sign. Cat pushed another button.

'You gotta walk up to catch the elevator goin' down,' he said with amusement. 'Security reasons.' They nodded approval and admiration.

It opened in the basement. One of the bodyguards waited by the open door of a clean white stretch limo, and Cat invited his guests in for a ride. They moved slowly past a row of Fleetwoods, several more limos, a Rolls, and an assortment of European luxury cars. 'They're all mine,' he said proudly.

The driver honked and a heavy door rolled up to reveal a one-way side street. 'Drive slow,' Cat yelled to the chauffeur and the bodyguard way up front. 'I wanna show you fellas around some.'

Carl Lee had received the tour a few years earlier during his last visit to Cat. There were rows of beaten and paintless shacks that the great man referred to as rental properties. There were ancient red-bricked warehouses with blackened or boarded windows and no clue as to what was stored inside. There was a church, a prosperous church, and a few blocks away, another one. He owned the preachers too, he said. There were dozens of corner taverns with open doors and groups of young blacks sitting on benches outside drinking quart bottles of Stag beer. He pointed proudly to a burned-out building near Beale and told with great zeal the story of a competitor who had attempted to gain a foothold in the topless business. He had no competitors, he said. And then there were the clubs, places with names like Angels and Cat's House and Black Paradise, places where a man could go for good drink, good food, good music, naked women, and possibly more, he said. The clubs had made him a very rich man. Eight of them in all.

They were shown all eight. Plus what seemed like most of the real estate in south Memphis. At the dead end of a nameless street near the river, the driver turned sharply between two of the red-bricked warehouses and drove through a narrow alley until a gate opened to the right. Past the gate a door opened next to a loading dock and the limo disappeared into the building. It stopped and the bodyguard got out.

'Keep your seats,' Cat said.

The trunk opened, then shut. In less than a minute the limo was again cruising the streets of Memphis.

'How 'bout lunch?' Cat asked. Before they answered he yelled at the driver, 'Black Paradise. Call and tell them I'm comin' for lunch.

'Got the best prime rib in Memphis, right here in one of my clubs. Course you won't read about it in the Sunday paper. I've been shunned by the critics. Can you imagine?'

'Sounds like discrimination,' Lester said.

'Yeah, I'm sure it is. But I don't use that until I'm indicted.'

'We ain't read about you lately, Cat,' Carl Lee said.

'It's been three years since my last trial. Tax evasion. Feds spent three weeks puttin' on proof, and the jury stayed out twenty-seven minutes and returned with the two most precious words in the Afro-English language – "Not guilty." '

'I've heard them myself,' Lester said.

A doorman waited under the canopy at the club, and a set of matching bodyguards, different bodyguards, escorted the great one and his guests to a private booth away from the dance floor. Drinks and food were served by a squad of waiters. Lester switched to Scotch and was drunk when the prime rib arrived. Carl Lee drank iced tea and swapped war stories with Cat.

When the food was gone, a bodyguard approached and whispered to Cat. He grinned and looked at Carl Lee. 'Y'all in the red Eldorado with Illinois plates?'

'Yeah. But we left it at the other place.'

'It's parked outside . . . in the trunk.'

'What?' said Lester. 'How –'

Cat roared and slapped him on the back. 'Don't ask, my man, don't ask. It's all taken care of, my man. Cat can do anything.'

As usual, Jake worked Saturday morning, after breakfast at the Coffee Shop. He enjoyed the tranquility of his office on Saturday – no phones, no Ethel. He locked the office, ignored the phone, and avoided clients.

He organized files, read recent decisions from the Supreme Court and planned strategy if a trial was approaching. His best thoughts and ideas came during quiet Saturday mornings.

At eleven he phoned the jail. 'Sheriff in?' he asked the dispatcher.

'Lemme check,' came the reply.

Moments passed before the sheriff answered. 'Sheriff Walls,' he announced.

'Ozzie, Jake Brigance. How are you?'

'Fine, Jake. You?'

'Fine. Will you be there for a while?'

'Coupla hours. What's up?'

'Not much. Just need to talk for a minute. I'll be there in thirty minutes.'

'I'll be waitin'.'

Jake and the sheriff had a mutual like and respect for each other. Jake had roughed him up a few times during cross-examinations, but Ozzie considered it business and nothing personal. Jake campaigned for Ozzie, and Lucien financed the campaigns, so Ozzie didn't mind a few sarcastic and pointed questions during trial. He liked to watch Jake at trial. And he liked to kid him about *the game*. In 1969, when Jake was a sophomore quarterback at Karaway, Ozzie was a senior all-conference, all-state tackle at Clanton. The two rivals, both undefeated, met in the final game at Clanton for the conference championship. For four long quarters Ozzie terrorized the Karaway offense, which was much smaller and led by a gutsy but battered sophomore quarterback. Late in the fourth quarter, leading 44–0, Ozzie broke Jake's leg on a blitz.

For years now he had threatened to break the other one. He always accused Jake of limping and asked about the leg.

'What's on your mind, buddy?' Ozzie asked as they sat in his small office.

'Carl Lee. I'm a little worried about him.'

'What way?'

'Look, Ozzie, whatever we say here is said in confidence. I don't want anyone to know about this conversation.'

'You sound serious, Jake.'

'I am serious. I talked to Carl Lee Wednesday after the hearing. He's out of his mind, and I understand that. I would be too. He was talking about killing the boys, and he sounded serious. I just think you ought to know.'

'They're safe, Jake. He couldn't get to them if he wanted to. We've had some phone calls, anonymous of course, with all kinds of threats. Black folks are bad upset. But the boys're safe. They're in a cell by themselves, and we're real careful.'

'That's good. I haven't been hired by Carl Lee, but I've represented all the Haileys at one time or another and I'm sure he considers me to be his lawyer, for whatever reason. I feel a responsibility to let you know.'

'I'm not worried, Jake.'

'Good. Let me ask you something. I've got a daughter, and you've got a daughter, right?'

'Got two of them.'

'What's Carl Lee thinking? I mean, as a black father?'

'Same thing you'd be thinkin'.'

'And what's that?'

Ozzie reared back in his chair and crossed his arms. He thought for a moment. 'He's wonderin' if she's okay, physically, I mean. Is she gonna live, and if she does, how bad is she hurt. Can she ever have kids? Then he's wonderin' if she's okay mentally and emotionally, and how will this affect her for the rest of her life. Thirdly, he wants to kill thc bastards.'

'Would you?'

'It's easy to say I would, but a man don't know what he'd do. I think my kids need me at home a whole lot more than Parchman needs me. What would you be thinkin', Jake?'

'About the same, I guess. I don't know what I'd do. Probably go crazy.' He paused and stared at the desk. 'But I might seriously plan to kill whoever did it. It'd be mighty hard to lie down at night knowing he was still alive.'

'What would a jury do?'

'Depends on who's on the jury. You pick the right jury and you walk. If the D.A. picks the right jury you get the gas. It depends strictly on the jury, and in this county you can pick the right folks. People are tired of raping and robbing and killing. I know white folks are.'

'Everbody is.'

'My point is that there'd be a lot of sympathy for a father who took matters into his own hands. People don't trust our judicial system. I think I could at least hang a jury. Just convince one or two that the bastard needed to die.'

'Like Monroe Bowie.'

'Exactly. Just like Monroe Bowie. He was a sorry nigger who needed killing and Lester took a walk. By the way, Ozzie, why do you suppose Lester drove from Chicago?'

'He's pretty close to his brother. We're watchin' him too.'

The conversation changed and Ozzie finally asked about the leg. They shook hands and Jake left. He drove straight home, where Carla was waiting with her list. She didn't mind the Saturdays at the office as long as he was home by noon and pretty much followed orders thereafter.

On Sunday afternoon a crowd gathered at the hospital and followed the little Hailey girl's wheelchair as it was pushed by her father down the hall, through the doors, and into the parking lot, where he gently raised her and sat her in the front seat. As she sat between her parents, with her three brothers in the back seat, he drove away, followed by a procession of friends and relatives and strangers. The caravan moved slowly, deliberately out of town and into the country.

She sat up in the front seat like a big girl. Her father was silent, her mother tearful, and her brothers mute and rigid.

Another throng waited at the house and rushed to the porch as the cars moved up the driveway and parked on the grass on the long front yard. The crowd hushed as he carried her up the steps, through the door, and laid her on the couch. She was glad to be home, but tired of the spectators. Her mother held her feet as cousins, uncles, aunts, neighbors, and everybody walked to her and touched her and smiled, some through tears, and said nothing. Her daddy went outside and talked to Uncle Lester and the men. Her brothers were in the kitchen with the crowd devouring the pile of food.

CHAPTER SEVEN

Rocky Childers had been the prosecutor for Ford County for more years than he cared to remember. The job paid fifteen thousand a year and required most of his time. It also destroyed any practice he hoped to build. At forty-two he was washed up as a lawyer, stuck in a dead-end part-time, full-time job, elected permanently every four years. Thankfully, he had a wife with a good job so they could drive new Buicks and afford the country club dues and in general put on the necessary airs of educated white people in Ford County. At a younger age he had political ambitions, but the voters dissuaded him, and he was malcontent to exhaust his career prosecuting drunks, shoplifters, and juvenile delinquents, and being abused by Judge Bullard, whom he despised. Excitement crept up occasionally when people like Cobb and Willard screwed up, and Rocky, by statutory authority, handled the preliminary and other hearings before the cases were sent to the grand jury and then to Circuit Court, and then to the real prosecutor, the big prosecutor, the district attorney, Mr. Rufus Buckley, from Polk County. It was Buckley who had disposed of Rocky's political career.

Normally, a bail hearing was no big affair for Childers, but this was a bit different. Since Wednesday he had received dozens of phone calls from blacks, all registered voters or claiming to be, who were very concerned about Cobb and Willard being released from jail. They wanted the boys locked up, just like the black ones who got in trouble and could not make bail before trial. Childers promised his best, but explained the bonds would be set by County Judge Percy Bullard, whose number was also in the phone book. On Bennington Street. They promised to be in court Monday to watch him and Bullard.

At twelve-thirty Monday, Childers was summoned to the judge's chambers, where the sheriff and Bullard were waiting. The judge was so nervous he could not sit.

'How much bond do you want?' he snapped at Childers.

'I dunno, Judge. I haven't thought much about it.'

'Don't you think it's about time you thought about it?' He paced rapidly back and forth behind his desk, then to the window, then back to his desk. Ozzie was amused and silent.

'Not really,' Childers answered softly. 'It's your decision. You're the judge.'

'Thanks! Thanks! Thanks! How much will you ask for?'

'I always ask for more than I expect,' replied Childers coolly, thoroughly enjoying the judge's neurosis.

'How much is that?'

'I dunno. I hadn't thought much about it.'

Bullard's neck turned dark red and he glared at Ozzie. 'Whatta you think, Sheriff?'

'Well,' Ozzie drawled, 'I would suggest pretty stiff bonds. These boys need to be in jail for their own safety. Black folk are restless out there. They might get hurt if they bond out. Better go high.'

'How much money they got?'

'Willard's broke. Can't tell about Cobb. Drug money's hard to trace. He might could find twenty, thirty thousand. I hear he's hired some big-shot Memphis lawyer. Supposed to be here today. He must have some money.'

'Damn, why don't I know these things. Who'd he hire?'

'Bernard. Peter K. Bernard,' answered Childers. 'He called me this morning.'

'Never heard of him,' retorted Bullard with an air of superiority, as though he memorized some kind of judicial rap sheet on all lawyers.

Bullard studied the trees outside the window as the sheriff and prosecutor exchanged winks. The bonds would be exorbitant, as always. The bail bondsmen loved Bullard for his outrageous bonds. They watched with delight as desperate families scraped and mortgaged to collect the ten percent premiums they charged to write the bonds. Bullard would be high, and he didn't care. It was politically safe to set them high and keep the criminals in jail. The blacks would appreciate it and that was important even if the county was seventy-four percent white. He owed the blacks a few favors.

'Let's go a hundred thousand on Willard and two hundred on Cobb. That oughtta satisfy them.'

'Satisfy who?' asked Ozzie.

'Er, uh, the people, the people out there. Sound okay to you?'

'Fine with me,' said Childers. 'But what about the hearing?' he asked with a grin.

'We'll give them a hearing, a fair hearing, then I'll set the bonds at a hundred and two hundred.'

'And I suppose you want me to ask for three hundred apiece so you can look fair?' asked Childers.

'I don't care what you ask for!' yelled the judge.

'Sounds fair to me,' said Ozzie as he headed for the door. 'Will you call me to testify?' he asked Childers.

'Naw, we don't need you. I don't guess the State will call anybody since we're having such a fair hearing.'

They left the chambers and Bullard stewed. He locked the door behind them and pulled a half pint of vodka from his briefcase, and gulped it furiously. Mr. Pate waited outside the door. Five minutes later Bullard barged into the packed courtroom.

'All rise for the court!' Mr. Pate shouted.

'Be seated!' screamed the judge before anyone could stand. 'Where are the defendants? Where?'

Cobb and Willard were escorted from the holding room and seated at the defense table. Cobb's new lawyer smiled at his client as the handcuffs were removed. Willard's lawyer, Tyndale, the public defender, ignored him.

The same crowd of blacks had returned from last Wednesday, and had brought some friends. They closely followed the movements of the two white boys. Lester saw them for the first time. Carl Lee was not in the courtroom.

From the bench Bullard counted deputies – nine in all. That had to be a record. Then he counted blacks – hundreds of them all bunched together, all glaring at the two rapists, who sat at the same table between their lawyers. The vodka felt good. He took a sip of what appeared to be ice water from a Styrofoam cup and managed a slight grin. It burned slowly downward and his cheeks flushed. What he ought to do was order the deputies out of the courtroom and throw Cobb and Willard to the niggers. That would be fun to watch, and justice would be served. He could just see the fat nigger women stomping up and down while their men carved on the boys with switchblades and machetes. Then, when they were finished, they would collect themselves and all march quietly from the courtroom. He smiled to himself.

He motioned for Mr. Pate, who approached the bench. 'I've got a half pint of ice water in my desk drawer,' he whispered. 'Pour me some in a Styrofoam cup.'

Mr. Pate nodded and disappeared.

'This is a bail hearing,' he declared loudly, 'and I don't intend for it to last long. Are the defendants ready?'

'Yes, sir,' said Tyndale.

'Yes, Your Honor,' said Mr. Bernard.

'The State ready?'

'Yes, sir,' answered Childers without standing.

'Good. Call your first witness.'

Childers addressed the judge. 'Your Honor, the State will call no witnesses. His Honor is well aware of the charges against these two defendants, since His Honor held the preliminary hearing last Wednesday. It is my understanding the victim is now home, so we do not anticipate further charges. The grand jury will be asked next Monday to indict the two defendants for rape, kidnapping, and aggravated assault. Because of the violent nature of these crimes, because of the age of the victim, and because Mr. Cobb is a convicted felon, the State would ask for the maximum bonds, and not a penny less.'

Bullard almost choked on his ice water. What maximum? There's no such thing as a maximum bond.

'What do you suggest, Mr. Childers?'

'Half a million apiece!' Childers announced proudly and sat down.

Half a million! Out of the question, thought Bullard. He sipped furiously and glared at the prosecutor. Half a million! Double-crossed in open court. He sent Mr. Pate after more ice water.

'The defense may proceed.'

Cobb's new lawyer stood purposefully. He cleared his throat and removed his horn-rimmed, academic, go-to-hell reading glasses. 'May it please the court, Your Honor, my name is Peter K. Bernard. I am from Memphis, and I have been retained by Mr. Cobb to represent him –'

'Do you have a license to practice in Mississippi?' interrupted Bullard.

Bernard was caught off-guard. 'Well, uh, not exactly, Your Honor.'

'I see. When you say "not exactly," do you mean something other than no?'

Several lawyers in the jury box snickered. Bullard was famous for this. He hated Memphis lawyers, and required them to associate local counsel before appearing in his court. Years before when he was practicing, a Memphis judge had kicked him out of court because he was not licensed in Tennessee. He had enjoyed revenge since the day he was elected.

'Your Honor, I am not licensed in Mississippi, but I am licensed in Tennessee.'

'I would hope so,' came the retort from the bench. More suppressed laughter from the jury box. 'Are you familiar with our local rules here in Ford County?' His Honor asked.

'Er, uh, yes, sir.'

'Do you have a copy of these rules?'

'Yes, sir.'

'And you read them carefully before you ventured into my courtroom?'

'Uh, yes, sir, most of them.'

'Did you understand Rule 14 when you read it?'

Cobb glanced up suspiciously at his new lawyer.

'Uh, I don't recall that one,' Bernard admitted.

'I didn't think so. Rule 14 requires out-of-state unlicensed attorneys to associate local counsel when appearing in my courtroom.'

'Yes, sir.'

From his looks and mannerisms, Bernard was a polished attorney, at least he was known as such in Memphis. He was, however, in the process of being totally degraded and humbled before a small-town, redneck judge with a quick tongue.

'Yes, sir, what?' snapped Bullard.

'Yes, sir, I think I've heard of that rule.'

'Then where's the local counsel?'

'There is none, but I planned –'

'Then you drove down here from Memphis, carefully read my rules, and deliberately ignored them. Right?'

Bernard lowered his head and stared at a blank yellow legal pad on the table.

Tyndale rose slowly. 'Your Honor, for the record, I show myself as associated counsel for Mr. Bernard for purposes of this hearing and for no other purpose.'

Bullard smiled. Slick move, Tyndale, slick move. The ice water warmed him and he relaxed. 'Very well. Call your first witness.'

Bernard stood straight again. He cocked his head. 'Your Honor, on behalf of Mr. Cobb, I would like to call his brother, Mr. Fred Cobb, to the stand.'

'Make it brief,' Bullard mumbled.

Cobb's brother was sworn and seated in the witness chair. Bernard assumed the podium and began a long, detailed direct examination. He was well prepared. He elicited proof that Billy Ray Cobb was gainfully employed, owned real estate in Ford County, grew up there, had most of his family there, and friends, and had no reason to leave. A solid citizen with deep roots with much to lose if he fled. A man who could be trusted to show up for court. A man worthy of a low bond.

Bullard sipped, tapped his pen, and searched the black faces in the audience.

Childers had no questions. Bernard called Cobb's mother, Cora, who repeated what her son Fred said about her son Billy Ray. She managed a couple of tears at an awkward moment, and Bullard shook his head.

Tyndale was next. He went through the same motions with Willard's family.

Half a million dollars bond! Anything less would be too little, and the blacks wouldn't like it. The judge had new reason to hate Childers. But he liked the blacks because they elected him last time. He received fifty-one percent of the vote countywide, but he got all the nigger vote.

'Anything else?' he asked when Tyndale finished.

The three lawyers looked blankly at each other, then at the judge. Bernard stood. 'Your Honor, I would like to summarize my client's position in regard to a reasonable bond –'

'Forget it, pal. I've heard enough from you and your client. Sit down.'

Bullard hesitated, then rapidly announced: 'Bond is hereby set at one hundred thousand for Pete Willard, and two hundred thousand for Billy Ray Cobb. Defendants will remain in the custody of the sheriff until they are able to make bail. Court's adjourned.' He rapped the gavel and disappeared into his chambers, where he finished the half pint and opened another one.

Lester was pleased with the bonds. His had been fifty thousand for the murder of Monroe Bowie. Of course, Bowie was black, and bonds were generally lower for those cases.

The crowd inched toward the rear door, but Lester did not move. He watched closely as the two white boys were handcuffed and taken through the door into the holding room. When they were out of sight, he placed his head in his hands and said a short prayer. Then he listened.

At least ten times a day Jake walked through the French doors and onto the balcony to inspect downtown Clanton. He sometimes puffed a cheap cigar and blew smoke over Washington Street. Even in the summer he left the windows open in the big office. The sounds of the busy small town made good company as he worked quietly. At times he was amazed at the volume of noise generated on the streets around the courthouse, and at other times he walked to the balcony to see why things were so quiet.

Just before 2:00 P.M., Monday, May 20, he walked to the balcony and lit a cigar. A heavy silence engulfed downtown Clanton, Mississippi.

Cobb went first down the stairs, cautiously, with his hands cuffed behind him, then Willard, then Deputy Looney. Ten steps down, then the landing, turn right, then ten steps to the first floor. Three other deputies waited outside by the patrol cars smoking cigarettes and watching reporters.

When Cobb reached the second step from the floor, and Willard was three steps behind, and Looney was one step off the landing, the small, dirty, neglected, unnoticed door to the janitor's closet burst open and Mr. Carl Lee Hailey sprung from the darkness with an M-16. At pointblank range he opened fire. The loud, rapid, clapping, popping gunfire shook the courthouse and exploded the silence. The rapists froze, then screamed as they were hit – Cobb first, in the stomach and chest, then Willard in the face, neck, and throat. They twisted vainly up the stairs, handcuffed and helpless, stumbling over each other as their skin and blood splashed together.

Looney was hit in the leg but managed to scramble up the stairs into the holding room, where he crouched and listened as Cobb and Willard screamed and moaned and the crazy nigger laughed. Bullets ricocheted between the walls of the narrow stairway, and Looney could see, looking down toward the landing, blood and flesh splashing on the walls and dripping down.

In short, sudden bursts of seven or eight rounds each, the enormous booming sound of the M-16 echoed through the courthouse for an eternity. Through the gunfire and the sounds of the bullets rattling around the walls of the stairway, the high-pitched, shrill, laughing voice of Carl Lee could be plainly heard.

When he stopped, he threw the rifle at the two corpses and ran. Into the restroom, he jammed the door with a chair, crawled out a window into the bushes, then onto the sidewalk. Nonchalantly, he walked to his pickup and drove home.

Lester froze when the shooting started. The gunfire was heard loudly in the courtroom. Willard's mother screamed and Cobb's mother screamed, and the deputies raced into the holding room, but did not venture down the stairs. Lester listened intently for the sounds of handguns, and hearing none, he left the courtroom.

With the first shot, Bullard grabbed the half pint and crawled under his desk while Mr. Pate locked the door.

Cobb, or what was left of him, came to rest on Willard. Their blood mixed and puddled on each step, then it overflowed and dripped to the next step, where it puddled before overflowing and dripping to the next. Soon the foot of the stairway was flooded with the mixture.

Jake sprinted across the street to the rear door of the courthouse. Deputy Prather crouched in front of the door, gun drawn, and cursed the reporters who pressed forward. The other deputies knelt fearfully on the doorsteps next to the patrol cars. Jake ran to the front of the courthouse, where more deputies were guarding the door and evacuating the county employees and courtroom spectators. A mass of bodies poured onto the front steps. Jake fought through the stampede and into the rotunda and found Ozzie directing people and yelling in all directions. He motioned for Jake, and they walked down the hall to the rear doors, where a half dozen deputies stood, guns in hand, gazing silently at the stairway. Jake felt nauseated. Willard had almost made it to the landing. The front of his head was missing, and his brains rolled out like jelly covering his face. Cobb had been able to twist over and absorb the bullets with his back. His face was buried in Willard's stomach, and his feet touched the fourth step from the floor. The blood continued from the lifeless bodies, and it covered completely the bottom six steps. The crimson pool on the floor inched quickly toward the deputies, who slowly backed away. The weapon was between Cobb's legs on the fifth step, and it too was covered with blood.

The group stood silently, mesmerized by the two bodies, which, though dead, continued to spew blood. The thick smell of gunfire hung over the stairway and drifted toward the hall into the rotunda, where the deputies continued to move people toward the front door.

'Jake, you'd better leave,' Ozzie said without looking from the bodies.

'Why?'

'Just leave.'

'Why?'

' 'Cause we gotta take pictures and collect evidence and stuff, and you don't need to be here.'

'Okay. But you don't interrogate him out of my presence. Understand?'

Ozzie nodded.

The photographs were taken, the mess cleaned, the evidence gathered, the bodies removed, and two hours later Ozzie left town followed by five patrol cars. Hastings drove and led the convoy into the country, toward the lake, past Bates Grocery, onto Craft Road. The Hailey driveway was empty except for Gwen's car, Carl Lee's pickup, and the red Cadillac from Illinois.

Ozzie expected no trouble as the patrol cars parked in a row across the front yard, and the deputies crouched behind the open doors, watching as the sheriff walked alone to the house. He stopped. The front door opened slowly and the Hailey family emerged. Carl Lee walked to the edge of the porch with Tonya in his arms. He looked down at his friend the sheriff, and behind him at the row of cars and deputies. To his right was Gwen, and to his left were his three sons, the smallest one crying softly but the older ones brave and proud. Behind them stood Lester.

The two groups watched each other, each waiting for the other to say or do something, each wanting to avoid what was about to happen. The only sounds were the soft sniffles of the little girl, her mother, and the youngest boy.

The children had tried to understand. Their daddy had explained to them what he had just done, and why. They understood that, but they could not comprehend why he had to be arrested and taken to jail.

Ozzie kicked at a clod of dirt, occasionally glancing at the family, then at his men.

Finally, he said, 'You better come with me.'

Carl Lee nodded slightly, but did not move. Gwen and the boy cried louder as Lester took the girl from her daddy. Then Carl Lee knelt before the three boys and whispered to them again that he must leave but wouldn't be gone long. He hugged them, and they all cried and clutched him. He turned and kissed his wife, then walked down the steps to the sheriff.

'You wanna handcuff me, Ozzie?'

'Naw, Carl Lee, just get in the car.'

CHAPTER EIGHT

Moss Junior Tatum, the chief deputy, and Jake talked quietly in Ozzie's office while deputies, reserves, trusties, and other jailhouse regulars gathered in the large, cluttered workroom next to the office and waited anxiously for the arrival of the new prisoner. Two of the deputies peered through the blinds at the reporters and cameramen waiting in the parking lot between the jail and the highway. The television vans were from Memphis, Jackson, and Tupelo, and they were parked in various directions throughout the crowded lot. Moss did not like this, so he walked slowly down the sidewalk and ordered the press to regroup in a certain area, and to move the vans.

'Will you make a statement?' yelled a reporter.

'Yeah, move the vans.'

'Can you say anything about the murders?'

'Yeah, two people got killed.'

'How about the details?'

'Nope. I wasn't there.'

'Do you have a suspect?'

'Yep.'

'Who is it?'

'I'll tell you when the vans are moved.'

The vans were immediately moved and the cameras and microphones were bunched together near the sidewalk. Moss pointed and directed until he was satisfied, then stepped to the crowd. He calmly chewed on a toothpick and stuck both thumbs in the front belt loops, just under the overlapping belly.

'Who did it?'

'Is he under arrest?'

'Was the girl's family involved?'

'Are both dead?'

Moss smiled and shook his head. 'One at a time. Yes we have a suspect. He's under arrest and will be here in a minute. Keep the vans outta the way. That's all I have.' Moss walked back to the jail as they continued to call at him. He ignored them and entered the crowded workroom.

'How's Looney?' he asked.

'Prather's with him at the hospital. He's fine – slight wound to the leg.'

'Yeah, that and a slight heart attack,' Moss said with a smile. The others laughed.

'Here they come!' a trusty shouted, and everyone inside moved to the windows as the line of blue lights rolled slowly into the parking lot. Ozzie drove the first car with Carl Lee seated, unhandcuffed, in the front. Hastings reclined in the back and waved at the cameras as the car passed them and continued through the crowd, past the vans and around to the rear of the jail, where Ozzie parked and the three walked casually inside. Carl Lee was given to the jailer, and Ozzie walked down the hall to his office where Jake was waiting.

'You can see him in a minute, Jake,' he said.

'Thanks. You sure he did it?'

'Yeah, I'm sure.'

'He didn't confess, did he?'

'No, he didn't say much of nothin'. I guess Lester coached him.'

Moss walked in. 'Ozzie, them reporters wanna talk to you. I said you'd be out in a minute.'

'Thanks, Moss,' Ozzie sighed.

'Anybody see it?' Jake asked.

Ozzie wiped his forehead with a red handkerchief. 'Yeah, Looney can I.D. him. You know Murphy, the little crippled man who sweeps floors in the courthouse?'

'Sure. Stutters real bad.'

'He saw the whole thing. He was sittin' on the east stairs, directly across from where it happened. Eatin' his lunch. Scared him so bad he couldn't talk for an hour.' Ozzie paused and eyed Jake. 'Why am I tellin' you all this?'

'What difference does it make? I'll find out sooner or later. Where's my man?'

'Down the hall in the jail. They gotta take his picture and all that. Be 'bout thirty minutes.'

Ozzie left and Jake used his phone to call Carla and remind her to watch the news and record it.

Ozzie faced the microphones and cameras. 'I ain't answerin' no questions. We have a suspect in custody. Name of Carl Lee Hailey from Ford County. Arrested for two counts of murder.'

'Is he the girl's father?'

'Yes, he is.'

'How do you know he did it?'

'We're very smart.'

'Any eyewitnesses?'

'None that we know of.'

'Has he confessed?'

'No.'

'Where'd you find him?'

'At his house.'

'Was a deputy shot?'

'Yes.'

'How is he?'

'He's fine. He's in the hospital, but he's okay.'

'What's his name?'

'Looney. DeWayne Looney.'

'When's the preliminary hearing?'

'I'm not the judge.'

'Any idea?'

'Maybe tomorrow, maybe Wednesday. No more questions, please. I have no further information to release at this time.'

The jailer took Carl Lee's wallet, money, watch, keys, ring, and pocketknife and listed the items on an inventory form that Carl Lee signed and dated. In a small room next to the jailer's station, he was photographed and fingerprinted, just as Lester said. Ozzie waited outside the door and led him down the hall to a small room where the drunks were taken to blow into the Intoxilyzer. Jake sat at a small table next to the machine. Ozzie excused himself.

The lawyer and client sat across the table and analyzed each other carefully. They grinned admiringly but neither spoke. They had last talked five days before, on Wednesday after the preliminary hearing, the day after the rape.

Carl Lee was not as troubled now. His face was relaxed and his eyes were clear. Finally he said: 'You didn't think I'd do it, Jake.'

'Not really. You did do it?'

'You know I did.'

Jake smiled, nodded, and crossed his arms. 'How do you feel?'

Carl Lee relaxed and sat back in the folding chair. 'Well, I feel better. I don't feel good 'bout the whole thing. I wish it didn't happen. But I wish my girl was okay too, you know. I didn't have nothin' against them boys till they messed with her. Now they got what they started. I feel sorry for their mommas and daddies, if they got daddies, which I doubt.'

'Are you scared?'

'Of what?'

'How about the gas chamber?'

'Naw, Jake, that's why I got you. I don't plan to go to no gas chamber. I saw you get Lester off, now just get me off. You can do it, Jake.'

'It's not quite that easy, Carl Lee.'

'Say what?'

'You just don't shoot a person, or persons, in cold blood, and then tell the jury they needed killing, and expect to walk out of the courtroom.'

'You did with Lester.'

'But every case is different. And the big difference here is that you killed two white boys and Lester killed a nigger. Big difference.'

'You scared, Jake?'

'Why should I be scared? I'm not facing the gas chamber.'

'You don't sound too confident.'

You big stupid idiot, thought Jake. How could he be confident at a time like this. The bodies were still warm. Sure, he was confident before the killings, but now it was different. His client was facing the gas for a crime which he admits he committed.

'Where'd you get the gun?'

'A friend in Memphis.'

'Okay. Did Lester help?'

'Nope. He knew 'bout what I's gonna do, and he wanted to help, but I wouldn't let him.'

'How's Gwen?'

'She's pretty crazy right now, but Lester's with her. She didn't know a thing about it.'

'The kids?'

'You know how kids are. They don't want their daddy in jail. They upset, but they'll make it. Lester'll take care of them.'

'Is he going back to Chicago?'

'Not for a while. Jake, when do we go to court?'

'The preliminary should be tomorrow or Wednesday, depends on Bullard.'

'Is he the judge?'

'He will be for the preliminary hearing. But he won't hear the trial. That'll be in Circuit Court.'

'Who's the judge there?'

'Omar Noose from Van Buren County; same judge who tried Lester.'

'Good. He's okay, ain't he?'

'Yeah, he's a good judge.'

'When will the trial be?'

'Late summer or early fall. Buckley will push for a quick trial.'

'Who's Buckley?'

'Rufus Buckley. District attorney. Same D.A. who prosecuted Lester. You remember him. Big, loud guy –'

'Yeah, yeah, I remember. Big bad Rufus Buckley. I'd forgot all about him. He's pretty mean, ain't he?'

'He's good, very good. He's corrupt and ambitious, and he'll eat this up because of the publicity.'

'You've beat him, ain't you?'

'Yeah, and he's beat me.'

Jake opened his briefcase and removed a file. Inside was a contract for legal services, which he studied although he had it memorized. His fees were based on the ability to pay, and the blacks generally could pay little unless there was a close and generous relative in St. Louis or Chicago with a good-paying job. Those were rare. In Lester's trial there had been a brother in California who worked for the post office but he'd been unwilling or unable to help. There were some sisters scattered around but they had their own problems and had offered only moral support for Lester. Gwen had a big family, and they stayed out of trouble, but they were not prosperous. Carl Lee owned a few acres around his house and had mortgaged it to help Lester pay Jake before.

He had charged Lester five thousand for his murder trial; half was paid before trial and the rest in installments over three years.

Jake hated to discuss fees. It was the most difficult part of practicing law. Clients wanted to know up front, immediately, how much he would cost, and they all reacted differently. Some were shocked, some just swallowed hard, a few had stormed out of his office. Some negotiated, but most paid or promised to pay.

He studied the file and the contract and thought desperately of a fair fee. There were other lawyers out there who would take such a case for almost nothing. Nothing but publicity. He thought about the acreage, and the job at the paper mill, and the family, and finally said, 'My fee is ten thousand.'

Carl Lee was not moved. 'You charged Lester five thousand.'

Jake anticipated this. 'You have three counts; Lester had one.'

'How many times can I go to the gas chamber?'

'Good point. How much can you pay?'

'I can pay a thousand now,' he said proudly. 'And I'll borrow as much as I can on my land and give it all to you.'

Jake thought a minute. 'I've got a better idea. Let's agree on a fee. You pay a thousand now and sign a note for the rest. Borrow on your land and pay against the note.'

'How much you want?' asked Carl Lee.

'Ten thousand.'

'I'll pay five.'

'You can pay more than that.'

'And you can do it for less than ten.'

'Okay, I can do it for nine.'

'Then I can pay six.'

'Eight?'

'Seven.'

'Can we agree on seventy-five hundred?'

'Yeah, I think I can pay that much. Depends on how much they'll loan me on my land. You want me to pay a thousand now and sign a note for sixty-five hundred?'

'That's right.'

'Okay, you got a deal.'

Jake filled in the blanks in the contract and promissory note, and Carl Lee signed both.

'Jake, how much would you charge a man with plenty of money?'

'Fifty thousand.'

'Fifty thousand! You serious?'

'Yep.'

'Man, that's a lotta money. You ever get that much?'

'No, but I haven't seen too many people on trial for murder with that kind of money.'

Carl Lee wanted to know about his bond, the grand jury, the trial, the witnesses, who would be on the jury, when could be get out of jail, could Jake speed up the trial, when could he tell his version, and a thousand other questions. Jake said they would have plenty of time to talk. He promised to call Gwen and his boss at the paper mill.

He left and Carl Lee was placed in his cell, the one next to the cell for state prisoners.

The Saab was blocked by a television van. Jake inquired as to who owned it. Most of the reporters had left but a few loitered about, expecting something. It was almost dark.

'Are you with the sheriff's department?' asked a reporter.

'No, I'm a lawyer,' Jake answered nonchalantly, attempting to seem disinterested.

'Are you Mr. Hailey's attorney?'

Jake turned and stared at the reporter as the others listened. 'Matter of fact, I am.'

'Will you answer some questions?'

'You can ask some. I won't promise any answers.'

'Will you step over here?'

Jake walked to the microphones and cameras and tried to act annoyed by the inconvenience. Ozzie and the deputies watched from inside. 'Jake loves cameras,' he said.

'All lawyers do,' added Moss.

'What is your name, sir?'

'Jake Brigance.'

'You're Mr. Hailey's attorney.'

'Correct,' Jake answered coolly.

'Mr. Hailey is the father of the young girl raped by the two men who were killed today?'

'Correct.'

'Who killed the two men?'

'I don't know.'

'Was it Mr. Hailey?'

'I said I don't know.'

'What's your client been charged with?'

'He's been arrested for the murders of Billy Ray Cobb and Pete Willard. He hasn't formally been charged with anything.'

'Do you expect Mr. Hailey to be indicted for the two murders?'

'No comment.'

'Why no comment?'

'Have you talked with Mr. Hailey?' asked another reporter.

'Yes, just a moment ago.'

'How is he?'

'What do you mean?'

'Well, uh, how is he?'

'You mean, how does he like jail?' Jake asked with a slight grin.

'Uh, yeah.'

'No comment.'

'When will he be in court?'

'Probably tomorrow or Wednesday.'

'Will he plead guilty?'

Jake smiled and replied, 'Of course not.'

After a cold supper, they sat in the swing on the front porch and watched the lawn sprinkler and talked about the case. The killings were big news across the country, and Carla recorded as many television reports as possible. Two of the networks covered the story live through their Memphis affiliates, and the Memphis, Jackson, and Tupelo stations replayed footage of Cobb and Willard being led into the courthouse surrounded by deputies, and seconds later, being carried from the courthouse under white sheets. One of the stations played the actual audio of the gunfire over film of the deputies scrambling for cover.

Jake's interview was too late for the evening news, so he and Carla waited, with the recorder, for the ten o'clock, and there he was, briefcase in hand, looking trim, fit, handsome, and arrogant, and very disgusted with the reporters for the inconvenience. Jake thought he looked great on TV, and he was excited to be there. There had been one other brief appearance, after Lester's acquittal, and the regulars at the Coffee Shop had kidded him for months.

He felt good. He relished the publicity and anticipated much more. He could not think of another case, another set of facts, another setting which could generate as much publicity as the trial of Carl Lee Hailey. And the acquittal of Carl Lee Hailey, for the murder of the two white men who raped his daughter, before an all-white jury in rural Mississippi –

'What're you smiling about?' Carla interrupted.

'Nothing.'

'Sure. You're thinking about the trial, and the cameras, the reporters, the acquittal, and walking out of the courthouse, arm around Carl Lee, reporters chasing you with the cameras rolling, people slapping you on the back, congratulations everywhere. I know exactly what you're thinking about.'

'Then why'd you ask?'

'To see if you'd admit it.'

'Okay, I admit it. This case could make me famous and make us a million bucks, in the long run.'

'If you win.'

'Yes, if I win.'

'And if you lose?'

'I'll win.'

'But if you don't?'

'Think positive.'

The phone rang and Jake spent ten minutes with the editor, owner, and only reporter of *The Clanton Chronicle*. It rang again, and Jake talked with a reporter with the Memphis morning paper. He hung up and called Lester and Gwen, then the foreman at the paper mill.

At eleven-fifteen it rang again, and Jake received his first death threat, anonymous of course. He was called a nigger-loving son of a bitch, one who would not live if the nigger walked.

CHAPTER NINE

Dell Perkins served more coffee and grits than usual Tuesday morning after the killings. All the regulars and some extras had gathered early to read the papers and talk about the killings, which had taken place less than three hundred feet from the front door of the Coffee Shop. Claude's and the Tea Shoppe were also crowded earlier than usual. Jake's picture made the front page of the Tupelo paper, and the Memphis and Jackson papers had front-page photos of Cobb and Willard, both before the shootings and afterward as the bodies were loaded into the ambulance. There were no pictures of Carl Lee. All three papers ran detailed accounts of the past six days in Clanton.

It was widely accepted around town that Carl Lee had done the killing, but rumors of additional gunmen surfaced and flourished until one table at the Tea Shoppe had a whole band of wild niggers in on the attack. However, the deputies in the Coffee Shop, though not talkative, throttled the gossip and kept it pretty much under control. Deputy Looney was a regular, and there was concern for his wounds, which appeared to be more serious than originally reported. He remained in the hospital, and he had identified the gunman as Lester Hailey's brother.

Jake entered at six and sat near the front with some farmers. He nodded at Prather and the other deputy, but they pretended not to see him. They'll be okay once Looney is released, he thought. There were some remarks about the front-page picture, but no one questioned Jake about his new client or the killings. He detected a certain coolness among some of the regulars. He ate quickly and left.

At nine Ethel called Jake. Bullard was holding.

'Hello, Judge. How are you?'

'Terrible. You represent Carl Lee Hailey?'

'Yes, sir.'

'When do you want the preliminary?'

'Why are you asking me, Judge?'

'Good question. Look, the funerals are tomorrow morning sometime, and I think it would be best to wait till they bury those bastards, don't you?'

'Yeah, Judge, good idea.'

'How 'bout tomorrow afternoon at two?'

'Fine.'

Bullard hesitated. 'Jake, would you consider waiving the preliminary and letting me send the case straight to the grand jury?'

'Judge, I never waive a preliminary, you know that.'

'Yeah, I know. Just thought I'd ask a favor. I won't hear this trial, and I have no desire to get near it. See you tomorrow.'

An hour later Ethel squawked through the intercom again: 'Mr. Brigance, there are some reporters here to see you.'

Jake was ecstatic. 'From where?'

'Memphis and Jackson, I believe.'

'Seat them in the conference room. I'll be down in a minute.'

He straightened his tie and brushed his hair, and checked the street below for television vans. He decided to make them wait, and after a couple of meaningless phone calls he walked down the stairs, ignored Ethel, and entered the conference room. They asked him to sit at one end of the long table, because of the lighting. He declined, told himself he would control things, and sat at one side with his back to the rows of thick, expensive law books.

The microphones were placed before him and the camera lights adjusted, and finally an attractive lady from Memphis with streaks of bright orange across her forehead and under her eyes cleared her throat and asserted herself. 'Mr. Brigance, you represent Carl Lee Hailey?'

'Yes, I do.'

'And he's been charged with the murders of Billy Ray Cobb and Pete Willard?'

'That's correct.'

'And Cobb and Willard were charged with raping Mr. Hailey's daughter?'

'Yes, that's correct.'

'Does Mr. Hailey deny killing Cobb and Willard?'

'He will plead not guilty to the charges.'

'Will he be charged for the shooting of the deputy, Mr. Looney?'

'Yes. We anticipate a third charge of aggravated assault against the officer.'

'Do you anticipate a defense of insanity?'

'I'm not willing to discuss the defense at this time because he has not been indicted.'

'Are you saying there's a chance he may not be indicted?'

A fat pitch, one Jake was hoping for. The grand jury would either indict him or not, and the grand jurors would not be selected until Circuit Court convened on Monday, May 27. So the future members of the grand jury were walking the streets of Clanton, tending their shops, working in the factories, cleaning house, reading newspapers, watching TV, and discussing whether or not he should be indicted.

'Yes, I think there's a chance he may not be indicted. It's up to the grand jury, or will be after the preliminary hearing.'

'When's the preliminary hearing?'

'Tomorrow. Two P.M.'

'You're assuming Judge Bullard will bind him over to the grand jury?'

'That's a pretty safe assumption,' replied Jake, knowing Bullard would be thrilled with the answer.

'When will the grand jury meet?'

'A new grand jury will be sworn in Monday morning. It could look at the case by Monday afternoon.'

'When do you anticipate a trial?'

'Assuming he's indicted, the case could be tried in late summer or early fall.'

'Which court?'

'Circuit Court of Ford County.'

'Who would be the judge?'

'Honorable Omar Noose.'

'Where's he from?'

'Chester, Mississippi. Van Buren County.'

'You mean the case will be tried here in Clanton?'

'Yes, unless venue is changed.'

'Will you request a change of venue?'

'Very good question, and one I'm not prepared to answer at this time. It's a bit premature to talk defense strategy.'

'Why would you want a change of venue?'

To find a blacker county, Jake thought. He answered thoughtfully, 'The usual reasons. Pretrial publicity, etc.'

'Who makes the decision to change venue?'

'Judge Noose. The decision is within his sole discretion.'

'Has bond been set?'

'No, and it probably won't be until after the indictments come down. He's entitled to a reasonable bond now, but as a matter of practice in this county bonds are not set in capital murder cases until after the indictment and arraignment in Circuit Court. At that point the bond will be set by Judge Noose.'

'What can you tell us about Mr. Hailey?'

Jake relaxed and reflected a minute while the cameras continued. Another fat pitch, with a golden chance to plant some seeds. 'He's thirty-seven years old. Married to the same woman for twenty years. Four kids – three boys and a girl. Nice guy with a clean record. Never been in trouble before. Decorated in Vietnam. Works fifty hours a week at the paper mill in Coleman. Pays his bills and owns a little land. Goes to church every Sunday with his family. Minds his own business and expects to be left alone.'

'Will you allow us to talk to him?'

'Of course not.'

'Wasn't his brother tried for murder several years ago?'

'He was, and he was acquitted.'

'You were his attorney?'

'Yes, I was.'

'You've handled several murder trials in Ford County, haven't you?'

'Three.'

'How many acquittals?'

'All of them,' he answered slowly.

'Doesn't the jury have several options in Mississippi?' asked the lady from Memphis.

'That's right. With a capital murder indictment, the jury at trial can find the defendant guilty of manslaughter, which carries twenty years, or capital murder, which carries life or death as determined by the jury. And the jury can find the defendant not guilty.' Jake smiled at the cameras. 'Again, you're assuming he'll be indicted.'

'How's the Hailey girl?'

'She's at home. Went home Sunday. She's expected to be fine.'

The reporters looked at each other and searched for other questions. Jake knew this was the dangerous part, when they ran out of things to ask and began serving up screwball questions.

He stood and buttoned his coat. 'Look, I appreciate you folks stopping by. I'm usually available, just give a little more notice and I'll be glad to talk to you anytime.'

They thanked him and left.

At ten Wednesday morning, in a no-frills double service at the funeral home, the rednecks buried their dead. The minister, a freshly ordained Pentecostal, struggled desperately for comforting and reassuring thoughts to lay upon the small crowd and over the two closed caskets. The service was brief with few tears.

The pickups and dirty Chevrolets moved slowly behind the single hearse as the procession left town and crawled into the country. They parked behind a small red brick church. The bodies were laid to rest one at a time at opposite ends of the tiny, overgrown cemetery. After a few additional words of inspiration, the crowd dispersed.

Cobb's parents had divorced when he was small, and his father drove from Birmingham for the funeral. After the burial he disappeared. Mrs. Cobb lived in a small, clean white frame house near the settlement of

Lake Village, ten miles south of Clanton. Her other two sons and their cousins and friends gathered under an oak tree in the backyard while the women made a fuss over Mrs. Cobb. The men talked about niggers in general, and chewed Red Man and sipped whiskey, and reminisced about the other days when niggers knew their place. Now they were just pampered and protected by the government and courts. And there was nothing white people could do. One cousin knew a friend or someone who used to be active in the Klan, and he might give him a call. Cobb's grandfather had been in the Klan long before his death, the cousin explained, and when he and Billy Ray were kids the old man would tell stories about hanging niggers in Ford and Tyler counties. What they should do was the same thing the nigger had done, but there were no volunteers. Maybe the Klan would be interested. There was a chapter farther down south near Jackson, near Nettles County, and the cousin was authorized to contact them.

The women prepared lunch. The men ate quietly, then returned to the whiskey under the shade tree. The nigger's hearing at 2:00 P.M. was mentioned, and they loaded up and drove to Clanton.

There was a Clanton before the killings, and there was a Clanton after the killings, and it would be months before the two resembled each other. One tragic, bloody event, the duration of which was less than fifteen seconds, transformed the quiet Southern town of eight thousand into a mecca for journalists, reporters, camera crews, photographers, some from neighboring towns, others from the national news organizations. Cameramen and TV reporters bumped into one another on the sidewalks around the square as they asked the man in the street for the hundredth time how he or she felt about the Hailey event and how he or she would vote if he or she was on the jury. There was no clear verdict from the man on the street. Television vans followed small, marked, imported television cars around the square and down the streets chasing leads, stories, and interviews. Ozzie was a favorite at first. He was interviewed a half dozen times the day after the shooting, then found other business and delegated the interviewing to Moss Junior, who enjoyed bantering with the press. He could answer twenty questions and not divulge one new detail. He also lied a lot, and the ignorant foreigners could not tell his lies from his truth.

'Sir, is there any evidence of additional gunmen?'

'Yes.'

'Really! Who?'

'We have evidence that the shootin's were authorized and financed by an offshoot of the Black Panthers,' Moss Junior replied with a straight face.

Half the reporters would either stutter or stare blankly while the other half repeated what he said and scribbled furiously.

Bullard refused to leave his office or take calls. He called Jake again and begged him to waive the preliminary. Jake refused. Reporters waited in the lobby of Bullard's office on the first floor of the courthouse, but he was safe with his vodka behind the locked door.

There was a request to film the funeral. The Cobb boys said yes, for a fee, but Mrs. Willard vetoed the proposal. The reporters waited outside the funeral home and filmed what they could. Then they followed the procession to the grave sites, and filmed the burials, and followed the mourners to Mrs. Cobb's, where Freddie, the oldest, cursed them and made them leave.

The Coffee Shop on Wednesday was silent. The regulars, including Jake, eyed the strangers who had invaded their sanctuary. Most of them had beards, spoke with unusual accents, and did not order grits.

'Aren't you Mr. Hailey's attorney?' shouted one from across the room.

Jake worked on his toast and said nothing.

'Aren't you? Sir?'

'What if I am?' shot Jake.

'Will he plead guilty?'

'I'm eating breakfast.'

'Will he?'

'No comment.'

'Why no comment?'

'No comment.'

'But why?'

'I don't comment during breakfast. No comment.'

'May I talk to you later?'

'Yeah, make an appointment. I talk at sixty bucks an hour.'

The regulars hooted, but the strangers were undaunted.

Jake consented to an interview, without charge, with a Memphis paper Wednesday, then barricaded himself in the war room and prepared for the preliminary hearing. At noon he visited his famous client at the jail. Carl Lee was rested and relaxed. From his cell he could see the coming and going of the reporters in the parking lot.

'How's jail?' Jake asked.

'Not that bad. Food's good. I eat with Ozzie in his office.'

'You what!'

'Yep. Play cards too.'

'You're kidding, Carl Lee.'

'Nope. Watch TV too. Saw you on the news last night. You looked real good. I'm gonna make you famous, Jake, ain't I?'

Jake said nothing.

'When do I get on TV? I mean, I did the killin' and you and Ozzie gettin' famous for it.' The client was grinning – the lawyer was not.

'Today, in about an hour.'

'Yeah, I heard we's goin' to court. What for?'

'Preliminary hearing. It's no big deal, at least it's not supposed to be. This one will be different because of the cameras.'

'What do I say?'

'Nothing! You don't say a word to anyone. Not to the judge, the prosecutor, the reporters, anyone. We just listen. We listen to the prosecutor and see what kind of case he's got. They're supposed to have an eyewitness, and he might testify. Ozzie will testify and tell the judge about the gun, the fingerprints, and Looney –'

'How's Looney?'

'Don't know. Worse than they thought.'

'Man, I feel bad 'bout shootin' Looney. I didn't even see the man.'

'Well, they're going to charge you with aggravated assault for shooting Looney. Anyway, the preliminary is just a formality. Its purpose is to allow the judge to determine if there's enough evidence to bind you over to the grand jury. Bullard always does that, so it's just a formality.'

'Then why do it?'

'We could waive it,' replied Jake, thinking of all the cameras he would miss. 'But I don't like to. It's a good chance to see what kind of case the State has.'

'Well, Jake, I'd say they gotta pretty good case, wouldn't you?'

'I would think so. But let's just listen. That's the strategy of a preliminary hearing. Okay?'

'Sounds good to me. You talked to Gwen or Lester today?'

'No, I called them Monday night.'

'They were here yesterday in Ozzie's office. Said they'd be in court today.'

'I think everyone will be in court today.'

Jake left. In the parking lot he brushed by some of the reporters who were awaiting Carl Lee's departure from jail. He had no comments for them and no comments for the reporters waiting outside his office. He was too busy at the moment for questions, but he was very aware of the cameras. At one-thirty he went to the courthouse and hid in the law library on the third floor.

Ozzie and Moss Junior and the deputies watched the parking lot and quietly cursed the mob of reporters and cameramen. It was one forty-five, time to transport the prisoner to court.

'Kinda reminds me of a buncha vultures waitin' for a dead dog beside the highway,' Moss Junior observed as he gazed through the blinds.

'Rudest buncha folks I ever saw,' added Prather. 'Won't take no for an answer. They expect the whole town to cater to them.'

'And that's only half of them – other half's waitin' at the courthouse.'

Ozzie hadn't said much. One newspaper had criticized him for the shooting, implying the security around the courthouse was intentionally relaxed. He was tired of the press. Twice Wednesday he had ordered reporters out of the jail.

'I got an idea,' he said.

'What?' asked Moss Junior.

'Is Curtis Todd still in jail?'

'Yep. Gets out next week.'

'He sorta favors Carl Lee, don't he?'

'Whatta you mean?'

'Well, I mean, he's 'bout as black as Carl Lee, roughly the same height and weight, ain't he?'

'Yeah, well, so what?' asked Prather.

Moss Junior grinned and looked at Ozzie, whose eyes never left the window. 'Ozzie, you wouldn't.'

'What?' asked Prather.

'Let's go. Get Carl Lee and Curtis Todd,' Ozzie ordered. 'Drive my car around back. Bring Todd here for some instructions.'

Ten minutes later the front door of the jail opened and a squad of deputies escorted the prisoner down the sidewalk. Two deputies walked in front, two behind, and one on each side of the man with the thick sunglasses and handcuffs, which were not fastened. As they approached the reporters, the cameras clicked and rolled. The questions flew:

'Sir, will you plead guilty?'

'Sir, will you plead not guilty?'

'Sir, how will you plead?'

'Mr. Hailey, will you plead insanity?'

The prisoner smiled and continued the slow walk to the waiting patrol cars. The deputies smiled grimly and ignored the mob. The photographers scrambled about trying to get the perfect shot of the most famous vigilante in the country.

Suddenly, with the nation watching, with deputies all around him, with dozens of reporters recording his every move, the prisoner broke and ran. He jolted, jumped, twisted, and squirmed, running wildly across the parking lot, over a ditch, across the highway, into some trees and out of sight. The reporters shouted and broke ranks and several even chased him for a moment. Curiously, the deputies ran back to the jail and slammed the door, leaving the vultures roaming in circles of disarray. In the woods, the prisoner removed the handcuffs and walked home. Curtis Todd had just been paroled one week early.

Ozzie, Moss Junior, and Carl Lee quickly left through the rear of the jail and drove down a back street to the courthouse, where more deputies waited to escort him into the courthouse.

'How many niggers out there?' Bullard screamed at Mr. Pate.

'A ton.'

'Wonderful! A ton of niggers. I guess there's a ton of rednecks too?'

'Quite a few.'

'Is the courtroom full?'

'Packed.'

'My God – it's only a preliminary!' Bullard screamed. He finished a half pint of vodka as Mr. Pate handed him another one.

'Take it easy, Judge.'

'Brigance. It's all his fault. He could waive this if he wanted to. I asked him to. Asked him twice. He knows I'll send it to the grand jury. He knows that. All lawyers know that. But now I gotta make all the niggers mad because I won't turn him loose, and I'll make all the rednecks mad because I won't execute him today in the courtroom. I'll get Brigance for this. He's playing for the cameras. I have to get reelected, but he doesn't, does he?'

'No, Judge.'

'How many officers out there?'

'Plenty. Sheriff's called in the reserves. You're safe.'

'How about the press?'

'They're lined up on the front rows.'

'No cameras!'

'No cameras.'

'Is Hailey here?'

'Yes, sir. He's in the courtroom with Brigance. Everbody's ready, just waitin' on you.'

His Honor filled a Styrofoam cup with straight vodka. 'Okay, let's go.'

Just like in the old days before the sixties, the courtroom was neatly segregated with the blacks and whites separated by the center aisle. The officers stood solemnly in the aisle and around the walls of the courtroom. Of particular concern was an assemblage of slightly intoxicated whites sitting together in two rows near the front. A couple were recognized as brothers or cousins of the late Billy Ray Cobb. They were watched closely. The two front rows, the one on the right in front of the blacks and the one on the left in front of the whites, were occupied by two dozen journalists of various sorts. Some took notes while some sketched the defendant, his lawyer, and now finally, the judge.

'They gonna make this nigger a hero,' mumbled one of the rednecks, loud enough for the reporters.

When Bullard assumed the bench, the deputies locked the rear door.

'Call your first witness,' he ordered in the direction of Rocky Childers.

'The State calls Sheriff Ozzie Walls.'

The sheriff was sworn and took the stand. He relaxed and began a long narrative describing the scene of the shooting, the bodies, the wounds, the gun, the fingerprints on the gun and the fingerprints of the defendant. Childers produced an affidavit signed by Officer Looney and witnessed by the sheriff and Moss Junior. It identified the gunman as Carl Lee. Ozzie verified Looney's signature and read the affidavit into the record.

'Sheriff, do you know of any other eyewitness?' asked Childers with no enthusiasm.

'Yes, Murphy, the janitor.'

'What's his first name?'

'Nobody knows. He's just Murphy.'

'Okay. Have you talked to him?'

'No, but my investigator did.'

'Who is your investigator?'

'Officer Rady.'

Rady was sworn and seated in the witness chair. Mr. Pate fetched the judge another cup of ice water from chambers. Jake took pages of notes. He would call no witnesses, and he chose not to cross-examine the sheriff. Occasionally, the State's witnesses would get their lies confused in a preliminary, and Jake would ask a few questions on cross-examination to nail down, for the record, the discrepancies. Later at trial when the lying started again, Jake would produce the testimony from the preliminary to further confuse the liars. But not today.

'Sir, have you had an occasion to talk with Murphy?' Childers asked.

'Murphy who?'

'I don't know – just Murphy, the janitor.'

'Oh him. Yes, sir.'

'Good. What did he say?'

'About what?'

Childers hung his head. Rady was new, and had not testified much. Ozzie thought this would be good practice.

'About the shooting! Tell us what he told you about the shooting.'

Jake stood. 'Your Honor. I object. I know hearsay is admissible in a preliminary, but this Murphy fella is available. He works here in the courthouse. Why not let him testify?'

'Because he stutters,' replied Bullard.

'What!'

'He stutters. And I don't want to hear him stutter for the next thirty minutes. Objection overruled. Continue, Mr. Childers.'

Jake sat in disbelief. Bullard snickered at Mr. Pate, who left for more ice water.

'Now, Mr. Rady, what did Murphy tell you about the shooting?'

'Well, he's hard to understand because he was so excited, and when he gets excited he stutters real bad. I mean he stutters anyway, but –'

'Just tell us what he said!' Bullard shouted.

'Okay. He said he saw a male black shoot the two white boys and the deputy.'

'Thank you,' said Childers. 'Now where was he when this took place?'

'Who?'

'Murphy!'

'He was sittin' on the stairs directly opposite the stairs where they got shot.'

'And he saw it all?'

'Said he did.'

'Has he identified the gunman?'

'Yes, we showed him photos of ten male blacks, and he identified the defendant, sittin' over there.'

'Good. Thank you. Your Honor, we have nothing further.'

'Any questions, Mr. Brigance?' asked the judge.

'No, sir,' Jake said as he stood.

'Any witnesses?'

'No, sir.'

'Any requests, motions, anything?'

'No, sir.'

Jake knew better than to request bail. First, it would do no good. Bullard would not set bail for capital murder. Second, it would make the judge look bad.

'Thank you, Mr. Brigance. The court finds sufficient evidence exists to hold this defendant for action by the Ford County grand jury. Mr. Hailey shall remain in the custody of the sheriff, without bond. Court's adjourned.'

Carl Lee was quickly handcuffed and escorted from the courtroom. The area around the rear door downstairs was sealed and guarded. The cameras outside caught a glimpse of the defendant between the door and the waiting patrol car. He was in jail before the spectators cleared the courtroom.

The deputies directed the whites on one side to leave first, followed by the blacks.

The reporters requested some of Jake's time, and they were instructed to meet him in the rotunda in a few minutes. He made them wait by first going to chambers and giving his regards to the judge. Then he walked to the third floor to check on a book. When the courtroom was empty and they had waited long enough, he walked through the rear door, into the rotunda and faced the cameras.

A microphone with red letters on it was thrust into his face. 'Why didn't you request bond?' a reporter demanded.

'That comes later.'

'Will Mr. Hailey plead an insanity defense?'

'As I've stated, it's too early to answer that question. We must now wait for the grand jury – he may not be indicted. If he is, we'll start planning his defense.'

'Mr. Buckley, the D.A., has stated he expects easy convictions. Any comment?'

'I'm afraid Mr. Buckley often speaks when he shouldn't. It's asinine for him to make any comment on this case until it is considered by the grand jury.'

'He also said he would vigorously oppose any request for a change of venue.'

'That request hasn't been made yet. He really doesn't care where the trial is held. He'd try it in the desert as long as the press showed up.'

'Can we assume there are hard feelings between you and the D.A.?'

'If you want to. He's a good prosecutor and a worthy adversary. He just talks when he shouldn't.'

He answered a few other assorted questions and excused himself.

Late Wednesday night the doctors cut below Looney's knee and removed the lower third of his leg. They called Ozzie at the jail, and he told Carl Lee.

CHAPTER TEN

Rufus Buckley scanned the Thursday morning papers and read with great interest the accounts of the preliminary hearing in Ford County. He was delighted to see his name mentioned by the reporters and by Mr. Brigance. The disparaging remarks were greatly outweighed by the fact that his name was in print. He didn't like Brigance, but he was glad Jake mentioned his name before the cameras and reporters. For two days the spotlight had been on Brigance and the defendant; it was about time the D.A. was mentioned. Brigance should not criticize anyone for seeking publicity. Lucien Wilbanks wrote the book on manipulating the press both before and during a trial, and he had taught Jake well. But Buckley held no grudge. He was pleased. He relished the thought of a long, nasty trial with his first opportunity at real, meaningful exposure. He looked forward to Monday, the first day of the May term of court in Ford County.

He was forty-one, and when he was first elected nine years earlier he had been the youngest D.A. in Mississippi. Now he was one year into his third term and his ambitions were calling. It was time to move on to another public office, say, attorney general, or possibly governor. And then to Congress. He had it all planned, but he was not well known outside the Twenty-second Judicial District (Ford, Tyler, Polk, Van Buren, and Milburn counties). He needed to be seen, and heard. He needed publicity. What Rufus needed more than anything else was a big, nasty, controversial, well-publicized conviction in a murder trial.

Ford County was directly north of Smithfield, the county seat of Polk County, where Rufus lived. He had grown up in Tyler County, near the Tennessee line, north of Ford County. He had a good base, politically. He was a good prosecutor. During elections he boasted of a ninety percent conviction rate, and of sending more men to death row than any prosecutor in the state. He was loud, abrasive, sanctimonious. His client was the people of the State of Mississippi, by God, and he took that obligation seriously. The people hated crime, and he hated crime, and together they could eliminate it.

He could talk to a jury; oh, how he could talk to a jury. He could preach, pray, sway, plead, beg. He could inflame a jury to the point it couldn't wait to get back to that jury room and have a prayer meeting, then vote and return with a rope to hang the defendant. He could talk like the blacks and he could talk like the rednecks, and that was enough to satisfy most of the jurors in the Twenty-second. And the juries were good to him in Ford County. He liked Clanton.

When he arrived at his office in the Polk County Courthouse, Rufus was delighted to see a camera crew waiting in his reception room. He was very busy, he explained, looking at his watch, but he might have a minute for a few questions.

He arranged them in his office and sat splendidly in his leather swivel behind the desk. The reporter was from Jackson.

'Mr. Buckley, do you have any sympathy for Mr. Hailey?'

He smiled seriously, obviously in deep thought. 'Yes, I do. I have sympathy for any parent whose child is raped. I certainly do. But what I cannot condone, and what our system cannot tolerate, is this type of vigilante justice.'

'Are you a parent?'

'I am. I have one small son and two daughters, one the age of the Hailey girl, and I'd be outraged if one of my daughters were raped. But I would hope our judicial system would deal effectively with the rapist. I have that much confidence in the system.'

'So you anticipate a conviction?'

'Certainly. I normally get a conviction when I go after one, and I intend to get a conviction in this case.'

'Will you ask for the death penalty?'

'Yes, it looks like a clear case of premeditated murder. I think the gas chamber would be appropriate.'

'Do you predict a death penalty verdict?'

'Of course. Ford County jurors have always been willing to apply the death penalty when I ask for it and it's appropriate. I get very good juries up there.'

'Mr. Brigance, the defendant's attorney, has stated the grand jury may not indict his client.'

Buckley chuckled at this. 'Well, Mr. Brigance should not be so foolish. The case will be presented to the grand jury Monday, and we'll have our indictments Monday afternoon. I promise you that. Really, he knows better.'

'You think the case will be tried in Ford County?'

'I don't care where it's tried. I'll get a conviction.'

'Do you anticipate the insanity defense?'

'I anticipate everything. Mr. Brigance is a most capable criminal defense attorney. I don't know what ploy he will use, but the State of Mississippi will be ready.'

'What about a plea bargain?'

'I don't much believe in plea negotiating. Neither does Brigance. I wouldn't expect that.'

'He said he's never lost a murder case to you.'

The smile disappeared instantly. He leaned forward on the desk and looked harshly at the reporter. 'True, but I bet he didn't mention a number of armed robberies and grand larcenies, did he? I've won my share. Ninety percent to be exact.'

The camera was turned off and the reporter thanked him for his time. No problem, said Buckley. Anytime.

Ethel waddled up the stairs and stood before the big desk. 'Mr. Brigance, my husband and I received an obscene phone call last night, and I've just taken the second one here at the office. I don't like this.'

He motioned to a chair. 'Sit down, Ethel. What did these people say?'

'They weren't really obscene. They were threatening. They threatened me because I work for you. Said I'd be sorry because I worked for a nigger lover. The ones here threaten to harm you and your family. I'm just scared.'

Jake was worried too, but shrugged it off for Ethel. He had called Ozzie on Wednesday and reported the calls to his house.

'Change your number, Ethel. I'll pay for it.'

'I don't want to change my number. I've had it for seventeen years.'

'Good, then don't. I've had my home number changed, and it's no big deal.'

'Well, I'll not do it.'

'Fine. What else do you want?'

'Well, I don't think you should have taken that case. I –'

'And I don't care what you think! You're not paid to think about my cases. If I want to know what you think, I'll ask. Until I do, keep quiet.'

She huffed and left. Jake called Ozzie again.

An hour later Ethel announced through the intercom: 'Lucien called this morning. He asked me to copy some recent cases, and he wants you to deliver them this afternoon. Said it had been five weeks since your last visit.'

'Four weeks. Copy the cases, and I'll take them this afternoon.'

Lucien stopped by the office or called once a month. He read cases and kept abreast of current developments in the law. He had little else to do except drink Jack Daniel's and play the stock market, both of which he did recklessly. He was a drunk, and he spent most of his time on the front porch of his big white house on the hill, eight blocks off the square, overlooking Clanton, sipping Jack in the Black and reading cases.

He had deteriorated since the disbarment. A full-time maid doubled as a nurse who served drinks on the porch from noon until midnight. He seldom ate or slept, preferring instead to rock away the hours.

Jake was expected to visit at least once a month. The visits were made out of some sense of duty. Lucien was a bitter, sick old man who cursed lawyers, judges, and especially the State Bar Association. Jake was his only friend, the only audience he could find and keep captive long enough to hear his sermons. Along with the preaching he also freely dispensed unsolicited advice on Jake's cases, a most annoying habit. He knew about the cases, although Jake never knew how Lucien knew so much. He was seldom seen downtown or anywhere in Clanton except at the package store in the black section.

The Saab parked behind the dirty, dented Porsche, and Jake handed the cases to Lucien. There were no hellos or other greetings, just the handing of the copies to Lucien, who said nothing. They sat in the wicker rockers on the long porch and looked out over Clanton. The top floor of the courthouse stood above the buildings and houses and trees around the square.

Finally he offered whiskey, then wine, then beer. Jake declined. Carla frowned on drinking, and Lucien knew it.

'Congratulations.'

'For what?' Jake asked.

'For the Hailey case.'

'Why am I to be congratulated?'

'I never had a case that big, and I had some big ones.'

'Big in terms of what?'

'Publicity. Exposure. That's the name of the game for lawyers, Jake. If you're unknown, you starve. When people get in trouble they call a lawyer, and they call someone they've heard of. You must sell yourself to the public, if you're a street lawyer. Of course it's different if you're in a big corporate or insurance firm where you sit on your ass and bill a hundred bucks an hour, ten hours a day, ripping off little people and –'

'Lucien,' Jake interrupted quietly, 'we've talked about this many times. Let's talk about the Hailey case.'

'All right, all right. I'll bet Noose refuses to change venue.'

'Who said I would request it?'

'You're stupid if you don't.'

'Why?'

'Simple statistics! This county is twenty-six percent black. Every other county in the Twenty-second is at least thirty percent black. Van Buren County is forty percent. That means more black jurors, potential jurors. If you get it moved, you have a better chance for blacks in the jury box. If it's tried here, you run the risk of an all-white jury, and believe me, I've seen enough all-white juries in this county. All you need is one black to hang it and get a mistrial.'

'But then it'll be retried.'

'Then hang it again. They'll give up after three trials. A hung jury is the same as a loss on Buckley's scorecard. He'll quit after the third trial.'

'So I simply tell Noose I want the trial moved to a blacker county so I can get a blacker jury.'

'You can if you want to, but I wouldn't. I'd go through the usual crap about pretrial publicity, a biased community, and on and on.'

'And you don't think Noose'll buy it.'

'Naw. This case is too big, and it'll get bigger. The press has intervened and already started the trial. Everyone's heard of it, and not just in Ford County. You couldn't find a person in this state without a preconceived notion of guilt or innocence. So why move it to another county?'

'Then why should I request it?'

'Because when that poor man is convicted, you'll need something to argue on appeal. You can claim he was denied a fair trial because venue was not changed.'

'Thanks for the encouragement. What're the chances of getting it moved to another district, say somewhere in the delta?'

'Forget it. You can request a change of venue, but you cannot request a certain location.'

Jake didn't know that. He usually learned something during these visits. He nodded confidently and studied the old man with the long, dirty gray beard. There had never been a time when he stumped Lucien on a point of criminal law.

'Sallie!' Lucien screamed, throwing his ice cubes into the shrubs.

'Who's Sallie?'

'My maid,' he replied as a tall, attractive black lady opened the screen door and smiled at Jake.

'Yeah, Lucien?' she answered.

'My glass is empty.'

She walked elegantly across the porch and took his glass. She was under thirty, shapely, pretty, and very dark. Jake ordered iced tea.

'Where'd you find her?' he asked.

Lucien stared at the courthouse.

'Where'd you find her?'

'I dunno.'

'How old is she?'

Lucien was silent.

'She live here?'

No response.

'How much do you pay her?'

'Why is it any of your business? More than you pay Ethel. She's a nurse too, you know.'

Sure, Jake thought with a grin. 'I'll bet she does a lot of things.'

'Don't worry about it.'

'I take it you're not thrilled with my chances for an acquittal.'

Lucien reflected a moment. The maid/nurse returned with the whiskey and tea.

'Not really. It will be difficult.'

'Why?'

'Looks like it was premeditated. From what I gather it was well planned. Right?'

'Yes.'

'I'm sure you'll plead insanity.'

'I don't know.'

'You must plead insanity,' Lucien lectured sternly. 'There is no other possible defense. You can't claim it was an accident. You can't say he shot those two boys, handcuffed and unarmed, with a machine gun in self-defense, can you?'

'No.'

'You won't create an alibi and tell the jury he was at home with his family?'

'Of course not.'

'Then what other defense do you have? You must say he was crazy!'

'But, Lucien, he was not insane, and there's no way I can find some bogus psychiatrist to say he was. He planned it meticulously, every detail.'

Lucien smiled and took a drink. 'That's why you're in trouble, my boy.'

Jake sat his tea on the table and rocked slowly. Lucien savored the moment. 'That's why you're in trouble,' he repeated.

'What about the jury? You know they'll be sympathetic.'

'That's exactly why you must plead insanity. You must give the jury a way out. You must show them a way to find him not guilty, if they are so inclined. If they're sympathetic, if they want to acquit, you must provide them with a defense they can use to do it. It makes no difference if they believe the insanity crap. That's not important in the jury room. What's important is that the jury have a legal basis for an acquittal, assuming they want to acquit.'

'Will they want to acquit?'

'Some will, but Buckley will make an awfully strong case of premeditated murder. He's good. He'll take away their sympathy. Hailey'll be just another black on trial for killing a white man when Buckley gets through with him.'

Lucien rattled his ice cubes and stared at the brown liquid. 'And what about the deputy? Assault with intent to kill a peace officer carries life, no parole. Talk your way out of that one.'

'There was no intent.'

'Great. That'll be real convincing when the poor guy hobbles to the witness stand and shows the jury his nub.'

'Nub?'

'Yes. Nub. They cut his leg off last night.'

'Looney!'

'Yes, the one Mr. Hailey shot.'

'I thought he was okay.'

'Oh he's fine. Just minus a leg.'

'How'd you find out?'

'I've got sources.'

Jake walked to the edge of the porch and leaned on a column. He felt weak. The confidence was gone, taken away again by Lucien. He was an expert at poking holes in every case Jake tried. It was sport to him, and he was usually right.

'Look, Jake, I don't mean to sound so hopeless. The case can be won – it's a long shot, but it can be won. You can walk him out of there, and you need to believe you can. Just don't get too cocky. You've said enough to the press for a while. Back off, and go to work.'

Lucien walked to the edge of the porch and spat in the shrubs. 'Always keep in mind that Mr. Hailey is guilty, guilty as hell. Most criminal defendants are, but especially this one. He took the law into his own hands, and he murdered two people. Planned it all, very carefully. Our legal system does not permit vigilante justice. Now, you can win the case, and if you do, justice will prevail. But if you lose it, justice will also prevail. Kind of a strange case, I guess. I just wish I had it.'

'You serious?'

'Sure I'm serious. It's a trial lawyer's dream. Win it and you're famous. The biggest gun in these parts. It could make you rich.'

'I'll need your help.'

'You've got it. I need something to do.'

After dinner, and after Hanna was asleep, Jake told Carla about the calls at the office. They had received a strange call before during one of the other murder trials, but no threats were made, just some groaning and breathing. But these were different. They mentioned Jake's name and his family, and promised revenge if Carl Lee was acquitted.

'Are you worried?' she asked.

'Not really. It's probably just some kids, or some of Cobb's friends. Does it scare you?'

'I would prefer they didn't call.'

'Everybody's getting calls. Ozzie's had hundreds. Bullard, Childers, everybody. I'm not worried about it.'

'What if it becomes more serious?'

'Carla, I would never endanger my family. It's not worth it. I'll withdraw from the case if I think the threats are legitimate. I promise.'

She was not impressed.

Lester peeled off nine one-hundred-dollar bills and laid them majestically on Jake's desk.

'That's only nine hundred,' Jake said. 'Our agreement was a thousand.'

'Gwen needed groceries.'

'You sure Lester didn't need some whiskey?'

'Come on, Jake, you know I wouldn't steal from my own brother.'

'Okay, okay. When's Gwen going to the bank to borrow the rest?'

'I'm goin' right now to see the banker. Atcavage?'

'Yeah, Stan Atcavage, next door at Security Bank. Good friend of mine. He loaned it before on your trial. You got the deed?'

'In my pocket. How much you reckon he'll give us?'

'No idea. Why don't you go find out.'

Lester left, and ten minutes later Atcavage was on the phone.

'Jake, I can't loan the money to these people. What if he's convicted – no offense, I know you're a good lawyer – my divorce, remember – but how's he gonna pay me sitting on death row?'

'Thanks. Look Stan, if he defaults you own ten acres, right?'

'Right, with a shack on it. Ten acres of trees and kudzu plus an old house. Just what my new wife wants. Come on, Jake.'

'It's a nice house, and it's almost paid for.'

'It's a shack, a clean shack. But it's not worth anything, Jake.'

'It's gotta be worth something.'

'Jake, I don't want it. The bank does not want it.'

'You loaned it before.'

'And he wasn't in jail before; his brother was, remember. He was working at the paper mill. Good job, too. Now he's headed for Parchman.'

'Thanks, Stan, for the vote of confidence.'

'Come on, Jake, I've got confidence in your ability, but I can't loan money on it. If anybody can get him off, you can. And I hope you do. But I can't make this loan. The auditors would scream.'

Lester tried the Peoples Bank and Ford National, with the same results. They hoped his brother was acquitted, but what if he wasn't.

Wonderful, thought Jake. Nine hundred dollars for a capital murder case.

CHAPTER ELEVEN

Claude had never seen the need for printed menus in his cafe. Years before when he first opened he couldn't afford menus, and now that he could he didn't need them because most folks knew what he served. For breakfast he cooked everything but rice and toast, and the prices varied. For Friday lunch he barbecued pork shoulder and spare ribs, and everybody knew it. He had few white customers during the week, but at noon Friday, every Friday, his small cafe was half white. Claude had known for some time that whites enjoyed barbecue as much as blacks; they just didn't know how to prepare it.

Jake and Atcavage found a small table near the kitchen. Claude himself delivered two plates of ribs and slaw. He leaned toward Jake and said softly, 'Good luck to you. Hope you get him off.'

'Thanks, Claude. I hope you're on the jury.'

Claude laughed and said louder, 'Can I volunteer?'

Jake attacked the ribs and chewed on Atcavage for not making the loan. The banker was steadfast, but did offer to lend five thousand if Jake would cosign. That would be unethical, Jake explained.

On the sidewalk a line formed and faces squinted through the painted letters on the front windows. Claude was everywhere, taking orders, giving orders, cooking, counting money, shouting, swearing, greeting customers, and asking them to leave. On Friday, the customers were allotted twenty minutes after the food was served, then Claude asked and sometimes demanded that they pay and leave so he could sell more barbecue.

'Quit talkin' and eat!' he would yell.

'I've got ten more minutes, Claude.'

'You got seven.'

On Wednesday he fried catfish, and allowed thirty minutes because of the bones. The white folks avoided Claude's on Wednesday, and he knew why. It was the grease, a secret recipe grease handed down by his grandmother, he said. It was heavy and sticky and wreaked havoc with the lower intestines of white people. It didn't faze the blacks, who piled in by the carloads every Wednesday.

Two foreigners sat near the cash register and watched Claude fearfully as he directed lunch. Probably reporters, thought Jake. Each time Claude drew nigh and glared, they obediently picked up and gnawed a rib. They had not experienced ribs before, and it was obvious to everyone they were from the North. They had wanted chef salads, but

Claude cursed them, and told them to eat barbecue or leave. Then he announced to the crowd these silly fools wanted chef salads.

'Here's your food. Hurry up and eat it,' he had demanded when he served them.

'No steak knives?' one had asked crisply.

Claude rolled his eyes and staggered away mumbling.

One noticed Jake, and, after staring for a few minutes, finally walked over and knelt by the table. 'Aren't you Jake Brigance, Mr. Hailey's attorney?'

'Yes, I am. Who are you?'

'I'm Roger McKittrick, with *The New York Times*.'

'Nice to meet you,' Jake said with a smile and a new attitude.

'I'm covering the Hailey case, and I'd like to talk with you sometime. As soon as possible, really.'

'Sure. I'm not too busy this afternoon. It's Friday.'

'I could do it late.'

'How about four?'

'Fine,' said McKittrick, who noticed Claude approaching from the kitchen. 'I'll see you then.'

'Okay, buddy,' Claude yelled at McKittrick. 'Time's up. Get your check and leave.'

Jake and Atcavage finished in fifteen minutes, and waited for the verbal assault from Claude. They licked their fingers and mopped their faces and commented on the tenderness of the ribs.

'This case'll make you famous, won't it?' asked Atcavage.

'I hope. Evidently it won't make any money.'

'Seriously, Jake, won't it help your practice?'

'If I win, I'll have more clients than I can handle. Sure it'll help. I can pick and choose my cases, pick and choose my clients.'

'Financially, what'll it mean?'

'I have no idea. There's no way to predict who or what it might attract. I'll have more cases to choose from, so that means more money. I could quit worrying about the overhead.'

'Surely you don't worry about the overhead.'

'Look, Stan, we're not all filthy rich. A law degree is not worth what it once was – too many of us. Fourteen in this little town. Competition is tough, even in Clanton – not enough good cases and too many lawyers. It's worse in the big towns, and the law schools graduate more and more, many of whom can't find jobs. I get ten kids a year knocking on my door looking for work. A big firm in Memphis laid off some lawyers a few months ago. Can you imagine? Just like a factory, they laid them off. I suppose they went down to the unemployment office and stood in line with the 'dozer operators. Lawyers now, not secretaries or truck drivers, but lawyers.'

'Sorry I asked.'

'Sure I worry about the overhead. It runs me four thousand a month, and I practice alone. That's fifty thousand a year before I clear a dime. Some months are good, others slow. They're all unpredictable. I wouldn't dare estimate what I'll gross next month. That's why this case is so important. There will never be another one like it. It's the biggest. I'll practice the rest of my life and never have another reporter from *The New York Times* stop me in a cafe and ask for an interview. If I win, I'll be the top dog in this part of the state. I can forget about the overhead.'

'And if you lose?'

Jake paused and glanced around for Claude. 'The publicity will be abundant regardless of the outcome. Win or lose, the case will help my practice. But a loss will really hurt. Every lawyer in the county is secretly hoping I blow it. They want him convicted. They're jealous, afraid I might get too big and take away their clients. Lawyers are extremely jealous.'

'You too?'

'Sure. Take the Sullivan firm. I despise every lawyer in that firm, but I'm jealous to an extent. I wish I had some of their clients, some of their retainers, some of their security. They know that every month they'll get a nice check, it's guaranteed almost, and every Christmas they'll get a big bonus. They represent old money, steady money. That would be enjoyable for a change. Me, I represent drunks, thugs, wife beaters, husband beaters, injured people, most of whom have little or no money. And I never know from one month to the next how many of these people will show up at my office.'

'Look, Jake,' Atcavage interrupted. 'I would really like to finish this discussion, but Claude just looked at his watch and then looked at us. I think our twenty minutes are up.'

Jake's check was seventy-one cents more than Atcavage's, and since both orders were identical, Claude was interrogated. No problem, he explained, Jake got an extra rib.

McKittrick was personable and precise, thorough and pushy. He had arrived in Clanton on Wednesday to investigate and write about what was billed as the most famous murder in the country, at the moment. He talked to Ozzie and Moss Junior, and they suggested he talk to Jake. He talked to Bullard, through the door, and the judge suggested he talk to Jake. He interviewed Gwen and Lester, but was not permitted to meet the girl. He visited with the regulars at the Coffee Shop and the Tea

Shoppe, and he visited with the regulars at Huey's and Ann's Lounge. He talked to Willard's ex-wife and mother, but Mrs. Cobb was through with reporters. One of Cobb's brothers offered to talk for a fee. McKittrick declined. He drove to the paper mill and talked to the co-workers, and he drove to Smithfield to interview the D.A. He would be in town for a few more days, then return for the trial.

He was from Texas, and retained, when convenient, a slight drawl, which impressed the locals and opened them up. He even said 'you all' and 'y'all' occasionally, and this distinguished him from most of the other reporters who clung to their crisp, precise, modern American pronunciation.

'What's that?' McKittrick pointed to the center of Jake's desk.

'That's a tape recorder,' Jake answered.

McKittrick sat his own recorder on the desk and looked at Jake's. 'May I ask why?'

'You may. It's my office, my interview, and if I want to record it, I will.'

'Are you expecting trouble?'

'I'm trying to prevent it. I hate to be misquoted.'

'I'm not known for misquoting.'

'Good. Then you won't mind if both of us record everthing.'

'You don't trust me, do you, Mr. Brigance?'

'Hell no. And my name is Jake.'

'Why don't you trust me?'

'Because you're a reporter, you're from a New York paper, you're looking for a sensational story, and if you're true to form, you'll write some well-informed, moralistic piece of trash depicting us all as racist, ignorant rednecks.'

'You're wrong. First of all, I'm from Texas.'

'Your paper is from New York.'

'But I consider myself a Southerner.'

'How long have you been gone?'

'About twenty years.'

Jake smiled and shook his head, as if to say: That's too long.

'And I don't work for a sensational newspaper.'

'We'll see. The trial is several months away. We'll have time to read your stories.'

'Fair enough.'

Jake punched the play button on his tape recorder, and McKittrick did likewise.

'Can Carl Lee Hailey receive a fair trial in Ford County?'

'Why couldn't he?' Jake asked.

'Well, he's black. He killed two white men, and he will be tried by a white jury.'

'You mean he will be tried by a bunch of white racists.'

'No, that's not what I said, nor what I implied. Why do you automatically assume I think you are all a bunch of racists?'

'Because you do. We're stereotyped, and you know it.'

McKittrick shrugged and wrote something on his steno pad. 'Will you answer the question?'

'Yes. He can receive a fair trial in Ford County, if he's tried here.'

'Do you want it tried here?'

'I'm sure we'll try to move it.'

'To where?'

'We won't suggest a place. That's up to the judge.'

'Where did he get the M-16?'

Jake chuckled and stared at the tape recorder. 'I do not know.'

'Would he be indicted if he were white?'

'He's black, and he has not been indicted.'

'But if he were white, would there be an indictment?'

'Yes, in my opinion.'

'Would he be convicted?'

'Would you like a cigar?' Jake opened a desk drawer and found a Roi-Tan. He unwrapped it, then lit it with a butane lighter.

'No thanks.'

'No, he would not be convicted if he were white. In my opinion. Not in Mississippi, not in Texas, not in Wyoming. I'm not sure about New York.'

'Why not?'

'Do you have a daughter?'

'No.'

'Then you wouldn't understand.'

'I think I do. Will Mr. Hailey be convicted?'

'Probably.'

'So the system does not work as fairly for blacks?'

'Have you talked with Raymond Hughes?'

'No. Who is he?'

'He ran for sheriff last time, and had the misfortune of making the runoff against Ozzie Walls. He's white. Ozzie, of course, is not. If I'm not mistaken, he got thirty-one percent of the vote. In a county that's seventy-four percent white. Why don't you ask Mr. Hughes if the system treats blacks fairly?'

'I was referring to the judicial system.'

'It's the same system. Who do you think sits in the jury box? The same registered voters who elected Ozzie Walls.'

'Well, if a white man would not be convicted, and Mr. Hailey will probably be convicted, explain to me how the system treats both fairly.'

'It doesn't.'

'I'm not sure I'm following you.'

'The system reflects society. It's not always fair, but it's as fair as the system in New York, or Massachusetts, or California. It's as fair as biased, emotional humans can make it.'

'And you think Mr. Hailey will be treated as fairly here as he would be in New York?'

'I'm saying there's as much racism in New York as in Mississippi. Look at our public schools – they're as desegregated as any.'

'By court order.'

'Sure, but what about the courts in New York. For years you pious bastards pointed your fingers and noses at us down here and demanded that we desegregate. It happened, and it has not been the end of the world. But you've conveniently ignored your own schools and neighborhoods, your own voting irregularities, your own all-white juries and city councils. We were wrong, and we've paid dearly for it. But we learned, and although the change has been slow and painful, at least we're trying. Y'all are still pointing fingers.'

'I didn't intend to refight Gettysburg.'

'I'm sorry. What defense will we use? I do not know at this point. Honestly, it's just too early. He hasn't even been indicted.'

'Of course he will?'

'Of course we don't know yet. More than likely. When will this be printed?'

'Maybe Sunday.'

'Makes no difference. No one here takes your paper. Yes, he will be indicted.'

McKittrick glanced at his watch, and Jake turned off his recorder.

'Look, I'm not a bad guy,' McKittrick said. 'Let's drink a beer sometime and finish this.'

'Off the record, I don't drink. But I accept your invitation.'

The First Presbyterian Church of Clanton was directly across the street from the First United Methodist Church of Clanton, and both churches were within sight of the much larger First Baptist Church. The Baptists had more members and money, but the Presbyterians and Methodists adjourned earlier on Sunday and outraced the Baptists to the restaurants for Sunday dinner. The Baptists would arrive at twelve-thirty and stand in line while the Presbyterians and Methodists ate slowly and waved at them.

Jake was content not to be a Baptist. They were a bit too narrow and strict, and they were forever preaching about Sunday night church, a ritual Jake had always struggled with. Carla was raised as a Baptist, Jake a Methodist, and during the courtship a compromise was negotiated, and they became Presbyterians. They were happy with their church and its activities, and seldom missed.

On Sunday, they sat in their usual pew, with Hanna asleep between them, and ignored the sermon. Jake ignored it by watching the preacher and picturing his confronting Buckley, in court, before twelve good and lawful citizens, as the nation watched and waited, and Carla ignored it by watching the preacher and mentally redecorating the dining room. Jake caught a few inquisitive stares during the worship service, and he figured his fellow church members were somewhat awed to have a celebrity among them. There were some strange faces in the congregation, and they were either long-lost repentant members or reporters. Jake was unsure until one persisted in staring at him – then he knew they were all reporters.

'Enjoyed your sermon, Reverend,' Jake lied as he shook hands with the minister on the steps outside the sanctuary.

'Good to see you, Jake,' replied the reverend. 'We've watched you all week on TV. My kids get excited every time they see you.'

'Thanks. Just pray for us.'

They drove to Karaway for Sunday lunch with Jake's parents. Gene and Eva Brigance lived in the old family house, a sprawling country home on five acres of wooded land in downtown Karaway, three blocks from Main Street and two blocks from the school where Jake and his sister put in twelve years. Both were retired, but young enough to travel the continent in a mobile home each summer. They would leave Monday for Canada and return after Labor Day. Jake was their only son. An older daughter lived in New Orleans.

Sunday lunch on Eva's table was a typical Southern feast of fried meats, fresh garden vegetables – boiled, battered, baked, and raw, homemade rolls and biscuits, two gravies, watermelon, cantaloupe, peach cobbler, lemon pie, and strawberry shortcake. Little of it would be eaten, and the leftovers would be neatly packaged by Eva and Carla and sent to Clanton, where it would last for a week.

'How are your parents, Carla?' Mr. Brigance asked as he passed the rolls.

'They're fine. I talked to Mother yesterday.'

'Are they in Knoxville?'

'No, sir. They're already in Wilmington for the summer.'

'Will y'all be going to visit them?' asked Eva as she poured the tea from a one-gallon ceramic pitcher.

Carla glanced at Jake, who was dipping butterbeans onto Hanna's plate. He did not want to discuss Carl Lee Hailey. Every meal since Monday night had centered around the case, and Jake was in no mood to answer the same questions.

'Yes, ma'am. We plan to. It depends on Jake's schedule. It could be a busy summer.'

'So we've heard,' Eva said flatly, slowly as if to remind her son he had not called since the killings.

'Is something wrong with your phone, son?' asked Mr. Brigance.

'Yes. We've had the number changed.'

The four adults ate slowly, apprehensively, while Hanna looked at the shortcake.

'Yes, I know. That's what the operator told us. To an unlisted number.'

'Sorry. I've been very busy. It's been hectic.'

'So we've read,' said his father.

Eva stopped eating and cleared her throat. 'Jake, do you really think you can get him off?'

'I'm worried about your family,' said his father. 'It could be a very dangerous case.'

'He shot them in cold blood,' Eva said.

'They raped his daughter, Mother. What would you do if someone raped Hanna?'

'What's rape?' asked Hanna.

'Never mind, dear,' Carla said. 'Could we please change the subject.' She looked firmly at the three Brigances, and they started eating again. The daughter-in-law had spoken, with wisdom, as usual.

Jake smiled at his mother without looking at Mr. Brigance. 'I just don't want to talk about the case, Mother. I'm tired of it.'

'I guess we'll have to read about it,' said Mr. Brigance.

They talked about Canada.

At about the time the Brigances finished lunch, the sanctuary of the Mt. Zion Chapel CME rocked and swayed as the Right Reverend Ollie Agee whipped the devotees into a glorified frenzy. Deacons danced. Elders chanted. Women fainted. Grown men screamed and raised their arms toward the heavens as the small children looked upward in holy terror. Choir members lurched and lunged and jerked, then broke down and shrieked different stanzas of the same song. The organist played one song, the pianist another, and the choir sang whatever came over it. The reverend hopped around the pulpit in his long white robe with purple trim, yelling, praying, screaming at God, and perspiring.

The bedlam rose and fell, rising it seemed with each new fainting, and falling with fatigue. Through years of experience Agee knew precisely when the fury reached its peak, when the delirium gave way to weariness, and when the flock needed a break. At that precise moment, he jigged to the pulpit and slapped it with the power of God Almighty. Instantly the music died, the convulsions ceased, the fainters awoke, the children stopped crying, and the multitude settled submissively into the pews. It was time for the sermon.

As the reverend was about to preach, the rear doors opened and the Haileys entered the sanctuary. Little Tonya walked by herself, limping, holding her mother's hand. Her brothers marched behind, and Uncle Lester followed. They moved slowly down the aisle and found a seat near the front. The reverend nodded at the organist, who began to play softly, then the choir began to hum and sway. The deacons stood and swayed with the choir. Not to be outdone, the elders stood and began to chant. Then, of all things, Sister Crystal fainted violently. Her fainting was contagious, and the other sisters began dropping like flies. The elders chanted louder than the choir, so the choir got excited. The organist could not be heard, so she increased the volume. The pianist joined in with a clanging rendition of a hymn unlike the hymn being played by the organist. The organist thundered back. Reverend Agee fluttered down from the podium and danced his way toward the Haileys. Everyone followed – the choir, the deacons, the elders, the women, the crying children – everyone followed the reverend to great the little Hailey girl.

Jail did not bother Carl Lee. Home was more pleasant, but under the circumstances, he found jail life tolerable. It was a new jail, built with federal money under the mandate of a prisoners' rights lawsuit. The food was cooked by two huge black women who knew how to cook and write bad checks. They were eligible for early release, but Ozzie had not bothered to tell them. The food was served to forty prisoners, give or take a few, by the trusties. Thirteen of the prisoners belonged at Parchman, but it was full. So they waited, never knowing if the next day would be their day for the dreaded trip to the sprawling, enclosed delta farm where the food was not as good, the beds were not as soft, the air conditioning was nonexistent, the mosquitoes immense, plentiful, and vicious, and where toilets were scarce and clogged.

Carl Lee's cell was next to Cell Two, where the state prisoners waited. With two exceptions, they were black, and with no exceptions, they were violent. But they were all afraid of Carl Lee. He shared Cell One with two shoplifters who were not just scared, but downright terrified of their famous cellmate. Each evening he was escorted to Ozzie's office, where he and the sheriff ate dinner and watched the news. He was a celebrity, and he liked that almost as much as did his lawyer and the D.A. He wanted to explain things to the reporters, tell them about his daughter and why he should not be in jail, but his lawyer said no.

After Gwen and Lester left late Sunday afternoon, Ozzie, Moss Junior, and Carl Lee sneaked out the rear of the jail and went to the hospital. It was Carl Lee's idea, and Ozzie saw no harm. Looney was alone in a private room when the three entered. Carl Lee took one look at the leg, then stared at Looney. They shook hands. With watery eyes and a breaking voice Carl Lee said he was sorry, that he had no intention of hurting anyone but the two boys, that he wished and prayed he could undo what he had done to Looney. Without hesitation, Looney accepted the apology.

Jake was waiting in Ozzie's office when they sneaked back into the jail. Ozzie and Moss Junior excused themselves, leaving the defendant with his lawyer.

'Where have y'all been?' Jake asked suspiciously.

'Went to the hospital to see Looney.'

'You what!'

'Nothin' wrong, is it?'

'I wish you would check with me before you make any more visits.'

'What's wrong with seein' Looney?'

'Looney will be the star witness for the State when they attempt to send you to the gas chamber. That's all. He ain't on our side, Carl Lee, and any talking you do with Looney should be with your attorney present. Understand?'

'Not really.'

'I can't believe Ozzie would do that,' Jake mumbled.

'It was my idea,' Carl Lee admitted.

'Well, if you get any more ideas, please let me know about them. Okay?'

'Okay.'

'You talked to Lester lately?'

'Yeah, him and Gwen came by today. Brought me goodies. Told me 'bout the banks.'

Jake planned to play hardball about his fee; no way he could represent Carl Lee for nine hundred dollars. The case would consume his practice for the next three months at least, and nine hundred would be less than minimum wage. It would not be fair to him or his family to work for nothing. Carl Lee would simply have to raise the money. There were plenty of relatives. Gwen had a big family. They would just have to sacrifice, maybe sell a few automobiles, maybe some land, but Jake would get his fee. If not, Carl Lee could find another lawyer.

'I'll give you the deed to my place,' Carl Lee offered.

Jake melted. 'I don't want your place, Carl Lee. I want cash. Sixty-five hundred dollars.'

'Show me how, and I'll do it. You the lawyer, you figure out a way. I'm with you.'

Jake was beat and he knew it. 'I can't do it for nine hundred dollars, Carl Lee. I can't let this case bankrupt me. I'm a lawyer. I'm supposed to make money.'

'Jake, I'll pay you the money. I promise. It may take a long time, but I'll pay you. Trust me.'

Not if you're on death row, thought Jake. He changed the subject. 'You know the grand jury meets tomorrow, and it'll take up your case.'

'So I go to court?'

'Naw, it means you'll be indicted tomorrow. The courthouse will be full of people and reporters. Judge Noose will be here to open the May term of court. Buckley'll be running around chasing cameras and blowing smoke. It's a big day. Noose starts an armed robbery trial in the afternoon. If you're indicted tomorrow, we'll be in court Wednesday or Thursday for the arraignment.'

'The what?'

'The arraignment. In a capital murder case, the judge is required by law to read the indictment to you in open court in front of God and everybody. They'll make a big deal out of it. We'll enter a plea of not guilty, and Noose sets the trial date. We ask for a reasonable bond, and he says no. When I mention bond Buckley'll scream and turn cartwheels. The more I think of him the more I hate him. He'll be a large pain in the ass.'

'Why don't I get a bond?'

'For capital murder, the judge does not have to set a bond. He can if he wants to, but most don't. Even if Noose set a bond, you couldn't pay it, so don't worry about it. You'll be in jail until trial.'

'I lost my job, you know.'

'When?'

'Gwen drove over Friday and got my paycheck. They told her. Nice, ain't it. Work there eleven years, miss five days, and they fire me. Guess they think I ain't comin' back.'

'I'm sorry to hear that, Carl Lee. Real sorry.'

CHAPTER TWELVE

The Honorable Omar Noose had not always been so honorable. Before he became the circuit judge for the Twenty-second Judicial District, he was a lawyer with meager talent and few clients, but he was a politician of formidable skills. Five terms in the Mississippi Legislature had corrupted him and taught him the art of political swindling and manipulation. Senator Noose prospered handsomely as chairman of the Senate Finance Committee, and few people in Van Buren County questioned how he and his family lived so affluently on his legislative salary of seven thousand dollars a year.

Like most members of the Mississippi Legislature, he ran for reelection one time too many, and in the summer of 1971 he was humiliated by an unknown opponent. A year later, Judge Loopus, his predecessor on the bench, died, and Noose persuaded his friends in the Legislature to persuade the governor to appoint him to serve the unexpired term. That's how ex-State Senator Noose became Circuit Judge Noose. He was elected in 1975, and reelected in 1979 and 1983.

Repentant, reformed, and very humbled by his rapid descent from power, Judge Noose applied himself to the study of the law, and after a shaky start, grew to the job. It paid sixty thousand a year, so he could afford to be honest. Now, at sixty-three, he was a wise old judge, well respected by most lawyers and by the state Supreme Court, which seldom reversed his rulings. He was quiet but charming, patient but strict, and he had a huge monument of a nose that was very long and very pointed and served as a throne for his black-rimmed, octagon-shaped reading glasses, which he wore constantly but never used. His nose, plus his tall, gawky frame, plus his wild, untamed, dense gray hair, plus his squeaky voice, had given rise to his secret nickname, whispered among lawyers, of Ichabod. Ichabod Noose. The Honorable Ichabod Noose.

He assumed the bench, and the crowded courtroom stood as Ozzie mumbled incoherently a statutorily required paragraph to officially open the May term of the Ford County Circuit Court. A long, flowery prayer was offered by a local minister, and the congregation sat down. Prospective jurors filled one side of the courtroom. Criminals and other litigants, their families and friends, the press, and the curious filled the other side. Noose required every lawyer in the county to attend the opening of the term, and the members of the bar sat in the jury box, all decked out in full regalia, all looking important. Buckley and his assistant, D.R. Musgrove, sat at the prosecution's table, splendidly representing the State.

Jake sat by himself in a wooden chair in front of the railing. The clerks and court reporters stood behind the large red docket books on the workbench, and with everyone else watched intently as Ichabod situated himself in his chair upon the bench, straightened his robe, adjusted his hideous reading glasses, and peered over them at the assemblage.

'Good morning,' he squeaked loudly. He pulled the microphone closer and cleared his throat. 'It's always nice to be in Ford County for the May term of court. I see most members of the bar found time to appear for the opening of court, and as usual, I will request Madam Clerk to note those absent attorneys so that I may personally contact them. I see a large number of potential jurors present, and I thank each of you for being here. I realize you had no choice, but your presence is vital to our judicial process. We will empanel a grand jury momentarily, and then we will select several trial juries to serve this week and next. I trust each member of the bar has a copy of the docket, and you will note it looks somewhat crowded. My calendar reveals at least two cases set for trial each day this week and next, but it's my understanding most of the criminal cases set for trial will go off on negotiated plea bargains. Nonetheless, we have many cases to move, and I request the diligent cooperation of the bar. Once the new grand jury is empaneled and goes to work, and once the indictments start coming down, I will schedule arraignments and first appearances. Let's quickly call the docket, criminal first, then civil; then the attorneys may be excused as we select a grand jury.

'State versus Warren Moke. Armed robbery, set for trial this afternoon.'

Buckley rose slowly, purposefully. 'The State of Mississippi is ready for trial, Your Honor,' he announced gloriously for the spectators.

'So's the defense,' said Tyndale, the court-appointed lawyer.

'How long do you anticipate for trial?' asked the judge.

'Day and a half,' answered Buckley. Tyndale nodded in agreement.

'Good. We'll select the trial jury this morning and start the trial at one P.M. today. State versus William Daal, forgery, six counts, set for tomorrow.'

'Your Honor,' answered D.R. Musgrove, 'there will be a plea in that case.'

'Good. State versus Roger Hornton, grand larceny, two counts, set for tomorrow.'

Noose continued through the docket. Each case drew the same response. Buckley would stand and proclaim the State ready for trial, or Musgrove would quietly inform the court that a plea had been negotiated. The defense attorneys would stand and nod. Jake had no cases in the May term, and although he tried his best to look bored, he enjoyed the call of the docket because he could learn who had the cases and what the competition was doing. It was also a chance to look good before some of the local folks. Half the members of the Sullivan firm were present, and they too looked bored as they sat arrogantly together in the front row of the jury box. The older partners of the Sullivan firm would not dare make an appearance at docket call, and they would lie and tell Noose they were in trial in Federal Court over in Oxford or perhaps before the Supreme Court in Jackson. Dignity prevented their mingling with the ordinary members of the bar, so the firm's younger lieutenants were sent to satisfy Noose and request that all the firm's civil cases be continued, postponed, delayed, stalled, or acted upon in such a way that the firm could drag them on forever and continue to bill by the hour. Their clients were insurance companies who generally preferred not to go to trial and would pay by the hour for legal maneuvering designed solely to keep the cases away from the juries. It would be cheaper and fairer to pay a reasonable settlement and avoid both litigation and the parasitic defense firms like Sullivan & O'Hare, but the insurance companies and their adjusters were too stupid and cheap, so street lawyers like Jake Brigance earned their livelihoods suing insurance companies and forcing them to pay more than what they would have paid had they dealt fairly from the beginning. Jake hated insurance companies, and he hated insurance defense attorneys, and he especially hated the Sullivan firm's younger members, all of whom were his age, and all of whom would gladly cut his throat, their associates' throats, their partners' throats, anyone's throat to make partner and earn two hundred thousand a year and skip docket calls.

Jake particularly hated Lotterhouse, or L. Winston Lotterhouse, as the letterhead proclaimed him, a little four-eyed wimp with a Harvard degree and a bad case of haughty self-importance who was next in line to make partner and thus had been especially indiscriminate with his throat cutting during the past year. He sat smugly between two other Sullivan associates and held seven files, each of which was being charged a hundred dollars per hour while he answered the docket call.

Noose began the civil docket. 'Collins versus Royal Consolidated General Mutual Insurance Company.'

Lotterhouse stood slowly. Seconds meant minutes. Minutes meant hours. Hours meant fees, retainers, bonuses, partnerships.

'Your Honor, sir, that case is set prime for a week from Wednesday.'

'I realize that,' Noose said.

'Yes, sir. Well, sir, I'm afraid I must ask for a continuance. A conflict has developed in my trial calendar for that Wednesday, and I have a pretrial conference in Federal Court in Memphis that the judge has refused to continue. I regret this. I field a motion this morning asking for a continuance.'

Gardner, the plaintiff's attorney, was furious. 'Your Honor, that case has been set prime for two months. It was set for trial in February, and Mr. Lotterhouse had a death in his wife's family. It was set for trial last November, and an uncle died. It was set for trial last August, and there was another funeral. I guess we should be thankful that this time no one has died.'

There were pockets of light laughter in the courtroom. Lotterhouse blushed.

'Enough is enough, Your Honor,' Gardner continued. 'Mr. Lotterhouse would prefer to postpone this trial forever. The case is ripe for trial, and my client is entitled to one. We strenuously oppose any motion for a continuance.'

Lotterhouse smiled at the judge and removed his glasses. 'Your Honor, If I may respond –'

'No, you may not, Mr. Lotterhouse,' interrupted Noose. 'No more continuances. The case is set for trial next Wednesday. There will be no more delays.'

Hallelujah, thought Jake. Noose was generally soft on the Sullivan firm. Jake smiled at Lotterhouse.

Two of Jake's civil cases were continued to the August term. When Noose finished the civil docket, he dismissed the attorneys, and turned his attention to the pool of prospective jurors. He explained the role of the grand jury, its importance and procedure. He distinguished it from the trial juries, equally important but not as time consuming. He began asking questions, dozens of questions, most of them required by law, all dealing with ability to serve as jurors, physical and moral fitness, exemptions, and age. A few were useless, but nonetheless required by some ancient statute. 'Are any of you common gamblers or habitual drunkards?'

There were laughs but no volunteers. Those over sixty-five were automatically excused, at their option. Noose granted the usual exemptions for illnesses, emergencies, and hardships, but he excused only a few of the many who requested pardons for economic reasons. It was amusing to watch the jurors stand, one at a time, and meekly explain to the judge how a few days of jury duty would cause irreparable damage to the farm, or the body shop, or the pulpwood cutting. Noose took a hard line and delivered several lectures on civic responsibility to the flimsier excuses.

From the venire of ninety or so prospects, eighteen would be selected for the grand jury, and the rest would remain available for selection as trial jurors. When Noose completed his questioning, the clerk drew eighteen names from a box and laid them on the bench before His Honor, who began calling names. The jurors, one by one, rose and walked slowly toward the front of the courtroom, through the gate in the railing, and into the cushioned, swivel rocking seats in the jury box. There were fourteen such seats, twelve for the jurors and two for the alternates. When the box was filled, Noose called four more who joined their colleagues in wooden chairs placed in front of the jury box.

'Stand and take the oath,' instructed Noose as the clerk stood before them holding and reading from a little black book that contained all the oaths. 'Raise your right hands,' she directed. 'Do you solemnly swear or affirm that you will faithfully discharge your duties as grand jurors; that you will fairly hear and decide all issues and matters brought before you, so help you God?'

A chorus of assorted 'I do's' followed and the grand jury was seated. Of the five blacks, two were women. Of the thirteen whites, eight were women, and most were rural. Jake recognized seven of the eighteen.

'Ladies and gentlemen,' Noose began his usual speech, 'you have been selected and duly sworn as grand jurors for Ford County, and you will serve in that capacity until the next grand jury is empaneled in August. I want to stress that your duties will not be time consuming. You will meet every day this week, then several hours each month until September. You have the responsibility of reviewing criminal cases, listening to law enforcement officials and victims, and determining whether or not reasonable grounds exist to believe the accused has committed the crime. If so, you issue an indictment, which is a formal charge placed against the accused. There are eighteen of you, and when at least twelve believe a person should be indicted, the indictment is issued, or returned, as we say. You have considerable power. By law, you can investigate any criminal act, any citizen suspected of wrongdoing, any public official; really anybody or anything that smells bad. You may convene yourself whenever you choose, but normally you meet whenever the district attorney, Mr. Buckley, wants you. You have the power to subpoena witnesses to testify before you, and you may also subpoena their records. Your deliberations are extremely private, with no one being present but yourselves, the D.A. and his staff, and the witnesses. The accused is not allowed to appear before you. You are expressly forbidden to discuss anything that is said or transpires in the grand jury room.

'Mr. Buckley, would you please stand. Thank you. This is Mr. Rufus Buckley, the district attorney. He's from Smithfield, in Polk County. He will sort of act as your supervisor while you deliberate. Thank you, Mr. Buckley. Mr. Musgrove, will you stand. This is D.R. Musgrove, assistant district attorney, also from Smithfield. He will assist Mr. Buckley while you are in session. Thank you, Mr. Musgrove. Now, these gentlemen represent the State of Mississippi, and they will present the cases to the grand jury.

'One final matter; the last grand jury in Ford County was empaneled in February, and the foreman was a white male. Therefore, in keeping with tradition and following the wishes of the Justice Department, I will appoint a black female as foreman of this grand jury. Let's see. Laverne Gossett. Where are you, Mrs. Gossett? There you are, good. I believe you are a schoolteacher, correct? Good. I'm sure you'll be able to handle your new duties. Now, it's time for you to get to work. I understand there are over fifty cases waiting on you. I will ask that you follow Mr. Buckley and Mr. Musgrove down the hall to the small courtroom that we use for a grand jury room. Thank you and good luck.'

Buckley proudly marched his new grand jury out of the courtroom and down the hall. He waved at reporters and had no comments – for the time being. In the small courtroom they seated themselves around two long, folding tables. A secretary rolled in boxes of files. An ancient half-crippled, half-deaf, long-retired deputy in a faded uniform took his position by the door. The room was secure. Buckley had second thoughts, excused himself, and met with the reporters in the hall. Yes, he said, the Hailey case would be presented that afternoon. In fact, he was calling a press conference for 4:00 P.M. on the front steps of the courthouse, and he would have the indictments at that time.

After lunch, the chief of the Karaway Police Department sat at one end of the long table and shuffled nervously through his files. He avoided looking at the grand jurors, who anxiously awaited their first case.

'State your name!' barked the D.A.

'Chief Nolan Earnhart, Karaway City Police.'

'How many cases do you have, Chief?'

'We have five from Karaway.'

'Let's hear the first one.'

'Okay, let's see, all right,' the chief mumbled and stuttered as he flipped through his paperwork. 'Okay, the first case is Fedison Bulow, male black, age twenty-five, got caught red-handed in the rear of Griffin's Feed Store in Karaway at two o'clock in the mornin', April 12. Silent alarm went off and we caught him in the store. Cash register had been broken into, and some fertilizer was gone. We found the cash and the goods in a car registered in his name parked behind the store. He gave a three-page confession at the jail, and I've got copies here.'

Buckley walked casually around the room smiling at everyone. 'And you want this grand jury to indict Fedison Bulow on one count of breaking and entering a commercial building, and one count of grand larceny?' Buckley asked helpfully.

'Yes, sir, that's right.'

'Now, members of the grand jury, you have the right to ask any questions. This is your hearing. Any questions?'

'Yes, does he have a record?' asked Mack Loyd Crowell, an unemployed truck driver.

'No,' replied the chief. 'This is his first offense.'

'Good question, always ask that question because if they have prior records we may need to indict them as habitual criminals,' lectured Buckley. 'Any more questions? None? Good. Now at this point, someone needs to make a motion that the grand jury return a true bill of indictment against Fedison Bulow.'

Silence. The eighteen stared at the table and waited for someone else to make a motion. Buckley waited. Silence. This is great, he thought. A soft grand jury. A bunch of timid souls afraid to speak. Liberals. Why couldn't he have a bloodthirsty grand jury eager to make motions to indict everybody for everything?

'Mrs. Gossett, would you like to make the first motion, since you're the foreman?'

'I so move,' she said.

'Thank you,' said Buckley. 'Now let's vote. How many vote to indict Fedison Bulow on one count of breaking and entering a commercial building and one count of grand larceny? Raise your hands.'

Eighteen hands went up, and Buckley was relieved.

The chief presented the other four cases from Karaway. Each involved defendants equally guilty as Bulow, and each received unanimous true bills. Buckley slowly taught the grand jury how to operate itself. He made them feel important, powerful, and laden with the heavy burden of justice. They became inquisitive:

'Does he have a record?'

'How much time does that carry?'

'When will he get out?'

'How many counts can we give him?'

'When will he be tried?'

'Is he out of jail now?'

With five indictments out of the way, with five true bills and no dissension, with the grand jury eager for the next case, whatever it might be, Buckley decided the mood was ripe. He opened the door and motioned for Ozzie, who was standing in the hall talking quietly with a deputy and watching the reporters.

'Present Hailey first,' Buckley whispered as the two met in the door.

'Ladies and gentlemen, this is Sheriff Walls. I'm sure most of you know him. He has several cases to present. What's first, Sheriff?'

Ozzie scrambled through his files, lost whatever he was looking for, and finally blurted, 'Carl Lee Hailey.'

The jurors became quiet again. Buckley watched them closely to gauge their reactions. Most of them stared at the table again. No one spoke while Ozzie reviewed the file, then excused himself to get another briefcase. He had not planned to present the Hailey case first.

Buckley prided himself on reading jurors, of watching their faces and knowing precisely their thoughts. He watched the jury constantly during a trial, always predicting to himself what each was thinking. He would cross-examine a witness and never take his eyes off the jury. He would sometimes stand and face the jury box and interrogate a witness and watch the faces react to the answers. After hundreds of trials he was good at reading jurors, and he knew instantly he was in trouble with Hailey. The five blacks grew tense and arrogant as if they welcomed the case and the inevitable argument. The foreman, Mrs. Gossett, looked particularly pious as Ozzie mumbled to himself and flipped papers. Most of the whites looked noncommittal, but Mack Loyd Crowell, a hard-looking middle-aged rural type, appeared as arrogant as the blacks. Crowell pushed back his chair and walked to the window, which looked over the north side of the courtyard. Buckley could not read him precisely, but he knew Crowell was trouble.

'Sheriff, how many witnesses do you have for the Hailey case?' Buckley asked, somewhat nervously.

Ozzie stopped shuffling paper and said, 'Well, uh, just me. We can get another if we need one.'

'All right, all right,' replied Buckley. 'Just tell us about the case.'

Ozzie reared back, crossed his legs, and said, 'Shoot, Rufus, everbody knows about this case. Been on TV for a week.'

'Just give us the evidence.'

'The evidence. Okay, one week ago today, Carl Lee Hailey, male black, age thirty-seven, shot and killed one Billy Ray Cobb and one Pete Willard, and he shot a peace officer, one DeWayne Looney, who's still in the hospital with his leg cut off. The weapon was an M-16 machine gun, illegal, which we recovered and matched the fingerprints with those of Mr. Hailey. I have an affidavit signed by Deputy Looney, and he states, under oath, that the man who did the shootin' was Carl Lee Hailey. There was an eyewitness, Murphy, the little crippled man that sweeps the courthouse and stutters real bad. I can get him here if you want.'

'Any questions?' interrupted Buckley.

The D.A. nervously watched the jurors, who nervously watched the sheriff. Crowell stood with his back to the others, looking through the window.

'Any questions?' Buckley repeated.

'Yeah,' answered Crowell as he turned and glared at the D.A., then at Ozzie. 'Those two boys he shot, they raped his little girl, didn't they, Sheriff?'

'We're pretty sure they did,' answered Ozzie.

'Well, one confessed, didn't he?'

'Yep.'

Crowell walked slowly, boldly, arrogantly across the room, and stood at the other end of the tables. He looked down at Ozzie. 'You got kids, Sheriff?'

'Yep.'

'You got a little girl?'

'Yep.'

'Suppose she got raped and you got your hands on the man who did it. What would you do?'

Ozzie paused and looked anxiously at Buckley, whose neck had turned a deep red.

'I don't have to answer that,' Ozzie replied.

'Is that so. You came before this grand jury to testify, didn't you? You're a witness, ain't you? Answer the question.'

'I don't know what I'd do.'

'Come on, Sheriff. Give us a straight answer. Tell the truth. What would you do?'

Ozzie felt embarrassed, confused, and angry at this stranger. He would like to tell the truth, and explain in detail how he would gladly castrate and mutilate and kill any pervert who touched his little girl. But he couldn't. The grand jury might agree and refuse to indict Carl Lee. Not that he wanted him indicted, but he knew the indictment was necessary. He looked sheepishly at Buckley, who was perspiring and seated now.

Crowell zeroed in on the sheriff with the zeal and fervor of a lawyer who had just caught a witness in an obvious lie.

'Come on, Sheriff,' he taunted. 'We're all listenin'. Tell the truth. What would you do to the rapist? Tell us. Come on.'

Buckley was near panic. The biggest case of his wonderful career was about to be lost, not at trial, but in the grand jury room, in the first round, at the hands of an unemployed truck driver. He stood and struggled for words. 'The witness does not have to answer.'

Crowell turned and shouted at Buckley, 'You sit down and shut up! We don't take orders from you. We can indict you if we want to, can't we?'

Buckley sat and looked blankly at Ozzie. Crowell was a ringer. He was too smart to be on a grand jury. Someone must have paid him. He knew too much. Yes, the grand jury could indict anyone.

Crowell retreated and returned to the window. They watched him until it appeared he was finished.

'Are you absolutely sure he done it, Ozzie?' asked Lemoyne Frady, an illegitimate distant cousin to Gwen Hailey.

'Yes, we're sure,' Ozzie answered slowly, with both eyes on Crowell.

'And you want us to indict him for what?' asked Mr. Frady, the admiration for the sheriff obvious.

'Two counts of capital murder, and one count of assault on a peace officer.'

'How much time you talkin' about?' asked Barney Flaggs, another black.

'Capital murder carries the gas chamber. Assault on a deputy carries life with no parole.'

'And that's what you want, Ozzie?' asked Flaggs.

'Yeah, Barney, I say this grand jury should indict Mr. Hailey. I sure do.'

'Any more questions?' interrupted Buckley.

'Not so fast,' replied Crowell as he turned from the window. 'I think you're tryin' to ram this case down our throats, Mr. Buckley, and I resent it. I wanna talk about it some. You sit down and if we need you, we'll ask you.'

Buckley glared fiercely and pointed his finger. 'I don't have to sit, and I don't have to say quiet!' he yelled.

'Yes. Yes, you do,' Crowell answered coolly with a caustic grin. 'Because if you don't we can make you leave, can't we, Mr. Buckley? We can ask you to leave this room, and if you refuse, we'll go ask the judge. He'll make you leave, won't he, Mr. Buckley?'

Rufus stood motionless, speechless, and stunned. His stomach turned flips and his knees were spongy, but he was frozen in place.

'So, if you would like to hear the rest of our deliberations, sit down and shut up.'

Buckley sat next to the bailiff, who was now awake.

'Thank you,' said Crowell. 'I wanna ask you folks a question. How many of you would do or wanna do what Mr. Hailey did if someone raped your daughter, or maybe your wife, or what about your mother? How many? Raise your hands.'

Seven or eight hands shot up, and Buckley dropped his head. Crowell smiled and continued, 'I admire him for what he did. It took guts. I'd hope I'd have the courage to do what he did,' 'cause Lord knows I'd want to. Sometimes a man's just gotta do what he's gotta do. This man deserves a trophy, not an indictment.'

Crowell walked slowly around the tables, enjoying the attention. 'Before you vote, I want you to do one thing. I want you to think about that poor little girl. I think she's ten. Try to picture her layin' there, hands tied behind her, cryin', beggin' for her daddy. And think of those two outlaws, drunk, doped up, takin' turns rapin' and beatin' and kickin' her. Hell, they even tried to kill her. Think of your own daughter. Put her in the place of the little Hailey girl.

'Now, wouldn't you say they got pretty much what they deserved? We should be thankful they're dead. I feel safer just knowin' those two bastards are no longer here to rape and kill other children. Mr. Hailey has done us a great service. Let's don't indict him. Let's send him home to his family, where he belongs. He's a good man who's done a good thing.'

Crowell finished and returned to the window. Buckley watched him fearfully, and when he was certain he was finished, he stood. 'Sir, are you finished?' There was no response.

'Good. Ladies and gentlemen of the grand jury. I would like to explain a few things. A grand jury is not supposed to try the case. That's what a trial jury is for. Mr. Hailey will get a fair trial before twelve fair and impartial jurors, and if he's innocent, he'll be acquitted. But his guilt or innocence is not supposed to be determined by the grand jury. You're supposed to decide, after listening to the State's version of the evidence, if there is a strong possibility a crime has been committed. Now, I submit to you that a crime has been committed by Carl Lee Hailey. Three crimes actually. He killed two men, and he wounded another. We have eye-witnesses.'

Buckley was warming as he circled the tables. The confidence was back. 'The duty of this grand jury is to indict him, and if he has a valid defense, he'll have a chance to present it at trial. If he has a legal reason for doing what he did, let him prove it at trial. That's what trials are for. The State charges him with a crime, and the State must prove at trial he committed the crime. If he has a defense, and if he can convince the trial jury, he will be acquitted, I assure you. Good for him. But it's not the duty of this grand jury to decide today that Mr. Hailey should go free. There'll be another day for that, right, Sheriff?'

Ozzie nodded and said, 'That's right. The grand jury is to indict if the evidence is presented. The trial jury will not convict him if the State can't prove its case, or if he puts a good defense. But the grand jury don't worry 'bout things like that.'

'Anything further from the grand jury?' Buckley asked anxiously. 'Okay, we need a motion.'

'I make a motion we don't indict him for anything,' yelled Crowell.

'Second,' mumbled Barney Flaggs.

Buckley's knees quivered. He tried to speak, but nothing came forth. Ozzie suppressed his joy.

'We have a motion and a second,' announced Mrs. Gossett. 'All in favor raise your hands.'

Five black hands went up, along with Crowell's. Six votes. The motion failed.

'Whatta we do now?' asked Mrs. Gossett.

Buckley spoke rapidly: 'Someone make a motion to indict Mr. Hailey for two counts of capital murder and one count of assault on a peace officer.'

'So move,' said one of the whites.

'Second,' said another.

'All in favor, raise your hands,' said Mrs. Gossett. 'I count twelve hands. All opposed – I count five plus mine makes six. Twelve to six. What does that mean?'

'That means he's been indicted,' Buckley replied proudly. He breathed normally again, and the color returned to his face. He whispered to a secretary, then addressed the grand jury. 'Let's take a ten-minute recess. We have about forty more cases to work on, so please don't be gone long. I would like to remind you of something Judge Noose said this morning. These deliberations are extremely confidential. You are not to discuss any of your work outside this room –'

'What he's tryin' to say,' interrupted Crowell, 'is that we can't tell anybody that he came within one vote of not gettin' the indictments. Ain't that right, Buckley?'

The D.A. quickly left the room and slammed the door.

Surrounded by dozens of cameras and reporters, Buckley stood on the front steps of the courthouse and waved copies of the indictments. He preached, lectured, moralized, praised the grand jury, sermonized against crime and vigilantes, and condemned Carl Lee Hailey. Bring on the trial. Put the jury in the box. He guaranteed a conviction. He guaranteed a death penalty. He was obnoxious, offensive, arrogant, self-righteous. He was himself. Vintage Buckley. A few of the reporters left, but he labored on. He extolled himself and his trial skills and his ninety, no, ninety-five percent conviction rate. More reporters left. More cameras were turned off. He praised Judge Noose for his wisdom and fairness. He acclaimed the intelligence and good judgement of Ford County jurors.

He outlasted them. They grew weary of him and they all left.

CHAPTER THIRTEEN

Stump Sisson was the Klan's Imperial Wizard for Mississippi, and he had called the meeting at the small cabin deep in the pine forest of Nettles County, two hundred and thirty miles south of Ford County. There were no robes, rituals, or speeches. The small group of Klansmen discussed the events in Ford County with a Mr. Freddie Cobb, brother of Billy Ray Cobb, deceased. Freddie had called a friend who called Stump to arrange the meeting.

Had they indicted the nigger? Cobb was not sure, but he had heard the trial would be in late summer, or early fall. What concerned him most was all the talk about the nigger pleading insanity and getting off. It wasn't right. The nigger killed his brother in cold blood, planned the shooting. He hid in a closet and waited for his brother. It was coldblooded murder, and now there was talk of the nigger walking free. What could the Klan do about it? The niggers have plenty of protection nowadays – the NAACP, ACLU, a thousand other civil rights groups, plus the courts and the government. Hell, white folks ain't got a chance, except for the Klan. Who else would march and stand up for white people. All the laws favor the niggers, and the liberal nigger-loving politicians keep making more laws against white people. Somebody's got to stand up for them. That's why he called the Klan.

Is the nigger in jail? Yes, and he's treated like a king. Got a nigger sheriff up there, Walls, and he likes this nigger. Gives him special privileges and extra protection. The sheriff's another story. Someone said Hailey might get out of jail this week on bond. Just a rumor. They hoped he got out.

What about your brother? Did he rape her? We're not sure, probably not. Willard, the other guy, confessed to rape, but Billy Ray never confessed. He had plenty of women. Why would he rape a little nigger girl? And if he did, what was the big deal?

Who's the nigger's lawyer? Brigance, a local boy in Clanton. Young, but pretty good. Does a lot of criminal work and has a good reputation. Won several murder trials. He told some reporters the nigger would plead insanity and get off.

Who's the judge? Don't know yet. Bullard was the county judge, but someone said he would not hear the case. There's talk of moving the case to another county, so who knows who will be the judge.

Sisson and the Kluxers listened intently to this ignorant redneck. They liked the part about the NAACP and the government and the politicians, but they had also read the papers and watched TV and they knew his brother had received justice. But at the hands of a nigger. It was unthinkable.

The case had real potential. With the trial several months away, there was time to plan a rebellion. They could march during the day around the courthouse in their white robes and pointed, hooded masks. They could make speeches to a captive audience and parade in front of the cameras. The press would love it – hate them, but love the altercations, the disruptions. And at night they could intimidate with burning crosses and threatening phone calls. The targets would be easy and unsuspecting. Violence would be unavoidable. They knew how to provoke it. They fully appreciated what the sight of marching white robes did to crowds of angry niggers.

Ford County could be their playground for hide and seek, search and destroy, and hit and run. They had time to organize and call in comrades from other states. What Kluxer would miss this golden moment? And new recruits? Why, this case could fuel the fires of racism and bring nigger haters out of the woods and onto the streets. Membership was down. Hailey would be their new battle cry, the rallying point.

'Mr. Cobb, can you get us the names and addresses of the nigger, his family, his lawyer, the judge, and the jurors?' asked Sisson.

Cobb pondered this task. 'Everbody but the jurors. They ain't been picked yet.'

'When will you know them?'

'Damned if I know. I guess at trial. What're y'all thinkin'?'

'We're not sure, but the Klan most likely will get involved. We need to flex our muscle a bit, and this could be a good opportunity.'

'Can I help?' Cobb asked eagerly.

'Sure, but you need to be a member.'

'We ain't got no Klan up there. It folded a long time ago. My granddaddy used to be a member.'

'You mean the grandfather of the victim was a Klansman?'

'Yep,' Cobb answered proudly.

'Well, then, we must get involved.' The Klansmen shook their heads in disbelief and vowed revenge. They explained to Cobb that if he could get five or six friends of similar thinking and motivation to agree to join, they would have a big, secret ceremony deep in the woods of Ford County with a huge burning cross and all sorts of rituals. They would be inducted as members, full-fledged members, of the Ku Klux Klan. Ford County Klavern. And they would all join in and make a spectacle of the trial of Carl Lee Hailey. They would raise so much hell in Ford County this summer that no juror with any common sense would consider voting to acquit the nigger. Just recruit half a dozen more, and they would make him the leader of the Ford County Klavern.

Cobb said he had enough cousins to start a klavern. He left the meeting drunk with excitement of being a Klansman, just like his grandfather.

Buckley's timing was a little off. His 4:00 P.M. press show was ignored by the evening news. Jake flipped the channels on a small black and white in his office, and laughed out loud when the networks and the Memphis, then Jackson, then Tupelo signed off with no news of the indictments. He could see the Buckley family in their den glued to the set, turning knobs and searching desperately for their hero while he yelled at them all to be quiet. And then at seven, after the Tupelo weather, the last weather, they backed away and left him alone in his recliner. Maybe at ten, he probably said.

At ten, Jake and Carla laid cross-legged and tangled in the dark on the sofa, waiting on the news. Finally, there he was, on the front steps, waving papers and shouting like a street preacher while the Channel 4 man on the scene explained that this was Rufus Buckley, the D.A. who would prosecute Carl Lee Hailey now that he had been indicted. After an awful glimpse of Buckley, the report panned around the square for a wonderful view of downtown Clanton, and then finally back to the reporter for two sentences about a trial in late summer.

'He's offensive,' Carla said. 'Why would he call a press conference to announce the indictments?'

'He's a prosecutor. We defense lawyers hate the press.'

'I've noticed. My scrapbook is rapidly filling up.'

'Be sure and make copies for Mom.'

'Will you autograph it for her?'

'Only for a fee. Yours, I will autograph for free.'

'Fine. And if you lose, I'll send you a bill for clipping and pasting.'

'I remind you, dear, that I have never lost a murder case. Three and oh, as a matter of fact.'

Carla punched the remote control and the weatherman remained but his volume disappeared. 'You know what I dislike most about your murder trials?' She kicked the cushions from her thin, bronze, almost perfect legs.

'The blood, the carnage, the gruesomeness?'

'No.' She unfolded her shoulder-length hair and let it fall around her on the arm of the sofa.

'The loss of life, regardless of how insignificant?'

'No.' She was wearing one of his old, starched-out, sixteen-by-thirty-four, pinpoint Oxford button-downs, and she began to play with the buttons.

'The horrible specter of an innocent man facing the gas chamber?'

'No.' She was unbuttoning it. The bluish gray rays from the television flashed like a strobe in the dark room as the anchorperson smiled and mouthed good night.

'The fear of a young family as the father walks into the courtroom and faces a jury of his peers?'

'No.' It was unbuttoned, and under it a thin, fluorescent band of white silk glittered against the brown skin.

'The latent unfairness of our judicial system?'

'No.' She slid an almost perfect bronze leg up, up, up to the back of the sofa where it gently came to rest.

'The unethical and unscrupulous tactics employed by cops and prosecutors to nail innocent defendants?'

'No.' She unsnapped the band of silk between the two almost perfect breasts.

'The fervor, the fury, the intensity, the uncontrolled emotions, the struggle of the human spirit, the unbridled passion?'

'Close enough,' she said. Shirts and shorts ricocheted off the lamps and coffee tables as the bodies meshed deep under the cushions. The old sofa, a gift from her parents, rocked and squeaked on the ancient hardwood floor. It was sturdy, and accustomed to the rocking and squeaking. Max the mix-breed instinctively ran down the hall to stand guard by Hanna's door.

CHAPTER FOURTEEN

Harry Rex Vonner was a huge slob of a lawyer who specialized in nasty divorce cases and perpetually kept some jerk in jail for back child support. He was vile and vicious, and his services were in great demand by divorcing parties in Ford County. He could get the children, the house, the farm, the VCR, and microwave, everything. One wealthy farmer kept him on retainer just so the current wife couldn't hire him for the next divorce. Harry Rex sent his criminal cases to Jake, and Jake sent his nasty divorces to Harry Rex. They were friends and disliked the other lawyers, especially the Sullivan firm.

Tuesday morning he barged in and growled at Ethel: 'Jake in?' He lumbered toward the stairs, glaring at her and daring her to speak. She nodded, knowing better than to ask if he was expected. He had cursed her before. He had cursed everybody before.

The stairway shook as he thundered upward. He was gasping for air as he entered the big office.

'Morning, Harry Rex. You gonna make it?'

'Why don't you get an office downstairs?' he demanded between breaths.

'You need the exercise. If it weren't for those stairs your weight would be over three hundred.'

'Thanks. Say, I just came from the courtroom. Noose wants you in chambers at ten-thirty if possible. Wants to talk about Hailey with you and Buckley. Set up arraignment, trial date, all that crap. He asked me to tell you.'

'Good. I'll be there.'

'I guess you heard about the grand jury?'

'Sure. I've got a copy of the indictment right here.'

Harry Rex smiled. 'No. No, I mean the vote on the indictment.'

Jake froze and looked at him curiously. Harry Rex moved in silent and dark circles like a cloud over the county. He was an endless source of gossip and rumor, and took great pride in spreading only the truth – most of the time. He was the first to know almost everything. The legend of Harry Rex began twenty years earlier with his first jury trial. The railroad he had sued for millions refused to offer a dime, and after three days of trial the jury retired to deliberate. The railroad lawyers became concerned when the jury failed to return with a quick verdict in their favor. They offered Harry Rex twenty-five thousand to settle when the deliberations went into the second day. With nerves of steel, he told them to go to hell. His client wanted the money. He told his client to go to hell. Hours later a weary and fatigued jury returned with a verdict for one hundred fifty thousand. Harry Rex shot the bird at the railroad lawyers, snubbed his clients and went to the bar at the Best Western. He bought drinks for everyone, and during the course of the long evening explained in detail exactly how he had wired the jury room and knew exactly what the jury was up to. Word spread, and Murphy found a series of wires running through the heating ducts to the jury room. The State Bar Association snooped around, but found nothing. For twenty years the judges had ordered the bailiffs to inspect the jury room when Harry Rex was in any way connected with a case.

'How do you know the vote?' Jake asked, suspicion hanging on every syllable.

'I got sources.'

'Okay, what was the vote?'

'Twelve to six. One fewer vote and you wouldn't be holding that indictment.'

'Twelve to six,' Jake repeated.

'Buckley near 'bout died. A guy named Crowell, white guy, took charge and almost convinced enough of them not to indict your man.'

'Do you know Crowell?'

'I handled his divorce two years ago. He lived in Jackson until his first wife was raped by a nigger. She went crazy and they got a divorce. She took a steak knife and sliced her wrists. Then he moved to Clanton and married some sleazebag out in the county. Lasted about a year. He ate Buckley's lunch. Told him to shut up and sit down. I wish I could've seen it.'

'Sounds like you did.'

'Naw. Just got a good source.'

'Who?'

'Jake, come on.'

'You been wiring rooms again?'

'Nope. I just listen. That's a good sign, ain't it?'

'What?'

'The close vote. Six outta eighteen voted to let him walk. Five niggers and Crowell. That's a good sign. Just get a couple of niggers on the jury and hang it. Right?'

'It's not that easy. If it's tried in this county there's a good chance we'll have an all-white jury. They're common here, and as you know, they're still very constitutional. Plus this guy Crowell sounds like he came outta nowhere.'

'That's what Buckley thought. You should see that ass. He's in the courtroom strutting around ready to sign autographs over his big TV splash last night. No one wants to talk about it, so he manages to work it into every conversation. He's like a kid begging for attention.'

'Be sweet. He may be your next governor.'

'Not if he loses Hailey. And he's gonna lose Hailey, Jake. We'll pick us a good jury, twelve good and faithful citizens, then we'll buy them.'

'I didn't hear that.'

'Works every time.'

A few minutes after ten-thirty, Jake entered the judge's chamber behind the courtroom and coolly shook hands with Buckley, Musgrove, and Ichabod. They had been waiting on him. Noose waved him toward a seat and sat behind the desk.

'Jake, this will take just a few minutes.' He peered down that nose. 'I would like to arraign Carl Lee Hailey in the morning at nine. Any problems with that?'

'No. That'll be fine,' replied Jake.

'We'll have some other arraignments in the morning, then we start a burglary case at ten. Right, Rufus?'

'Yes, sir.'

'Okay. Now let's discuss a trial date for Mr. Hailey. As you know, the next term of court here is in late August – third Monday – and I'm sure the docket will be just as crowded then. Because of the nature of this case and, frankly, because of the publicity, I think it would be best if we had a trial as soon as practical.'

'The sooner the better,' inserted Buckley.

'Jake, how long will you need to prepare for trial?'

'Sixty days.'

'Sixty days!' Buckley repeated in disbelief. 'Why so long?'

Jake ignored him and watched Ichabod adjust his reading glasses and study his calendar. 'Would it be safe to anticipate a request for a change of venue?' he asked.

'Yes.'

'Won't make any difference,' Buckley said. 'We'll get a conviction anywhere.'

'Save it for the cameras, Rufus,' Jake said quietly.

'You shouldn't talk about cameras,' Buckley shot back. 'You seem to enjoy them yourself.'

'Gentlemen, please,' Noose said. 'What other pretrial motions can we expect from the defense?'

Jake thought for a moment. 'There will be others.'

'May I inquire about the others?' asked Noose with a hint of irritation.

'Judge, I really don't care to discuss my defense at this time. We just received the indictment and I haven't discussed it with my client. We obviously have some work to do.'

'How much time do you need?'

'Sixty days.'

'Are you kidding!' Buckley shouted. 'Is this a joke? The State could try it tomorrow, Judge. Sixty days is ridiculous.'

Jake began to burn but said nothing. Buckley walked to the window and mumbled to himself in disbelief.

Noose studied his calendar. 'Why sixty days?'

'It could be a complicated case.'

Buckley laughed and continued shaking his head.

'Then we can expect a defense of insanity?' asked the judge.

'Yes, sir. And it will take time to have Mr. Hailey examined by a psychiatrist. Then the State will of course want him examined by its doctors.'

'I see.'

'And we may have other pretrial matters. It's a big case, and I want to make sure we have time to adequately prepare.'

'Mr. Buckley?' said the judge.

'Whatever. It makes no difference to the State. We'll be ready. We could try it tomorrow.'

Noose scribbled on his calendar and adjusted his reading glasses, which were perched on the tip of that nose and held in place by a tiny wart located perfectly at the foot of the beak. Due to the size of the nose and the odd shape of the head, specially built reading glasses with extra long stems were required for His Honor, who never used them for reading or any other purpose except in a vain effort to distract from the size and shape of the nose. Jake had always suspected this, but lacked the courage to inform His Honor that the ridiculous, orange-tinted hexagonal glasses diverted attention from everything else directly to the nose.

'How long do you anticipate for trial, Jake?' Noose asked.

'Three or four days. But it could take three days to pick the jury.'

'Mr. Buckley?'

'Sounds about right. But I don't understand why it takes sixty days to prepare for a three-day trial. I think it should be tried sooner.'

'Relax, Rufus,' Jake said calmly. 'The cameras will be here in sixty days, even ninety days. They won't forget about you. You can give interviews, hold press conferences, preach sermons, everything. The works. But don't worry so much. You'll get your chance.'

Buckley's eyes narrowed and his face reddened. He took three steps in Jake's direction. 'If I'm not mistaken, Mr. Brigance, you've given more interviews and seen more cameras than I have during the past week.'

'I know, and you're jealous, aren't you?'

'No, I'm not jealous! I don't care about the cameras –'

'Since when?'

'Gentlemen, please,' Noose interrupted. 'This promises to be a long, emotional case. I expect my attorneys to act like professionals. Now, my calendar is congested. The only opening I have is the week of July 22. Does that present a problem?'

'We can try it that week,' said Musgrove.

Jake smiled at Buckley and flipped through his pocket calendar. 'Looks good to me.'

'Fine. All motions must be filed and pretrial matters disposed of by Monday, July 8. Arraignment is set for tomorrow at nine. Any questions?'

Jake stood and shook hands with Noose and Musgrove, and left.

After lunch he visited his famous client in Ozzie's office at the jail. A copy of the indictment had been served on Carl Lee in his cell. He had some questions for his lawyer.

'What's capital murder?'

'The worst kind.'

'How many kinds are there?'

'Basically three. Manslaughter, regular murder, and capital murder.'

'What's manslaughter?'

'Twenty years.'

'What's regular murder?'

'Twenty to life.'

'What's capital murder?'

'Gas chamber.'

'What's aggravated assault on an officer?'

'Life. No parole.'

Carl Lee studied the indictment carefully. 'You mean I got two gas chambers and a life sentence.'

'Not yet. You're entitled to a trial first. Which, by the way, has been set for July 22.'

'That's two months away! Why so long?'

'We need the time. It'll take that long to find a psychiatrist who'll say you were crazy. Then Buckley gets to send you to Whitfield to be examined by the State's doctors, and they'll all say you were not crazy at the time. We file motions, Buckley files motions, we have a bunch of hearings. It takes time.'

'No way to have it sooner?'

'We don't want it sooner.'

'What if I do?' Carl Lee snapped.

Jake studied him carefully. 'What's the matter, big man?'

'I gotta get outta here, and fast.'

'I thought you said jail wasn't so bad.'

'It ain't, but I need to get home. Gwen's outta money, can't find a job. Lester's in trouble with his wife. She's callin' all the time, so he won't last much longer. I hate to ask my folk for help.'

'But they will, won't they?'

'Some. They got their own problems. You gotta get me outta here, Jake.'

'Look, you'll be arraigned in the morning at nine. The trial is July 22, and the date won't be changed, so forget about that. Have I explained the arraignment to you?'

Carl Lee shook his head.

'It won't last twenty minutes. We appear before Judge Noose in the big courtroom. He'll ask you some questions, then ask me some questions. He'll read the indictment to you in open court, and ask if you've received a copy. Then he'll ask you to plead guilty or not guilty. When you answer not guilty, he'll set the trial date. You'll sit down, and me and Buckley will get into a big fight over your bond. Noose will refuse to set a bond, then they'll bring you back to the jail, where you'll stay until the trial.'

'What about after the trial?'

Jake smiled. 'Naw, you won't be in jail after the trial.'

'You promise?'

'Nope. No promises. Any questions about tomorrow?'

'No. Say, Jake, uh, how much money did I pay you?'

Jake hesitated and smelled trouble. 'Why do you ask?'

'Just thinkin'.'

'Nine hundred, plus a note.'

Gwen had less than a hundred dollars. Bills were due and food was low. She had visited on Sunday and cried for an hour. Panic was a part of her life, her makeup, her composition. But he knew they were broke and she was scared. Her family would be of little help, maybe some vegetables from the garden and a few bucks for milk and eggs. When it came to funerals and hospital stays they were very dependable. They were generous and gave of their time freely to wail and moan and put on a show. But when real money was needed they scattered like chickens. He had little use for her family, and his wasn't much better.

He wanted to ask Jake for a hundred dollars, but decided to wait until Gwen was completely broke. It would be easier then.

Jake flipped through his legal pad and waited for Carl Lee to ask for money. Criminal clients, especially the blacks, always asked for some of the fee back after it was paid. He doubted he would ever see more than nine hundred dollars, and he was not about to return any. Besides, the blacks always took care of their own. The families would be there and the churches would get involved. No one would starve.

He waited and placed the legal pad and file in his briefcase. 'Any questions, Carl Lee?'

'Yeah. What can I say tomorrow?'

'What do you want to say?'

'I wanna tell that judge why I shot them boys. They raped my daughter. They needed shootin'.'

'And you want to explain that to the judge tomorrow?'

'Yeah.'

'And you think he'll turn you loose once you explain it all?'

Carl Lee said nothing.

'Look, Carl Lee, you hired me to be your lawyer. And you hired me because you have confidence in me, right? And if I want you to say something tomorrow, I'll tell you. If I don't, you stay quiet. When you go to trial in July you'll have the chance to tell your side. But in the meantime, I'll do the talking.'

'You got that right.'

Lester and Gwen piled the boys and Tonya in the red Cadillac and drove to the doctor's building next to the hospital. The rape was two weeks in the past. Tonya walked with a slight limp and wanted to run and climb steps with her brothers. But her mother held her hand. The soreness in her legs and buttocks was almost gone, the bandages on her wrists and ankles had been removed by the doctor last week, and the cuts were healing nicely. The gauze and cotton between her legs remained.

In a small room she undressed and sat next to her mother on a padded table. Her mother hugged her and helped her stay warm. The doctor poked in her mouth and rubbed her jaw. He held her wrists and ankles and inspected them. He laid her on the table and touched between her legs. She cried and clutched her mother, who leaned over her.

She was hurting again.

CHAPTER FIFTEEN

At five Wednesday morning, Jake sipped coffee in his office and stared through the French doors across the dark courtyard square. He had slept fitfully, and several hours earlier had given up and left his warm bed in a desperate effort to find a nameless Georgia case that, as he thought he remembered from law school, required the judge to allow bail in a capital murder case if the defendant had no prior criminal record, owned property in the county, had a stable job, and had plenty of relatives nearby. It had not been found. He did find a battery of recent, well-reasoned, clear, and unambiguous Mississippi cases allowing the judge complete discretion in denying bail to such defendants. That was the law and Jake now knew it well, but he needed something to argue to Ichabod. He dreaded asking bail for Carl Lee. Buckley would scream and preach and cite those wonderful cases, and Noose would smile and listen, then deny bail. Jake would get his tail kicked in the first skirmish.

'You're here early this morning, sweetheart,' Dell said to her favorite customer as she poured his coffee.

'At least I'm here.' He had missed a few mornings since the amputation. Looney was popular, and there was resentment at the Coffee Shop and around town for Hailey's lawyer. He was aware of it and tried to ignore it.

There was resentment among many for any lawyer who would defend a nigger for killing two white men.

'You got a minute?' Jake asked.

'Sure,' Dell said, looking around. At five-fifteen, the cafe was not yet full. She sat across from Jake in a small booth and poured coffee.

'What's the talk in here?' he asked.

'The usual. Politics, fishing, farming. It never changes. I've been here for twenty-one years, serving the same food to the same people, and they're still talking about the same things.'

'Nothing new?'

'Hailey. We get a lotta talk about that. Except when the strangers are here, then it goes back to the usual.'

'Why?'

'Because if you act like you know anything about the case, some reporter will follow you outside with a bunch of questions.'

'That bad, huh?'

'No. It's great. Business has never been better.'

Jake smiled and buttered his grits, then added Tabasco.

'How do you feel about the case?'

Dell scratched her nose with long, red, fake fingernails and blew into her coffee. She was famous for her bluntness, and he was hoping for a straight answer.

'He's guilty. He killed them. It's cut and dried. But he had the best damned excuse I've ever seen. There's some sympathy for him.'

'Let's say you're on the jury. Guilty or innocent?'

She watched the front door and waved at a regular. 'Well, my instinct is to forgive anyone who kills a rapist. Especially a father. But, on the other hand, we can't allow people to grab guns and hand out their own justice. Can you prove he was crazy when he did it?'

'Let's assume I can.'

'Then I would vote not guilty, even though I don't think he was crazy.'

He smeared strawberry preserves on dry toast and nodded his approval.

'But what about Looney?' she asked. 'He's a friend of mine.'

'It was an accident.'

'Is that good enough?'

'No. No, it's not. The gun did not go off by accident. Looney was accidentally shot, but I doubt if that's a valid defense. Would you convict him for shooting Looney?'

'Maybe,' she answered slowly. 'He lost a leg.'

How could he be insane when he shot Cobb and Willard, and not when he shot Looney, Jake thought, but didn't ask. He changed the subject.

'What's the gossip on me?'

'About the same. Someone was asking where you were the other day, and said you don't have time for us now that you're a celebrity. I've heard some mumbling, about you and the nigger, but it's pretty quiet. They don't criticize you loudly. I won't let them.'

'You're a sweetheart.'

'I'm a mean bitch and you know it.'

'No. You just try to be.'

'Yeah, watch this.' She jumped from the booth and shouted abuse at a table of farmers who had motioned for more coffee. Jake finished alone, and returned to the office.

When Ethel arrived at eight-thirty, two reporters were loitering on the sidewalk outside the locked door. They followed Ethel inside and demanded to see Mr. Brigance. She refused, and asked them to leave. They refused, and repeated their demand. Jake heard the commotion downstairs and locked his door. Let Ethel fight with them.

From his office he watched a camera crew set up by the rear door of the courthouse. He smiled and felt a wonderful surge of adrenaline. He could see himself on the evening news walking briskly, stern, businesslike, across the street followed by reporters begging for dialogue but getting no comments. And this was just the arraignment. Imagine the trial! Cameras everywhere, reporters yelling questions, front page stories, perhaps magazine covers. An Atlanta paper had called it the most sensational murder in the South in twenty years. He would have taken the case for free, almost.

Moments later he interrupted the argument downstairs, and warmly greeted the reporters. Ethel disappeared into the conference room.

'Could you answer some questions?' one of them asked.

'No,' Jake answered politely. 'I have to meet with Judge Noose.'

'Just a couple of questions?'

'No. But there will be a press conference at three P.M.' Jake opened the door, and the reporters followed him onto the sidewalk.

'Where's the press conference?'

'In my office.'

'What's the purpose?'

'To discuss the case.'

Jake walked slowly across the street and up the short driveway to the courthouse answering questions along the way.

'Will Mr. Hailey be at the press conference?'

'Yes, along with his family.'

'The girl, too?'

'Yes, she will be there.'

'Will Mr. Hailey answer questions?'

'Maybe. I haven't decided.'

Jake said good day, and disappeared into the courthouse, leaving the reporters to chat and gossip about the press conference.

Buckley entered the courthouse through the huge wooden front doors, amid no fanfare. He had hoped for a camera or two, but was dismayed to learn they were gathering at the rear door to catch a glimpse of the defendant. He would use the rear door in the future.

Judge Noose parked by a fire hydrant in front of the post office and loped along the east sidewalk across the courtyard square and into the courthouse. He, too, attracted no attention, except for a few curious stares.

Ozzie peered through the front windows of the jail and watched the mob waiting for Carl Lee in the parking lot. The ploy of another end run crossed his mind, but he dismissed it. His office had received two dozen death threats on Carl Lee, and Ozzie took a few seriously. They were specific, with dates and places. But most were just general, everyday death threats. And this was just the arraignment. He thought of the trial, and mumbled something to Moss Junior. They surrounded Carl Lee with uniformed bodies and marched him down the sidewalk, past the press and into a rented step van. Six deputies and a driver piled in. Escorted by Ozzie's three newest patrol cars, the van drove quickly to the courthouse.

Noose had scheduled a dozen arraignments for 9:00 A.M., and when he settled into the chair on the bench he shifted through the files until he found Hailey's. He looked to the front row in the courtroom and saw a somber group of suspicious-looking men, all newly indicted. At the far end of the front row, two deputies sat next to a handcuffed defendant, and Brigance was whispering to him. Must be Hailey.

Noose picked up a red court file and adjusted his reading glasses so they would not hinder his reading. 'State versus Carl Lee Hailey, case number 3889. Will Mr. Hailey come forward?'

The handcuffs were removed, and Carl Lee followed his attorney to the bench, where they stood looking up to His Honor, who quietly and nervously scanned the indictment in the file. The courtroom grew silent. Buckley rose and strutted slowly to within a few feet of the defendant. The artists near the railing busily sketched the scene.

Jake glared at Buckley, who had no reason to stand before the bench during the arraignment. The D.A. was dressed in his finest black three-piece polyester suit. Every hair on his huge head had been meticulously combed and plastered in place. He had the appearance of a television evangelist.

Jake walked to Buckley and whispered, 'That's a nice suit, Rufus.'

'Thanks,' he replied, somewhat off-guard.

'Does it glow in the dark?' Jake asked, then returned to the side of his client.

'Are you Carl Lee Hailey?' asked the judge.

'Yes.'

'Mr. Brigance your attorney?'

'Yes.'

'I'm holding here a copy of an indictment returned against you by the grand jury. Have you been served a copy of this?'

'Yes.'

'Have you read it?'

'Yes.'

'Have you discussed it with your attorney?'

'Yes.'

'Do you understand it?'

'Yes.'

'Good. I'm required by law to read it to you in open court.' Noose cleared his throat. 'The grand jurors of the State of Mississippi, taken from the body of good and lawful citizens of Ford County thereof, duly elected, empaneled, sworn, and charged to inquire in and for said county and state aforesaid, in the name and under the authority of the State of Mississippi, upon their oaths present that Carl Lee Hailey, late of the county and state aforesaid, within the jurisdiction of this court, did unlawfully, willfully, and feloniously and intentionally and with malice aforethought, kill and murder Billy Ray Cobb, a human being, and Pete Willard, a human being, and did shoot and attempt to kill DeWayne Looney, a peace officer, in direct violation of the Mississippi Code, and against the peace and dignity of the State of Mississippi. A true bill. Signed, Laverne Gossett, foreman of the grand jury.'

Noose caught his breath. 'Do you understand the charges against you?'

'Yes.'

'Do you understand that if convicted you could be put to death in the gas chamber at the state penitentiary at Parchman?'

'Yes.'

'Do you wish to plead guilty or not guilty?'

'Not guilty.'

Noose reviewed his calendar as the audience watched intently. The reporters took notes. The artists focused on the principals, including Buckley, who had managed to enter the picture and stand sideways, allowing for a profile shot. He was anxious to say something. He scowled contemptuously at the rear of Carl Lee's head, as if he could not wait to fry this murderer. He swaggered to the table where Musgrove was sitting and the two whispered importantly. He marched across the courtroom and engaged in hushed conversation with one of the clerks. Then he returned to the bench where the defendant stood motionless next to his attorney, who was aware of Buckley's show and was trying desperately to ignore it.

'Mr. Hailey,' Noose squeaked, 'your trial is set for Monday, July 22. All pretrial motions and matters must be filed by June 24, and disposed of by July 8.'

Carl Lee and Jake nodded.

'Anything further?'

'Yes, Your Honor,' Buckley boomed loud enough for the reporters in the rotunda. 'The State opposes any request for bail by this defendant.'

Jake gripped his fists and wanted to scream. 'Your Honor, the defendant has not yet asked for bail. Mr. Buckley, as usual, is confused about the procedure. He cannot oppose a request until it is made. He should've learned that in law school.'

Buckley was stung, but continued. 'Your Honor, Mr. Brigance always requests bail, and I'm sure he'll request it today. The State will oppose any such request.'

'Well, why don't you wait until he makes his request?' Noose asked the D.A. with a touch of irritation.

'Very well,' Buckley said. His face had reddened and he glared at Jake.

'Do you plan to request bail?' Noose asked.

'I had planned to at the proper time, but before I got a chance Mr. Buckley intervened with his theatrics –'

'Never mind Mr. Buckley,' Noose interrupted.

'I know, Judge, he's just confused.'

'Bail, Mr. Brigance?'

'Yes, I had planned to request it.'

'I thought so, and I've already considered whether bail should be allowed in this case. As you know, it is completely within my discretion, and I never allow bail in a capital murder case. I don't feel as though an exception is in order in this case.'

'You mean you've decided to deny bail?'

'Yes.'

Jake shrugged his shoulders and laid a file on the table. 'Good enough.'

'Anything further?' Noose asked.

'No, Your Honor,' Jake said.

Buckley shook his head in silence.

'Good. Mr. Hailey, you are hereby ordered to remain in the custody of the Ford County sheriff until trial. You are dismissed.'

Carl Lee returned to the front row, where a deputy waited with the handcuffs. Jake opened his briefcase, and was stuffing it with files and papers when Buckley grabbed his arm.

'That was a cheap shot, Brigance,' he said through clenched teeth.

'You asked for it,' Jake replied. 'Let go of my arm.'

Buckley released his arm. 'I don't appreciate it.'

'Too bad, big man. You shouldn't talk so much. Big mouths get burned.'

Buckley had three inches and fifty pounds on Jake, and his irritation was growing. The exchange had drawn attention, and a deputy moved between them. Jake winked at Buckley and left the courtroom.

At two the Hailey clan, led by Uncle Lester, entered Jake's office through the rear door. Jake met them in a small office next to the conference room downstairs. They talked about the press conference. Twenty minutes later, Ozzie and Carl Lee strolled nonchalantly through the rear door, and Jake led them to the office, where Carl Lee was reunited with his family. Ozzie and Jake left the room.

The press conference was carefully orchestrated by Jake, who marveled at his ability to manipulate the press and its willingness to be manipulated. On one side of the long conference table he sat with the three Hailey boys standing behind him. Gwen was seated to his left, Carl Lee to his right holding Tonya.

Legal etiquette forbade revealing the identity of a child rape victim, but Tonya was different. Her name, face, and age were well known because of her daddy. She had already been exposed to the world, and Jake wanted her to be seen and photographed in her best white Sunday dress sitting on her daddy's knee. The jurors, whoever they were and wherever they lived, would be watching.

Reporters crammed into the room, which overflowed and trailed down the hall to the reception area, where Ethel rudely ordered them to sit and leave her alone. A deputy guarded the front door, and two others sat on the rear steps. Sheriff Walls and Lester stood awkwardly behind the Haileys and their lawyer. Microphones were clustered on the table in front of Jake, and the cameras clicked and flashed under the warm television lights.

'I have a few prefatory remarks,' Jake began. 'First, all questions will be answered by me. No questions are to be directed to Mr. Hailey or any member of his family. If he is asked a question, I will instruct him not to answer. Second, I would like to introduce his family. To my left is his wife, Gwen Hailey. Standing behind us are his sons, Carl Lee, Jr., Jarvis, and Robert. Behind the boys is Mr. Hailey's brother, Lester Hailey.'

Jake paused and smiled at Tonya. 'Sitting in her daddy's lap is Tonya Hailey. Now I'll answer questions.'

'What happened in court this morning?'

'Mr. Hailey was arraigned, he pled not guilty, and his trial was set for July 22.'

'Was there an altercation between you and the district attorney?'

'Yes. After the arraignment, Mr. Buckley approached me, grabbed my arm, and looked as if he planned to assault me when a deputy intervened.'

'What caused it?'

'Mr. Buckley has a tendency to crack under pressure.'

'Are you and Mr. Buckley friends?'

'No.'

'Will the trial be in Clanton?'

'A motion to change venue will be filed by the defense. The location of the trial will be determined by Judge Noose. No predictions.'

'Could you describe what this has done to the Hailey family?'

Jake thought a minute while the cameras rolled. He glanced at Carl Lee and Tonya. 'You're looking at a very nice family. Two weeks ago life was good and simple. There was a job at the paper mill, a little money in the bank, security, stability, church every Sunday together, a loving family. Then, for reasons known only to God, two drunk, drugged punks committed a horrible, violent act against this little ten-year-old girl. They shocked us, and made us all feel sick. They ruined her life, and the lives of her parents and family. It was too much for her father. He snapped. He broke. Now he's in jail facing trial and the prospect of the gas chamber. The job is gone. The money is gone. The innocence is gone. The children face the possibility of growing up without their father. Their mother must now find a job to support them, and she'll have to beg and borrow from friends and relatives in order to survive.

'To answer your question, sir, the family has been devastated and destroyed.'

Gwen began crying quietly, and Jake handed her a handkerchief.

'Are you hinting at a defense of insanity?'

'Yes.'

'Will there in fact be a plea of insanity?'

'Yes.'

'Can you prove it?'

'That will be left for the jury. We will provide them experts in the field of psychiatry.'

'Have you already consulted with these experts?'

'Yes,' lied Jake.

'Could you give us their names?'

'No, that would be inappropriate at this point.'

'We've heard rumors of death threats against Mr. Hailey. Could you confirm?'

'There continue to be threats against Mr. Hailey, his family, my family, the sheriff, the judge, just about everyone involved. I don't know how serious they are.'

Carl Lee patted Tonya on the leg and looked blankly at the table. He looked scared, pitiful, and in need of sympathy. His boys looked scared too, but, according to strict orders, they stood at attention, afraid to move. Carl Lee, Jr., the oldest at fifteen, stood behind Jake. Jarvis, the middle son at thirteen, stood behind his daddy. And Robert, age eleven, stood behind his mother. They wore identical navy suits with white shirts and little red bow ties. Robert's suit was once Carl Lee, Jr.'s, then Jarvis's, and now his, and it looked a bit more worn than the other two. But it was clean, neatly pressed, and perfectly cuffed. The boys looked sharp.

How could any juror vote to force these children to live without their father?

The press conference was a hit. Segments of it ran on the networks and local stations, both on the evening and late news. The Thursday papers ran front page pictures of the Haileys and their lawyer.

CHAPTER SIXTEEN

The Swede had called several times during the two weeks her husband had been in Mississippi. She didn't trust him down there. There were old girlfriends he had confessed to. Each time she called, Lester was not around, and Gwen lied and explained that he was fishing or cutting pulpwood so they could buy groceries. Gwen was tired of lying, and Lester was tired of carousing, and they were tired of each other. When the phone rang before dawn Friday morning, Lester answered it. It was the Swede.

Two hours later the red Cadillac was parked at the jail. Moss Junior led Lester into Carl Lee's cell. The brothers whispered above the sleep of the inmates.

'Gotta go home,' Lester mumbled, somewhat ashamed, somewhat timid.

'Why?' Carl Lee asked as if he had been expecting it.

'My wife called this mornin'. I gotta be at work tomorrow or I'm fired.'

Carl Lee nodded approvingly.

'I'm sorry, bubba. I feel bad about goin', but I ain't got no choice.'

'I understand. When you comin' back?'

'When you want me back?'

'For the trial. It'll be real hard on Gwen and the kids. Can you be back then?'

'You know I'll be here. I got some vacation time and all. I'll be here.'

They sat on the edge of Carl Lee's bunk and watched each other in silence. The cell was dark and quiet. The two bunks opposite Carl Lee's were empty.

'Man, I forgot how bad this place is,' Lester said.

'I just hope I ain't here much longer.'

They stood and embraced, and Lester called for Moss Junior to open the cell. 'I'm proud of you, bubba,' he said to his older brother, then left for Chicago.

Carl Lee's second visitor of the morning was his attorney, who met him in Ozzie's office. Jake was red eyed and irritable.

'Carl Lee, I talked to two psychiatrists in Memphis yesterday. Do you know what the minimum fee is to evaluate you for trial purposes? Do you?'

'Am I supposed to know?' asked Carl Lee.

'One thousand dollars,' Jake shouted. 'One thousand dollars. Where can you find a thousand dollars?'

'I gave you all the money I got. I even offered –'

'I don't want the deed to your land. Why? Because nobody wants to buy it, and if you can't sell it, it's no good. We've got to have cash, Carl Lee. Not for me, but for the psychiatrists.'

'Why?'

'Why!' Jake repeated in disbelief. 'Why? Because I'd like to keep you away from the gas chamber, and it's only a hundred miles from here. It's not that far. And to do that, we've got to convince the jury that you were insane when you shot those boys. I can't tell them you were crazy. You can't tell them you were crazy. It takes a psychiatrist. An expert. A doctor. And they don't work for free. Understand?'

Carl Lee leaned on his knees and watched a spider crawl across the dusty carpet. After twelve days in jail and two court appearances, he had had enough of the criminal justice system. He thought of the hours and minutes before the killings. What was he thinking? Sure the boys had to die. He had no regrets. But did he contemplate jail, or poverty, or lawyers, or psychiatrists? Maybe, but only in passing. Those unpleasantries were only by-products to be encountered and endured temporarily before he was set free. After the deed, the system would process him, vindicate him, and send him home to his family. It would be easy, just as Lester's episode had been virtually painless.

But the system was not working now. It was conspiring to keep him in jail, to break him, to make orphans of his children. It seemed determined to punish him for performing an act he considered unavoidable. And now, his only ally was making demands he could not meet. His lawyer asked the impossible. His friend Jake was angry and yelling.

'Get it,' Jake shouted as he headed for the door. 'Get it from your brothers and sisters, from Gwen's family, get it from your friends, get it from your church. But get it. And as soon as possible.'

Jake slammed the door and marched out of the jail.

Carl Lee's third visitor of the morning arrived before noon in a long black limousine with a chauffeur and Tennessee plates. It maneuvered through the small parking lot and came to rest straddling three spaces. A large black bodyguard emerged from behind the wheel and opened the door to release his boss. They strutted up the sidewalk and into the jail.

The secretary stopped typing and smiled suspiciously. 'Good mornin'.'

'Mornin',' said the smaller one, the one with the patch. 'My name is Cat Bruster, and I'd like to see Sheriff Walls.'

'May I ask what for?'

'Yes ma'am. It's regardin' a Mr. Hailey, a resident of your fine facility.'

The sheriff heard his name mentioned, and appeared from his office to greet this infamous visitor. 'Mr. Bruster, I'm Ozzie Walls.' They shook hands. The bodyguard did not move.

'Nice to meet you, Sheriff. I'm Cat Bruster, from Memphis.'

'Yes. I know who you are. Seen you in the news. What brings you to Ford County?'

'Well, I gotta buddy in bad trouble. Carl Lee Hailey, and I'm here to help.'

'Okay. Who's he?' Ozzie asked, looking up at the bodyguard. Ozzie was six feet four, and at least five inches shorter than the bodyguard. He weighed at least three hundred pounds, most of it in his arms.

'This here is Tiny Tom,' Cat explained. 'We just call him Tiny for short.'

'I see.'

'He's sort of like a bodyguard.'

'He's not carryin' a gun, is he?'

'Naw, Sheriff, he don't need a gun.'

'Fair enough. Why don't you and Tiny step into my office?'

In the office, Tiny closed the door and stood by it while his boss took a seat across from the sheriff.

'He can sit if he wants to,' Ozzie explained to Cat.

'Naw, Sheriff, he always stands by the door. That's the way he's been trained.'

'Sorta like a police dog?'

'Right.'

'Fine. What'd you wanna talk about?'

Cat crossed his legs and laid a diamond-clustered hand on his knee. 'Well, Sheriff, me and Carl Lee go way back. Fought together in 'Nam. We was pinned down near Da Nang, summer of '71. I got hit in the head, and, bam!, two seconds later he got hit in the leg. Our squad disappeared, and the gooks was usin' us for target practice. Carl Lee limped to where I's layin', put me on his shoulders, and ran through the gunfire to a ditch next to a trail. I hung on his back while he crawled two miles. Saved my life. He got a medal for it. You know that?'

'No.'

'It's true. We laid next to each other in a hospital in Saigon for two months, then got our black asses outta Vietnam. Don't plan to go back.'

Ozzie was listening intently.

'And now that my man is in trouble, I'd like to help.'

'Did he get the M-16 from you?'

Tiny grunted and Cat smiled. 'Of course not.'

'Would you like to see him?'

'Why sure. It's that easy?'

'Yep. If you can move Tiny away from that door, I'll get him.'

Tiny stepped aside, and two minutes later Ozzie was back with the prisoner. Cat yelled at him, hugged him, and they patted each other like boxers. Carl Lee looked awkwardly at Ozzie, who took the hint and left. Tiny again closed the door and stood guard. Carl Lee moved two chairs together so they could face each other closely and talk.

Cat spoke first. 'I'm proud of you, big man, for what you did. Real proud. Why didn't you tell me that's why you wanted the gun?'

'Just didn't.'

'How was it?'

'Just like 'Nam, except they couldn't shoot back.'

'That's the best way.'

'Yeah, I guess. I just wish none of this had to happen.'

'You ain't sorry, are you?'

Carl Lee rocked in his chair and studied the ceiling. 'I'd do it over, so I got no regrets about that. I just wish they hadn't messed with my little girl. I wish she was the same. I wish none of it ever happened.'

'Right, right. It's gotta be tough on you here.'

'I ain't worried 'bout me. I'm real concerned with my family.'

'Right, right. How's the wife?'

'She's okay. She'll make it.'

'I saw in the paper where the trial's in July. You been in the paper more than me here lately.'

'Yeah, Cat. But you always get off. I ain't so sure 'bout me.'

'You gotta good lawyer, don't you?'

'Yeah. He's good.'

Cat stood and walked around the office, admiring Ozzie's trophies and certificates. 'That's the main reason I came to see you, my man.'

'What's that?' Carl Lee asked, unsure of what his friend had in mind, but certain his visit had a purpose.

'Carl Lee, you know how many times I been on trial?'

'Seems like all the time.'

'Five! Five times they put me on trial. The federal boys. The state boys. The city boys. Dope, gamblin', bribery, guns, racketeerin', whores. You name it, and they've tried me for it. And you know somethin', Carl Lee, I've been guilty of it all. Evertime I've gone to trial, I've been guilty as hell. You know how many times I been convicted?'

'No.'

'None! Not once have they got me. Five trials, five not guilties.'

Carl Lee smiled with admiration.

'You know why they can't convict me?'

Carl Lee had an idea, but he shook his head anyway.

'Because, Carl Lee, I got the smartest, meanest, crookedest criminal lawyer in these parts. He cheats, he plays dirty, and the cops hate him. But I'm sittin' here instead of some prison. He'll do whatever it takes to win a case.'

'Who is he?' Carl Lee asked eagerly.

'You've seen him on television walkin' in and outta court. He's in the papers all the time. Evertime some bigshot crook gets in trouble, he's there. He gets the drug dealers, the politicians, me, all the big-time thugs.'

'What's his name?'

'He handles nothin' but criminal cases, mainly dope, bribery, extortion, stuff like that. But you know what his favorite is?'

'What?'

'Murder. He loves murder cases. Ain't never lost one. Gets all the big ones in Memphis. Remember when they caught those two niggers throwin' a dude off the bridge into the Mississippi. Caught them redhanded. 'Bout five years ago?'

'Yeah, I remember.'

'Had a big trial for two weeks, and they got off. He was the man. Walked them outta there. Not guilty.'

'I think I remember seein' him on TV.'

'Sure you did. He's a bad dude, Carl Lee. I'm tellin' you the man never loses.'

'What's his name?'

Cat landed in his chair and stared solemnly into Carl Lee's face. 'Bo Marsharfsky,' he said.

Carl Lee gazed upward as if he remembered the name. 'So what?'

Cat laid five fingers with eight carats on Carl Lee's knee. 'So he wants to help you, my man.'

'I already got one lawyer I can't pay. How I'm gonna pay another?'

'You ain't gotta pay, Carl Lee. That's where I come in. He's on my retainer all the time. I own him. Paid the guy 'bout a hundred thousand last year just to keep me outta trouble. You don't pay.'

Suddenly, Carl Lee had a keen interest in Bo Marsharfsky. 'How does he know 'bout me?'

'Because he reads the paper and watches the tube. You know how lawyers are. I was in his office yesterday and he was studyin' the paper with your picture on the front. I told him 'bout me and you. He went crazy. Said he had to have your case. I said I would help.'

'And that's why you're here?'

'Right, right. He said he knew just the folks to get you off.'

'Like who?'

'Doctors, psychiatrists, folks like that. He knows them all.'

'They cost money.'

'I'll pay for it, Carl Lee! Listen to me! I'll pay for it all. You'll have the best lawyer and doctors money can buy, and your old pal Cat will pay the tab. Don't worry 'bout money!'

'But I gotta good lawyer.'

'How old is he?'

'I guess 'bout thirty.'

Cat rolled his eyes in amazement. 'He's a child, Carl Lee. He ain't been outta school long enough. Marsharfsky's fifty, and he's handled more murder cases than your boy'll ever see. This is your life, Carl Lee. Don't trust it to no rookie.'

Suddenly, Jake was awful young. But then there was Lester's trial when Jake had been even younger.

'Look, Carl Lee, I been in many trials, and that crap is complicated and technical. One mistake and your ass is gone. If this kid misses one trick, it might be the difference between life and death. You can't afford to have no young kid in there hopin' he don't mess up. One mistake,' Cat snapped his fingers for special effect, 'and you're in the gas chamber. Marsharfsky don't make mistakes.'

Carl Lee was on the ropes. 'Would he work with my lawyer?' he asked, seeking compromise.

'No! No way. He don't work with nobody. He don't need no help. Your boy'd be in the way.'

Carl Lee placed his elbows on his knees and stared at his feet. A thousand bucks for a doctor would be impossible. He did not understand the need for one since he had not felt insane at the time, but evidently one would be necessary. Everyone seemed to think so. A thousand bucks for a cheap doctor. Cat was offering the best money could buy.

'I hate to do this to my lawyer,' he muttered quietly.

'Don't be stupid, man,' Cat scolded. 'You better be lookin' out for Carl Lee and to hell with this child. This ain't no time to worry 'bout hurtin' feelin's. He's a lawyer, forget him. He'll get over it.'

'But I already paid him –'

'How much?' Cat demanded, snapping his fingers at Tiny.

'Nine hundred bucks.'

Tiny produced a wad of cash, and Cat peeled off nine one-hundred-dollar bills and stuffed them in Carl Lee's shirt pocket. 'Here's somethin' for the kids,' he said as he unraveled a one-thousand-dollar bill and stuffed it with the rest.

Carl Lee's pulse jumped as he thought of the cash covering his heart. He felt it move in the pocket and press gently against his chest. He wanted to look at the big bill and hold it firmly in his hand. Food, he thought, food for his kids.

'We gotta deal?' Cat asked with a smile.

'You want me to fire my lawyer and hire yours?' he asked carefully.

'Right, right.'

'And you gonna pay for everthing?'

'Right, right.'

'What about this money?'

'It's yours. Lemme know if you need more.'

'Mighty nice of you, Cat.'

'I'm a very nice man. I'm helpin' two friends. One saved my life many years ago, and the other saves my ass ever two years.'

'Why does he want my case so bad?'

'Publicity. You know how lawyers are. Look at how much press this kid's already made off you. It's a lawyer's dream. We gotta deal?'

'Yeah. It's a deal.'

Cat struck him on the shoulder with an affectionate blow, and walked to the phone on Ozzie's desk. He punched the numbers. 'Collect to 901-566-9800. From Cat Bruster. Person to person to Bo Marsharfsky.'

On the twentieth floor in a downtown office building, Bo Marsharfsky hung up the phone and asked his secretary if the press release was prepared. She handed it to him, and he read it carefully.

'This looks fine,' he said. 'Get it to both newspapers immediately. Tell them to use the file photograph, the new one. See Frank Fields at the *Post.* Tell him I want it on the front page in the morning. He owes me a favor.'

'Yes, sir. What about the TV stations?' she asked.

'Deliver them a copy. I can't talk now, but I'll hold a news conference in Clanton next week.'

Lucien called at six-thirty Saturday morning. Carla was buried deep under the blankets and did not respond to the phone. Jake rolled toward the wall and grappled with the lamp until he found the receiver. 'Hello,' he managed weakly.

'What're you doing?' Lucien asked.

'I was sleeping until the phone rang.'

'You seen the paper?'

'What time is it?'

'Go get the paper and call me after you read it.'

The phone was dead. Jake stared at the receiver, then placed it on the table. He sat on the edge of the bed, rubbed the fog from his eyes, and tried to remember the last time Lucien called his house. It must be important.

He made the coffee, turned out the dog, and walked quickly in his gym shorts and sweatshirt to the edge of the street where the three morning papers had fallen within ten inches of each other. He rolled the rubber bands off onto the kitchen table and spread the papers next to his coffee. Nothing in the Jackson paper. Nothing from Tupelo. *The Memphis Post* carried a headline of death in the Middle East, and, then, he saw it. On the bottom half of the front page he saw himself, and under his picture was the caption: 'Jake Brigance – Out.' Next was a picture of Carl Lee, and then a splendid picture of a face he had seen before. Under it, the words: 'Bo Marsharfsky – In.' The headline announced that the noted Memphis criminal attorney had been hired to represent the 'vigilante killer.'

He was stunned, weak, and confused. Surely it was a mistake. He had seen Carl Lee only yesterday. He read the story slowly. There were few details, just a history of Marsharfsky's greatest verdicts. He promised a news conference in Clanton. He said the case would present new challenges, etc. He had faith in the jurors of Ford County.

Jake slipped silently into starched khakis and a buttondown. His wife was still lost somewhere deep in the bed. He would tell her later. He took the paper and drove to the office. The Coffee Shop would not be safe. At Ethel's desk he read the story again and stared at his picture on the front page.

Lucien had a few words of comfort. He knew Marsharfsky, or 'The Shark,' as he was known. He was a sleazy crook with polish and finesse. Lucien admired him.

Moss Junior led Carl Lee into Ozzie's office, where Jake waited with a newspaper. The deputy quickly left and closed the door. Carl Lee sat on the small black vinyl couch.

Jake threw the newspaper at him. 'Have you seen this?' he demanded.

Carl Lee glared at him and ignored the paper.

'Why, Carl Lee?'

'I don't have to explain, Jake.'

'Yes, you do. You didn't have the guts to call me like a man and tell me. You let me read it in the paper. I demand an explanation.'

'You wanted too much money, Jake. You're always gripin' over the money. Here I am sittin' in jail and you're bitchin' 'bout somethin' I can't help.'

'Money. You can't afford to pay me. How can you afford Marsharfsky?'

'I ain't gotta pay him.'

'What!'

'You heard me. I ain't payin' him.'

'I guess he works for free.'

'Nope. Somebody else is payin'.'

'Who!' Jake shouted.

'I ain't tellin'. It ain't none of your business, Jake.'

'You've hired the biggest criminal lawyer in Memphis, and someone else is payin' his bill?'

'Yep.'

The NAACP, thought Jake. No, they wouldn't hire Marsharfsky. They've got their own lawyers. Besides, he was too expensive for them. Who else?

Carl Lee took the newspaper and folded it neatly. He was ashamed, and felt bad, but the decision had been made. He had asked Ozzie to call Jake and convey the news, but the sheriff wanted no part of it. He should have called, but he was not going to apologize. He studied his picture on the front page. He liked the part about the vigilante business.

'And you're not going to tell me who?' Jake said, somewhat quieter.

'Naw, Jake. I ain't tellin'.'

'Did you discuss it with Lester?'

The glare returned to his eyes. 'Nope. He ain't on trial, and it ain't none of his business.'

'Where is he?'

'Chicago. Left yesterday. And don't you go call him. I've made up my mind, Jake.'

We'll see, Jake said to himself. Lester would find out shortly.

Jake opened the door. 'That's it. I'm fired. Just like that.'

Carl Lee stared at his picture and said nothing.

Carla was eating breakfast and waiting. A reporter from Jackson had called looking for Jake, and had told her about Marsharfsky.

There were no words, just motions. He filled a cup with coffee and went to the back porch. He sipped from the steaming cup and surveyed the unkempt hedges that lined the boundary of his long and narrow backyard. A brilliant sun baked the rich green Bermuda and dried the dew, creating a sticky haze that drifted upward and hung to his shirt. The hedges and grass were waiting on their weekly grooming. He kicked off his loafers – no socks – and walked through the soggy turf to inspect a broken birdbath near a scrawny crepe myrtle, the only tree of any significance.

She followed the wet footprints and stood behind him. He took her hand and smiled. 'You okay?' she asked.

'Yeah, I'm fine.'

'Did you talk to him?'

'Yes.'

'What did he say?'

He shook his head and said nothing.

'I'm sorry, Jake.'

He nodded and stared at the birdbath.

'There will be other cases,' she said without confidence.

'I know.' He thought of Buckley, and could hear the laughter. He thought of the guys at the Coffee Shop, and vowed not to return. He thought of the cameras and reporters, and a dull pain moved through his stomach. He thought of Lester, his only hope of retrieving the case.

'Would you like some breakfast?' she asked.

'No. I'm not hungry. Thanks.'

'Look on the bright side,' she said. 'We won't be afraid to answer the phone.'

'I think I'll cut the grass,' he said.

CHAPTER SEVENTEEN

The Council of Ministers was a group of black preachers that had been formed to coordinate political activities in the black communities of Ford County. It met infrequently during the off years, but during election years it met weekly, on Sunday afternoons, to interview candidates and discuss issues, and, more importantly, to determine the benevolence of each office seeker. Deals were cut, strategies developed, money exchanged. The council had proven it could deliver the black vote. Gifts and offerings to black churches rose dramatically during elections.

The Reverend Ollie Agee called a special meeting of the council for Sunday afternoon at his church. He wrapped up his sermon early, and by 4:00 P.M. his flock had scattered when the Cadillacs and Lincolns began filling his parking lot. The meetings were secret, with only ministers who were council members invited. There were twenty-three black churches in Ford County, and twenty-two members were present when Reverend Agee called the meeting to order. The meeting would be brief, since some of the ministers, especially from the Church of Christ, would begin their evening services shortly.

The purpose of the meeting, he explained, was to organize moral, political, and financial support of Carl Lee Hailey, a member in good standing of his church. A legal defense fund must be established to assure the best legal representation. Another fund must be established to provide support for his family. He, Reverend Agee, would chair the fund-raising efforts, with each minister responsible for his own congregation, as usual. A special offering would be taken during the morning and evening services, starting next Sunday. Agee would use his discretion in disbursing the money to the family. Half of the proceeds would go to the defense fund. Time was important. The trial was next month. The money had to be raised quickly while the issue was hot, and the people were in a giving mood.

The council unanimously agreed with Reverend Agee. He continued.

The NAACP must become active in the Hailey case. He would not be on trial if he was white. Not in Ford County. He was on trial only because he was black, and this must be addressed by the NAACP. The national director had been called. The Memphis and Jackson chapters had promised help. Press conferences would be held. Demonstrations and marches would be important. Maybe boycotts of white-owned businesses – that was a popular tactic at the moment, and it worked with amazing results.

This must be done immediately, while the people were willing and in a giving mood. The ministers unanimously agreed and left for their evening services.

In part due to fatigue, and in part due to embarrassment, Jake slept through church. Carla fixed pancakes, and they enjoyed a long breakfast with Hanna on the patio. He ignored the Sunday papers after he found, on the front page of the second section of *The Memphis Post,* a full-page spread on Marsharfsky and his famous new client. The story was complete with pictures and quotes from the great lawyer. The Hailey case presented his biggest challenge, he said. Serious legal and social issues would be addressed. A novel defense would be employed, he promised. He had not lost a murder case in twelve years, he boasted. It would be difficult, but he had confidence in the wisdom and fairness of Mississippi jurors.

Jake read the article without comment and laid the paper in the trash can.

Carla suggested a picnic, and although he needed to work he knew better than to mention it. They loaded the Saab with food and toys and drove to the lake. The brown, muddy waters of Lake Chatulla had crested for the year, and within days would begin their slow withdrawal to the center. The high water attracted a flotilla of skiboats, bass rigs, catamarans, and dinghies.

Carla threw two heavy quilts under an oak on the side of a hill while Jake unloaded the food and doll house. Hanna arranged her large family with pets and automobiles on one quilt and began giving orders and setting up house. Her parents listened and smiled. Her birth had been a harrowing, gut-wrenching nightmare, two and a half months premature and shrouded with conflicting symptoms and prognoses. For eleven days Jake sat by the incubator in ICU and watched the tiny, purple, scrawny, beautiful three-pound body cling to life while an army of doctors and nurses studied the monitors and adjusted tubes and needles, and shook their heads. When he was alone he touched the incubator and wiped tears from his cheeks. He prayed as he had never prayed. He slept in a rocking chair near his daughter and dreamed of a beautiful blue-eyed, dark-haired little girl playing with dolls and sleeping on his shoulder. He could hear her voice.

After a month the nurses smiled and the doctors relented. The tubes were removed one at a time each day for a week. Her weight ballooned to a hearty four and a half pounds, and the proud parents took her home. The doctors suggested no more children, unless adopted.

She was perfect now, and the sound of her voice could still bring tears to his eyes. They ate and chuckled as Hanna lectured her dolls on proper hygiene.

'This is the first time you've relaxed in two weeks,' Carla said as they lay on their quilt. Wildly colored catamarans crisscrossed the lake below dodging a hundred roaring boats pulling half-drunken skiers.

'We went to church last Sunday,' he replied.

'And all you thought about was the trial.'

'Still thinking about it.'

'It's over, isn't it?'

'I don't know.'

'Will he change his mind?'

'He might, if Lester talks to him. It's hard to say. Blacks are so unpredictable, especially when they're in trouble. He's got a good deal, really. He's got the best criminal lawyer in Memphis, and he's free.'

'Who's paying the bill?'

'An old friend of Carl Lee's from Memphis, a guy by the name of Cat Bruster.'

'Who's he?'

'A very rich pimp, dope pusher, thug, thief. Marsharfsky's his lawyer. A couple of crooks.'

'Did Carl Lee tell you this?'

'No. He wouldn't tell me, so I asked Ozzie.'

'Does Lester know?'

'Not yet.'

'What do you mean by that? You're not going to call him, are you?'

'Well, yes, I had planned to.'

'That's going a bit far, isn't it?'

'I don't think so. Lester has a right to know, and –'

'Then Carl Lee should tell him.'

'He should, but he won't. He's made a mistake, and he does not realize it.'

'But it's his problem, not yours. At least not anymore.'

'Carl Lee's too embarrassed to tell Lester. He knows Lester will cuss him and tell him he's made another mistake.'

'So it's up to you to intervene in their family affairs.'

'No. But I think Lester should know.'

'I'm sure he'll see it in the papers.'

'Maybe not,' Jake said without any conviction. 'I think Hanna needs some more orange juice.'

'I think you want to change the subject.'

'The subject doesn't bother me. I want the case, and I intend to get it back. Lester's the only person who can retrieve it.'

Her eyes narrowed and he could feel them. He watched a bass rig drift into a mud bar on the near shore.

'Jake, that's unethical, and you know it.' Her voice was calm, yet controlled and firm. The words were slow and scornful.

'That's not true, Carla. I'm a very ethical attorney.'

'You've always preached ethics. But at this moment you're scheming to solicit the case. That's wrong, Jake.'

'Retrieve, not solicit.'

'What's the difference?'

'Soliciting is unethical. I've never seen a prohibition against retrieving.'

'It's not right, Jake. Carl Lee's hired another lawyer and it's time for you to forget it.'

'And I suppose you think Marsharfsky reads ethics opinions. How do you think he got the case? He's been hired by a man who's never heard of him. He chased the case, and he's got it.'

'So that makes it okay if you chase it now?'

'Retrieve, not chase.'

Hanna demanded cookies, and Carla searched through the picnic basket. Jake reclined on an elbow and ignored them both. He thought of Lucien. What would he do in this situation? Probably rent a plane, fly to Chicago, get Lester, slip him some money, bring him home, and convince him to browbeat Carl Lee. He would assure Lester that Marsharfsky could not practice in Mississippi, and since he was a foreigner, the rednecks on the jury wouldn't believe him anyway. He would call Marsharfsky and curse him for chasing cases and threaten him with an ethics complaint the minute he stepped into Mississippi. He would get his black cronies to call Gwen and Ozzie and persuade them that the only lawyer with a dog's chance in hell of winning the case was Lucien Wilbanks. Finally, Carl Lee would knuckle under and send for Lucien.

That's exactly what Lucien would do. Talk about ethics.

'Why are you smiling?' Carla interrupted.

'Just thinking about how nice it is out here with you and Hanna. We don't do this enough.'

'You're disappointed, aren't you?'

'Sure. There will never be another case like this one. Win it, and I'm the greatest lawyer in these parts. We would never have to worry about money again.'

'And if you lost it?'

'It would still be a drawing card. But I can't lose what I don't have.'

'Embarrassed?'

'A little. It's hard to accept. Every lawyer in the county is laughing about it, except maybe Harry Rex. But I'll get over it.'

'What should I do with the scrapbook?'

'Save it. You might fill it up yet.'

The cross was a small one, nine feet long and four feet wide, made to fit inconspicuously in the long bed of a pickup. Much larger crosses were used for the rituals, but the small ones worked better in the nocturnal raids into residential areas. They were not used often, or often enough according to their builders. In fact, it had been many years since one had been used in Ford County. The last one was planted in the yard of a nigger accused of raping a white woman.

Several hours before dawn on Monday morning, the cross was lifted quietly and quickly from the pickup and thrust into a ten-inch, freshly dug slot in the front yard of the quaint Victorian house on Adams Street. A small torch was thrown at the foot of the cross, and in seconds it was in flames. The pickup disappeared into the night and stopped at a pay phone at the edge of town, where a call was placed to the dispatcher.

Moments later, Deputy Marshall Prather turned down Adams and instantly saw the blazing cross in Jake's front yard. He turned into the driveway and parked behind the Saab. He punched the doorbell and stood on the porch watching the flames. It was almost three-thirty. He punched it again. Adams was dark and silent except for the glow of the cross and the snapping and crackling of the wood burning fifty feet away. Finally, Jake stumbled through the front door and froze, wild-eyed and stunned, next to the deputy. The two stood side by side on the porch, mesmerized not only by the burning cross, but by its purpose.

'Mornin', Jake,' Prather finally said without looking from the fire.

'Who did it?' Jake asked with a scratchy, dry throat.

'Don't know. They didn't leave a name. Just called and told us about it.'

'When did they call?'

'Fifteen minutes ago.'

Jake ran his fingers through his hair in an effort to keep it from blowing wild in the soft breeze. 'How long will it burn?' he asked, knowing Prather knew as little or even less than he about burning crosses.

'No tellin'. Probably soaked in kerosene. Smells like it anyway. Might burn for a couple of hours. You want me to call a fire truck?'

Jake looked up and down the street. Every house was silent and dark.

'Naw. No need to wake everybody. Let it burn. It won't hurt anything, will it?'

'It's your yard.'

Prather never moved; just stood there, hands in his pockets, his belly hanging over his belt. 'Ain't had one of these in a long time around here. Last one I remember was in Karaway, nineteen-sixty –'

'Nineteen sixty-seven.'

'You remember?'

'Yeah. I was in high school. We drove out and watched it burn.'

'What was that nigger's name?'

'Robinson, something Robinson. Said he raped Velma Thayer.'

'Did he?' asked Prather.

'The jury thought so. He's in Parchman chopping cotton for the rest of his life.'

Prather seemed satisfied.

'Let me get Carla,' Jake mumbled as he disappeared. He returned with his wife behind him.

'My God, Jake! Who did it?'

'Who knows.'

'Is it the KKK?' she asked.

'Must be,' answered the deputy. 'I don't know anybody else who burns crosses, do you, Jake?'

Jake shook his head.

'I thought they left Ford County years ago,' said Prather.

'Looks like they're back,' said Jake.

Carla stood frozen, her hand over her mouth, terrified. The glow of the fire reddened her face. 'Do something, Jake. Put it out.'

Jake watched the fire and again glanced up and down the street. The snapping and popping grew louder and the orange flames reached higher into the night. For a moment he hoped it would die quickly without being seen by anyone other than the three of them, and that it would simply go away and be forgotten and no one in Clanton would ever know. Then he smiled at his foolishness.

Prather grunted, and it was obvious he was tired of standing on the porch. 'Say, Jake, uh, I don't mean to bring this up, but accordin' to the papers they got the wrong lawyer. That true?'

'I guess they can't read,' Jake muttered.

'Probably not.'

'Tell me, Prather, do you know of any active Klan members in this county?'

'Not a one. Got some in the southern part of the state, but none around here. Not that I know of. FBI told us the Klan was a thing of the past.'

'That's not very comforting.'

'Why not?'

'Because these guys, if they're Klan members, are not from around here. Visitors from parts unknown. It means they're serious, don't you think, Prather?'

'I don't know. I'd worry more if it was local people workin' with the Klan. Could mean the Klan's comin' back.'

'What does it mean, the cross?' Carla asked the deputy.

'It's a warnin'. Means stop what you're doin', or the next time we'll do more than burn a little wood. They used these things for years to intimidate whites who were sympathetic to niggers and all that civil rights crap. If the whites didn't stop their nigger lovin', then violence followed. Bombs, dynamite, beatings, even murder. But that was a long time ago, I thought. In your case, it's their way of tellin' Jake to stay away from Hailey. But since he ain't Hailey's lawyer no more, I don't know what it means.'

'Go check on Hanna,' Jake said to Carla, who went inside.

'If you got a water hose, I'll be glad to put it out,' offered Prather.

'That's a good idea,' Jake said. 'I'd hate for the neighbors to see it.'

Jake and Carla stood on the porch in their bathrobes and watched the deputy spray the burning cross. The wood fizzed and smoked as the water covered the cross and snuffed out the flames. Prather soaked it for fifteen minutes, then neatly rolled the hose and placed it behind the shrubs in the flower bed next to the front steps.

'Thanks, Marshall. Let's keep this quiet, okay?'

Prather wiped his hands on his pants and straightened his hat. 'Sure. Y'all lock up good. If you hear anything, call the dispatcher. We'll keep a close watch on it for the next few days.'

He backed from the driveway and drove slowly down Adams Street toward the square. They sat in the swing and watched the smoking cross.

'I feel like I'm looking at an old issue of Life magazine,' Jake said.

'Or a chapter from a Mississippi history textbook. Maybe we should tell them you got fired.'

'Thanks.'

'Thanks?'

'For being so blunt.'

'I'm sorry. Should I say discharged, or terminated, or –'

'Just say he found another lawyer. You're really scared aren't you?'

'You know I'm scared. I'm terrified. If they can burn a cross in our front yard, what's to stop them from burning the house? It's not worth it, Jake. I want you to be happy and successful and all that wonderful stuff, but not at the expense of our safety. No case is worth this.'

'You're glad I got fired?'

'I'm glad he found another lawyer. Maybe they'll leave us alone now.'

Jake put his arm around her, and pulled her into his lap. The swing rocked gently. She was beautiful, at three-thirty in the morning in her bathrobe.

'They won't be back, will they?' she asked.

'Naw. They're through with us. They'll find out I'm off the case, then they'll call and apologize.'

'It's not funny, Jake.'

'I know.'

'Do you think people will know?'

'Not for another hour. When the Coffee Shop opens at five, Dell Perkins will know every detail before she pours the first cup of coffee.'

'What're you going to do with it?' she asked, nodding at the cross, now barely visible under the half moon.

'I've got an idea. Let's load it up, take it to Memphis, and burn it in Marsharfsky's yard.'

'I'm going to bed.'

By 9:00 A.M. Jake had finished dictating his motion to withdraw as counsel of record. Ethel was typing it with zest when she interrupted him: 'Mr. Brigance, there's a Mr. Marsharfsky on the phone. I told him you were in conference, and he said he would hold.'

'I'll talk to him.' Jake gripped the receiver. 'Hello.'

'Mr. Brigance, Bo Marsharfsky in Memphis. How are you?'

'Terrific.'

'Good. I'm sure you saw the morning paper Saturday and Sunday. You do get the paper in Clanton?'

'Yes, and we have telephones and mail.'

'So you saw the stories on Mr. Hailey?'

'Yes. You write some very nice articles.'

'I'll ignore that. I wanted to discuss the Hailey case if you have a minute.'

'I would love to.'

'As I understand Mississippi procedure, out-of-state counsel must associate local counsel for trial purposes.'

'You mean you don't have a Mississippi license?' Jake asked incredulously.

'Well, no, I don't.'

'That wasn't mentioned in your articles.'

'I'll ignore that too. Do the judges require local counsel in all cases?'

'Some do, some don't.'

'I see. What about Noose?'

'Sometimes.'

'Thanks. Well, I usually associate local counsel when I try cases out in the country. The locals feel better with one of their own sitting there at counsel table with me.'

'That's real nice.'

'I don't suppose you'd be interested in –'

'You must be kidding!' Jake yelled. 'I've just been fired and now you want me to carry your briefcase. You're crazy. I wouldn't have my name associated with yours.'

'Wait a minute, hayseed –'

'No, you wait a minute, counselor. This may come as a surprise to you, but in this state we have ethics and laws against soliciting litigation and clients. Champerty – ever hear of it? Of course not. It's a felony in Mississippi, as in most states. We have canons of ethics that prohibit ambulance chasing and solicitation. Ethics, Mr. Shark, ever hear of them?'

'I don't chase cases, sonny. They come to me.'

'Like Carl Lee Hailey. I'm supposed to believe he picked your name out of the yellow pages. I'm sure you have a full-page ad, next to the abortionists.'

'He was referred to me.'

'Yeah, by your pimp. I know exactly how you got him. Outright solicitation. I may file a complaint with the bar. Better yet, I might have your methods reviewed by the grand jury.'

'Yeah, I understand you and the D.A. are real close. Good day, counselor.'

Marsharfsky got the last word before he hung up. Jake fumed for an hour before he could concentrate on the brief he was writing. Lucien would have been proud of him.

Just before lunch Jake received a call from Walter Sullivan, of the Sullivan firm.

'Jake, my boy, how are you?'

'Wonderful.'

'Good. Listen, Jake, Bo Marsharfsky is an old friend of mine. We defended a couple of bank officials years ago on fraud charges. Got them off, too. He's quite a lawyer. He's associated me as local counsel for Carl Lee Hailey. I was just wanting to know –'

Jake dropped the receiver and walked out of his office. He spent the afternoon on Lucien's front porch.

CHAPTER EIGHTEEN

Gwen did not have Lester's number. Neither did Ozzie, nor did anyone else. The operator said there were two pages of Haileys in the Chicago phone book, at least a dozen Lester Haileys, and several L. S.'s. Jake asked for the first five Lester Haileys and called each one. They were all white. He called Tank Scales, the owner of one of the safer and finer black honky tonks in the county. Tank's Tonk, as it was known. Lester was especially fond of the place. Tank was a client and often provided Jake with valuable and confidential information on various blacks, their dealings and whereabouts.

Tank stopped by the office Tuesday morning on the way to the bank.

'Have you seen Lester Hailey in the past two weeks?' Jake asked.

'Sure. Spent several days at the place shootin' pool, drinkin' beer. Went back to Chicago last weekend, I heard. Must've I didn't see him all weekend.'

'Who was he with?'

'Hisself mostly.'

'What about Iris?'

'Yeah, he brung her a couple of times when Henry was outta town. Makes me nervous when he brings her. Henry's a bad dude. He'd cut them both if he knew they's datin'.'

'They've been doing it for ten years, Tank.'

'Yeah, she got two kids by Lester. Everybody knows it but Henry. Poor old Henry. He'll find out one day, and you'll have another murder case.'

'Listen, Tank, can you talk to Iris?'

'She don't come in too often.'

'That's not what I asked. I need Lester's phone number in Chicago. I figure Iris knows it.'

'I'm sure she does. I think he sends her money.'

'Can you get it for me? I need to talk to Lester.'

'Sure, Jake. If she's got it, I'll get it.'

By Wednesday Jake's office had returned to normal. Clients began to reappear. Ethel was especially sweet, or as sweet as possible for a cranky old nag. He went through the motions of practicing law, but the pain showed. He skipped the Coffee Shop each morning and avoided the courthouse by making Ethel do the filing or checking or whatever business required his presence across the street. He was embarrassed, humiliated, and troubled. It was difficult to concentrate on other cases. He contemplated a long vacation, but couldn't afford it. Money was tight, and he was not motivated to work. He spent most of his time in his office doing little but watching the courthouse and the town square below.

He dwelt on Carl Lee, sitting in his cell a few blocks away, and asked himself a thousand times why he had been betrayed. He had pushed too hard for money, and forgot there were other lawyers willing to take the case for free. He hated Marsharfsky. He recalled the many times he had seen Marsharfsky parade in and out of Memphis courtrooms proclaiming the innocence and mistreatment of his pitiful, oppressed clients. Dope dealers, pimps, crooked politicians, and slimy corporate thugs. All guilty, all deserving of long prison terms, or perhaps even death. He was a yankee, with an obnoxious twang from somewhere in the upper Midwest. It would irritate anybody south of Memphis. An accomplished actor, he would look directly into the cameras and whine: 'My client has been horribly abused by the Memphis police.' Jake had seen it a dozen times. 'My client is completely, totally, absolutely innocent. He should not be on trial. My client is a model citizen, a taxpayer.' What about his four prior convictions for extortion? 'He was framed by the FBI. Set up by the government. Besides, he's paid his debt. He's innocent this time.' Jake hated him, and to his recollection, he had lost as many as he had won.

By Wednesday afternoon, Marsharfsky had not been seen in Clanton. Ozzie promised to notify Jake if he showed up at the jail.

Circuit Court would be in session until Friday, and it would be respectful to meet briefly with Judge Noose and explain the circumstances of his departure from the case. His Honor was presiding over a civil case, and there was a good chance Buckley would be absent. He had to be absent. He could not be seen or heard.

Noose usually recessed for ten minutes around three-thirty, and precisely at that time Jake entered chambers through the side door. He had not been seen. He sat patiently by the window waiting for Ichabod to descend from the bench and stagger into the room. Five minutes later the door flung open, and His Honor walked in.

'Jake, how are you?' he asked.

'Fine, Judge. Can I have a minute?' Jake asked as he closed the door.

'Sure, sit down. What's on your mind?' Noose removed his robe, threw it over a chair, and lay on top of the desk, knocking off books, files, and the telephone in the process. Once his gawky frame had ceased moving, he slowly folded his hands over his stomach, closed his eyes, and breathed deeply. 'It's my back, Jake. My doctor tells me to rest on a hard surface when possible.'

'Uh, sure, Judge. Should I leave?'

'No, no. What's on your mind?'

'The Hailey case.'

'I thought so. I saw your motion. Found a new lawyer, huh?'

'Yes, sir. I had no idea it was coming. I expected to try the case in July.'

'You owe no apologies, Jake. The motion to withdraw will be granted. It's not your fault. Happens all the time. Who's the new guy, Marsharfsky?'

'Yes, sir. From Memphis.'

'With a name like that he should be a hit in Ford County.'

'Yes, sir.' Almost as bad as Noose, thought Jake.

'He has no Mississippi license,' Jake explained, helpfully.

'That's interesting. Is he familiar with our procedure?'

'I'm not sure he's ever tried a case in Mississippi. He told me he normally associates a local boy when he's out in the country.'

'In the country?'

'That's what he said.'

'Well, he'd better associate if he comes into my court. I've had some bad experiences with out-of-state attorneys, especially from Memphis.'

'Yes, sir.'

Noose was breathing harder, and Jake decided to leave. 'Judge, I need to go. If I don't see you in July, I'll see you during the August term of court. Take care of your back.'

'Thanks, Jake. Take care.'

Jake almost made it to the rear door of the small office when the main door from the courtroom opened and the Honorable L. Winston Lotterhouse and another hatchet man from the Sullivan firm strutted into chambers.

'Well, hello, Jake,' Lotterhouse announced. 'You know K. Peter Otter, our newest associate.'

'Nice to meet you, K. Peter,' replied Jake.

'Are we interrupting anything?'

'No, I was just leaving. Judge Noose is resting his back, and I was on my way out.'

'Sit down, gentlemen,' Noose said.

Lotterhouse smelled blood. 'Say, Jake, I'm sure Walter Sullivan has informed you that our firm will serve as local counsel for Carl Lee Hailey.'

'I have heard.'

'I'm sorry it happened to you.'

'Your grief is overwhelming.'

'It does present an interesting case for our firm. We don't get too many criminal cases, you know.'

'I know,' Jake said, looking for a hole to crawl in. 'I need to run. Nice chatting with you, L. Winston. Nice meeting you, K. Peter. Tell J. Walter and F. Robert and all the boys I said hello.'

Jake slid out of the rear door of the courthouse and cursed himself for showing his face where he could get it slapped. He ran to his office.

'Has Tank Scales called?' he asked Ethel as he started up the stairs.

'No. But Mr. Buckley is waiting.'

Jake stopped on the first step. 'Waiting where?' he asked without moving his jaws.

'Upstairs. In your office.'

He walked slowly to her desk and leaned across to within inches of her face. She had sinned, and she knew it.

He glared at her fiercely. 'I didn't know he had an appointment.' Again, the jaws did not move.

'He didn't,' she replied, her eyes glued to the desk.

'I didn't know he owned this building.'

She didn't move, didn't answer.

'I didn't know he had a key to my office.'

Again, no movement, no answer.

He leaned closer. 'I should fire you for this.'

Her lip quivered and she looked helpless.

'I'm sick of you, Ethel. Sick of your attitude, your voice, your insubordination. Sick of the way you treat people, sick of everything about you.'

Her eyes watered. 'I'm sorry.'

'No you're not. You know, and have known for years, that no one, no one in the world, not even my wife, goes up those stairs into my office if I'm not here.'

'He insisted.'

'He's an ass. He gets paid for pushing people around. But not in this office.'

'Shhh. He can hear you.'

'I don't care. He knows he's an ass.'

He leaned even closer until their noses were six inches apart. 'Would you like to keep your job, Ethel?'

She nodded, unable to speak.

'Then do exactly as I say. Go upstairs to my office, fetch Mr. Buckley, and lead him into the conference room, where I'll meet him. And don't ever do it again.'

Ethel wiped her face and ran up the stairs. Moments later the D.A. was seated in the conference room with the door closed. He waited.

Jake was next door in the small kitchen drinking orange juice and assessing Buckley. He drank slowly. After fifteen minutes he opened the door and entered the room. Buckley was seated at one end of the long conference table. Jake sat at the other end, far away.

'Hello, Rufus. What do you want?'

'Nice place you have here. Lucien's old offices, I believe.'

'That's right. What brings you here?'

'Just wanted to visit.'

'I'm very busy.'

'And I wanted to discuss the Hailey case.'

'Call Marsharfsky.'

'I was looking forward to the battle, especially with you on the other side. You're a worthy adversary, Jake.'

'I'm honored.'

'Don't get me wrong. I don't like you, and I haven't for a long time.'

'Since Lester Hailey.'

'Yeah, I guess you're right. You won, but you cheated.'

'I won, that's all that counts. And I didn't cheat. You got caught with your pants down.'

'You cheated and Noose let you by with it.'

'Whatever. I don't like you either.'

'Good. That makes me feel better. What do you know about Marsharfsky?'

'Is that the reason you're here?'

'Could be.'

'I've never met the man, but if he was my father I wouldn't tell you anything. What else do you want?'

'Surely you've talked to him.'

'We had some words on the phone. Don't tell me you're worried about him.'

'No. Just curious. He's got a good reputation.'

'Yes, he does. You didn't come here to discuss his reputation.'

'No, not really. I wanted to talk about the case.'

'What about it?'

'Chances for an acquittal, possible defenses, was he really insane. Things like that.'

'I thought you guaranteed a conviction. In front of the cameras, remember? Just after the indictment. One of your press conferences.'

'Do you miss the cameras already, Jake?'

'Relax, Rufus. I'm out of the game. The cameras are all yours, at least yours and Marsharfsky's, and Walter Sullivan's. Go get them, tiger. If I've stolen some of your spotlight, then I'm deeply sorry. I know how it hurts you.'

'Apology accepted. Has Marsharfsky been to town?'

'I don't know.'

'He promised a press conference this week.'

'And you came here to talk about his press conference, right?'

'No, I wanted to discuss Hailey, but obviously you're too busy.'

'That's right. Plus I have nothing to discuss with you, Mr. Governor.'

'I resent that.'

'Why? You know it's true. You'd prosecute your mother for a couple of headlines.'

Buckley stood and began pacing back and forth behind his chair. 'I wish you were still on this case, Brigance,' he said, the volume increasing.

'So do I.'

'I'd teach you a few things about prosecuting murderers. I really wanted to clean your plow.'

'You haven't been too successful in the past.'

'That's why I wanted you on this one, Brigance. I wanted you so bad.' His face had returned to the deep red that was so familiar.

'There'll be others, Governor.'

'Don't call me that,' he shouted.

'It's true, isn't it, Governor. That's why you chase the cameras so hard. Everybody knows it. There goes old Rufus, chasing cameras, running for governor. Sure it's true.'

'I'm doing my job. Prosecuting thugs.'

'Carl Lee Hailey's no thug.'

'Watch me burn him.'

'It won't be that easy.'

'Watch me.'

'It takes twelve out of twelve.'

'No problem.'

'Just like your grand jury?'

Buckley froze in his tracks. He squinted his eyes and frowned at Jake. Three huge wrinkles creased neatly across his mammoth forehead. 'What do you know about the grand jury?'

'As much as you do. One vote less and you'd have sucked eggs.'

'That's not true!'

'Come on, Governor. You're not talking to a reporter. I know exactly what happened. Knew it within hours.'

'I'll tell Noose.'

'And I'll tell the newspapers. That'll look good before the trial.'

'You wouldn't dare.'

'Not now. I have no reason to. I've been fired, remember? That's the reason you're here, right, Rufus? To remind me that I'm no longer on the case, but you are. To rub a little salt in the wounds. Okay, you've done it. Now I wish you'd leave. Go check on the grand jury. Or maybe there's a reporter hanging around the courthouse. Just leave.'

'Gladly. I'm sorry I bothered.'

'Me too.'

Buckley opened the door leading into the hall, then stopped. 'I lied, Jake. I'm tickled to death you're not on this case.'

'I know you lied. But don't count me out.'

'What does that mean?'

'Good day, Rufus.'

The Ford County grand jury had been busy, and by Thursday of the second week of the term Jake had been retained by two freshly indicted defendants. One was a black who cut another black at Massey's Tonk back in April. Jake enjoyed the stabbings because acquittals were possible; just get an all-white jury full of rednecks who could care less if all niggers stabbed each other. They were just having a little fun down at the tonk, things got out of hand, one got stabbed, but didn't die. No harm, no conviction. It was similar to the strategy Jake had learned with Lester Hailey. The new client promised fifteen hundred dollars, but first had to post bond.

The other new indictee was a white kid caught driving a stolen pickup. It was the third time he'd been caught in a stolen pickup, and there was no way to keep him out of Parchman for seven years.

Both were in jail, and their presence there afforded Jake the opportunity, and duty, to visit them and check with Ozzie. Late Thursday afternoon he found the sheriff in his office.

'Are you busy?' Jake asked. A hundred pounds of paper was strewn over the desk and onto the floor.

'No, just paperwork. Any more burnin' crosses?'

'No, thank God. One's enough.'

'I haven't seen your friend from Memphis.'

'That's strange,' said Jake. 'I thought he would be here by now. Have you talked to Carl Lee?'

'Every day. He's gettin' nervous. The lawyer ain't even called, Jake.'

'Good. Let him sweat. I don't feel sorry for him.'

'You think he made a mistake?'

'I know he did. I know these rednecks around here, Ozzie, and I know how they act when you put them on a jury. They won't be impressed by some slick-talking foreigner. You agree?'

'I don't know. You're the lawyer. I don't doubt what you say, Jake. I've seen you work.'

'He's not even licensed to practice in Mississippi. Judge Noose is laying for him. He hates out-of-state lawyers.'

'You're kiddin'?'

'Nope. I talked to him yesterday.'

Ozzie looked disturbed and eyed Jake carefully. 'You wanna see him?'

'Who?'

'Carl Lee.'

'No! I have no reason to see him.' Jake glanced in his briefcase. 'I need to see Leroy Glass, aggravated assault.'

'You got Leroy?'

'Yeah. His folks came in this morning.'

'Follow me.'

Jake waited in the Intoxilyzer room while a trusty went for the new client. Leroy wore the standard Ford County jail issue of glow-in-the-dark orange coveralls. Pink sponge rollers shot in all directions from his scalp, and two long greasy cornrows clung to the back of his neck. His black leathery feet were protected from the dirty linoleum by a pair of lime green terrycloth slides. No socks. A wicked, aged scar started next to his right ear lobe, made the ridge over his cheekbone, and connected neatly with his right nostril. It proved beyond a reasonable doubt that Leroy was no stranger to stabbings and carvings. He wore it like a medal. He smoked Kools.

'Leroy, I'm Jake Brigance,' the lawyer introduced himself and pointed to a folding chair next to the Pepsi machine. 'Your momma and brother hired me this morning.'

'Good to know you, Mr. Jake.'

A trusty waited in the hall by the door as Jake asked questions. He filled three pages of notes on Leroy Glass. Of primary interest, at least at this point, was money. How much did he have, and where could he find more. They would talk about the stabbing later. Aunts, uncles, brothers, sisters, friends, anyone with a job who might be able to make a loan. Jake took phone numbers.

'Who referred you to me?' Jake asked.

'Saw you on TV, Mr. Jake. You and Carl Lee Hailey.'

Jake was proud, but did not smile. Television was just part of his job. 'You know Carl Lee?'

'Yeah, know Lester too. You's Lester's lawyer, wasn't you?'

'Yes.'

'Me and Carl Lee in the same cell. Moved me last night.'

'You don't say.'

'Yeah. He don't talk much. He said you's a real good lawyer and all, but he found somebody else from Memphis.'

'That's right. What does he think of his new lawyer?'

'I don't know, Mr. Jake. He was fussin' this mornin' cause the new lawyer ain't been to see him yet. He say you come to see him all the time and talk 'bout the case, but the new lawyer, some funny name, ain't even been down to meet him yet.'

Jake concealed his delight with a grim face, but it was difficult. 'I'll tell you something if you promise you won't tell Carl Lee.'

'Okay.'

'His new lawyer can't come to see him.'

'No! Why not?'

'Because he doesn't have a license to practice law in Mississippi. He's a Tennessee lawyer. He'll get thrown out of court if he comes down here by himself. I'm afraid Carl Lee's made a big mistake.'

'Why don't you tell him?'

'Because he's already fired me. I can't give him advice anymore.'

'Somebody ought to.'

'You just promised you won't, okay?'

'Okay. I won't.'

'Promise?'

'I swear.'

'Good. I gotta go. I'll meet with the bondsman in the morning, and maybe we'll have you out in a day or so. Not a word to Carl Lee, right?'

'Right.'

Tank Scales was leaning on the Saab in the parking lot when Jake left the jail. He stepped on a cigarette butt and pulled a piece of paper from his shirt pocket. 'Two numbers. Top one's for home, bottom for work. But don't call at work unless you have to.'

'Good work, Tank. Did you get them from Iris?'

'Yeah. She didn't want to. She stopped by the tonk last night and I got her drunk.'

'I owe you one.'

'I'll get it, sooner or later.'

It was dark, almost eight o'clock. Dinner was cold, but that was not unusual. That's why he had bought her a microwave. She was accustomed to the hours and the warmed-over dinners, and she did not complain. They would eat when he came home, whether it was six or ten.

Jake drove from the jail to his office. He wouldn't dare call Lester from home, not with Carla listening. He settled behind his desk and stared at the numbers Tank had located. Carl Lee had told him not to make this call. Why should he do it? Would it be solicitation? Unethical? Would it be unethical to call Lester and tell him that Carl Lee had fired him and hired another lawyer? No. And to answer Lester's questions about the new lawyer? No. And to express concern? No. And to criticize the new lawyer? Probably not. Would it be unethical to encourage Lester to talk to his brother? No. And convince him to fire Marsharfsky? Probably so. And to rehire Jake? Yes, no doubt about it. That would be very unethical. What if he just called Lester and talked about Carl Lee and allowed the conversation to follow its own course.

'Hello.'

'Is there a Lester Hailey there?'

'Yes. Who's calling?' came the accented reply from the Swede.

'Jake Brigance, from Mississippi.'

'One moment.'

Jake checked his watch. Eight-thirty. It was the same time in Chicago, wasn't it?

'Jake!'

'Lester, how are you?'

'Fine, Jake. Tired, but fine. How 'bout you?'

'Great. Listen, have you talked to Carl Lee this week?'

'No. I left Friday, and I've been workin' two shifts since Sunday. I ain't had time for nothin'.'

'You seen the newspapers?'

'No. What's happened?'

'You won't believe it, Lester.'

'What is it, Jake?'

'Carl Lee fired me and hired a big-shot lawyer from Memphis.'

'What! You're kiddin'? When?'

'Last Friday. I guess after you left. He didn't bother to tell me. I read it in the Memphis paper Saturday morning.'

'He's crazy. Why'd he do it, Jake? Who'd he hire?'

'You know a guy named Cat Bruster from Memphis?'

'Of course.'

'It's his lawyer. Cat's paying for it. He drove down from Memphis last Friday and saw Carl Lee at the jail. Next morning I saw my picture in the paper and read where I've been fired.'

'Who's the lawyer?'

'Bo Marsharfsky.'

'He any good?'

'He's a crook. He defends all the pimps and drug dealers in Memphis.'

'Sounds like a Polack.'

'He is. I think he's from Chicago.'

'Yeah, bunch of Polacks up here. Does he talk like these?'

'Like he's got a mouthful of hot grease. He'll go over big in Ford County.'

'Stupid, stupid, stupid. Carl Lee never was too bright. I always had to think for him. Stupid, stupid.'

'Yeah, he's made a mistake, Lester. You know what a murder trial is like because you've been there. You realize how important that jury is when they leave the courtroom and go to the jury room. Your life is in their hands. Twelve local people back there fighting and arguing over your case, your life. The jury's the most important part. That's why you gotta be able to talk to the jury.'

'That's right, Jake. You can do it too.'

'I'm sure Marsharfsky can do it in Memphis, but not Ford County. Not in rural Mississippi. These people won't trust him.'

'You're right, Jake. I can't believe he did it. He's screwed up again.'

'He did it, Lester, and I'm worried about him.'

'Have you talked to him?'

'Last Saturday, after I saw the newspaper, I went straight to the jail. I asked him why, and he could not answer. He felt bad about it. I haven't talked to him since then. But neither has Marsharfsky. He hasn't found Clanton yet, and I understand Carl Lee's upset. As far as I can tell, nothing has been done on the case this week.'

'Has Ozzie talked to him?'

'Yeah, but you know Ozzie. He's not gonna say too much. He knows Bruster's a crook and Marsharfsky's a crook, but he won't lean on Carl Lee.'

'Man oh man. I can't believe it. He's stupid if he thinks those rednecks'll listen to some shyster from Memphis. Hell, Jake, they don't trust the lawyers from Tyler County and it's next door. Man oh man.'

Jake smiled at the receiver. So far, nothing unethical.

'What should I do, Jake?'

'I don't know, Lester. He needs some help, and you're the only one he'll listen to. You know how headstrong he is.'

'I guess I'd better call him.'

No, thought Jake, it would be easier for Carl Lee to say no over the phone. Confrontation was needed between the brothers. A drive from Chicago would make an impact.

'I don't think you'll get very far over the phone. His mind's made up. Only you can change it, and you can't do it over the phone.'

Lester paused a few seconds while Jake waited anxiously. 'What's today?'

'Thursday, June 6.'

'Let's see,' Lester mumbled. 'I'm ten hours away. I work the four-to-midnight shift tomorrow and again Sunday. I could leave here midnight tomorrow, and be in Clanton by ten Saturday mornin'. Then I could leave early Sunday mornin' and be back by four. That's a lot of drivin', but I can handle it.'

'It's very important, Lester. I think it's worth the trip.'

'Where will you be Saturday, Jake?'

'Here at the office.'

'Okay. I'll go to the jail, and if I need you I'll call the office.'

'Sounds good. One other thing, Lester. Carl Lee told me not to call you. Don't mention it.'

'What'll I tell him?'

'Tell him you called Iris, and she gave you the story.'

'Iris who?'

'Come on, Lester. It's been common knowledge around here for years. Everybody knows it but her husband, and he'll find out.'

'I hope not. We'll have us another murder. You'll have another client.'

'Please. I can't keep the ones I've got. Call me Saturday.'

He ate from the microwave at ten-thirty. Hanna was asleep. They talked about Leroy Glass and the white kid in the stolen pickup. About Carl Lee, but not about Lester. She felt better, safer now that Carl Lee Hailey was behind them. No more calls. No more burning crosses. No more stares at church. There would be other cases, she promised. He said little; just ate and smiled.

CHAPTER NINETEEN

Just before the courthouse closed on Friday. Jake called the clerk to see if a trial was in progress. No, she said, Noose was gone. Buckley, Musgrove, everybody was gone. The courtroom was deserted. Secure with that knowledge, Jake eased across the street, through the rear door of the courthouse, and down the hall to the clerk's office. He flirted with the clerks and secretaries while he located Carl Lee's file. He held his breath as he flipped through the pages. Good! Just as he had hoped. Nothing had been added to the file all week, with the exception of his motion to withdraw as counsel. Marsharfsky and his local counsel had not touched the file. Nothing had been done. He flirted some more and eased back to his office.

Leroy Glass was still in jail. His bond was ten thousand dollars, and his family couldn't raise the thousand-dollar premium to pay a bondsman. So he continued to share the cell with Carl Lee. Jake had a friend who was a bondsman and who took care of Jake's clients. If a client needed out of jail, and there was little danger of him disappearing once he was sprung, the bond would be written. Terms were available for Jake's clients. Say, five percent down and so much a month. If Jake wanted Leroy Glass out of jail, the bond could be written anytime. But Jake needed him in jail.

'Look, Leroy, I'm sorry. I'm working with the bondsman,' Jake explained to his client in the Intoxilyzer room.

'But you said I'd be out by now.'

'Your folks don't have the money, Leroy. I can't pay it myself. We'll get you out, but it'll take a few days. I want you out so you can go to work, make some money and pay me.'

Leroy seemed satisfied. 'Okay, Mr. Jake, just do what you can.'

'Food's pretty good here, isn't it?' Jake asked with a smile.

'It ain't bad. Better at home.'

'We'll get you out,' Jake promised.

'How's the nigger I stabbed?'

'Not sure. Ozzie said he's still in the hospital. Moss Tatum says he's been released. Who knows. I don't think he's hurt too bad.'

'Who was the woman?' Jake asked, unable to remember the details.

'Willie's woman.'

'Willie who?'

'Willie Hoyt.'

Jake thought for a second and tried to recall the indictment. 'That's not the man you stabbed.'

'Naw, he's Curtis Sprawling.'

'You mean, y'all were fighting over another man's woman?'

'That's right.'

'Where was Willie?'

'He was fightin' too.'

'Who was he fighting?'

'Some other dude.'

'You mean the four of you were fighting over Willie's woman?'

'Yeah, you got it.'

'What caused the fight?'

'Her husband was outta town.'

'She's married?'

'That's right.'

'What's her husband's name?'

'Johnny Sands. When he's outta town, there's normally a fight.'

'Why is that?'

' 'Cause she ain't got no kids, can't have any, and she likes to have company. Know what I mean? When he leaves, everybody knows it. If she shows up at a tonk, look out for a fight.'

What a trial, thought Jake. 'But I thought you said she showed up with Willie Hoyt?'

'That's right. But that don't mean nothin' because everybody at the tonk starts easin' up on her, buyin' drinks, wantin' to dance. You can't help it.'

'Some woman, huh?'

'Oh, Mr. Jake, she looks so good. You oughtta see her.'

'I will. On the witness stand.'

Leroy gazed at the wall, smiling, dreaming, lusting after the wife of Johnny Sands. Never mind that he stabbed a man and could get twenty years. He had proven, in hand-to-hand combat, that he was worthy.

'Listen, Leroy, you haven't talked to Carl Lee, have you?'

'Sure. I'm still in his cell. We talk all the time. Ain't much else to do.'

'You haven't told him what we discussed yesterday?'

'Oh no. I told you I wouldn't.'

'Good.'

'But I'll tell you this, Mr. Jake, he's some kinda worried. He ain't heard from his new lawyer. He's bad upset. I had to bite my tongue to keep from tellin' him, but I didn't. I did tell him you were my lawyer.'

'That's okay.'

'He said you was good 'bout comin' by the jail and talkin' 'bout the case and all. He said I hired a good lawyer.'

'Not good enough for him, though.'

'I think Carl Lee's confused. He ain't sure who to trust or anything. He's a good dude.'

'Well, don't be telling him what we discussed, right? It's confidential.'

'Right. But somebody needs to.'

'He didn't consult with me or anyone else before he fired me and hired his new lawyer. He's a grown man. He made the decision. It's his baby.' Jake paused and moved closer to Leroy. He lowered his voice. 'And I'll tell you something else, but you can't tell it. I checked his court file thirty minutes ago. His new lawyer hasn't touched the case all week. Not one thing has been filed. Nothing.'

Leroy frowned and shook his head. 'Man oh man.'

His lawyer continued. 'These big shots operate like that. Talk a lot, blow a lot of smoke, fly by the seat of their pants. Take more cases than they can handle, and end up losing more than they win. I know them. I watch them all the time. Most are overrated.'

'Is that why he ain't been to see Carl Lee?'

'Sure. He's too busy. Plus he's got plenty of other big cases. He don't care about Carl Lee.'

'That's bad. Carl Lee deserves better.'

'It was his choice. He'll have to live with it.'

'You think he'll be convicted, Mr. Jake?'

'No doubt about it. He's looking at the gas chamber. He's hired a bogus big-shot lawyer who doesn't have time to work on his case, doesn't even have the time to talk to him in jail.'

'Are you sayin' you could get him off?'

Jake relaxed and crossed his legs. 'No, I never make that promise, and I won't make it for your trial. A lawyer is stupid if he promises an acquittal. Too many things can go wrong at trial.'

'Carl Lee said his lawyer promised a not guilty in the newspaper.'

'He's a fool.'

'Where you been?' Carl Lee asked his cellmate as the jailer locked the door.

'Talkin' to my lawyer.'

'Jake?'

'Yeah.'

Leroy sat on his bunk directly across the cell from Carl Lee, who was rereading a newspaper. He folded the paper and laid it under his bunk.

'You look worried,' Carl Lee said. 'Bad news about your case?'

'Naw. Just can't make my bail. Jake says it'll be a few days.'

'Jake talk about me?'

'Naw. Not much.'

'Not much? What'd he say?'

'Just ask how you was.'

'That all?'

'Yeah.'

'He's not mad at me?'

'Naw. He might be worried about you, but I don't think he's mad.'

'Why's he worried about me?'

'I don't know,' Leroy answered as he stretched out on his bunk, folding his hands behind his head.

'Come on, Leroy. You know somethin' you ain't tellin'. What'd Jake say about me?'

'Jake said I can't tell you what we talk about. He says it's confidential. You wouldn't want your lawyer repeatin' what y'all talk about, would you?'

'I ain't seen my lawyer.'

'You had a good lawyer till you fired him.'

'I gotta good one now.'

'How do you know? You ain't ever met him. He's too busy to come talk to you, and if he's that busy, he ain't got time to work on your case.'

'How do you know about him?'

'I asked Jake.'

'Yeah. What'd he say?'

Leroy was silent.

'I wanna know what he said,' demanded Carl Lee as he sat on the edge of Leroy's bunk. He glared at his smaller, weaker cellmate. Leroy decided he was frightened and now had a good excuse to tell Carl Lee. Either talk or get slapped.

'He's a crook,' Leroy said. 'He's a big-shot crook who'll sell you out. He don't care about you or your case. He just wants the publicity. He hasn't touched your case all week. Jake knows, he checked in the courthouse this afternoon. Not a sign of Mr. Big Shot. He's too busy to leave Memphis and check on you. He's got too many other crooked clients in Memphis, includin' your friend Mr. Bruster.'

'You're crazy, Leroy.'

'Okay, I'm crazy. Wait and see who pleads insaneness. Wait and see how hard he works on your case.'

'What makes you such an expert?'

'You asked me and I'm tellin' you.'

Carl Lee walked to the door and grabbed the bars, gripping them tightly with his huge hands. The cell had shrunk in three weeks, and the smaller it became the harder it was for him to think, to reason, to plan, to react. He could not concentrate in jail. He knew only what was told to him and had no one to trust. Gwen was irrational. Ozzie was noncommittal. Lester was in Chicago. There was no other person he trusted except Jake, and for some reason he had found a new lawyer. Money, that was the reason. Nineteen hundred dollars cash, paid by the biggest pimp and dope dealer in Memphis, whose lawyer specialized in defending pimps and dope dealers, and all kinds of cutthroats and hoodlums. Did Marsharfsky represent decent people? What would the jury think when they watched Carl Lee sit at the defense table next to Marsharfsky? He was guilty, of course. Why else would he hire a famous, big-city crook like Marsharfsky?

'You know what them rednecks on the jury'll say when they see Marsharfsky?' Leroy asked.

'What?'

'They're gonna think this poor nigger is guilty, and he's sold his soul to hire the biggest crook in Memphis to tell us he ain't guilty.'

Carl Lee mumbled something through the bars.

'They're gonna fry you, Carl Lee.'

Moss Junior Tatum was on duty at six-thirty Saturday morning when the phone rang in Ozzie's office. It was the sheriff.

'What're you doing awake?' asked Moss.

'I'm not sure I'm awake,' answered the sheriff. 'Listen, Moss, do you remember an old black preacher named Street, Reverend Isaiah Street?'

'Not really.'

'Yeah you do. He preached for fifty years at Springdale Church, north of town. First member of the NAACP in Ford County. He taught all the blacks around here how to march and boycott back in the sixties.'

'Yeah, now I remember. Didn't the Klan catch him once?'

'Yeah, they beat him and burned his house, but nothin' serious. Summer of '65.'

'I thought he died a few years back.'

'Naw, he's been half dead for ten years, but he still moves a little. He called me at five-thirty and talked for an hour. Reminded me of all the political favors I owe him.'

'What's he want?'

'He'll be there at seven to see Carl Lee. Why, I don't know. But treat him nice. Put them in my office and let them talk. I'll be in later.'

'Sure, Sheriff.'

In his heyday in the sixties, the Reverend Isaiah Street had been the moving force behind civil rights activity in Ford County. He walked with Martin Luther King in Memphis and Montgomery. He organized marches and protests in Clanton and Karaway and other towns in north

Mississippi. In the summer of '64 he greeted students from the North and coordinated their efforts to register black voters. Some had lived in his home that memorable summer, and they still visited him from time to time. He was no radical. He was quiet, compassionate, intelligent, and had earned the respect of all blacks and most whites. His was a calm, cool voice in the midst of hatred and controversy. He unofficially officiated the great public school desegregation in '69, and Ford County saw little trouble.

A stroke in '75 deadened the right side of his body but left his mind untouched. Now, at seventy-eight, he walked by himself, slowly and with a cane. Proud, dignified, erect as possible. He was ushered into the sheriff's office and seated. He declined coffee, and Moss Junior left to get the defendant.

'You awake, Carl Lee?' he whispered loudly, not wanting to wake the other prisoners, who would begin screaming for breakfast, medicine, lawyers, bondsmen, and girlfriends.

Carl Lee sat up immediately. 'Yeah, I didn't sleep much.'

'You have a visitor. Come on.' Moss quietly unlocked the cell.

Carl Lee had met the reverend years earlier when he addressed the last senior class at East High, the black school. Desegregation followed, and East became the junior high. He had not seen the reverend since the stroke.

'Carl Lee, do you know Reverend Isaiah Street?' Moss asked properly.

'Yes, we met years ago.'

'Good, I'll close the door and let y'all talk.'

'How are you, sir?' Carl Lee asked. They sat next to each other on the couch.

'Fine, my son, and you?'

'As good as possible.'

'I've been in jail too, you know. Years ago. It's a terrible place, but I guess it's necessary. How are they treating you?'

'Fine, just fine. Ozzie lets me do as I please.'

'Yes, Ozzie. We're very proud of him, aren't we?'

'Yes, suh. He's a good man.' Carl Lee studied the frail, feeble old man with the cane. His body was weak and tired, but his mind was sharp, his voice strong.

'We're proud of you too, Carl Lee. I don't condone violence, but at times it's necessary too, I guess. You did a good deed, my son.'

'Yes, suh,' answered Carl Lee, uncertain of the appropriate response.

'I guess you wonder why I'm here.'

Carl Lee nodded. The reverend tapped his cane on the floor.

'I'm concerned about your acquittal. The black community is concerned. If you were white, you would most likely go to trial, and most likely be acquitted. The rape of a child is a horrible crime, and who's to blame a father for rectifying the wrong? A white father, that is. A black father evokes the same sympathy among blacks, but there's one problem: the jury will be white. So a black father and a white father would not have equal chances with the jury. Do you follow me?'

'I think so.'

'The jury is all important. Guilt versus innocence. Freedom versus prison. Life versus death. All to be determined by the jury. It's a fragile system, this trusting of lives to twelve average, ordinary people who do not understand the law and are intimidated by the process.'

'Yes, suh.'

'Your acquittal by a white jury for the killings of two white men will do more for the black folk of Mississippi than any event since we integrated the schools. And it's not just Mississippi; it's black folk everywhere. Yours is a most famous case, and it's being watched carefully by many people.'

'I just did what I had to do.'

'Precisely. You did what you thought was right. It was right; although it was brutal and ugly, it was right. And most folks, black and white, believe that. But will you be treated as though you were white? That's the question.'

'And if I'm convicted?'

'Your conviction would be another slap at us; a symbol of deep-seated racism; of old prejudices, old hatreds. It would be a disaster. You must not be convicted.'

'I'm doin' all I can do.'

'Are you? Let's talk about your attorney, if we may.'

Carl Lee nodded.

'Have you met him?'

'No.' Carl Lee lowered his head and rubbed his eyes. 'Have you?'

'Yes, I have.'

'You have? When?'

'In Memphis in 1968. I was with Dr. King. Marsharfsky was one of the attorneys representing the garbage workers on strike against the city. He asked Dr. King to leave Memphis, claimed he was agitating the whites and inciting the blacks, and that he was impeding the contract negotiations. He was arrogant and abusive. He cursed Dr. King – in private, of course. We thought he was selling out the workers and getting money under the table from the city. I think we were right.'

Carl Lee breathed deeply and rubbed his temples.

'I've followed his career,' the reverend continued. 'He's made a name for himself representing gangsters, thieves, and pimps. He gets some of them off, but they're always guilty. When you see one of his clients, you know he's guilty. That's what worrics me most about you. I'm afraid you'll be considered guilty by association.'

Carl Lee sunk lower, his elbows resting on his knees. 'Who told you to come here?' he asked softly.

'I had a talk with an old friend.'

'Who?'

'Just an old friend, my son. He's concerned about you too. We're all concerned about you.'

'He's the best lawyer in Memphis.'

'This isn't Memphis, is it?'

'He's an expert on criminal law.'

'That could be because he's a criminal.'

Carl Lee stood abruptly and walked across the room, his back to the reverend.

'He's free. He's not costin' me a dime.'

'His fee won't seem important when you're on death row, my son.'

Moments passed and neither spoke. Finally, the reverend lowered his cane and struggled to his feet. 'I've said enough. I'm leaving. Good luck, Carl Lee.'

Carl Lee shook his hand. 'I do appreciate your concern and I thank you for visitin'.'

'My point is simply this, my son. Your case will be difficult enough to win. Don't make it more difficult with a crook like Marsharfsky.'

Lester left Chicago just before midnight Friday. He headed south alone, as usual. Earlier his wife went north to Green Bay for a weekend with her family. He liked Green Bay much less than she liked Mississippi, and neither cared to visit the other's family. They were nice people, the Swedes, and they would treat him like family if he allowed it. But they were different, and it wasn't just their whiteness. He grew up with whites in the South and knew them. He didn't like them all and didn't like most of their feelings toward him, but at least he knew them. But the Northern whites, especially the Swedes, were different. Their customs, speech, food, almost everything was foreign to him, and he would never feel comfortable with them.

There would be a divorce, probably within a year. He was black, and his wife's older cousin had married a black in the early seventies and received a lot of attention. Lester was a fad, and she was tired of him. Luckily, there were no kids. He suspected someone else. He had someone else too, and Iris had promised to marry him and move to Chicago once she ditched Henry.

Both sides of Interstate 57 looked the same after midnight – scattered lights from the small, neat farms strewn over the countryside, and occasionally a big town like Champaign or Effingham. The north was where he lived and worked, but it wasn't home. Home was where Momma was, in Mississippi, although he would never live there again. Too much ignorance and poverty. He didn't mind the racism; it wasn't as bad as it once was and he was accustomed to it. It would always be there, but gradually becoming less visible. The whites still owned and controlled everything, and that in itself was not unbearable. It was not about to change. What he found intolerable was the ignorance and stark poverty of many of the blacks; the dilapidated, shotgun houses, the high infant mortality rate, the hopelessly unemployed, the unwed mothers and their unfed babies. It was depressing to the point of being intolerable, and intolerable to the point he fled Mississippi like thousands of others and migrated north in search of a job, any decent-paying job which could ease the pain of poverty.

It was both pleasant and depressing to return to Mississippi. Pleasant in that he would see his family; depressing because he would see their poverty. There were bright spots. Carl Lee had a decent job, a clean house, and well-dressed kids. He was an exception, and now it was all in jeopardy because of two drunk, low-bred pieces of white trash. Blacks had an excuse for being worthless, but for whites in a white world, there were no excuses. They were dead, thank God, and he was proud of his big brother.

Six hours out of Chicago the sun appeared as he crossed the river at Cairo. Two hours later he crossed it again at Memphis. He drove southeast into Mississippi, and an hour later circled the courthouse in Clanton. He'd been awake for twenty hours.

'Carl Lee, you have a visitor,' Ozzie said through the iron bars in the door.

'I'm not surprised. Who is it?'

'Just follow me. I think you better use my office. This could take a while.'

Jake loitered at his office waiting on the phone to ring. Ten o'clock. Lester should be in town, if he's coming. Eleven. Jake riffled through some stale files and made notes for Ethel. Noon. He called Carla and lied about meeting a new client at one o'clock, so forget lunch. He would work in the yard later. One o'clock. He found an ancient case from Wyoming where a husband was acquitted after tracking down the man who raped his wife. In 1893. He copied the case, then threw it in the garbage. Two o'clock. Was Lester in town? He could go visit Leroy and snoop around the jail. No, that didn't feel right. He napped on the couch in the big office.

At two-fifteen the phone rang. Jake bolted upright and scrambled from the couch. His heart was pounding as he grabbed the phone. 'Hello!'

'Jake, this is Ozzie.'

'Yeah, Ozzie, what's up?'

'Your presence is requested here at the jail.'

'What?' Jake asked, feigning innocence.

'You're needed down here.'

'By who?'

'Carl Lee wants to talk to you.'

'Is Lester there?'

'Yeah. He wants you too.'

'Be there in a minute.'

'They've been in there for over four hours,' Ozzie said, pointing to the office door.

'Doing what?' asked Jake.

'Talkin', cussin', shoutin'. Things got quiet about thirty minutes ago. Carl Lee came out and asked me to call you.'

'Thanks. Let's go in.'

'No way, man. I ain't goin' in there. They didn't send for me. You're on your own.'

Jake knocked on the door.

'Come in!'

He opened it slowly, walked inside and closed it. Carl Lee was sitting behind the desk. Lester was lying on the couch. He stood and shook Jake's hand. 'Good to see you, Jake.'

'Good to see you, Lester. What brings you home?'

'Family business.'

Jake looked at Carl Lee, then walked to the desk and shook his hand. The defendant was clearly irritated.

'Y'all sent for me?'

'Yeah, Jake, sit down. We need to talk,' said Lester. 'Carl Lee's got somethin' to tell you.'

'You tell him,' Carl Lee said.

Lester sighed and rubbed his eyes. He was tired and frustrated. 'I ain't sayin' another word. This is between you and Jake.' Lester closed his eyes and relaxed on the couch. Jake sat in a padded, folding chair that he leaned against the wall opposite the couch. He watched Lester carefully, but did not look at Carl Lee, who rocked slowly in Ozzie's swivel chair. Carl Lee said nothing. Lester said nothing. After three minutes of silence, Jake was annoyed.

'Who sent for me?' he demanded.

'I did,' answered Carl Lee.

'Well, what do you want?'

'I wanna give you my case back.'

'You assume I want it back.'

'What!' Lester sat up and looked at Jake.

'It's not a gift you give or take away. It's an agreement between you and your attorney. Don't act as though you're doing me a great favor.' Jake's voice was rising, his anger apparent.

'Do you want the case?' asked Carl Lee.

'Are you trying to rehire me, Carl Lee?'

'That's right.'

'Why do you want to rehire me?'

' 'Cause Lester wants me to.'

'Fine, then I don't want your case.' Jake stood and started for the door. 'If Lester wants me and you want Marsharfsky, then stick with Marsharfsky. If you can't think for yourself, you need Marsharfsky.'

'Wait, Jake. Be cool, man,' Lester said as he met Jake at the door. 'Sit down, sit down. I don't blame you for bein' mad at Carl Lee for firin' you. He was wrong. Right, Carl Lee?'

Carl Lee picked at his fingernails.

'Sit down, Jake, sit down and let's talk,' Lester pleaded as he led him back to the folding chair. 'Good. Now, let's discuss this situation. Carl Lee, do you want Jake to be your lawyer?'

Carl Lee nodded. 'Yeah.'

'Good. Now, Jake –'

'Explain why,' Jake asked Carl Lee.

'What?'

'Explain why you want me to handle your case. Explain why you're firing Marsharfsky.'

'I don't have to explain.'

'Yes! Yes, you do. You at least owe me an explanation. You fired me a week ago and didn't have the guts to call me. I read it in the newspaper. Then I read about your new high-priced lawyer who evidently can't find his way to Clanton. Now you call me and expect me to drop everything because you might change your mind again. Explain, please.'

'Explain, Carl Lee. Talk to Jake,' Lester said.

Carl Lee leaned forward and placed his elbows on the desk. He buried his face in his hands and spoke between his palms. 'I'm just confused. This place is drivin' me crazy. My nerves are shot. I'm worried about my little girl. I'm worried about my family. I'm worried about my own skin. Everbody's tellin' me to do somethin' different. I ain't ever been in a situation like this and I don't know what to do. All I can do is trust people. I trust Lester, and I trust you, Jake. That's all I can do.'

'You trust my advice?' asked Jake.

'I always have.'

'And you trust me to handle your case?'

'Yeah, Jake, I want you to handle it.'

'Good enough.'

Jake relaxed, and Lester eased into the couch. 'You'll need to notify Marsharfsky. Until you do, I can't work on your case.'

'We'll do that this afternoon,' Lester said.

'Good. Once you talk to him, give me a call. There's a lot of work to do, and the time will disappear.'

'What about the money?' asked Lester.

'Same fee. Same arrangements. Is that satisfactory?'

'Okay with me,' replied Carl Lee. 'I'll pay you any way I can.'

'We'll discuss that later.'

'What about the doctors?' asked Carl Lee.

'We'll make some arrangements. I don't know. It'll work out.'

The defendant smiled. Lester snored loudly and Carl Lee laughed at his brother. 'I figured you called him, but he swears you didn't.'

Jake smiled awkwardly but said nothing. Lester was a smooth liar, a talent which had proved extremely beneficial during his murder trial.

'I'm sorry, Jake. I was wrong.'

'No apologies. There's too much work to spend time apologizing.'

Next to the parking lot outside the jail, a reporter stood under a shade tree waiting for something to happen.

'Excuse me, sir, aren't you Mr. Brigance?'

'Who wants to know?'

'I'm Richard Flay, with *The Jackson Daily*. You're Jake Brigance.'

'Yes.'

'Mr. Hailey's ex-lawyer.'

'No. Mr. Hailey's lawyer.'

'I thought he had retained Bo Marsharfsky. In fact, that's why I'm here. I heard a rumor Marsharfsky would be here this afternoon.'

'If you see him, tell him he's too late.'

Lester slept hard on the couch in Ozzie's office. The dispatcher woke him at 4:00 A.M. Sunday, and after filling a tall Styrofoam cup with black coffee, he left for Chicago. Late Saturday night he and Carl Lee had called Cat in his office above the club and informed him of Carl Lee's conversion. Cat was indifferent and busy. He said he would call Marsharfsky. There was no mention of the money.

CHAPTER TWENTY

Not long after Lester disappeared, Jake staggered down his driveway in his bathrobe to get the Sunday papers. Clanton was an hour southeast of Memphis, three hours north of Jackson, and forty-five minutes from Tupelo. All three cities had daily papers with fat Sunday editions that were available in Clanton. Jake had long subscribed to all three, and was now glad he did so Carla would have plenty of material for her scrapbook. He spread the papers and began the task of plowing through five inches of print.

Nothing in the Jackson paper. He hoped Richard Flay had reported something. He should have spent more time with him outside the jail. Nothing from Memphis. Nothing from Tupelo. Jake was not surprised, just hopeful that somehow the story had been discovered. But it happened too late yesterday. Maybe Monday. He was tired of hiding; tired of feeling embarrassed. Until it was in the papers and read by the boys at the Coffee Shop, and the people at church, and the other lawyers, including Buckley and Sullivan and Lotterhouse, until everybody knew it was his case again, he would stay quiet and out of view. How should he tell Sullivan? Carl Lee would call Marsharfsky, or the pimp, probably the pimp, who would then call Marsharfsky with the news. What kind of press release would Marsharfsky write for that? Then the great lawyer would call Walter Sullivan with the wonderful news. That should happen Monday morning, if not sooner. Word would spread quickly throughout the Sullivan firm, and the senior partners, junior partners, and little associates would all gather in the long, mahogany-laced conference room and curse Brigance and his low ethics and tactics. The associates would try to impress their bosses by spouting rules and code numbers of ethics Brigance probably violated. Jake hated them, every one of them. He would send Sullivan a short, curt letter with a copy to Lotterhouse.

He wouldn't call or write Buckley. He would be in shock after he saw the paper. A letter to Judge Noose with a copy to Buckley would work fine. He would not honor him with a personal letter.

Jake had a thought, then hesitated, then dialed Lucien's number. It was a few minutes after seven. The nurse/maid/bartender answered the phone.

'Sallie?'

'Yes.'

'This is Jake. Is Lucien awake?'

'Just a moment.' She rolled over and handed the phone to Lucien.

'Hello.'

'Lucien, it's Jake.'

'Yeah, whatta you want?'

'Good news. Carl Lee Hailey rehired me yesterday. The case is mine again.'

'Which case?'

'The Hailey case!'

'Oh, the vigilante. He's yours?'

'As of yesterday. We've got work to do.'

'When's the trial? July sometime?'

'Twenty-second.'

'That's pretty close. What's priority?'

'A psychiatrist. A cheap one who'll say anything.'

'I know just the man,' said Lucien.

'Good. Get busy. I'll call in a couple of days.'

Carla awoke at a decent hour and found her husband in the kitchen with newspapers strewn over and under the breakfast table. She made fresh coffee and, without a word, sat across the table. He smiled at her and continued reading.

'What time did you get up?' she asked.

'Five-thirty.'

'Why so early? It's Sunday.'

'I couldn't sleep.'

'Too excited?'

Jake lowered the paper. 'As a matter of fact, I am excited. Very excited. It's too bad the excitement will not be shared.'

'I'm sorry about last night.'

'You don't have to apologize. I know how you feel. Your problem is that you only look at the negative, never the positive. You have no idea what this case can do for us.'

'Jake, this case scares me. The phone calls, the threats, the burning cross. If the case means a million dollars, is it worth it if something happens?'

'Nothing will happen. We'll get some more threats and they'll stare at us at church and around town, but nothing serious.'

'But you can't be sure.'

'We went through this last night and I don't care to rehash it this morning. I do have an idea, though.'

'I can't wait to hear it.'

'You and Hanna fly to North Carolina and stay with your parents until after the trial. They'd love to have you, and we wouldn't worry about the Klan or whoever likes to burn crosses.'

'But the trial is six weeks away! You want us to stay in Wilmington for six weeks?'

'Yes.'

'I love my parents, but that's ridiculous.'

'You don't see enough of them, and they don't see enough of Hanna.'

'And we don't see enough of you. I'm not leaving for six weeks.'

'There's a ton of preparation. I'll eat and sleep this case until the trial is over. I'll work nights, weekends –'

'What else is new?'

'I'll ignore y'all and think of nothing but this case.'

'We're used to that.'

Jake smiled at her. 'You're saying you can handle it?'

'I can handle you. It's those crazies out there that scare me.'

'When the crazies get serious, I'll back off. I will run from this case if my family is in danger.'

'You promise?'

'Of course I promise. Let's send Hanna.'

'If we're not in danger, why do you want to send anybody?'

'Just for safety. She'd have a great time spending the summer with her grandparents. They'd love it.'

'She wouldn't last a week without me.'

'And you wouldn't last a week without her.'

'That's true. It's out of the question. I don't worry about her as long as I can hold her and squeeze her.'

The coffee was ready and Carla filled their cups. 'Anything in the paper?'

'No. I thought the Jackson paper might run something, but it happened too late, I guess.'

'I guess your timing is a little rusty after a week's layoff.'

'Just wait till in the morning.'

'How do you know?'

'I promise.'

She shook her head and searched for the fashion and food sections. 'Are you going to church?'

'No.'

'Why not? You've got the case. You're a star again.'

'Yeah, but no one knows it yet.'

'I see. Next Sunday.'

'Of course.'

At Mount Hebron, Mount Zion, Mount Pleasant, and at Brown's Chapel, Green's Chapel, and Norris Road, Section Line Road, Bethel Road, and at God's Temple, Christ's Temple, and Saints' Temple, the buckets and baskets and plates were passed and re-passed and left at the altars and front doors to collect the money for Carl Lee Hailey and his family. The large, family-size Kentucky Fried Chicken buckets were used in many of the churches. The bigger the bucket, or basket, the smaller the individual offerings appeared as they fell to the bottom, thus allowing the minister just cause to order another passing through the flock. It was a special offering, separate from the regular giving, and was preceded in virtually every church with a heart-wrenching account of what happened to the precious little Hailey girl, and what would happen to her daddy and family if the buckets were not filled. In many instances the sacred name of the NAACP was invoked and the effect was a loosening of the wallets and purses.

It worked. The buckets were emptied, the money counted, and the ritual repeated during the evening services. Late Sunday night the morning offerings and evening offerings were combined and counted by each minister, who would then deliver a great percentage of the total to the Reverend Agee sometime Monday. He would keep the money somewhere in his church, and a great percentage of it would be spent for the benefit of the Hailey family.

From two to five each Sunday afternoon, the prisoners in the Ford County jail were turned out into a large fenced yard across the small back street behind the jail. A limit of three friends and/or relatives for each prisoner was allowed inside for no more than an hour. There were a couple of shade trees, some broken picnic tables, and a well-maintained basketball hoop. Deputies and dogs watched carefully from the other side of the fence.

A routine was established. Gwen and the kids would leave church after the benediction around three, and drive to the jail. Ozzie allowed Carl Lee early entrance to the recreation area so he could assume the best picnic table, the one with four legs and a shade tree. He would sit there by himself, speaking to no one, and watch the basketball skirmish until his family arrived. It wasn't basketball, but a hybrid of rugby, wrestling, judo, and basketball. No one dared officiate. No blood, no foul. And, surprisingly, no fights. A fight meant quick admittance to solitary and no recreation for a month.

There were a few visitors, some girlfriends and wives, and they would sit in the grass by the fence with their men and quietly watch the mayhem under the basketball hoop. One couple asked Carl Lee if they could use his table for lunch. He shook his head, and they ate in the grass.

Gwen and the kids arrived before three. Deputy Hastings, her cousin, unlocked the gate and the children ran to meet their daddy. Gwen spread the food. Carl Lee was aware of the stares from the less fortunate, and he enjoyed the envy. Had he been white, or smaller and weaker, or perhaps charged with a lesser crime, he would have been asked to share his food. But he was Carl Lee Hailey, and no one stared too long. The game returned to its fury and violence, and the family ate in peace. Tonya always sat next to her daddy.

'They started an offerin' for us this mornin',' Gwen said after lunch.

'Who did?'

'The church. Reverend Agee said all the black churches in the county are gonna take up money ever Sunday for us and for the lawyer fees.'

'How much?'

'Don't know. He said they gonna pass the bucket ever Sunday until the trial.'

'That's mighty nice. What'd he say 'bout me?'

'Just talked about your case and all. Said how expensive it would be, and how we'd need help from the churches. Talked about Christian givin' and all that. Said you're a real hero to your people.'

What a pleasant surprise, thought Carl Lee. He expected some help from his church, but nothing financial. 'How many churches?'

'All the black ones in the county.'

'When do we get the money?'

'He didn't say.'

After he got his cut, thought Carl Lee. 'Boys, y'all take your sister and go play over there by the fence. Me and Momma needs to talk. Be careful now.'

Carl Lee, Jr., and Robert took their little sister by the hand and did exactly as ordered.

'What does the doctor say?' Carl Lee asked as he watched the children walk away.

'She's doin' good. Her jaw's healin' good. He might take the wire off in a month. She can't run and jump and play yet, but it won't be long. Still some soreness.'

'What about the, uh, the other?'

Gwen shook her head and covered her eyes. She began crying and wiping her eyes. She spoke and her voice cracked. 'She'll never have kids. He told me . . .' She stopped, wiped her face and tried to continue. She began sobbing loudly, and buried her face in a paper towel.

Carl Lee felt sick. He placed his forehead in his palms. He ground his teeth together as his eyes watered. 'What'd he say?'

Gwen raised her head and spoke haltingly, fighting back tears. 'He told me Tuesday there was too much damage . . .' She wiped her wet face with her fingers. 'But he wants to send her to a specialist in Memphis.'

'He's not sure?'

She shook her head. 'Ninety percent sure. But he thinks she should be examined by another doctor in Memphis. We're supposed to take her in a month.'

Gwen tore off another paper towel and wiped her face. She handed one to her husband, who quickly dabbed his eyes.

Next to the fence, Tonya sat listening to her brothers argue about which one would be a deputy and which one would be in jail. She watched her parents talk and shake their heads and cry. She knew something was wrong with her. She rubbed her eyes and started crying too.

'The nightmares are gettin' worse,' Gwen said, interrupting the silence. 'I have to sleep with her ever night. She dreams about men comin' to get her, men hidin' in the closets, chasin' her through the woods. She wakes up screamin' and sweatin'. The doctor says she needs to see a psychiatrist. Says it'll get worse before it gets better.'

'How much will it cost?'

'I don't know. I haven't called yet.'

'Better call. Where is this psychiatrist?'

'Memphis.'

'Figures.'

'How are the boys treatin' her?'

'They've been great. They treat her special. But the nightmares keep them scared. When she wakes up screamin' she wakes everybody. The boys run to her bed and try to help, but it scares them. Last night she wouldn't go back to sleep unless the boys slept on the floor next to her. We all laid there wide awake with the lights on.'

'The boys'll be all right.'

'They miss their daddy.'

Carl Lee managed a forced smile. 'It won't be much longer.'

'You really think so?'

'I don't know what to think anymore. But I don't plan to spend the rest of my life in jail. I hired Jake back.'

'When?'

'Yesterday. That Memphis lawyer never showed up, never even called. I fired him and hired Jake again.'

'But you said Jake is too young.'

'I was wrong. He is young, but he's good. Ask Lester.'

'It's your trial.'

Carl Lee walked slowly around the yard, never leaving the fence. He thought of the two boys, somewhere out there, dead and buried, their flesh rotting by now, their souls burning in hell. Before they died, they met his little girl, only briefly, and within two hours wrecked her little body and ruined her mind. So brutal was their attack that she could never have children; so violent the encounter that she now saw them hiding for her, waiting in closets. Could she ever forget about it, block it out, erase it from her mind so her life would be normal? Maybe a psychiatrist could do that. Would other children allow her to be normal?

She was just a little nigger, they probably thought. Somebody's little nigger kid. Illegitimate, of course, like all of them. Rape would be nothing new.

He remembered them in court. One proud, the other scared. He remembered them coming down the stairs as he awaited the execution. Then, the looks of horror as he stepped forward with the M-16. The sound of the gunfire, the cries for help, the screams as they fell backward together, one on top of the other, handcuffed, screaming and twisting, going nowhere. He remembered smiling, even laughing, as he watched them struggle with their heads half blown away, and when their bodies were still, he ran.

He smiled again. He was proud of it. The first gook he killed in Vietnam had bothered him more.

The letter to Walter Sullivan was to the point:

Dear J. Walter:

By now it's safe to assume Mr. Marsharfsky has informed you that his employment by Carl Lee Hailey has been terminated. Your services as local counsel will, of course, no longer be needed. Have a nice day.

Sincerely,

Jake

A copy was sent to L. Winston Lotterhouse. The letter to Noose was just as short:

Dear Judge Noose:

Please be advised that I have been retained by Carl Lee Hailey. We are preparing for trial on July 22. Please show me as counsel of record.

Sincerely,

Jake

A copy was sent to Buckley.

Marsharfsky called at nine-thirty Monday. Jake watched the hold button blink for two minutes before he lifted the receiver. 'Hello.'

'How'd you do it?'

'Who is this?'

'Your secretary didn't tell you? This is Bo Marsharfsky, and I want to know how you did it.'

'Did what?'

'Hustled my case.'

Stay cool, thought Jake. He's an agitator. 'As I recall, it was hustled from me,' replied Jake.

'I never met him before he hired me.'

'You didn't have to. You sent your pimp, remember?'

'Are you accusing me of chasing cases?'

'Yes.'

Marsharfsky paused and Jake braced for the obscenities.

'You know something, Mr. Brigance, you're right. I chase cases every day. I'm a pro at hustling cases. That's how I make so much money. If there's a big criminal case, I intend to get it. And I'll use whatever method I find necessary.'

'Funny, that wasn't mentioned in the paper.'

'And if I want the Hailey case, I'll get it.'

'Come on down.' Jake hung up and laughed for ten minutes. He lit a cheap cigar, and began working on his motion for a change of venue.

Two days later Lucien called and instructed Ethel to instruct Jake to come see him. It was important. He had a visitor Jake needed to meet.

The visitor was Dr. W.T. Bass, a retired psychiatrist from Jackson. He had known Lucien for years, and they had collaborated on a couple of insane criminals during their friendship. Both of the criminals were still in Parchman. His retirement had been one year before the disbarment and had been precipitated by the same thing that contributed heavily to the disbarment, to wit, a strong affection for Jack Daniel's. He visited Lucien occasionally in Clanton, and Lucien visited him more frequently in Jackson, and they enjoyed their visits because they enjoyed staying drunk together. They sat on the big porch and waited on Jake.

'Just say he was insane,' instructed Lucien.

'Was he?' asked the doctor.

'That's not important.'

'What is important?'

'It's important to give the jury an excuse to acquit the man. They won't care if he's crazy or not. But they'll need some reason to acquit him.'

'It would be nice to examine him.'

'You can. You can talk to him all you want. He's at the jail just waiting on someone to talk to.'

'I'll need to meet with him several times.'

'I know that.'

'What if I don't think he was insane at the time of the shooting?'

'Then you won't get to testify at trial, and you won't get your name and picture in the paper, and you won't be interviewed on TV.'

Lucien paused long enough to take a long drink. 'Just do as I say. Interview him, take a bunch of notes. Ask stupid questions. You know what to do. Then say he was crazy.'

'I'm not so sure about this. It hasn't worked too well in the past.'

'Look, you're a doctor, aren't you? Then act proud, vain, arrogant. Act like a doctor's supposed to act. Give your opinion and dare anyone to question it.'

'I don't know. It hasn't worked too well in the past.'

'Just do as I say.'

'I've done that before, and they're both at Parchman.'

'They were hopeless. Hailey's different.'

'Does he have a chance?'

'Slim.'

'I thought you said he was different.'

'He's a decent man with a good reason for killing.'

'Then why are his chances slim?'

'The law says his reason is not good enough.'

'That's par for the law.'

'Plus he's black, and this is a white county. I have no confidence in these bigots around here.'

'And if he were white?'

'If he were white and he killed two blacks who raped his daughter, the jury would give him the courthouse.'

Bass finished one glass and poured another. A fifth and a bucket of ice sat on the wicker table between the two.

'What about his lawyer?' he asked.

'He should be here in a minute.'

'He used to work for you?'

'Yeah, but I don't think you met him. He was in the firm about two years before I left. He's young, early thirties. Clean, aggressive, works hard.'

'And he used to work for you?'

'That's what I said. He's got trial experience for his age. This is not his first murder case, but, if I'm not mistaken, it's his first insanity case.'

'That's nice to hear. I don't want someone asking a lot of questions.'

'I like your confidence. Wait till you meet the D.A.'

'I just don't feel good about this. We tried it twice, and it didn't work.'

Lucien shook his head in bewilderment. 'You've got to be the humblest doctor I've known.'

'And the poorest.'

'You're supposed to be pompous and arrogant. You're the expert. Act like one. Who's gonna question your professional opinion in Clanton, Mississippi?'

'The State will have experts.'

'They will have one psychiatrist from Whitfield. He'll examine the defendant for a few hours, and then drive up for trial and testify that the defendant is the sanest man he's ever met. He's never seen a legally insane defendant. To him no one is insane. Everybody's blessed with perfect mental health. Whitfield is full of sane people, except when it applies for government money, then half the state's crazy. He'd get fired if he started saying defendants are legally insane. So that's who you're up against.'

'And the jury will automatically believe me?'

'You act as though you've never been through one of these before.'

'Twice, remember. One rapist, one murderer. Neither was insane, in spite of what I said. Both are now locked away where they belong.'

Lucien took a long drink and studied the light brown liquid and the floating ice cubes. 'You said you would help me. God knows you owe me the favor. How many divorces did I handle for you?'

'Three. And I got cleaned out every time.'

'You deserved it every time. It was either give in or go to trial and have your habits discussed in open court.'

'I remember.'

'How many clients, or patients, have I sent you over the years?'

'Not enough to pay my alimony.'

'Remember the malpractice case by the lady whose treatment consisted primarily of weekly sessions on your couch with the foldaway bed? Your malpractice carrier refused to defend, so you called your dear friend Lucien who settled it for peanuts and kept it out of court.'

'There were no witnesses.'

'Just the lady herself. And the court files showing where your wives had sued for divorce on the grounds of adultery.'

'They couldn't prove it.'

'They didn't get a chance. We didn't want them to try, remember?'

'All right, enough, enough. I said I would help. What about my credentials?'

'Are you a compulsive worrier?'

'No. I just get nervous when I think of courtrooms.'

'Your credentials are fine. You've been qualified before as an expert witness. Don't worry so much.'

'What about this?' He waved his drink at Lucien.

'You shouldn't drink so much,' he said piously.

The doctor dropped his drink and exploded in laughter. He rolled out of his chair and crawled to the edge of the porch, holding his stomach and shaking in laughter.

'You're drunk,' Lucien said as he left for another bottle.

When Jake arrived an hour later, Lucien was rocking slowly in his huge wicker rocker. The doctor was asleep in the swing at the far end of the porch. He was barefoot, and his toes had disappeared into the shrubbery that lined the porch. Jake walked up the steps and startled Lucien.

'Jake, my boy, how are you?' he slurred.

'Fine, Lucien. I see you're doing quite well.' He looked at the empty bottle and one not quite empty.

'I wanted you to meet that man,' he said, trying to sit up straight.

'Who is he?'

'He's our psychiatrist. Dr. W.T. Bass, from Jackson. Good friend of mine. He'll help us with Hailey.'

'Is he good?'

'The best. We've worked together on several insanity cases.'

Jake took a few steps in the direction of the swing and stopped. The doctor was lying on his back with his shirt unbuttoned and his mouth wide open. He snored heavily, with an unusual guttural gurgling sound. A horsefly the size of a small sparrow buzzed around his nose and retreated to the top of the swing with each thunderous exhalation. A rancid vapor emanated with the snoring and hung like an invisible fog over the end of the porch.

'He's a doctor?' Jake asked as he sat next to Lucien.

'Psychiatry,' Lucien said proudly.

'Did he help you with those?' Jake nodded at the bottles.

'I helped him. He drinks like a fish, but he's always sober at trial.'

'That's comforting.'

'You'll like him. He's cheap. Owes me a favor. Won't cost a dime.'

'I like him already.'

Lucien's face was as red as his eyes. 'Wanna drink?'

'No. It's three-thirty in the afternoon.'

'Really! What day is it?'

'Wednesday, June 12. How long have y'all been drinking?'

' 'Bout thirty years.' Lucien laughed and rattled his ice cubes.

'I mean today.'

'We drank our breakfast. What difference does it make?'

'Does he work?'

'Naw, he's retired.'

'Was his retirement voluntary?'

'You mean, was he disbarred, so to speak?'

'That's right, so to speak.'

'No. He still has his license, and his credentials are impeccable.'

'He looks impeccable.'

'Booze got him a few years ago. Booze and alimony. I handled three of his divorces. He reached the point where all of his income went for alimony and child support, so he quit working.'

'How does he manage?'

'We, uh, I mean, he stashed some away. Hid it from his wives and their hungry lawyers. He's really quite comfortable.'

'He looks comfortable.'

'Plus he peddles a little dope, but only to a rich clientele. Not really dope, but narcotics which he can legally prescribe. It's not really illegal; just a little unethical.'

'What's he doing here?'

'He visits occasionally. He lives in Jackson but hates it. I called him Sunday after I talked to you. He wants to meet Hailey as soon as possible, tomorrow if he can.'

The doctor grunted and rolled to his side, causing the swing to move suddenly. It swung a few times, and he moved again, still snoring. He stretched his right leg, and his foot caught a thick branch in the shrubbery. The swing jerked sideways and threw the good doctor onto the porch. His head crashed onto the wooden floor while his right foot remained lodged through the end of the swing. He grimaced and coughed, then began snoring again. Jake instinctively started toward him, but stopped when it was apparent he was unharmed and still asleep.

'Leave him alone!' ordered Lucien between laughs.

Lucien slid an ice cube down the porch and just missed the doctor's head. The second cube landed perfectly on the tip of his nose. 'Perfect shot!' Lucien roared. 'Wake up, you drunk!'

Jake walked down the steps toward his car, listening to his former boss laugh and curse and throw ice cubes at Dr. W.T. Bass, psychiatrist, witness for the defense.

Deputy DeWayne Looney left the hospital on crutches, and drove his wife and three children to the jail, where the sheriff, the other deputies, the reserves, and a few friends waited with a cake and small gifts. He would be a dispatcher now, and would retain his badge and uniform and full salary.

CHAPTER TWENTY-ONE

The fellowship hall of the Springdale Church had been thoroughly cleaned and shined, and the folding tables and chairs dusted and placed in perfect rows around the room. It was the largest black church in the county and it was in Clanton, so the Reverend Agee deemed it necessary to meet there. The purpose of the press conference was to get vocal, to show support of the local boy who made good, and to announce the establishment of the Carl Lee Hailey Legal Defense Fund. The national director of the NAACP was present with a five-thousand-dollar check and a promise of serious money later. The executive director of the Memphis branch brought five thousand and grandly laid it on the table. They sat with Agee behind the two folding tables in the front of the room with every member of the council seated behind them and two hundred black church members in the crowded audience. Gwen sat next to Agee. A few reporters and cameras, much fewer than expected, grouped in the center of the room and filmed away.

Agee spoke first and was inspired by the cameras. He talked of the Haileys and their goodness and innocence, and of baptizing Tonya when she was only eight. He talked of a family wrecked by racism and hatred. There were sniffles in the audience. Then he got mean. He tore into the judicial system and its desire to prosecute a good and decent man who had done no wrong; a man, who, if white, would not be on trial; a man who was on trial only because he was black and that was what was so wrong with the prosecution and persecution of Carl Lee Hailey. He found his rhythm and the crowd joined in, and the press conference took on the fervor of a tent revival. He lasted for forty-five minutes.

He was a hard act to follow. But the national director did not hesitate. He delivered a thirty-minute oratorical condemnation of racism. He seized the moment and spouted national statistics on crime and arrests and convictions and inmate population and summed it all up by declaring that the criminal justice system was controlled by white people who unfairly persecuted black people. Then in a bewildering flurry of rationale he brought the national statistics to Ford County and pronounced the system unfit to deal with Carl Lee Hailey. The lights from the TV cameras produced a line of sweat above his eyebrows and he warmed to the task. He got angrier than Reverend Agee and pounded the podium and made the cluster of microphones jump and shake. He exhorted the blacks of Ford County and of Mississippi to give until it hurt. He promised demonstrations and marches. The trial would be a battle cry for black and oppressed folk everywhere.

He answered questions. How much money would be raised? At least fifty thousand, they hoped. It would be expensive to defend Carl Lee Hailey and fifty thousand may not be enough, but they would raise whatever it took. But time was running short. Where would the money go? Legal fees and litigation expenses. A battery of lawyers and doctors would be needed. Would NAACP lawyers be used? Of course. The legal staff in Washington was already at work on the case. The capital defense unit would handle all aspects of the trial. Carl Lee Hailey had become their top priority and all available resources would be devoted to his defense.

When he finished, Reverend Agee retook the podium and nodded at a piano player in the corner. The music started. They all stood, hand in hand, and sang a stirring rendition of 'We Shall Overcome.'

Jake read about the defense fund in Tuesday's paper. He had heard rumors of the special offering being administered by the council, but was told the money was for the support of the family. Fifty thousand for legal fees! He was angry, but interested. Would he be fired again? Suppose Carl Lee refused to hire the NAACP lawyers, what would happen to the money? The trial was five weeks away, plenty of time for the capital defense team to descend on Clanton. He had read about these guys; a team of six capital murder specialists who toured the South defending blacks accused of heinous and notorious crimes. 'The Death Squad' was their nickname. They were very bright, very talented, very educated lawyers dedicated to rescuing black murderers from the various gas chambers and electric chairs around the South. They handled nothing but capital murder cases and were very, very good at their work. The NAACP ran their interference, raising money, organizing local blacks, and generating publicity. Racism was their best, and sometimes only, defense and though they lost much more than they won, their record was not bad. The cases they handled were supposed to be lost, all of them. Their goal was to martyr the defendant before the trial and hopefully hang the jury.

Now they were coming to Clanton.

A week earlier Buckley had filed the proper motions to have Carl Lee examined by the State's doctors. Jake requested the doctors be required to conduct their examinations in Clanton, preferably in Jake's office. Noose declined, and ordered the sheriff to transport Carl Lee to the Mississippi State Mental Hospital at Whitfield. Jake requested that he be allowed to accompany his client and be present during the examinations. Again, Noose declined.

Early Wednesday morning, Jake and Ozzie sipped coffee in the sheriff's office and waited for Carl Lee to shower and change clothes. Whitfield was three hours away, and he was to check in at nine. Jake had final instructions for his client.

'How long will y'all be there?' Jake asked Ozzie.

'You're the lawyer. How long will it take?'

'Three or four days. You've been there before, haven't you?'

'Sure, we've had to transport plenty of crazy people. But nothin' like this. Where do they keep him?'

'They've got all kinds of cells.'

Deputy Hastings casually entered the office, sleepy-eyed and crunching on a stale doughnut. 'How many cars we takin'?'

'Two,' answered Ozzie. 'I'll drive mine and you drive yours. I'll take Pirtle and Carl Lee, you take Riley and Nesbit.'

'Guns?'

'Three shotguns in each car. Plenty of shells. Everbody wears a vest, includin' Carl Lee. Get the cars ready. I'd like to leave by five-thirty.'

Hastings mumbled something and disappeared.

'Are you expecting trouble?' Jake asked.

'We've had some phone calls. Two in particular mentioned the trip to Whitfield. Lot of highway between here and there.'

'How are you going?'

'Most folks take 22 to the interstate, wouldn't you say? It might be safer to take some smaller highways. We'll probably run 14 south to 89.'

'That would be unexpected.'

'Good. I'm glad you approve.'

'He's my client, you know.'

'For right now, anyway.'

Carl Lee quickly devoured the eggs and biscuits as Jake briefed him on what to expect during the stay at Whitfield.

'I know, Jake. You want me to act crazy, right?' Carl Lee said with a laugh. Ozzie thought it was funny too.

'This is serious, Carl Lee. Listen to me.'

'Why? You said yourself it won't matter what I say or do down there. They won't say I was insane when I shot them. Them doctors work for the State, right? The State's prosecutin' me, right? What difference does it make what I say or do? They've already made up their minds. Ain't that right, Ozzie?'

'I'm not gettin' involved. I work for the State.'

'You work for the County,' said Jake.

'Name, rank, and serial number. That's all they're gettin' outta me,' Carl Lee said as he emptied a small paper sack.

'Very funny,' said Jake.

'He's crackin' up, Jake,' Ozzie said.

Carl Lee stuck two straws up his nose and began tiptoeing around the office, staring at the ceiling and then grabbing at something above his head. He put it in the sack. He lunged at another one and put it in the sack. Hastings returned and stopped in the door. Carl Lee grinned at him with wild eyes, then grabbed at another one toward the ceiling.

'What the hell he's doin'?' Hastings asked.

'Catchin' butterflies,' Carl Lee said.

Jake grabbed his briefcase and headed for the door. 'I think you should leave him at Whitfield.' He slammed the door and left the jail.

Noose had scheduled the venue hearing for Monday, June 24, in Clanton. The hearing would be long and well publicized. Jake had requested the change of venue, and he had the burden of proving Carl Lee could not receive a fair and impartial trial in Ford County. He needed witnesses. Persons with credibility in the community who were willing to testify that a fair trial was not possible. Atcavage said he might do it as a favour, but the bank might not want him involved. Harry Rex had eagerly volunteered. Reverend Agee said he would be glad to testify, but that was before the NAACP announced its lawyers would be handling the case. Lucien had no credibility, and Jake did not seriously consider asking him.

Buckley, on the other hand, would line up a dozen credible witnesses – elected officials, lawyers, businessmen, maybe other sheriffs – all of whom would testify that they had vaguely heard of Carl Lee Hailey and he could most certainly receive a fair trial in Clanton.

Jake personally preferred the trial to be in Clanton, in his courthouse across the street from his office, in front of his people. Trials were pressure-filled, tedious, sleepless ordeals. It would be nice to have this one in a friendly arena, three minutes from his driveway. When the trial recessed, he could spend the free moments in his office doing research, preparing witnesses or relaxing. He could eat at the Coffee Shop or Claude's or even run home for a quick lunch. His client could remain in the Ford County jail, near his family.

And, of course, his media exposure would be much greater. The reporters would gather in front of his office each morning of the trial and follow him as he walked slowly toward the courthouse. That thought was exciting.

Did it matter where they tried Carl Lee Hailey? Lucien was correct: the publicity had reached every resident of every county in Mississippi. So why change venue? His guilt or innocence had already been prejudged by every prospective juror in the state.

Sure it mattered. Some prospective jurors were white and some were black. Percentage-wise, there would be more white ones in Ford County than the surrounding counties. Jake loved black jurors, especially in criminal cases and especially when the criminal was black. They were not as anxious to convict. They were open minded. He preferred them in civil cases, too. They felt for the underdog against the big corporation or insurance company, and they were more liberal with other people's money. As a rule, he picked all the black jurors he could find, but they were scarce in Ford County.

It was imperative the case be tried in another county, a blacker county. One black could hang the jury. A majority could force, maybe, an acquittal. Two weeks in a motel and strange courthouse was not appealing, but the small discomforts were greatly outweighed by the need to have black faces in the jury box.

The venue question had been thoroughly researched by Lucien. As instructed, Jake arrived promptly, although reluctantly, at 8.00 A.M. Sallie served breakfast on the porch. Jake drank coffee and orange juice; Lucien bourbon and water. For three hours they covered every aspect of a change of venue. Lucien had copies of every Supreme Court case for the past eighty years, and lectured like a professor. The pupil took notes, argued once or twice, but mainly listened.

Whitfield was located a few miles from Jackson in a rural part of Rankin County. Two guards waited by the front gate and argued with reporters. Carl Lee was scheduled to arrive at nine, that was all the guards knew. At eight-thirty two patrol cars with Ford County insignia rolled to a stop at the gate. The reporters and their cameramen ran to the driver of the first car. Ozzie's window was down.

'Where's Carl Lee Hailey?' a reporter shouted in a panic.

'He's in the other car,' Ozzie drawled, winking at Carl Lee in the back seat.

'He's in the second car!' someone shouted, and they ran to Hastings' car.

'Where's Hailey?' they demanded.

Pirtle, in the front seat, pointed to Hastings, the driver. 'That's him.'

'Are you Carl Lee Hailey?' a reporter screamed at Hastings.

'Yep.'

'Why are you driving?'

'What's with the uniform?'

'They made me a deputy,' answered Hastings with a straight face. The gate opened, and the two cars sped through.

Carl Lee was processed in the main building and led, along with

Ozzie and the deputies, to another building where he was checked into his cell, or room, as it was called. The door was locked behind him. Ozzie and his men were excused and returned to Clanton.

After lunch, an assistant of some sort with a clipboard and white jacket arrived and began asking questions. Starting with birth, he asked Carl Lee about every significant event and person in his life. It lasted two hours. At 4:00 P.M., two security guards handcuffed Carl Lee and rode him in a golf cart to a modern brick building a half mile from his room. He was led to the office of Dr. Wilbert Rodeheaver, head of staff. The guards waited in the hall by the door.

CHAPTER TWENTY-TWO

It had been five weeks since the shootings of Billy Ray Cobb and Pete Willard. The trial was four weeks away. The three motels in Clanton were booked solid for the week of the trial and the week before. The Best Western was the largest and nicest, and had attracted the Memphis and Jackson press. The Clanton Court had the best bar and restaurant, and was booked by reporters from Atlanta, Washington, and New York. At the less than elegant East Side Motel the rates had curiously doubled for the month of July but it had nonetheless sold out.

The town had been friendly at first to these outsiders, most of whom were rude and spoke with different accents. But some of the descriptions of Clanton and its people had been less than flattering, and most of the locals now honored a secret code of silence. A noisy cafe would become instantly silent when a stranger walked in and took a seat. Merchants around the square offered little assistance to anyone they did not recognize. The employees in the courthouse had become deaf to questions asked a thousand times by nosy intruders. Even the Memphis and Jackson reporters had to struggle to extract anything new from the locals. The people were tired of being described as backward, redneck, and racist. They ignored the outsiders whom they could not trust and went about their business.

The bar at the Clanton Court became the watering hole for the reporters. It was the one place in town they could go to find a friendly face and good conversation. They sat in the booths under the big-screen TV and gossiped about the small town and the upcoming trial. They compared notes and stories and leads and rumors, and drank until they were drunk because there was nothing else to do in Clanton after dark.

The motels filled Sunday night, June 23, the night before the venue hearing. Early Monday morning they gathered in the restaurant at the Best Western to drink coffee and speculate. The hearing was the first major skirmish, and could likely be the only courtroom action until the trial. A rumor surfaced that Noose was ill and did not want to hear the case, and that he would ask the Supreme Court to appoint another judge. Just a rumor, with no source and nothing more definite, said a reporter from Jackson. At eight they packed their cameras and microphones and left for the square. One group set up outside the jail, another at the rear of the courthouse, but most headed for the courtroom. By eight-thirty it was filled.

From the balcony of his office, Jake watched the activity around the courthouse. His heart beat faster than normal, and his stomach tingled. He smiled. He was ready for Buckley, ready for the cameras.

Noose looked down past the end of his nose, over his reading glasses, and around the packed courtroom. Everyone was in place.

'The court has before it,' he began, 'the defendant's motion for a change of venue. The trial in this matter has been set for Monday, July 22. That's four weeks from today, according to my calendar. I have set a deadline for filing motions and disposing of same, and I believe those are the only two deadlines between now and trial.'

'That's correct, Your Honor,' thundered Buckley, half standing behind his table. Jake rolled his eyes and shook his head.

'Thank you, Mr. Buckley,' Noose said dryly. 'The defendant has filed the proper notice that he intends to use an insanity defense. Has he been examined at Whitfield?'

'Yes sir, Your Honor, last week,' Jake answered.

'Will he employ his own psychiatrist?'

'Of course, Your Honor.'

'Has he been examined by his own?'

'Yes, sir.'

'Good. So that's out of the way. What other motions do you anticipate filing?'

'Your Honor, we expect to file a motion requesting the clerk to summons more than the usual number of prospective jurors –'

'The State will oppose that motion,' Buckley yelled as he jumped to his feet.

'Sit down, Mr. Buckley!' Noose said sternly, ripping off his glasses and glaring at the D.A. 'Please don't yell at me again. Of course you will oppose it. You will oppose any motion filed by the defense. That's your job. Don't interrupt again. You'll have ample opportunity after we adjourn to perform for the media.'

Buckley slumped in his chair and hid his red face. Noose had never screamed at him before.

'Continue, Mr. Brigance.'

Jake was startled by Ichabod's meanness. He looked tired and ill. Perhaps it was the pressure.

'We may have some written objections to anticipated evidence.'

'Motions *in limine*?'

'Yes, sir.'

'We'll hear those at trial. Anything else?'

'Not at this time.'

'Now, Mr. Buckley, will the State file any motions?'

'I can't think of any,' Buckley answered meekly.

'Good. I want to make sure there are no surprises between now and trial. I will be here one week before trial to hear and decide any pretrial matters. I expect any motions to be filed promptly, so that we can tie up any loose ends well before the twenty-second.'

Noose flipped through his file and studied Jake's motion for a change of venue. Jake whispered to Carl Lee, whose presence was not required for the hearing, but he insisted. Gwen and the three boys sat in the first row behind their daddy. Tonya was not in the courtroom.

'Mr. Brigance, your motion appears to be in order. How many witnesses?'

'Three, Your Honor.'

'Mr. Buckley, how many will you call?'

'We have twenty-one,' Buckley said proudly.

'Twenty-one!' yelled the judge.

Buckley cowered and glanced at Musgrove. 'B-but, we probably won't need them all. In fact, I know we won't call all of them.'

'Pick your best five, Mr. Buckley. I don't plan to be here all day.'

'Yes, Your Honor.'

'Mr. Brigance, you've asked for a change of venue. It's your motion. You may proceed.'

Jake stood and walked slowly across the courtroom, behind Buckley, to the wooden podium in front of the jury box. 'May it please the court, Your Honor, Mr. Hailey has requested that his trial be moved from Ford County. The reason is obvious: the publicity in this case will prevent a fair trial. The good people of this county have prejudged the guilt or innocence of Carl Lee Hailey. He is charged with killing two men, both of whom were born here and left families here. Their lives were not famous, but their deaths certainly have been. Mr. Hailey was known by few outside his community until now. Now everyone in this county knows who he is, knows about his family and his daughter and what happened to her, and knows most of the details of his alleged crimes. It will be impossible to find twelve people in Ford County who have not already prejudged this case. This trial should be held in another part of the state where the people are not so familiar with the facts.'

'Where would you suggest?' interrupted the judge.

'I wouldn't recommend a specific county, but it should be as far away as possible. Perhaps the Gulf Coast.'

'Why?'

'Obvious reasons, Your Honor. It's four hundred miles away, and I'm sure the people down there do not know as much as the people around here.'

'And you think the people in south Mississippi haven't heard about it?'

'I'm sure they have. But they are much further away.'

'But they have televisions and newspapers, don't they, Mr. Brigance?'

'I'm sure they do.'

'Do you believe you could go to any county in this state and find twelve people who haven't heard the details of this case?'

Jake looked at his legal pad. He could hear the artists sketching on their pads behind him. He could see Buckley grinning out of the corner of his eye. 'It would be difficult,' he said quietly.

'Call your first witness.'

Harry Rex Vonner was sworn in and took his seat on the witness stand. The wooden swivel chair popped and creaked under the heavy load. He blew into the microphone and a loud hiss echoed around the courtroom. He smiled at Jake and nodded.

'Would you state your name?'

'Harry Rex Vonner.'

'And your address?'

'Eighty-four ninety-three Cedarbrush, Clanton, Mississippi.'

'How long have you lived in Clanton?'

'All my life. Forty-six years.'

'Your occupation?'

'I'm a lawyer. I've had my license for twenty-two years.'

'Have you ever met Carl Lee Hailey?'

'Once.'

'What do you know about him?'

'He supposedly shot two men, Billy Ray Cobb and Pete Willard, and he wounded a deputy, DeWayne Looney.'

'Did you know either of those boys?'

'Not personally. I knew of Billy Ray Cobb.'

'How did you learn of the shootings?'

'Well, it happened on a Monday, I believe. I was in the courthouse, on the first floor, checking title on some land in the clerk's office, when I heard the gunshots. I ran out into the hall and bedlam had broken loose. I asked a deputy and he told me that the boys had been killed near the back door of the courthouse. I hung around here for a while, and pretty soon there was a rumor that the killer was the father of the little girl who got raped.'

'What was your initial reaction?'

'I was shocked, like most people. But I was shocked when I first heard of the rape too.'

'When did you learn that Mr. Hailey had been arrested?'

'Later that night. It was all over the television.'

'What did you see on TV?'

'Well, I watched as much of it as I could. There were news reports from the local stations in Memphis and Tupelo. We've got the cable, you know, so I watched the news out of New York, Chicago, and Atlanta. Just about every channel had something about the shootings and the arrest. There was footage from the courthouse and jail. It was a big deal. Biggest thing that ever happened in Clanton, Mississippi.'

'How did you react when you learned that the girl's father had supposedly done the shooting?'

'It was no big surprise to me. I mean, we all sort of figured it was him. I admired him. I've got kids, and I sympathize with what he did. I still admire him.'

'How much do you know about the rape?'

Buckley leapt to his feet. 'Objection! The rape is irrelevant!'

Noose ripped off his glasses again and stared angrily at the D.A. Seconds passed and Buckley glanced at the table. He shifted his weight from one foot to the next, then sat down. Noose leaned forward and glared down from the bench.

'Mr. Buckley, don't yell at me. If you do it again, so help me God, I will hold you in contempt. You may be correct, the rape may be irrelevant. But this is not the trial, is it? This is simply a hearing, isn't it? We don't have a jury in the box, do we? You're overruled and out of order. Now stay in your seat. I know it's hard with this sort of audience, but I instruct you to stay in your seat unless you have something truly worthy to say. At that point, you may stand and politely and quietly tell me what's on your mind.'

'Thank you, Your Honor,' Jake said as he smiled at Buckley. 'Now, Mr. Vonner, as I was saying, how much do you know about the rape?'

'Just what I've heard.'

'And what's that?'

Buckley stood and bowed like a Japanese sumo wrestler. 'If Your Honor please,' he said softly and sweetly, 'I would like to object at this point, if it pleases the court. The witness may testify to only what he knows from first-hand knowledge, not from what he's heard from other people.'

Noose answered just as sweetly. 'Thank you, Mr. Buckley. Your objection is noted, and you are overruled. Please continue, Mr. Brigance.'

'Thank you, Your Honor.'

'What have you heard about the rape?'

'Cobb and Willard grabbed the little Hailey girl and took her out in the woods somewhere. They were drunk, they tied her to a tree, raped her repeatedly and tried to hang her. They even urinated on her.'

'They what!' asked Noose.

'They pissed on her, Judge.'

The courtroom buzzed at this revelation. Jake had never heard it, Buckley hadn't heard it, and evidently no one knew it but Harry Rex. Noose shook his head and lightly rapped his gavel.

Jake scribbled something on his legal pad and marveled at his friend's esoteric knowledge. 'Where did you learn about the rape?'

'All over town. It's common knowledge. The cops were giving the details the next morning at the Coffee Shop. Everybody knows it.'

'Is it common knowledge throughout the county?'

'Yes. I haven't talked to anybody in a month who did not know the details of the rape.'

'Tell us what you know about the shootings.'

'Well, like I said, it was a Monday afternoon. The boys were here in this courtroom for a bail hearing, I believe, and when they left the courtroom they were handcuffed and led by the deputies down the back stairs. When they got down the stairs, Mr. Hailey jumped out of a closet with an M-16. They were killed and DeWayne Looney was shot. Part of his leg was amputated.'

'Exactly where did this take place?'

'Right below us here, at the rear entrance of the courthouse. Mr. Hailey was hiding in a janitor's closet and just stepped out and opened fire.'

'Do you believe this to be true?'

'I know it's true.'

'Where did you learn all this?'

'Here and there. Around town. In the newspapers. Everybody knows about it.'

'Where have you heard it discussed?'

'Everywhere. In bars, in churches, at the bank, at the cleaners, at the Tea Shoppe, at the cafes around town, at the liquor store. Everywhere.'

'Have you talked to anyone who believes Mr. Hailey did not kill Billy Ray Cobb and Pete Willard?'

'No, You won't find a single person in this county who believes he didn't do it.'

'Have most folks around here made up their minds about his guilt or innocence?'

'Every single one of them. There are no fence straddlers on this one. It's a hot topic, and everyone has an opinion.'

'In your opinion, could Mr. Hailey receive a fair trial in Ford County?'

'No. sir. You couldn't find three people in this county of thirty thousand who have not already made up their minds, one way or the other. Mr. Hailey has been judged already. There's just no way to find an impartial jury.'

'Thank you, Mr. Vonner. No further questions, Your Honor.' Buckley patted his pompadour and ran his fingers over his ears to make sure every hair was in place. He walked purposefully to the podium.

'Mr. Vonner,' he bellowed magnificently, 'have you already prejudged Carl Lee Hailey?'

'Damn right I have.'

'Your language, please,' said Noose.

'And what would your judgment be?'

'Mr. Buckley, let me explain it this way. And I'll do so very carefully and slowly so that even you will understand it. If I was the sheriff, I would not have arrested him. If I was on the grand jury, I would not have indicted him. If I was the judge, I would not try him. If I was the D.A., I would not prosecute him. If I was on the trial jury, I would vote to give him a key to the city, a plaque to hang on his wall, and I would send him home to his family. And, Mr. Buckley, if my daughter is ever raped, I hope I have the guts to do what he did.'

'I see. You think people should carry guns and settle their disputes in shootouts?'

'I think children have a right not to be raped, and their parents have the right to protect them. I think little girls are special, and if mine was tied to a tree and gang raped by two dopeheads I'm sure it would make me crazy. I think good and decent fathers should have a constitutional right to execute any pervert who touches their children. And I think you're a lying coward when you claim you would not want to kill the man who raped your daughter.'

'Mr. Vonner, please!' Noose said.

Buckley struggled, but kept his cool. 'You obviously feel very strongly about this case, don't you?'

'You're very perceptive.'

'And you want to see him acquitted, don't you?'

'I would pay money, if I had any.'

'And you think he stands a better chance of acquittal in another county, don't you?'

'I think he's entitled to a jury made up of people who don't know everything about the case before the trial starts.'

'You would acquit him, wouldn't you?'

'That's what I said.'

'And you've no doubt talked to other people who would acquit him?'

'I have talked to many.'

'Are there folks in Ford County who would vote to convict him?'

'Of course. Plenty of them. He's black, isn't he?'

'In all your discussions around the county, have you detected a clear majority one way or the other?'

'Not really.'

Buckley looked at his legal pad and made a note. 'Mr. Vonner, is Jake Brigance a close friend of yours?'

Harry Rex smiled and rolled his eyes at Noose. 'I'm a lawyer, Mr. Buckley, my friends are few and far between. But he is one of them. Yes, sir.'

'And he asked you to come testify?'

'No. I just happened to stumble through the courtroom a few moments ago and landed here in this chair. I had no idea you guys were having a hearing this morning.'

Buckley threw his legal pad on the table and sat down. Harry Rex was excused.

'Call your next witness,' Noose ordered.

'Reverend Ollie Agee,' Jake said.

The reverend was led from the witness room and seated in the witness stand. Jake had met him at his church the day before with a list of questions. He wanted to testify. They did not discuss the NAACP lawyers.

The reverend was an excellent witness. His deep, graveled voice needed no microphone as it carried around the courtroom. Yes, he knew the details of the rape and the shooting. They were members of his church. He had known them for years, they were family almost, and he had held their hands and suffered with them after the rape. Yes, he had talked to countless people since it happened and everyone had an opinion on guilt or innocence. He and twenty-two other black ministers were members of the council and they had all talked about the Hailey case. And, no, there were no unmade minds in Ford County. A fair trial was not possible in Ford County, in his opinion.

Buckley asked one question. 'Reverend Agee, have you talked to any black who would vote to convict Carl Lee Hailey?'

'No, suh, I have not.'

The reverend was excused. He took a seat in the courtroom between two of his brethren on the council.

'Call your next witness,' Noose said.

Jake smiled at the D.A., and announced, 'Sheriff Ozzie Walls.'

Buckley and Musgrove immediately locked heads and whispered. Ozzie was on their side, the side of law and order, the prosecution's side. It was not his job to help the defense. Proves you can't trust a nigger, thought Buckley. They take up for each other when they know they're guilty.

Jake led Ozzie through a discussion of the rape and the backgrounds of Cobb and Willard. It was boring and repetitious, and Buckley wanted to object. But he'd been embarrassed enough for one day. Jake sensed that Buckley would remain in his seat so he dwelt on the rape and the gory details. Finally, Noose had enough.

'Move on please, Mr. Brigance.'

'Yes, Your Honor. Sheriff Walls, did you arrest Carl Lee Hailey?'

'I did.'

'Do you believe he killed Billy Ray Cobb and Pete Willard?'

'I do.'

'Have you met anybody in this county who believes he did not shoot them?'

'No, sir.'

'Is it widely believed in this county that Mr. Hailey killed them?'

'Yes. Everbody believes it. At least everbody I've talked to.'

'Sheriff, do you circulate in this county?'

'Yes, sir. It's my job to know what's goin' on.'

'And you talk to a lot of people?'

'More than I would like.'

'Have you run across anyone who hasn't heard of Carl Lee Hailey?'

Ozzie paused and answered slowly. 'A person would have to be deaf, dumb, and blind not to know of Carl Lee Hailey.'

'Have you met anyone without an opinion on his guilt or innocence?'

'There's no such person in this county.'

'Can he get a fair trial here?'

'I don't know about that. I do know you can't find twelve people who don't know all about the rape and the shootin'.'

'No further questions,' Jake said to Noose.

'Is he your last witness?'

'Yes, sir.'

'Any cross-examination, Mr. Buckley?'

Buckley remained in his seat and shook his head.

'Good,' said His Honor. 'Let's take a short recess. I would like to see the attorneys in chambers.'

The courtroom erupted in conversation as the attorneys followed Noose and Mr. Pate through the door beside the bench. Noose closed the door to his chambers and removed his robe. Mr. Pate brought him a cup of black coffee.

'Gentlemen, I am considering imposing a gag order from now until the trial is over. I am disturbed by the publicity, and I don't want this case tried by the press. Any comments?'

Buckley looked pale and shaken. He opened his mouth, but nothing happened.

'Good idea, Your Honor,' Jake said painfully. 'I had considered requesting such an order.'

'Yes, I'm sure you have. I've noticed how you run from publicity. What about you, Mr. Buckley?'

'Uh, who would it apply to?'

'You, Mr. Buckley. You, and Mr. Brigance, would be ordered not to discuss any aspect of the case or the trial with the press. It would apply to everyone, at least everyone under the control of this court. The attorneys, the clerks, the court officials, the sheriff.'

'But why?' asked Buckley.

'I don't like the idea of the two of you trying this case through the media. I'm not blind. You've both fought for the spotlight, and I can only imagine what the trial will be like. A circus, that's what it will be. Not a trial, but a three-ring circus.' Noose walked to the window and mumbled something to himself. He paused for a moment, then continued mumbling. The attorneys looked at each other, then at the awkward frame standing in the window.

'I'm imposing a gag order, effective immediately, from now until the trial is over. Violation of the order will result in contempt of court proceedings. You are not to discuss any aspect of this case with any member of the press. Any questions?'

'No, sir,' Jake said quickly.

Buckley looked at Musgrove and shook his head.

'Now, back to this hearing. Mr. Buckley, you said you have over twenty witnesses. How many do you really need?'

'Five or six.'

'That's much better. Who are they?'

'Floyd Loyd.'

'Who's he?'

'Supervisor, First District, Ford County.'

'What's his testimony?'

'He's lived here for fifty years, been in office ten years or so. In his opinion a fair trial is possible in this county.'

'I suppose he's never heard of this case?' Noose said sarcastically.

'I'm not sure.'

'Who else?'

'Nathan Baker. Justice of the Peace, Third District, Ford County.'

'Same testimony?'

'Well, basically, yes.'

'Who else?'

'Edgar Lee Baldwin, former supervisor, Ford County.'

'He was indicted a few years back, wasn't he?' Jake asked.

Buckley's face turned redder than Jake had ever seen it. His huge mouth dropped open and his eyes glazed over.

'He was not convicted,' shot Musgrove.

'I didn't say he was. I simply said he was indicted. FBI, wasn't it?'

'Enough, enough,' said Noose. 'What will Mr. Baldwin tell us?'

'He's lived here all his life. He knows the people of Ford County, and thinks Mr. Hailey can receive a fair trial here,' Musgrove answered. Buckley remained speechless as he stared at Jake.

'Who else?'

'Sheriff Harry Bryant, Tyler County.'

'Sheriff Bryant? What'll he say?'

Musgrove was talking for the State now. 'Your Honor, we have two theories we are submitting in opposition to the motion for a change of venue. First, we contend a fair trial is possible here in Ford County. Second, if the court is of the opinion that a fair trial is not possible here, the State contends that the immense publicity has reached every prospective juror in this state. The same prejudices and opinions, for and against, which exist in this county exist in every county. Therefore, nothing will be gained by moving the trial. We have witnesses to support this second theory.'

'That's a novel concept, Mr. Musgrove. I don't think I've heard it before.'

'Neither have I,' added Jake.

'Who else do you have?'

'Robert Kelly Williams, district attorney for the Ninth District.'

'Where's that?'

'Southwestern tip of the state.'

'He drove all the way up here to testify that everyone in his neck of the woods has already prejudged the case?'

'Yes, sir.'

'Who else?'

'Grady Liston, district attorney, Fourteenth District.'

'Same testimony?'

'Yes, sir.'

'Is that all?'

'Well, Your Honor, we have several more. But their testimony will pretty much follow the other witnesses'.'

'Good, then we can limit your proof to these six witnesses?'

'Yes, sir.'

'I will hear your proof. I will allow each of you five minutes to conclude your arguments, and I will rule on this motion within two weeks. Any questions?'

CHAPTER TWENTY-THREE

It hurt to say no to the reporters. They followed Jake across Washington Street, where he excused himself, offered his no comments, and sought refuge in his office. Undaunted, a photographer from *Newsweek* pushed his way inside and asked if Jake would pose for a photograph. He wanted one of those important ones with a stern look and thick leather books in the background. Jake straightened his tie and showed the photographer into the conference room, where he posed in court-ordered silence. The photographer thanked him and left.

'May I have a few minutes of your time?' Ethel asked politely as her boss headed for the stairs.

'Certainly.'

'Why don't you sit down. We need to talk.'

She's finally quitting, Jake thought as he took a seat by the front window.

'What's on your mind?'

'Money.'

'You're the highest-paid legal secretary in town. You got a raise three months ago.'

'Not my money. Please listen. You don't have enough in the bank to pay this month's bills. June is almost gone, and we've grossed seventeen hundred dollars.'

Jake closed his eyes and rubbed his forehead.

'Look at these bills,' she said, waving a stack of invoices. 'Four thousand dollars worth. How am I supposed to pay these?'

'How much is in the bank?'

'Nineteen hundred dollars, as of Friday. Nothing came in this morning.'

'Nothing?'

'Not a dime.'

'What about the settlement on the Liford case? That's three thousand in fees.'

'Ethel shook her head. 'Mr. Brigance, that file has not been closed. Mr. Liford has not signed the release. You were to take it by his house. Three weeks ago, remember?'

'No, I don't remember. What about Buck Britt's retainer? That's a thousand dollars.'

'His check bounced. The bank returned it, and it's been on your desk for two weeks.'

She paused and took a deep breath. 'You've stopped seeing clients. You don't return phone calls, and –'

'Don't lecture me, Ethel!'

'And you're a month behind on everything.'

'That's enough.'

'Ever since you took the Hailey case. That's all you think about. You're obsessed with it. It's going to break us.'

'Us! How many paychecks have you missed, Ethel? How many of those bills are past due? Huh?'

'Several.'

'But no more than usual, right?'

'Yes, but what about next month? The trial is four weeks away.'

'Shut up, Ethel. Just shut up. If you can't take the pressure, then quit. If you can't keep your mouth shut, then you're fired.'

'You'd like to fire me, wouldn't you?'

'I could care less.'

She was a tough, hard woman. Fourteen years with Lucien had toughened her skin and hardened her conscience, but she was a woman nonetheless, and at this moment her lip started to quiver, and her eyes watered. She dropped her head.

'I'm sorry,' she muttered. 'I'm just worried.'

'Worried about what?'

'Me and Bud.'

'What's wrong with Bud?'

'He's a very sick man.'

'I know that.'

'His blood pressure keeps acting up. Especially after the phone calls. He's had three strokes in five years, and he's due for another one. He's scared; we're both scared.'

'How many phone calls?'

'Several. They threaten to burn our house or blow it up. They always tell us they know where we live, and if Hailey is acquitted, then they'll burn it or stick dynamite under it while we are asleep. A couple have threatened to kill us. It's just not worth it.'

'Maybe you should quit.'

'And starve? Bud hasn't worked in ten years, you know that. Where else would I work?'

'Look, Ethel, I've had threats too. I don't take them seriously. I promised Carla I'd give up the case before I endangered my family, and you should be comforted by that. You and Bud should relax. The threats are not serious. There are a lot of nuts out there.'

'That's what worries me. People are crazy enough to do something.'

'Naw, you worry too much. I'll tell Ozzie to watch your house a bit closer.'

'Will you do that?'

'Sure. They've been watching mine. Take my word, Ethel, there's nothing to worry about. Probably just some young punks.'

She wiped her eyes. 'I'm sorry for crying, and I'm sorry for being so irritable lately.'

You've been irritable for forty years, Jake thought. 'That's okay.'

'What about these?' she asked, pointing to the invoices.

'I'll get the money. Don't worry about it.'

Willie Hastings finished the second shift at 10.00 P.M. and punched the clock next to Ozzie's office. He drove straight to the Hailey house. It was his night to sleep on the couch. Someone slept on Gwen's couch every night; a brother, a cousin, or a friend. Wednesday was his night.

It was impossible to sleep with the lights on. Tonya refused to go near the bed unless every light in the house was on. Those men could be in the dark, waiting for her. She had seen them many times crawling along the floor toward her bed, and lurking in the closets. She had heard their voices outside her window, and she had seen their bloodshot eyes peering in, watching her as she got ready for bed. She heard noises in the attic, like the footsteps of the bulky cowboy boots they had kicked her with. She knew they were up there, waiting for everyone to go to sleep so they could come down and take her back to the woods. Once a week her mother and oldest brother climbed the folding stairs and inspected the attic with a flashlight and a pistol.

Not a single room in the house could be dark when she went to bed. One night, as she lay wide awake next to her mother, a light in the hall burned out. She screamed violently until Gwen's brother drove to Clanton to an all-night quick shop for more bulbs.

She slept with her mother, who held her firmly for hours until the demons faded into the night and she drifted away. At first, Gwen had trouble with the lights, but after five weeks she napped periodically through the night. The small body next to her wiggled and jerked even while it slept.

Willie said good night to the boys and kissed Tonya. He showed her his gun and promised to stay awake on the couch. He walked through the house and checked the closets. When Tonya was satisfied, she lay next to her mother and stared at the ceiling. She cried softly.

Around midnight, Willie took off his boots and relaxed on the couch. He removed his holster and placed the gun on the floor. He was almost asleep when he heard the scream. It was the horrible, high-pitched cry of a child being tortured. He grabbed his gun and ran to the bedroom. Tonya was sitting on the bed, facing the wall, screaming and shaking. She had seen them in the window, waiting for her. Gwen hugged her. The three boys ran to the foot of the bed and watched helplessly. Carl Lee, Jr., went to the window and saw nothing. They had been through it many times in five weeks, and knew there was little they could do.

Gwen soothed her and laid her head gently on the pillow. 'It's okay, baby, Momma's here and Uncle Willie's here. Nobody's gonna get you. It's okay, baby.'

She wanted Uncle Willie to sit under the window with his gun and the boys to sleep on the floor around the bed. They took their positions. She moaned pitifully for a few moments, then grew quiet and still.

Willie sat on the floor by the window until they were all asleep. He carried the boys one at a time to their beds and tucked them in. He sat under her window and waited for the morning sun.

Jake and Atcavage met for lunch at Claude's on Friday. They ordered ribs and slaw. The place was packed as usual, and for the first time in four weeks there were no strange faces. The regulars talked and gossiped like old times. Claude was in fine form – ranting and scolding and cursing his loyal customers. Claude was one of those rare people who could curse a man and make him enjoy it.

Atcavage had watched the venue hearing, and would have testified had he been needed. The bank had discouraged his testifying, and Jake did not want to cause trouble. Bankers have an innate fear of courtrooms, and Jake admired his friend for overcoming this paranoia and attending the hearing. In doing so, he became the first banker in the history of Ford County to voluntarily appear in a courtroom without a subpoena while court was in session. Jake was proud of him.

Claude raced by and told them they had ten minutes, so shut up and eat. Jake finished a rib and mopped his face. 'Say, Stan, speaking of loans, I need to borrow five thousand for ninety days, unsecured.'

'Who said anything about loans?'

'You said something about banks.'

'I thought we were condemning Buckley. I was enjoying it.'

'You shouldn't criticize, Stan. It's an easy habit to acquire and an impossible one to break. It robs your soul of character.'

'I'm terribly sorry. How can you ever forgive me?'

'About the loan?'

'Okay. Why do you need it?'

'Why is that relevant?'

'What do you mean, "Why is that relevant?" '

'Look Stan, all you should worry about is whether or not I can repay the money in ninety days.'

'Okay. Can you repay the money in ninety days?'

'Good question. Of course I can.'

The banker smiled. 'Hailey's got you bogged down, huh?'

The lawyer smiled. 'Yeah,' he admitted. 'It's hard to concentrate on anything else. The trial is three weeks from Monday, and until then I won't concentrate on anything else.'

'How much will you make off this case?'

'Nine hundred minus ten thousand.'

'Nine hundred dollars!'

'Yeah, he couldn't borrow on his land, remember?'

'Cheap shot.'

'Of course, if you'd loan Carl Lee the money on his land, then I wouldn't have to borrow any.'

'I prefer to loan it to you.'

'Great. When can I get a check?'

'You sound desperate.'

'I know how long you guys take, with your loan committees and auditors and vice-presidents here and vice-presidents there, and maybe a vice-president will finally approve my loan in a month or so, if the manual says he can and if the home office is in the right mood. I know how you operate.'

Atcavage looked at his watch. 'Three o'clock soon enough?'

'I guess.'

'Unsecured?'

Jake wiped his mouth and leaned across the table. He spoke quietly. 'My house is a landmark with landmark mortgages, and you've got the lien on my car, remember? I'll give you the first mortgage on my daughter, but if you try to foreclose I'll kill you. Now what security do you have in mind?'

'Sorry I asked.'

'When can I get the check?'

'Three P.M.'

Claude appeared and refilled the tea glasses. 'You got five minutes,' he said loudly.

'Eight,' replied Jake.

'Listen Mr. Big Shot,' Claude said with a grin. 'This ain't no courtroom, and your picture in the paper ain't worth two cents in here. I said five minutes.'

'Just as well. My ribs were tough anyway.'

'I notice you didn't leave any.'

'Might as well eat them, as much as they cost.'

'They cost more if you complain.'

'We're leaving,' Atcavage said as he stood and threw a dollar on the table.

Sunday afternoon the Haileys picnicked under the tree away from the violence under the basketball goal. The first heatwave of the summer had settled in, and the heavy, sticky humidity hung close to the ground and penetrated the shade. Gwen swatted flies as the children and their daddy ate warm fried chicken and sweated. The children ate hurriedly and ran to a new swing Ozzie had installed for the children of his inmates.

'What'd they do at Whitfield?' Gwen asked.

'Nothin' really. Asked a bunch of questions, made me do some tests. Bunch of crap.'

'How'd they treat you?'

'With handcuffs and padded walls.'

'No kiddin'. They put you in a room with padded walls?' Gwen was amused and managed a rare giggle.

'Sure did. They watched me like I was some animal. Said I was famous. My guards told me they was proud of me – one was white and one was black. Said that I did the right thing and they hoped I got off. They was nice to me.'

'What'd the doctors say?'

'They won't say nothin' till we get to trial, and then they'll say I'm fine.'

'How do you know what they'll say?'

'Jake told me. He ain't been wrong yet.'

'Has he found you a doctor?'

'Yeah, some crazy drunk he drug up somewhere. Says he's a psychiatrist. We've talked a couple of times in Ozzie's office.'

'What'd he say?'

'Not much. Jake said he'll say whatever we want him to say.'

'Must be a real good doctor.'

'He'd fit in good with those folks in Whitfield.'

'Where's he from?'

'Jackson, I think. He wasn't too sure of anything. He acted like I was gonna kill him too. I swear he was drunk both times we talked. He asked some questions that neither one of us understood. Took some notes like a real big shot. Said he thought he could help me. I asked Jake about him. Jake said not to worry, that he would be sober at the trial. But I think Jake's worried too.'

'Then why are we usin' him?'

''Cause he's free. Owes somebody some favors. A real shrink'd cost over a thousand dollars just to evaluate me, and then another thousand or so to come testify at trial. A cheap shrink. Needless to say, I can't pay it.'

Gwen lost her smile and looked away. 'We need some money around the house,' she said without looking at him.

'How much?'

'Coupla hundred for groceries and bills.'

'How much you got?'

'Less than fifty.'

'I'll see what I can do.'

She looked at him. 'What does that mean? What makes you think you can get money while you're in jail?'

Carl Lee raised his eyebrows and pointed at his wife. She was not to question him. He still wore the pants, even though he put them on in jail. He was the boss.

'I'm sorry,' she whispered.

CHAPTER TWENTY-FOUR

Reverend Agee peered through a crack in one of the huge stained glass windows of his church and watched with satisfaction as the clean Cadillacs and Lincolns arrived just before five Sunday afternoon. He had called a meeting of the council to assess the Hailey situation and plan strategy for the final three weeks before the trial, and to prepare for the arrival of the NAACP lawyers. The weekly collections had gone well – over seven thousand dollars had been gathered throughout the county and almost six thousand had been deposited by the reverend in a special account for the Carl Lee Hailey Legal Defense Fund. None had been given to the family. Agee was waiting for the NAACP to direct him in spending the money, most of which, he thought, should go to the defense fund. The sisters in the church could feed the family if they got hungry. The cash was needed elsewhere.

The council talked of ways to raise more money. It was not easy getting money from poor people, but the issue was hot and the time was right, and if they didn't raise it now it would not be raised. They agreed to meet the following day at the Springdale Church in Clanton. The NAACP people were expected in town by morning. No press; it was to be a work session.

Norman Reinfeld was a thirty-year-old genius in criminal law who held the record for finishing Harvard's law school at the age of twenty-one, and after graduation declined a most generous offer to join his father and grandfather's prestigious Wall Street law factory, opting instead to take a job with the NAACP and spend his time fighting furiously to keep Southern blacks off death row. He was very good at what he did although, through no fault of his own, he was not very successful at what he did. Most Southern blacks along with most Southern whites who faced the gas chamber deserved the gas chamber. But Reinfeld and his team of capital murder defense specialists won more than their share, and even in the ones they lost they usually managed to keep the convicts alive through a myriad of exhausting delays and appeals. Four of his former clients had either been gassed, electrocuted, or lethally injected, and that was four too many for Reinfeld. He had watched them all die, and with each execution he renewed his vow to break any law, violate any ethic, contempt any court, disrespect any judge, ignore any mandate, or do whatever it took to prevent a human from legally killing another human. He didn't worry much about the illegal killings of humans, such as those killings so artfully and cruelly achieved by his clients. It wasn't his business to think about those killings, so he didn't. Instead he vented his righteous and sanctimonious anger and zeal at the legal killings.

He seldom slept more than three hours a night. Sleep was difficult with thirty-one clients on death row. Plus seventeen clients awaiting trial. Plus eight egotistical attorneys to supervise. He was thirty and looked forty-five. He was old, abrasive, and ill-tempered. In the normal course of his business, he would have been much too busy to attend a gathering of local black ministers in Clanton, Mississippi. But this was not the normal case. This was Hailey. The vigilante. The father driven to revenge. The most famous criminal case in the country at the moment. This was Mississippi, where for years whites shot blacks for any reason or no reason and no one cared; where whites raped blacks and it was considered sport; where blacks were hanged for fighting back. And now a black father had killed two white men who raped his daughter, and faced the gas chamber for something that thirty years earlier would have gone unnoticed had he been white. This was the case, his case, and he would handle it personally.

On Monday he was introduced to the council by Reverend Agee, who opened the meeting with a lengthy and detailed review of the activities in Ford County. Reinfeld was brief. He and his team could not represent Mr. Hailey because he had not been hired by Mr. Hailey, so a meeting was imperative. Today, preferably. Tomorrow morning at the latest, because he had a flight out of Memphis at noon. He was needed in a murder trial somewhere in Georgia. Reverend Agee promised to arrange a meeting with the defendant as soon as possible. He was friends with the sheriff. Fine, said Reinfeld, just get it done.

'How much money have you raised?' Reinfeld asked.

'Fifteen thousand from you folks,' Agee answered.

'I know that. How much locally?'

'Six thousand,' Agee said proudly.

'Six thousand!' repeated Reinfeld. 'Is that all? I thought you people were organized. Where's all this great local support you were talking about? Six thousand! How much more can you raise? We've only got three weeks.'

The council members were silent. This Jew had a lot of nerve. The only white man in the group and he was on the attack.

'How much do we need?' asked Agee.

'That depends, Reverend, on how good a defense you want for Mr. Hailey. I've only got eight other attorneys on my staff. Five are in trial at this very moment. We've got thirty-one capital murder convictions at various stages of appeal. We've got seventeen trials scheduled in ten states over the next five months. We get ten requests each week to represent defendants, eight of which we turn down because we simply don't have the staff or the money. For Mr. Hailey, fifteen thousand has been contributed by two local chapters and the home office. Now you tell me that only six thousand has been raised locally. That's twenty-one thousand. For that amount you'll get the best defense we can afford. Two attorneys, at least one psychiatrist, but nothing fancy. Twenty-one thousand gets a good defense, but not what I had in mind.'

'What exactly did you have in mind?'

'A first-class defense. Three or four attorneys. A battery of psychiatrists. Half dozen investigators. A jury psychologist, just to name a few. This is not your run-of-the-mill murder case. I want to win. I was led to believe that you folks wanted to win.'

'How much?' asked Agee.

'Fifty thousand, minimum. A hundred thousand would be nice.'

'Look, Mr. Reinfeld, you're in Mississippi. Our people are poor. They've given generously so far, but there's no way we can raise another thirty thousand here.'

Reinfeld adjusted his horn-rimmed glasses and scratched his graying beard. 'How much more can you raise?'

'Another five thousand, maybe.'

'That's not much money.'

'Not to you, but it is to the black folk of Ford County.'

Reinfeld studied the floor and continued stroking his beard. 'How much has the Memphis chapter given?'

'Five thousand,' answered someone from Memphis.

'Atlanta?'

'Five thousand.'

'How about the state chapter?'

'Which state?'

'Mississippi.'

'None.'

'None?'

'None.'

'Why not?'

'Ask him,' Agee said, pointing at Reverend Henry Hillman, the state director.

'Uh, we tryin' to raise some money now,' Hillman said weakly. 'But –'

'How much have you raised so far?' asked Agee.

'Well, uh, we got –'

'Nothin', right? You ain't raised nothin', have you, Hillman?' Agee said loudly.

'Come on, Hillman, tell us how much you raised,' chimed in Reverend Roosevelt, vice-chairman of the council.

Hillman was dumbfounded and speechless. He had been sitting quietly on the front pew minding his own business, half asleep. Suddenly he was under attack.

'The state chapter will contribute.'

'Sure you will, Hillman. You folks at state are constantly badgerin' us locals to contribute here and donate there for this cause and that cause, and we never see any of the money. You always cryin' about bein' so broke, and we're always sendin' money to state. But when we need help, state don't do a thing but show up here and talk.'

'That's not true.'

'Don't start lyin', Hillman.'

Reinfeld was embarrassed and immediately aware that a nerve had been touched. 'Gentlemen, gentlemen, let's move on,' he said diplomatically.

'Good idea,' Hillman said.

'When can we meet with Mr. Hailey?' Reinfeld asked.

'I'll arrange a meetin' for in the mornin',' Agee said.

'Where can we meet?'

'I suggest we meet in Sheriff Walls' office in the jail. He's black, you know, the only black sheriff in Mississippi.'

'Yes, I've heard.'

'I think he'll let us meet in his office.'

'Good. Who is Mr. Hailey's attorney?'

'Local boy. Jake Brigance.'

'Make sure he's invited. We'll ask him to help us on the case. It'll ease the pain.'

Ethel's obnoxious, high-pitched, bitchy voice broke the tranquility of the late afternoon and startled her boss. 'Mr. Brigance, Sheriff Walls is on line two,' she said through the intercom.

'Okay.'

'Do you need me for anything else, sir?'

'No. See you in the morning.'

Jake punched line two. 'Hello, Ozzie. What's up?'

'Listen Jake, we've got a bunch of NAACP big shots in town.'

'What else is new?'

'No, this is different. They wanna meet with Carl Lee in the mornin'.'

'Why?'

'Some guy named Reinfeld.'

'I've heard of him. He heads up their capital murder team. Norman Reinfeld.'

'Yeah, that's him.'

'I've been waiting for this.'

'Well, he's here, and he wants to talk to Carl Lee.'

'Why are you involved?'

'Reverend Agee called me. He wants a favor, of course. He asked me to call you.'

'The answer is no. Emphatically no.'

Ozzie paused a few seconds. 'Jake, they want you to be present.'

'You mean I'm invited?'

'Yes. Agee said Reinfeld insisted on it. He wants you to be here.'

'Where?'

'In my office. Nine A.M.'

Jake breathed deeply and replied slowly. 'Okay, I'll be there. Where's Carl Lee?'

'In his cell.'

'Get him in your office. I'll be there in five minutes.'

'What for?'

'We need to have a prayer meeting.'

Reinfeld and Reverends Agee, Roosevelt, and Hillman sat in a perfect row of folding chairs and faced the sheriff, the defendant, and Jake, who puffed a cheap cigar in a determined effort to pollute the small office. He puffed mightily and stared nonchalantly at the floor, trying his best to show nothing but absolute contempt for Reinfeld and the reverends. Reinfeld was no pushover when it came to arrogance, and his disdain for this simple, small-time lawyer was not well hidden because he made no attempt to hide it. He was arrogant and insolent by nature. Jake had to work at it.

'Who called this meeting?' Jake asked impatiently, after a long, uncomfortable silence.

'Uh, well, I guess we did,' answered Agee as he searched Reinfeld for guidance.

'Well, get on with it. What do you want?'

'Take it easy now, Jake,' Ozzie said. 'Reverend Agee asked me to arrange the meeting so Carl Lee could meet Mr. Reinfeld here.'

'Fine. They've met. Now what, Mr. Reinfeld?'

'I'm here to offer my services, and the services of my staff and the entire NAACP to Mr. Hailey,' said Reinfeld.

'What type of services?' asked Jake.

'Legal, of course.'

'Carl Lee, did you ask Mr. Reinfeld to come here?' asked Jake.

'Nope.'

'Sounds like solicitation to me, Mr. Reinfeld.'

'Skip the lecture, Mr. Brigance. You know what I do, and you know why I'm here.'

'So you chase all your cases?'

'We don't chase anything. We're called in by local NAACP members and other civil rights activists. We handle only capital murder cases, and we're very good at what we do.'

'I suppose you're the only attorney competent to handle a case of this magnitude?'

'I've handled my share.'

'And lost your share.'

'Most of my cases are supposed to be lost.'

'I see. Is that your position on this case? Do you expect to lose it?'

Reinfeld picked at his beard and glared at Jake. 'I didn't come here to argue with you, Mr. Brigance.'

'I know. You came here to offer your formidable legal skills to a defendant who's never heard of you and happens to be satisfied with his attorney. You came here to take my client. I know exactly why you're here.'

'I'm here because the NAACP invited me. Nothing more or less.'

'I see. Do you get all your cases from the NAACP?'

'I work for the NAACP, Mr. Brigance. I'm in charge of its capital murder defense team. I go where the NAACP sends me.'

'How many clients do you have?'

'Several dozen. Why is that important?'

'Did they all have attorneys before you pushed yourself into their cases?'

'Some did, some didn't. We always try to work with the local attorney.'

Jake smiled. 'That's marvelous. You're offering me a chance to carry your briefcase and chauffeur you around Clanton. I might even get to fetch you a sandwich during the noon recess. What a thrill.'

Carl Lee sat frozen with arms crossed and his eyes fixed on a spot in the rug. The reverends watched him closely, waiting for him to say something to his lawyer, to tell him to shut up, that he was fired and the NAACP lawyers would handle the case. They watched and waited, but Carl Lee just sat calmly and listened.

'We have a lot to offer, Mr. Hailey,' Reinfeld said. It was best to stay calm until the defendant decided who would represent him. A tantrum might ruin things.

'Such as?' Jake asked.

'Staff, resources, expertise, experienced trial lawyers who do nothing but capital defense. Plus we have a number of highly competent doctors we use in these cases. You name it, we have it.'

'How much money do you have to spend?'

'That's none of your business.'

'Is that so? Is it Mr. Hailey's business? After all, it's his case. Perhaps Mr. Hailey would like to know how much you have to spend in his defense. Would you, Mr. Hailey?'

'Yep.'

'All right, Mr. Reinfeld, how much do you have to spend?'

Reinfeld squirmed and looked hard at the reverends, who looked hard at Carl Lee.

'Approximately twenty thousand, so far,' Reinfeld admitted sheepishly.

Jake laughed and shook his head in disbelief. 'Twenty thousand! Y'all are really serious about this, aren't you? Twenty thousand! I thought you guys played in the big leagues. You raised a hundred and fifty thousand for the cop killer in Birmingham last year. And he was convicted, by the way. You spent a hundred thousand for the whore in Shreveport who killed her customer. And she, too, was convicted, I might add. And you think this case is worth only twenty thousand.'

'How much do you have to spend?' asked Reinfeld.

'If you can explain to me how that's any of your business, I'll be glad to discuss it with you.'

Reinfeld started to speak, then leaned forward and rubbed his temples. 'Why don't you talk to him, Reverend Agee.'

The reverends stared at Carl Lee. They wished they were alone with him, with no white folks around. They could talk to him like he was a nigger. They could explain things to him; tell him to fire this young white boy and get him some real lawyers. NAACP lawyers. Lawyers who knew how to fight for blacks. But they were not alone with him, and they couldn't curse him. They had to show respect for the white folks present. Agee spoke first.

'Look here, Carl Lee, we tryin' to help you. We brought in Mr. Reinfeld here, and he's got all his lawyers and everbody at your disposal, to help you now. We ain't got nothin' against Jake here; he's a fine young lawyer. But he can work with Mr. Reinfeld. We don't want you to fire Jake; we just want you to hire Mr. Reinfeld too. They can all work together.'

'Forget that,' said Jake.

Agee paused and looked helplessly at Jake.

'Come on, Jake. We ain't got nothin' against you. It's a big chance for you. You can work with some real big lawyers. Get some real good experience. We –'

'Let me make it real clear, Reverend. If Carl Lee wants your lawyers, fine. But I'm not playing gofer for anyone. I'm either in or out. Nothing in between. My case or your case. The courtroom is not big enough for me, Reinfeld, and Rufus Buckley.'

Reinfeld rolled his eyes and looked at the ceiling, shaking his head slowly and grinning with an arrogant little smirk.

'You sayin' it's up to Carl Lee?' asked Reverend Agee.

'Of course it's up to him. He's hired me. He can fire me. He's already done it once. I'm not the one facing the gas chamber.'

'How 'bout it, Carl Lee?' asked Agee.

Carl Lee uncrossed his arms and stared at Agee. 'This twenty thousand, what's it for?'

'Really, it's more like thirty thousand,' answered Reinfeld. 'The local folks have pledged another ten thousand. The money will be used for your defense. None of it's attorney fees. We'll need two or three investigators. Two, maybe three, psychiatric experts. We often use a jury psychologist to assist us in selecting the jury. Our defenses are very expensive.'

'Uh huh. How much money has been raised by local people?' asked Carl Lee.

'About six thousand,' answered Reinfeld.

'Who collected this money?'

Reinfeld looked at Agee. 'The churches,' answered the reverend.

'Who collected the money from the churches?' asked Carl Lee.

'We did,' answered Agee.

'You mean, you did,' said Carl Lee.

'Well, uh, right. I mean, each church gave the money to me, and I deposited it in a special bank account.'

'Yeah, and you deposited every nickel you received?'

'Of course I did.'

'Of course. Let me ask you this. How much of the money have you offered to my wife and kids?'

Agee looked a bit pale, or as pale as possible, and quickly searched the faces of the other reverends, who, at the moment, were preoccupied with a stink bug on the carpet. They offered no help. Each knew Agee had been taking his cut, and each knew the family had received nothing. Agee had profited more than the family. They knew it, and Carl Lee knew it.

'How much, Reverend?' repeated Carl Lee.

'Well, we thought the money –'

'How much, Reverend?'

'The money is gonna be spent on lawyer fees and stuff like that.'

'That ain't what you told your church, is it? You said it was for the support of the family. You almost cried when you talked about how my family might starve to death if the folks didn't donate all they could. Didn't you, Reverend?'

'The money's for you, Carl Lee. You and your family. Right now we think it could be better spent on your defense.'

'And what if I don't want your lawyers? What happens to the twenty thousand?'

Jake chuckled. 'Good question. What happens to the money if Mr. Hailey doesn't hire you, Mr. Reinfeld?'

'It's not my money,' answered Reinfeld.

'Reverend Agee?' asked Jake.

The reverend had had enough. He grew defiant and belligerent. He pointed at Carl Lee. 'Listen here, Carl Lee. We busted our butts to raise this money. Six thousand bucks from the poor people of this county, people who didn't have it to give. We worked hard for this money, and it was given by poor people, your people, people on food stamps and welfare and Medicaid, people who couldn't afford to donate a dime. But they gave for one reason, and only one reason: they believe in you and what you did, and they want you to walk outta that courtroom a free man. Don't say you don't want the money.'

'Don't preach to me,' Carl Lee replied softly. 'You say the poor folks of this county gave six thousand?'

'Right?'

'Where'd the rest of the money come from?'

'NAACP. Five thousand from Atlanta, five from Memphis, and five from national. And it's strictly for your defense fees.'

'If I use Mr. Reinfeld here?'

'Right.'

'And if I don't use him, the fifteen thousand disappears?'

'Right.'

'What about the other six thousand?'

'Good question. We ain't discussed that yet. We thought you'd appreciate us for raisin' money and tryin' to help. We're offerin' the best lawyers and obviously you don't care.'

The room was silent for an eternity as the preachers, the lawyers, and the sheriff waited for some message from the defendant. Carl Lee chewed on his lower lip and stared at the floor. Jake lit another cigar. He had been fired before, and he could handle it again.

'You gotta know right now?' Carl Lee asked finally.

'No,' said Agee.

'Yes,' said Reinfeld. 'The trial is less than three weeks away, and we're two months behind already. My time is too valuable to wait on you, Mr. Hailey. Either you hire me now or forget it. I've got a plane to catch.'

'Well, I'll tell you what you do, Mr. Reinfeld. You go and catch your plane and don't ever worry 'bout comin' back to Clanton on my behalf. I'll take my chances with my friend Jake.'

CHAPTER TWENTY-FIVE

The Ford County Klavern was founded at midnight, Thursday, July 11, in a small pasture next to a dirt road deep in a forest somewhere in the northern part of the county. The six inductees stood nervously before the huge burning cross and repeated strange words offered by a wizard. A dragon and two dozen white-robed Klansmen watched and chanted when appropriate. A guard with a gun stood quietly down the road, occasionally watching the ceremony but primarily watching for uninvited guests. There were none.

Precisely at midnight the six fell to their knees and closed their eyes as the white hoods were ceremoniously placed onto their heads. They were Klansmen now, these six. Freddie Cobb, brother of the deceased, Jerry Maples, Clifton Cobb, Ed Wilburn, Morris Lancaster, and Terrell Grist. The grand dragon hovered above each one and chanted the sacred vows of klanhood. The flames from the cross scorched the faces of the new members as they knelt and quietly suffocated under the heavy robes and hoods. Sweat dripped from their red faces as they prayed fervently for the dragon to shut up with his nonsense and finish the ceremony. When the chanting stopped, the new members rose and quickly retreated from the cross. They were embraced by their new brothers, who grabbed their shoulders firmly and pounded primal incantations onto their sweaty collar-bones. The heavy hoods were removed, and the Klansmen, both new members and old, walked proudly from the pasture and into the rustic cabin across the dirt road. The same guard sat on the front steps as the whiskey was poured around the table and plans were made for the trial of Carl Lee Hailey.

Deputy Pirtle pulled the graveyard shift, ten to six, and had stopped for coffee and pie at Gurdy's all-night diner on the highway north of town when his radio blared out the news that he was wanted at the jail. It was three minutes after midnight, Friday morning.

Pirtle left his pie and drove a mile south to the jail. 'What's up?' he asked the dispatcher.

'We got a call a few minutes ago, anonymous, from someone lookin' for the sheriff. I explained that he was not on duty, so they asked for whoever was on duty. That's you. They said it was very important, and they'd call back in fifteen minutes.'

Pirtle poured some coffee and relaxed in Ozzie's big chair. The phone rang. 'It's for you,' yelled the dispatcher.

'Hello,' answered Pirtle.

'Who's this?' asked the voice.

'Deputy Joe Pirtle. Who's this?'

'Where's the sheriff?'

'Asleep, I reckon.'

'Okay listen, and listen real good because this is important and I ain't callin' again. You know that Hailey nigger?'

'Yeah.'

'You know his lawyer, Brigance?'

'Yeah.'

'Then listen. Sometime between now and three A.M., they're gonna blow up his house.'

'Who?'

'Brigance.'

'No, I mean who's gonna blow up his house?'

'Don't worry about that, Deputy, just listen to me. This ain't no joke, and if you think it's a joke, just sit there and wait for his house to go up. It may happen any minute.'

The voice became silent but did not disappear. Pirtle listened. 'You still there?'

'Good night, Deputy.' The receiver clicked.

Pirtle jumped to his feet and ran to the dispatcher. 'Did you listen?'

'Of course I did.'

'Call Ozzie and tell him to get down here. I'll be at the Brigance house.'

Pirtle hid his patrol car in a driveway on Monroe Street and walked across the front lawns to Jake's house. He saw nothing. It was 12:55 A.M. He walked around the house with his flashlight and noticed nothing unusual. Every house on the street was dark and asleep. He unscrewed the light bulb on the front porch and took a seat in a wicker chair. He waited. The odd-looking foreign car was parked next to the Oldsmobile under the veranda. He would wait and ask Ozzie about notifying Jake.

Headlights appeared at the end of the street. Pirtle slumped lower in the chair, certain he could not be seen. A red pickup moved suspiciously toward the Brigance house but did not stop. He sat up and watched it disappear down the street.

Moments later he noticed two figures jogging from the direction of the square. He unbuttoned his holster and removed his service revolver. The first figure was much larger than the second, and seemed to run with more ease and grace. It was Ozzie. The other was Nesbit. Pirtle met the two in the driveway and they retreated into the darkness of the front porch. They whispered and watched the street.

'What exactly did he say?' asked Ozzie.

'Said someone's gonna blow up Jake's house between now and three A.M. Said it was no joke.'

'Is that all?'

'Yep. He wasn't real friendly.'

'How long you been here?'

'Twenty minutes.'

Ozzie turned to Nesbit. 'Give me your radio and go hide in the backyard. Stay quiet and keep your eyes open.'

Nesbit scurried to the rear of the house and found a small opening between the shrubs along the back fence. Crawling on all fours, he disappeared into the shrubs. From his nest he could see the entire rear of the house.

'You gonna tell Jake?' asked Pirtle.

'Not yet. We might in a minute. If we knock on the door, they'll be turnin' on lights and we don't need that right now.'

'Yeah, but what if Jake hears us and comes through the door firin' away. He might think we're just a couple of niggers tryin' to break in.'

Ozzie watched the street and said nothing.

'Look, Ozzie, put yourself in his place. The cops have your house surrounded at one o'clock in the mornin' waitin' for somebody to throw a bomb. Now, would you wanna stay in bed asleep or would you wanna know about it?'

Ozzie studied the houses in the distance.

'Listen, Sheriff, we better wake them up. What if we don't stop whoever's plannin' this, and somebody inside the house gets hurt? We get blamed, right?'

Ozzie stood and punched the doorbell. 'Unscrew that light bulb,' he ordered, pointing at the porch ceiling.

'I already did.'

Ozzie punched the doorbell again. The wooden door swung open, and Jake walked to the storm door and stared at the sheriff. He was wearing a wrinkled nightshirt that fell just below his knees, and he held a loaded .38 in his right hand. He slowly opened the storm door.

'What is it, Ozzie?' he asked.

'Can I come in?'

'Yeah. What's going on?'

'Stay here on the porch,' Ozzie told Pirtle. 'I'll be just a minute.'

Ozzie closed the front door behind them and turned off the light in the foyer. They sat in the dark living room overlooking the porch and the front yard.

'Start talking,' Jake said.

''Bout a half hour ago we took an anonymous call from someone who said that someone planned to blow up your house between now and three A.M. We're takin' it serious.'

'Thanks.'

'I've got Pirtle on the front porch and Nesbit in the backyard. 'Bout ten minutes ago Pirtle saw a pickup drive by real interested like, but that's all we've seen.'

'Have you searched around the house?'

'Yeah, nothin'. They ain't been here yet. But somethin' tells me this is the real thing.'

'Why?'

'Just a hunch.'

Jake laid the .38 beside him on the couch and rubbed his temples. 'What's your suggestion?'

'Sit and wait. That's all we can do. You got a rifle?'

'I've got enough guns to invade Cuba.'

'Why don't you get it and get dressed. Take a position in one of those cute little windows upstairs. We'll hide outside and wait.'

'Have you got enough men?'

'Yeah, I figure there'll only be one or two of them.'

'Who's them?'

'Don't know. Could be the Klan, could be some freelancers. Who knows?'

Both men sat in deep thought and stared at the dark street. They could see the top of Pirtle's head as he slumped in the wicker chair just outside the window.

'Jake, you remember those three civil rights workers killed by the Klan back in '64? Found them buried in a levee down around Philadelphia.'

'Sure. I was a kid, but I remember.'

'Those boys would've never been found if someone hadn't told where they was. That someone was in the Klan. An informant. Seems like that always happened to the Klan. Somebody on the inside was always squealin'.'

'You think it's the Klan?'

'Sure looks like it. If it was just one or two freelancers, then who else would know about it? The bigger the group, the better the chance of someone tippin' us off.'

'That makes sense, but for some reason I'm not comforted by it.'

'Of course, it could be a joke.'

'Nobody's laughing.'

'You gonna tell your wife?'

'Yeah. I'd better go do that.'

'I would too. But don't be turnin' on lights. You might scare them off.'

'But I would like to scare them off.'

'And I'd like to catch them. If we don't catch them now, they'll try again, and next time they might forget to call us ahead of time.'

Carla dressed hurriedly in the dark. She was terrified. Jake laid Hanna on the couch in the den, where she mumbled something and went back to sleep. Carla held her head and watched Jake load a rifle.

'I'll be upstairs in the guest room. Don't turn on any lights. The cops have the place surrounded, so don't worry.'

'Don't worry! Are you crazy?'

'Try to go back to sleep.'

'Sleep! Jake, you've lost your mind.'

They didn't wait long. From his vantage point somewhere deep in the shrubs in front of the house, Ozzie saw him first: a lone figure walking casually down the street from the direction opposite the square. He had in his hand a small box or case of some sort. When he was two houses away, he left the street and cut through the front lawns of the neighbors. Ozzie pulled his revolver and nightstick and watched the man walk directly toward him. Jake had him in the scope of his deer rifle. Pirtle crawled like a snake across the porch and into the shrubs, ready to strike.

Suddenly, the figure darted across the front lawn next door and to the side of Jake's house. He carefully laid the small suitcase under Jake's bedroom window. As he turned to run, a huge black nightstick crashed across the side of his head, ripping his right ear in two places, each barely hanging to his head. He screamed and fell to the ground.

'I got him!' Ozzie yelled. Pirtle and Nesbit sprinted to the side of the house. Jake calmly walked down the stairs.

'I'll be back in a minute,' he told Carla.

Ozzie grabbed the suspect by the neck and sat him next to the house. He was conscious but dazed. The suitcase was inches away.

'What's your name?' Ozzie demanded.

He moaned and clutched his head and said nothing.

'I asked you a question,' Ozzie said as he hovered over his suspect. Pirtle and Nesbit stood nearby, guns drawn, too frightened to speak or move. Jake stared at the suitcase.

'I ain't sayin',' came the reply.

Ozzie raised the nightstick high over his head and drove it solidly against the man's right ankle. The crack of the bone was sickening.

He howled and grabbed his leg. Ozzie kicked him in the face. He fell backward and his head smashed into the side of the house. He rolled to his side and groaned in pain.

Jake knelt above the suitcase and put his ear next to it. He jumped and retreated. 'It's ticking,' he said weakly.

Ozzie bent over the suspect and laid the nightstick softly against his nose. 'I've got one more question before I break ever bone in your body. What's in the box?'

No answer.

Ozzie recoiled the nightstick and broke the other ankle. 'What's in the box!' he shouted.

'Dynamite!' came the anguished reply.

Pirtle dropped his gun. Nesbit's blood pressure shot through his cap and he leaned on the house. Jake turned white and his knees vibrated. He ran through the front door yelling at Carla. 'Get the car keys! Get the car keys!'

'What for?' she asked nervously.

'Just do as I say. Get the car keys and get in the car.'

He lifted Hanna and carried her through the kitchen, into the carport, and laid her in the back seat of Carla's Cutlass. He took Carla by the arm and helped her into the car. 'Leave, and don't come back for thirty minutes.'

'Jake, what's going on?' she demanded.

'I'll tell you later. There's no time now. Just leave. Go drive around for thirty minutes. Stay away from this street.'

'But why, Jake? What have you found?'

'Dynamite.'

She backed out of the driveway and disappeared.

When Jake returned to the side of the house, the suspect's left hand had been handcuffed to the gas meter next to the window. He was moaning, mumbling, cursing. Ozzie carefully lifted the suitcase by the handle and sat it neatly between the suspect's broken legs. Ozzie kicked both legs to spread them. He groaned louder. Ozzie, the deputies, and Jake backed away slowly and watched him. He began to cry.

'I don't know how to defuse it,' he said through clenched teeth.

'You'd better learn fast,' Jake said, his voice somewhat stronger.

The suspect closed his eyes and lowered his head. He bit his lip and breathed loudly and rapidly. Sweat dripped from his chin and eyebrows. His ear was shredded and hung like a falling leaf. 'Give me a flashlight.'

Pirtle handed him a flashlight.

'I need both hands,' he said.

'Try it with one,' Ozzie said.

He placed his fingers gently on the latch and closed his eyes.

'Let's get outta here,' Ozzie said. They ran around the corner of the house and into the carport, as far away as possible.

'Where's your family?' Ozzie asked.

'Gone. Recognize him?'

'Nope,' said Ozzie.

'I never seen him,' said Nesbit.

Pirtle shook his head.

Ozzie called the dispatcher, who called Deputy Riley, the self-trained explosives man for the county.

'What if he passes out and the bomb goes off?' Jake asked.

'You got insurance, don't you, Jake?' asked Nesbit.

'That's not funny.'

'We'll give him a few minutes, then Pirtle can go check on him,' said Ozzie.

'Why me?'

'Okay, Nesbit can go.'

'I think Jake should go,' said Nesbit. 'It's his house.'

'Very funny,' said Jake.

They waited and chatted nervously. Nesbit made another stupid remark about insurance. 'Quiet!' Jake said. 'I heard something.'

They froze. Seconds later the suspect yelled again. They ran back across the front yard, then slowly turned the corner. The empty suitcase had been tossed a few feet away. Next to the man was a neat pile of a dozen sticks of dynamite. Between his legs was a large, round-faced clock with wires bound together with silver electrical tape.

'Is it defused?' Ozzie asked anxiously.

'Yeah,' he replied between heavy, rapid breaths.

Ozzie knelt before him and removed the clock and the wires. He did not touch the dynamite. 'Where are your buddies?'

No response.

He removed his nightstick and moved closer to the man. 'I'm gonna start breakin' ribs one at a time. You better start talkin'. Now where are your buddies?'

'Kiss my ass.'

Ozzie stood and quickly looked around, not at Jake and the deputies, but at the house next door. Seeing nothing, he raised the nightstick. The suspect's left arm hung from the gas meter, and Ozzie planted the stick just below the left armpit. He squealed and jerked to the left. Jake almost felt sorry for him.

'Where are they?' Ozzie demanded.

No response.

Jake turned his head as the sheriff landed another blow to the ribs.

'Where are they?'

No response.

Ozzie raised the nightstick.

'Stop . . . please stop,' the suspect begged.

'Where are they?'

'Down that way. A couple of blocks.'

'How many?'

'One.'

'What vehicle?'

'Pickup. Red GMC.'

'Get the patrol cars,' Ozzie ordered.

Jake waited impatiently under the carport for his wife to return. At two-fifteen she drove slowly into the driveway and parked.

'Is Hanna asleep?' Jake asked as he opened the door.

'Yes.'

'Good. Leave her there. We'll be leaving in a few minutes.'

'Where are we going?'

'We'll discuss it inside.'

Jake poured the coffee and tried to act calm. Carla was scared and shaking and angry and making it difficult to act calm. He described the bomb and suspect and explained that Ozzie was searching for the accomplice.

'I want you and Hanna to go to Wilmington and stay with your parents until after the trial,' he said.

She stared at the coffee and said nothing.

'I've already called your dad and explained everything. They're scared too, and they insist you stay with them until this thing is over.'

'And what if I don't want to go?'

'Please, Carla. How can you argue at a time like this?'

'What about you?'

'I'll be fine. Ozzie will give me a bodyguard and they'll watch the house around the clock. I'll sleep at the office some. I'll be safe, I promise.'

She was not convinced.

'Look, Carla, I've got a thousand things on my mind right now. I've got a client facing the gas chamber and his trial is ten days away. I can't lose it. I'll work night and day from now until the twenty-second, and once the trial starts you won't see me anyway. The last thing I need is to be worried about you and Hanna. Please go.'

'They were going to kill us, Jake. They tried to kill us.'

He couldn't deny it.

promised to withdraw if the danger became real.'

'It's out of the question. Noose would never allow me to withdraw at this late date.'

'I feel as though you've lied to me.'

'That's not fair. I think I underestimated this thing, and now it's too late.'

She walked to the bedroom and began packing.

'The plane leaves Memphis at six-thirty. Your father will meet you at the Raleigh airport at nine-thirty.'

'Yes, sir.'

Fifteen minutes later they left Clanton. Jake drove and Carla ignored him. At five, they ate breakfast in the Memphis airport. Hanna was sleepy but excited about seeing her grandparents. Carla said little. She had much to say, but as a rule, they didn't argue in front of Hanna. She ate quietly and sipped her coffee and watched her husband casually read the paper as if nothing had happened.

Jake kissed them goodbye and promised to call every day. The plane left on time. At seven-thirty he was in Ozzie's office.

'Who is he?' Jake asked the sheriff.

'We have no idea. No wallet, no identification, nothin'. And he ain't talkin'.'

'Does anybody recognize him?'

Ozzie thought for a second. 'Well, Jake, he's kinda hard to recognize right now. Got a lot of bandages on his face.'

Jake smiled. 'You play rough, don't you, big guy?'

'Only when I have to. I didn't hear you object.'

'No, I wanted to help. What about his friend?'

'We found him sleepin' in a red GMC 'bout a half a mile from your house. Terrell Grist. Local redneck. Lives out from Lake Village. I think he's a friend of the Cobb family.'

Jake repeated the name a few times. 'Never heard of him. Where is he?'

'Hospital. Same room with the other.'

'My God, Ozzie, did you break his legs too?'

'Jake, my friend, he resisted arrest. We had to subdue him. Then we had to interrogate him. He didn't want to cooperate.'

'What did he say?'

'Not much. Don't know nothin'. I'm convinced he doesn't know the guy with the dynamite.'

'You mean they brought in a professional?'

'Could be. Riley looked at the firecrackers and timin' device and said it was pretty good work. We'd have never found you, your wife, your daughter, probably never found your house. It was set for t[illegible] Without the tip, you'd be dead, Jake. So would your family.'

Jake felt dizzy and sat on the couch. Reaction set in like a hard kick to the groin. A case of diarrhea almost manifested itself, and he was nauseated.

'You get your family off?'

'Yeah,' he said weakly.

'I'm gonna assign a deputy to you full-time. Got a preference?'

'Not really.'

'How 'bout Nesbit?'

'Fine. Thanks.'

'One other thing. I guess you want this kept quiet?'

'If possible. Who knows about it?'

'Just me and the deputies. I think we can keep it under wraps until after the trial, but I can't guarantee anything.'

'I understand. Try your best.'

'I will, Jake.'

'I know you will, Ozzie. I appreciate you.'

Jake drove to the office, made the coffee and lay on the couch in his office. He wanted a quick nap, but sleep was impossible. His eyes burned, but he could not close them. He stared at the ceiling fan.

'Mr. Brigance,' Ethel called over the intercom.

No response.

'Mr. Brigance!'

Somewhere in the deep recesses of his subconscious, Jake heard himself being paged. He bolted upright. 'Yes!' he yelled.

'Judge Noose is on the phone.'

'Okay, okay,' he mumbled as he staggered to his desk. He checked his watch. Nine A.M. He had slept for an hour.

'Good morning, Judge,' he said cheerfully, trying to sound alert and awake.

'Good morning, Jake. How are you?'

'Just fine, Judge. Busy getting ready for the big trial.'

'I thought so. Jake, what is your schedule today?'

What's today, he thought. He grabbed his appointment book. 'Nothing but office work.'

'Good. I would like to have lunch with you at my home. Say around eleven-thirty.'

'I would be delighted, Judge. What's the occasion?'

'I want to discuss the Hailey case.'

'Fine, Judge. I'll see you at eleven-thirty.'

The Nooses lived in a stately antebellum home off the town square in Chester. The home had been in the wife's family for over a century, and although it could stand some maintenance and repair, it was in decent condition. Jake had never been a guest in the house, and had never met Mrs. Noose, although he had heard she was a snobby blue blood whose family at one time had money but lost it. She was as unattractive as Ichabod, and Jake wondered what the children looked like. She was properly polite when she met Jake at the door and attempted small talk as she led him to the patio, where His Honor was drinking iced tea and reviewing correspondence. A maid was preparing a small table nearby.

'Good to see you, Jake,' Ichabod said warmly. 'Thanks for coming over.'

'My pleasure, Judge. Beautiful place you have here.'

They discussed the Hailey trial over soup and chicken salad sandwiches. Ichabod was dreading the ordeal, although he didn't admit it. He seemed tired, as if the case was already a burden. He surprised Jake with an admission that he detested Buckley. Jake said he felt the same way.

'Jake, I'm perplexed over this venue ruling,' he said. 'I've studied your brief and Buckley's brief, and I've researched the law myself. It's a tough question. Last weekend I attended a judges' conference on the Gulf Coast, and I had a few drinks with Judge Denton on the Supreme Court. He and I were in law school together, and we were colleagues in the state senate. We're very close. He's from Dupree County in south Mississippi, and he says that everybody down there talks about the case. People on the street ask him how he's gonna rule if the case winds up on appeal. Everybody's got an opinion, and that's almost four hundred miles away. Now, if I agree to change venue, where do we go? We can't leave the state, and I'm convinced that everyone has not only heard about your client, but already prejudged him. Would you agree?'

'Well, there's been a lot of publicity,' Jake said carefully.

'Talk to me, Jake. We're not in court. That's why I invited you here. I want to pick your brain. I know there's been a lot of publicity. If we move it, where do we go?'

'How about the delta?'

Noose smiled. 'You'd like that, wouldn't you?'

'Of course. We could pick us a good jury over there. One that would truly understand the issues.'

'Yeah, and one that would be half black.'

'I hadn't thought about that.'

'Do you really believe those folks haven't already prejudged this defendant?'

'I suppose so.'

'So where do we go?'

'Did Judge Denton have a suggestion?'

'Not really. We discussed the court's traditional refusal to allow changes of venue except in the most heinous of cases. It's a difficult issue with a notorious crime that arouses passion both for and against the defendant. With television and all the press nowadays, these crimes are instant news, and everyone knows the details long before the trial. And this case tops them all. Even Denton admitted he'd never seen a case with this much publicity, and he admitted it would be impossible to find a fair and impartial jury anywhere in Mississippi. Suppose I leave it in Ford County and your man is convicted. Then you appeal claiming venue should have been changed. Denton indicated he would be sympathetic with my decision not to move it. He thinks a majority of the court would uphold my denial of the venue change. Of course, that's no guarantee, and we discussed it over several long drinks. Would you like a drink?'

'No thanks.'

'I just don't see any reason to move the trial from Clanton. If we did, we'd be fooling ourselves if we thought we could find twelve people who are undecided about Mr. Hailey's guilt.'

'Sounds like you've already made up your mind, Judge.'

'I have. We're not changing venue. The trial will be held in Clanton. I'm not comfortable with it, but I see no reason to move the trial. Besides, I like Clanton. It's close to home and the air conditioning works in the courthouse.'

Noose reached for a file and found an envelope. 'Jake, this is an order, dated today, overruling the request to change venue. I've sent a copy to Buckley, and there's a copy for you. The original is in here, and I would appreciate you filing this with the clerk in Clanton.'

'I'll be glad to.'

'I just hope I'm doing the right thing. I've really struggled with this.'

'It's a tough job,' Jake offered, attempting sympathy.

Noose called the maid and ordered a gin and tonic. He insisted that Jake view his rose garden, and they spent an hour in the sprawling rear lawn admiring His Honor's flowers. Jake thought of Carla, and Hanna, and his home, and the dynamite, but gallantly remained interested in Ichabod's handiwork.

Friday afternoons often reminded Jake of law school, when, depending on the weather, he and his friends would either group in their favorite bar in Oxford and guzzle happy-hour beer and debate their new-found theories of law or curse the insolent, arrogant, terroristic law professors, or, if the weather was warm and sunny, pile the beer in Jake's well-used convertible Beetle and head for the beach at Sardis Lake, where the women from sorority row plastered their beautiful, bronze bodies with oil and sweated in the sun and coolly ignored the catcalls from the drunken law students and fraternity rats. He missed those innocent days. He hated law school – every law student with any sense hated law school – but he missed the friends and good times, especially the Fridays. He missed the pressureless lifestyle, although at times the pressure had seemed unbearable, especially during the first year when the professors were more abusive than normal. He missed being broke, because when he had nothing he owed nothing and most of his classmates were in the same boat. Now that he had an income he worried constantly about mortgages, the overhead, credit cards, and realizing the American dream of becoming affluent. Not wealthy, just affluent. He missed his Volkswagen because it had been his first new car, a gift at high school graduation, and it was paid for, unlike the Saab. He missed being single, occasionally, although he was happily married. And he missed beer, either from a pitcher, can, or bottle. It didn't matter. He had been a social drinker, only with friends, and he spent as much time as possible with his friends. He didn't drink every day in law school, and he seldom got drunk. But there had been several painful, memorable hangovers.

Then came Carla. He met her at the beginning of his last semester, and six months later they married. She was beautiful, and that's what got his attention. She was quiet, and a little snobby at first, like most of the wealthy sorority girls at Ole Miss. But he found her to be warm and personable and lacking in self-confidence. He had never understood how someone as beautiful as Carla could be insecure. She was a Dean's List scholar in liberal arts with no intention of ever doing more than teaching school for a few years. Her family had money, and her mother had never worked. This appealed to Jake – the family money and the absence of a career ambition. He wanted a wife who would stay home and stay beautiful and have babies and not try to wear the pants. It was love at first sight.

But she frowned on drinking, any type of drinking. Her father drank heavily when she was a child, and there were painful memories. So Jake dried out his last semester in law school and lost fifteen pounds. He looked great, felt great, and he was madly in love. But he missed beer.

There was a country grocery a few miles out of Chester with a Coors sign in the window. Coors had been his favorite in law school, although at that time it was not for sale east of the river. It was a delicacy at Ole Miss, and the bootlegging of Coors had been profitable around the campus. Now that it was available everywhere most folks had returned to Budweiser.

It was Friday, and hot. Carla was nine hundred miles away. He had no desire to go to the office, and anything there could wait until tomorrow. Some nut just tried to kill his family and remove his landmark from the National Register of Historic Places. The biggest trial of his career was ten days away. He was not ready and the pressure was mounting. He had just lost his most critical pretrial motion. And he was thirsty. Jake stopped and bought a six-pack of Coors.

It took almost two hours to travel the sixty miles from Chester to Clanton. He enjoyed the diversion, the scenery, the beer. He stopped twice to relieve himself and once to get another six-pack. He felt great.

There was only one place to go in his condition. Not home, not the office, certainly not the courthouse to file Ichabod's villainous order. He parked the Saab behind the nasty little Porsche and glided up the sidewalk with cold beer in hand. As usual, Lucien was rocking slowly on the front porch, drinking and reading a treatise on the insanity defense. He closed the book and, noticing the beer, smiled at his former associate. Jake just grinned at him.

'What's the occasion, Jake?'

'Nothing, really. Just got thirsty.'

'I see. What about your wife?'

'She doesn't tell me what to do. I'm my own man. I'm the boss. If I want beer, I'll drink some beer, and she'll say nothing.' Jake took a long sip.

'She must be outta town.'

'North Carolina.'

'When did she leave?'

'Six this morning. Flew from Memphis with Hanna. She'll stay with her parents in Wilmington until the trial's over. They've got a fancy little beach house where they spend their summers.'

'She left this morning, and you're drunk by mid-afternoon.'

'I'm not drunk,' Jake answered. 'Yet.'

'How long you been drinkin'?'

'Coupla hours. I bought a six-pack when I left Noose's house around one-thirty. How long have you been drinking?'

'I normally drink my breakfast. Why were you at his house?'

'We discussed the trial over lunch. He refused to change venue.'

'He what?'

'You heard me. The trial will be in Clanton.'

Lucien took a drink and rattled his ice. 'Sallie!' he screamed.

'Did he give any reason?'

'Yeah. Said it would be impossible to find jurors anywhere who hadn't heard of the case.'

'I told you so. That's a good common sense reason not to move it, but it's a poor legal reason. Noose is wrong.'

Sallie returned with a fresh drink and took Jake's beer to the refrigerator. Lucien took a slug and smacked his lips. He wiped his mouth with his arm, and took another long drink.

'You know what that means, don't you?' he asked.

'Sure. An all-white jury.'

'That, plus a reversal on appeal if he's convicted.'

'Don't bet on it. Noose has already consulted with the Supreme Court. He thinks the Court will affirm him if challenged. He thinks he's on solid ground.'

'He's an idiot. I can show him twenty cases that say the trial should be moved. I think he's afraid to move it.'

'Why would Noose be afraid?'

'He's taking some heat.'

'From who?'

Lucien admired the golden liquid in his large glass and slowly stirred the ice cubes with a finger. He grinned and looked as though he knew something but wouldn't tell unless he was begged.

'From who?' Jake demanded, glaring at his friend with shiny, pink eyes.

'Buckley,' Lucien said smugly.

'Buckley,' Jake repeated. 'I don't understand.'

'I knew you wouldn't.'

'Do you mind explaining?'

'I guess I could. But you can't repeat it. It's very confidential. Came from good sources.'

'Who?'

'Can't tell.'

'Who are your sources?' Jake insisted.

'I said I can't tell. Won't tell. Okay?'

'How can Buckley put pressure on Noose?'

'If you'll listen, I'll tell you.'

'Buckley has no influence over Noose. Noose despises him. Told me so himself. Today. Over lunch.'

'I realize that.'

'Then how can you say Noose is feeling some heat from Buckley?'

'If you'll shut up, I'll tell you.'

Jake finished a beer and called for Sallie.

'You know what a cutthroat and political whore Buckley is.'

Jake nodded.

'You know how bad he wants to win this trial. If he wins, he thinks it will launch his campaign for attorney general.'

'Governor,' said Jake.

'Whatever. He's ambitious, okay?'

'Okay.'

'Well, he's been getting political chums throughout the district to call Noose and suggest that the trial be held in Ford County. Some have been real blunt with Noose. Like, move the trial, and we'll get you in the next election. Leave it in Clanton, and we'll help you get reelected.'

'I don't believe that.'

'Fine. But it's true.'

'How do you know?'

'Sources.'

'Who's called him?'

'One example. Remember that thug that used to be sheriff in Van Buren County? Motley? FBI got him, but he's out now. Still a very popular man in that county.'

'Yeah, I remember.'

'I know for a fact he went to Noose's house with a couple of sidekicks and suggested very strongly that Noose leave the trial here. Buckley put them up to it.'

'What did Noose say?'

'They all cussed each other real good. Motley told Noose he wouldn't get fifty votes in Van Buren County next election. They promised to stuff ballot boxes, harass the blacks, rig the absentee ballots, the usual election practices in Van Buren County. And Noose knows they'll do it.'

'Why should he worry about it?'

'Don't be stupid, Jake. He's an old man who can do nothing but be a judge. Can you imagine him trying to start a law practice. He makes sixty thousand a year and would starve if he got beat. Most judges are like that. He's got to keep that job. Buckley knows it, so he's talking to the local bigots and pumping them up and telling how this no-good nigger might be acquitted if the trial is moved and that they should put a little heat on the judge. That's why Noose is feeling some pressure.'

They drank for a few minutes in silence, both rocking quietly in the tall wooden rockers. The beer felt great.

'There's more,' Lucien said.

'To what?'

'To Noose.'

'What is it?'

'He's had some threats. Not political threats, but death threats. I hear he's scared to death. Got the police over there guarding his house. Carries a gun now.'

'I know the feeling,' Jake mumbled.

'Yeah, I heard.'

'Heard what?'

'About the dynamite. Who was he?'

Jake was flabbergasted. He stared blankly at Lucien, unable to speak.

'Don't ask. I got connections. Who was he?'

'No one knows.'

'Sounds like a pro.'

'Thanks.'

'You're welcome to stay here. I've got five bedrooms.'

The sun was gone by eight-fifteen when Ozzie parked his patrol car behind the Saab, which was still parked behind the Porsche. He walked to the foot of the steps leading up to the porch. Lucien saw him first.

'Hello, Sheriff,' he attempted to say, his tongue thick and ponderous.

'Evenin', Lucien. Where's Jake?'

Lucien nodded toward the end of the porch, where Jake lay sprawled on the swing.

'He's taking a nap,' Lucien explained helpfully.

Ozzie walked across the squeaking boards and stood above the comatose figure snoring peacefully. He punched him gently in the ribs. Jake opened his eyes, and struggled desperately to sit up.

'Carla called my office lookin' for you. She's worried sick. She's been callin' all afternoon and couldn't find you. Nobody's seen you. She thinks you're dead.'

Jake rubbed his eyes as the swing rocked gently. 'Tell her I'm not dead. Tell her you've seen me and talked to me and you are convinced beyond a shadow of a doubt that I am not dead. Tell her I'll call her tomorrow. Tell her, Ozzie, please tell her.'

'No way, buddy. You're a big boy, you call her and tell her.' Ozzie walked off the porch. He was not amused.

Jake struggled to his feet and staggered into the house. 'Where's the phone?' he yelled at Sallie. As he dialed, he could hear Lucien on the porch laughing uncontrollably.

CHAPTER TWENTY-SIX

The last hangover had been in law school, six or seven years earlier; he couldn't remember. The date, that is. He couldn't remember the date, but the pounding head, dry mouth, short breath, and burning eyes brought back painful, vivid memories of long and unforgettable bouts with the tasty brown stuff

He knew he was in trouble immediately, when his left eye opened. The eyelids on the right one were matted firmly together, and they would not open, unless manually opened with fingers, and he did not dare move. He lay there in the dark room on a couch, fully dressed, including shoes, listening to his head pound and watching the ceiling fan rotate slowly. He felt nauseated. His neck ached because there was no pillow. His feet throbbed because of the shoes. His stomach rolled and flipped and promised to erupt. Death would have been welcome.

Jake had problems with hangovers because he could not sleep them off. Once his eyes opened and his brain awoke and began spinning again, and the throbbing between his temples set in, he could not sleep. He had never understood this. His friends in law school could sleep for days with a hangover, but not Jake. He never managed more than a few hours after the last can or bottle was empty.

Why? That was always the question the next morning. Why did he do it? A cold beer was refreshing. Maybe two or three. But ten, fifteen, even twenty? He had lost count. After six, beer lost its taste, and from then on the drinking was just for the sake of drinking and getting drunk. Lucien had been very helpful. Before dark he had sent Sallie to the store for a whole case of Coors, which he gladly paid for, then encouraged Jake to drink. There were a few cans left. It was Lucien's fault.

Slowly he lifted his legs, one at a time, and placed his feet on the floor. He gently rubbed his temples, to no avail. He breathed deeply, but his heart pounded rapidly, pumping more blood to his brain and fueling the small jackhammers at work on the inside of his head. He had to have water. His tongue was dehydrated and puffed to the point where it was easier to leave his mouth open like a dog in heat. Why, oh why?

He stood, carefully, slowly, retardedly, and crept into the kitchen. The light above the stove was shielded and dim, but it penetrated the darkness and pierced his eyes. He rubbed his eyes and tried to clean them with his smelly fingers. He drank the warm water slowly and allowed it to run from his mouth and drip on the floor. He didn't care. Sallie would clean it. The clock on the counter said it was two-thirty.

Gaining momentum, he walked awkwardly yet quietly through the living room, past the couch with no pillow, and out the door. The porch was littered with empty cans and bottles. Why?

He sat in the hot shower in his office for an hour, unable to move. It relieved some of the aches and soreness, but not the violence swirling around his brain. Once in law school, he had managed to crawl from his bed to the refrigerator for a beer. He drank it, and it helped; then he drank another, and felt much better. He remembered this now while sitting in the shower, and the thought of another beer made him vomit.

He lay on the conference table in his underwear and tried his best to die. He had plenty of life insurance. They would leave his house alone. The new lawyer could get a continuance.

Nine days to trial. Time was scarce, precious, and he had just wasted one day with a massive hangover. Then he thought of Carla, and his head pounded harder. He had tried to sound sober. Told her he and Lucien had spent the afternoon reviewing insanity cases, and he would have called earlier but the phones weren't working, at least Lucien's weren't. But his tongue was heavy and his speech slow, and she knew he was drunk. She was furious – a controlled fury. Yes, her house was still standing. That was all she believed.

At six-thirty he called her again. She might be impressed if she knew he was at the office by dawn working diligently. She wasn't. With great pain and fortitude, he sounded cheerful, even hyper. She was not impressed.

'How do you feel?' she insisted.

'Great!' he answered with closed eyes.

'What time did you go to bed?'

What bed, thought Jake. 'Right after I called you.'

She said nothing.

'I got to the office at three o'clock this morning,' he said proudly.

'Three o'clock!'

'Yeah, I couldn't sleep.'

'But you didn't sleep any Thursday night.' A touch of concern edged through her icy words, and he felt better.

'I'll be okay. I may stay with Lucien some this week and next. It might be safer over there.'

'What about the bodyguard?'

'Yeah, Deputy Nesbit. He's parked outside asleep in his car.'

She hesitated and Jake could feel the phone lines thawing. 'I'm worried about you,' she said warmly.

'I'll be fine, dear. I'll call tomorrow. I've got work to do.'

He replaced the receiver, ran to the restroom and vomited again.

The knocking persisted at the front door. Jake ignored it for fifteen minutes, but whoever it was knew he was there and kept knocking.

He walked to the balcony. 'Who is it?' he yelled at the street.

The woman walked from the sidewalk under the balcony and leaned on a black BMW parked next to the Saab. Her hands were thrust deep into the pockets of faded, starched, well-fitting jeans. The noon sun burned brightly and blinded her as she looked up in his direction. It also illuminated her light, goldish red hair.

'Are you Jake Brigance?' she asked, shielding her eyes with a forearm.

'Yeah. Whatta you want?'

'I need to talk to you.'

'I'm very busy.'

'It's very important.'

'You're not a client, are you?' he asked, focusing his eyes on the slender figure and knowing she was indeed not a client.

'No. I just need five minutes of your time.'

Jake unlocked the door. She walked in casually as if she owned the place. She shook his hand firmly.

'I'm Ellen Roark.'

He pointed to a seat by the door. 'Nice to meet you. Sit down.'

Jake sat on the edge of Ethel's desk. 'One syllable or two?'

'I beg your pardon.'

She had a quick, cocky Northeast accent, but tempered with some time in the South.

'Is it Rork or Row Ark?'

'R-o-a-r-k. That's Rork in Boston, and Row Ark in Mississippi.'

'Mind if I call you Ellen?'

'Please do, with two syllables. Can I call you Jake?'

'Yes, please.'

'Good, I hadn't planned to call you Mister.'

'Boston, huh?'

'Yeah, I was born there. Went to Boston College. My dad is Sheldon Roark, a notorious criminal lawyer in Boston.'

'I guess I've missed him. What brings you to Mississippi?'

'I'm in law school at Ole Miss.'

'Ole Miss! How'd you wind up down here?'

'My mother's from Natchez. She was a sweet little sorority girl at Ole Miss, then moved to New York, where she met my father.'

'I married a sweet little sorority girl from Ole Miss.'

'They have a great selection.'

'Would you like coffee?'

'No thanks.'

'Well, now that we know each other, what brings you to Clanton?'

'Carl Lee Hailey.'

'I'm not surprised.'

'I'll finish law school in December, and I'm killing time in Oxford this summer. I'm taking criminal procedure under Guthrie, and I'm bored.'

'Crazy George Guthrie.'

'Yeah, he's still crazy.'

'He flunked me in constitutional law my first year.'

'Anyway, I'd like to help you with the trial.'

Jake smiled and took a seat in Ethel's heavy-duty, rotating secretarial chair. He studied her carefully. Her black cotton polo shirt was fashionably weathered and neatly pressed. The outlines and subtle shadows revealed a healthy bustline, no bra. The thick, wavy hair fell perfectly on her shoulders.

'What makes you think I need help?'

'I know you practice alone, and I know you don't have a law clerk.'

'How do you know all this?'

'*Newsweek*.'

'Ah, yes. A wonderful publication. It was a good picture, wasn't it?'

'You looked a bit stuffy, but it was okay. You look better in person.'

'What credentials do you bring with you?'

'Genius runs in my family. I finished *summa cum laude* at BC, and I'm second in my law class. Last summer I spent three months with the Southern Prisoners Defense League in Birmingham and played gofer in seven capital trials. I watched Elmer Wayne Doss die in the Florida electric chair and I watched Willie Ray Ash get lethally injected in Texas. In my spare time at Ole Miss I write briefs for the ACLU and I'm working on two death penalty appeals for a law firm in Spartanburg, South Carolina. I was raised in my father's law office, and I was proficient in legal research before I could drive. I've watched him defend murderers, rapists, embezzlers, extortionists, terrorists, assassins, child abusers, child fondlers, child killers, and children who killed their parents. I worked forty hours a week in his office when I was in high school and fifty when I was in college. He has eighteen lawyers in his firm, all very bright, very talented. It's a great training ground for criminal lawyers, and I've been there for fourteen years. I'm twenty-five years old, and when I grow up I want to be a radical criminal lawyer like my dad and spend a glorious career stamping out the death penalty.'

'Is that all?'

'My dad's filthy rich, and even though we're Irish Catholic I'm an only child. I've got more money than you do so I'll work for free. No charge. A free law clerk for three weeks. I'll do all the research, typing, answering the phone. I'll even carry your briefcase and make the coffee.'

'I was afraid you'd want to be a law partner.'

'No. I'm a woman, and I'm in the South. I know my place.'

'Why are you so interested in this case?'

'I want to be in the courtroom. I love criminal trials, big trials where there's a life on the line and pressure so thick you can see it in the air. Where the courtroom's packed and security is tight. Where half the people hate the defendant and his lawyers and the other half pray he gets off. I love it. And this is the trial of all trials. I'm not a Southerner and I find this place bewildering most of the time, but I have developed a perverse love for it. It'll never make sense to me, but it is fascinating. The racial implications are enormous. The trial of a black father for killing two white men who raped his daughter – my father said he would take the case for free.'

'Tell him to stay in Boston.'

'It's a trial lawyer's dream. I just want to be there. I'll stay out of the way, I promise. Just let me work in the background and watch the trial.'

'Judge Noose hates women lawyers.'

'So does every male lawyer in the South. Besides, I'm not a lawyer, I'm a law student.'

'I'll let you explain that to him.'

'So I've got the job.'

Jake stopped staring at her and breathed deeply. A minor wave of nausea vibrated through his stomach and lungs and took his breath. The jackhammers had returned with a fury and he needed to be near the restroom.

'Yes, you've got the job. I could use some free research. These cases are complicated, as I'm sure you are aware.'

She flashed a comely, confident smile. 'When do I start?'

'Now.'

Jake led her through a quick tour of the office, and assigned her to the war room upstairs. They laid the Hailey file on the conference table and she spent an hour copying it.

At two-thirty Jake awoke from a nap on his couch. He walked downstairs to the conference room. She had removed half the books from the shelves and had them scattered the length of the table with page markers sticking up every fifty or so pages. She was busy taking notes.

'Not a bad library,' she said.

'Some of these books haven't been used in twenty years.'

'I noticed the dust.'

'Are you hungry?'

'Yes. I'm starving.'

'There's a little cafe around the corner where the specialty is grease and fried corn meal. My system needs a shot of grease.'

'Sounds delicious.'

They walked around the square to Claude's, where the crowd was thin for a Saturday afternoon. There were no other whites in the place. Claude was absent and the silence was deafening. Jake ordered a cheeseburger, onion rings, and three headache powders.

'Got a headache?' Ellen asked.

'Massive.'

'Stress?'

'Hangover.'

'Hangover? I thought you were a teetotaler.'

'And where'd you hear that?'

'*Newsweek*. The article said you were a clean-cut family man, workaholic, devout Presbyterian who drank nothing and smoked cheap cigars. Remember? How could you forget, right?'

'You believe everything you read?'

'No.'

'Good, because last night I got plastered, and I've puked all morning.'

The law clerk was amused. 'What do you drink?'

'I don't – remember. At least I didn't until last night. This is my first hangover since law school, and I hope it's my last. I'd forgotten how terrible these things are.'

'Why do lawyers drink so much?'

'They learn how in law school. Does your dad drink?'

'Are you kidding? We're Catholic. He's careful, though.'

'Do you drink?'

'Sure, all the time,' she said proudly.

'Then you'll make a great lawyer.'

Jake carefully mixed the three powders in a glass of ice water and slugged it down. He grimaced and wiped his mouth. She watched intently with an amused smile.

'What'd your wife say?'

'About what?'

'The hangover, from such a devout and religious family man.'

'She doesn't know about it. She left me early yesterday morning.'

'I'm sorry.'

'She went to stay with her parents until the trial is over. We've had anonymous phone calls and death threats for two months now, and early yesterday morning they planted dynamite outside our bedroom window.

The cops found it in time and they caught the men, probably the Klan. Enough dynamite to level the house and kill all of us. That was a good excuse to get drunk.'

'I'm sorry to hear that.'

'The job you've just taken could be very dangerous. You should know that at this point.'

'I've been threatened before. Last summer in Dothan, Alabama, we defended two black teenagers who had sodomized and strangled an eighty-year-old woman. No lawyer in the state would take the case so they called the Defense League. We rode into town on black horses and the mere sight of us would cause lynch mobs to form instantly on street corners. I've never felt so hated in my life. We hid in a motel in another town and felt safe, until one night two men cornered me in the motel lounge and tried to abduct me.'

'What happened?'

'I carry a snub-nosed .38 in my purse and I convinced them I knew how to use it.'

'A snub-nosed .38?'

'My father gave it to me for my fifteenth birthday. I have a license.'

'He must be a hell of a guy.'

'He's been shot at several times. He takes very controversial cases, the kind you read about in the papers where the public is outraged and demanding that the defendant be hanged without a trial or a lawyer. Those are the cases he likes best. He has a full-time bodyguard.'

'Big deal. So do I. His name is Deputy Nesbit, and he couldn't hit the side of a barn with a shotgun. He was assigned to me yesterday.'

The food arrived. She removed the onions and tomatoes from her Claudeburger, and offered him the french fries. She cut it in half and nibbled around the edges like a bird. Hot grease dripped to her plate. With each small bite, she carefully wiped her mouth.

Her face was gentle and pleasant with an easy smile that belied the ACLU, ERA, burn-the-bra, I-can-outcuss-you bitchiness Jake knew was lurking somewhere near the surface. There was not a trace of makeup anywhere on the face. None was needed. She was not beautiful, not cute, and evidently determined not to be so. She had the pale skin of a redhead, but it was healthy skin with seven or eight freckles splattered about the small, pointed nose. With each frequent smile, her lips spread wonderfully and folded her cheeks into neat, transient, hollow dimples. The smiles were confident, challenging, and mysterious. The metallic green eyes radiated a soft fury and were fixed and unblinking when she talked.

It was an intelligent face, attractive as hell.

Jake chewed on his burger and tried to nonchalantly ignore her eyes. The heavy food settled his stomach, and for the first time in ten hours he began to think he might live.

'Seriously, why'd you choose Ole Miss?' he asked.

'It's a good law school.'

'It's my school. But we don't normally attract the brightest students from the Northeast. That's Ivy League country. We send our smartest kids up there.'

'My father hates every lawyer with an Ivy League degree. He was dirt poor and scratched his way through law school at night. He's endured the snubs from rich, well-educated, and incompetent lawyers all his life. Now he laughs at them. He told me I could go to law school anywhere in the country, but if I chose an Ivy League school he would not pay for it. Then there's my mother. I was raised on these enchanting stories of life in the Deep South, and I had to see for myself. Plus, the Southern states seemed determined to practice the death penalty, so I think I'll end up here.'

'Why are you so opposed to the death penalty?'

'And you're not?'

'No, I'm very much in favor of it.'

'That's incredible! Coming from a criminal defense lawyer.'

'I'd like to go back to public hangings on the courthouse lawn.'

'You're kidding, aren't you? I hope. Tell me you are.'

'I am not.'

She stopped chewing and smiling. The eyes glowed fiercely and watched him for a signal of weakness. 'You are serious.'

'I am very serious. The problem with the death penalty is that we don't use it enough.'

'Have you explained that to Mr. Hailey?'

'Mr. Hailey does not deserve the death penalty. But the two men who raped his daughter certainly did.'

'I see. How do you determine who gets it and who doesn't?'

'That's very simple. You look at the crime and you look at the criminal. If it's a dope dealer who guns down an undercover narcotics officer, then he gets the gas. If it's a drifter who rapes a three-year-old girl, drowns her by holding her little head in a mudhole, then throws her body off a bridge, then you take his life and thank God he's gone. If it's an escaped convict who breaks into a farmhouse late at night and beats and tortures an elderly couple before burning them with their house, then you strap him in a chair, hook up a few wires, pray for his soul, and pull the switch. And if it's two dopeheads who gang-rape a ten-year-old girl and kick her with pointed-toe cowboy boots until her jaws break, then you happily, merrily, thankfully, gleefully lock them in a gas chamber and listen to them squeal. It's very simple.'

'It's barbaric.'

'Their crimes were barbaric. Death is too good for them, much too good.'

'And if Mr. Hailey is convicted and sentenced to die?'

'If that happens, I'm sure I'll spend the next ten years cranking out appeals and fighting furiously to save his life. And if they ever strap him in the chair, I'm sure I'll be outside the prison with you and the Jesuits and a hundred other kindly souls marching and holding candles and singing hymns. And then I'll stand beside his grave behind his church with his widow and children and wish I'd never met him.'

'Have you ever witnessed an execution?'

'Not that I recall.'

'I've watched two. You'd change your mind if you saw one.'

'Good. I won't see one.'

'It's a horrible thing to watch.'

'Were the victims' families there?'

'Yes, in both instances.'

'Were they horrified? Were their minds changed? Of course not. Their nightmares were over.'

'I'm surprised at you.'

'And I'm bewildered by people like you. How can you be so zealous and dedicated in trying to save people who have begged for the death penalty and according to the law should get it?'

'Whose law? It's not the law in Massachusetts.'

'You don't say. What do you expect from the only state McGovern carried in 1972? You folks have always been tuned in with the rest of the country.'

The Claudeburgers were being ignored and their voices had grown too loud. Jake glanced around and caught a few stares. Ellen smiled again, and took one of his onion rings.

'What do you think of the ACLU?' she asked, crunching.

'I suppose you've got a membership card in your purse.'

'I do.'

'Then you're fired.'

'I joined when I was sixteen.'

'Why so late? You must've been the last one in your Girl Scout troop to join.'

'Do you have any respect for the Bill of Rights?'

'I adore the Bill of Rights. I despise the judges who interpret them. Eat.'

They finished the burgers in silence, watching each other carefully. Jake ordered coffee and two more headache powders.

'So how do we plan to win this case?' she asked.

'We?'

'I still have the job, don't I?'

'Yes. Just remember that I'm the boss and you're the clerk.'

'Sure, boss. What's your strategy?'

'How would you handle it?'

'Well, from what I gather, our client carefully planned the killings and shot them in cold blood, six days after the rape. It sounds exactly like he knew what he was doing.'

'He did.'

'So we have no defense and I think you should plead him guilty for a life sentence and avoid the gas chamber.'

'You're a real fighter.'

'Just kidding. Insanity is our only defense. And it sounds impossible to prove.'

'You're familiar with the M'Naghten Rule?' Jake asked.

'Yes. Do we have a psychiatrist?'

'Sort of. He'll say anything we want him to say; that is, if he's sober at trial. One of your more difficult tasks as my new law clerk will be to make sure he is sober at trial. It won't be easy, believe me.'

'I live for new challenges in the courtroom.'

'All right Row Ark, take a pen. Here's a napkin. Your boss is about to give you instructions.'

She began making notes on a paper napkin.

'I want a brief on the M'Naghten decisions rendered by the Mississippi Supreme Court in the past fifty years. There's probably a hundred. There's a big case from 1976, *State vs. Hill,* where the court was bitterly divided five to four, with the dissenters opting for a more liberal definition of insanity. Keep the brief short, less than twenty pages. Can you type?'

'Ninety words a minute.'

'I should've known. I'd like it by Wednesday.'

'You'll have it.'

'There are some evidentiary points I need researched. You saw those gruesome pictures of the two bodies. Noose normally allows the jury to see the blood and gore, but I'd like to keep them away from the jury. See if there's a way.'

'It won't be easy.'

'The rape is crucial to his defense. I want the jury to know details. This needs to be researched thoroughly. I've got two or three cases you can start from, and I think we can prove to Noose that the rape is very relevant.'

'Okay. What else?'

'I don't know. When my brain is alive again I'll think of more, but that will do it for now.'

'Do I report Monday morning?'

'Yes, but no sooner than nine. I like my quiet time.'

'What's the dress code?'

'You look fine.'

'Jeans and no socks?'

'I have one other employee, a secretary by the name of Ethel. She's sixty-four, top heavy, and thankfully she wears a bra. It wouldn't be a bad idea for you.'

'I'll think about it.'

'I don't need the distraction.'

CHAPTER TWENTY-SEVEN

Monday, July 15. One week until trial. Over the weekend word spread quickly that the trial would be in Clanton, and the small town braced for the spectacle. The phones rang steadily at the three motels as the journalists and their crews confirmed reservations. The cafes buzzed with anticipation. A county maintenance crew swarmed around the courthouse after breakfast and began painting and polishing. Ozzie sent the yardboys from the jail with their mowers and weed-eaters. The old men under the Vietnam monument whittled cautiously and watched all this activity. The trusty who supervised the yard work asked them to spit their Red Man in the grass, not on the sidewalk. He was told to go to hell. The thick, dark Bermuda was given an extra layer of fertilizer, and a dozen lawn sprinklers were hissing and splashing by 9:00 A.M.

By 10:00 A.M. the temperature was ninety-two. The merchants in the small shops around the square opened their doors to the humidity and ran their ceiling fans. They called Memphis and Jackson and Chicago for inventory to be sold at special prices next week.

Noose had called Jean Gillespie, the Circuit Court clerk, late Friday and informed her that the trial would be in her courtroom. He instructed her to summon one hundred and fifty prospective jurors. The defense had requested an enlarged panel from which to select the twelve, and Noose agreed. Jean and two deputy clerks spent Saturday combing the voter registration books randomly selecting potential jurors. Following Noose's specific instructions, they culled those over sixty-five. One thousand names were chosen, and each name along with its address was written on a small index card and thrown into a cardboard box. The two deputy clerks then took turns drawing cards at random from the box. One clerk was white, one black. Each would pull a card blindly from the box and arrange it neatly on a folding table with the other cards. When the count reached one hundred and fifty, the drawing ceased and a master list was typed. These were the jurors for State *vs.* Hailey. Each step of their selection had been carefully dictated by the Honorable Omar Noose, who knew exactly what he was doing. If there was an all-white jury, and a conviction, and a death sentence, every single elementary step of the jury selection procedure would be attacked on appeal. He had been through it before, and had been reversed. But not this time.

From the master list, the name and address of each juror was typed on a separate jury summons. The stack of summonses was kept in Jean's office under lock until eight Monday morning when Sheriff Ozzie Walls arrived. He drank coffee with Jean and received his instructions.

'Judge Noose wants these served between four P.M. and midnight tonight,' she said.

'Okay.'

'The jurors are to report to the courtroom promptly by nine next Monday.'

'Okay.'

'The summons does not indicate the name or nature of the trial, and the jurors are not to be told anything.'

'I reckon they'll know.'

'Probably so, but Noose was very specific. Your men are to say nothing about the case when the summonses are served. The names of the jurors are very confidential, at least until Wednesday. Don't ask why – Noose's orders.'

Ozzie flipped through the stack. 'How many do we have here?'

'One fifty.'

'A hundred and fifty! Why so many?'

'It's a big case. Noose's orders.'

'It'll take ever man I've got to serve these papers.'

'I'm sorry.'

'Oh well. If that's what His Honor wants.'

Ozzie left, and within seconds Jake was standing at the counter flirting with the secretaries and smiling at Jean Gillespie. He followed her back to her office. He closed the door. She retreated behind her desk and pointed at him. He kept smiling.

'I know why you're here,' she said sternly, 'and you can't have it.'

'Give me the list, Jean.'

'Not until Wednesday. Noose's orders.'

'Wednesday? Why Wednesday?'

'I don't know. But Omar was very specific.'

'Give me the list, Jean.'

'Jake, I can't. Do you want me to get in trouble?'

'You won't get in trouble because no one will know it. You know how well I can keep a secret.' He was not smiling now. 'Jean, give me the damned list.'

'Jake, I just can't.'

'I need it, and I need it now. I can't wait until Wednesday. I've got work to do.'

'It wouldn't be fair to Buckley,' she said weakly.

'To hell with Buckley. Do you think he plays fair? He's a snake and you dislike him as much as I do.'

'Probably more.'

'Give me the list, Jean.'

'Look, Jake, we've always been close. I think more of you than any lawyer I know. When my son got in trouble I called you, right? I trust you and I want you to win this case. But I can't defy a judge's orders.'

'Who helped you get elected last time, me or Buckley?'

'Come on, Jake.'

'Who kept your son out of jail, me or Buckley?'

'Please.'

'Who tried to put your son in jail, me or Buckley?'

'That's not fair, Jake.'

'Who stood up for your husband when everybody, and I mean everybody, in the church wanted him gone when the books didn't balance?'

'It's not a question of loyalty, Jake. I love you and Carla and Hanna, but I just can't do it.'

Jake slammed the door and stormed out of the office. Jean sat at her desk and wiped tears from her cheeks.

At 10:00 A.M. Harry Rex barged into Jake's office and threw a copy of the jury list on his desk. 'Don't ask,' he said. Beside each name he had made notes, such as 'Don't know' or 'Former client – hates niggers' or 'Works at the shoe factory, might be sympathetic.'

Jake read each name slowly, trying to place it with a face or a reputation. There was nothing but names. No addresses, ages, occupations. Nothing but names. His fourth-grade schoolteacher from Karaway. One of his mother's friends from the Garden Club. A former client, shoplifting, he thought. A name from church. A regular at the Coffee Shop. A prominent farmer. Most of the names sounded white. There was a Willie Mae Jones, Leroy Washington, Roosevelt Tucker, Bessie Lou Bean, and a few other black names. But the list looked awfully pale. He recognized thirty names at most.

'Whatta you think?' asked Harry Rex.

'Hard to tell. Mostly white, but that's to be expected. Where'd you get this?'

'Don't ask. I made notes by twenty-six names. That's the best I can do. The rest I don't know.'

'You're a true friend, Harry Rex.'

'I'm a prince. Are you ready for trial?'

'Not yet. But I've found a secret weapon.'

'What?'

'You'll meet her later.'

'Her?'

'Yeah. You busy Wednesday night?'

'I don't think so. Why?'

'Good. Meet here at eight. Lucien will be here. Maybe one or two others. I want to take a couple of hours and talk about the jury. Who do we want? Let's get a profile of the model juror, and go from there. We'll cover each name and hopefully identify most of these people.'

'Sounds like fun. I'll be here. What's your model juror?'

'I'm not sure. I think the vigilante would appeal to rednecks. Guns, violence, protection of women. The rednecks would eat it up. But my man is black, and a bunch of rednecks would fry him. He killed two of their own.'

'I agree. I'd stay away from women. They would have no sympathy for the rapists, but they place a higher value on life. Taking an M-16 and blowing their heads off is something women just don't understand. You and I understand it because we're fathers. It appeals to us. The violence and blood doesn't bother us. We admire him. You've got to pick some admirers on that jury. Young fathers with some education.'

'That's interesting. Lucien said he would stick with women because they're more sympathetic.'

'I don't think so. I know some women who'd cut your throat if you crossed them.'

'Some of your clients?'

'Yeah, and one is on that list. Frances Burdeen. Pick her, and I'll tell her how to vote.'

'You serious?'

'Yep. She'll do anything I tell her.'

'Can you be in court Monday? I want you to watch the jury during the selection process, then help me decide on the twelve.'

'I wouldn't miss it.'

Jake heard voices downstairs and pressed his finger to his lips. He listened, then smiled and motioned for Harry Rex to follow him. They tiptoed to the top of the stairs and listened to the commotion around Ethel's desk.

'You most certainly do not work here,' Ethel insisted.

'I most certainly do. I was hired Saturday by Jake Brigance, who I believe is your boss.'

'Hired for what?' Ethel demanded.

'As a law clerk.'

'Well, he didn't discuss it with me.'

'He discussed it with me, and gave me the job.'

'How much is he paying you?'

'A hundred bucks an hour.'

'Oh my God! I'll have to speak with him first.'

'I've already spoken with him, Ethel.'

'It's Mrs. Twitty to you.' Ethel studied her carefully from head to toe. Acid-washed jeans, penny loafers, no socks, an oversized white cotton button-down with, evidently, nothing on underneath. 'You're not dressed appropriately for this office. You're, you're indecent.'

Harry Rex raised his eyebrows and smiled at Jake. They watched the stairs and listened.

'My boss, who happens to be your boss, said I could dress like this.'

'But you forgot something, didn't you?'

'Jake said I could forget it. He told me you hadn't worn a bra in twenty years. He said most of the women in Clanton go braless, so I left mine at home.'

'He what?' Ethel screamed with arms crossed over her chest.

'Is he upstairs?' Ellen asked coolly.

'Yes, I'll call him.'

'Don't bother.'

Jake and Harry Rex retreated into the big office and waited for the law clerk. She entered carrying a large briefcase.

'Good morning, Row Ark,' Jake said. 'I want you to meet a good friend, Harry Rex Vonner.'

Harry Rex shook her hand and stared at her shirt. 'Nice to meet you. What was your first name?'

'Ellen.'

'Just call her Row Ark,' Jake said. 'She'll clerk here until Hailey's over.'

'That's nice,' said Harry Rex, still staring.

'Harry Rex is a local lawyer, Row Ark, and one of the many you cannot trust.'

'What'd you hire a female law clerk for, Jake?' he asked bluntly.

'Row Ark's a genius in criminal law, like most third-year law students. And she works very cheap.'

'You have something against females, sir?' Ellen asked.

'No ma'am. I love females. I've married four of them.'

'Harry Rex is the meanest divorce lawyer in Ford County,' Jake explained. 'In fact, he's the meanest lawyer, period. Come to think of it, he's the meanest man I know.'

'Thanks,' said Harry Rex. He had stopped staring at her.

She looked at his huge, dirty, scuffed, worn wingtips, his ribbed nylon socks that had drooped into thick wads around his ankles, his soiled and battered khaki pants, his frayed navy blazer, his brilliant pink wool tie that fell eight inches above his belt, and she said, 'I think he's cute.'

'I might make you wife number five,' Harry Rex said.

'The attraction is purely physical,' she said.

'Watch it,' Jake said. 'There's been no sex in this office since Lucien left.'

'A lot of things left with Lucien,' said Harry Rex.

'Who's Lucien?'

Jake and Harry Rex looked at each other. 'You'll meet him soon enough,' Jake explained.

'Your secretary is very sweet,' Ellen said.

'I knew y'all would hit it off. She's really a doll once you get to know her.'

'How long does that take?'

'I've known her for twenty years,' said Harry Rex, 'and I'm still waiting.'

'How's the research coming?' Jake asked.

'Slow. There are dozens of M'Naghten cases, and they are all very long. I'm about half through. I planned to work on it all day here; that is, if that pit bull downstairs doesn't attack me.'

'I'll take care of her,' Jake said.

Harry Rex headed for the door. 'Nice meetin' you, Row Ark. I'll see you around.'

'Thanks, Harry Rex,' said Jake. 'See you Wednesday night.'

The dirt and gravel parking lot of Tank's Tonk was full when Jake finally found it after dark. There had been no reason to visit Tank's before, and he was not thrilled about seeing the place now. It was well hidden off a dirt road, six miles out of Clanton. He parked far away from the small cinderblock building and toyed with the idea of leaving the engine running in case Tank was not there and a quick escape became necessary. But he quickly dismissed the stupid idea because he liked his car, and theft was not only likely but highly probable. He locked it, then double-checked it, almost certain that all or part of it would be missing when he returned.

The juke box blasted from the open windows, and he thought he heard a bottle crash on the floor, or across a table or someone's head. He hesitated beside his car and decided to leave. No, it was important. He sucked in his stomach, held his breath, and opened the ragged wooden door.

Forty sets of black eyes immediately focused on this poor lost white boy with a coat and tie who was squinting and trying to focus inside the vast blackness of their tonk. He stood there awkwardly, desperately searching for a friend. There were none. Michael Jackson conveniently finished his song on the juke box, and for an eternity the tonk was silent. Jake stayed close to the door. He nodded and smiled and tried to act like one of the gang. There were no other smiles.

Suddenly, there was movement at the bar and Jake's knees began vibrating. 'Jake! Jake!' someone shouted. It was the sweetest two words he had ever heard. From behind the bar he saw his friend Tank removing his apron and heading for him. They shook hands warmly.

'What brings you here?'

'I need to talk to you for a minute. Can we step outside?'

'Sure. What's up?'

'Just business.'

Tank flipped on a light switch by the front door. 'Say, everbody, this here is Carl Lee Hailey's lawyer, Jake Brigance. A good friend of mine. Let's hear it for him.'

The small room exploded in applause and bravos. Several of the boys at the bar grabbed Jake and shook his hand. Tank reached in a drawer under the bar and pulled out a handful of Jake's cards, which he passed out like candy. Jake was breathing again and the color returned to his face.

Outside, they leaned on the hood of Tank's yellow Cadillac. Lionel Richie echoed through the windows and the crowd returned to normal. Jake handed Tank a copy of the list.

'Look at each name. See how many of these folks you know. Ask around and find out what you can.'

Tank held the list near his eyes. The light from the Michelob sign in the window glowed over his shoulder. 'How many are black?'

'You tell me. That's one reason I want you to look at it. Circle the black ones. If you're not sure, find out. If you know any of the white folks, make a note.'

'I'll be glad to, Jake. This ain't illegal, is it?'

'Naw, but don't tell anybody. I need it back by Wednesday morning.'

'You're the boss.'

Tank got the last list, and Jake headed for the office. It was almost ten. Ethel had retyped the list from the initial one provided by Harry Rex, and a dozen copies had been hand-delivered to selected, trusted friends. Lucien, Stan Atcavage, Tank, Dell at the Coffee Shop, a lawyer in Karaway named Roland Isom, and a few others. Even Ozzie got a list.

Less than three miles from the tonk was a small, neat white-framed country house where Ethel and Bud Twitty had lived for almost forty years. It was a pleasant house with pleasant memories of raising children who were now scattered up North. The retarded son, the one who greatly resembled Lucien, lived in Miami for some reason. The house was quieter now. Bud hadn't worked in years, not since his first stroke in '75. Then a heart attack, followed by two more major strokes and several small ones. His days were numbered, and he had long since accepted the fact that he would most likely catch the big one and die on his front porch shelling butterbeans. That's what he hoped for, anyway.

Monday night he sat on the porch shelling butterbeans and listening to the Cardinals on the radio. Ethel was working in the kitchen. In the bottom of the eighth with the Cards at bat and two on, he heard a noise from the side of the house. He turned the volume down. Probably just a dog. Then another noise. He stood and walked to the end of the porch. Suddenly, a huge figure dressed in solid black with red, white, and black war paint smeared wickedly across his face jumped from the bushes, grabbed Bud and yanked him off the porch. Bud's anguished cry was not heard in the kitchen. Another warrior joined in and they dragged the old man to the foot of the steps leading up to the front porch. One maneuvered him into a half-nelson while the other pounded his soft belly and bloodied his face. Within seconds, he was unconscious.

Ethel heard noises and scurried through the front door. She was grabbed by a third member of the gang, who twisted her arm tightly behind her and wrapped a huge arm around her throat. She couldn't scream or talk or move, and was held there on the porch, terrified, watching below as the two thugs took turns with her husband. On the front sidewalk ten feet behind the violence stood three figures, each garbed in a full, flowing, white robe with red garnishment, each with a tall, white, pointed headdress from which fell a red and white mask that loosely covered each face. They emerged from the darkness and watched over the scene as though they were the three wise men attending the manger.

After a long, agonizing minute, the beating grew monotonous. 'Enough,' said the ruler in the middle. The three terrorists in black ran. Ethel rushed down the steps and slumped over her battered husband. The three in white disappeared.

Jake left the hospital after midnight with Bud still alive but everyone pessimistic. Along with the broken bones he had suffered another major heart attack. Ethel had made a scene and blamed it all on Jake.

'You said there was no danger!' she screamed. 'Tell that to my husband! It's all your fault!'

He had listened to her rant and rave, and the embarrassment turned to anger. He glanced around the small waiting room at the friends and relatives. All eyes were on him. Yes, they seemed to say, it was all his fault.

CHAPTER TWENTY-EIGHT

Gwen called the office early Tuesday morning and the new secretary, Ellen Roark, answered the phone. She fumbled with the intercom until she broke it, then walked to the stairs and yelled: 'Jake, it's Mr. Hailey's wife.'

He slammed a book shut and angrily picked up the receiver. 'Hello.'

'Jake, are you busy?'

'Very. What's on your mind?'

She started crying. 'Jake, we need money. We're broke, and the bills are past due. I haven't paid the house note in two months and the mortgage company is callin'. I don't know who else to turn to.'

'What about your family?'

'They're poor folks, Jake, you know that. They'll feed us and do what they can, but they can't make our house notes and pay the utilities.'

'Have you talked to Carl Lee?'

'Not about money. Not lately. There's not much he can do except worry, and Lord knows he's got enough to worry about.'

'What about the churches?'

'Ain't seen a dime.'

'How much do you need?'

'At least five hundred, just to catch up. I don't know 'bout next month. I'll guess I'll worry then.'

Nine hundred minus five hundred left Jake with four hundred dollars for a capital murder defense. That had to be a record. Four hundred dollars! He had an idea.

'Can you be at my office at two this afternoon?'

'I'll have to bring the kids.'

'That's okay. Just be here.'

'I'll be there.'

He hung up and quickly searched the phone book for Reverend Ollie Agee. He found him at the church. Jake fed him a line about meeting to discuss the Hailey trial and covering Agee's testimony. Said the reverend would be an important witness. Agee said he would be there at two.

The Hailey clan arrived first, and Jake seated them around the conference table. The kids remembered the room from the press conference and were awed by the long table, thick swivel chairs, and impressive rows of books. When the reverend arrived he hugged Gwen and made a fuss over the kids, especially Tonya.

'I'll be very brief, Reverend,' started Jake. 'There are some things we need to discuss. For several weeks now, you and the other black ministers in this county have been raising money for the Haileys. And you've done a real good job. Over six thousand, I believe. I don't know where the money is, and it's none of my business. You offered the money to the NAACP lawyers to represent Carl Lee, but as you and I know, those lawyers won't be involved in this case. I'm the lawyer, the only lawyer, and so far none of the money has been offered to me. I don't expect any of it. Evidently you don't care about what kind of defense he gets if you can't pick his lawyer. That's fine. I can live with that. What really bothers me, Reverend, is the fact that none, and I repeat none, of the money has been given to the Haileys. Right, Gwen?'

The empty look on her face had turned to one of amazement, then disbelief, then anger as she glared at the reverend.

'Six thousand dollars,' she repeated.

'Over six thousand, at last reported count,' said Jake. 'And the money is lying in some bank while Carl Lee sits in jail, Gwen's not working, the bills are past due, the only food comes from friends, and foreclosure is a few days away. Now, tell us, Reverend, what're your plans with the money?'

Agee smiled and said with an oily voice, 'That's none of your business.'

'But it's my business!' Gwen said loudly. 'You used my name and my family's name when you raised that money, didn't you, Reverend. I heard it myself. Told all the church folk that the love offerin', as you called it, was for my family. I figured you had done spent the money on lawyers' fee or somethin' like that. And now, today, I find out you've got it stuck in the bank. I guess you plan to keep it.'

Agee was unmoved. 'Now wait a minute, Gwen. We thought the money could best be spent on Carl Lee. He declined the money when he refused to hire the NAACP lawyers. So I asked Mr. Reinfeld, the head lawyer, what to do with the money. He told me to save it because Carl Lee will need it for his appeal.'

Jake cocked his head sideways and clenched his teeth. He started to rebuke this ignorant fool, but realized Agee did not understand what he was saying. Jake bit his lip.

'I don't understand,' said Gwen.

'It's simple,' said the reverend with an accommodating smile. 'Mr. Reinfeld said that Carl Lee would be convicted because he didn't hire him. So then we've got to appeal, right? And after Jake here loses the trial, you and Carl Lee will of course be lookin' for another lawyer who can save his life. That's when we'll need Reinfeld and that's when we'll need the money. So you see, it's all for Carl Lee.'

Jake shook his head and silently cursed. He cursed Reinfeld more than Agee.

Gwen's eyes flooded and she clenched her fists. 'I don't understand all that, and I don't want to understand it. All I know is that I'm tired of beggin' for food, tired of dependin' on others, and tired of worryin' about losin' my house.'

Agee looked at her sadly. 'I understand, Gwen, but –'

'And if you got six thousand dollars of our money in the bank, you're wrong not to give it to us. We've got enough sense to spend it right.'

Carl Lee, Jr., and Jarvis stood next to their mother and comforted her. They stared at Agee.

'But it's for Carl Lee,' the reverend said.

'Good,' Jake said. 'Have you asked Carl Lee how he wants his money spent?'

The dirty little grin left Agee's face and he squirmed in his chair. 'Carl Lee understands what we're doin',' he said without much conviction.

'Thank you. That's not what I asked. Listen to me carefully. Have you asked Carl Lee how he wants his money spent?'

'I think it's been discussed with him,' Agee lied.

'Let's see,' Jake said. He stood and walked to the door leading to the small office next to the conference room. The reverend watched nervously, almost in panic. Jake opened the door and nodded to someone. Carl Lee and Ozzie casually walked in. The kids yelled and ran to their father. Agee looked devastated.

After a few awkward minutes of hugs and kisses, Jake moved in for the kill. 'Now, Reverend, why don't you ask Carl Lee how he wants to spend his six thousand dollars.'

'It ain't exactly his,' said Agee.

'And it ain't exactly yours,' shot Ozzie.

Carl Lee removed Tonya from his knee and walked to the chair where Agee was sitting. He sat on the edge of the table, above the reverend, poised and ready to strike if necessary. 'Let me make it real simple, preacher, so you won't have trouble understandin' it. You raised that money in my name, for the benefit of my family. You took it from the black folk of this county, and you took it with the promise that it'd go to help me and my family. You lied. You raised it so you could impress the NAACP, not to help my family. You lied in church, you lied in the newspapers, you lied everwhere.'

Agee looked around the room and noticed that everyone, including the kids, was staring at him and nodding slowly.

Carl Lee put his foot in Agee's chair and leaned closer. 'If you don't give us that money, I'll tell ever nigger I know that you're a lyin' crook. I'll call ever member of your church, and I'm one too, remember, and tell them we ain't got a dime from you, and when I get through you won't be able to raise two dollars on Sunday mornin'. You'll lose your fancy Cadillacs and your fancy suits. You may even lose your church, 'cause I'll ask everbody to leave.'

'You finished?' Agee asked. 'If you are, I just wanna say that I'm hurt. Hurt real bad that you and Gwen feel this way.'

'That's the way we feel, and I don't care how hurt you are.'

Ozzie stepped forward. 'I agree with them, Reverend Agee, you ain't done right, and you know it.'

'That hurts, Ozzie, comin' from you. It really hurts.'

'Lemme tell you what's gonna hurt a whole lot worse than that. Next Sunday me and Carl Lee will be in your church. I'll sneak him outta the jail early Sunday and we'll take a little drive. Just about the time you get ready to preach, we'll walk in the front door, down the aisle and up to the pulpit. If you get in my way, I'll put handcuffs on you. Carl Lee will do the preachin'. He'll tell all your people that the money they've given so generously has so far not left your pocket, that Gwen and the kids are about to lose their house 'cause you're tryin' to big-shot with the NAACP. He'll tell them that you lied to them. He may preach for an hour or so. And when he gets through, I'll say a few words. I'll tell them what a lyin', sleazy nigger you are. I'll tell them about the time you bought that stolen Lincoln in Memphis for a hundred dollars and almost got indicted. I'll tell them about the kickbacks from the funeral home. I'll tell them about the DUI charge in Jackson I got dismissed for you two years ago. And, Reverend, I'll tell –'

'Don't say it, Ozzie,' Agee begged.

'I'll tell them a dirty little secret that only you and me and a certain woman of ill repute know about.'

'When do y'all want the money?'

'How soon can you get it?' Carl Lee demanded.

'Awfully damned quick.'

Jake and Ozzie left the Haileys to themselves and went upstairs to the big office, where Ellen was buried in law books. Jake introduced Ozzie to his law clerk, and the three sat around the big desk.

'How are my buddies?' Jake asked.

'The dynamite boys? They're recuperatin' nicely. We'll keep them in the hospital until the trial's over. We fixed a lock on the door, and I keep a deputy in the hall. They ain't goin' anywhere.'

'Who's the main man?'

'We still don't know. Fingerprint tests haven't come back yet. There may be no prints to match. He ain't talkin'.'

'The other is a local boy, isn't he?' asked Ellen.

'Yeah. Terrell Grist. He wants to sue because he got hurt during the arrest. Can you imagine?'

'I can't believe it's been kept quiet so far,' Jake said.

'Me neither. Of course, Grist and Mr. X ain't talkin'. My men are quiet. That leaves you and your clerk here.'

'And Lucien, but I didn't tell him.'

'Figures.'

'When will you process them?'

'After the trial we'll move them to the jail and start the paperwork. It's up to us.'

'How's Bud?' Jake asked.

'I stopped by this mornin' to check on the other two, and I went downstairs to see Ethel. He's still critical. No changes.'

'Any suspects?'

'Gotta be the Klan. With the white robes and all. It all adds up. First there was the burnin' cross in your yard, then the dynamite, and now Bud. Plus all the death threats. I figure it's them. And we got an informant.'

'You what!'

'You heard me. Calls himself Mickey Mouse. He called me at home Sunday and told me that he saved your life. "That nigger's lawyer" is what he called you. Said the Klan has officially arrived in Ford County. They've set up a klavern, whatever that is.'

'Who's in it?'

'He ain't much on details. He promised to call me only if someone is about to get hurt.'

'How nice. Can you trust him?'

'He saved your life.'

'Good point. Is he a member?'

'Didn't say. They've got a big march planned Thursday.'

'The Klan?'

'Yep. NAACP has a rally tomorrow in front of the courthouse. Then they're gonna march for a while. The Klan's supposed to show up for a peaceful march on Thursday.'

'How many?'

'The Mouse didn't say. Like I said, he ain't much on details.'

'The Klan, marching in Clanton. I can't believe it.'

'This is heavy stuff,' Ellen said.

'It'll get heavier,' Ozzie replied. 'I've asked the governor to keep the highway patrol on standby. It could be a rough week.'

'Can you believe Noose is willing to try this case in this town?' asked Jake.

'It's too big to move, Jake. It would draw marches, and protests, and Klansmen anywhere you tried it.'

'Maybe you're right. How about your jury list?'

'I'll have it tomorrow.'

After supper Tuesday Joe Frank Perryman sat on his front porch with the evening paper and a fresh chew of Red Man, and spat carefully, neatly through a small hand-carved hole in the porch. This was the evening ritual. Lela would finish the dishes and fix them a tall glass of iced tea, and they would sit on the porch until dark and talk about the crops, the grandchildren, the humidity. They lived out from Karaway on eighty acres of neatly trimmed and cultivated farmland that Joe Frank's father had stolen during the Depression. They were quiet, hardworking Christian folks.

After a few discharges through the hole, a pickup slowed out on the highway and turned into the Perrymans' long gravel driveway. It parked next to the front lawn, and a familiar face emerged. It was Will Tierce, former president of the Ford County Board of Supervisors. Will had served his district for twenty-four years, six consecutive terms, but had lost the last election in '83 by seven votes. The Perrymans had always supported Tierce because he took care of them with an occasional load of gravel or a culvert for the driveway.

'Evenin', Will,' said Joe Frank as the ex-supervisor walked across the lawn and up the steps.

'Evenin', Joe Frank.' They shook hands and relaxed on the porch.

'Gimme a chew,' Tierce said.

'Sure. What brings you around here?'

'Just passin' by. Thought about Lela's iced tea and got real thirsty. Hadn't seen you folks in a while.'

They sat and talked, chewed and spat, and drank iced tea until it was dark and time for the mosquitoes. The drought required most of their time and Joe Frank talked at length of the dry spell and how it was the worst in ten years. Hadn't had a drop of rain since the third week of June. And if it didn't let up, he could forget the cotton crop. The beans might make it, but he was worried about the cotton.

'Say, Joe Frank, I hear you got one of those jury summons for the trial next week.'

'Yeah, afraid so. Who told you?'

'I don't know. I just heard it around.'

'I didn't know it was public knowledge.'

'Well, I guess I must've heard it in Clanton today. I had business at the courthouse. That's where I heard it. It's that nigger's trial, you know.'

'That's what I figured.'

'How do you feel about that nigger shootin' them boys like he did?'

'I don't blame him,' inserted Lela.

'Yeah, but you can't take the law into your own hands,' explained Joe Frank to his wife. 'That's what the court system is for.'

'I'll tell you what bothers me,' said Tierce, 'is this insanity crap. They're gonna say the nigger was crazy and try to get him off by insanity. Like that nut who shot Reagan. It's a crooked way to get off. Plus it's a lie. That nigger planned to kill them boys, and just sat there and waited on them. It was cold-blooded murder.'

'What if it was your daughter, Will?' asked Lela.

'I'd let the courts handle it. When we catch a rapist around here, especially a nigger, we generally lock him up. Parchman's full of rapists who'll never get out. This ain't New York or California or some crazy place where criminals go free. We've got a good system, and old Judge Noose hands down tough sentences. You gotta let the courts handle it. Our system won't survive if we allow people, especially niggers, to take the law into their own hands. That's what really scares me. Suppose this nigger gets off, walks out of the courthouse a free man. Everbody in the country will know it, and the niggers will go crazy. Evertime somebody crosses a nigger, he'll just kill him, then say he was insane, and try to get off. That's what's dangerous about this trial.'

'You gotta keep the niggers under control,' agreed Joe Frank.

'You better believe it. And if Hailey gets off, none of us will be safe. Ever nigger in this county'll carry a gun and just look for trouble.'

'I hadn't really thought about that,' admitted Joe Frank.

'I hope you do the right thing, Joe Frank. I just hope they put you in that jury box. We need some people with some sense.'

'Wonder why they picked me?'

'I heard they fixed up a hundred and fifty summonses. They're expectin' about a hundred to show up.'

'What're my chances of gettin' picked?'

'One in a hundred,' said Lela.

'I feel better then. I really ain't got time to serve, what with my farmin' and all.'

'We sure need you on that jury,' said Tierce.

The conversation drifted to local politics and the new supervisor and what a sorry job he was doing with the roads. Darkness meant bedtime for the Perrymans. Tierce said good night and drove home. He sat at his kitchen table with a cup of coffee and reviewed the jury list. His friend Rufus would be proud. Six names had been circled on Will's list, and he had talked to all six. He put an okay by each name. They would be good jurors, people Rufus could count on to keep law and order in Ford County. A couple had been noncommittal at first, but their good and trusted friend Will Tierce had explained justice to them and they were now ready to convict.

Rufus would be real proud. And he had promised that young Jason Tierce, a nephew, would never be tried on those dope charges.

Jake picked at the greasy pork chops and butterbeans, and watched Ellen across the table do the same thing. Lucien sat at the head of the table, ignored his food, fondled his drink, and flipped through the jury list offering comments on every name he recognized. He was drunker than normal. Most of the names he didn't recognize, but he commented on them anyway. Ellen was amused and winked repeatedly at her boss.

He dropped the list, and knocked his fork off the table.

'Sallie!' he yelled.

'Do you know how many ACLU members are in Ford County?' he asked Ellen.

'At least eighty percent of the population,' she said.

'One. Me. I was the first in history and evidently the last. These people are fools around here, Row Ark. They don't appreciate civil liberties. They're a bunch of right-wing knee-jerk conservative Republican fanatics, like our friend Jake here.'

'That's not true. I eat at Claude's at least once a week,' Jake said.

'So that makes you progressive?' asked Lucien.

'It makes me a radical.'

'I still think you're a Republican.'

'Look, Lucien, you can talk about my wife, or my mother, or my ancestors, but don't call me a Republican.'

'You look like a Republican,' said Ellen.

'Does he look like a Democrat?' Jake asked, pointing at Lucien.

'Of course. I knew he was a Democrat the moment I saw him.'

'Then I'm a Republican.'

'See! See!' yelled Lucien. He dropped his glass on the floor and it shattered.

'Sallie!'

'Row Ark, guess who was the third white man in Mississippi to join the NAACP?'

'Rufus Buckley,' said Jake.

'Me. Lucien Wilbanks. Joined in 1967. White people thought I was crazy.'

'Can you imagine,' Jake said.

'Of course, black folks, or Negroes as we called them back then, thought I was crazy too. Hell, everybody thought I was crazy back then.'

'Have they ever changed their minds?' Jake asked.

'Shut up, Republican. Row Ark, why don't you move to Clanton and We'll start us a law firm handling nothing but ACLU cases. Hell, bring your old man down from Boston and we'll make him a partner.'

'Why don't you just go to Boston?' Jake asked.

'Why don't you just go to hell?'

'What will we call it?' asked Ellen.

'The nut house,' said Jake.

'Wilbanks, Row and Ark. Attorneys at law.'

'None of whom have licenses,' said Jake.

Lucien's eyelids weighed several pounds each. His head nodded forward involuntarily. He slapped Sallie on the rear as she cleaned up his mess.

'That was a cheap shot, Jake,' he said seriously.

'Row Ark,' Jake said, imitating Lucien, 'guess who was the last lawyer permanently disbarred by the Mississippi Supreme Court?'

Ellen gracefully smiled at both men and said nothing.

'Row Ark,' Lucien said loudly, 'guess who will be the next lawyer in this county to be evicted from his office?' He roared with laughter, screaming and shaking. Jake winked at her.

When he settled down, he asked, 'What's this meeting tomorrow night?'

'I want to cover the jury list with you and a few others.'

'Who?'

'Harry Rex, Stan Atcavage, maybe one other.'

'Where?'

'Eight o'clock. My office. No alcohol.'

'It's my office, and I'll bring a case of whiskey if I want to. My grandfather built the building, remember?'

'How could I forget.'

'Row Ark, let's get drunk.'

'No thanks, Lucien. I've enjoyed dinner, and the conversation, but I need to get back to Oxford.'

They stood and left Lucien at the table. Jake declined the usual invitation to sit on the porch. Ellen left, and he went to his temporary room upstairs. He had promised Carla he would not sleep at home. He called her. She and Hanna were fine. Worried, but fine. He didn't mention Bud Twitty.

CHAPTER TWENTY-NINE

A convoy of converted school buses, each with an original paint job of white and red or green and black or a hundred other combinations and the name of a church emblazoned along the sides under the windows, rolled slowly around the Clanton square after lunch Wednesday. There were thirty-one in all, each packed tightly with elderly black people who waved paper fans and handkerchiefs in a futile effort to overcome the stifling heat. After three trips around the courthouse, the lead bus stopped by the post office and thirty-one doors flew open. The buses emptied in a frenzy. The people were directed to a gazebo on the courthouse lawn, where Reverend Ollie Agee was shouting orders and handing out blue and white FREE CARL LEE placards.

The side streets leading into the square became congested as cars from all directions inched toward the courthouse and finally parked when they could move no closer. Hundreds of blacks left their vehicles in the streets and walked solemnly toward the square. They mingled around the gazebo and waited for their placards, then wandered through the oaks and magnolias looking for shade and greeting friends. More church buses arrived and were unable to circle the square because of the traffic. They unloaded next to the Coffee Shop.

For the first time that year the temperature hit a hundred and promised to go higher. The sky produced no clouds for protection, and there were no winds or breezes to weaken the burning rays or to blow away the humidity. A man's shirt would soak and stick to his back in fifteen minutes under a shade tree; five minutes without shade. Some of the weaker old folks found refuge inside the courthouse.

The crowd continued to grow. It was predominantly elderly, but there were many younger, militant, angry-looking blacks who had missed the great civil rights marches and demonstrations of the sixties and now realized that this might be a rare opportunity to shout and protest and sing 'We Shall Overcome,' and in general celebrate being black and oppressed in a white world. They meandered about waiting for someone to take charge. Finally, three students marched to the front steps of the courthouse, lifted their placards, and shouted, 'Free Carl Lee. Free Carl Lee.'

Instantly, the mob repeated the war cry:

'Free Carl Lee!'

'Free Carl Lee!'

'Free Carl Lee!'

They left the shade trees and courthouse and moved closer together near the steps where a makeshift podium and PA system had been set up. They yelled in unison at no one or no place or nothing in particular, just howled the newly established battle cry in a perfect chorus:

'Free Carl Lee!'

'Free Carl Lee!'

The windows of the courthouse flew open as the clerks and secretaries gawked at the happening below. The roar could be heard for blocks and the small shops and offices around the square emptied. The owners and customers filled the sidewalks and watched in astonishment. The demonstrators noticed their spectators, and the attention fueled the chanting, which increased in tempo and volume. The vultures had loitered about waiting and watching, and the noise excited them. They descended upon the front lawn of the courthouse with cameras and microphones.

Ozzie and his men directed traffic until the highway and the streets were hopelessly gridlocked. They maintained a presence, although there was no hint they would be needed.

Agee and every full-time, part-time, retired, and prospective black preacher in three counties paraded through the dense mass of black screaming faces and made their way to the podium. The sight of the ministers pumped up the celebrants, and their unified chants reverberated around the square, down the side streets into the sleepy residential districts and out into the countryside. Thousands of blacks waved their placards and yelled their lungs out. Agee swayed with the crowd. He danced across the small podium. He slapped hands with the other ministers. He led the rhythmic noise like a choir director. He was a sight.

'Free Carl Lee!'

'Free Carl Lee!'

For fifteen minutes, Agee whipped the crowd into a frenzied, coalescent mob. Then, when with his finely trained ear he detected the first hint of fatigue, he walked to the microphones and asked for quiet. The panting, sweating faces yelled on but with less volume. The chants of freedom died quickly. Agee asked for room near the front so the press could congregate and do its job. He asked for stillness so they could go to the Lord in prayer. Reverend Roosevelt offered a marathon to the Lord, an eloquent, alliterative oratorical fiesta that brought tears to the eyes of many.

When he finally said 'Amen,' an enormous black woman with a sparkling red wig stepped to the microphones and opened her vast mouth. The opening stanza of 'We Shall Overcome' flowed forth in a deep, rich, mellow river of glorious a cappella. The ministers behind her immediately clasped hands and began to sway. Spontaneity swept the crowd and two thousand voices joined her in surprising harmony. The mournful, promising anthem rose above the small town.

When they finished, someone shouted 'Free Carl Lee!' and ignited another round of chanting. Agee quieted them again, and stepped to the microphones. He pulled an index card from his pocket, and began his sermon.

As expected, Lucien arrived late and half loaded. He brought a bottle and offered a drink to Jake, Atcavage, and Harry Rex, and each declined.

'It's a quarter till nine, Lucien,' Jake said. 'We've been waiting for almost an hour.'

'I'm being paid for this, am I?' he asked.

'No, but I asked you to be here at eight sharp.'

'And you also told me not to bring a bottle. And I informed you this was my building, built by my grandfather, leased to you as my tenant, for a very reasonable rent I might add, and I will come and go as I please, with or without a bottle.'

'Forget it. Did you –'

'What're those blacks doing across the street walking around the courthouse in the dark?'

'It's called a vigil,' explained Harry Rex. 'They've vowed to walk around the courthouse with candles, keeping a vigil until their man is free.'

'That could be an awfully long vigil. I mean, those poor people could be walking until they die. I mean, this could be a twelve-, fifteen-year vigil. They might set a record. They might have candle wax up to their asses. Evenin', Row Ark.'

Ellen sat at the rolltop desk under William Faulkner. She looked at a well-marked copy of the jury list. She nodded and smiled at Lucien.

'Row Ark,' Lucien said, 'I have all the respect in the world for you. I view you as an equal. I believe in your right to equal pay for equal work. I believe in your right to choose whether to have a child or abort. I believe in all that crap. You are a woman and entitled to no special privileges because of your gender. You should be treated just like a man.' Lucien reached in his pocket and pulled out a clip of cash. 'And since you are a law clerk, genderless in my eyes, I think you should be the one to go buy a case of cold Coors.'

'No, Lucien,' Jake said.

'Shut up, Jake.'

Ellen stood and stared at Lucien. 'Sure, Lucien. But I'll pay for the beer.'

She left the office.

Jake shook his head and fumed at Lucien. 'This could be a long night.'

Harry Rex changed his mind and poured a shot of whiskey into his coffee cup.

'Please don't get drunk,' Jake begged. 'We've got work to do.'

'I work better when I'm drunk,' said Lucien.

'Me too,' said Harry Rex.

'This could be interesting,' said Atcavage.

Jake laid his feet on his desk and puffed on a cigar. 'Okay, the first thing I want to do is decide on a model juror.'

'Black,' said Lucien.

'Black as old Coaly's ass,' said Harry Rex.

'I agree,' said Jake. 'But we won't get a chance. Buckley will save his peremptory challenges for the blacks. We know that. We've got to concentrate on white people.'

'Women,' said Lucien. 'Always pick women for criminal trials. They have bigger hearts, bleeding hearts, and they're much more sympathetic. Always go for women.'

'Naw,' said Harry Rex. 'Not in this case. Women don't understand things like taking a gun and blowing people away. You need fathers, young fathers who would want to do the same thing Hailey did. Daddies with little girls.'

'Since when did you get to be such an expert on picking juries?' asked Lucien. 'I thought you were a sleazy divorce lawyer.'

'I am a sleazy divorce lawyer, but I know how to pick juries.'

'And listen to them through the wall.'

'Cheap shot.'

Jake raised his arms. 'Fellas, please. How about Victor Onzell? You know him, Stan?'

'Yeah, he banks with us. He's about forty, married, three or four kids. White. From somewhere up North. Runs the truck stop on the highway north of town. He's been here about five years.'

'I wouldn't take him,' Lucien said. 'If he's from up North, he doesn't think like we do. Probably in favor of gun control and all that crap. Yankees always scare me in criminal cases. I've always thought we should have a law in Mississippi that no certified yankee could sit on a jury down here regardless of how long he's lived here.'

'Thank you so much,' said Jake.

'I'd take him,' said Harry Rex.

'Why?'

'He's got kids, probably a daughter. If he's from the North he's probably not as prejudiced. Sounds good to me.'

'John Tate Aston.'

'He's dead,' said Lucien.

'What?'

'I said he's dead. Been dead for three years.'

'Why's he on the list?' asked Atcavage, the non-lawyer.

'They don't purge the voter registration list,' explained Harry Rex, between drinks. 'Some die and some move away, and it's impossible to keep the list up to date. They've issued a hundred and fifty summons, and you can expect a hundred to a hundred and twenty to show up. The rest have died or moved away.'

'Caroline Baxter. Ozzie says she's black,' Jake said flipping through his notes. 'Works at the carburetor plant in Karaway.'

'Take her,' said Lucien.

'I wish,' said Jake.

Ellen returned with the beer. She dropped it in Lucien's lap and tore a sixteen-ounce can out of a six-pack. She popped the top and returned to the rolltop desk. Jake declined, but Atcavage decided he was thirsty. Jake remained the non-drinker.

'Joe Kitt Shepherd.'

'Sounds like a redneck,' said Lucien.

'Why do you say that?' asked Harry Rex.

'The double first name,' Lucien explained. 'Most rednecks have double first names. Like Billy Ray, Johnny Ray, Bobby Lee, Harry Lee, Jesse Earl, Billy Wayne, Jerry Wayne, Eddie Mack. Even their women have double first names. Bobbie Sue, Betty Pearl, Mary Belle, Thelma Lou, Sally Faye.'

'What about Harry Rex?' asked Harry Rex.

'Never heard of a woman named Harry Rex.'

'I mean for a male redneck.'

'I guess it'll do.'

Jake interrupted. 'Dell Perry said he used to own a bait shop down by the lake. I take it no one knows him.'

'No, but I bet he's a redneck,' said Lucien. 'Because of his name. I'd scratch him.'

'Aren't you given their addresses, ages, occupations, basic information like that?' asked Atcavage.

'Not until the day of trial. On Monday each prospective juror fills out a questionnaire in the courtroom. But until then we have only the names.'

'What kind of juror are we looking for, Jake?' Ellen asked.

'Young to middle-aged men with families. I would prefer to have no one over fifty.'

'Why?' Lucien asked belligerently.

'Younger whites are more tolerant of blacks.'

'Like Cobb and Willard,' Lucien said.

'Most of the older folks will always dislike blacks, but the younger generation has accepted an integrated society. Less bigotry, as a rule, with youth.'

'I agree,' said Harry Rex, 'and I would stay away from women and rednecks.'

'That's my plan.'

'I think you're wrong,' said Lucien. 'Women are more sympathetic. Just look at Row Ark. She's sympathetic toward everyone. Right, Row Ark?'

'Right, Lucien.'

'She has sympathy for criminals, child pornographers, atheists, illegal immigrants, gays. Don't you, Row Ark?'

'Right, Lucien.'

'She and I hold the only two ACLU cards existing at this very moment in Ford County, Mississippi.'

'That's sick,' said Atcavage, the banker.

'Clyde Sisco,' Jake said loudly, trying to minimize controversy.

'He can be bought,' Lucien said smugly.

'What do you mean "He can be bought"?' Jake asked.

'Just what I said. He can be bought.'

'How do you know?' asked Harry Rex.

'Are you kidding? He's a Sisco. Biggest bunch of crooks in the eastern part of the county. They all live around the Mays community. They're professional thieves and insurance defrauders. They burn their houses every three years. You've never heard of them?' He was shouting at Harry Rex.

'No. How do you know he can be bought?'

'Because I bought him once. In a civil case, ten years ago. He was on the jury list, and I got word to him that I'd give him ten percent of the jury verdict. He's very persuasive.'

Jake dropped the jury lists and rubbed his eyes. He knew this was probably true, but didn't want to believe it.

'And?' asked Harry Rex.

'And he was selected for the jury, and I got the largest verdict in the history of Ford County. It's still the record.'

'Stubblefield?' Jake asked in disbelief.

'That's it, my boy. Stubblefield versus North Texas Pipeline. September 1974. Eight hundred thousand dollars. Appealed and affirmed by the Supreme Court.'

'Did you pay him?' asked Harry Rex.

Lucien finished a long drink and smacked his lips. 'Eighty thousand cash, in one-hundred-dollar bills,' he said proudly. He built a new house, then burned it down.'

'What was your cut?' asked Atcavage.

'Forty percent, minus eighty thousand.'

The room was silent as everybody but Lucien made the calculation.

'Wow,' Atcavage mumbled.

'You're kidding, aren't you, Lucien?' Jake asked half-heartedly.

'You know I'm serious, Jake. You know I lie compulsively, but never about things like this. I'm telling the truth, and I'm telling you this guy can be bought.'

'How much?' asked Harry Rex.

'Forget it!' said Jake.

'Five thousand cash, just guessing.'

'Forget it!'

There was a pause as each one looked at Jake to make sure he was not interested in Clyde Sisco, and when it was obvious he was not interested, they took a drink and waited for the next name. Around ten-thirty Jake had his first beer, and an hour later the case was gone and forty names remained. Lucien staggered to the balcony and watched the blacks carry their candles along the sidewalks next to the streets around the courthouse.

'Jake, why is this deputy sitting in his car in front of my office?' he asked.

'That's my bodyguard.'

'What's his name?'

'Nesbit.'

'Is he awake?'

'Probably not.'

Lucien leaned dangerously over the railing. 'Hey, Nesbit,' he yelled.

Nesbit opened the door of his patrol car. 'Yeah, what is it?'

'Jake here wants you to go to the store and get us some more beer. He's very thirsty. Here's a twenty. He'd like a case of Coors.'

'I can't buy it when I'm on duty,' Nesbit protested.

'Since when?' Lucien laughed at himself.

'I can't do it.'

'It's not for you, Nesbit. It's for Mr. Brigance, and he really needs it. He's already called the sheriff, and it's okay.'

'Who called the sheriff?'

'Mr. Brigance,' lied Lucien. 'Sheriff said he didn't care what you did as long as you didn't drink any.'

Nesbit shrugged and appeared satisfied. Lucien dropped a twenty from the balcony. Within minutes Nesbit was back with a case minus one which had been opened and was sitting on his radar gun. Lucien ordered Atcavage to fetch the beer from below and distribute the first six-pack.

An hour later the list was finished and the party was over. Nesbit loaded Harry Rex, Lucien, and Atcavage into his patrol car and took them home. Jake and his clerk sat on the balcony, sipping and watching the candles flicker and move slowly around the courthouse. Several cars were parked on the west side of the square, and a small group of blacks sat nearby in lawn chairs waiting to take their turns with the candles.

'We didn't do bad,' Jake said quietly, staring at the vigil. 'We made notes on all but twenty of the hundred and fifty.'

'What's next?'

'I'll try to find something on the other twenty, then we'll make an index card for each juror. We'll know them like family by Monday.'

Nesbit returned to the square and circled twice, watching the blacks. He parked between the Saab and the BMW.

'The M'Naghten brief is a masterpiece. Our psychiatrist, Dr. Bass, will be here tomorrow, and I want you to review M'Naghten with him. You need to outline in detail the necessary questions to ask him at trial, and cover these with him. He worries me. I don't know him, and I'm relying on Lucien. Get his résumé and investigate his background. Make whatever phone calls are necessary. Check with the state medical association to make sure he has no history of disciplinary problems. He is very important to our case, and I don't want any surprises.'

'Okay, boss.'

Jake finished his last beer. 'Look, Row Ark, this is a very small town. My wife left five days ago, and I'm sure people will know it soon. You look suspicious. People love to talk, so be discreet. Stay in the office and do your research and tell anyone who asks that you're Ethel's replacement.'

'That's a big bra to fill.'

'You could do it if you wanted to.'

'I hope you know that I'm not nearly as sweet as I'm being forced to act.'

'I know that.'

They watched the blacks change shifts and a new crew take up the candles. Nesbit threw an empty beer can onto the sidewalk.

'You're not driving home are you?' Jake asked.

'It would not be a good idea. I'd register at least .20.'

'You can sleep on the couch in my office.'

'Thanks. I will.'

Jake said good night, locked the office, and spoke briefly to Nesbit. Then he placed himself carefully behind the wheel of the Saab. Nesbit followed him to his home on Adams. He parked under the carport, next to Carla's car, and Nesbit parked in the driveway. It was 1:00 A.M., Thursday, July 18.

CHAPTER THIRTY

They arrived in groups of two and three and came from all over the state. They parked along the gravel road by the cabin deep in the woods. They entered the cabin dressed as normal working men, but once inside they slowly and meticulously changed into their neatly pressed and neatly folded robes and headdresses. They admired one another's uniforms and helped each other into the bulky outfits. Most of them knew each other, but a few introductions were necessary. They were forty in number; a good turnout.

Stump Sisson was pleased. He sipped whiskey and moved around the room like a head coach reassuring his team before the kickoff. He inspected the uniforms and made adjustments. He was proud of his men, and told them so. It was the biggest meeting of its kind in years, he said. He admired them and their sacrifices in being there. He knew they had jobs and families, but this was important. He talked about the glory days when they were feared in Mississippi and had clout. Those days must return, and it was up to this very group of dedicated men to take a stand for white people. The march could be dangerous, he explained. Niggers could march and demonstrate all day long and no one cared. But let white folks try and march and it was dangerous. The city had issued a permit, and the nigger sheriff promised order, but most Klan marches nowadays were disrupted by roving bands of young wild nigger punks. So be careful, and keep ranks. He, Stump, would do the talking.

They listened intently to Stump's pep talk, and when he finished they loaded into a dozen cars and followed him to town.

Few if any people in Clanton had ever seen the Klan march, and as 2:00 P.M. approached a great wave of excitement rippled around the square. The merchants and their customers found excuses to inspect the sidewalks. They milled about importantly and watched the side streets. The vultures were out in full force and had congregated near the gazebo on the front lawn. A group of young blacks gathered nearby under a massive oak. Ozzie smelled trouble. They assured him they had only come to watch and listen. He threatened them with jail if trouble started. He stationed his men at various points around the courthouse.

'Here they come!' someone yelled, and the spectators strained to get a glimpse of the marching Klansmen as they strutted importantly from a small street onto Washington Avenue, the north border of the square. They walked cautiously, but arrogantly, their faces hidden by the sinister red and white masks hanging from the royal headdresses. The spectators gawked at the faceless figures as the procession moved slowly along Washington, then south along Caffey Street, then east along Jackson Street. Stump waddled proudly in front of his men. When he neared the front of the courthouse, he made a sharp left turn and led his troops down the long sidewalk in the center of the front lawn. They closed ranks in a loose semicircle around the podium on the courthouse steps.

The vultures had scrambled and fallen over themselves following the march, and when Stump stopped his men the podium was quickly adorned with a dozen microphones trailing wires in all directions to the cameras and recorders. Under the tree the group of blacks had grown larger, much larger, and some of them walked to within a few feet of the semicircle. The sidewalks emptied as the merchants and shopkeepers, their customers, and the other curious streamed across the streets onto the lawn to hear what the leader, the short fat one, was about to say. The deputies walked slowly through the crowd, paying particular attention to the group of blacks. Ozzie placed himself under the oak, in the midst of his people.

Jake watched intently from the window in Jean Gillespie's second floor office. The sight of the Klansmen, in full regalia, their cowardly faces hidden behind the ominous masks, gave him a sick feeling. The white hood, for decades a symbol of hatred and violence in the South, was back. Which one of those men had burned the cross in his yard? Were they all active in planning the bombing of his home? Which one would try something next? From the second floor, he could see the blacks inch closer.

'You niggers were not invited to this rally!' Stump screamed into the microphone, pointing at the blacks. 'This is a Klan meetin', not a meetin' for a buncha niggers!'

From the side streets and small alleys behind the rows of red brick buildings, a steady stream of blacks moved toward the courthouse. They joined the others, and in seconds Stump and his boys were outnumbered ten to one. Ozzie radioed for backup.

'My name's Stump Sisson,' he said as he removed his mask. 'And I'm proud to say I'm the Mississippi Imperial Wizard for the Invisible Empire of the Ku Klux Klan. I'm here to say that the law-abidin' white folks of Mississippi are sick and tired of niggers stealin', rapin', killin', and gettin' by with it. We demand justice, and we demand that this Hailey nigger be convicted and his black ass sent to the gas chamber!'

'Free Carl Lee!' screamed one of the blacks.

'Free Carl Lee!' they repeated in unison.

'Free Carl Lee!'

'Shut up, you wild niggers!' Stump shrieked back. 'Shut up, you animals!' His troops stood facing him, frozen, with their backs to the screaming crowd. Ozzie and six deputies moved between the groups.

'Free Carl Lee!'

'Free Carl Lee!'

Stump's naturally colorful face had turned an even deeper red. His teeth nearly touched the microphones. 'Shut up, you wild niggers! You had your rally yesterday and we didn't disturb you. We have a right to assemble in peace, just like you do! Now, shut up!'

The chanting intensified. 'Free Carl Lee! Free Carl Lee!'

'Where's the sheriff? He's supposed to keep law and order. Sheriff, do your job. Shut those niggers up so we can assemble in peace. Can't you do your job, Sheriff? Can't you control your own people? See, folks, that's what you get when you elect niggers to public office.'

The shouting continued and Stump stepped back from the microphones and watched the blacks. The photographers and TV crews spun in circles trying to record it all. No one noticed a small window on the third floor of the courthouse. It opened slowly, and from the darkness within a crude firebomb was thrown onto the podium below. It landed perfectly at Stump's feet and exploded, engulfing the wizard in flames.

The riot was on. Stump screamed and rolled wildly down the front steps. Three of his men shed their heavy robes and masks and attempted to cover him and smother the flames. The wooden podium and platform burned with the thick, unmistakable smell of gasoline. The blacks charged, wielding sticks and knives and hacking at anything with a white face or white robe. Under each white robe was a short black nightstick, and the Klansmen proved ready for the assault. Within seconds of the explosion, the front lawn of the Ford County Courthouse was a battlefield as men screamed and cursed and howled in pain through thick, heavy smoke. The air was filled with rocks and stones and nightsticks as the two groups brawled in hand-to-hand combat.

Bodies began falling on the lush, green grass. Ozzie fell first; the victim of a wicked smash to the base of his skull with a wrecking bar. Nesbit, Prather, Hastings, Pirtle, Tatum, and other deputies ran here and there attempting unsuccessfully to separate various combatants before they killed each other. Instead of running for cover, the vultures darted crazily through the midst of the smoke and violence valiantly trying to capture yet a better shot of the blood and gore. They were sitting ducks. One cameraman, his right eye buried deep in his camera, caught a jagged piece of brick with his left eye. He and his camera dropped quickly to the sidewalk, where, after a few seconds, another cameraman appeared and filmed his fallen comrade. A fearless, busy female reporter from a Memphis station charged into the melee with her microphone in hand and her cameraman at her heels. She dodged a brick, then maneuvered too close to a large Klansman who was just finishing off a couple of black teenagers, when, with a loud piercing scream, he slapped her pretty head with his nightstick, kicked her as she fell, then brutally attacked her cameraman.

Fresh troops from the Clanton City Police arrived. In the center of the battle, Nesbit, Prather, and Hastings came together, stood with their backs to each other, and began firing their Smith & Wesson .357 magnum service revolvers into the air. The sound of the gunfire quelled the riot. The warriors froze and searched for the gunfire, then quickly separated and glared at each other. They retreated slowly to their own groups. The officers formed a dividing line between the blacks and the Klansmen, all of whom were thankful for the truce.

A dozen wounded bodies were unable to retreat. Ozzie sat dazed, rubbing his neck. The lady from Memphis was unconscious and bleeding profusely from the head. Several Klansmen, their white robes soiled and bloody, lay sprawled near the sidewalk. The fire continued to burn.

The sirens drew closer and finally the fire trucks and ambulances arrived and drove onto the battlefield. Firemen and medics attended the wounded. None were dead. Stump Sisson was taken away first. Ozzie was half dragged and half carried to a patrol car. More police arrived and broke up the crowd.

Jake, Harry Rex, and Ellen ate a lukewarm pizza and watched intently as the small television in the conference room broadcasted the day's events in Clanton, Mississippi. CBS ran the story halfway through the news. The reporter had apparently escaped the riot unscathed, and he narrated the video with a play by play of the march, the shouting, the firebomb, and the melee. 'As of late this afternoon,' he reported, 'the exact number of casualties is unknown. The most serious injuries are believed to be the extensive burns suffered by a Mr. Sisson, who identified himself as an imperial wizard of the Ku Klux Klan. He is listed in serious condition at the Mid South Burn Hospital in Memphis.'

The video showed a closeup of Stump burning while all hell broke loose. He continued: 'The trial of Carl Lee Hailey is scheduled to start Monday here in Clanton. It is unknown at this time what effect, if any, today's riot will have on this trial. There is some speculation the trial will be postponed and/or moved to another county.'

'That's news to me,' said Jake.

'You haven't heard anything?' asked Harry Rex.

'Not a word. And I presume I would be notified before CBS.'

The reporter disappeared and Dan Rather said he would return in a moment.

'What does this mean?' asked Ellen.

'It means Noose is stupid for not changing venue.'

'Be glad he didn't,' said Harry Rex. 'It'll give you something to argue on appeal.'

'Thanks, Harry Rex. I appreciate your confidence in my ability as a trial lawyer.'

The phone rang. Harry Rex grabbed it and said hello to Carla. He handed it to Jake. 'It's your wife. Can we listen?'

'No! Go get another pizza. Hello dear.'

'Jake, are you all right?'

'Of course I'm all right.'

'I just saw it on the news. It's awful. Where were you?'

'I was wearing one of those white robes.'

'Jake, please. This is not funny.'

'I was in Jean Gillespie's office on the second floor. We had wonderful seats. Saw the whole thing. It was very exciting.'

'Who are those people?'

'Same ones who burned the cross in our front yard and tried to blow up the house.'

'Where are they from?'

'Everywhere. Five are in the hospital and their addresses are scattered all over the state. One is a local boy. How's Hanna?'

'She's fine. She wants to come home. Will the trial be postponed?'

'I doubt it.'

'Are you safe?'

'Sure. I've got a full-time bodyguard and I carry a .38 in my briefcase. Don't worry.'

'But I'm worried, Jake. I need to be home with you.'

'No.'

'Hanna can stay here until it's over, but I want to come home.'

'No, Carla. I know you're safe out there. You won't be safe if you're here.'

'Then you're not safe either.'

'I'm as safe as I can get. But I'm not taking chances with you and Hanna. It's out of the question. That's final. How are your parents?'

'I didn't call to talk about my parents. I called because I'm scared and I want to be with you.'

'And I want to be with you, but not now. Please understand.'

She hesitated. 'Where are you staying?'

'At Lucien's most of the time. Occasionally at home, with my bodyguard in the driveway.'

'How's my house?'

'It's still there. Dirty, but still there.'

'I miss it.'

'Believe me, it misses you.'

'I love you, Jake, and I'm scared.'

'I love you, and I'm not scared. Just relax and take care of Hanna.'

'Goodbye.'

'Goodbye.'

Jake handed the receiver to Ellen. 'Where is she?'

'Wilmington, North Carolina. Her parents spend the summers there.'

Harry Rex had left for another pizza.

'You miss her, don't you?' asked Ellen.

'In more ways than you can imagine.'

'Oh, I can imagine.'

At midnight they were in the cabin drinking whiskey, cussing niggers, and comparing wounds. Several had returned from the hospital in Memphis where they had visited briefly with Stump Sisson. He told them to proceed as planned. Eleven had been released from the Ford County Hospital with various cuts and bruises, and the others admired their wounds as each took his turn describing to the last detail how he had gallantly battled multiple niggers before being wounded, usually from the rear or blind side. They were the heroes, the ones with the bandages. Then the others told their stories and the whiskey flowed. They heaped praise upon the largest one when he told of his attack on the pretty television reporter and her nigger cameraman.

After a couple of hours of drinking and storytelling the talk turned to the task at hand. A map of the county was produced, and one of the locals pinpointed the targets. There were twenty homes this night – twenty names taken from the list of prospective jurors someone had furnished.

Five teams of four each left the cabin in pickups and headed into the darkness to further their mischief. In each pickup were four wooden crosses, the smaller models, nine feet by four feet, each soaked with kerosene. They avoided Clanton and the small towns in the county and instead kept to the dark countryside. The targets were in isolated areas, away from traffic and neighbors, out in the country where things go unnoticed and people go to bed early and sleep soundly.

The plan of attack was simple: a truck would stop a few hundred feet down the road, out of sight, no headlights, and the driver remained with engine running while the other three carried the cross to the front yard, stuck it in the ground, and threw a torch on it. The pickup then met them in front of the house for a quiet getaway and joyride to the next target.

The plan worked simply and with no complications at nineteen of the twenty targets. But at Luther Pickett's residence a strange noise earlier in the night had aroused Luther, and he sat in the darkness of his front porch waiting for nothing in particular when he saw a strange pickup move suspiciously along the gravel road out beyond his pecan tree. He grabbed his shotgun and listened as the truck turned around and stopped down the road. He heard voices, and then saw three figures carrying a pole or something into his front yard, next to the gravel road. Luther crouched behind a shrub next to the porch, and aimed.

The driver took a slug of cold beer and watched to see the cross go up in flames. He heard a shotgun instead. His buddies abandoned the cross and the torch and the front yard, and jumped into a small ditch next to the road. Another shotgun blast. The driver could hear the screams and obscenities. They had to be rescued! He threw down his beer and stepped on the gas.

Old Luther fired again as he came off the porch, and again as the truck appeared and stopped by the shallow ditch. The three scrambled desperately from the mud, stumbling and sliding, cussing and yelling as they attacked the truck and furiously fought to jump into the bed.

'Hang on!' yelled the driver just as old Luther fired again, this time spraying the pickup. He watched with a smile as the truck sped away, spinning gravel and fishtailing from ditch to ditch. Just a bunch of drunk kids, he thought.

From a pay phone, a Kluxer held the list of twenty names and twenty phone numbers. He called them all, simply to ask them to take a look in their front yards.

CHAPTER THIRTY-ONE

Friday morning Jake phoned the Noose home and was informed by Mrs. Ichabod that His Honor was presiding over a civil trial in Polk County. Jake gave instructions to Ellen and left for Smithfield, an hour away. He nodded at His Honor as he entered the empty courtroom and sat on the front row. Except for the jurors, there were no other spectators. Noose was bored, the jurors were bored, the lawyers were bored, and after two minutes Jake was bored. After the witness finished Noose called for a short recess, and Jake went to his chambers.

'Hello, Jake. Why're you here?'

'You heard what happened yesterday.'

'I saw it on the news last night.'

'Have you heard what happened this morning?'

'No.'

'Evidently someone gave the Klan a list of the prospective jurors. Last night they burned crosses in the yards of twenty of the jurors.'

Noose was shocked. 'Our jurors!'

'Yes, sir.'

'Did they catch anybody?'

'Of course not. They were too busy putting out fires. Besides, you don't catch these people.'

'Twenty of our jurors,' Noose repeated.

'Yes, sir.'

Noose pawed at his mangled mass of brilliant gray hair and walked slowly around the small room, shaking his head and occasionally scratching his crotch.

'Sounds like intimidation to me,' he muttered.

What a mind, thought Jake. A real genius. 'I would say so.'

'So what am I supposed to do?' he asked with a touch of frustration.

'Change venue.'

'To where?'

'Southern part of the state.'

'I see. Perhaps Carey County. I believe it's sixty percent black. That would generate at least a hung jury, wouldn't it? Or maybe you would like Brower County. I think it's even blacker. You'd probably get an acquittal there, wouldn't you?'

'I don't care where you move it. It's not fair to try him in Ford County. Things were bad enough before the war yesterday. Now the white folks are really in a lynching mood, and my man's got the nearest available neck. The situation was terrible before the Klan started decorating the country with Christmas trees. Who knows what else they'll try before Monday. There's no way to pick a fair and impartial jury in Ford County.'

'You mean black jury?'

'No, sir! I mean a jury that hasn't prejudged this case. Carl Lee Hailey is entitled to twelve people who haven't already decided his guilt or innocence.'

Noose lumbered toward his chair and fell into it. He removed those glasses from that nose and picked at the end of it.

'We could excuse the twenty,' he wondered aloud.

'That won't help. The entire county knows about it or will know about it within a few hours. You know how fast word travels. The entire panel will feel threatened.'

'Then we could disqualify the entire panel and summon a new one.'

'Won't work,' Jake answered sharply, frustrated by Noose's stubbornness. 'All jurors must come from Ford County, and everybody in the county knows about it. And how do you keep the Klan from harassing the next panel? It won't work.'

'What makes you so confident the Klan won't follow the case if I move it to another county?' The sarcasm dripped from every word.

'I think they will follow it,' Jake admitted. 'But we don't know that for sure. What we do know is that the Klan is already in Ford County, that it's quite active now, and that it has already intimidated some potential jurors. That's the issue. The question is, what will you do about it?'

'Nothing,' Noose said bluntly.

'Sir?'

'Nothing. I will do nothing but dismiss the twenty. I will carefully interrogate the panel next Monday, when the trial starts in Clanton.'

Jake stared in disbelief. Noose had a reason, a motive, a fear, something he was not telling. Lucien was right – someone had gotten to him.

'May I ask why?'

'I don't think it matters where we try Carl Lee Hailey. I don't think it matters who we put in the jury box. I don't think it matters what color they are. Their minds are made up. All of them, wherever and whoever they are. They've already made up their minds, Jake, and it's your job to pick those who think your man is a hero.'

That's probably true, thought Jake, but he wouldn't admit it. He continued staring at the trees outside. 'Why are you afraid to move it?'

Ichabod's eyes narrowed, and he glared at Jake. 'Afraid? I'm not afraid of any ruling I make. Why are you afraid to try it in Ford County?'

'I thought I just explained it.'

'Mr. Hailey will be tried in Ford County starting Monday. That's three days from today. And he will be tried there not because I'm afraid to move it, but because it wouldn't do any good to move it. I've considered all this very carefully, Mr. Brigance, many times, and I feel comfortable with the trial in Clanton. It will not be moved. Anything further?'

'No, sir.'

'Good. See you Monday.'

Jake entered his office through the rear door. The front door had been locked for a week now, and there was always someone banging on it and yelling at it. Most of them were reporters, but many were friends just stopping by to gossip and find out what they could about the big trial. Clients were a thing of the past. The phone rang constantly. Jake never touched it and Ellen grabbed it if she was nearby.

He found her in the conference room up to her elbows in law books. The M'Naghten brief was a masterpiece. He had requested no more than twenty pages. She gave him seventy-five perfectly typed and plainly worded pages, and explained there was no way to cover the Mississippi version of M'Naghten in fewer words. Her research was painstaking and detailed. She had started with the original M'Naghten case in England in the 1800's and worked through a hundred and fifty years of insanity law in Mississippi. She discarded insignificant or confusing cases, and explained in wonderful simplicity the complicated, major cases. The brief concluded with a summary of current law, and applied it to the trial of Carl Lee Hailey.

In a smaller brief, only fourteen pages, she had reached the unmistakable conclusion that the jury would see the sickening pictures of Cobb and Willard with their brains splattered about the stairway. Mississippi admitted such inflammatory evidence, and she had found no way around it.

She had typed thirty-one pages of research on the defense of justifiable homicide, something Jake had considered briefly after the killings. She reached the same conclusion Jake had reached – it wouldn't work. She had found an old Mississippi case where a man had caught and killed an escaped convict who was armed. He had been acquitted, but the differences in that case and Carl Lee's case were enormous. Jake had not asked for the brief, and was irritated that so much energy had been spent on it. He said nothing, however, since she had produced everything he had asked for.

The most pleasant surprise had been her work with Dr. W.T. Bass.

She had met with him twice during the week, and they had covered M'Naghten in great detail. She prepared a twenty-five-page script of the questions to be asked by Jake and the answers to be given by Bass. It was a skillfully crafted dialogue, and he marveled at her seasoning. When he was her age, he was an average student more concerned with romance than research. She, on the other hand, as a third-year law student was writing briefs that read like treatises.

'How'd it go?' she asked.

'As expected. He did not budge. The trial will start here Monday with the same panel, minus the twenty who received their subtle warnings.'

'He's crazy.'

'What're you working on?'

'I'm finishing the brief to support our position that the details of the rape should be discussed before the jury. It looks good, at this point.'

'When will you finish it?'

'Is there some hurry?'

'By Sunday, if possible. I've got another chore, something a little different.'

She slid her legal pad away and listened.

'The State's psychiatrist will be Dr. Wilbert Rodeheaver, head of staff at Whitfield. He's been there forever, and has testifed in hundreds of cases. I want you to dig a little and see how often his name appears in court decisions.'

'I've already run across his name.'

'Good. As you know, the only cases we read about from the Supreme Court are the ones where the defendant at trial was convicted and has appealed. The acquittals are not reported. I'm more interested in these.'

'Where are you coming from?'

'I have a hunch Rodeheaver is very reluctant to give an opinion that a defendant was legally insane. There's a chance he's never done it. Even in cases where the defendant was clearly crazy and did not know what he was doing. I'd like to ask Rodeheaver, on cross-examination, about some of the cases in which he's said there's nothing wrong with an obviously sick man, and the jury acquitted him.'

'Those cases will be very hard to find.'

'I know, but you can do it, Row Ark. I've watched you work for a week now, and I know you can do it.'

'I'm flattered, boss.'

'You may have to make phone calls to attorneys around the state who've crossed Rodeheaver before. It'll be hard, Row Ark, but get it done.'

'Yes, boss. I'm sure you wanted it yesterday.'

'Not really. I doubt if we'll get to Rodeheaver next week, so you have some time.'

'I don't know how to act. You mean it's not urgent?'

'No, but that rape brief is.'

'Yes, boss.'

'Have you had lunch?'

'I'm not hungry.'

'Good. Don't make any plans for dinner.'

'What does that mean?'

'It means I've got an idea.'

'Sort of like a date?'

'No, sort of like a business lunch with two professionals.'

Jake packed two briefcases and left. 'I'll be at Lucien's,' he told her, 'but don't call unless it's a dire emergency. Don't tell anyone where I am.'

'What are you working on?'

'The jury.'

Lucien had passed out drunk in the swing on the porch, and Sallie was not around. Jake helped himself to the spacious study upstairs. Lucien had more law books in his home than most lawyers had in their offices. He unpacked his mess in a chair, and on the desk he placed an alphabetical list of the jurors, a stack of three-by-five notecards, and several Magic Markers.

The first name was Acker, Barry Acker. The last name was written in large print across the top of a notecard with a blue Magic Marker. Blue for men, red for women, black for blacks, regardless of gender. Under Acker's name he made notes with a pencil. Age, about forty. Married to his second wife, three children, two daughters. Runs a small unprofitable hardware store on the highway in Clanton. Wife, secretary at a bank. Drives a pickup. Likes to hunt. Wears cowboy boots. Pretty nice guy. Atcavage had gone to the hardware store Thursday to get a look at Barry Acker. Said he looked okay, talked like he had some education. Jake wrote the number nine by the name Acker.

Jake was impressed with his research. Surely Buckley would not be as thorough.

The next name was Bill Andrews. What a name. There were six of them in the phonebook. Jake knew one, Harry Rex knew another one, and Ozzie knew a black one, but nobody knew which one got the summons. He put a question mark by the name.

Gerald Ault. Jake smiled when he wrote the name on the notecard. Ault had passed through his office a few years back when the bank foreclosed on his house in Clanton. His wife was stricken with kidney disease, and the medical bills broke them. He was an intellectual, educated at Princeton, where he met his wife. She was from Ford County, the only child of a once prominent family of fools who had invested all their money in railroads. He arrived in Ford County just in time for his in-laws to go under, and the easy life he had married dissolved into one of struggle. He taught school for a while, then ran the library, then worked as a clerk in the courthouse. He developed an aversion to hard work. Then his wife got sick, and they lost their modest house. He now worked in a convenience store.

Jake knew something about Gerald Ault that no one else knew. As a child in Pennsylvania, his family lived in a farmhouse near the highway. One night while they slept, the house caught fire. A passing motorist stopped, kicked in the front door and began rescuing the Aults. The fire spread quickly, and when Gerald and his brother awoke they were trapped in their upstairs bedroom. They ran to the window and screamed. Their parents and siblings yelled helplessly from the front lawn. Flames poured from every window in the house except for their bedroom. Suddenly, the rescuer soaked himself with water from the garden hose, dashed into the burning house, fought the flames and smoke as he raced upstairs, then bolted through the bedroom door. He kicked out the window, grabbed Gerald and his brother, and jumped to the ground. Miraculously, they were not hurt. They thanked him, through tears and embraces. They thanked this stranger, whose skin was black. He was the first Negro the children had ever seen.

Gerald Ault was one of the few white people in Ford County who truly loved black people. Jake put a ten by his name.

For six hours he went through the jury list, making notecards, concentrating on each name, envisioning each juror in the box and in deliberation, talking to each one. He rated them. Every black got an automatic ten; the whites were not so easy. The men rated higher than the women; the young men higher than the old men; the educated slightly higher than the uneducated; the liberals, both of them, received the highest ratings.

He eliminated the twenty Noose planned to exclude. He knew something about one hundred and eleven of the prospective jurors. Surely, Buckley could not know so much.

Ellen was typing on Ethel's machine when Jake returned from Lucien's. She turned it off, closed the law books she was typing from, and watched him.

'Where's dinner?' she asked with a wicked smile.

'We're taking a road trip.'

'All right! Where to?'

'Have you ever been to Robinsonville, Mississippi?'

'No, but I'm ready. What's there?'

'Nothing but cotton, soybeans, and a great little restaurant.'

'What's the dress code?'

Jake inspected her. She wore the usual – jeans, neatly starched and faded, no socks, a navy button-down that was four sizes too big but tucked in nicely above her slender hips.

'You look fine,' he said.

They turned off the copier and the lights and left Clanton in the Saab. Jake stopped at a liquor store in the black section of town and bought a six-pack of Coors and a tall, cold bottle of Chablis.

'You have to bring your own bottle to this place,' he explained as they left town. The sun was setting into the highway ahead, and Jake flipped down the sun visors. Ellen played bartender and opened two cans.

'How far is this place?' she asked.

'Hour and a half.'

'Hour and a half! I'm starving.'

'Then fill up on beer. Believe me it's worth it.'

'What's on the menu?'

'Barbecued, sautéed shrimp, frog legs, and charbroiled catfish.'

She sipped on the beer. 'We'll see.'

Jake stepped on the gas, and they raced across bridges over the countless tributaries of Lake Chatulla. They climbed steep hills covered with layers of dark green kudzu. They flew around corners and dodged pulpwood trucks making their last runs of the day. Jake opened the sunroof, lowered the windows and let the wind blow. Ellen leaned back in the seat and closed her eyes. Her thick, wavy hair swirled around her face.

'Look, Row Ark, this dinner is strictly business –'

'Sure, sure,'

'I mean it. I'm the employer, you're the employee, and this is a business meal. Nothing more or less. So don't get any lustful ideas in your ERA, sexually liberated brain.'

'Sounds like you're the one with the ideas.'

'Nope. I just know what you're thinking.'

'How do you know what I'm thinking? Why do you assume you're so irresistible and that I'm planning a big seduction scene?'

'Just keep your hands to yourself. I'm a wonderfully happily married man with a gorgeous wife who'd kill if she thought I was fooling around.'

'Okay, let's pretend to be friends. Just two friends having dinner.'

'That doesn't work in the South. A male friend cannot have dinner with a female friend if the male friend has a wife. It just doesn't work down here.'

'Why not?'

'Because men don't have female friends. No way. I don't know of a single man in the entire South who is married and has a female friend. I think it goes back to the Civil War.'

'I think it goes back to the Dark Ages. Why are Southern women so jealous?'

'Because that's the way we've trained them. They learned from us. If my wife met a male friend for lunch or dinner, I'd tear his head off and file for divorce. She learned it from me.'

'That makes absolutely no sense.'

'Of course it doesn't.'

'Your wife has no male friends?'

'None that I know of. If you learn of any, let me know.'

'And you have no female friends?'

'Why would I want female friends? They can't talk about football, or duck hunting, or politics, or lawsuits, or anything that I want to talk about. They talk about kids, clothes, recipes, coupons, furniture, stuff I know nothing about. No, I don't have any female friends. Don't want any.'

'That's what I love about the South. The people are so tolerant.'

'Thank you.'

'Do you have any Jewish friends?'

'I don't know of any in Ford County. I had a real good friend in law school, Ira Tauber, from New Jersey. We were very close. I love Jews. Jesus was a Jew, you know. I've never understood anti-Semitism.'

'My God, you are a liberal. How about, uh, homosexuals?'

'I feel sorry for them. They don't know what they're missing. But that's their problem.'

'Could you have a homosexual friend?'

'I guess, as long as he didn't tell me.'

'Nope, you're a Republican.'

She took his empty can and threw it in the back seat. She opened two more. The sun was gone, and the heavy, humid air felt cool at ninety miles an hour.

'So we can't be friends?' she said.

'Nope.'

'Nor lovers.'

'Please. I'm trying to drive.'

'So what are we?'

'I'm the lawyer, you're the law clerk. I'm the employer, you're the employee. I'm the boss, you're the gofer.'

'You're the male, I'm the female.'

Jake admired her jeans and bulky shirt. 'There's not much doubt about that.'

Ellen shook her head and stared at the mountains of kudzu flying by. Jake smiled, drove faster, and sipped his beer. He negotiated a series of intersections on the rural, deserted highways and, suddenly, the hills disappeared and the land became flat.

'What's the name of the restaurant?' she asked.

'The Hollywood.'

'The what?'

'The Hollywood.'

'Why is it called that?'

'It was once located in a small town a few miles away by the name of Hollywood, Mississippi. It burned, and they moved it to Robinsonville. They still call it the Hollywood.'

'What's so great about it?'

'Great food, great music, great atmosphere, and it's a thousand miles from Clanton and no one will see me having dinner with a strange and beautiful woman.'

'I'm not a woman, I'm a gofer.'

'A strange and beautiful gofer.'

Ellen smiled to herself and ran her fingers through her hair. At another intersection, he turned left and headed west until they found a settlement near a railroad. A row of wooden buildings sat empty on one side of the road, and across the street, all by itself, was an old dry goods store with a dozen cars parked around it and music rolling softly out the windows. Jake grabbed the bottle of Chablis and escorted his law clerk up the steps, onto the front porch, and inside the building.

Next to the door was a small stage, where a beautiful old black lady, Merle, sat at her piano and sang 'Rainy Night in Georgia.' Three long rows of tables ran to the front and stopped next to the stage. The tables were half full, and a waitress in the back poured beer from a pitcher and motioned for them to come on in. She seated them in the rear, at a small table with a red-checkered tablecloth.

'Y'all want some fried dill pickles, honey?' she asked Jake.

'Yes! Two orders.'

Ellen frowned and looked at Jake. 'Fried dill pickles?'

'Yes, of course. They don't serve them in Boston?'

'Do you people fry everything?'

'Everything that's worth eating. If you don't like them, I'll eat them.'

A yell went up from the table across the aisle. Four couples toasted something or somebody, then broke into riotous laughing. The restaurant maintained a constant roar of yelling and talking.

'The good thing about the Hollywood,' Jake explained, 'is that you can make all the noise you want and stay as long as you want, and nobody cares. When you get a table here, it's yours for the night. They'll start singing and dancing in a minute.'

Jake ordered sautéed shrimp and charbroiled catfish for both of them. Ellen passed on the frog legs. The waitress hurried back with the Chablis and two chilled glasses. They toasted Carl Lee Hailey and his insane mind.

'Whatta you think of Bass?' Jake asked.

'He's the perfect witness. He'll say anything we want him to say.'

'Does that bother you?'

'It would if he was a fact witness. But he's an expert, and he can get by with his opinions. Who will challenge him?'

'Is he believable?'

'When he's sober. We talked twice this week. On Tuesday he was lucid and helpful. On Wednesday, he was drunk and indifferent. I think he'll be as helpful as any psychiatrist we could find. He doesn't care what the truth is, and he'll tell us what we want to hear.'

'Does he think Carl Lee was legally insane?'

'No. Do you?'

'No. Row Ark, Carl Lee told me five days before the killings that he would do it. He showed me the exact place where he would ambush them, although at the time I didn't realize it. Our client knew exactly what he was doing.'

'Why didn't you stop him?'

'Because I didn't believe him. His daughter had just been raped and was fighting for her life.'

'Would you have stopped him if you could?'

'I did tell Ozzie. But at the time neither of us dreamed it could happen. No, I would not have stopped him if I knew for certain. I would have done the same thing.'

'How?'

'Exactly as he did it. It was very easy.'

Ellen approached a fried dill pickle with her fork and played with it suspiciously. She cut it in half, pierced it with the fork, and sniffed it carefully. She put it in her mouth and chewed slowly. She swallowed, then pushed her pile of pickles across the table toward Jake.

'Typical yankee,' he said. 'I don't understand you, Row Ark. You don't like fried dill pickles, you're attractive, very bright, you could go to work with any blue-chip law firm in the country for megabucks, yet you want to spend your career losing sleep over cutthroat murderers who are on death row and about to get their just rewards. What makes you tick, Row Ark?'

'You lose sleep over the same people. Now it's Carl Lee Hailey. Next year it'll be some other murderer who everybody hates but you'll lose sleep over him because he happens to be your client. One of these days, Brigance, you'll have a client on death row, and you'll learn how terrible it is. When they strap him in the chair and he looks at you for the last time, you'll be a changed man. You'll know how barbaric the system is, and you'll remember Row Ark.'

'Then I'll grow a beard and join the ACLU.'

'Probably, if they would accept you.'

The sautéed shrimp arrived in a small black skillet. It simmered in butter and garlic and barbeque sauce. Ellen dipped spoonfuls onto her plate and ate like a refugee. Merle lit into a stirring rendition of 'Dixie,' and the crowd sang and clapped along.

The waitress ran by and threw a platter of battered and crunchy frog legs on the table. Jake finished a glass of wine and grabbed a handful of the frog legs. Ellen tried to ignore them. When they were full of appetizers, the catfish was served. The grease popped and fizzed and they did not touch the china. It was charbroiled to a deep brown crisp with black squares from the grill burned on each side. They ate and drank slowly, watching each other and savoring the delicious entree.

At midnight, the bottle was empty and the lights were dimmed. They said good night to the waitress and to Merle. They walked carefully down the steps and to the car. Jake buckled his seat belt.

'I'm too drunk to drive,' he said.

'So am I. I saw a little motel not far down the road.'

'I saw it too, and there were no vacancies. Nice try, Row Ark. Get me drunk and try to take advantage of me.'

'I would if I could, mister.'

For a moment their eyes met. Ellen's face reflected the red light cast by the neon sign that flashed HOLLYWOOD atop the restaurant.

The moment grew longer and then the sign was turned off. The restaurant had closed.

Jake started the Saab, let it warm, and raced away into the darkness.

Mickey Mouse called Ozzie early Saturday morning at his home and promised more trouble from the Klan. The riot on Thursday had not been their fault, he explained, yet they were being blamed for it. They had marched in peace, and now their leader lay near death with seventy percent of his body covered with third-degree burns. There would be retaliation; it had been ordered from above. Reinforcements were on the way from other states, and there would be violence. No specifics now, but he would call later when he knew more.

Ozzie sat on the side of his bed, rubbed the swollen hump on the back of his neck and called the mayor. And he called Jake. An hour later they met in Ozzie's office.

'The situation is about to get outta hand,' Ozzie said, holding an ice pack to his neck and grimacing with every word. 'I've got it from a reliable informant that the Klan plans to retaliate for what happened Thursday. They're supposed to bring fresh troops from other states.'

'Do you believe it?' asked the mayor.

'I'm afraid not to believe it.'

'Same informant?' asked Jake.

'Yep.'

'Then I believe it.'

'Somebody said there was talk of movin' or postponin' the trial,' Ozzie said. 'Any chance of it?'

'No. I met with Judge Noose yesterday. It won't be moved and it'll start Monday.'

'Did you tell him about the burnin' crosses?'

'I told him everything.'

'Is he crazy?' asked the mayor.

'Yes, and stupid. But don't quote me on that.'

'Is he on solid legal ground?' asked Ozzie.

Jake shook his head. 'More like quicksand.'

'What have you got in mind?' asked the mayor.

Ozzie changed ice packs and carefully rubbed his neck. He spoke with pain. 'I have a strong desire to prevent another riot. Our hospital is not big enough to allow this crap to continue. We must do something. The blacks are angry and volatile, and it wouldn't take much to ignite them. Some blacks are just lookin' for a reason to start shootin', and those white robes are good targets. I've got a hunch the Klan may do somethin' really stupid, like try to kill somebody. They're gettin' more national exposure off this than they've had in ten years. The informant told me that after Thursday they've had calls from all over the country from volunteers wantin' to come down here and join the fun.'

He slowly rolled his head around his shoulders and changed ice packs again. 'I hate to say it, Mayor, but I think you should call the governor and ask for the National Guard. I know it's a drastic step, but I'd hate to get someone killed.'

'The National Guard!' the mayor repeated in disbelief.

'That's what I said.'

'Occupying Clanton?'

'Yep. Protectin' your people.'

'Patrolling the streets?'

'Yep. With guns and everthing.'

'Oh my, this is drastic. Aren't you overreacting a bit?'

'No. It's evident I don't have enough men to keep peace around here. We couldn't even stop a riot that happened right in front of us. The Klan's burnin' crosses all over the county, and we can't do anything about it. What will we do when the blacks decide to start some trouble? I don't have enough men, Mayor. I need some help.'

Jake thought it was a marvelous idea. How could a fair and impartial jury be chosen when the National Guard had the courthouse surrounded? He thought of the jurors arriving for court Monday and walking past the soldiers with guns and jeeps and maybe even a tank or two parked in front of the courthouse. How could they be fair and impartial? How could Noose insist on trying the case in Clanton? How could the Supreme Court refuse to reverse if, heaven forbid, there was a conviction? It was a great idea.

'Whatta you think, Jake?' asked the mayor, looking for help.

'I don't think you have a choice, Mayor. We can't stand another riot. It could hurt you politically.'

'I'm not worried about politics,' the mayor replied angrily, knowing Jake and Ozzie knew better. The mayor had been reelected last time by less than fifty votes and did not make a move without weighing the political fallout. Ozzie caught a grin from Jake as the mayor squirmed with the thought of having his quiet little town occupied by the army.

After dark Saturday, Ozzie and Hastings led Carl Lee out the rear door of the jail and into the sheriff's patrol car. They talked and laughed as Hastings drove in slow motion out into the country, past Bates Grocery and onto Craft Road. The Haileys' front yard was covered with cars when they arrived, so he parked in the road. Carl Lee walked through his front door like a free man and was immediately embraced by a mob of kinfolks, friends, and his children. They had not been told he was coming. He hugged them desperately, all four at the same time in one long bear hug as if there might be no more for a long time. The crowd watched in silence as this huge man knelt on the floor and buried his head among his weeping children. Most of those in the crowd wept too.

The kitchen was covered with food, and the guest of honor was seated in his usual chair at the head of the table with his wife and children seated around him. Reverend Agee returned thanks with short prayer of hope and homecoming. A hundred friends waited on the family. Ozzie and Hastings filled their plates and retreated to the front porch, where they swatted mosquitoes and planned strategy for the trial. Ozzie was deeply concerned about Carl Lee's safety while they moved him from the jail to court and back each day. The defendant himself had proven clearly that such journeys are not always safe.

After supper the crowd spilled out into the front yard. The children played while the adults stayed on the porch, as close as possible to Carl Lee. He was their hero, the most famous man most of them would ever see, and they knew him personally. To his people he was on trial for one reason only. Sure he killed those boys, but that wasn't the issue. If he was white, he would receive civic awards for what he did. They would half-heartedly prosecute him, but with a white jury the trial would be a joke. Carl Lee was on trial because he was black. And if they convicted him, it would be because he was black. No other reason. They believed that. They listened carefully as he talked about the trial. He wanted their prayers and support, and wanted them all to be there and watch it and to protect his family.

They sat for hours in the sweltering humidity; Carl Lee and Gwen in the swing rocking slowly, surrounded by admirers all wanting to be near this great man. When they began to leave they all embraced him and promised to be there Monday. They wondered if they would see him again sitting on his front porch.

At midnight Ozzie said it was time to go. Carl Lee hugged Gwen and the kids one last time, then took his seat in Ozzie's car.

Bud Twitty died during the night. The dispatcher called Nesbit, who told Jake. He made a note to send flowers.

CHAPTER THIRTY-TWO

Sunday. One day before trial. Jake awoke at 5:00 A.M. with a knot in his stomach that he attributed to the trial, and a headache that he attributed to the trial and a late Saturday night session on Lucien's porch with his law clerk and former boss. Ellen had decided to sleep in a guest room at Lucien's, so Jake spent the night on his couch in the office.

He lay on the couch and heard voices from the street below. He staggered in the dark to the balcony, and stopped in amazement at the scene around the courthouse. D-Day! The war was on! Patton had arrived! The streets around the square were lined with transport trucks, jeeps, and soldiers busy running here and there in an effort to get organized and look military. Radios squawked, and potbellied commanders yelled to their men to hurry and get organized. A command post was set up near the gazebo on the front lawn. Three squads of soldiers hammered on stakes and pulled ropes and strung up three enormous canvas camouflage pavilions. Barricades were set up on the four corners of the square, and sentries took their positions. They smoked cigarettes and leaned on the street lights.

Nesbit sat on the trunk of his car and watched the fortifying of downtown Clanton. He chatted with a few of the guardsmen. Jake made coffee and took him a cup. He was awake now, safe and secure, and Nesbit could go home and rest until dark. Jake returned to the balcony and watched the activity until dawn. Once the troops were unloaded, the transport trucks were moved to the National Guard armory north of town, where the men would sleep. He estimated their number at two hundred. They piddled around the courthouse and walked in small groups around the square, looking in shops, waiting for daylight and the hope of some excitement.

Noose would be furious. How dare they call the National Guard without asking him. It was his trial. The mayor had mentioned this, and Jake had explained that it was the mayor's responsibility to keep Clanton safe, not the trial judge's. Ozzie concurred, and Noose was not called.

The sheriff and Moss Junior Tatum arrived and met with the colonel in the gazebo. They walked around the courthouse, inspecting troops and pavilions. Ozzie pointed in various directions and the colonel seemed to agree with whatever he wanted. Moss Junior unlocked the courthouse so the troops would have drinking water and toilet facilities. It was after nine before the first of the vultures stumbled onto the occupation of downtown

Clanton. Within an hour they were running everywhere with cameras and microphones gathering important words from a sergeant or a corporal.

'What is your name, sir?'

'Sergeant Drumwright.'

'Where are you from?'

'Booneville.'

'Where's that?'

' 'Bout a hundred miles from here.'

'Why are you here?'

'Governor called us.'

'Why did he call you?'

'Keep things under control.'

'Are you expecting trouble?'

'No.'

'How long will you be here?'

'Don't know.'

'Will you be here until the trial's over?'

'Don't know.'

'Who knows?'

'The governor, I reckon.'

And so on.

Word of the invasion spread quickly through the quiet Sunday morning, and after church the townfolk streamed to the square to verify for themselves that the army had indeed captured the courthouse. The sentries removed the barricades and allowed the curious to drive around their square and gawk at the real live soldiers with their rifles and jeeps. Jake sat on the balcony, drinking coffee and memorizing the notecards of his jurors.

He called Carla and explained that the National Guard had been deployed, but he was still safe. In fact, he had never felt so safe. As he talked to her, he explained, there were hundreds of heavily armed army militiamen across Washington Street just waiting to protect him. Yes, he still had his bodyguard. Yes, the house was still standing. He doubted if the death of Bud Twitty had been reported yet, so he did not tell her. Maybe she would not hear of it. They were going fishing on her father's boat, and Hanna wanted her daddy to go. He said goodbye, and missed the two women in his life more than ever.

Ellen Roark unlocked the rear door of the office and placed a small grocery sack on the table in the kitchen. She pulled a file out of her briefcase and began looking for her boss. He was on the balcony, staring at notecards and watching the courthouse. 'Evenin', Row Ark.'

'Good evening, boss.' She handed him a brief an inch thick. 'It's the research you requested on the admissibility of the rape. It's a tough issue, and it got involved. I apologize for the size of it.'

It was as neat as her other briefs, complete with a table of contents, bibliography, and numbered pages. He flipped through it. 'Damn, Row Ark, I didn't ask for a textbook.'

'I know you're intimidated by scholarly work, so I made a conscious effort to use words with fewer than three syllables.'

'My, aren't we frisky today. Could you summarize this in a dissertation of, say, thirty pages or so?'

'Look, it's a thorough study of the law by a gifted law student with a remarkable ability to think and write clearly. It's a work of genius, and it's yours, and it's absolutely free. So quit bitching.'

'Yes, ma'am. Does your head hurt?'

'Yes. It's been aching since I woke up this morning. I've typed on that brief for ten hours, and I need a drink. Do you have a blender?'

'A what?'

'Blender. It's a new invention we have up North. They're kitchen appliances.'

'There's one in the shelves next to the microwave.'

She disappeared. It was almost dark, and the traffic had thinned around the square as the Sunday drivers had grown bored with the sight of soldiers guarding their courthouse. After twelve hours of suffocating heat and foglike humidity in downtown Clanton, the troops were weary and homesick. They sat under trees and on folding canvas chairs, and cursed the governor. As it grew darker, they strung wires from inside the courthouse and hung floodlights around the pavilions. By the post office a carload of blacks arrived with lawn chairs and candles to start the nightly vigil. They began pacing the sidewalk along Jackson Street under the suddenly aroused stares of two hundred heavily armed guardsmen. The lead walker was Miss Rosia Alfie Gatewood, a two-hundred-pound widow who had raised eleven children and sent nine to college. She was the first black known to have sipped cold water from the public fountain on the square and live to tell about it. She glared at the soldiers. They did not speak.

Ellen returned with two Boston College beer mugs filled with a pale green liquid. She sat them on the table and pulled up a chair.

'What's that?'

'Drink it. It'll help you relax.'

'I'll drink it. But I'd like to know what it is.'

'Margaritas.'

Jake studied the top of his mug. 'Where's the salt?'

'I don't like salt on mine.'

'Well, I don't either then. Why margaritas?'

'Why not?'

Jake closed his eyes and took a long drink. And then another. 'Row Ark, you are a talented woman.'

'Gofer.'

He took another long drink. 'I haven't had a margarita in eight years.'

'I'm very sorry.' Her twenty-ounce mug was half empty.

'What kind of rum?'

'I would call you a dumbass if you weren't my boss.'

'Thank you.'

'It's not rum. It's tequila, with lime juice and Cointreau. I thought every law student knew that.'

'How can you ever forgive me? I'm sure I knew it when I was a law student.'

She gazed around the square.

'This is incredible! It looks like a war zone.'

Jake drained his glass and licked his lips. Under the pavilions they played cards and laughed. Others sought refuge from the mosquitoes in the courthouse. The candles turned the corner and made a pass down Washington Street.

'Yes,' Jake said with a smile. 'It's beautiful, isn't it? Think of our fair and impartial jurors as they arrive in the morning and are confronted with that. I'll renew my motion for a change of venue. It'll be denied. I'll ask for a mistrial, and Noose will say no. And then I'll make sure the court reporter records the fact that this trial is being conducted in the middle of a three-ring circus.'

'Why are they here?'

'The sheriff and the mayor called the governor, and convinced him the National Guard was needed to preserve peace in Ford County. They told him our hospital is not large enough for this trial.'

'Where are they from?'

'Booneville and Columbus. I counted two hundred and twenty around lunch.'

'They've been here all day?'

'They woke me at five this morning. I've followed their movements all day. They were pinned down a couple of times, but reinforcements arrived. A few minutes ago they met the enemy when Miss Gatewood and her friends arrived with their candles. She stared them down, so now they're playing cards.'

Ellen finished her drink and left for more. Jake picked up the stack of notecards for the hundredth time and flashed them on the table. Name, age, occupation, family, race, education – he had read and repeated the information since early morning. Round Two arrived with haste, and she took the cards.

'Correen Hagan,' she said, sipping.

He thought a second. 'Age, about fifty-five. Secretary for an insurance agent. Divorced, two grown children. Education, probably high school, no more. Native of Florida, for what that's worth.'

'Rating?'

'I think I gave her a six.'

'Very good. Millard Sills.'

'Owns a pecan orchard near Mays. About seventy years old. His nephew was shot in the head by two blacks during a robbery in Little Rock several years ago. Hates blacks. He will not be on the jury.'

'Rating?'

'Zero, I believe.'

'Clay Bailey.'

'Age, about thirty. Six kids. Devout Pentecostal. Works at the furniture plant west of town.'

'You've given him a ten.'

'Yeah. I'm sure he's read that part in the Bible about an eye for an eye, etc. Plus, out of six kids, I'd think at least two would be daughters.'

'Do you have all of them memorized?'

He nodded and took a drink. 'I feel like I've known them for years.'

'How many will you recognize?'

'Very few. But I'll know more about them than Buckley.'

'I'm impressed.'

'What! What did you say! I have impressed you with my intellect!'

'Among other things.'

'I feel so honored. I've impressed a genius in criminal law. The daughter of Sheldon Roark, whoever he is. A real live *summa cum laude*. Wait'll I tell Harry Rex.'

'Where is that elephant? I miss him. I think he's cute.'

'Go call him. Ask him to join us for a patio party as we watch the troops prepare for the Third Battle of Bull Run.'

She headed for the phone on Jake's desk. 'What about Lucien?'

'No! I'm tired of Lucien.'

Harry Rex brought a fifth of tequila he found somewhere deep in his liquor cabinet. He and the law clerk argued violently over the proper ingredients of a good margarita. Jake voted with his clerk.

They sat on the balcony, calling names from index cards, drinking the tangy concoction, yelling at the soldiers, and singing Jimmy Buffet songs. At midnight, Nesbit loaded Ellen in his patrol car and took her to Lucien's. Harry Rex walked home. Jake slept on the couch.

CHAPTER THIRTY-THREE

Monday, July 22. Not long after the last margarita Jake bolted from the couch and stared at the clock on his desk. He had slept for three hours. A swarm of wild butterflies fought violently in his stomach. A nervous pain shot through his groin. He had no time for a hangover.

Nesbit slept like an infant behind the wheel. Jake roused him and jumped in the back seat. He waved at the sentries, who watched curiously from across the street. Nesbit drove two blocks to Adams, released his passenger, and waited in the driveway as instructed. He showered and shaved quickly. He chose a charcoal worsted wool suit, a white pinpoint button-down, and a very neutral, noncontroversial, expressionless burgundy silk tie with a few narrow navy stripes for good measure. The pleated pants hung perfectly from his trim waist. He looked great, much more stylish than the enemy.

Nesbit was asleep again when Jake released the dog and jumped in the back seat.

'Everything okay in there?' Nesbit asked, wiping the saliva from his chin.

'I didn't find any dynamite, if that's what you mean.'

Nesbit laughed at this, with the same irritating, laughing response he made to almost everything. They circled the square and Jake got out in front of his office. Thirty minutes after he left, he turned on the front lights and made the coffee.

He took four aspirin and drank a quart of grapefruit juice. His eyes burned and his head ached from abuse and fatigue, and the tiring part had not yet begun. On the conference table he spread out his file on Carl Lee Hailey. It had been organized and indexed by his law clerk, but he wanted to break it down and put it back together. If a document or case can't be found in thirty seconds, it's no good. He smiled at her talent for organization. She had files and sub-files on everything, all ten seconds away at a fingertip. In a one-inch, three-ring notebook she had a summary of Dr. Bass's qualifications and the outline of his testimony. She had made notes on anticipated objections from Buckley, and provided case authority to fight his objections. Jake took great pride in his trial preparation, but it was humbling to learn from a third-year law student.

He repacked the file in his trial briefcase, the heavy black leather one with his initials in gold on the side. Nature called, and he sat on the toilet flipping through the index cards. He knew them all. He was ready.

A few minutes after five, Harry Rex knocked on the door. It was dark and he looked like a burglar.

'Whatta you doing up so early?' Jake asked.

'I couldn't sleep. I'm kinda nervous.' He thrust forward a loaded paper sack with grease spots. 'Dell sent these over. They're fresh and hot. Sausage biscuits, bacon and cheese biscuits, chicken and cheese biscuits, you name it. She's worried about you.'

'Thanks, Harry Rex, but I'm not hungry. My system is in revolt.'

'Nervous?'

'As a whore in church.'

'You look pretty haggard.'

'Thanks.'

'Nice suit though.'

'Carla picked it out.'

Harry Rex reached into the sack and produced a handful of biscuits wrapped in foil. He piled them on the conference table and fixed his coffee. Jake sat across from him and flipped through Ellen's brief on M'Naghten.

'She write that?' Harry Rex asked with both cheeks full and his jaws grinding rapidly.

'Yeah, it's a seventy-five-page summary of the insanity defense in Mississippi. It took her three days.'

'She seems very bright.'

'She's got the brains, and she writes fluidly. The intellect is there, but she has trouble applying what she knows to the real world.'

'Whatta you know about her?' Crumbs fell from his mouth and bounced on the table. He brushed them onto the floor with a sleeve.

'She's solid. Number two in her class at Ole Miss. I called Nelson Battles, Assistant Dean of the Law School, and she checked out fine. She has a good chance of finishing number one.'

'I finished ninety-third outta ninety-eight. I would've finished ninety-second but they caught me cheating on an exam. I started to protest, but I figured ninety-third was just as good. Hell, I figured, who cares in Clanton. These people were just glad I came back here to practice when I graduated instead of going to Wall Street or some place like that.'

Jake smiled at the story he had heard a hundred times.

Harry Rex unwrapped a chicken and cheese biscuit. 'You look nervous, buddy.'

'I'm okay. The first day is always the hardest. The preparation has been done. I'm ready. It's just a matter of waiting now.'

'What time does Row Ark make her entrance?'

'I don't know.'

'Lord, I wonder what she'll wear.'

'Or not wear. I just hope she's decent. You know what a prude Noose is.'

'You're not gonna let her sit at counsel table are you?'

'I don't think so. She'll stay in the background, sort of like you. She might offend some of the women jurors.'

'Yeah, keep her there, but outta sight.'

Harry Rex wiped his mouth with a huge paw. 'You sleeping with her?'

'No! I'm not crazy, Harry Rex.'

'You're crazy if you don't. That woman could be had.'

'Then have her. I've got enough on my mind.'

'She thinks I'm cute, don't she?'

'She says she does.'

'I think I'll give it a shot,' he said with a straight face, then he smiled, then he burst into laughter with crumbs spraying the bookshelves.

The phone rang. Jake shook his head, and Harry Rex picked up the receiver. 'He's not here, but I'll be glad to give him the message.' He winked at Jake. 'Yes sir, yes sir, uh huh, yes sir. It's a terrible thing, ain't it. Can you believe a man would do it? Yes sir, yes sir, I agree one hundred percent. Yes sir, and what's your name, sir? Sir?' Harry Rex smiled at the receiver and laid it down.

'What'd he want?'

'Said you was a shame to the white race for being that nigger's lawyer, and that he didn't see how any lawyer could represent a nigger such as Hailey. And that he hoped the Klan got ahold of you, and if they didn't he hoped the bar association looked into it and took away your license for helping niggers. Said he knew you were no 'count because you were trained by Lucien Wilbanks who lives with a nigger woman.'

'And you agreed with him!'

'Why not? He was really sincere, not hateful, and he feels better now that it's off his chest.'

The phone rang again. Harry Rex snatched the receiver. 'Jake Brigance, Attorney, Counselor, Consultant, Adviser, and Guru at Law.'

Jake left for the restroom. 'Jake, it's a reporter!' Harry Rex yelled.

'I'm on the potty.'

'He's got the runs!' Harry Rex told the reporter.

At six – seven in Wilmington – Jake called Carla. She was awake, reading the paper, drinking coffee. He told her about Bud Twitty, and Mickey Mouse, and the promise of more violence. No, he wasn't afraid of that. It did not bother him. He was afraid of the jury, of the twelve who would be chosen, and their reaction to him and his client. His only fear, at the moment, was of what the jury might do to his client. Everything else was irrelevant. For the first time, she did not mention coming home. He promised to call that night.

When he hung up, he heard a commotion downstairs. Ellen had arrived, and Harry Rex was talking loudly. She's wearing a see-through blouse with a miniskirt, thought Jake as he walked downstairs. She was not. Harry Rex was congratulating her on dressing like a Southern woman with all the accessories. She was wearing a gray glen plaid suit with a V-necked jacket and short slim skirt. The silk blouse was black, and apparently the necessary garment was underneath. Her hair was pulled back and braided in some fashion. Incredibly, traces of mascara, eyeliner, and lipstick were visible. In the words of Harry Rex, she looked as much like a lawyer as a woman could look.

'Thanks, Harry Rex,' she said. 'I wish I had your taste in clothes.'

'You look nice, Row Ark,' Jake said.

'So do you,' she said. She looked at Harry Rex, but said nothing.

'Please forgive us, Row Ark,' Harry Rex said. 'We're impressed because we had no idea you owned so many types of garments. We apologize for admiring you and we know how much this infuriates your little liberated heart. Yes, we're sexist pigs, but you chose to come to the South. And in the South we, as a rule, drool over well-dressed attractive females, liberated or not.'

'What's in the sack?' she said.

'Breakfast.'

She tore it open and unwrapped a sausage and biscuit. 'No bagels?' she asked.

'What's that?' asked Harry Rex.

'Forget it.'

Jake rubbed his hands together and tried to sound enthusiastic. 'Well, now that we've gathered here three hours before trial, what would y'all like to do?'

'Let's make some margaritas,' said Harry Rex.

'No!' said Jake.

'It'll take the edge off.'

'Not me,' said Ellen. 'This is business.'

Harry Rex unwrapped a biscuit, the last of the sack. 'What happens first today?'

'After the sun comes up, we start the trial. At nine, Noose will say a few words to the jurors and we start the selection process.'

'How long will it take?' asked Ellen.

'Two or three days. In Mississippi, we have the right to interrogate each juror individually in chambers. That takes time.'

'Where do I sit and what do I do?'

'She certainly sounds experienced,' Harry Rex said to Jake. 'Does she know where the courthouse is?'

'You do not sit at counsel table,' said Jake. 'Just me and Carl Lee.'

She wiped her mouth. 'I see. Just you and the defendant sitting alone, surrounded by the forces of evil, facing death alone.'

'Something like that.'

'My father uses that tactic occasionally.'

'I'm glad you approve. You'll sit behind me, next to the railing. I'll ask Noose to allow you into chambers for the private discussions.'

'What about me?' asked Harry Rex.

'Noose doesn't like you, Harry Rex. He never has. He'd have a stroke if I asked if you could go in chambers. It'd be best if you pretended we'd never met.'

'Thanks.'

'But we do appreciate your assistance,' Ellen said.

'Up yours, Ellie Mae.'

'And you can still drink with us,' she said.

'And furnish the tequila.'

'There will be no more alcohol in this office,' Jake said.

'Until the noon recess,' said Harry Rex.

'I want you to stand behind the clerk's table, just loiter about like you always do, and take notes on the jury. Try to match them with the notecards. There'll probably be a hundred and twenty.'

'Whatever you say.'

Daybreak brought the army out in force. The barricades were reinstalled, and on each corner of the square soldiers clustered around the orange and white barrels blocking the street. They were poised and anxious, watching every car intently, waiting for the enemy to attack, wanting some excitement. Things stirred a little when a few of the vultures in their compact wagons and minivans with fancy logos on the doors appeared at seven-thirty. The troops surrounded the vehicles and informed everyone there would be no parking around the courthouse during the trial. The vultures disappeared down the side streets, then moments later reappeared on foot with their bulky cameras and equipment. Some set up camp on the front steps of the courthouse, others by the back door, and another group in the rotunda outside the main door of the courtroom on the second floor.

Murphy, the janitor and only real eyewitness to the killings of Cobb and Willard, informed the press, as best he could, that the courtroom would be opened at eight, and not a minute before. A line formed and soon circled the rotunda.

The church buses parked somewhere off the square, and the marchers were led slowly down Jackson Street by the ministers. They carried FREE CARL LEE signs and sang 'We Shall Overcome' in a perfect chorus. As they neared the square, the soldiers heard them and the radios began squawking. Ozzie and the colonel conferred quickly, and the soldiers relaxed. The marchers were led by Ozzie to a section of the front lawn where they milled about and waited under the watchful eyes of the Mississippi National Guard.

At eight, a metal detector was moved to the front doors of the courtroom, and a trio of heavily armed deputies began slowly searching and admitting the crowd of spectators that now filled the rotunda and trailed off into the halls. Inside the courtroom, Prather directed traffic, seating people on the long pews on one side of the aisle while reserving the other side for the jurors. The front pew was reserved for the family, and the second row was filled with courtroom artists who immediately began sketching the bench and the bar and the portraits of Confederate heroes.

The Klan felt obligated to make its presence known on opening day, especially to the prospective jurors as they arrived. Two dozen Kluxers in full parade dress walked quietly onto Washington Street. They were immediately stopped and surrounded by soldiers. The potbellied colonel swaggered across the street and for the first time in his life came face to face with a white-robed and white-hooded Ku Klux Klansman, who happened to be a foot taller. He then noticed the cameras, which had gravitated to this confrontation, and the bully in him vanished. His usual bark and growl was instantly replaced by a high-pitched, nervous, trembling stutter that was incomprehensible even to himself.

Ozzie arrived and saved him. 'Good mornin', fellas,' he said coolly as he stepped beside the faltering colonel. 'We've got you surrounded, and we've got you outnumbered. We also know we can't keep you from being here.'

'That's right,' said the leader.

'If you'll just follow me and do as I say, we won't have any trouble.'

They followed Ozzie and the colonel to a small area on the front lawn, where it was explained that this was their turf for the trial. Stay there and stay quiet, and the colonel would personally keep the troops off them. They agreed.

As expected, the sight of the white robes aroused the blacks who were some two hundred feet away. They began shouting: 'Free Carl Lee! Free Carl Lee! Free Carl Lee!'

The Klansmen shook their fists and shouted back:

'Fry Carl Lee!'

'Fry Carl Lee!'

'Fry Carl Lee!'

Two rows of troops lined the main sidewalk that divided the lawn and led to the front steps. Another row stood between the sidewalk and the Klansmen, and one between the sidewalk and the blacks.

As the jurors began arriving, they walked briskly through the rows of soldiers. They clutched their summonses and listened in disbelief as the two groups screamed at each other.

The Honorable Rufus Buckley arrived in Clanton and politely informed the guardsmen of who he was and what that meant, and he was allowed to park in his spot marked RESERVED FOR D.A. next to the courthouse. The reporters went wild. This must be important, someone had broken through the barricade. Buckley sat in his well-used Cadillac for a moment to allow the reporters to catch him. They surrounded him as he slammed the door. He smiled and smiled and made his way ever so slowly to the front door of the courthouse. The rapid fire of questions proved irresistible, and Buckley violated the gag order at least eight times, each time smiling and explaining that he could not answer the question he had just answered. Musgrove trailed behind carrying the great man's briefcase.

Jake paced nervously in his office. The door was locked. Ellen was downstairs working on another brief. Harry Rex was at the Coffee Shop eating another breakfast and gossiping. The notecards were scattered on his desk, and he was tired of them. He flipped through a brief, then walked to the French doors. The shouting echoed through the open windows. He returned to the desk and studied the outline of the opening comments to the prospective jurors. The first impression was critical.

He lay on the couch, closed his eyes, and thought of a thousand things he'd rather be doing. For the most part, he enjoyed his work. But there were moments, frightening moments like this one, when he wished he'd become an insurance agent or a stockbroker. Or maybe even a tax lawyer. Surely those guys didn't regularly suffer from nausea and diarrhea at critical moments in their careers.

Lucien had taught him that fear was good; fear was an ally; that every lawyer was afraid when he stood before a new jury and presented his case. It was okay to be afraid – just don't show it. Jurors would not follow the lawyer with the quickest tongue or prettiest words. They would not follow the sharpest dresser. They would not follow a clown or court jester. They would not follow the lawyer who preached the loudest or fought the hardest. Lucien had convinced him that jurors followed the lawyer who told the truth, regardless of his looks, words, or superficial abilities. A lawyer had to be himself in the courtroom, and if he was afraid, so be it. The jurors were afraid too.

Make friends with fear, Lucien always said, because it will not go away, and it will destroy you if left uncontrolled.

The fear hit deep in his bowels, and he walked carefully downstairs to the rest room.

'How are you, boss?' Ellen asked when he checked on her.

'Ready, I guess. We'll leave in a minute.'

'There are some reporters waiting outside. I told them you had withdrawn from the case and left town.'

'At this moment, I wish I had.'

'Have you heard of Wendall Solomon?'

'Not right off hand.'

'He's with the Southern Prisoner Defense Fund. I worked under him last summer. He's tried over a hundred capital cases all over the South. He gets so nervous before a trial he can neither eat nor sleep. His doctor gives him sedatives, but he's still so jumpy no one speaks to him on opening day. And that's after a hundred of these trials.'

'How does your father handle it?'

'He has a couple of martinis with a Valium. Then he lies on his desk with the door locked and the lights off until it's time for court. His nerves are ragged and he's ill-tempered. Of course, a lot of that is natural.'

'So you know the feeling?'

'I know it well.'

'Do I look nervous?'

'You look tired. But you'll do.'

Jake checked his watch. 'Let's go.'

The reporters on the sidewalk pounced on their prey. 'No comment,' he insisted as he moved slowly across the street toward the courthouse. The barrage continued.

'Is it true you plan to ask for a mistrial?'

'I can't do that until the trial starts.'

'Is it true the Klan has threatened you?'

'No comment.'

'Is it true you sent your family out of town until after the trial?'

Jake hesitated and glanced at the reporter. 'No comment.'

'What do you think of the National Guard?'

'I'm proud of them.'

'Can your client get a fair trial in Ford County?'

Jake shook his head, then added, 'No comment.'

A deputy stood guard a few feet from where the bodies had come to rest. He pointed at Ellen. 'Who's she, Jake?'

'She's harmless. She's with me.'

They ran up the rear stairs. Carl Lee sat alone at the defense table, his back to the packed courtroom. Jean Gillespie was busy checking in jurors while deputies roamed the aisles looking for anything suspicious. Jake greeted his client warmly, taking special care to shake his hand, smile broadly at him, and put his hand on his shoulder. Ellen unpacked the briefcases and neatly arranged the files on the table.

Jake whispered to his client and looked around the courtroom. All eyes were on him. The Hailey clan sat handsomely in the front row. Jake smiled at them and nodded at Lester. Tonya and the boys were decked out in their Sunday clothes, and they sat between Lester and Gwen like perfect little statues. The jurors sat across the aisle, and they were carefully studying Hailey's lawyer. Jake thought this would be a good time for the jurors to see the family, so he walked through the swinging gate in the railing and went to speak to the Haileys. He patted Gwen on the shoulder, shook hands with Lester, pinched each of the boys, and, finally, hugged Tonya, the little Hailey girl, the one who had been raped by the two rednecks who got what they deserved. The jurors watched every move of this production, and paid special attention to the little girl.

'Noose wants us in chambers,' Musgrove whispered to Jake as he returned to the defense table.

Ichabod, Buckley, and the court reporter were chatting when Jake and Ellen entered chambers. Jake introduced his clerk to His Honor and Buckley and Musgrove, and to Norma Gallo, the court reporter. He explained that Ellen Roark was a third-year law student at Ole Miss who was clerking in his office, and requested that she be allowed to sit near counsel table and participate in the proceedings in chambers. Buckley had no objections. It was common practice, Noose explained, and he welcomed her.

'Preliminary matters, gentlemen?' Noose asked.

'None,' said the D.A.

'Several,' said Jake as he opened a file. 'I want this on the record.'

Norma Gallo started writing.

'First of all, I want to renew my motion for a change of venue –'

'We object,' interrupted Buckley.

'Shut up, Governor!' Jake yelled. 'I'm not through, and don't interrupt me again!'

Buckley and the others were startled by this loss of composure. It's all those margaritas, thought Ellen.

'I apologize, Mr. Brigance,' Buckley said calmly. 'Please don't refer to me as governor.'

'Let me say something at this point,' Noose started. 'This trial will be a long and arduous ordeal. I can appreciate the pressure you're both under. I've been in your shoes many times myself, and I know what you're going through. You're both excellent lawyers, and I'm thankful that I have two fine lawyers for a trial of this magnitude. I can also detect a certain amount of ill will between you. That's certainly not uncommon, and I will not ask you to shake hands and be good friends. But I will insist that when you're in my courtroom or in these chambers that you refrain from interrupting each other, and that the shouting be held to a bare minimum. You will refer to each other as Mr. Brigance, and Mr. Buckley, and Mr. Musgrove. Now do each of you understand what I'm saying?'

'Yes, sir.'

'Yes, sir.'

'Good. Then continue, Mr. Brigance.'

'Thank you, Your Honor, I appreciate that. As I was saying, the defendant renews his motion for a change of venue. I want the record to reflect that as we sit here now in chambers, at nine-fifteen, July twenty-second, as we are about to select a jury, the Ford County Courthouse is surrounded by the Mississippi National Guard. On the front lawn a group of Ku Klux Klansmen, in white robes, is at this very moment yelling at a group of black demonstrators, who are, of course, yelling back. the two groups are separated by heavily armed National Guardsmen. As the jurors arrived for court this morning, they witnessed this circus on the courthouse lawn. It will be impossible to select a fair and impartial jury.'

Buckley watched with a cocky grin on his huge face, and when Jake finished he said, 'May I respond, Your Honor?'

'No,' Noose said bluntly. 'Motion is overruled. What else do you have?'

'The defense moves to strike this entire panel.'

'On what grounds?'

'On the grounds that there has been an overt effort by the Klan to intimidate this panel. We know of at least twenty cross burnings.'

'I intend to excuse those twenty, assuming they all showed up,' said Noose.

'Fine,' Jake replied sarcastically. 'What about the threats we don't know about? What about the jurors who've heard of the cross burnings?'

Noose wiped his eyes and said nothing. Buckley had a speech but didn't want to interrupt.

'I've got a list here,' Jake said, reaching into a file, 'of the twenty jurors who received visits. I've also got copies of the police reports, and an affidavit from Sheriff Walls in which he details the acts of intimidation. I am submitting these to the court in support of my motion to strike this panel. I want this made a part of the record so the Supreme Court can see it in black and white.'

'Expecting an appeal, Mr. Brigance?' asked Mr. Buckley.

Ellen had just met Rufus Buckley, and now, seconds later, she understood exactly why Jake and Harry Rex hated him.

'No, Governor, I'm not expecting an appeal. I'm trying to insure that my man gets a fair trial from a fair jury. You should understand that.'

'I'm not going to strike this panel. That would cost us a week,' Noose said.

'What's time when a man's life is at stake? We're talking about justice. The right to a fair trial, remember, a most basic constitutional right. It's a travesty not to strike this panel when you know for a fact that some of these people have been intimidated by a bunch of goons in white robes who want to see my client hanged.'

'Your motion is overruled,' Noose said flatly. 'What else do you have?'

'Nothing, really. I request that when you do excuse the twenty, you so do in such a way that the other jurors don't know the reason.'

'I can handle that, Mr. Brigance.'

Mr. Pate was sent to find Jean Gillespie. Noose handed her a list of the twenty names. She returned to the courtroom and read the list. They were not needed for jury duty, and were free to go. She returned to chambers.

'How many jurors do we have?' Noose asked her.

'Ninety-four.'

'That's enough. I'm sure we can find twelve who are fit to serve.'

'You couldn't find two,' Jake mumbled to Ellen, loud enough for Noose to hear and Norma Gallo to record. His Honor excused them and they took their places in the courtroom.

Ninety-four names were written on small strips of paper that were placed in a short wooden cylinder. Jean Gillespie spun the cylinder, stopped it, and picked a name at random. She handed it to Noose, who sat above her and everyone else on his throne, or bench, as it was called. The courtroom watched in dead silence as he squinted down that nose and looked at the first name.

'Carlene Malone, juror number one,' he shrieked in his loudest voice. The front row had been cleared, and Mrs. Malone took her seat next to the aisle. Each pew would seat ten, and there were ten pews, all to be filled with jurors. The ten pews on the other side of the aisle were packed with family, friends, spectators, but mainly reporters who scribbled down the name of Carlene Malone. Jake wrote her name too. She was white, fat, divorced, lower income. She was a two on the Brigance scale. Zero for one, he thought.

Jean spun again.

'Marcia Dickens, juror number two,' yelled Noose. White, fat, over sixty with a rather unforgiving look. Zero for two.

'Jo Beth Mills, number three.'

Jake sank a little in his seat. She was white, about fifty, and worked for minimum wage at a shirt factory in Karaway. Thanks to affirmative action, she had a black boss who was ignorant and abusive. She had a zero by her name on the Brigance notecard. Zero for three.

Jake stared desperately at Jean as she spun again. 'Reba Betts, number four.'

He sunk lower and began pinching his forehead. Zero for four. 'This is incredible,' he mumbled in the direction of Ellen. Harry Rex shook his head.

'Gerald Ault, number five.'

Jake smiled as his number-one juror took a seat next to Reba Betts. Buckley placed a nasty black mark by his name.

'Alex Summers, number six.'

Carl Lee managed a weak smile as the first black emerged from the rear and took a seat next to Gerald Ault. Buckley smiled too as he neatly circled the name of the first black.

The next four were white women, none of whom rated above three on the scale. Jake was worried as the first pew filled. By law he had twelve peremptory challenges, free strikes with no reason required. The luck of the draw would force him to use at least half of his peremptories on the first pew.

'Walter Godsey, number eleven,' announced Noose, his voice declining steadily in volume. Godsey was a middle-aged sharecropper with no compassion and no potential.

When Noose finished the second row, it contained seven white women, two black men, and Godsey. Jake sensed a disaster. Relief didn't come until the fourth row when Jean hit a hot streak and pulled the names of seven men, four of whom were black.

It took almost an hour to seat the entire panel. Noose recessed for fifteen minutes to allow Jean time to type a numerical list of names. Jake and Ellen used the break to review their notes and place the names with the faces. Harry Rex had sat at the counter behind the red docket books and feverishly taken notes while Noose called the names. He huddled with Jake and agreed things were not going well.

At eleven, Noose reassumed the bench, and the courtroom was silenced. Someone suggested he should use the mike, and he placed it within inches of his nose. He spoke loudly, and his fragile, obnoxious voice rattled violently around the courtroom as he asked a lengthy series of statutorily required questions. He introduced Carl Lee and asked if any juror was kin to him or knew him. They all knew of him, and Noose assumed that, but only two of the panel admitted knowing him prior to May. Noose introduced the lawyers, then explained briefly the nature of the charges. Not a single juror confessed to being ignorant of the Hailey case.

Noose rambled on and on, and mercifully finished at twelve-thirty. He recessed until two.

Dell delivered hot sandwiches and iced tea to the conference room. Jake hugged and thanked her, and told her to send him the bill. He ignored his food, and laid the notecards on the table in the order the jurors had been seated. Harry Rex attacked a roast beef and cheddar sandwich. 'We got a terrible draw,' he kept repeating with both cheeks stretched to the limit. 'We got a terrible draw.'

When the ninety-fourth card was in place, Jake stood back and studied them. Ellen stood beside him and nibbled on a french fry. She studied the cards.

'We got a terrible draw,' Harry Rex said, washing it all down with a pint of tea.

'Would you shut up,' Jake snapped.

'Of the first fifty, we have eight black men, three black women, and thirty white women. That leaves nine white men, and most are unattractive. Looks like a white female jury,' Ellen said.

'White females, white females,' Harry Rex said. 'The worst possible jurors in the world. White females!'

Ellen stared at him. 'I think fat white men are the worst jurors.'

'Don't get me wrong, Row Ark, I love white females. I've married four of them, remember. I just hate white female jurors.'

'I wouldn't vote to convict him.'

'Row Ark, you're an ACLU communist. You wouldn't vote to convict anybody of anything. In your little demented mind you think child pornographers and PLO terrorists are really swell people who've been abused by the system and should be given a break.'

'And in your rational, civilized, and compassionate mind, what do you think we should do with them?'

'Hang them by their toes, castrate them, and let them bleed to death, without a trial.'

'And the way you understand the law, that would be constitutional?'

'Maybe not, but it'd stop a lot of child pornography and terrorism. Jake, are you gonna eat this sandwich?'

'No.'

Harry Rex unwrapped a ham and cheese. 'Stay away from number one, Carlene Malone. She's one of those Malones from Lake Village. White trash and mean as hell.'

'I'd like to stay away from this entire panel,' Jake said, still staring at the table.

'We got a terrible draw.'

'Whatta you think, Row Ark?' Jake asked.

Harry Rex swallowed quickly. 'I think we oughtta plead him guilty and get the hell outta there. Run like a scalded dog.'

Ellen stared at the cards. 'It could be worse.'

Harry Rex forced a loud laugh. 'Worse! The only way it could be worse would be if the first thirty were sitting there wearing white robes with pointed hats and little masks.'

'Harry Rex, would you shut up,' Jake said.

'Just trying to help. Do you want your french fries?'

'No. Why don't you put all of them in your mouth and chew on them for a long time?'

'I think you're wrong about some of these women,' Ellen said. 'I'm inclined to agree with Lucien. Women, as a very general rule, will have more sympathy. We're the ones who get raped, remember?'

'I have no response to that,' Harry Rex said.

'Thanks,' replied Jake. 'Which one of these girls is your former client who'll supposedly do anything for you if you'll simply wink at her?'

Ellen snickered. 'Must be number twenty-nine. She's five feet tall and weighs four hundred pounds.'

Harry Rex wiped his mouth with a sheet of paper. 'Very funny. Number seventy-four. She's too far back. Forget her.'

Noose rapped his gavel at two and the courtroom came to order.

'The State may examine the panel,' he said.

The magnificent district attorney rose slowly and walked importantly to the bar, where he stood and gazed pensively at the spectators and jurors. He realized the artists were sketching him, and he seemed to pose for just a moment. He smiled sincerely at the jurors, then introduced himself. He explained that he was the people's lawyer; his client, the State of Mississippi. He had served as their prosecutor for nine years now, and it was an honor for which he would always be grateful to the fine folks of Ford County. He pointed at them and told them that they, the very ones sitting there, were the folks who had elected him to represent them. He thanked them, and hoped he did not let them down.

Yes, he was nervous and frightened. He had prosecuted thousands of criminals, but he was always scared with each trial. Yes! He was scared, and not ashamed to admit it. Scared because of the awesome responsibility the people had bestowed upon him as the man responsible for sending criminals to jail and protecting the people. Scared because he might fail to adequately represent his client, the people of this great state.

Jake had heard all this crap many times before. He had it memorized. Buckley the good guy, the state's lawyer, united with the people to seek justice, to save society. He was a smooth, gifted orator who one moment could chat softly with a jury, much like a grandfather giving advice to his grandchildren. The next moment he would launch into a tirade and deliver a sermon that any black preacher would envy. A split second later, in a fluid burst of eloquence, he could convince a jury that the stability of our society, yes, even the future of the human race, depended upon a guilty verdict. He was at his best in big trials, and this was his biggest. He spoke without notes, and held the courtroom captivated as he portrayed himself as the underdog, the friend and partner of the jury, who, together with him, would find the truth, and punish this man for his monstrous deed.

After ten minutes, Jake had enough. He stood with a frustrated look. 'Your Honor, I object to this. Mr. Buckley is not selecting a jury. I'm not sure what he's doing; but he's not interrogating the panel.'

'Sustained!' Noose yelled into the mike. 'If you don't have any questions for the panel, Mr. Buckley, then please sit down.'

'I apologize, Your Honor,' Buckley said awkwardly, pretending to be hurt. Jake had drawn first blood.

Buckley picked up a legal pad and launched into a list of a thousand questions. He asked if anyone on the panel had ever served on a jury before. Several hands went up. Civil or criminal? Did you vote to acquit or convict? How long ago? Was the defendant black or white? Victim, black or white? Had anyone been the victim of a violent crime? Two hands. When? Where? Was the assailant caught? Convicted? Black or white? Jake, Harry Rex, and Ellen took pages of notes. Any member of your family been the victim of a violent crime? Several more hands. When? Where? What happened to the criminal? Any member of your family ever been charged with a crime? Indicted? Put on trial? Convicted? Any friends or family members employed in law enforcement? Who? Where?

For three nonstop hours Buckley probed and picked like a surgeon. He was masterful. The preparation was obvious. He asked questions that Jake had not considered. And he asked virtually every question Jake had written in his outline. He delicately pried details of personal feelings and opinions. And when the time was right, he would say something funny so everyone could laugh and relieve the tension. He held the courtroom in his palm, and when Noose stopped him at five o'clock he was in full stride. He would finish in the morning.

His Honor adjourned until nine the next morning. Jake talked to his client for a few moments while the crowd moved toward the rear. Ozzie stood nearby with the handcuffs. When Jake finished, Carl Lee knelt before his family on the front row and hugged them all. He would see them tomorrow, he said. Ozzie led him into the holding room and down the stairs, where a swarm of deputies waited to take him to jail.

CHAPTER THIRTY-FOUR

For Day Two the sun rose quickly in the east and in seconds burned the dew off the thick green Bermuda around the Ford County Courthouse. A sticky, invisible fog smoldered from the grass and clung to the heavy boots and bulky pants of the soldiers. The sun baked them as they nonchalantly paced the sidewalks of downtown Clanton. They loitered under shade trees and the canopies of small shops. By the time breakfast was served under the pavilions, the soldiers had stripped to their pale green undershirts and were drenched in sweat.

The black preachers and their followers went directly to their spot and set up camp. They unfolded lawn chairs under oak trees and placed coolers of ice water on card tables. Blue and white FREE CARL LEE placards were tacked on tomato stakes and stuck in the ground like neat fencerows. Agee had printed some new posters with an enlarged black and white photo of Carl Lee in the center and a red, white, and blue border. They were slick and professional.

The Klansmen went obediently to their section of the front lawn. They brought their own placards – white backgrounds with bold red letters screaming FRY CARL LEE, FRY CARL LEE. They waved them at the blacks across the lawn, and the two groups started shouting. The soldiers formed neat lines along the sidewalk, and stood armed but casual as obscenities and chants flew over their heads. It was 8:00 A.M. of Day Two.

The reporters were giddy with all the newsworthiness. They rushed to the front lawn when the yelling started. Ozzie and the colonel walked around and around the courthouse, pointing here and there and yelling into their radios.

At nine, Ichabod said good morning to the standing-room-only crowd. Buckley stood slowly and with great animation informed His Honor that he had no further questions for the panel.

Lawyer Brigance rose from his seat with rubber knees and turbulence in his stomach. He walked to the railing and gazed into the anxious eyes of ninety-four prospective jurors.

The crowd listened intently to this young, cocky mouthpiece who had once boasted of never having lost a murder case. He appeared relaxed and confident. His voice was loud, yet warm. His words were educated, yet colloquial. He introduced himself again, and his client, then his client's family, saving the little girl for last. He complimented the D.A. for such an exhaustive interrogation yesterday afternoon, and confessed that most of his questions had already been asked. He glanced at his notes. His first question was a bombshell.

'Ladies and gentlemen, do any of you believe that the insanity defense should not be used under any circumstances?'

They squirmed a little, but no hands. He caught them off-guard, right off the bat. Insanity! Insanity! The seed had been planted.

'If we prove Carl Lee Hailey was legally insane when he shot Billy Ray Cobb and Pete Willard, is there a person on this panel who cannot find him not guilty?'

The question was hard to follow – intentionally so. There were no hands. A few wanted to respond, but they were not certain of the appropriate response.

Jake eyed them carefully, knowing most of them were confused, but also knowing that for this moment every member of the panel was thinking about his client being insane. That's where he would leave them.

'Thank you,' he said with all the charm he had ever mustered in his life. 'I have nothing further, Your Honor.'

Buckley looked confused. He stared at the judge, who was equally bewildered.

'Is that all?' Noose asked incredulously. 'Is that all, Mr. Brigance?'

'Yes, sir, Your Honor, the panel looks fine to me,' Jake said with an air of trust, as opposed to Buckley, who had grilled them for three hours. The panel was anything but acceptable to Jake, but there was no sense repeating the same questions Buckley had asked.

'Very well. Let me see the attorneys in chambers.'

Buckley, Musgrove, Jake, Ellen, and Mr. Pate followed Ichabod through the door behind the bench and sat around the desk in chambers. Noose spoke: 'I assume, gentlemen, that you want each juror questioned individually on the death penalty.'

'Yes, sir,' said Jake.

'That's correct, Your Honor,' said Buckley.

'Very well. Mr. Bailiff, would you bring in juror number one, Carlene Malone.'

Mr. Pate left, walked to the courtroom and yelled for Carlene Malone. Moments later she followed him into chambers. She was terrified. The attorneys smiled but said nothing: Noose's instructions.

'Please have a seat,' Noose offered as he removed his robe. 'This will only take a minute, Mrs. Malone. Do you have any strong feelings one way or the other about the death penalty?' asked Noose.

She shook her head nervously and stared at Ichabod. 'Uh, no, sir.'

'You realize that if you're selected for this jury and Mr. Hailey is convicted, you will be called upon to sentence him to death?'

'Yes, sir.'

'If the State proves beyond a reasonable doubt that the killings were premeditated, and if you believe Mr. Hailey was not legally insane at the time of the killings, could you consider imposing the death penalty?'

'Certainly. I think it should be used all the time. Might stop some of this meanness. I'm all for it.'

Jake continued smiling and nodding politely at juror number one. Buckley smiled too, and winked at Musgrove.

'Thank you, Mrs. Malone. You may return to your seat in the courtroom,' Noose said.

'Bring in number two,' Noose ordered Mr. Pate. Marcia Dickens, an elderly white woman with a hard frown, was led to chambers. Yes, sir, she said, she was very much in favor of the death penalty. Would have no problems voting for it. Jake sat there and smiled. Buckley winked again. Noose thanked her and called for number three.

Three and four were equally unforgiving, ready to kill if the proof was there. Then number five, Gerald Ault, Jake's secret weapon, was seated in chambers.

'Thank you Mr. Ault, this will only take a minute,' Noose repeated. 'First of all, do you have strong feelings for or against the death penalty?'

'Oh, yes, sir.' Ault answered eagerly, his voice and face radiating compassion. 'I'm very much against it. It's cruel and unusual. I'm ashamed I live in a society which permits the legal killing of a human being.'

'I see. Could you, under any circumstances, if you were a juror, vote to impose the death penalty?'

'Oh, no, sir. Under no circumstances. Regardless of the crime. No, sir.'

Buckley cleared his throat and somberly announced, 'Your Honor, the State would challenge Mr. Ault for cause and move to excuse him under the authority of State vs. Witherspoon.'

'Motion sustained. Mr. Ault, you are excused from jury duty,' Noose said. 'You may leave the courtroom if you wish. If you choose to remain in the courtroom, I ask that you not sit with the other jurors.'

Ault was puzzled and looked helplessly at his friend Jake, who at the moment was staring at the floor with a tight mouth.

'May I ask why?' Gerald asked.

Noose removed his glasses and became the professor. 'Under the law, Mr. Ault, the court is required to excuse any potential juror who admits he or she cannot consider, and the key word is consider, the death penalty. You see, whether you like it or not, the death penalty is a legal method of punishment in Mississippi and in most states. Therefore, it is unfair to select jurors who cannot follow the law.'

The curiosity of the crowd was piqued when Gerald Ault emerged from behind the bench, walked through the small gate in the railing, and left the courtroom. The bailiff fetched number six, Alex Summers, and led him to chambers. He returned moments later and took his seat on the first row. He lied about the death penalty. He opposed it as did most blacks, but he told Noose he had no objections to it. No problem. Later during a recess, he quietly met with other black jurors and explained how the questions in chambers should be answered.

The slow process continued until mid-afternoon, when the last juror left chambers. Eleven had been excused due to reservations about capital punishment. Noose recessed at three-thirty and gave the lawyers until four to review their notes.

In the library on the third floor, Jake and his team stared at the jury lists and notecards. It was time to decide. He had dreamed about names written in blue and red and black with numbers beside them. He had watched them in the courtroom for two full days now. He knew them. Ellen wanted women. Harry Rex wanted men.

Noose stared at his master list, with the jurors renumbered to reflect the dismissals for cause, and looked at his lawyers. 'Gentlemen, are you ready? Good. As you know this is a capital case, so each of you have twelve peremptory challenges. Mr. Buckley, you are required to submit a list of twelve jurors to the defense. Please start with juror number one and refer to each juror only by number.'

'Yes sir. Your Honor, the State will accept jurors number one, two, three, four, use our first challenge on number five, accept numbers six, seven, eight, nine, use our second challenge on number ten, accept numbers eleven, twelve, thirteen, use our third challenge on number fourteen, and accept number fifteen. That's twelve, I believe.'

Jake and Ellen circled and made notes on their lists. Noose methodically recounted. 'Yes, that's twelve. Mr. Brigance.'

Buckley submitted twelve white females. Two blacks and a white male had been stricken.

Jake studied his list and scratched names. 'The defense will strike jurors number one, two, three, accept four, six, and seven, strike eight, nine, eleven, twelve, accept thirteen, strike fifteen. I believe that's eight of our challenges.'

His Honor drew lines and check marks down his list, calculating slowly as he went. 'Both of you have accepted jurors number four, six, seven, and thirteen. Mr. Buckley, it's back to you. Give us eight more jurors.'

'The State will accept sixteen, use our fourth challenge on seventeen, accept eighteen, nineteen, twenty, strike twenty-one, accept twenty-two, strike twenty-three, accept twenty-four, strike twenty-five and twenty-six, and accept twenty-seven and twenty-eight. That's twelve with four challenges remaining.'

Jake was flabbergasted. Buckley had again stricken all the blacks and all the men. He was reading Jake's mind.

'Mr. Brigance, it's back to you.'

'May we have a moment to confer, Your Honor?'

'Five minutes,' Noose replied.

Jake and his clerk stepped next door to the coffee room, where Harry Rex was waiting. 'Look at this,' Jake said as he laid the list on a table and the three huddled around it. 'We're down to twenty-nine. I've got four challenges left and so does Buckley. He's struck every black and every male. It's an all-white female jury right now. The next two are white females, thirty-one is Clyde Sisco, and thirty-two is Barry Acker.'

'Then four of the next six are black,' Ellen said.

'Yeah, but Buckley won't take it that far. In fact, I'm surprised he's let us get this close to the fourth row.'

'I know you want Acker. What about Sisco?' asked Harry Rex.

'I'm afraid of him. Lucien said he's a crook who could be bought.'

'Great! Let's get him, then go buy him.'

'Very funny. How do you know Buckley hasn't already bought him?'

'I'd take him.'

Jake studied the list, counting and recounting. Ellen wanted to strike both men – Acker and Sisco.

They returned to chambers and sat down. The court reporter was ready. 'Your Honor, we will strike number twenty-two and number twenty-eight, with two challenges remaining.'

'Back to you, Mr. Buckley. Twenty-nine and thirty.'

'The State will take them both. That's twelve with four challenges left.'

'Back to you, Mr. Brigance.'

'We will strike twenty-nine and thirty.'

'And you're out of challenges, correct?' Noose asked.

'Correct.'

'Very well. Mr. Buckley, thirty-one and thirty-two.'

'The State will take them both,' Buckley said quickly, looking at the names of the blacks coming after Clyde Sisco.

'Good. That's twelve. Let's select two alternates. You will both have two challenges for the alternates. Mr. Buckley, thirty-three and thirty-four.'

Juror thirty-three was a black male. Thirty-four was a white female Jake wanted. The next two were black males.

'We'll strike thirty-three, accept thirty-four and thirty-five.'

'The defense will accept both,' Jake said.

Mr. Pate brought the courtroom to order as Noose and the lawyers took their places. His Honor called the names of the twelve and they slowly, nervously made their way to the jury box, where they were seated in order by Jean Gillespie. Ten women, two men, all white. The blacks in the courtroom mumbled and eyed each other in disbelief.

'Did you pick that jury?' Carl Lee whispered to Jake.

'I'll explain later,' Jake said.

The two alternates were called and seated next to the jury box.

'What's the black dude for?' Carl Lee whispered, nodding at the alternate.

'I'll explain later,' Jake said.

Noose cleared his throat and looked down at his new jury. 'Ladies and gentlemen, you have been carefully selected to serve as jurors in this case. You have been sworn to fairly try all issues presented before you and to follow the law as I instruct. Now, according to Mississippi law, you will be sequestered until this trial is over. This means you will be housed in a motel and will not be allowed to return home until it's over. I realize this is an extreme hardship, but it's one the law requires. In just a few moments we will recess until in the morning, and you will be given the chance to call home and order your clothes, toiletries, and whatever else you need. Each night you will stay in a motel at an undisclosed location outside of Clanton. Any questions?'

The twelve appeared dazed, bewildered by the thought of not going home for several days. They thought of families, kids, jobs, laundry. Why them? Out of all those people in the courtroom, why them?

With no response, Noose banged his gavel and the courtroom began to empty. Jean Gillespie escorted the first juror to the judge's chambers, where she called home and ordered clothes and a toothbrush.

'Where are we going?' she asked Jean.

'It's confidential,' Jean said.

'It's confidential,' she repeated over the phone to her husband.

By seven, the families had responded with a wild assortment of luggage and boxes. The chosen ones loaded a chartered Greyhound bus outside the rear door. Preceded by two patrol cars and an army jeep and followed by three state troopers, the bus circled the square and left Clanton.

Stump Sisson died Tuesday night at the burn hospital in Memphis. His short, fat body had been neglected over the years and proved itself deficient in resisting the complications bred by the serious burns. His death brought to four the number of fatalities related to the rape of Tonya Hailey. Cobb, Willard, Bud Twitty, and now Sisson.

Immediately, word of his death reached the cabin deep in the woods where the patriots met, ate, and drank each night after the trial. Revenge, they vowed, an eye for an eye and so on. There were new recruits from Ford County – five in all – making a total of eleven local boys. They were eager and hungry, and wanted some action.

The trial had been too quiet so far. It was time for excitement.

Jake paced in front of the couch and delivered his opening statement for the hundredth time. Ellen listened intently. She had listened, interrupted, objected, criticized, and argued for two hours. She was tired now. He had it perfect. The margaritas had calmed him and plated his tongue silver. The words flowed smoothly. He was gifted. Especially after a drink or two.

When he finished they sat on the balcony and watched the candles inch slowly in the darkness around the square. The laughter from the poker games under the pavilions echoed softly through the night. There was no moon.

Ellen left for the final round of drinks. She returned with her same beer mugs filled with ice and margaritas. She sat them on the table and stood behind her boss. She placed her hands on his shoulders and began rubbing the lower part of his neck with her thumbs. He relaxed and moved his head from side to side. She massaged his shoulders and upper back, and pressed her body against his.

'Ellen, it's ten-thirty, and I'm sleepy. Where are you staying tonight?'

'Where do you think I should stay?'

'I think you should stay at your apartment at Ole Miss.'

'I'm too drunk to drive.'

'Nesbit will drive you.'

'Where, may I ask, are you staying?'

'At the house my wife and I own on Adams Street.'

She stopped rubbing and grabbed her drink. Jake stood and leaned over the rail and yelled at Nesbit. 'Nesbit! Wake up! You're driving to Oxford!'

CHAPTER THIRTY-FIVE

Carla found the story on the second page of the front section. 'All White Jury Chosen for Hailey' read the headline. Jake had not called Tuesday night. She read the story and ignored her coffee.

The beach house sat by itself in a semisecluded area of the beach. The nearest neighbor was two hundred yards away. Her father owned the land in between and had no plans to sell it. He had built the house ten years earlier when he sold his company in Knoxville and retired wealthy. Carla was the only child, and now Hanna would be the only grandchild. The house – with four bedrooms and four bathrooms scattered over three levels – had room for a dozen grandchildren.

She finished the article and walked to the bay windows in the breakfast room overlooking the beach, and then the ocean. The brilliant orange mass of the sun had just cleared the horizon. She preferred the warmth of the bed until well after daybreak, but life with Jake had brought new adventure to the first seven hours of each day. Her body was conditioned to at least wake up at five-thirty. He once told her his goal was to go to work in the dark and return from work in the dark. He usually achieved this goal. He took great pride in working more hours each day than any lawyer in Ford County. He was different, but she loved him.

Forty-eight miles northeast of Clanton, the Milburn county seat of Temple lay peacefully beside the Tippah River. It had three thousand people and two motels. The Temple Inn was deserted, there being no moral reason to be there this time of year. At the end of one secluded wing, eight rooms were occupied and guarded by soldiers and a couple of state troopers. The ten women had paired off nicely, as had Barry Acker and Clyde Sisco. The black alternate, Ben Lester Newton, was awarded a room to himself, as was the other alternate, Francie Pitts. The televisions had been disconnected and no newspapers were allowed. Supper Tuesday night had been delivered to the rooms, and Wednesday's breakfast arrived promptly at seven-thirty while the Greyhound warmed and blew diesel fumes all over the parking lot. Thirty minutes later the fourteen loaded aboard and the entourage set out for Clanton.

They talked on the bus about their families and jobs. Two or three had known each other prior to Monday; most were strangers. They awkwardly avoided any mention of why they were all together and the task before them. Judge Noose had been very plain on this point; no discussions about the case. They wanted to talk about many things: the rape, the rapists, Carl Lee, Jake, Buckley, Noose, the Klan, lots of things. Everyone knew of the burning crosses, but they weren't discussed, at least they weren't discussed on the bus. There had been many discussions back in the motel rooms.

The Greyhound arrived at the courthouse five minutes before nine, and the jurors stared through dark windows to see how many blacks and how many Klansmen and how many others were being separated by the guardsmen. It eased past the barricades and parked at the rear of the courthouse, where the deputies were waiting to escort them upstairs as soon as possible. They went up the back stairs to the jury room, where coffee and doughnuts were waiting. The bailiff informed them it was nine, and His Honor was ready to start. He led them into the crowded courtroom and into the jury box, where they sat in their designated seats.

'All rise for the court,' Mr. Pate yelled.

'Please be seated,' Noose said as he fell into the tall leather chair behind the bench. 'Good morning, ladies and gentlemen,' he said warmly to the jurors. 'I trust you're all feeling well this morning, and ready to go.'

They all nodded.

'Good. I'm going to ask you this question every morning: Did anybody attempt to contact you, talk to you, or influence you in any way last night?'

They all shook their heads.

'Good. Did you discuss this case among yourselves?'

They all lied and shook their heads.

'Good. If anyone attempts to contact you and discuss this case or influence you in any way, I expect you to notify me as soon as possible. Do you understand?'

They nodded.

'Now at this time we are ready to start the trial. The first order of business is to allow the attorneys to make opening statements. I want to caution you that nothing the attorneys say is testimony and is not to be taken as evidence. Mr. Buckley, do you wish to make an opening statement?'

Buckley rose and buttoned his shiny polyester coat. 'Yes, Your Honor.'

'I thought so. You may proceed.'

Buckley lifted the small, wooden podium and moved it squarely in front of the jury box, where he stood behind it and breathed deeply and slowly flipped through some notes on a legal pad. He enjoyed the brief period of quietness with all eyes on him and all ears anxious for his words.

He started by thanking the jurors for being there, for their sacrifices, for their citizenship (as if they had a choice, thought Jake). He was proud of them and honored to be associated with them in this most important case. Again, he was their lawyer. His client, the State of Mississippi. He expressed fear at this awesome responsibility that they, the people, had given to him, Rufus Buckley, a simple country lawyer from Smithfield. He rambled on about himself and his thoughts on the trial and his hopes and prayers that he would do a good job for the people of this state.

He gave pretty much the same spiel in all of his opening statements, but this was a better performance. It was refined and polished garbage, and objectionable. Jake wanted to burn him, but from experience he knew Ichabod would not sustain an objection during an opening statement unless the offense was flagrant, and Buckley's rhetoric did not qualify – yet. All this fake sincerity and gushiness irritated Jake to no end, primarily because the jury listened to it and, more often than not, fell for it. The prosecutor was always the good guy, seeking to right an injustice and punish a criminal for some heinous crime; to lock him away forever so he could sin no more. Buckley was master at convincing a jury, right off the mark, during the opening statement, that it was up to them, He and The Twelve Chosen Ones, to search diligently for the truth, together as a team, united against evil. It was the truth they were after, nothing but the truth. Find the truth and justice would win. Follow him, Rufus Buckley, the people's lawyer, and they would find the truth.

The rape was a terrible deed. He was a father, in fact had a daughter the same age of Tonya Hailey, and when he first heard of the rape he was sick at his stomach. He grieved for Carl Lee and his wife. Yes, he thought of his own little girls and had thoughts of retribution.

Jake smiled quickly at Ellen. This was interesting. Buckley had chosen to confront the rape instead of keeping it from the jury. Jake was expecting a critical confrontation with him on the admissibility of any testimony regarding the rape. Ellen's research found the law to be clear that the lurid details were inadmissible, but it wasn't so clear as to whether it could be mentioned or referred to. Evidently Buckley felt it was better to acknowledge the rape than try to hide it. Good move, thought Jake, since all twelve and the rest of the world knew the details anyway.

Ellen smiled too. The rape of Tonya Hailey was about to be tried for the first time.

Buckley explained it would be natural for any parent to want revenge. He would too, he admitted. But, he continued with his voice growing heavier, there is a mighty distinction between wanting revenge and getting revenge.

He was warming up now as he paced deliberately back and forth, ignoring the podium, getting his rhythm. He launched himself into a twenty-minute discourse on the criminal justice system and how it was practiced in Mississippi, and how many rapists that he, Rufus Buckley, had personally sent to Parchman, for life, most of them. The system worked because Mississippians had enough good common sense to make it work, and it would collapse if people like Carl Lee Hailey were allowed to short-circuit the system and dispense justice according to their own terms. Imagine that. A lawless society where vigilantes roamed at will. No police, no jails, no courts, no trials, no juries. Every man for himself.

It was sort of ironic, he said, winding down for a moment. Carl Lee Hailey now sat before them asking for due process and a fair trial, yet he did not believe in such things. Ask the mothers of Billy Ray Cobb and Pete Willard. Ask them what kind of fair trials their sons received.

He paused to allow the jury and the courtroom to absorb and ponder that last thought. It sunk in heavy, and every person in the jury box looked at Carl Lee Hailey. They were not looks of compassion. Jake cleaned his fingernails with a small knife and looked thoroughly bored. Buckley pretended to review his notes at the podium, then checked his watch. He started again, this time in a most confident businesslike tone of voice. The State would prove that Carl Lee Hailey carefully planned the killings. He waited for almost an hour in a small room next to the stairs where he knew the boys would eventually be led as they were taken back to jail. He somehow managed to sneak an M-16 into the courthouse. Buckley walked to a small table by the court reporter and hoisted the M-16. 'This is the M-16!' he announced to the jury, waving it wildly about with one hand. He sat it on the podium and talked about how it was carefully selected by Carl Lee Hailey because he had used one before in close combat, and he knew how to kill with it. He had been trained with an M-16. It's an illegal weapon. You can't buy one down at the Western Auto. He had to go find it. He planned it.

The proof would be clear: premeditated, carefully planned, cold-blooded murder.

And then there was Deputy DeWayne Looney. A fourteen-year veteran of the Sheriff's Department. A family man – one of the finest law enforcement officers he had ever known. Gunned down in the line of duty by Carl Lee Hailey. His leg was partially amputated. What was his sin? Perhaps the defense would say it was accidental, that it shouldn't count. That's no defense in Mississippi.

There's no excuse, ladies and gentlemen, for any of this violence. The verdict must be guilty.

They each had an hour for their openings, and the lure of that much time proved irresistible for the D.A., whose remarks were becoming repetitive. He lost himself twice during his condemnation of the insanity ruse. The jurors began to look bored and searched for other points of interest around the courtroom. The artists quit sketching, the reporters quit writing, and Noose cleaned his glasses seven or eight times. It was a known fact that Noose cleaned the glasses to stay awake and fight boredom, and he usually cleaned them throughout the trial. Jake had seen him rub them with a handkerchief or tie or shirttail while witnesses broke down and cried and lawyers screamed and flailed their arms at each other. He didn't miss a word or objection or trick; he was just bored with it all, even a case of this magnitude. He never slept on the bench, although he was sorely tempted at times. Instead he removed his glasses, held them upward in the light, blew on them, rubbed them as though they were caked with grease, then remounted them just north of the wart. No more than five minutes later they would be dirty again. The longer Buckley droned on, the more they were cleaned.

Finally, after an hour and a half, Buckley shut up and the courtroom sighed.

'Ten-minute recess,' Noose announced, and lunged off the bench, through the door, past chambers to the men's room.

Jake had planned a brief opening, and after Buckley's marathon, he decided to make it even shorter. Most people don't like lawyers to begin with, especially long-winded, tall-talking, wordy lawyers who feel that every insignificant point must be repeated at least three times, and the major ones have to be hammered and drilled by constant repetition into whoever happened to be listening. Jurors especially dislike lawyers who waste time, for two very good reasons. First, they can't tell the lawyers to shut up. They're captives. Outside the courtroom a person can curse a lawyer and shut him up, but in the jury box they become trapped and forbidden to speak. Thus, they must resort to sleeping, snoring, glaring, squirming, checking their watches, or any one of a dozen signals which boring lawyers never recognize. Second, jurors don't like long trials. Cut the crap and get it over with. Give us the facts and we'll give you a verdict.

He explained this to his client during the recess.

'I agree. Keep it short,' said Carl Lee.

He did. Fourteen minutes worth of opening statement, and the jury appreciated every word. He began by talking about daughters and how special they are. How they are different from little boys and need special protection. He told them of his own daughter and the special bond that exists between father and daughter, a bond that could not be explained and should not be tampered with. He admitted admiration for Mr.

Buckley and his alleged ability to be so forgiving and compassionate to any drunken pervert who might rape his daughter. He was a big man indeed. But in reality, could they, as jurors, as parents, be so tender and trusting and indulging if their daughter had been raped – by two drunk, stoned, brutal animals who tied her to a tree and –'

'Objection!' shouted Buckley.

'Sustained,' Noose shouted back.

He ignored the shouting and continued softly. He asked them to try to imagine, throughout the trial, how they would feel had it been their daughter. He asked them not to convict Carl Lee but to send him home to his family. He didn't mention insanity. They knew it was coming.

He finished shortly after he started, and left the jury with a marked contrast in the two styles.

'Is that all?' Noose asked in amazement.

Jake nodded as he sat by his client.

'Very well. Mr. Buckley, you may call your first witness.'

'The State calls Cora Cobb.'

The bailiff went to the witness room and fetched Mrs. Cobb. He led her through the door by the jury box, into the courtroom where she was sworn by Jean Gillespie, and then he seated her in the witness chair.

'Speak into the microphone,' he instructed.

'You are Cora Cobb?' Buckley asked with full volume as he situated the podium near the railing.

'Yes, sir.'

'Where do you live?'

'Route 3, Lake Village, Ford County.'

'You are the mother of Billy Ray Cobb, deceased?'

'Yes, sir,' she said as her eyes watered. She was a rural woman whose husband had left when the boys were small. They had raised themselves while she worked two shifts at a cheap furniture factory between Karaway and Lake Village. She lost control over them at an early age. She was about fifty, tried to look forty with hair dye and makeup, but could easily pass for early sixties.

'How old was your son at the time of his death?'

'Twenty-three.'

'When did you last see him alive?'

'Just a few seconds before he was kilt.'

'Where did you see him?'

'Here in this courtroom.'

'Where was he killed?'

'Downstairs.'

'Did you hear the shots that killed your son?'

She began to cry. 'Yes, sir.'

'Where did you last see him?'

'At the funeral home.'

'And what was his condition?'

'He was dead.'

'Nothing further,' Buckley announced.

'Cross-examination, Mr. Brigance?'

She was a harmless witness, called to establish that the victim was indeed dead, and to evoke a little sympathy. Nothing could be gained by cross-examination, and normally she would have been left alone. But Jake saw an opportunity he couldn't pass. He saw a chance to set the tone for the trial, to wake Noose and Buckley and the jury; to just get everyone aroused. She was not really that pitiful; she was faking some. Buckley had probably instructed her to cry if possible.

'Just a few questions,' Jake said as he walked behind Buckley and Musgrove to the podium. The D.A. was immediately suspicious.

'Mrs. Cobb, is it true that your son was convicted of selling marijuana?'

'Objection!' Buckley roared, springing to his feet. 'The criminal record of the victim is inadmissible!'

'Sustained!'

'Thank you, Your Honor,' Jake said properly, as if Noose had done him a favor.

She wiped her eyes and cried harder.

'You say your son was twenty-three when he died?'

'Yes.'

'In his twenty-three years, how many other children did he rape?'

'Objection! Objection!' yelled Buckley, waving his arms and looking desperately at Noose, who was yelling, 'Sustained! Sustained! You're out of order, Mr. Brigance! You're out of order!'

Mrs. Cobb burst into tears and bawled uncontrollably as the shouting erupted. She managed to keep the microphone in her face, and her wailing and carrying on resounded through the stunned courtroom.

'He should be admonished, Your Honor!' Buckley demanded, his face and eyes glowing with violent anger and his neck a deep purple.

'I'll withdraw the question,' Jake replied loudly as he returned to his seat.

'Cheap shot, Brigance,' Musgrove mumbled.

'Please admonish him,' Buckley begged, 'and instruct the jury to disregard.'

'Any redirect?' asked Noose.

'No,' answered Buckley as he dashed to the witness stand with a handkerchief to rescue Mrs. Cobb, who had buried her head in her hands and was sobbing and shaking violently.

'You are excused, Mrs. Cobb,' Noose said. 'Bailiff, please assist the witness.'

The bailiff lifted her by the arm, with Buckley's assistance, and led her down from the witness stand, in front of the jury box, through the railing, down the center aisle. She shrieked and whined every step of the way, and her noises increased as she neared the back door until she was roaring at full throttle when she made her exit.

Noose glared at Jake until she was gone and the courtroom was quiet again. Then he turned to the jury and said: 'Please disregard the last question by Mr. Brigance.'

'What'd you do that for?' Carl Lee whispered to his lawyer.

'I'll explain later.'

'The State calls Earnestine Willard,' Buckley announced in a quieter tone and with much more hesitation.

Mrs. Willard was brought from the witness room above the courtroom. She was sworn and seated.

'You are Earnestine Willard?' asked Buckley.

'Yes, sir,' She said in a fragile voice. Life had been rough on her too, but she had a certain dignity that made her more pitiful and believable than Mrs. Cobb. The clothes were inexpensive, but clean and neatly pressed. The hair was minus the cheap black dye that Mrs. Cobb relied on so heavily. The face was minus the layers of makeup. When she began crying, she cried to herself.

'And where do you live?'

'Out from Lake Village.'

'Pete Willard was your son?'

'Yes, sir.'

'When did you last see him alive?'

'Right here in this room, just before he was killed.'

'Did you hear the gunfire that killed him?'

'Yes, sir.'

'Where did you last see him?'

'At the funeral home.'

'And what was his condition?'

'He was dead,' she said, wiping tears with a Kleenex.

'I'm very sorry,' Buckley offered. 'No further questions,' he added, eyeing Jake carefully.

'Any cross-examination?' Noose asked, also eyeing Jake suspiciously.

'Just a couple,' Jake said.

'Mrs. Willard, I'm Jake Brigance.' He stood behind the podium and looked at her without compassion.

She nodded.

'How old was your son when he died?'

'Twenty-seven.'

Buckley pushed his chair from the table and sat on its edge, ready to spring. Noose removed his glasses and leaned forward. Carl Lee lowered his head.

'During his twenty-seven years, how many other children did he rape?'

Buckley bolted upright. 'Objection! Objection! Objection!'

'Sustained! Sustained! Sustained!'

The yelling frightened Mrs. Willard, and she cried louder.

'Admonish him, Judge! He must be admonished!'

'I'll withdraw the question,' Jake said on his way back to his seat.

Buckley pleaded with his hands. 'But that's not good enough, Judge! He must be admonished!'

'Let's go into chambers,' Noose ordered. He excused the witness and recessed until one.

Harry Rex was waiting on the balcony of Jake's office with sandwiches and a pitcher of margaritas. Jake declined and drank grapefruit juice. Ellen wanted just one, a small one she said to calm her nerves. For the third day, lunch had been prepared by Dell and personally delivered to Jake's office. Compliments of the Coffee Shop.

They ate and relaxed on the balcony and watched the carnival around the courthouse. What happened in chambers? Harry Rex demanded. Jake nibbled on a Reuben. He said he wanted to talk about something other than the trial.

'What happened in chambers, dammit?'

'Cardinals are three games out, did you know that, Row Ark?'

'I thought it was four.'

'What happened in chambers!'

'Do you really want to know?'

'Yes! Yes!'

'Okay. I've got to go use the rest room. I'll tell you when I get back.' Jake left.

'Row Ark, what happened in chambers?'

'Not much. Noose rode Jake pretty good, but no permanent damage. Buckley wanted blood, and Jake said he was sure some was forthcoming if Buckley's face got any redder. Buckley ranted and screamed and condemned Jake for intentionally inflaming the jury, as he called it. Jake just smiled at him and said he was sorry, Governor. Every time he would say governor, Buckley would scream at Noose, 'He's calling me governor, Judge, do something.' And Noose would say, 'Please, gentlemen, I expect you to act like professionals.' And Jake would say, 'Thank you, Your Honor.' Then he would wait a few minutes and call him governor again.'

'Why did he make those two old ladies cry?'

'It was a brilliant move, Harry Rex. He showed the jury, Noose, Buckley, everybody, that it's his courtroom and he's not afraid of a damned person in it. He drew first blood. He's got Buckley so jumpy right now he'll never relax. Noose respects him because he's not intimidated by His Honor. The jurors were shocked, but he woke them up and told them in a not so subtle way that this is war. A brilliant move.'

'Yeah, I thought so myself.'

'It didn't hurt us. Those women were asking for sympathy, but Jake reminded the jury of what their sweet little boys did before they died.'

'The scumbags.'

'If there's any resentment by the jury, they'll forget by the time the last witness testifies.'

'Jake's pretty smooth, ain't he?'

'He's good. Very good. He's the best I've seen for his age.'

'Wait till his closing argument. I've heard a couple. He could get sympathy out of a drill sergeant.'

Jake returned and poured a small margarita. Just a very small one, for his nerves. Harry Rex drank like a sailor.

Ozzie was the first State witness after lunch. Buckley produced large, multicolored plats of the first and second floors of the courthouse, and together they traced the precise, last movements of Cobb and Willard.

Then Buckley produced a set of ten 16 × 24 color photographs of Cobb and Willard lying freshly dead on the stairs. They were gruesome. Jake had seen lots of pictures of dead bodies, and although none were particularly pleasant given their nature, some weren't so bad. In one of his cases, the victim had been shot in the heart with a .357 and simply fell over dead on his porch. He was a large, muscular old man, and the bullet never found its way out of the body. So there was no blood, just a small hole in his overalls, and then a small sealed hole in his chest. He looked as though he could have fallen asleep and slumped over, or passed out drunk on the porch, like Lucien. It was not a spectacular scene, and Buckley had not been proud of those photographs. They had not been enlarged. He had just handed the small Polaroids to the jury and looked disgusted because they were so clean.

But most murder pictures were grisly and sickening, with blood splashed on walls and ceilings, and parts of bodies blown free and scattered everywhere. Those were always enlarged by the D.A. and entered into evidence with great fanfare, then waved around the courtroom by Buckley as he and the witness described the scenes in the pictures. Finally, with the jurors fidgeting with curiosity, Buckley would politely ask the judge for permission to show the photographs to the jury, and the judge would always consent. Then Buckley and everybody else would watch their faces intently as they were shocked, horrified, and occasionally nauseated. Jake had actually seen two jurors vomit when handed photos of a badly slashed corpse.

Such pictures were highly prejudicial and highly inflammatory, and also highly admissible. 'Probative' was the word used by the Supreme Court. Such pictures could aid the jury, according to ninety years of decisions from the Court. It was well settled in Mississippi that murder pictures, regardless of their impact on the jury, were always admissible.

Jake had seen the Cobb and Willard photographs weeks earlier, and had filed the standard objection and received the standard denial.

These were mounted professionally on heavy posterboard, something the D.A. had not done before. He handed the first one into the jury box to Reba Betts. It was the one of Willard's head and brains taken at close range.

'My God!' she gasped, and shoved it to the next juror, who gawked in horror, and passed it on. They handed it to one another, then to the alternates. Buckley took it, and gave Reba another one. The ritual continued for thirty minutes until all the pictures were returned to the D.A.

Then he grabbed the M-16 and thrust it at Ozzie. 'Can you identify this?'

'Yes, it's the weapon found at the scene.'

'Who picked it up at the scene?'

'I did.'

'And what did you do with it?'

'Wrapped it in a plastic bag and placed it in the vault at the jail. Kept it locked up until I handed it to Mr. Laird with the crime lab in Jackson.'

'Your Honor, the State would offer the weapon, Exhibit S-13, into evidence,' Buckley said, waving it wildly.

'No objections,' Jake said.

'We have nothing further of this witness,' Buckley announced.

'Cross-examination?'

Jake flipped through his notes as he walked slowly to the podium. He had just a few questions for his friend.

'Sheriff, did you arrest Billy Ray Cobb and Pete Willard?'

Buckley pushed his chair back and perched his ample frame on the edge, poised to leap and scream if necessary.

'Yes I did,' answered the sheriff.

'For what reason?'

'For the rape of Tonya Hailey,' he answered perfectly.

'And how old was she at the time she was raped by Cobb and Willard?'

'She was ten.'

'Is it true, Sheriff, that Pete Willard signed a written confession in –'

'Objection! Objection! Your Honor! That's inadmissible and Mr. Brigance knows it.'

Ozzie nodded affirmatively during the objection.

'Sustained.'

Buckley was shaking. 'I ask that the question be stricken from the record and the jury be instructed to disregard it.'

'I'll withdraw the question,' Jake said to Buckley with a smile.

'Please disregard the last question from Mr. Brigance,' Noose instructed the jury.

'No further questions,' said Jake.

'Any redirect examination, Mr. Buckley?'

'No, sir.'

'Very well. Sheriff, you may step down.'

Buckley's next witness was a fingerprint man from Washington who spent an hour telling the jurors what they had known for weeks. His dramatic final conclusion unmistakably linked the prints on the M-16 to those of Carl Lee Hailey. Then came the ballistics expert from the state crime lab whose testimony was as boring and uninformative as his predecessor on the stand. Yes, without a doubt, the fragments recovered from the crime scene were fired from the M-16 lying there on the table. That was his final opinion, and with the charts and diagrams, it took Buckley an hour to get it to the jury. Prosecutorial overkill, as Jake called it; a debility suffered by all prosecutors.

The defense had no questions for either expert, and at five-fifteen Noose said goodbye to the jurors with strict instructions against discussing the case. They nodded politely as they filed from the courtroom. Then he banged his gavel and adjourned until nine in the morning.

CHAPTER THIRTY-SIX

The great civic duty of jury service had grown old rapidly. The second night in the Temple Inn had seen the telephones removed – judge's orders. Some old magazines donated by the Clanton library were circulated and quickly discarded, there being little interest among the group in *The New Yorker, The Smithsonian,* and *Architectural Digest.*

'Got any *Penthouses*?' Clyde Sisco had whispered to the bailiff as he made the rounds. He said no, but he'd see what he could do.

Confined to their rooms with no television, newspapers, or phones, they did little but play cards and talk about the trial. A trip to the end of the hall for ice and a soft drink became a special occasion, something the roommates planned and rotated. The boredom descended heavily.

At each end of the hall two soldiers guarded the darkness and solitude, the stillness interrupted only by the systematic emergence of the jurors with change for the drink machine.

Sleep came early, and when the sentries knocked on the doors at 6:00 A.M., all the jurors were awake, some even dressed. They devoured Thursday's breakfast of pancakes and sausage, and eagerly boarded the Greyhound at eight for the trip back home.

For the fourth straight day the rotunda was crowded by eight o'clock. The spectators had learned that all seats were taken by eight-thirty. Prather opened the door and the crowd filed slowly through the metal detector, past the careful eyes of the deputies and finally into the courtroom, where the blacks filled the left side and the whites the right. The front row was again reserved by Hastings for Gwen, Lester, the kids, and other relatives. Agee and other council members sat in the second row with the kinfolks who couldn't fit up front. Agee was in charge of alternating courtroom duty and outside demonstration duty for the ministers. Personally, he preferred the courtroom duty, where he felt safer, but he did miss the cameras and reporters which were so abundant on the front lawn. To his right, across the aisle, sat the families and friends of the victims. They had behaved so far.

A few minutes before nine, Carl Lee was escorted from the small holding room. The handcuffs were removed by one of the many officers surrounding him. He flashed a big smile at his family and sat in his chair. The lawyers took their places and the courtroom grew quiet. The bailiff poked his head through the door beside the jury box, and, satisfied with whatever he saw, opened the door and released the jurors to their assigned seats. Mr. Pate was watching all this from the door leading to chambers, and when all was perfect, he stepped forward and yelled: 'All rise for the Court!'

Ichabod, draped in his favorite wrinkled and faded black robe, loped to the bench and instructed everyone to have a seat. He greeted the jury and questioned them about what happened or didn't happen since yesterday's adjournment.

He looked at the lawyers. 'Where's Mr. Musgrove?'

'He's running a bit late, Your Honor. We are ready to proceed,' Buckley announced.

'Call your next witness,' Noose ordered Buckley.

The pathologist from the state crime lab was located in the rotunda and entered the courtroom. Normally, he would have been much too busy for a simple trial and would have sent one of his underlings to explain to the jury precisely what killed Cobb and Willard. But this was the Hailey case, and he felt compelled to do the job himself. It was actually the simplest case he had seen in a while; the bodies were found as they were dying, the weapon was with the bodies, and there were enough holes in the boys to kill them a dozen times. Everybody in the world knew how those boys died. But the D.A. had insisted on the most thorough pathological workup, so the doctor took the stand Thursday morning laden with photos of the autopsies and multicolored anatomy charts.

Earlier in chambers, Jake had offered to stipulate to the causes of death, but Buckley would have no part of it. No sir, he wanted the jury to hear and know how they died.

'We will admit that they died by multiple wounds from bullets fired from the M-16,' Jake had stated precisely.

'No, sir. I have a right to prove it,' Buckley said stubbornly.

'But he's offering to stipulate to the causes of death,' Noose said incredulously.

'I have the right to prove it,' Buckley hung on.

So he proved it. In a classic case of prosecutorial overkill, Buckley proved it. For three hours the pathologist talked about how many bullets hit Cobb and how many hit Willard, and what each bullet did upon penetration, and the ghastly damage thereafter. The anatomy charts were placed on easels before the jury, and the expert took a plastic, numbered pellet that represented a bullet, and moved it ever so slowly through the body. Fourteen pellets for Cobb and eleven for Willard. Buckley would ask a question, elicit a response, then interrupt to belabor a point.

'Your Honor, we would be glad to stipulate as to the causes of death,' Jake announced with great frustration every thirty minutes.

'We won't,' Buckley replied tersely, and moved to the next pellet.

Jake fell into his chair, shook his head, and looked at the jurors, those who were awake.

The doctor finished at noon and Noose, tired and numb with boredom, awarded a two-hour lunch break. The jurors were awakened by the bailiff and led to the jury room where they dined on barbeque specials on plastic plates, then struck up card games. They were forbidden to leave the courthouse.

In every small Southern town there's a kid who was born looking for the quick buck. He was the kid who at the age of five set up the first lemonade stand on his street and charged twenty-five cents a cup for four ounces of artificially flavored water. He knew it tasted awful, but he knew the adults thought he was adorable. He was the first kid on the street to purchase a lawn mower on credit at the Western Auto and knock on doors in February to line up yard work for the summer. He was the first kid to pay for his own bike, which he used for morning and afternoon paper routes. He sold Christmas cards to old ladies in August. He sold fruitcakes door to door in November. On Saturday mornings when his friends were watching cartoons, he was at the flea markets at the courthouse selling roasted peanuts and corn dogs. At the age of twelve he bought his first certificate of deposit. He had his own banker. At fifteen, he paid cash for his new pickup the same day he passed his driver's license exam. He bought a trailer to follow the truck and filled it with lawn equipment. He sold T-shirts at high school football games. He was a hustler; a millionaire to be.

In Clanton, his name was Hinky Myrick, age sixteen. He waited nervously in the rotunda until Noose broke for lunch, then moved past the deputies and entered the courtroom. Seating was so precious that almost none of the spectators left for lunch. Some would stand, glare at their neighbors, point at their seats and make sure everybody knew it was theirs for the day, then leave for the rest room. But most of them sat in their highly treasured spaces on the pews, and suffered through lunch.

Hinky could smell opportunity. He could sense people in need. On Thursday, just as he had on Wednesday, he rolled a shopping cart down the aisle to the front of the courtroom. It was filled with a wide assortment of sandwiches and plate lunches in plastic containers. He began yelling toward the far end of the rows, then passing food down to his customers. He worked his way slowly toward the rear of the courtroom. He was a vicious scalper. A tuna salad on white bread went for two dollars; his cost, eighty cents. A plate lunch of cold chicken with a few peas went for three dollars; his cost, a buck twenty-five. A canned soft drink was one-fifty. But they gladly paid his prices and kept their seats. He sold out before he reached the fourth row from the front, and began taking orders from the rest of the courtroom. Hinky was the man of the hour.

With a fistful of orders, he raced from the courthouse, across the lawn, through the crowd of blacks, across Caffey Street and into Claude's. He ran to the kitchen, shoved a twenty-dollar bill at the cook and handed him the orders. He waited and watched his watch. The cook moved slowly. Hinky gave him another twenty.

The trial ushered a wave of prosperity Claude had never dreamed of. Breakfast and lunch in his small cafe became happenings as demand greatly exceeded the number of chairs and the hungry lined the sidewalk, waiting in the heat and haze for a table. After the lunch recess on Monday, he had dashed around Clanton buying every folding card table and matching chair set he could find. At lunch the aisles disappeared, forcing his waitresses to maneuver nimbly among and between the rows of people, virtually all of whom were black.

The trial was the only topic of conversation. On Wednesday, the composition of the jury had been hotly condemned. By Thursday, the talk centered on the growing dislike for the prosecutor.

'I hear tell he wants to run for governor.'

'He Democrat or Republican?'

'Democrat.'

'He can't win without the black vote, not in this state.'

'Yeah, and he ain't likely to get much after this trial.'

'I hope he tries.'

'He acts more like a Republican.'

In pretrial Clanton, the noon hour began ten minutes before twelve when the young, tanned, pretty, coolly dressed secretaries from the banks, law offices, insurance agencies, and courthouse left their desks and took to the sidewalks. During lunch they ran errands around the square. They went to the post office. They did their banking. They shopped. Most of them bought their food at the Chinese Deli and ate on the park benches under the shade trees around the courthouse. They met friends and gossiped. At noon the gazebo in front of the courthouse attracted more beautiful women than the Miss Mississippi pageant. It was an unwritten rule in Clanton that an office girl on the square got a headstart on lunch and did not have to return until one. The men followed at twelve, and watched the girls.

But the trial changed things. The shade trees around the courthouse were in a combat zone. The cafes were full from eleven to one with soldiers and strangers who couldn't get seats in the courtroom. The Chinese Deli was packed with foreigners. The office girls ran their errands and ate at their desks.

At the Tea Shoppe the bankers and other white collars discussed the trial more in terms of its publicity and how the town was being perceived. Of particular concern was the Klan. Not a single customer knew anyone connected with the Klan, and it had long been forgotten in north Mississippi. But the vultures loved the white robes, and as far as the outside world knew, Clanton, Mississippi, was the home of the Ku Klux Klan. They hated the Klan for being there. They cussed the press for keeping them there.

For lunch Thursday, the Coffee Shop offered the daily special of country-fried pork chops, turnip greens, and either candied yams, creamed corn, or fried okra. Dell served the specials to a packed house that was evenly divided among locals, foreigners, and soldiers. The unwritten but firmly established rule of not speaking to anyone with a beard or funny accent was strictly enforced, and for a friendly people it was awkward not to smile and carry on with those from the outside. A tight-lipped arrogance had long since replaced the warm reception given to the visitors in the first few days after the shootings. Too many of the press hounds had betrayed their hosts and printed unkind, unflattering, and unfair words about the county and its people. It was amazing how they could arrive in packs from all over and within twenty-four hours become experts on a place they had never heard of and a people they had never met.

The locals had watched them as they scrambled like idiots around the square chasing the sheriff, the prosecutor, the defense lawyer, or anybody who might know anything. They watched them wait at the rear of the courthouse like hungry wolves to pounce on the defendant, who was invariably surrounded by cops, and who invariably ignored them as they yelled the same ridiculous questions at him. The locals watched with distaste as they kept their cameras on the Kluxers and the rowdier blacks, always searching for the most radical elements, and then making those elements appear to be the norm.

They watched them, and they hated them.

'What's that orange crap all over her face?' Tim Nunley asked, looking at a reporter sitting in a booth by the window. Jack Jones crunched on his okra and studied the orange face.

'I think it's something they use for the cameras. Makes her face look white on TV.'

'But it's already white.'

'I know, but it don't look white on TV unless it's painted orange.'

Nunley was not convinced. 'Then what do the niggers use on TV?' he asked.

No one could answer.

'Did you see her on TV last night?' asked Jack Jones.

'Nope. Where's she from?'

'Channel Four, Memphis. Last night she interviewed Cobb's mother, and of course she kept on pushing till the old woman broke down. All they showed on TV was the cryin'. It was sickenin'. Night before she had some Klansmen from Ohio talkin' about what we need here in Mississippi. She's the worst.'

The State finished its case against Carl Lee Thursday afternoon. After lunch Buckley put Murphy on the stand. It was gut-wrenching, nerve-wracking testimony as the poor little man stuttered uncontrollably for an hour.

'Calm down, Mr. Murphy,' Buckley said a hundred times.

He would nod, and take a drink of water. He nodded affirmatively and shook negatively as much as possible, but the court reporter had an awful time picking up the nods and shakes.

'I didn't get that,' she would say, her back to the witness stand. So he would try to answer and get hung, usually on a hard consonant like a 'P' or 'T'. He would blurt out something, then stutter and spit incoherently.

'I didn't get that,' she would say helplessly when he finished. Buckley would sigh. The jurors rocked furiously. Half the spectators chewed their fingernails.

'Could you repeat that?' Buckley would say with as much patience as he could find.

'I'm s-s-s-s-s-s-s-s-sorry,' he would say frequently. He was pitiful.

Through it all, it was determined that he had been drinking a Coke on the rear stairs, facing the stairs where the boys were killed. He had noticed a black man peeking out of a small closet some forty feet away. But he didn't think much about it. Then when the boys came down, the black man just stepped out and opened fire, screaming and laughing. When he stopped shooting, he threw down the gun and took off. Yes, that was him, sitting right there. The black one.

Noose rubbed holes in his glasses listening to Murphy. When Buckley sat down, His Honor looked desperately at Jake. 'Any cross-examination?' he asked painfully.

Jake stood with a legal pad. The court reporter glared at him. Harry Rex hissed at him. Ellen closed her eyes. The jurors wrung their hands and watched him carefully.

'Don't do it,' Carl Lee whispered firmly.

'No, Your Honor, we have no questions.'

'Thank you, Mr. Brigance,' Noose said, breathing again.

The next witness was Officer Rady, the investigator for the Sheriff's Department. He informed the jury that he found a Royal Crown Cola can in the closet next to the stairs, and the prints on the can matched those of Carl Lee Hailey.

'Was it empty or full?' Buckley asked dramatically.

'It was completely empty.'

Big deal, thought Jake, so he was thirsty. Oswald had a chicken dinner waiting on Kennedy. No, he had no questions for this witness.

'We have one final witness, Your Honor,' Buckley said with great finality at 4:00 P.M. 'Officer DeWayne Looney.'

Looney limped with a came into the courtroom and to the witness stand. He removed his gun and handed it to Mr. Pate.

Buckley watched him proudly. 'Would you state your name, please, sir?'

'DeWayne Looney.'

'And your address?'

'Fourteen sixty-eight Bennington Street, Clanton, Mississippi.'

'How old are you?'

'Thirty-nine.'

'Where are you employed?'

'Ford County Sheriff's Department.'

'And what do you do there?'

'I'm a dispatcher.'

'Where did you work on Monday, May 20?'

'I was a deputy.'

'Were you on duty?'

'Yes. I was assigned to transport two subjects from the jail to court and back.'

'Who were those two subjects?'

'Billy Ray Cobb and Pete Willard.'

'What time did you leave court with them?'

'Around one-thirty, I guess.'

'Who was on duty with you?'

'Marshall Prather. He and I were in charge of the two subjects. There were some other deputies in the courtroom helpin' us, and we had two or three men outside waitin' on us. But me and Marshall were in charge.'

'What happened when the hearing was over?'

'We immediately handcuffed Cobb and Willard and got them outta here. We took them to that little room over there and waited a second or two, and Prather walked on down the stairs.'

'Then what happened?'

'We started down the back stairs. Cobb first, then Willard, then me. Like I said, Prather had already gone on down. He was out the door.'

'Yes, sir. Then what happened?'

'When Cobb was near 'bout to the foot of the stairs, the shootin' started. I was on the landing, fixin' to go on down. I didn't see anybody at first for a second, then I seen Mr. Hailey with the machine gun firin' away. Cobb was blown backward into Willard, and they both screamed and fell in a heap, tryin' to get back up where I was.'

'Yes, sir. Describe what you saw.'

'You could hear the bullets bouncin' off the walls and hittin' everywhere. It was the loudest gun I ever heard and seemed like he kept shootin' forever. The boys just twisted and thrashed about, screamin' and squealin'. They were handcuffed, you know.'

'Yes, sir. What happened to you?'

'Like I said, I never made it past the landing. I think one of the bullets ricocheted off the wall and caught me in the leg. I was tryin' to get back up the steps when I felt my leg burn.'

'And what happened to your leg?'

'They cut it off,' Looney answered matter-of-factly, as if an amputation happened monthly. 'Just below the knee.'

'Did you get a good look at the man with the gun?'

'Yes, sir.'

'Can you identify him for the jury?'

'Yes, sir. It's Mr. Hailey, the man sittin' over there.'

That answer would have been a logical place to end Looney's testimony. He was brief, to the point, sympathetic and positive of the identification. The jury had listened to every word so far. But Buckley and Musgrove retrieved the large diagrams of the courthouse and arranged them before the jury so that Looney could limp around for a while. Under Buckley's direction, he retraced everybody's exact movements just before the killings.

Jake rubbed his forehead and pinched the bridge of his nose. Noose cleaned and recleaned his glasses. The jurors fidgeted.

'Any cross-examination, Mr. Brigance?' Noose asked at last.

'Just a few questions,' Jake said as Musgrove cleared the debris from the courtroom.

'Officer Looney, who was Carl Lee looking at when he was shooting?'

'Them boys, as far as I could tell.'

'Did he ever look at you?'

'Well, now, I didn't spend a lotta time tryin' to make eye contact with him. In fact, I was movin' in the other direction.'

'So he didn't aim at you?'

'Oh, no, sir. He just aimed at those boys. Hit them too.'

'What did he do when he was shooting?'

'He just screamed and laughed like he was crazy. It was the weirdest thing I ever heard, like he was some kinda madman or something. And you know, what I'll always remember is that with all the noise, the gun firin', the bullets whistlin', the boys screamin' as they got hit, over all the noise I could hear him laughin' that crazy laugh.'

The answer was so perfect Jake had to fight off a smile. He and Looney had worked on it a hundred times, and it was a thing of beauty. Every word was perfect. Jake busily flipped through his legal pad and glanced at the jurors. They all stared at Looney, enthralled by his answer. Jake scribbled something, anything, nothing, just to kill a few more seconds before the most important questions of the trial.

'Now, Deputy Looney, Carl Lee Hailey shot you in the leg.'

'Yes, sir, he did.'

'Do you think it was intentional?'

'Oh, no, sir. It was an accident.'

'Do you want to see him punished for shooting you?'

'No, sir. I have no ill will toward the man. He did what I would've done.'

Buckley dropped his pen and slumped in his chair. He looked sadly at his star witness.

'What do you mean by that?'

'I mean I don't blame him for what he did. Those boys raped his little girl. I gotta little girl. Somebody rapes her and he's a dead dog. I'll blow him away, just like Carl Lee did. We oughtta give him a trophy.'

'Do you want the jury to convict Carl Lee?'

Buckley jumped and roared, 'Objection! Objection! Improper question!'

'No!' Looney yelled. 'I don't want him convicted. He's a hero. He –'

'Don't answer, Mr. Looney!' Noose said loudly. 'Don't answer!'

'Objection! Objection!' Buckley continued, on his tiptoes.

'He's a hero! Turn him loose!' Looney yelled at Buckley.

'Order! Order!' Noose banged his gavel.

Buckley was silent. Looney was silent. Jake walked to his chair and said, 'I'll withdraw the question.'

'Please disregard,' Noose instructed the jury.

Looney smiled at the jury and limped from the courtroom.

'Call your next witness,' Noose said, removing his glasses.

Buckley rose slowly and with a great effort at drama, said, 'Your Honor, the State rests.'

'Good,' Noose replied, looking at Jake. 'I assume you have a motion or two, Mr. Brigance.'

'Yes, Your Honor.'

'Very well, we'll take those up in chambers.'

Noose excused his jury with the same parting instructions and adjourned until nine Friday.

CHAPTER THIRTY-SEVEN

Jake awoke in the darkness with a slight hangover, a headache due to fatigue and Coors, and the distant but unmistakable sound of his doorbell ringing continually as if held firmly in place by a large and determined thumb. He opened the front door in his nightshirt and tried to focus on the two figures standing on the porch. Ozzie and Nesbit, it was finally determined.

'Can I help you?' he asked as he opened the door. They followed him into the den.

'They're gonna kill you today,' Ozzie said.

Jake sat on the couch and massaged his temples. 'Maybe they'll succeed.'

'Jake, this is serious. They plan to kill you.'

'Who?'

'The Klan.'

'Mickey Mouse?'

'Yeah. He called yesterday and said something was up. He called back two hours ago and said you're the lucky man. Today is the big day. Time for some excitement. They bury Stump Sisson this morning in Loydsville, and it's time for the eye-for-an-eye, tooth-for-a-tooth routine.'

'Why me? Why don't they kill Buckley or Noose or someone more deserving?'

'We didn't get a chance to talk about that.'

'What method of execution?' Jake asked, suddenly feeling awkward sitting there in his nightshirt.

'He didn't say.'

'Does he know?'

'He ain't much on details. He just said they'd try to do it sometime today.'

'So what am I supposed to do? Surrender?'

'What time you goin' to the office?'

'What time is it?'

'Almost five.'

'As soon as I can shower and dress.'

'We'll wait.'

At five-thirty, they rushed him into his office and locked the door. At eight, a platoon of soldiers gathered on the sidewalk under the balcony and waited for the target. Harry Rex and Ellen watched from the second floor of the courthouse. Jake squeezed between Ozzie and Nesbit, and the three of them crouched in the center tight formation. Off they went across Washington Street in the direction of the courthouse. The vultures sniffed something and surrounded the entourage.

The abandoned feed mill sat near the abandoned railroad tracks halfway down the tallest hill in Clanton, two blocks north and east of the square. Beside it was a neglected asphalt and gravel street that ran downhill and intersected Cedar Street, after which it became much smoother and wider and continued downward until finally it terminated and merged into Quincy Street, the eastern boundary of the Clanton square.

From his position inside an abandoned silo, the marksman had a clear but distant view of the rear of the courthouse. He crouched in the darkness and aimed through a small opening, confident no one in the world could see him. The whiskey helped the confidence, and the aim, which he practiced a thousand times from seven-thirty until eight, when he noticed activity around the nigger's lawyer's office.

A comrade waited in a pickup hidden in a run-down warehouse next to the silo. The engine was running and the driver chain-smoked Lucky Strikes, waiting anxiously to hear the clapping sounds from the deer rifle.

As the armored mass stepped its way across Washington, the marksman panicked. Through the scope he could barely see the head of the nigger's lawyer as it bobbed and weaved awkwardly among the sea of green, which was surrounded and chased by a dozen reporters. Go ahead, the whiskey said, create some excitement. He timed the bobbing and weaving as best he could, and pulled the trigger as the target approached the rear door of the courthouse.

The rifle shot was clear and unmistakable.

Half the soldiers hit the ground rolling and the other half grabbed Jake and threw him violently under the veranda. A guardsman screamed in anguish. The reporters and TV people crouched and stumbled to the ground, but valiantly kept the cameras rolling to record the carnage. The soldier clutched his throat and screamed again. Another shot. Then another.

'He's hit!' someone yelled. The soldiers scrambled on all fours across the driveway to the fallen one. Jake escaped through the doors to the safety of the courthouse. He fell onto the floor of the rear entrance and buried his head in his hands. Ozzie stood next to him, watching the soldiers through the door.

The gunman dropped from the silo, threw his gun behind the back seat, and disappeared with his comrade into the countryside. They had a funeral to attend in south Mississippi.

'He's hit in the throat!' someone screamed as his buddies waded around the reporters. They lifted him and dragged him to a jeep.

'Who got hit?' Jake asked without removing his palms from his eyes.

'One of the guardsmen,' Ozzie said. 'You okay?'

'I guess,' he answered as he clasped his hands behind his head and stared at the floor. 'Where's my briefcase?'

'It's out there on the driveway. We'll get it in a minute.' Ozzie removed his radio from his belt and barked orders to the dispatcher, something about all men to the courthouse.

When it was apparent the shooting was over, Ozzie joined the mass of soldiers outside. Nesbit stood next to Jake. 'You okay?' he asked.

The colonel rounded the corner, yelling and swearing. 'What the hell happened?' he demanded. 'I heard some shots.'

'Mackenvale got hit.'

'Where is he?' the colonel said.

'Off to the hospital,' a sergeant replied, pointing at a jeep flying away in the distance.

'How bad is he?'

'Looked pretty bad. Got him in the throat.'

'Throat! Why did they move him?'

No one answered.

'Did anybody see anything?' the colonel demanded.

'Sounded like it came from up the hill,' Ozzie said looking up past Cedar Street. 'Why don't you send a jeep up there to look around.'

'Good idea.' The colonel addressed his eager men with a string of terse commands, punctuated liberally with obscenities. The soldiers scattered in all directions, guns drawn and ready for combat, in search of an assassin they could not identify, who was, in fact, in the next county when the foot patrol began exploring the abandoned feed mill.

Ozzie laid the briefcase on the floor next to Jake. 'Is Jake okay?' he whispered to Nesbit. Harry Rex and Ellen stood on the stairs where Cobb and Willard had fallen.

'I don't know. He ain't moved in ten minutes,' Nesbit said.

'Jake, are you all right?' the sheriff asked.

'Yes,' he said slowly without opening his eyes. The soldier had been on Jake's left shoulder. 'This is kinda silly, ain't it?' he had just said to Jake when a bullet ripped through his throat. He fell into Jake, grabbing at his neck, gurgling blood and screaming. Jake fell, and was tossed to safety.

'He's dead, isn't he?' Jake asked softly.

'We don't know yet,' replied Ozzie. 'He's at the hospital.'

'He's dead. I know he's dead. I heard his neck pop.'

Ozzie looked at Nesbit, then at Harry Rex. Four or five coin-sized drops of blood were splattered on Jake's light gray suit. He hadn't noticed them yet, but they were apparent to everyone else.

'Jake, you've got blood on your suit,' Ozzie finally said. 'Let's go back to your office so you can change clothes.'

'Why is that important?' Jake mumbled to the floor. They stared at each other.

Dell and the others from the Coffee Shop stood on the sidewalk and watched as they led Jake from the courthouse, across the street, and into his office, ignoring the absurdities thrown by the reporters. Harry Rex locked the front door, leaving the bodyguards on the sidewalk. Jake went upstairs and removed his coat.

'Row Ark, why don't you make some margaritas,' Harry Rex said. 'I'll go upstairs and stay with him.'

'Judge, we've had some excitement,' Ozzie explained as Noose unpacked his briefcase and removed his coat.

'What is it?' Buckley asked.

'They tried to kill Jake this mornin'.'

'What!'

'When?' asked Buckley.

' 'Bout an hour ago, somebody shot at Jake as he was comin' into the courthouse. It was a rifle at long range. We have no idea who did it. They missed Jake and hit a guardsman. He's in surgery now.'

'Where's Jake?' asked His Honor.

'Over in his office. He's pretty shook up.'

'I would be too,' Noose said sympathetically.

'He wanted you to call him when you got here.'

'Sure.' Ozzie dialed the number and handed the phone to the judge.

'It's Noose,' Harry Rex said, handing the phone to Jake.

'Hello.'

'Are you okay, Jake?'

'Not really. I won't be there today.'

Noose struggled for a response. 'Do what?'

'I said I won't be in court today. I'm not up to it.'

'Well, uh, Jake, where does that leave the rest of us?'

'I don't care, really,' Jake said, sipping on his second margarita.

'Beg your pardon?'

'I said I don't care, Judge. I don't care what you do, I won't be there.'

Noose shook his head and looked at the receiver. 'Are you hurt?' he asked with feeling.

'You ever been shot at, Judge?'

'No, Jake.'

'You ever seen a man get shot, hear him scream?'

'No, Jake.'

'You ever had somebody else's blood splashed on your suit?'

'No, Jake.'

'I won't be there.'

Noose paused and thought for a moment. 'Come on over, Jake, and let's talk about it.'

'No. I'm not leaving my office. It's dangerous out there.'

'Suppose we stand in recess until one. Will you feel better then?'

'I'll be drunk by then.'

'What!'

'I said I'll be drunk by then,'

Harry Rex covered his eyes. Ellen left for the kitchen.

'When do you think you might be sober?' Noose asked sternly. Ozzie and Buckley looked at each other.

'Monday.'

'What about tomorrow?'

'Tomorrow's Saturday.'

'Yes, I know, and I'd planned to hold court tomorrow. We've got a jury sequestered, remember?'

'Okay, I'll be ready in the morning.'

'That's good to hear. What do I tell the jury right now? They're sitting in the jury room waiting on us. The courtroom is packed. Your client is sitting out there by himself waiting on you. What do I tell these people?'

'You'll think of something, Judge. I've got faith in you.' Jake hung up. Noose listened to the unbelievable until it was evident that he had in fact been hung up on. He handed the phone to Ozzie.

His Honor looked out the window and removed his glasses. 'He says he ain't comin' today.'

Uncharacteristically, Buckley remained silent.

Ozzie was defensive. 'It really got to him, Judge.'

'Has he been drinking?'

'Naw, not Jake,' Ozzie replied. 'He's just tore up over that boy gettin' shot like he did. He was right next to Jake, and caught the bullet that was aimed for him. It would upset anybody, Judge.'

'He wants us to remain in recess until tomorrow morning,' Noose said to Buckley, who shrugged and again said nothing.

As word spread, a regular carnival developed on the sidewalk outside Jake's office. The press set up camp and pawed at the front window in hopes of seeing someone or something newsworthy inside. Friends stopped by to check on Jake, but were informed by various of the reporters that he was locked away inside and would not come out. Yes, he was unhurt.

Dr. Bass had been scheduled to testify Friday morning. He and Lucien entered the office through the rear door a few minutes after ten, and Harry Rex left for the liquor store.

With all the crying, the conversation with Carla had been difficult. He called after three drinks, and things did not go well. He talked to her father, told him he was safe, unhurt, and that half of the Mississippi National Guard had been assigned to protect him. Settle her down, he said, and he would call back later.

Lucien was furious. He had fought with Bass to keep him sober Thursday night so he could testify Friday. Now that he would testify Saturday, there was no way to keep him sober two days in a row. He thought of all the drinking they had missed Thursday, and was furious.

Harry Rex returned with a gallon of liquor. He and Ellen mixed drinks and argued over the ingredients. She rinsed the coffeepot, filled it with Bloody Mary mix and a disproportionate helping of Swedish vodka. Harry Rex added a lavish dose of Tabasco. He made the rounds in the conference room and refilled each cup with the delightful mixture.

Dr. Bass gulped frantically and ordered more. Lucien and Harry Rex debated the likely identity of the gunman. Ellen silently watched Jake, who sat in the corner and stared at the bookshelves.

The phone rang. Harry Rex grabbed it and listened intently. He hung up and said, 'That was Ozzie. The soldier's outta surgery. Bullet's lodged in the spine. They think he'll be paralyzed.'

They all sipped in unison and said nothing. They made great efforts to ignore Jake as he rubbed his forehead with one hand and sloshed his drink with the other. The faint sound of someone knocking at the rear door interrupted the brief memorial.

'Go see who it is,' Lucien ordered Ellen, who left to see who was knocking.

'It's Lester Hailey,' she reported to the conference room.

'Let him in,' Jake mumbled, almost incoherently.

Lester was introduced to the party and offered a Bloody Mary. He declined and asked for something with whiskey in it.

'Good idea,' said Lucien. 'I'm tired of light stuff. Let's get some Jack Daniel's.'

'Sounds good to me,' added Bass as he gulped the remnants in his cup.

Jake managed a weak smile at Lester, then returned to the study of the bookshelves. Lucien threw a hundred-dollar bill on the table, and Harry Rex left for the liquor store.

When she awoke hours later, Ellen was on the couch in Jake's office. The room was dark and deserted, with an acrid, intoxicating smell to it. She moved cautiously. She found her boss peacefully snoring away in the war room, on the floor, partially under the war desk. There were no lights to extinguish, so she carefully walked down the stairs. The conference room was littered with empty liquor bottles, beer cans, plastic cups and chicken dinner boxes. It was 9:30 P.M. She had slept five hours.

She could stay at Lucien's, but needed to change clothes. Her friend Nesbit would drive her to Oxford, but she was sober. Plus, Jake needed all the protection he could get. She locked the front door and walked to her car.

Ellen almost made it to Oxford when she saw the blue lights behind her. As usual, she was driving seventy-five. She parked on the shoulder and walked to her taillights, where she searched her purse and waited on the trooper.

Two plainsclothesmen approached from the blue lights.

'You drunk, ma'am?' one of them asked, spewing tobacco juice.

'No, sir. I'm trying to find my license.'

She crouched before the taillights and fished for the license. Suddenly, she was knocked to the ground. A heavy quilt was thrown over her and both men held her down. A rope was wrapped around her chest and waist. She kicked and cursed, but could offer little resistance. The quilt covered her head and trapped her arms underneath. They pulled the rope tightly.

'Be still, bitch! Be still!'

One of them removed her keys from the ignition and opened the trunk. They threw her inside and slammed it shut. The blue lights were unplugged in the old Lincoln and it roared away, trailed by the BMW. They found a gravel road and followed it deep into the woods. It turned into a dirt road that led to a small pasture where a large cross was being burned by a handful of Kluxers.

The two assailants quickly donned their robes and masks and removed her from the trunk. She was thrown to the ground and the quilt removed. They bound and gagged her, and dragged her to a large pole a few feet from the cross where she was tied, her back to the Kluxers, her face to the pole.

She saw the white robes and pointed hats, and tried desperately to spit out the oily, cotton rag crammed in her mouth. She managed only to gag and cough.

The flaming cross illuminated the small pasture, discharging a glowing wave of heat that began to roast her as she wrestled with the pole and emitted strange, guttural noises.

A hooded figure left the others and approached her. She could hear him walking and breathing. 'You nigger-loving bitch,' he said in a crisp Midwestern voice. He grabbed the rear of her collar and ripped the white silk blouse until it hung in shreds around her neck and shoulders. Her hands were tied firmly around the pole. He removed a bowie knife from under the robe, and began cutting the remainder of the blouse from her body. 'You nigger-loving bitch. You nigger-loving bitch.'

Ellen cursed him, but her words were muffled groans.

He unzipped the navy linen skirt on the right side. She tried to kick, but the heavy rope around her ankles held her feet to the pole. He placed the tip of the knife at the bottom of the zipper, and cut downward through the hem. He grabbed around the waist and pulled it off like a magician. The Kluxers stepped forward.

He slapped her on the butt, and said, 'Nice, very nice.' He stepped back to admire his handiwork. She grunted and twisted but could not resist. The slip fell to mid-thigh. With great ceremony, he cut the straps, then sliced it neatly down the back. He yanked it off and threw it at the foot of the burning cross. He cut the bra straps and removed it. She jerked and the moans became louder. The silent semicircle inched forward and stopped ten feet away.

The fire was hot now. Her bare back and legs were covered with sweat. The light red hair was drenched around her neck and shoulders. He reached under his robe again and brought out a bullwhip. He popped it loudly near her, and she flinched. He marched backward, carefully measuring the distance to the pole.

He cocked the bullwhip and aimed at the bare back. The tallest one stepped forward with his back to her. He shook his head. Nothing was said, but the whip disappeared.

He walked to her and grabbed her head. With his knife, he cut her hair. He grabbed handfuls and hacked away until her scalp was gapped and ugly. It piled gently around her feet. She moaned and did not move.

They headed for their cars. A gallon of gasoline was splashed inside the BMW with Massachusetts tags and somebody threw a match.

When he was certain they were gone, Mickey Mouse slid from the bushes. He untied her and carried her to a small clearing away from the pasture. He gathered the remains of her clothing and tried to cover her. When her car finished burning beside the dirt road, he left her. He drove to Oxford, to a pay phone, and called the Lafayette County sheriff.

CHAPTER THIRTY-EIGHT

Saturday court was unusual but not unheard of, especially in capital cases where the jury was locked up. The participants didn't mind because Saturday brought the end one day nearer.

The locals didn't mind either. It was their day off, and for most Ford Countians it was their only chance to watch the trial, or if they couldn't get a seat, at least hang around the square and see it all first-hand. Who knows, there may even be some more shooting.

By seven, the cafes downtown were at full capacity serving nonregulars. For every customer who was awarded a seat, two were turned away and left to loiter around the square and the courthouse and wait for a seat in the courtroom. Most of them paused for a moment in front of the lawyer's office, hoping to catch a glimpse of the one they tried to kill. The braggarts told of being clients of this famous man.

Upward, a few feet, the target sat at his desk and sipped a bloody concoction left from yesterday's party. He smoked a Roi-Tan, ate headache powders, and rubbed the cobwebs from his brain. Forget about the soldier, he had told himself for the past three hours. Forget about the Klan, the threats, forget everything but the trial, and specifically Dr. W.T. Bass. He uttered a short prayer, something about Bass being sober on the witness stand. The expert and Lucien had stayed through the afternoon, drinking and arguing, accusing each other of being a drunk and receiving a dishonorable discharge from their respective professions. Violence flared briefly at Ethel's desk when they were leaving. Nesbit intervened and escorted them to the patrol car for the ride home. The reporters burned with curiosity as the two blind drunks were led from Jake's office by the deputy and put in the car, where they continued to rage and cuss at each other, Lucien in the back seat, Bass in the front.

He reviewed Ellen's masterpiece on the insanity defense. Her outline of questions for Bass needed only minor changes. He studied his expert's résumé, and though unimpressive, it would suffice for Ford County. The nearest psychiatrist was eighty miles away.

Judge Noose glanced at the D.A. and looked sympathetically at Jake, who sat next to the door and watched the faded portrait of some dead judge hanging over Buckley's shoulder.

'How do you feel this morning, Jake?' Noose asked warmly.

'I'm fine.'

'How's the soldier?' asked Buckley.

'Paralyzed.'

Noose, Buckley, Musgrove, and Mr. Pate looked at the same spot on the carpet and grimly shook their heads in a quiet moment of respect.

'Where's your law clerk?' Noose asked, looking at the clock on the wall.

Jake looked at his watch. 'I don't know. I expected her by now.'

'Are you ready?'

'Sure.'

'Is the courtroom ready, Mr. Pate?'

'Yes, sir.'

'Very well. Let's proceed.'

Noose seated the courtroom, and for ten minutes offered a rambling apology to the jurors for yesterday's delay. They were the only fourteen in the county who did not know what happened Friday morning, and it might be prejudicial to tell them. Noose droned on about emergencies and how sometimes during trials things conspire to cause delays. When he finally finished, the jurors were completely bewildered and praying that somebody would call a witness.

'You may call your first witness,' Noose said in Jake's direction.

'Dr. W.T. Bass,' Jake announced as he moved to the podium. Buckley and Musgrove exchanged winks and silly grins.

Bass was seated next to Lucien on the second row in the middle of the family. He stood noisily and made his way to the center aisle, stepping on feet and assaulting people with his heavy, leather, empty briefcase. Jake heard the commotion behind him and continued smiling at the jury.

'I do, I do,' Bass said rapidly at Jean Gillespie during his swearing in.

Mr. Pate led him to the witness stand and delivered the standard orders to speak up and use the microphone. Though mortified and hung over, the expert looked remarkably arrogant and sober. He wore his most expensive dark gray hand-sewn wool suit, a perfectly starched white buttondown, and a cute little red paisley bow tie that made him appear rather cerebral. He looked like an expert, in something. He also wore, over Jake's objections, a pair of light gray ostrich skin cowboy boots that he had paid over a thousand for and worn less than a dozen times. Lucien had insisted on the boots eleven years earlier in the first insanity case. Bass wore them, and the very sane defendant went to Parchman. He wore them in the second insanity trial, again at Lucien's behest; again, Parchman. Lucien referred to them as Bass's good luck charm.

Jake wanted no part of the damned boots. But the jury could relate to them, Lucien had argued. Not expensive ostrich skin, Jake countered. They're too dumb to know the difference, replied Lucien. Jake could not be swayed. The rednecks will trust someone with boots, Lucien had explained. Fine, said Jake, let him wear a pair of those camouflage squirrel-hunting boots with a little mud on the heels and soles, some boots they could really identify with. Those wouldn't complement his suit, Bass had inserted.

He crossed his legs, laying the right boot on his left knee, flaunting it. He grinned at it, then grinned at the jury. The ostrich would have been proud.

Jake looked from his notes on the podium and saw the boot, which was plainly visible above the rail of the witness stand. Bass was admiring it, the jurors pondering it. He choked and returned to his notes.

'State your name, please.'

'Dr. W.T. Bass,' he replied, his attention suddenly diverted from the boot. He looked grimly, importantly at Jake.

'What is your address?'

'Nine-oh-eight West Canterbury, Jackson, Mississippi.'

'What is your profession?'

'I am a physician.'

'Are you licensed to practice in Mississippi?'

'Yes.'

'When were you licensed?'

'February 8, 1963.'

'Are you licensed to practice medicine in any other state?'

'Yes.'

'Where?'

'Texas.'

'When did you obtain that license?'

'November 3, 1962.'

'Where did you go to college?'

'I received my bachelor's degree from Millsaps College in 1956, and received my M.D., or Doctor of Medicine, from the University of Texas Health Science Center in Dallas, Texas, in 1960.'

'Is that an accredited medical school?'

'Yes.'

'By whom?'

'By the Council of Medical Education and Hospitals of the American Medical Association, the recognized accrediting agency of our profession, and by the educational authority of the State of Texas.'

Bass relaxed a bit, uncrossed and recrossed his legs, and displayed his left boot. He rocked gently and turned the comfortable swivel chair partially toward the jury.

'Where did you intern and for how long?'

'After graduation from medical school, I spent twelve months as an intern at the Rocky Mountain Medical Center in Denver.'

'What is your medical specialty?'

'Psychiatry.'

'Explain to us what that means.'

'Psychiatry is that branch of medicine concerned with the treatment of disorders of the mind. It usually, but not always, deals with mental malfunction, the organic basis of which is unknown.'

Jake breathed for the first time since Bass took the stand. His man was sounding good.

'Now, Doctor,' he said as he casually walked to within a foot of the jury box, 'describe to the jury the specialized training you received in the field of psychiatry.'

'My specialized training in psychiatry consisted of two years as a resident in psychiatry at the Texas State Mental Hospital, an approved training center. I engaged in clinical work with psychoneurotic and psychotic patients. I studied psychology, psychopathology, psychotherapy, and the physiological therapies. This training, supervised by competent psychiatric teachers, included instruction in the psychiatric aspects of children, adolescents, and adults.'

It was doubtful if a single person in the courtroom comprehended any of what Bass had just said, but it came from the mouth of a man who suddenly appeared to be a genius, an expert, for he had to be a man of great wisdom and intelligence to pronounce those words. With the bow tie and vocabulary, and in spite of the boots, Bass was gaining credibility with each answer.

'Are you a diplomate of the American Board of Psychiatry?'

'Of course,' he answered confidently.

'In which branch are you certified?'

'I am certified in psychiatry.'

'And when were you certified?'

'April of 1967.'

'What does it take to become certified by the American Board of Psychiatry?'

'A candidate must pass oral and practical exams, as well as a written test at the direction of the Board.'

Jake glanced at his notes and noticed Musgrove winking at Buckley.

'Doctor, do you belong to any professional groups?'

'Yes.'

'Name them please.'

'I am a member of the American Medical Association, American Psychiatric Association, and the Mississippi Medical Association.'

'How long have you been engaged in the practice of psychiatry?'

'Twenty-two years.'

Jake walked three steps in the direction of the bench and eyed Noose, who was watching intently.

'Your Honor, the defense offers Dr. Bass as an expert in the field of psychiatry.'

'Very well,' replied Noose. 'Do you wish to examine this witness, Mr. Buckley?'

The D.A. stood with his legal pad. 'Yes, Your Honor, just a few questions.'

Surprised but not worried, Jake took his seat next to Carl Lee. Ellen was still not in the courtroom.

'Dr. Bass, in your opinion, are you an expert in the field of psychiatry?' asked Buckley.

'Yes.'

'Have you ever taught psychiatry?'

'No.'

'Have you ever published any articles on psychiatry?'

'No.'

'Have you ever published any books on psychiatry?'

'No.'

'Now, I believe you testified that you are a member of the A.M.A., M.M.A., and the American Psychiatric Association?'

'Yes.'

'Have you ever served as an officer in any of these organizations?'

'No.'

'What hospital positions do you currently hold, as of today?'

'None.'

'Has your experience in psychiatry included any work under the auspices of the federal government or any state government?'

'No.'

The arrogance was beginning to fade from his face, and the confidence from his voice. He shot a glance at Jake, who was digging through a file.

'Dr. Bass, are you now engaged in the practice of psychiatry full-time?'

The expert hesitated, and looked briefly at Lucien on the second row. 'I see patients on a regular basis.'

'How many patients and how regular?' Buckley retorted with an enormous air of confidence.

'I see from five to ten patients per week.'

'One or two a day?'

'Something like that.'

'And you consider that a full-time practice?'

'I'm as busy as I want to be.'

Buckley threw his legal pad on the table and looked at Noose. 'Your Honor, the State objects to this man testifying as an expert in the field of psychiatry. It's obvious he's not qualified.'

Jake was on his feet with his mouth open.

'Overruled, Mr. Buckley. You may proceed, Mr. Brigance.'

Jake gathered his legal pads and returned to the podium, well aware of the suspicion the D.A. had just artfully thrown over his star witness. Bass shifted boots.

'Now, Dr. Bass, have you examined the defendant, Carl Lee Hailey?'

'Yes.'

'How many times?'

'Three.'

'When was your first examination?'

'June 10.'

'What was the purpose of this examination?'

'I examined him to determine his current mental condition as well as his condition on May 20, when he allegedly shot Mr. Cobb and Mr. Willard.'

'Where did this examination take place?'

'Ford County Jail.'

'Did you conduct this examination alone?'

'Yes. Just Mr. Hailey and myself.'

'How long did the examination last?'

'Three hours.'

'Did you review his medical history?'

'In a roundabout way, you could say. We talked at great length about his past.'

'What did you learn?'

'Nothing remarkable, except for Vietnam.'

'What about Vietnam?'

Bass folded his hands over his slightly overweight stomach and frowned intelligently at the defense attorney. 'Well, Mr. Brigance, like many Vietnam vets I've worked with, Mr. Hailey had some rather horrible experiences over there.'

War is hell, thought Carl Lee. He listened intently. Now, Vietnam was bad. He'd been shot. He'd lost friends. He'd killed people, many people. He'd killed children, Vietnamese children carrying guns and grenades. It was bad. He wished he'd never seen the place. He dreamed about it, had flashbacks and nightmares occasionally. But he didn't feel warped or insane because of it. He didn't feel warped or insane because of Cobb and Willard. In fact, he felt quite satisfied because they were dead. Just like those in Vietnam.

He had explained all this to Bass once at the jail, and Bass had seemed unimpressed by it. And they had talked only twice, and never more than an hour.

Carl Lee eyed the jury and listened suspiciously to the expert, who talked at length of Carl Lee's dreadful experiences in the war. Bass's vocabulary jumped several octaves as he explained to the laymen in nonlaymen terms the effects of Vietnam on Carl Lee. It sounded good. There had been nightmares over the years, dreams Carl Lee had never worried much about, but to hear Bass explain it, were extremely significant events.

'Did he talk freely of Vietnam?'

'Not really,' replied Bass, then explaining in great detail the tremendous task he confronted in dragging out the war from this complex, burdened, probably unstable mind. Carl Lee didn't remember it that way. But he dutifully listened with a pained expression, wondering for the first time in his life if perhaps he could be a little off.

After an hour, the war had been refought and its effects flogged thoroughly. Jake decided to move on.

'Now, Dr. Bass,' Jake said, scratching his head. 'Other than Vietnam, what other significant events did you note regarding his mental history?'

'None, except the rape of his daughter.'

'Did you discuss the rape with Carl Lee?'

'At great length, during each of the three examinations.'

'Explain to the jury what the rape did to Carl Lee Hailey.'

Bass stroked his chin and looked perplexed. 'Quite frankly, Mr. Brigance, it would take a great deal of time to explain what the rape did to Mr. Hailey.'

Jake thought a moment, and seemed to thoroughly analyze this last statement. 'Well, could you summarize it for the jury?'

Bass nodded gravely. 'I'll try.'

Lucien grew weary of listening to Bass, and began watching the jury in hopes of eyeing Clyde Sisco, who had also lost interest but appeared to be admiring the boots. Lucien watched intently from the corner of his eye, waiting for Sisco to gaze around the courtroom.

Finally, as Bass rambled on, Sisco left the testimony and looked at Carl Lee, then Buckley, then one of the reporters on the front row. Then his line of vision locked solidly into a wild-eyed, bearded old man who had once handed him eighty thousand cash for performing his civic duty and returning a just verdict. They focused unmistakably on each other, and both managed a slight grin. How much? was the look in Lucien's eyes. Sisco returned to the testimony, but seconds later he was staring at Lucien. How much? Lucien said, his lips actually moving but with no sound.

Sisco looked away and watched Bass, thinking of a fair price. He looked in Lucien's direction, scratched his beard, then suddenly, while staring at Bass, flashed five fingers across his face and coughed. He coughed again and studied the expert.

Five hundred or five thousand? Lucien asked himself. Knowing Sisco, it was five thousand, maybe fifty thousand. It made no difference; Lucien would pay it. He was worth a ton.

By ten-thirty, Noose had cleaned his glasses a hundred times and consumed a dozen cups of coffee. His bladder pressed forward toward the spillway. 'Time for the morning recess. We'll adjourn until eleven.' He rapped the gavel and disappeared.

'How'm I doing?' Bass asked nervously. He followed Jake and Lucien to the law library on the third floor.

'You're doing fine,' Jake said. 'Just keep those boots outta sight.'

'The boots are critical,' Lucien protested.

'I needa drink,' Bass said desperately.

'Forget it,' Jake said.

'So do I,' Lucien added. 'Let's run over to your office for a quick one.'

'Great idea!' Bass said.

'Forget it,' Jake repeated. 'You're sober and you're doing great.'

'We got thirty minutes,' Bass said as he and Lucien were leaving the library and heading for the stairs.

'No! Don't do it, Lucien!' Jake demanded.

'Just one,' Lucien replied, pointing a finger at Jake. 'Just one.'

'You've never had just one.'

'Come with us, Jake. It'll settle your nerves.'

'Just one,' Bass yelled as he disappeared down the steps.

At eleven, Bass sat himself in the witness chair and looked through glazed eyes at the jury. He smiled, and almost giggled. He was aware of the artists on the front row, so he looked as expert as possible. His nerves were indeed settled.

'Dr. Bass, are you familiar with the criminal responsibility test relative to the M'Naghten Rule?' Jake asked.

'I certainly am!' Bass replied with a sudden air of superiority.

'Would you explain this rule to the jury?'

'Of course. The M'Naghten Rule is the standard for criminal

responsibility in Mississippi, as in fifteen other states. It goes back to England, in the year 1843, when a man by the name of Daniel M'Naghten attempted to assassinate the prime minister, Sir Robert Peel. He mistakenly shot and killed the prime minister's secretary, Edward Drummond. During his trial the evidence plainly showed M'Naghten was suffering from what we would call paranoid schizophrenia. The jury returned a verdict of not guilty, by reason of insanity. From this the M'Naghten Rule was established. It is still followed in England and sixteen states.'

'What does the M'Naghten Rule mean?'

'The M'Naghten Rule is fairly simple. Every man is presumed to be sane, and to establish a defense on the ground of insanity, it must be clearly proven that when the defendant did what he did he was laboring under such a defect of reason, from a mental disease, that he did not know the nature and quality of the act he was doing, or if he did know what he was doing, he did not know it was wrong.'

'Could you simplify that?'

'Yes. If a defendant cannot distinguish right from wrong, he is legally insane.'

'Define insanity, please.'

'It has no significance, medically. It is strictly a legal standard for a person's mental state or condition.'

Jake breathed deeply and plowed forward. 'Now, Doctor, based upon your examination of the defendant, do you have an opinion as to the mental condition of Carl Lee Hailey on May 20 of this year, at the time of the shooting?'

'Yes, I do.'

'And what is that opinion?'

'It is my opinion,' Bass said slowly, 'that the defendant had a total break with reality when his daughter was raped. When he saw her immediately after the rape he didn't recognize her, and when someone told him she'd been gang-raped, and beaten, and almost hanged, something just snapped in Carl Lee's mind. That's a very elementary way of putting it, but that's what happened. Something snapped. He broke with reality.

'They had to be killed. He told me once that when he first saw them in court, he could not understand why the deputies were protecting them. He kept waiting for one of the cops to pull a gun and blow their heads off. A few days went by and nobody killed them, so he figured it was up to him. I mean, he felt as though someone in the system would executive the two for raping his little girl.

'What I'm saying, Mr. Brigance, is that, mentally, he left us. He was in another world. He was suffering from delusions. He broke.'

Bass knew he was sounding good. He was talking to the jury now, not the lawyer.

'The day after the rape he spoke with his daughter in the hospital. She could barely talk, with the broken jaws and all, but she said she saw him in the woods running to save her, and she asked him why he disappeared. Now, can you imagine what that would do to a father? She later told him she begged for her daddy, and the two men laughed at her and told her she didn't have a daddy.'

Jake let those words sink in. He studied Ellen's outline and saw only two more questions.

'Now, Dr. Bass, based upon your observations of Carl Lee Hailey, and your diagnosis of his mental condition at the time of the shooting, do you have an opinion, to a reasonable degree of medical certainty, as to whether Carl Lee Hailey was capable of knowing the difference between right and wrong when he shot these men?'

'I have.'

'And what is that opinion?'

'That due to his mental condition, he was totally incapable of distinguishing right from wrong.'

'Do you have an opinion, based upon the same factors, as to whether Carl Lee Hailey was able to understand and appreciate the nature and quality of his actions?'

'I do.'

'And what is that opinion?'

'In my opinion, as an expert in the field of psychiatry, Mr. Hailey was totally incapable of understanding and appreciating the nature and quality of what he was doing.'

'Thank you, Doctor. I tender the witness.'

Jake gathered his legal pad and strolled confidently back to his seat. He glanced at Lucien, who was smiling and nodding. He glanced at the jury. They were watching Bass and thinking about his testimony. Wanda Womack, a young woman with a sympathetic glow about her, looked at Jake and smiled ever so slightly. It was the first positive signal he received from the jury since the trial started.

'So far so good,' Carl Lee whispered.

Jake smiled at his client. 'You're a real psycho, big man.'

'Any cross-examination?' Noose asked Buckley.

'Just a few questions,' Buckley said as he grabbed the podium.

Jake could not imagine Buckley arguing psychiatry with an expert, even if it was W.T. Bass.

But Buckley had no plans to argue psychiatry. 'Dr. Bass, what is your full name?'

Jake froze. The question had an ominous hint to it. Buckley asked it with a great deal of suspicion.

'William Tyler Bass.'

'What do you go by?'

'W.T. Bass.'

'Have you ever been known as Tyler Bass?'

The expert hesitated. 'No,' he said meekly.

An immense feeling of anxiety hit Jake and felt like a hot spear tearing into his stomach. The question could only mean trouble.

'Are you positive?' Buckley asked with raised eyebrows and an enormous amount of distrust in his voice.

Bass shrugged. 'Maybe when I was younger.'

'I see. Now, I believe you testified that you studied medicine at the University of Texas Health Science Center?'

'That's correct.'

'And where is that?'

'Dallas.'

'And when were you a student there?'

'From 1956 to 1960.'

'And under what name were you registered?'

'William T. Bass.'

Jake was numb with fear. Buckley had something, a dark secret from the past known only to Bass and himself.

'Did you ever use the name Tyler Bass while you were a medical student?'

'No.'

'Are you positive?'

'I certainly am.'

'What is your social security number?'

'410-96-8585.'

Buckley made a check mark beside something on his legal pad.

'And what is your date of birth?' he asked carefully.

'September 14, 1934.'

'And what was your mother's name?'

'Jonnie Elizabeth Bass.'

'And her maiden name?'

'Skidmore.'

Another check mark. Bass looked nervously at Jake.

'And your place of birth?'

'Carbondale, Illinois.'

Another check mark.

An objection to the relevance of these questions was in order and sustainable, but Jake's knees were like Jell-O and his bowels were suddenly fluid. He feared he would embarrass himself if he stood and tried to speak.

Buckley studied his check marks and waited a few seconds. Every ear in the courtroom waited for the next question, knowing it would be brutal. Bass watched the D.A. like a prisoner watching the firing squad, hoping and praying the guns would somehow misfire.

Finally, Buckley smiled at the expert. 'Dr. Bass, have you ever been convicted of a felony?'

The question echoed throughout the silence and landed from all directions on the trembling shoulders of Tyler Bass. Even a cursory look at his face revealed the answer.

Carl Lee squinted and looked at his lawyer.

'Of course not!' Bass answered loudly, desperately.

Buckley just nodded and walked slowly to the table, where Musgrove, with much ceremony, handed him some important-looking papers.

'Are you certain?' Buckley thundered.

'Of course I'm certain,' Bass protested as he eyed the important-looking papers.

Jake knew he needed to rise and say something or do something to stop the carnage that was seconds away, but his mind was paralyzed.

'You're certain?' Buckley asked.

'Yes,' Bass answered through clenched teeth.

'You've never been convicted of a felony?'

'Of course not.'

'Are you as certain of that as you are the rest of your testimony before this jury?'

That was the trap, the killer, the deadliest question of all; one Jake had used many times, and when he heard it, he knew Bass was finished. And so was Carl Lee.

'Of course,' Bass answered with feigned arrogance.

Buckley moved in for the kill. 'You're telling this jury that on October 17, 1956, in Dallas, Texas, you were not convicted of a felony under the name of Tyler Bass?'

Buckley asked the question while looking at the jury and reading from the important-looking documents.

'That's a lie,' Bass said quietly, and unconvincingly.

'Are you sure it's a lie?' Buckley asked.

'A bald-faced lie.'

'Do you know a lie from the truth, Dr. Bass?'

'Damn right I do.'

Noose placed his glasses on his nose and leaned forward. The jurors quit rocking. The reporters quit scribbling. The deputies along the back wall stood still and listened.

Buckley picked out one of the important-looking documents and studied it. 'You're telling this jury that on October 17, 1956, you were not convicted of statutory rape?'

Jake knew it was important, in the midst of any great courtroom crisis, even this one, to maintain a straight, poker face. It was important for the jurors, who missed nothing, to see the defendant's lawyer with a positive look about him. Jake had practiced this positive, everything's-wonderful, I'm-in-control look through many trials and many surprises, but with the 'statutory rape' the positive and confident and certain look was immediately replaced by a sickly, pale, pained expression that was being scrutinized by at least half of those in the jury box.

The other half scowled at the witness on the stand.

'Were you convicted of statutory rape, Doctor?' Buckley asked again after a lengthy silence.

No answer.

Noose uncoiled and leaned downward in the direction of the witness. 'Please answer the question, Dr. Bass.'

Bass ignored His Honor and stared at the D.A., then said, 'You've got the wrong man.'

Buckley snorted and walked to Musgrove, who was holding some more important-looking papers. He opened a large white envelope and removed something that resembled an 8 × 10 photograph.

'Well, Dr. Bass, I've got some photographs of you taken by the Dallas Police Department on September 11, 1956. Would you like to see them?'

No answer.

Buckley held them out to the witness. 'Would you like to see these, Dr. Bass? Perhaps they could refresh your memory.'

Bass slowly shook his head, then lowered it and stared blankly at his boots.

'Your Honor, the State would introduce into evidence these copies, certified under the Acts of Congress, of the Final Judgement and Sentencing Order in the case styled State of Texas versus Tyler Bass, said records being obtained by the State from the proper officials in Dallas, Texas, and showing that on October 17, 1956, a one Tyler Bass pled guilty to the charge of statutory rape, a felony under the laws of the State of Texas. We can prove that Tyler Bass and this witness, Dr. W.T. Bass, are one and the same.'

Musgrove politely handed Jake a copy of everything Buckley was waving.

'Any objections to this introduction into evidence?' Noose asked in Jake's direction.

A speech was needed. A brilliant, emotional explanation that would touch the hearts of the jurors and make them weep with pity for Bass and his patient. But the rules of procedure did not permit one at this point. Of course the evidence was admissible. Unable to stand, Jake waved in the negative. No objections.

'We have no further questions,' Buckley announced.

'Any redirect, Mr. Brigance?' Noose asked.

In the split second available, Jake could not think of a single thing he could ask Bass to improve the situation. The jury had heard enough from the defence expert.

'No,' Jake said quietly.

'Very well, Dr. Bass, you are excused.'

Bass made a quick exit through the small gate in the railing, down the center aisle, and out of the courtroom. Jake watched his departure intently, conveying as much hatred as possible. It was important for the jury to see how shocked the defendant and his lawyer were. The jury had to believe a convicted felon was not knowingly put on the stand.

When the door closed and Bass was gone, Jake scanned the courtroom in hopes of finding an encouraging face. There were none. Lucien stroked his beard and stared at the floor. Lester sat with his arms folded and a disgusted look on his face. Gwen was crying.

'Call your next witness,' Noose said.

Jake continued searching. In the third row, between Reverend Ollie Agee and Reverend Luther Roosevelt, sat Norman Reinfeld. When his eyes met Jake's he frowned and shook his head as if to say 'I told you so.' On the other side of the courtroom, most of the whites looked relaxed and a few even grinned at Jake.

'Mr. Brigance, you may call your next witness.'

Against his better judgment, Jake attempted to stand. His knees buckled and he leaned forward with his palms flat against the table. 'Your Honor,' he said in a high-pitched, shrill, defeated voice, 'could we recess till one?'

'But Mr. Brigance, it's only eleven-thirty.'

A lie seemed appropriate. 'Yes, Your Honor, but our next witness is not here, and will not arrive until one.'

'Very well. We'll stand in recess until one. I need to see the attorneys in chambers.'

Next to chambers was a coffee room where the lawyers loitered and gossiped by the hour, and next to it was a small rest room. Jake closed and locked the rest room door and removed his coat, throwing it to the floor. He knelt beside the toilet, waited momentarily, then vomited.

Ozzie stood before the judge and attempted small talk while Musgrove and the D.A. smiled at each other. They waited on Jake. Finally, he entered chambers and apologized.

'Jake, I have some bad news,' Ozzie said.

'Let me sit down.'

'I got a call an hour ago from the sheriff of Lafayette County. Your law clerk, Ellen Roark, is in the hospital.'

'What happened!'

'The Klan got her last night. Somewhere between here and Oxford. They tied her to a tree and beat her.'

'How is she?' Jake asked.

Stable but serious.'

'What happened?' Buckley asked.

'We ain't sure. They stopped her car somehow and took her out in the woods. Cut her clothes off her and cut her hair. She's got a concussion and cuts on the head, so they figure she was beat.'

Jake needed to vomit again. He couldn't speak. He massaged his temples and thought how nice it would be to tie Bass to a tree and beat him.

Noose studied the defense attorney with compassion. 'Mr. Brigance, are you okay?'

No response.

'Let's recess until two. I think we could all use the break,' Noose said.

Jake walked slowly up the front steps with an empty Coors bottle and for a moment gave serious thought to smashing it against Lucien's head. He realized the injury would not be felt.

Lucien rattled his ice cubes and stared off in the distance, in the direction of the square, which had long been deserted except for the soldiers and the regular crowd of teenagers flocking to the theater for the Saturday night double feature.

They said nothing. Lucien stared away. Jake glared at him with the empty bottle. Bass was hundreds of miles away.

After a minute or so, Jake asked, 'Where's Bass?'

'Gone.'

'Gone where?'

'Gone home.'

'Where's his home?'

'Why do you wanna know?'

'I'd like to see his home. I'd like to see him in his home. I'd like to beat him to death with a baseball bat in his home.'

Lucien rattled some more. 'I don't blame you.'

'Did you know?'

'Know what?'

'About the conviction?'

'Hell no. No one knew. The record was expunged.'

'I don't understand.'

'Bass told me the record of the conviction in Texas was expunged three years after it was entered.'

Jake placed the beer bottle on the porch beside his chair. He grabbed a dirty glass, blew into it, then filled it with ice cubes and Jack Daniel's.

'Do you mind explaining, Lucien?'

'According to Bass, the girl was seventeen, and the daughter of a prominent judge in Dallas. They fell in heat, and the judge caught them screwing on the couch. He pressed charges, and Bass didn't have a chance. He pled guilty to the statutory rape. But the girl was in love. They kept seeing each other and she comes up pregnant. Bass married her, and gives the judge a perfect baby boy for his first grandchild. The old man has a change of heart, and the record is expunged.'

Lucien drank and watched the lights from the square.

'What happened to the girl?'

'According to Bass, a week before he finished medical school, his wife, who's pregnant again, and the little boy were killed in a train wreck in Fort Worth. That's when he started drinking, and quit living.'

'And he's never told you this before?'

'Don't interrogate me. I told you I knew nothing about it. I put him on the witness stand twice myself, remember. If I had known it, he would never have testified.'

'Why didn't he ever tell you?'

'I guess because he thought the record was erased. I don't know. Technically, he's right. There is no record after the expungement. But he was convicted.'

Jake took a long, bitter drink of whiskey. It was nasty.

They sat in silence for ten minutes. It was dark and the crickets were in full chorus. Sallie walked to the screen door and asked Jake if he wanted supper. He said no thanks.

'What happened this afternoon?' Lucien asked.

'Carl Lee testified, and we adjourned at four. Buckley didn't have his psychiatrist ready. He'll testify Monday.'

'How'd he do?'

'Fair. He followed Bass, and you could feel the hatred from the jurors. He was stiff and sounded rehearsed. I don't think he scored too many points.'

'What'd Buckley do?'

'Went wild. Screamed at Carl Lee for an hour. Carl Lee kept getting smart with him, and they sniped back and forth. I think they both got hurt. On redirect, I propped him up some and he came across pitiful and sympathetic. Almost cried at the end.'

'That's nice.'

'Yeah, real nice, But they'll convict him, won't they?'

'I would imagine.'

'After we adjourned, he tried to fire me. Said I'd lost his case and he wanted a new lawyer.'

Lucien walked to the edge of the porch and unzipped his pants. He leaned on a column and sprayed the shrubs. He was barefoot and looked like a flood victim. Sallie brought him a fresh drink.

'How's Row Ark?' he asked.

'Stable, they say. I called her room and a nurse said she couldn't talk. I'll go over tomorrow.'

'I hope she's okay. She's a fine girl.'

'She's a radical bitch, but a very smart one. I feel like it's my fault, Lucien.'

'It's not your fault. It's a crazy world, Jake. Full of crazy people. Right now I think half of them are in Ford County.'

'Two weeks ago, they planted dynamite outside my bedroom window. They beat to death my secretary's husband. Yesterday they shot at me and hit a guardsman. Now they grab my law clerk, tie her to a pole, rip her clothes off, cut her hair, and she's in the hospital with a concussion. I wonder what's next.'

'I think you should surrender.'

'I would. I would march down to the courthouse right now and surrender my briefcase, lay down my arms, give up. But to whom? The enemy is invisible.'

'You can't quit, Jake. Your client needs you.'

'To hell with my client. He tried to fire me today.'

'He needs you. This thing ain't over till it's over.'

Nesbit's head hung halfway out the window and the saliva dripped down the left side of his chin, down the door, forming a small puddle over the 'O' in the Ford of the Sheriff's Department insignia on the side of the car. An empty beer can moistened his crotch. After two weeks of bodyguard duty he had grown accustomed to sleeping with the mosquitoes in his patrol car while protecting the nigger's lawyer.

Moments after Saturday turned into Sunday, the radio violated his rest. He grabbed the mike while wiping his chin on his left sleeve.

'S.O. 8,' he responded.

'What's your 10-20?'

'Same place it was two hours ago.'

'The Wilbanks house?'

'10-4.'

'Is Brigance still there?'

'10-4.'

'Get him and take him to his house on Adams. It's an emergency.'

Nesbit walked past the empty bottles on the porch, through the unlocked door, where he found Jake sprawled on the couch in the front room.

'Get up, Jake! You gotta go home! It's an emergency!'

Jake jumped to his feet and followed Nesbit. They stopped on the front steps and looked past the dome of the courthouse. In the distance a boiling funnel of black smoke rose above an orange glow and drifted peacefully toward the half moon.

Adams Street was blocked with an assortment of volunteer vehicles, mostly pickups. Each had a variety of red and yellow emergency lights, at least a thousand in all. They spun and flashed and streaked through the darkness in a silent chorus, illuminating the street.

The fire engines were parked haphazardly in front of the house. The firemen and volunteers worked frantically laying lines and getting organized, responding occasionally to the commands of the chief. Ozzie, Prather, and Hastings stood near an engine. Some guardsmen lingered benignly near a jeep.

The fire was brilliant. Flames roared from every window across the front of the house, upstairs and down. The carport was completely engulfed. Carla's Cutlass burned inside and out – the four tires emitting a darker glow of their own. Curiously, another, smaller car, not the Saab, burned next to the Cutlass.

The thundering, crackling noise of the fire, plus the rumbling of the fire engines, plus the loud voices, attracted neighbors from several blocks. They crowded together in the lawns across the street and watched.

Jake and Nesbit ran down the street. The chief spotted them and came running.

'Jake! Is anybody in the house?'

'No!'

'Good. I didn't think so.'

'Just a dog.'

'A dog!'

Jake nodded and watched the house.

'I'm sorry,' said the chief.

They gathered at Ozzie's car in front of Mrs. Pickle's house. Jake answered questions.

That's not your Volkswagen under there, is it, Jake?'

Jake stared in stunned silence at Carla's landmark. He shook his head.

I didn't think so. Looks like that's where it started.'

'I don't understand,' said Jake.

'If it ain't your car, then somebody parked it there, right? Notice how the floor of the carport is burnin'? Concrete don't normally burn. It's gasoline. Somebody loaded the VW with gasoline, parked it and ran away. Probably had some kinda device which set the thing off.'

Prather and two volunteers agreed.

'How long's it been burning?' Jake asked.

'We got here ten minutes ago,' the chief said, 'and it was well involved. I'd say thirty minutes. It's a good fire. Somebody knew what they's doin'.'

'I don't suppose we could get anything out of there, could we?' Jake asked in general, knowing the answer.

'No way, Jake. It's too involved. My men couldn't go in there if people were trapped. It's a good fire.'

'Why do you say that?'

'Well, look at it. It's burnin' evenly through the house. You can see flames in every window. Downstairs and up. That's very unusual. In just a minute, it'll burn through the roof.'

Two squads inched forward with the lines, shooting water in the direction of the windows by the front porch. A smaller line was aimed at a window upstairs. After watching for a minute or two as the water disappeared into the flames with no noticeable effect, the chief spat and said, 'It'll burn to the ground.' With that he disappeared around an engine and began shouting.

Jake looked at Nesbit. Will you do me a favor?'

'Sure, Jake.'

'Drive over to Harry Rex's and bring him back. I'd hate for him to miss this.'

'Sure.'

For two hours Jake, Ozzie, Harry Rex, and Nesbit sat on the patrol car and watched the fire fulfill the chief's prediction. From time to time a neighbor would stop by and extend sympathies and ask about the family. Mrs. Pickle, the sweet old woman next door, cried loudly when informed by Jake that Max had been consumed.

By three, the deputies and other curious had disappeared, and by four the quaint little Victorian had been reduced to smoldering rubble.

The last of the firemen smothered any sign of smoke from the ruins. Only the chimney and burnt frames of two cars stood above the remains as the heavy rubber boots kicked and plowed through the waste looking for sparks or hidden flames that might somehow leap from the dead and burn the rest of the wreckage.

They rolled up the last of the lines as the sun began to appear. Jake thanked them when they left. He and Harry Rex walked through the backyard and surveyed the damage.

'Oh well,' Harry Rex said. 'It's just a house.'

'Would you call Carla and tell her that?'

'No. I think you should.'

'I think I'll wait.'

Harry Rex looked at his watch. It's about breakfast time, isn't it?'

'It's Sunday morning, Harry Rex. Nothing's open.'

'Ah, Jake, you're an amateur, and I'm a professional. I can find hot food at any time of any day.'

'The truck stop?'

'The truck stop!'

'Okay. And when we finish we'll go to Oxford to check on Row Ark.'

'Great. I can't wait to see her with a butch haircut.'

Sallie grabbed the phone and threw it at Lucien, who fumbled with it until it was arranged properly next to his head.

'Yeah, who is it?' he asked, squinting through the window into the darkness.

'Is this Lucien Wilbanks?'

'Yeah, who's this?'

'Do you know Clyde Sisco?'

'Yeah.'

'It's fifty thousand.'

'Call me back in the morning.'

CHAPTER THIRTY-NINE

Sheldon Roark sat in the window with his feet on the back of a chair, reading the Memphis Sunday paper's version of the Hailey trial. On the bottom of the front page was a picture of his daughter and the story about her encounter with the Klan. She rested comfortably in the bed a few feet away. The left side of her head was shaved and covered with a thick bandage. The left ear was sewn with twenty-eight stitches. The severe concussion had been downgraded to a mild concussion, and the doctors had promised she could leave by Wednesday.

She had not been raped or whipped. When the doctors called him in Boston they were short on details. He had flown for seven hours not knowing what they had done to her, but expecting the worst. Late Saturday night, the doctors ran more X rays and told him to relax. The scars would fade and the hair would grow back. She had been frightened and roughed up, but it could have been much worse.

He heard a commotion in the hall. Someone was arguing with a nurse. He laid the paper on her bed and opened the door.

A nurse had caught Jake and Harry Rex sneaking down the hall. She explained that visiting hours started at 2:00 P.M., and that happened to be six hours away; that only family members were allowed; and that she would call security if they didn't leave. Harry Rex explained that he didn't give a damn about visiting hours or any other silly rules of the hospital; that it was his fiancée and that he would see her one last time before she died; and that if the nurse didn't shut up he would sue her for harassment because he was a lawyer and hadn't sued anybody in a week and was getting anxious.

'What's going on here?' Sheldon said.

Jake looked at the small man with the red hair and green eyes, and said, 'You must be Sheldon Roark.'

'I am.'

'I'm Jake Brigance. The one –'

'Yes, I've been reading about you. It's okay, nurse, they're with me.'

'Yeah,' Harry Rex said. 'It's okay. We're with him. Now would you please leave us alone before I garnishee your check.'

She vowed to call security, and stormed down the hall.

'I'm Harry Rex Vonner,' he said, shaking hands with Sheldon Roark.

'Step inside,' he said. They followed him into the small room and stared at Ellen. She was still asleep.

'How bad is she?' Jake asked.

'Mild concussion. Twenty-eight stitches in her ear, and eleven in her head. She'll be fine. Doctor said she might leave by Wednesday. She was awake last night and we talked for a long time.'

'Her hair looks awful,' Harry Rex observed.

'They yanked it and cut it with a dull knife, she said. They also cut her clothes off, and at one time threatened to bullwhip her. The head injuries are self-inflicted. She thought they would either kill her or rape her, or both. So she banged her brains out against the pole she was tied to. Must have scared them.'

'You mean they didn't beat her?'

'No. They didn't hurt her. Just scared the hell out of her.'

'What did she see?'

'Not much. Burning cross, white robes, about a dozen men. Sheriff said it was a pasture eleven miles east of here. Owned by some paper company.'

'Who found her?' Harry Rex asked.

'The sheriff received an anonymous phone call from a fella by the name of Mickey Mouse.'

'Ah yes. My old friend.'

Ellen moaned softly and stretched.

'Let's step outside,' Sheldon said.

'Does this place have a cafeteria?' Harry Rex asked. 'I get hungry when I get near a hospital.'

'Sure. Let's have coffee.'

The cafeteria on the first floor was empty. Jake and Mr. Roark drank black coffee. Harry Rex started with three sweet rolls and a pint of milk.

'According to the paper, things aren't going too well,' Sheldon said.

'The paper is very kind,' Harry Rex said with a mouthful. 'Jake here is gettin' his ass kicked all over the courtroom. And life ain't so great outside the courtroom, either. When they're not shooting at him, or kidnapping his law clerk, they're burning his house.'

'They burned your house!'

Jake nodded. 'Last night. It's still smoldering.'

'I thought I detected the smell of smoke.'

'We watched it burn to the ground. It took four hours.'

'I'm sorry to hear that. They've threatened me with that before, but the worst I've had was slashed tires. I've never been shot at either.'

'I've been shot at a couple of times.'

'Do y'all have the Klan in Boston?' asked Harry Rex.

'Not that I know of.'

'It's a shame. Those folks add a real dimension to your law practice.'

'Sounds like it. We saw the television reports of the riot around the courthouse last week. I've watched it pretty close since Ellen became involved. It's a famous case. Even up there. I wish I had it.'

'It's all yours,' said Jake. 'I think my client is looking for a new lawyer.'

'How many shrinks will the State call?'

'Just one. He'll testify in the morning, and we'll have closing arguments. The jury should get it by late tomorrow afternoon.'

'I hate that Ellen will miss it. She called me every day and talked about the case.'

'Where did Jake go wrong?' Harry Rex asked.

'Don't talk with your mouth full,' Jake said.

'I think Jake has done a good job. It's a lousy set of facts to begin with. Hailey committed the murders, planned them carefully, and is relying on a rather weak plea of insanity. Juries in Boston would not be too sympathetic.'

'Nor in Ford County,' added Harry Rex.

'I hope you have a soul-stirring final summation up your sleeve,' Sheldon said.

'He doesn't have any sleeves,' said Harry Rex. 'They've all been burned. Along with his pants and underwear.'

'Why don't you come over tomorrow and watch?' Jake asked. 'I'll introduce you to the judge and ask that you have privileges of chambers.'

'He wouldn't do that for me,' Harry Rex said.

'I can understand why,' Sheldon said with a smile. 'I might just do that. I had planned to stay until Tuesday anyway. Is it safe over there?'

'Not really.'

Woody Mackenvale's wife sat on a plastic bench in the hall next to his room and cried quietly while trying to be brave for her two small sons seated next to her. Each boy squeezed a well-used wad of Kleenexes, occasionally wiping their cheeks and blowing their noses. Jake knelt before her and listened intently as she described what the doctors had said. The bullet had lodged in the spine – the paralysis was severe and permanent. He was a foreman at a plant in Booneville. Good job. Good life. She didn't work, at least until now. They would make it somehow, but she wasn't sure how. He coached his sons' Little League team. He was very active.

She cried louder and the boys wiped their cheeks.

'He saved my life,' Jake said to her, and looked at the boys.

She closed her eyes and nodded. 'He was doing his job. We'll make it.'

Jake took a Kleenex from the box on the bench and wiped his eyes.

A group of relatives stood nearby and watched. Harry Rex paced nervously at the end of the hall.

Jake hugged her and patted the boys on the head. He gave her his phone number – office – and told her to call if he could do anything. He promised to visit Woody when the trial was over.

The beer stores opened at noon on Sunday, as if the church folks needed it then and would stop on the way home from the Lord's house to pick up a couple of six-packs, then on to Grandmother's for Sunday dinner and an afternoon of hell-raising. Oddly, they would close again at six in the afternoon, as if the same folks should then be denied beer as they returned to church for the Sunday night services. On the other six days beer was sold from six in the morning until midnight. But on Sunday, the selling was curtailed in honor of the Almighty.

Jake bought a six-pack at Bates Grocery and directed his chauffeur toward the lake. Harry Rex's antique Bronco carried three inches of dried mud across the doors and fenders. The tires were imperceptible. The windshield was cracked and dangerous, with thousands of splattered insects caked around the edges. The inspection sticker was four years old and unseen from the outside. Dozens of empty beer cans and broken bottles littered the floorboard. The air conditioner had not worked in six years. Jake had suggested use of the Saab. Harry Rex had cursed him for his stupidity. The red Saab was an easy target for snipers. No one would suspect the Bronco.

They drove slowly in the general direction of the lake, to no place in particular. Willie Nelson wailed from the cassette. Harry Rex tapped the steering wheel and sang along. His normal speaking voice was coarse and unrefined. With song, it was heinous. Jake sipped his beer and searched for daylight through the windshield.

The heat wave was about to be broken. Dark clouds loomed to the southwest, and when they passed Huey's Lounge the rains fell and showered the parched earth. It cleansed and removed the dust from the kudzu that lined the roadbeds and hung like Spanish moss from the trees. It cooled the scorched pavement and created a sticky fog that rose three feet above the highway. The red baked gullies absorbed the water, and when full began to carry tiny streams downward to the larger field drains and road ditches. The rains drenched the cotton and soybeans, and pounded the crop rows until small puddles formed between the stalks.

Remarkably, the windshield wipers worked. They slapped back and forth furiously and removed the mud and insect collection. The storm grew. Harry Rex increased the volume of the stereo.

The blacks with their cane poles and straw hats camped under the bridges and waited for the storm to blow over. Below them, the still creeks came to life. Muddy water from the fields and gullies rushed downward and stirred the small streams and brooks. The water rose and moved forward. The blacks ate bologna and crackers and told fishing stories.

Harry Rex was hungry. He stopped at Treadway's Grocery near the lake, and bought more beer, two catfish dinners, and a large bag of Cajun-spiced red-hot barbecue pork skins. He threw them at Jake.

They crossed the dam in a blinding downpour. Harry Rex parked next to a small pavilion over a picnic area. They sat on the concrete table and watched the rain batter Lake Chatulla. Jake drank beer while Harry Rex ate the catfish dinners.

'When you gonna tell Carla?' he asked, slurping beer.

The tin roof roared above. 'About what?'

'The house.'

'I'm not gonna tell her. I think I can have it rebuilt before she gets back.'

'You mean by the end of the week?'

'Yeah.'

'You're cracking up, Jake. You're drinking too much, and you're losing your mind.'

'I deserve it. I've earned it. I'm two weeks away from bankruptcy. I'm about to lose the biggest case of my career, for which I have been paid nine hundred dollars. My beautiful home that everyone took pictures of and the old ladies from the Garden Club tried to get written up in *Southern Living* has been reduced to rubble. My wife has left me, and when she hears about the house, she'll divorce me. No question about that. So I'll lose my wife. And once my daughter learns that her damned dog died in the fire, she'll hate me forever. There's a contract on my head. I've got Klan goons looking for me. Snipers shooting at me. There's a soldier lying up in the hospital with my bullet in his spine. He'll be a vegetable, and I'll think about him every hour of every day for the rest of my life. My secretary's husband was killed because of me. My last employee is in the hospital with a punk haircut and a concussion because she worked for me. The jury thinks I'm a lying crook because of my expert witness. My client wants to fire me. When he's convicted, everybody will blame me. He'll hire another lawyer for the appeal, one of those ACLU types, and they'll sue me claiming ineffective trial counsel. And they'll be right. So I'll get my ass sued for malpractice. I'll have no wife, no daughter, no house, no practice, no clients, no money, nothing.'

'You need psychiatric help, Jake. I think you should make an appointment with Dr. Bass. Here, have a beer.'

'I guess I'll move in with Lucien and sit on the porch all day.'

'Can I have your office?'

'Do you think she'll divorce me?'

'Probably so. I've had four divorces, and they'll file for damned near anything.'

'Not Carla. I worship the ground she walks on, and she knows it.'

'She'll be sleeping on the ground when she gets back to Clanton.'

'Naw, we'll get a nice, cozy little double-wide trailer. It'll do us fine until the bankruptcy is over. Then we'll find another old house and start over.'

'You'll probably find you another wife and start over. Why would she leave a swanky cottage on the beach and return to a house trailer in Clanton?'

'Because I'll be in the house trailer.'

'That's not good enough, Jake. You'll be a drunk, bankrupt, disbarred lawyer, living in a house trailer. You will be publicly disgraced. All of your friends, except me and Lucien, will forget about you. She'll never come back. It's over, Jake. As your friend and divorce lawyer, I advise you to file first. Do it now, tomorrow, so she'll never know what hit her.'

'Why would I sue her for divorce?'

'Because she's gonna sue you. We'll file first and allege that she deserted you in your hour of need.'

'Is that grounds for divorce?'

'No. But we'll also claim that you're crazy, temporary insanity. Just let me handle it. The M'Naghten Rule. I'm the sleazy divorce lawyer, remember.'

'How could I forget?'

Jake poured hot beer from his neglected bottle, and opened another. The rain slackened and the clouds lightened. A cool wind blew up from the lake.

'They'll convict him, won't they, Harry Rex?' he asked, staring at the lake in the distance.

He quit chomping and wiped his mouth. He laid the paper plate on the table, and took a long drink of beer. The wind blew light drops of water onto his face. He wiped it with a sleeve.

'Yeah, Jake. Your man is about to be sent away. I can see it in their eyes. The insanity crap just didn't work. They didn't want to believe Bass to begin with, and after Buckley yanked his pants down, it was all over. Carl Lee didn't help himself any. He seemed rehearsed and too sincere. Like he was begging for sympathy. He was a lousy witness. I watched the jury while he testified. I saw no support for him. They'll convict, Jake. And quickly.'

'Thanks for being so blunt.'

'I'm your friend, and I think you should start preparing for a conviction and a long appeal.'

'You know, Harry Rex, I wish I'd never heard of Carl Lee Hailey.'

'I think it's too late, Jake.'

Sallie answered the door and told Jake she was sorry about the house. Lucien was upstairs in his study, working and sober. He pointed to a chair and instructed Jake to sit down. Legal pads littered his desk.

'I've spent all afternoon working on a closing argument,' he said, waving at the mess before him. 'Your only hope of saving Hailey is with a spellbinding performance on final summation. I mean, we're talking about the greatest closing argument in the history of jurisprudence. That's what it'll take.'

'And I assume you've created such a masterpiece.'

'As a matter of fact, I have. It's much better than anything you could come up with. And I assumed – correctly – that you would spend your Sunday afternoon mourning the loss of your home and drowning your sorrows with Coors. I knew you would have nothing prepared. So I've done it for you.'

'I wish I could stay as sober as you, Lucien.'

'I was a better lawyer drunk than you are sober.'

'At least I'm a lawyer.'

Lucien tossed a legal pad at Jake. 'There it is. A compilation of my greatest closing arguments. Lucien Wilbanks at his best, all rolled into one for you and your client. I suggest you memorize it and use it word for word. It's that good. Don't try to modify it, or improvise. You'll just screw it up.'

'I'll think about it. I've done this before, remember?'

'You'd never know it.'

'Dammit, Lucien! Get off my back!'

'Take it easy, Jake. Let's have a drink. Sallie! Sallie!'

Jake threw the masterpiece on the couch and walked to the window overlooking the backyard. Sallie ran up the stairs. Lucien ordered whiskey and beer.

'Were you up all night?' Lucien asked.

'No. I slept from eleven to twelve.'

'You look terrible. You need a good night's rest.'

'I feel terrible, and sleep will not help. Nothing will help, except the end of this trial. I don't understand, Lucien. I don't understand how everything has gone so wrong. Surely to God we're entitled to a little good luck. The case should not even be tried in Clanton. We were dealt the worst possible jury – a jury that's been tampered with. But I can't prove it. Our star witness was completely destroyed. The defendant made a lousy witness. And the jury does not trust me. I don't know what else could go wrong.'

'You can still win the case, Jake. It'll take a miracle, but those things happen sometimes. I've snatched victory from the jaws of defeat many times with an effective closing argument. Zero in on one or two jurors. Play to them. Talk to them. Remember, it just takes one to hang the jury.'

'Should I make them cry?'

'If you can. It's not that easy. But I believe in tears in the jury box. It's very effective.'

Sallie brought the drinks, and they followed her downstairs to the porch. After dark, she fed them sandwiches and fried potatoes. At ten, Jake excused himself and went to his room. He called Carla and talked for an hour. There was no mention of the house. His stomach cramped when he heard her voice and realized that one day very soon he would be forced to tell her that the house, her house, no longer existed. He hung up and prayed she didn't read about it in the newspaper.

CHAPTER FORTY

Clanton returned to normal Monday morning as the barricades were put in place around the square and the ranks of the soldiers swelled to preserve the public peace. They loitered about in loose formation, watching as the Kluxers returned to their appointed ground on one side, and the black protestors on the other. The day of rest brought renewed energy to both groups, and by eight-thirty they were in full chorus. The collapse of Dr. Bass had been big news, and the Kluxers smelled victory. Plus they had scored a direct hit on Adams Street. They appeared to be louder than normal.

At nine, Noose summoned the attorneys to chambers. 'Just wanted to make sure you were all alive and well.' He grinned at Jake.

'Why don't you kiss my ass, Judge?' Jake said under his breath, but loud enough to be heard. The prosecutors froze. Mr. Pate cleared his throat.

Noose cocked his head sideways as if hard of hearing. 'What did you say, Mr. Brigance?'

'I said, "Why don't we get started, Judge?" '

'Yes, that's what I thought you said. How's your clerk, Ms. Roark?'

'She'll be fine.'

'Was it the Klan?'

'Yes, Judge. The same Klan that tried to kill me. Same Klan that lit up the county with crosses and who knows what else for our jury panel. Same Klan that's probably intimidated most of those jurors sitting out there. Yes, sir, it's the same Klan.'

Noose ripped off his glasses. 'Can you substantiate that?'

'You mean, do I have written, signed, notarized confessions from the Klansmen? No, sir. They're most uncooperative.'

'If you can't prove it, Mr. Brigance, then leave it alone.'

'Yes, Your Honor.'

Jake left chambers and slammed the door. Seconds later Mr. Pate called the place to order and everyone rose. Noose welcomed his jury back and promised the ordeal was almost over. No one smiled at him. It had been a lonely weekend at the Temple Inn.

'Does the State have any rebuttal?' he asked Buckley.

'One witness, Your Honor.'

Dr. Rodeheaver was fetched from the witness room. He carefully situated himself in the witness chair and nodded warmly at the jury. He looked like a psychiatrist. Dark suit, no boots.

Buckley assumed the podium and smiled at the jury. 'You are Dr. Wilbert Rodeheaver?' he thundered, looking at the jury as if to say, 'Now you'll meet a real psychiatrist.'

'Yes, sir.'

Buckley asked questions, a million questions, about his educational and professional background. Rodeheaver was confident, relaxed, prepared, and accustomed to the witness chair. He talked at great length about his broad educational training, his vast experience as a practicing physician, and more recently, the enormous magnitude of his job as head of staff at the state mental hospital. Buckley asked him if he had written any articles in his field. He said yes, and for thirty minutes they discussed the writings of this very learned man. He had received research grants from the federal government and from various states. He was a member of all the organizations Bass belonged to, and a few more. He had been certified by every association remotely touching the study of the human mind. He was polished, and sober.

Buckley tendered him as an expert, and Jake had no questions.

Buckley continued. 'Dr. Rodeheaver, when did you first examine Carl Lee Hailey?'

The expert checked his notes. 'June 19.'

'Where did the examination take place?'

'In my office at Whitfield.'

'How long did you examine him?'

'Couple of hours.'

'What was the purpose of this examination?'

'To try and determine his mental condition at that time and also at the time he killed Mr. Cobb and Mr. Willard.'

'Did you obtain his medical history?'

'Most of the information was taken by an associate at the hospital. I reviewed it with Mr. Hailey.'

'What did the history reveal?'

'Nothing remarkable. He talked a lot about Vietnam, but nothing remarkable.'

'Did he talk freely about Vietnam?'

'Oh yes. He wanted to talk about it. It was almost like he had been told to discuss it as much as possible.'

'What else did you discuss at the first examination?'

'We covered a wide variety of topics. His childhood, family, education, various jobs, just about everything.'

'Did he discuss the rape of his daughter?'

'Yes, in great detail. It was painful for him to talk about it, the same as it would have been for me had it been my daughter.'

'Did he discuss with you the events leading up to the shootings of Cobb and Willard?'

'Yes, we talked about that for quite a while. I tried to ascertain the degree of knowledge and understanding he had about those events.'

'What did he tell you?'

'Initially, not much. But with time, he opened up and explained how he inspected the courthouse three days before the shooting and picked a good place to attack.'

'What about the shootings?'

'He never told me much about the actual killings. Said he didn't remember much, but I suspect otherwise.'

Jake sprang to his feet. 'Objection! The witness can only testify as to what he actually knows. He cannot speculate.'

'Sustained. Please continue, Mr. Buckley.'

'What else did you observe concerning his mood, attitude, and manner of speech?'

Rodeheaver crossed his legs and rocked gently. He lowered his eyebrows in deep thought. 'Initially, he was distrustful of me and had difficulty looking me in the eye. He gave short answers to my questions. He was very resentful of the fact that he was guarded and sometimes handcuffed while at our facility. He questioned the padded walls. But after a while, he opened up and talked freely about most everything. He flatly refused to answer a few questions, but other than that I would say he was fairly cooperative.'

'When and where did you examine him again?'

'The next day, same place.'

'What was his mood and attitude?'

'About the same as the day before. Cool at first, but he opened up eventually. He discussed basically the same topics as the day before.'

'How long did this examination last?'

'Approximately four hours.'

Buckley reviewed something on a legal pad, then whispered to Musgrove. 'Now, Dr. Rodeheaver, as a result of your examinations of Mr. Hailey on June 19 and 20, were you able to arrive at a medical diagnosis of the defendant's psychiatric condition on those dates?'

'Yes, sir.'

'And what is that diagnosis?'

'On June 19 and 20, Mr. Hailey appeared to be of sound mind. Perfectly normal, I would say.'

'Thank you. Based on your examinations, were you able to arrive at a diagnosis of Mr. Hailey's mental condition on the day he shot Billy Ray Cobb and Pete Willard?'

'Yes.'

'And what is that diagnosis?'

'At that time his mental condition was sound, no defects of any nature.'

'Upon what factors do you base this?'

Rodeheaver turned to the jury and became a professor. 'You must look at the level of premeditation involved in this crime. Motive is an element of premeditation. He certainly had a motive for doing what he did, and his mental condition at that time did not prevent him from entertaining the requisite premeditation. Frankly, Mr. Hailey carefully planned what he did.'

'Doctor, you are familiar with the M'Naghten Rule as a test for criminal responsibility?'

'Certainly.'

'And you are aware that another psychiatrist, a Dr. W.T. Bass, has told this jury that Mr. Hailey was incapable of knowing the difference between right and wrong, and, further, that he was unable to understand and appreciate the nature and quality of his actions.'

'Yes, I am aware of that.'

'Do you agree with that testimony?'

'No. I find it preposterous, and I am personally offended by it. Mr. Hailey himself has testified he planned the murders. He's admitted, in effect, that his mental condition at the time did not prevent him from possessing the ability to plan. That's called premeditation in every legal and medical book. I've never heard of someone planning a murder, admitting he planned it, then claiming he did not know what he was doing. It's absurd.'

At that moment, Jake felt it was absurd too, and as it echoed around the courtroom it sounded mighty absurd. Rodeheaver sounded good and infinitely credible. Jake thought of Bass and cursed to himself.

Lucien sat with the blacks and agreed with every word of Rodeheaver's testimony. When compared to Bass, the State's doctor was terribly believable. Lucien ignored the jury box. From time to time he would cut his eyes without moving his head and catch Clyde Sisco blatantly and openly staring directly at him. But Lucien would not allow their eyes to meet. The messenger had not called Monday morning as instructed. An affirmative nod or wink from Lucien would consummate the deal, with payment to be arranged later, after the verdict. Sisco knew the rules, and he watched for an answer. There was none. Lucien wanted to discuss it with Jake.

'Now, Doctor, based upon these factors and your diagnosis of his mental condition as of May 20, do you have an opinion, to a reasonable degree of medical certainty, as to whether Mr. Hailey was capable of knowing the difference between right and wrong when he shot Billy Ray Cobb, Pete Willard, and Deputy DeWayne Looney?'

'I have.'

'And what is that opinion?'

'His mental condition was sound, and he was very capable of distinguishing right from wrong.'

'And do you have an opinion, based upon the same factors, as to whether Mr. Hailey was able to understand and appreciate the nature and quality of his actions?'

'I have.'

'And what is that opinion?'

'That he fully appreciated what he was doing.'

Buckley snatched his legal pad and bowed politely. 'Thank you, Doctor. I have no further questions.'

'Any cross-examination, Mr. Brigance?' Noose asked.

'Just a few questions.'

'I thought so. Let's take a fifteen-minute recess.'

Jake ignored Carl Lee, and moved quickly out of the courtroom, up the stairs, and into the law library on the third floor. Harry Rex was waiting, and smiling.

'Relax, Jake. I've called every newspaper in North Carolina, and there's no story about the house. There's nothing about Row Ark. The Raleigh morning paper ran a story about the trial, but it was in real general terms. Nothing else. Carla doesn't know about it, Jake. As far as she knows, her pretty little landmark is still standing. Isn't that great?'

'Wonderful. Just wonderful. Thanks, Harry Rex.'

'Don't mention it. Look, Jake, I sorta hate to bring this up.'

'I can't wait.'

'You know I hate Buckley. Hate him worse than you do. But me and Musgrove get along okay. I can talk to Musgrove. I was thinking last night that it might be a good idea to approach them – me through Musgrove – and explore the possibilities of a plea bargain.'

'No!'

'Listen, Jake. What harm will it do? None! If you can plead him guilty to murder with no gas chamber, then you know you have saved his life.'

'No!'

'Look, Jake. Your man is about forty-eight hours away from a death penalty conviction. If you don't believe that, then you're blind, Jake. My blind friend.'

'Why should Buckley cut a deal? He's got us on the ropes.'

'Maybe he won't. But let me at least find out.'

'No, Harry Rex. Forget it.'

Rodeheaver returned to his seat after the recess, and Jake looked at him from behind the podium. In his brief legal career, he had never won an argument, in court or out, with an expert witness. And the way his luck was running, he decided not to argue with this one.

'Dr. Rodeheaver, psychiatry is the study of the human mind, is it not?'

'It is.'

'And it is an inexact science at best, is it not?'

'That is correct.'

'You might examine a person and reach a diagnosis, and the next psychiatrist might reach a completely different diagnosis?'

'That's possible, yes.'

'In fact, you could have ten psychiatrists examine a mental patient, and arrive at ten different opinions about what's wrong with the patient.'

'That's unlikely.'

'But it could happen, couldn't it, Doctor?'

'Yes, it could. Just like legal opinions, I guess.'

'But we're not dealing with legal opinions in this case, are we, Doctor?'

'No.'

'The truth is, Doctor, in many cases psychiatry cannot tell us what is wrong with a person's mind?'

'That is true.'

'And psychiatrists disagree all the time, don't they, Doctor?'

'Of course.'

'Now, who do you work for, Doctor?'

'The State of Mississippi.'

'And for how long?'

'Eleven years.'

'And who is prosecuting Mr. Hailey?'

'The State of Mississippi.'

'During your eleven-year career with the State, how many times have you testified in trials where the insanity defense was used?'

Rodeheaver thought for a moment. 'I think this is my forty-third trial.'

Jake checked something in a file and eyed the doctor with a nasty little smile. 'Are you sure it's not your forty-sixth?'

'It could be, yes. I'm not certain.'

The courtroom became still. Buckley and Musgrove hovered over their legal pads, but watched their witness carefully.

'Forty-six times you've testified for the State in insanity trials?'

'If you say so.'

'And forty-six times you've testified that the defendant was not legally insane. Correct, Doctor?'

'I'm not sure.'

'Well, let me make it simple. You've testified forty-six times, and forty-six times it has been your opinion the defendant was not legally insane. Correct?'

Rodeheaver squirmed just a little, and a hint of discomfort broke around his eyes. 'I'm not sure.'

'You've never seen a legally insane criminal defendant, have you, Doctor?'

'Of course I have.'

'Good. Would you then, please, sir, tell us the name of the defendant and where he was tried?'

Buckley rose and buttoned his coat. 'Your Honor, the State objects to these questions. Dr. Rodeheaver cannot be required to remember the names and places of the trials he has testified in.'

'Overruled. Sit down. Answer the question, Doctor.'

Rodeheaver breathed deeply and studied the ceiling. Jake glanced at the jurors. They were awake and waiting on an answer.

'I can't remember,' he finally said.

Jake lifted a thick stack of papers and waved it at the witness. 'Could it be, Doctor, that the reason you can't remember is that in eleven years, forty-six trials, you have never testified in favor of the defendant?'

'I honestly can't remember.'

'Can you honestly name us one trial in which you found the defendant to be legally insane?'

'I'm sure there are some.'

'Yes or no, Doctor. One trial?'

The expert looked briefly at the D.A. 'No. My memory fails me. I cannot at this time.'

Jake walked slowly to the defense table and picked up a thick file.

'Dr. Rodeheaver, do you recall testifying in the trial of a man by the name of Danny Booker in McMurphy County in December of 1975? A rather gruesome double homicide?'

'Yes, I recall that trial.'

'And you testified to the effect that he was not legally insane, did you not?'

'That is correct.'

'Do you recall how many psychiatrists testified in his behalf?'

'Not exactly. There were several.'

'Do the names Noel McClacky, M.D.; O.G. McGuire, M.D.; and Lou Watson, M.D., ring a bell?'

'Yes.'

'They're all psychiatrists, aren't they?'

'Yes.'

'They're all qualified, aren't they?'

'Yes.'

'And they all examined Mr. Booker and testified at trial that in their opinions the poor man was legally insane?'

'That's correct.'

'And you testified he was not legally insane?'

'That's correct.'

'How many other doctors supported your position?'

'None, that I recall.'

'So it was three against one?'

'Yes, but I'm still convinced I was right.'

'I see. What did the jury do, Doctor?'

'He, uh, was found not guilty by reason of insanity.'

'Thank you. Now, Dr. Rodeheaver, you're the head doctor at Whitfield, aren't you?'

'Yes, so to speak.'

'Are you directly or indirectly responsible for the treatment of every patient at Whitfield?'

'I'm directly responsible, Mr. Brigance. I may not personally see every patient, but their doctors are under my supervision.'

'Thank you. Doctor, where is Danny Booker today?'

Rodeheaver shot a desperate look at Buckley, and immediately covered it with a warm, relaxed grin for the jury. He hesitated for a few seconds, then hesitated one second too long.

'He's at Whitfield, isn't he?' Jake asked in a tone of voice that informed everyone that the answer was yes.

'I believe so,' Rodeheaver said.

'So, he's directly under your care, then, Doctor?'

'I suppose.'

'And what is his diagnosis, Doctor?'

'I really don't know. I have a lot of patients and –'

'Paranoid schizophrenic?'

'It's possible, yes.'

Jake walked backward and sat on the railing. He turned up the volume. 'Now, Doctor, I want to make this clear for the jury. In 1975 you testified that Danny Booker was legally sane and understood exactly what he was doing when he committed his crime, and the jury disagreed with you and found him not guilty, and since that time he has been a patient in your hospital, under your supervision, and treated by you as a paranoid schizophrenic. Is that correct?'

The smirk on Rodeheaver's face informed the jury that it was indeed correct.

Jake picked up another piece of paper and seemed to review it. 'Do you recall testifying in the trial of a man by the name of Adam Couch in Dupree County in May of 1977?'

'I remember that case.'

'It was a rape case, wasn't it?'

'Yes.'

'And you testified on behalf of the State against Mr. Couch?'

'That's correct.'

'And you told the jury that he was not legally insane?'

'That was my testimony.'

'Do you recall how many doctors testified on his behalf and told the jury he was a very sick man, that he was legally insane?'

'There were several.'

'Have you ever heard of the following doctors: Felix Perry, Gene Shumate, and Hobny Wicker?'

'Yes.'

'Are they all qualified psychiatrists?'

'They are.'

'And they all testified on behalf of Mr. Couch, didn't they?'

'Yes.'

'And they all said he was legally insane, didn't they?'

'They did.'

'And you were the only doctor in the trial who said he was not legally insane?'

'As I recall, yes.'

'And what did the jury do, Doctor?'

'He was found not guilty.'

'By reason of insanity?'

'Yes.'

'And where is Mr. Couch today, Doctor?'

'I think he's at Whitfield.'

'And how long has he been there?'

'Since the trial, I believe.'

'I see. Do you normally admit patients and keep them for several years if they are of perfectly sound mind?'

Rodeheaver shifted his weight and began a slow burn. He looked at his lawyer, the people's lawyer, as if to say he was tired of this, do something to stop it.

Jake picked up more papers. 'Doctor, do you recall the trial of a man by the name of Buddy Wooddall in Cleburne County, May of 1979?'

'Yes, I certainly do.'

'Murder, wasn't it?'

'Yes.'

'And you testified as an expert in the field of psychiatry and told the jury that Mr. Wooddall was not insane?'

'I did.'

'Do you recall how many psychiatrists testified on his behalf and told the jury the poor man was legally insane?'

'I believe there were five, Mr. Brigance.'

'That's correct, Doctor. Five against one. Do you recall what the jury did?'

The anger and frustration was building in the witness stand. The wise old grandfather/professor with all the right answers was becoming rattled. 'Yes, I recall. He was found not guilty by reason of insanity.'

'How do you explain that, Dr. Rodeheaver? Five against one, and the jury finds against you?'

'You just can't trust juries,' he blurted, then caught himself. He fidgeted and grinned awkwardly at the jurors.

Jake stared at him with a wicked smile, then looked at the jury in disbelief. He folded his arms and allowed the last words to sink in. He waited, staring and grinning at the witness.

'You may proceed, Mr. Brigance,' Noose finally said.

Moving slowly and with great animation, Jake gathered his files and notes while staring at Rodeheaver. 'I think we've heard enough from this witness, Your Honor.'

'Any redirect, Mr. Buckley?'

'No, sir. The State rests.'

Noose addressed the jury. 'Ladies and gentlemen, this trial is almost over. There will be no more witnesses. I will now meet with the attorneys to cover some technical areas, then they will be allowed to make their final arguments to you. That will begin at two o'clock and take a couple of hours. You will finally get the case around four, and I will allow you to deliberate until six. If you do not reach a verdict today, you will be taken back to your rooms until tomorrow. It is now almost eleven, and we'll recess until two. I need to see the attorneys in chambers.'

Carl Lee leaned over and spoke to his lawyer for the first time since Saturday's adjournment. 'You tore him up pretty good, Jake.'

'Wait till you hear the closing argument.'

Jake avoided Harry Rex, and drove to Karaway. His childhood home was an old country house in downtown, surrounded by ancient oaks and maples and elms that kept it cool in spite of the summer heat. In the back, past the trees, was a long open field which ran for an eighth of a mile and disappeared over a small hill. A chickenwire backstop stood over the weeds in one corner. Here, Jake had taken his first steps, rode his first bike, thrown his first football and baseball. Under an oak beside the field, he had buried three dogs, a raccoon, a rabbit, and some ducks. A tire from a '54 Buick swung not far from the small cemetery.

The house had been locked and deserted for two months. A neighborhood kid cut the grass and tended the lawn. Jake checked the house once a week. His parents were somewhere in Canada in a camper – the summer ritual. He wished he were with them.

He unlocked the door and walked upstairs to his room. It would never change. The walls were covered with team pictures, trophies, baseball caps, posters of Pete Rose, Archie Manning, and Hank Aaron. A row of baseball gloves hung above the closet door. A cap and gown picture sat on the dresser. His mother still cleaned it weekly. She once told him she often went to his room and expected to find him doing homework or sorting baseball cards. She would flip through his scrapbooks, and get all teary eyed.

He thought of Hanna's room, with the stuffed animals and Mother Goose wallpaper. A thick knot formed in his throat.

He looked out the window, past the trees, and saw himself swinging in the tire near the three white crosses where he buried his dogs. He remembered each funeral, and his father's promises to get another dog. He thought of Hanna and her dog, and his eyes watered.

The bed was much smaller now. He removed his shoes and lay down. A football helmet hung from the ceiling. Eighth grade, Karaway Mustangs. He scored seven touchdowns in five games. It was all on film downstairs under the bookshelves. The butterflies floated wildly through his stomach.

He carefully placed his notes – his notes, not Lucien's – on the dresser. He studied himself in the mirror.

He addressed the jury. He began by facing his biggest problem, Dr. W.T. Bass. He apologized. A lawyer walks into a courtroom, faces a strange jury, and has nothing to offer but his credibility. And if he does anything to hurt his credibility, he has hurt his cause, his client. He asked them to believe that he would never put a convicted felon on the stand as an expert witness in any trial. He did not know of the conviction, he raised his hand and swore to this. The world is full of psychiatrists, and he could easily have found another if he had known Bass had a problem, but he simply did not know. And he was sorry.

But what about Bass's testimony. Thirty years ago he had sex with a girl under eighteen in Texas. Does that mean he is lying now in this trial? Does that mean you cannot trust his professional opinion? Please be fair to Bass the psychiatrist, forget Bass the person. Please be fair to his patient, Carl Lee Hailey. He knew nothing of the doctor's past.

There was something about Bass they might like to know. Something that was not mentioned by Mr. Buckley when he was ripping the doctor to pieces. The girl he had sex with was seventeen. She later became his wife, bore him a son, and was pregnant when she and the boy were killed in a train –

'Objection!' Buckley shouted. 'Objection, Your Honor. That evidence is not in the record!'

'Sustained. Mr. Brigance, you are not to refer to facts not in evidence. The jury will disregard the last statements by Mr. Brigance.'

Jake ignored Noose and Buckley and stared painfully at the jury.

When the shouting died, he continued. What about Rodeheaver? He wondered if the State's doctor had ever engaged in sex with a girl under eighteen. Seemed silly to think about such things, didn't it? Bass and Rodeheaver in their younger days – it seemed so unimportant now in this courtroom almost thirty years later.

The State's doctor is a man with an obvious bias. A highly trained specialist who treats thousands for all sorts of mental illnesses, yet when crimes are involved he cannot recognize insanity. His testimony should be carefully weighed.

They watched him, listened to every word. He was not a courtroom preacher, like his opponent. He was quiet, sincere. He looked tired, almost hurt.

Lucien was sober, and he sat with folded arms and watched the jurors, all except Sisco. It was not his closing, but it was good. It was coming from the heart.

Jake apologized for his inexperience. He had not been in many trials, not nearly as many as Mr. Buckley. And if he seemed a little green, or if he made mistakes, please don't hold it against Carl Lee. It wasn't his fault. He was just a rookie trying his best against a seasoned adversary who tried murder cases every month. He made a mistake with Bass, and he made other mistakes, and he asked the jury to forgive him.

He had a daughter, the only one he would ever have. She was four, almost five, and his world revolved around her. She was special; she was a little girl, and it was up to him to protect her. There was a bond there, something he could not explain. He talked about little girls.

Carl Lee had a daughter. Her name was Tonya. He pointed to her on the front row next to her mother and brothers. She's a beautiful little girl, ten years old. And she can never have children. She can never have a daughter because –'

'Objection,' Buckley said without shouting.

'Sustained,' Noose said.

Jake ignored the commotion. He talked about rape for a while, and explained how rape is much worse than murder. With murder, the victim is gone, and not forced to deal with what happened to her. The family must deal with it, but not the victim. But rape is much worse. The victim has a lifetime of coping, of trying to understand, of asking questions, and, the worst part, of knowing the rapist is still alive and may someday escape or be released. Every hour of every day, the victim thinks of the rape and asks herself a thousand questions. She relives it, step by step, minute by minute, and it hurts just as bad.

Perhaps the most horrible crime of all is the violent rape of a child. A woman who is raped has a pretty good idea why it happened. Some animal was filled with hatred, anger and violence. But a child? A ten-year-old child? Suppose you're a parent. Imagine yourself trying to explain to your child why she was raped. Imagine yourself trying to explain why she cannot bear children.

'Objection.'

'Sustained. Please disregard that last statement, ladies and gentlemen.'

Jake never missed a beat. Suppose, he said, your ten-year-old daughter is raped, and you're a Vietnam vet, very familiar with an M-16, and you get your hands on one while your daughter is lying in the hospital fighting for her life. Suppose the rapist is caught, and six days later you manage to maneuver to within five feet of him as he leaves court. And you've got the M-16.

What do you do?

Mr. Buckley has told you what he would do. He would mourn for his daughter, turn the other cheek, and hope the judicial system worked. He would hope the rapist would receive justice, be sent to Parchman, and hopefully never paroled. That's what he would do, and they should admire him for being such a kind, compassionate, and forgiving soul. But what would a reasonable father do?

What would Jake do? If he had the M-16? Blow the bastard's head off!

It was simple. It was justice.

Jake paused for a drink of water, then shifted gears. The pained and humble look was replaced with an air of indignation. Let's talk about Cobb and Willard. They started this mess. It was their lives the State was attempting to justify. Who would miss them except their mothers? Child rapists. Drug pushers. Would society miss such productive citizens? Wasn't Ford County safer without them? Were not the other children in the county better off now that two rapists and pushers had been removed? All parents should feel safer. Carl Lee deserves a medal, or at least a round of applause. He was a hero. That's what Looney said. Give the man a trophy. Send him home to his family.

He talked about Looney. He had a daughter. He also had one leg, thanks to Carl Lee Hailey. If anyone had a right to be bitter, to want blood, it was DeWayne Looney. And he said Carl Lee should be sent home to his family.

He urged them to forgive as Looney had forgiven. He asked them to follow Looney's wishes.

He became much quieter, and said he was almost through. He wanted to leave them with one thought. Picture this if they could. When she was lying there, beaten, bloodied, legs spread and tied to trees, she looked into the woods around her. Semiconscious and hallucinating, she saw someone running toward her. It was her daddy, running desperately to save her. In her dreams she saw him when she needed him the most. She cried out for him, and he disappeared. He was taken away.

She needs him now, as much as she needed him then. Please don't take him away. She waits on the front row for her daddy.

Let him go home to his family.

The courtroom was silent as Jake sat next to his client. He glanced at the jury, and saw Wanda Womack brush away a tear with her finger. For the first time in two days he felt a flicker of hope.

At four, Noose bid farewell to his jury. He told them to elect a foreman, get organized, and get busy. He told them they could deliberate until six, maybe seven, and if no verdict was reached he would recess until nine Tuesday morning. They stood and filed slowly from the courtroom. Once out of sight, Noose recessed until six and instructed the attorneys to remain close to the courtroom or leave a number with the clerk.

The spectators held their seats and chatted quietly. Carl Lee was allowed to sit on the front row with his family. Buckley and Musgrove waited in chambers with Noose. Harry Rex, Lucien, and Jake left for the office and a liquid supper. No one expected a quick verdict.

The bailiff locked them in the jury room and instructed the two alternates to take a seat in the narrow hallway. Inside, Barry Acker was elected foreman by acclamation. He laid the jury instructions and exhibits on a small table in a corner. They sat anxiously around two folding tables placed end to end.

'I suggest we take an informal vote,' he said. 'Just to see where we are. Any objections to that?'

There were none. He had a list of twelve names.

'Vote guilty, not guilty, or undecided. Or you can pass for now.'

'Reba Betts.'

'Undecided.'

'Bernice Toole.'

'Guilty.'

'Carol Corman.'

'Guilty.'

'Donna Lou Peck.'

'Undecided.'

'Sue Williams.'

'Pass.'

'Jo Ann Gates.'

'Guilty.'

'Rita Mae Plunk.'

'Guilty.'

'Frances McGowan.'

'Guilty.'

'Wanda Womack.'

'Undecided.'

'Eula Dell Yates.'

'Undecided, for now. I wanna talk about it.'

'We will. Clyde Sisco.'

'Undecided.'

'That's eleven. I'm Barry Acker, and I vote not guilty.'

He tallied for a few seconds and said, 'That's five guilties, five undecideds, one pass, and one not guilty. Looks like we've got our work cut out for us.'

They worked through the exhibits, photographs, fingerprints, and ballistics reports. At six, they informed the judge they had not reached a verdict. They were hungry and wanted to go. He recessed until Tuesday morning.

CHAPTER FORTY-ONE

They sat for hours on the porch, saying little, watching as darkness surrounded the town below and ushered in the mosquitoes. The heat wave had returned. The soggy air clung to their skin and moistened their shirts. The sounds of a hot summer night echoed softly across the front lawn. Sallie had offered to cook. Lucien declined and ordered whiskey. Jake had no appetite for food, but the Coors filled his system and satisfied any hunger pangs stirring within. When things were good and dark, Nesbit emerged from his car, walked across the porch, through the front screen door, and into the house. A moment later he slammed the door, walked past them with a cold beer, and disappeared down the driveway in the direction of his car. He never said a word.

Sallie stuck her head through the door and made one last offer of food. Both declined.

'Jake, I got a call this afternoon. Clyde Sisco wants twenty-five thousand to hang the jury, fifty thousand for an acquittal.'

Jake began shaking his head.

'Before you say no, listen to me. He knows he can't guarantee an acquittal, but he can guarantee a hung jury. It just takes one. That's twenty-five thousand. I know it's a lot of money, but you know I've got it. I'll pay it and you can repay me over the years. Whenever, I don't care. If you never repay it, I don't care. I've got a bankful of C.D.'s. You know money means nothing to me. If I were you I'd do it in a minute.'

'You're crazy, Lucien.'

'Sure I'm crazy. You haven't been acting so good yourself. Trial work'll drive you crazy. Just take a look at what this trial has done to you. No sleep, no food, no routine, no house. Plenty of booze, though.'

'But I've still got ethics.'

'And I have none. No ethics, no morals, no conscience. But I won, bubba. I won more than anybody has ever won around here, and you know it.'

'It's corrupt, Lucien.'

'And I guess you think Buckley's not corrupt. He would lie, cheat, bribe, and steal to win this case. He's not worried about fancy ethics, rules, and opinions. He's not concerned about morality. He's concerned with one thing and only one thing – winning! And you've got a golden chance to beat him at his own game. I'd do it, Jake.'

'Forget it, Lucien. Please, just forget it.'

An hour passed with no words. The lights of the town below slowly disappeared. Nesbit's snoring was audible in the darkness. Sallie brought one last drink and said good night.

'This is the hardest part,' Lucien said. 'Waiting on twelve average, everyday people to make sense of all this.'

'It's a crazy system, isn't it?'

'Yes, it is. But it usually works. Juries are right ninety percent of the time.'

'I just don't feel lucky. I'm waiting on the miracle.'

'Jake, my boy, the miracle happens tomorrow.'

'Tomorrow?'

'Yes. Early tomorrow morning.'

'Would you care to elaborate?'

'By noon tomorrow, Jake, there will be ten thousand angry blacks swarming like ants around the Ford County Courthouse. Maybe more.'

'Ten thousand! Why?'

'To scream and shout and chant 'Free Carl Lee, Free Carl Lee.' To raise hell, to scare everybody, to intimidate the jury. To just disrupt the hell out of everything. There'll be so many blacks, white folks will run for cover. The governor will send in more troops.'

'And how do you know all this?'

'Because I planned it, Jake.'

'You?'

'Listen, Jake, when I was in my prime I knew every black preacher in fifteen counties. I've been in their churches. Prayed with them, marched with them, sang with them. They sent me clients, and I sent them money. I was the only white radical NAACP lawyer in north Mississippi. I filed more race discrimination lawsuits than any ten firms in Washington. These were my people. I've just made a few phone calls. They'll start arriving in the morning, and by noon you won't be able to stir niggers with a stick in downtown Clanton.'

'Where will they come from?'

'Everywhere. You know how blacks love to march and protest. This will be great for them. They're looking forward to it.'

'You're crazy, Lucien. My crazy friend.'

'I win, bubba.'

In Room 163, Barry Acker and Clyde Sisco finished their last game of gin rummy and made preparations for bed. Acker gathered some coins and announced he wanted a soft drink. Sisco said he was not thirsty.

Acker tiptoed past a guardsman asleep in the hall. The machine informed him it was out of order, so he quietly opened the exit door and walked up the stairs to the second floor, where he found another machine next to an ice maker. He inserted his coins. The machine responded with a diet Coke. He bent over to pick it up.

Out of the darkness two figures charged. They knocked him to the floor, kicked him and pinned him in a dark corner beside the ice maker, next to a door with a chain and padlock. The large one grabbed Acker's collar and threw him against the cinder block wall. The smaller one stood by the Coke machine and watched the dark hall.

'You're Barry Acker!' said the large one through clenched teeth.

'Yeah! Let go of me!' Acker attempted to shake free, but his assailant lifted him by the throat and held him to the wall with one hand. He used the other hand to unsheathe a shiny hunting knife, which he placed next to Acker's nose. The wiggling stopped.

'Listen to me,' he demanded in a loud whisper, 'and listen good. We know you're married and you live at 1161 Forrest Drive. We know you got three kids, and we know where they play and go to school. Your wife works at the bank.'

Acker went limp.

'If that nigger walks free, you'll be sorry. Your family will be sorry. It may take years, but you'll be awfully sorry.'

He dropped him to the floor and grabbed his hair. 'You breathe one word of this to anyone, and you'll lose a kid. Understand?'

They vanished. Acker breathed deeply, almost gasping for breath. He rubbed his throat and the back of his head. He sat in the darkness, too scared to move.

CHAPTER FORTY-TWO

At hundreds of small black churches across north Mississippi, the faithful gathered before dawn and loaded picnic baskets, coolers, lawn chairs, and water jugs into converted school buses and church vans. They greeted friends and chatted nervously about the trial. For weeks they had read and talked about Carl Lee Hailey; now, they were about to go help. Many were old and retired, but there were entire families with children and playpens. When the buses were full, they piled into cars and followed their preachers. They sang and prayed. The preachers met other preachers in small towns and county seats, and they set out in force down the dark highways. When daylight materialized, the highways and roads leading to Ford County were filled with caravans of pilgrims.

They jammed the side streets for blocks around the square. They parked where they stopped and unloaded.

The fat colonel had just finished breakfast and stood in the gazebo watching intently. Buses and cars, many with horns honking, were coming from all directions to the square. The barricades held firm. He barked commands and the soldiers jumped into high gear. More excitement. At seven-thirty, he called Ozzie and told him of the invasion. Ozzie arrived immediately and found Agee, who assured him it was a peaceful march. Sort of like a sit-in. How many were coming? Ozzie asked. Thousands, said Agee. Thousands.

They set up camp under the stately oaks, and milled around the lawn inspecting things. They arranged tables and chairs and playpens. They were indeed peaceful, until a group began the familiar cry of 'Free Carl Lee!' They cleared their throats and joined in. It was not yet eight o'clock.

A black radio station in Memphis flooded the airwaves early Tuesday with a call for help. Black bodies were needed to march and demonstrate in Clanton, Mississippi, an hour away. Hundreds of cars met at a mall and headed south. Every civil rights activist and black politician in the city made the trip.

Agee was a man possessed. He used a bullhorn to shout orders here and there. He herded new arrivals into their places. He organized the black preachers. He assured Ozzie and the colonel everything was okay.

Everything was okay until a handful of Klansmen made their routine appearance. The sight of the white robes was new to many of the blacks, and they reacted loudly. They inched forward, screaming and jeering. The troops surrounded the robes and protected them. The Kluxers were stunned and scared, and did not yell back.

By eight-thirty, the streets of Clanton were gridlocked. Deserted cars, vans, and buses were scattered haphazardly through parking lots and along the quiet residential streets. A steady stream of blacks walked toward the square from all directions. Traffic did not move. Driveways were blocked. Merchants parked blocks away from their shops. The mayor stood in the center of the gazebo, wringing his hands and begging Ozzie to do something. Around him thousands of blacks swarmed and yelled in perfect unison. Ozzie asked the mayor if he wanted him to start arresting everybody on the courthouse lawn.

Noose parked at a service station a half mile south of the jail, and walked with a group of blacks to the courthouse. They watched him curiously, but said nothing. No one would suspect he was a person of authority. Buckley and Musgrove parked in a driveway on Adams Street. They cursed and walked toward the square. They noticed the pile of rubble that had been Jake's house but said nothing. They were too busy cursing. With state troopers leading the way, the Greyhound from Temple reached the square at twenty minutes after nine. Through the dark windows, the fourteen passengers stared in disbelief at the carnival around the courthouse.

Mr. Pate called the packed courtroom to order, and Noose welcomed his jury. He apologized for the trouble outside, but there was nothing he could do. If there were no problems to report, they could continue deliberations.

'Very well, you may retire to the jury room and get to work. We will meet again just before lunch.'

The jurors filed out and went to the jury room. The Hailey children sat with their father at the defense table. The spectators, now predominantly black, remained seated and struck up conversations. Jake returned to his office.

Foreman Acker sat at the end of the long, dusty table and thought of the hundreds, perhaps thousands, of Ford Countians who had served in this room and sat around this table and argued about justice over the past century. Any pride he may have felt for serving on the jury of the most famous case was greatly overshadowed by what happened last night. He wondered how many of his predecessors had been threatened with death. Probably a few, he decided.

The others fixed their coffee and slowly found seats around the tables. The room brought back fond memories for Clyde Sisco. Prior jury duty had proved lucrative for him, and he relished the thought of another handsome payoff for another just and true verdict. His messenger had not contacted him.

'How would y'all like to proceed?' the foreman asked.

Rita Mae Plunk had an especially hard and unforgiving look about her. She was a rough woman with a house trailer, no husband, and two outlaws for sons, both of whom had expressed hatred for Carl Lee Hailey. She had a few things she wanted to get off her large chest.

'I got a few things I wanna say,' she informed Acker.

'Fine. Why don't we start with you, Miss Plunk, and go around the table.'

'I voted guilty yesterday in the first vote, and I'll vote guilty next time. I don't see how anybody could vote not guilty, and I want just one of you to explain to me how you could vote in favor of this nigger!'

'Don't say that word again!' yelled Wanda Womack.

'I'll say "nigger" if I wanna say "nigger," and there ain't a damned thing you can do,' replied Rita Mae.

'Please don't use that word,' said Frances McGowan.

'I find it personally offensive,' said Wanda Womack.

'Nigger, Nigger, Nigger, Nigger, Nigger, Nigger,' Rita Mae yelled across the table.

'Come on,' said Clyde Sisco.

'Oh boy,' said the foreman. 'Look, Miss Plunk, let's be honest, okay. Most of us use that word, from time to time. I'm sure some of us use it more than others. But it's offensive to many people, and I think it'd be a good idea not to use it during our deliberations. We've got enough to worry about as it is. Can we all agree not to use that word?'

Everyone nodded but Rita Mae.

Sue Williams decided to answer. She was well dressed, attractive, about forty. She worked for the county welfare department. 'I didn't vote yesterday. I passed. But I tend to sympathize with Mr. Hailey. I have a daughter, and if she was raped, it would greatly affect my mental stability. I can understand how a parent might crack in that situation, and I think it's unfair for us to judge Mr. Hailey as if he was supposed to act completely rational.'

'You think he was legally insane?' asked Reba Betts, an undecided.

'I'm not sure. But I know he wasn't stable. He couldn't have been.'

'So you believe that nut of a doctor who testified for him?' asked Rita Mae.

'Yes. He was as believable as the State's doctor.'

'I liked his boots,' said Clyde Sisco. No one laughed.

'But he's a convict,' said Rita Mae. 'He lied and tried to cover it up. You can't believe a word he said.'

'He had sex with a girl under eighteen,' Clyde said. 'If that's a crime, then a bunch of us should've been indicted.'

Again, no one appreciated the attempt at humor. Clyde decided to stay quiet for a while.

'He later married the girl,' said Donna Lou Peck, an undecided.

They went around the table, one at a time, expressing opinions and answering questions. The N word was carefully avoided by those wanting a conviction. The battle lines became clearer. Most of the undecideds leaned toward guilty, it seemed. The careful planning by Carl Lee, knowing the exact movements of the boys, the M-16 – it all seemed so premeditated. If he had caught them in the act and killed them on the spot, he would not be held accountable. But to plan it so carefully for six days did not indicate an insane mind.

Wanda Womack, Sue Williams, and Clyde Sisco leaned toward acquittal – the rest toward conviction. Barry Acker was noticeably noncommittal.

Agee unfurled a long blue and white FREE CARL LEE banner. The ministers gathered fifteen abreast behind it, and waited for the parade to form behind them. They stood in the center of Jackson Street, in front of the courthouse, while Agee screamed instructions to the masses. Thousands of blacks packed tightly behind them, and off they went. They inched down Jackson, and turned left on Caffey, up the west side of the square. Agee led the marchers in their now familiar battle cry of 'Free Carl Lee! Free Carl Lee!' They screamed it in an endless, repetitive, numbing chorus. As the crowd moved around the square, it grew in number and volume.

Smelling trouble, the merchants locked up and headed for home and safety. They checked their policies to see if they were insured for riot damage. The green soldiers were lost in a sea of black. The colonel, sweating and nervous, ordered his troops to circle the courthouse and stand firm. While Agee and the marchers were turning onto Washington Street, Ozzie met with the handful of Kluxers. In a sincere and diplomatic way, he convinced them things could get out of hand, and he could no longer guarantee their safety. He acknowledged their right to assemble, said they had made their point, and asked them to get away from the square before there was trouble. They huddled quickly, and disappeared.

When the banner passed under the jury room, all twelve gaped from the window. The incessant chanting rattled the glass panes. The bullhorn sounded like a loudspeaker hanging from the ceiling. The jurors stared in disbelief at the mob, the black mob which filled the street and trailed around the corner onto Caffey. A varied assortment of homemade signs bobbed above the masses and demanded that the man be freed.

'I didn't know there were this many niggers in Ford County,' Rita Mae Plunk said. At that moment, the other eleven held the same thought.

Buckley was furious. He and Musgrove watched from a third-floor window in the library. The roar below had disrupted their quiet conversation.

'I didn't know there were this many niggers in Ford County,' Musgrove said.

'There ain't. Somebody shipped these niggers in here. I wonder who put them up to it.'

'Probably Brigance.'

'Yeah, probably so. It's mighty convenient that they start all this hell-raising when the jury is deliberating. There must be five thousand niggers down there.'

'At least.'

Noose and Mr. Pate watched and listened from a second-floor window in chambers. His Honor was not happy. He worried about his jury. 'I don't see how they can concentrate on much with all this going on.'

'Pretty good timing, ain't it, Judge?' Mr. Pate said.

'It certainly is.'

'I didn't know we had that many blacks in the whole county.'

It took twenty minutes for Mr. Pate and Jean Gillespie to find the attorneys and bring the courtroom to order. When it was quiet, the jurors filed into their seats. There were no smiles.

Noose cleared his throat. 'Ladies and gentlemen, it is time for lunch. I don't suppose you have anything to report.'

Barry Acker shook his head.

'That's what I figured. Let's break for lunch, until one-thirty. I realize you cannot leave the courthouse, but I want you to eat for a while without working on the case. I apologize for the disturbance outside, but, frankly, I can't do anything about it. We'll be in recess until one-thirty.'

In chambers, Buckley went wild. 'This is crazy, Judge! There's no way the jury can concentrate on this case with all that noise out there. This is a deliberate effort to intimidate the jury.'

'I don't like it,' Noose said.

'It was planned, Judge! It's intentional!' Buckley yelled.

'It looks bad,' Noose added.

'I'm almost ready for a mistrial!'

'I won't grant one. What do you say, Jake?'

Jake grinned for a moment, and said, 'Free Carl Lee.'

'Very funny,' Buckley growled. 'You probably planned all this.'

'No. If you will recall, Mr. Buckley, I tried to prevent it. I have repeatedly asked for a change of venue. I have repeatedly said the trial should not be held in this courthouse. You wanted it here, Mr. Buckley, and you kept it here, Judge Noose. You both now look foolish complaining.'

Jake was impressed with his arrogance. Buckley growled and stared out the window. 'Look at them. Wild niggers. Must be ten thousand out there.'

During lunch the ten thousand grew to fifteen thousand. Cars from a hundred miles away – some with Tennessee plates – parked on the shoulders of the highways outside the city limits. The people hiked for two and three miles under a blistering sun to join the festivities around the courthouse. Agee broke for lunch, and the square quieted.

The blacks were peaceful. They opened their coolers and picnic baskets, and shared with each other. They congregated in the shade, but there were not enough trees to go around. They filled the courthouse in search of cold water and rest rooms. They walked the sidewalks and gazed in the windows of the closed shops and stores. Fearing trouble from the horde, the Coffee Shop and the Tea Shoppe closed during lunch. Outside of Claude's, they lined the sidewalk for a block and a half.

Jake, Harry Rex, and Lucien relaxed on the balcony and enjoyed the circus below. A pitcher of fresh, slushy margaritas sat on the table and slowly disappeared. At times they participated in the rally, yelling 'Free Carl Lee' or humming along with 'We Shall Overcome.' No one knew the words but Lucien. He had learned them during the glorious civil rights days of the sixties, and still claimed to be the only white in Ford County who knew all the words to every stanza. He had even joined a black church back then, he explained between drinks, after his church voted to exclude black members. He dropped out after a three-hour sermon ruptured a disc. He had decided white people were not cut out for that kind of worship. He still contributed, however.

Occasionally, a crew of TV people would stray near Jake's office and serve up a question. Jake would pretend not to hear, then finally yell 'Free Carl Lee.'

Precisely at one-thirty, Agee found his bullhorn, unfurled his banner, lined up the ministers and gathered his marchers. He started with the hymn, sung directly into the bullhorn, and the parade crawled down Jackson, then onto Caffey, and around and around the square. Each lap attracted more people and made more noise.

The jury room was silent for fifteen minutes after Reba Betts was converted from an undecided to a not guilty. If a man raped her, she just might blow his head off if she got the chance. It was now five to five with two undecideds, and a compromise looked hopeless. The foreman continued to straddle the fence. Poor old Eula Dell Yates had cried one way, then cried the other, and everyone knew she would eventually go with the majority. She had burst into tears at the window, and was led to her seat by Clyde Sisco. She wanted to go home. Said she felt like a prisoner.

The shouting and marching had taken its toll. When the bullhorn passed nearby, the anxiety level in the small room reached a frenzied peak. Acker would ask for quiet, and they would wait impatiently until the racket faded to the front of the courthouse. It never disappeared completely. Carol Corman was the first to inquire about their safety. For the first time in a week, the quiet motel was awfully attractive.

Three hours of nonstop chanting had unraveled whatever nerves were left. The foreman suggested they talk about their families and wait until Noose sent for them at five.

Bernice Toole, a soft guilty, suggested something they had all thought about but no one had mentioned. 'Why don't we just tell the judge we are hopelessly deadlocked?'

'He'd declare a mistrial, wouldn't he?' asked Jo Ann Gates.

'Yes,' answered the foreman. 'And he would be retried in a few months. Why don't we call it a day, and try again tomorrow?'

They agreed. They were not ready to quit. Eula Dell cried softly.

At four, Carl Lee and the kids walked to one of the tall windows lining each side of the courtroom. He noticed a small knob. He turned it, and the windows swung open to a tiny platform hanging over the west lawn. He nodded at a deputy, and stepped outside. He held Tonya and watched the crowd.

They saw him. They yelled his name and rushed to the building under him. Agee led the marchers off the street and across the lawn. A wave of black humanity gathered under the small porch and pressed forward for a closer look at their champion.

'Free Carl Lee!'

'Free Carl Lee!'

'Free Carl Lee!'

He waved at his fans below him. He kissed his daughter and hugged his sons. He waved and told the kids to wave.

Jake and his small band of hombres used the diversion to stagger across the street to the courthouse. Jean Gillespie had called. Noose wanted to see the lawyers in chambers. He was disturbed. Buckley was raging.

'I demand a mistrial! I demand a mistrial!' he yelled at Noose the second Jake walked in.

'You move for a mistrial, Governor. You don't demand,' Jake said through glassy eyes.

'You go to hell, Brigance! You planned all this. You plotted this insurrection. Those are your niggers out there.'

'Where's the court reporter?' Jake asked. 'I want this on the record.'

'Gentlemen, gentlemen,' Noose said. 'Let's be professionals.'

'Judge, the State moves for a mistrial,' Buckley said, somewhat professionally.

'Overruled.'

'All right, then. The State moves to allow the jury to deliberate at someplace other than the courthouse.'

'Now that's an interesting idea,' Noose said.

'I see no reason why they can't deliberate at the motel. It's quiet and few people know where it is,' Buckley said confidently.

'Jake?' Noose said.

'Nope, it won't work. There is no statutory provision giving you the authority to allow deliberations outside the courthouse.' Jake reached in his pocket and found several folded papers. He threw them on the desk. 'State versus Dubose, 1963 case from Linwood County. The air conditioning in the Linwood County Courthouse quit during a heat wave. The circuit judge allowed the jury to deliberate in a local library. The defense objected. Jury convicted. On appeal, the Supreme Court ruled the judge's decision was improper and an abuse of discretion. The court went on to hold that the jury deliberations must take place in the jury room in the courthouse where the defendant is being tried. You can't move them.'

Noose studied the case and handed it to Musgrove.

'Get the courtroom ready,' he said to Mr. Pate.

With the exception of the reporters, the courtroom was solid black. The jurors looked haggard and strained.

'I take it you do not have a verdict,' Noose said.

'No, sir,' replied the foreman.

'Let me ask you this. Without indicating any numerical division, have you reached a point where you can go no further?'

'We've talked about that, Your Honor. And we'd like to leave, get a good night's rest, and try again tomorrow. We're not ready to quit.'

'That's good to hear. I apologize for the distractions, but, again, there's nothing I can do. I'm sorry. You'll just have to do your best. Anything further?'

'No, sir.'

'Very well. We'll stand adjourned until nine A.M. tomorrow.'

Carl Lee pulled Jake's shoulder. 'What does all this mean?'

'It means they're deadlocked. It could be six to six, or eleven to one against you, or eleven to one for acquittal. So don't get excited.'

Barry Acker cornered the bailiff and handed him a folded sheet of paper. It read:

Luann:

Pack the kids and go to your mother's. Don't tell anyone. Stay there until this thing is over. Just do as I say. Things are dangerous.

Barry

'Can you get this to my wife today? Our number is 881-0774.'

'Sure,' said the bailiff.

Tim Nunley, mechanic down at the Chevrolet place, former client of Jake Brigance, and Coffee Shop regular, sat on a couch in the cabin deep in the woods and drank a beer. He listened to his Klan brothers as they got drunk and cursed niggers. Occasionally, he cursed them too. He had noticed whispering for the past two nights now, and felt something was up. He listened carefully.

He stood to get another beer. Suddenly, they jumped him. Three of his comrades pinned him against the wall and pounded him with fists and feet. He was beaten badly, then gagged, bound, and dragged outside, across the gravel road, and into the field where he had been inducted as a member. A cross was lit as he was tied to a pole and stripped. A bullwhip lashed him until his shoulders, back, and legs were solid crimson.

Two dozen of his ex-brethren watched in mute horror as the pole and limp body were soaked with kerosene. The leader, the one with the bullwhip, stood next to him for an eternity. He pronounced the death sentence, then threw a match.

Mickey Mouse had been silenced.

They packed their robes and belongings, and left for home. Most would never return to Ford County.

CHAPTER FORTY-THREE

Wednesday. For the first time in weeks Jake slept more than eight hours. He had fallen asleep on the couch in his office, and he awoke at five to the sounds of the military preparing for the worst. He was rested, but the nervous throbbing returned with the thought that this day would probably be the big day. He showered and shaved downstairs, and ripped open a new pack of Fruit of the Loom he had purchased at the drug store. He dressed himself in Stan Atcavage's finest navy all-season suit, which was an inch too short and a bit loose, but not a bad fit under the circumstances. He thought of the rubble on Adams Street, then Carla, and the knot in his stomach began to churn. He ran for the newspapers.

On the front pages of the Memphis, Jackson, and Tupelo papers were identical photos of Carl Lee standing on the small porch over the mob, holding his daughter and waving to his people. There was nothing about Jake's house. He was relieved, and suddenly hungry.

Dell hugged him like a lost child. She removed her apron and sat next to him in a corner booth. As the regulars arrived and saw him, they stopped by and patted him on the back. It was good to see him again. They had missed him, and they were for him. He looked gaunt, she said, so he ordered most of the menu.

'Say, Jake, are all those blacks gonna be back today?' asked Bert West.

'Probably,' he said as he stabbed a chunk of pancakes.

'I heard they's plannin' to bring more folks this mornin',' said Andy Rennick. 'Ever nigger radio station in north Mississippi is tellin' folks to come to Clanton.'

Great, thought Jake. He added Tabasco to his scrambled eggs.

'Can the jury hear all that yellin'?' asked Bert.

'Sure they can,' Jake answered. 'That's why they're doing it. They're not deaf.'

'That's gotta scare them.'

Jake certainly hoped so.

'How's the family?' Dell asked quietly.

'Fine, I guess. I talked to Carla every night.'

'She scared?'

'Terrified.'

'What have they done to you lately?'

'Nothing since Sunday morning.'

'Does Carla know?'

Jake chewed and shook his head.

'I didn't think so. You poor thing.'

'I'll be okay. What's the talk in here?'

'We closed at lunch yesterday. There were so many blacks outside, and we were afraid of a riot. We'll watch it close this morning, and we may close again. Jake, what if there's a conviction?'

'It could get hairy.'

He stayed for an hour and answered their questions. Strangers arrived, and Jake excused himself.

There was nothing to do but wait. He sat on the balcony, drank coffee, smoked a cigar, and watched the guardsmen. He thought of the clients he once had; of a quiet little Southern law office with a secretary and clients waiting to see him. Of docket calls and interviews at the jail. Of normal things, like a family, a home, and church on Sunday mornings. He was not meant for the big time.

The first church bus arrived at seven-thirty and was halted by the soldiers. The doors flew open and an endless stream of blacks with lawn chairs and food baskets headed for the front lawn. For an hour Jake blew smoke into the heavy air and watched with great satisfaction as the square filled beyond capacity with noisy yet peaceful protestors. The reverends were out in full force, directing their people and assuring Ozzie and the colonel they were nonviolent folk. Ozzie was convinced. The colonel was nervous. By nine, the streets were crammed with demonstrators. Someone spotted the Greyhound. 'Here they come!' Agee screamed into the loudspeaker. The mob pushed to the corner of Jackson and Quincy, where the soldiers, troopers, and deputies formed a mobile barricade around the bus and walked it through the crowd to the rear of the courthouse.

Eula Dell Yates cried openly. Clyde Sisco sat next to the window and held her hand. The others stared in fear as the bus inched around the square. A heavily armed passageway was cleared from the bus to the courthouse, and Ozzie came aboard. The situation was under control, he assured them over the roar. Just follow him and walk as fast as possible.

The bailiff locked the door as they gathered around the coffeepot. Eula Dell sat by herself in the corner crying softly and flinching as each 'Free Carl Lee!' boomed from below.

'I don't care what we do,' she said. 'I really don't care, but I just can't take any more of this. I haven't seen my family in eight days, and now this madness. I didn't sleep any last night.' She cried louder. 'I think I'm close to a nervous breakdown. Let's just get outta here.'

Clyde handed her a Kleenex and rubbed her shoulder.

Jo Ann Gates was a soft guilty who was ready to crack. 'I didn't sleep either last night. I can't take another day like yesterday. I wanna go home to my kids.'

Barry Acker stood by the window and thought of the riot that would follow a guilty verdict. There wouldn't be a building left downtown, including the courthouse. He doubted if anybody would protect the jurors in the aftermath of a wrong verdict. They probably wouldn't make it back to the bus. Thankfully, his wife and kids had fled to safety in Arkansas.

'I feel like a hostage,' said Bernice Toole, a firm guilty. 'That mob would storm the courthouse in a split second if we convict him. I feel intimidated.'

Clyde handed her a box of Kleenexes.

'I don't care what we do,' Eula Dell whined in desperation. 'Let's just get outta here. I honestly don't care if we convict him or cut him loose, let's just do something. My nerves can't take it.'

Wanda Womack stood at the end of the table and nervously cleared her throat. She asked for attention. 'I have a proposal,' she said slowly, 'that just might settle this thing.'

The crying stopped, and Barry Acker returned to his seat. She had their complete attention.

'I thought of something last night when I couldn't sleep, and I want you to consider it. It may be painful. It may cause you to search your heart and take a long look at your soul. But I'll ask you to do it anyway. And if each of you will be honest with yourself, I think we can wrap this up before noon.'

The only sounds came from the street below.

'Right now we are evenly divided, give or take a vote. We could tell Judge Noose that we are hopelessly deadlocked. He would declare a mistrial, and we would go home. Then in a few months this entire spectacle would be repeated. Mr. Hailey would be tried again in this same courtroom, with the same judge, but with a different jury, a jury drawn from this county, a jury of our friends, husbands, wives, and parents. The same kind of people who are now in this room. That jury will be confronted with the same issues before us now, and those people will not be any smarter than we are.

'The time to decide this case is now. It would be morally wrong to shirk our responsibilities and pass the buck to the next jury. Can we all agree on that?'

They silently agreed.

'Good. This is what I want you to do. I want you to pretend with me for a moment. I want you to use your imaginations. I want you to close your eyes and listen to nothing but my voice.'

They obediently closed their eyes. Anything was worth a try.

Jake lay on the couch in his office and listened to Lucien tell stories about his prestigious father and grandfather, and their prestigious law firm, and all the people they screwed out of money and land.

'My inheritance was built by my promiscuous ancestors!' he yelled. 'They screwed everybody they could!'

Harry Rex laughed uncontrollably. Jake had heard the stories before, but they were always funny, and different.

'What about Ethel's retarded son?' Jake asked.

'Don't talk that way about my brother,' Lucien protested. 'He's the brightest one in the family. Sure he's my brother. Dad hired her when she was seventeen, and believe it or not, she looked good back then. Ethel Twitty was the hottest thing in Ford County. My dad couldn't keep his hands off her. Sickening to think about now, but it's true.'

'It's disgusting,' Jake said.

'She had a houseful of kids, and two of them looked just like me, especially the dunce. It was very embarrassing back then.'

'What about your mother?' asked Harry Rex.

'She was one of those dignified old Southern ladies whose main concern was who had blue blood and who didn't. There's not much blue blood around here, so she spent most of her time in Memphis trying to impress and be accepted by the cotton families. I spent a good part of my childhood at the Peabody Hotel all starched out with a little red bow tie, trying to act polished around the rich kids from Memphis. I hated it, and I didn't care much for my mother either. She knew about Ethel, but she accepted it. She told the old man to be discreet and not embarrass the family. He was discreet, and I wound up with a retarded half-brother.'

'When did she die?'

'Six months before my father was killed in the plane crash.'

'How'd she die?' asked Harry Rex.

'Gonorrhea. Caught it from the yard boy.'

'Lucien! Seriously?'

'Cancer. Carried it for three years, but she was dignified to the very end.'

'Where'd you go wrong?' Jake asked.

'I think it started in the first grade. My uncle owned the big plantation south of town, and he owned several black families. This was in the Depression, right? I spent most of my childhood there because my father was too busy right here in this office and my mother was too busy with her hot-tea-drinkers clubs. All of my playmates were black. I'd been raised by black servants. My best friend was Willie Ray Wilbanks. No kidding. My great-grandfather purchased his great-grandfather. And when the slaves were freed, most of them just kept the family name. What were they supposed to do? That's why you've got so many black Wilbankses around here. We owned all the slaves in Ford County, and most of them became Wilbankses.'

'You're probably kin to some,' Jake said.

'Given the proclivities of my forefathers, I'm probably kin to all of them.'

The phone rang. They froze and stared at it. Jake sat up and held his breath. Harry Rex picked up the receiver, then hung up. 'Wrong number,' he said.

They studied each other, then smiled.

'Anyway, back to the first grade,' Jake said.

'Okay. When it came time to start school, Willie Ray and the rest of my little buddies got on the bus headed for the black school. I jumped on the bus too, and the driver very carefully took my hand and made me get off. I cried and screamed, and my uncle took me home and told my mother, "Lucien got on the nigger school bus." She was horrified, and beat my little ass. The old man beat me too, but years later admitted it was funny. So I went to the white school where I was always the little rich kid. Everybody hated the little rich kid, especially in a poor town like Clanton. Not that I was lovable to begin with, but everyone got a kick out of hating me just because we had money. That's why I've never thought much of money. That's where the nonconformity started. In the first grade. I decided not to be like my mother because she frowned all the time and looked down on the world. And my old man was always too busy to enjoy himself. I said piss on it. I'm gonna have some fun.'

Jake stretched and closed his eyes.

'Nervous?' Lucien asked.

'I just want it to be over.'

The phone rang again, and Lucien grabbed it. He listened, then hung up.

'What is it?' Harry Rex demanded.

Jake sat up and glared at Lucien. The moment had arrived.

'Jean Gillespie. The jury is ready.'

'Oh my God,' Jake said as he rubbed his temples.

'Listen to me, Jake,' Lucien lectured. 'Millions of people will see what is about to happen. Keep your cool. Be careful what you say.'

'What about me?' Harry Rex moaned. 'I need to go vomit.'

'That's strange advice coming from you, Lucien,' Jake said as he buttoned Stan's coat.

'I've learned a lot. Show your class. If you win, watch what you say to the press. Be sure and thank the jury. If you lose –'

'If you lose,' Harry Rex said, 'run like hell, because those niggers will storm the courthouse.'

'I feel weak,' Jake admitted.

Agee took the platform on the front steps and announced the jury was ready. He asked for quiet, and instantly the mob grew still. They moved toward the front columns. Agee asked them to fall to their knees and pray. They knelt obediently and prayed earnestly. Every man, woman, and child on the front lawn bowed before God and begged him to let their man go.

The soldiers stood bunched together and also prayed for an acquittal.

Ozzie and Moss Junior seated the courtroom and lined deputies and reserves around the walls and down the aisle. Jake entered from the holding room and stared at Carl Lee at the defense table. He glanced at the spectators. Many were praying. Many were biting their fingers. Gwen was wiping tears. Lester looked fearfully at Jake. The children were confused and scared.

Noose assumed the bench and an electrified silence engulfed the courtroom. There was no sound from the outside. Twenty thousand blacks knelt on the ground like Muslims. Perfect stillness inside the courtroom and out.

'I have been advised that the jury has reached a verdict, is that correct, Mr. Bailiff? Very well. We will soon seat the jury, but before we do so I have some instructions. I will not tolerate any outbursts or displays of emotion. I will direct the sheriff to remove any person who creates a disturbance. If need be, I will clear the courtroom. Mr. Bailiff, will you seat the jury.'

The door opened, and it seemed like an hour before Eula Dell Yates appeared first with tears in her eyes. Jake dropped his head. Carl Lee stared gamely at the portrait of Robert E. Lee above Noose. They awkwardly filled the jury box. They seemed jittery, tense, scared. Most had been crying. Jake felt sick. Barry Acker held a piece of paper that attracted the attention of everyone.

'Ladies and gentlemen, have you reached a verdict?'

'Yes, sir, we have,' answered the foreman in a high-pitched, nervous voice.

'Hand it to the clerk, please.'

Jean Gillespie took it and handed it to His Honor, who studied it forever. 'It is technically in order,' he finally said.

Eula Dell was flooding, and her sniffles were the only sounds in the courtroom. Jo Ann Gates and Bernice Toole padded their eyes with handkerchiefs. The crying could mean only one thing. Jake had vowed to ignore the jury before the verdict was read, but it was impossible. In his first criminal trial, the jurors had smiled as they took their seats. At that moment, Jake had become confident of an acquittal. Seconds later he learned that the smiles were because a criminal was about to be removed from the streets. Since that trial, he had vowed never to look at the jurors. But he always did. It would be nice to see a wink or a thumbs up, but that never happened.

Noose looked at Carl Lee. 'Will the defendant please rise.'

Jake knew there were probably more terrifying requests known to the English tongue, but to a criminal lawyer that request at that particular moment had horrible implications. His client stood awkwardly, pitifully. Jake closed his eyes and held his breath. His hands shook and his stomach ached.

Noose handed the verdict back to Jean Gillespie. 'Please read it, Madam Clerk.'

She unfolded it and faced the defendant. 'As to each count of the indictment, we the jury find the defendant not guilty by reason of insanity.'

Carl Lee turned and bolted for the railing. Tonya and the boys sprang from the front pew and grabbed him. The courtroom exploded in pandemonium. Gwen screamed and burst into tears. She buried her head in Lester's arms. The reverends stood, looked upward, and shouted 'Hallelujah!' and 'Praise Jesus!' and 'Lord! Lord! Lord!'

Noose's admonition meant nothing. He rapped the gavel half-heartedly and said, 'Order, order, order in the courtroom.' He was inaudible in the midst of the roar, and seemed content to allow a little celebration.

Jake was numb, lifeless, paralyzed. His only movement was a weak smile in the direction of the jury box. His eyes watered and his lip quivered, and he decided not to make a spectacle of himself. He nodded at Jean Gillespie, who was crying, and just sat at the defense table nodding and trying to smile, unable to do anything else. From the corner of his eye he could see Musgrove and Buckley removing files, legal pads, and important-looking papers, and throwing it all into their briefcases. Be gracious, he told himself.

A teenager darted between two deputies, through the door, and ran through the rotunda screaming 'Not guilty! Not guilty!' He ran to a small balcony over the front steps and screamed to the masses below *'Not guilty! Not guilty!'* Bedlam erupted.

'Order, order in the court,' Noose was saying when the delayed reaction from the outside came thundering through the windows.

'Order, order in the courtroom.' He tolerated the excitement for another minute, then asked the sheriff to restore order. Ozzie raised his hands and spoke. The clapping, hugging and praising died quickly. Carl Lee released his children and returned to the defense table. He sat close to his attorney and put his arm around him, grinning and crying at the same time.

Noose smiled at the defendant. 'Mr. Hailey, you have been tried by a jury of your peers and found not guilty. I do not recall any expert testimony that you are now dangerous or in need of further psychiatric treatment. You are a free man.'

His Honor looked at the attorneys. 'If there is nothing further, this court will stand adjourned until August 15.'

Carl Lee was smothered by his family and friends. They hugged him, hugged each other, hugged Jake. They wept unashamedly and praised the Lord. They told Jake they loved him.

The reporters pressed against the railing and began firing questions at Jake. He held up his hands, and said he would have no comment. But there would be a full-blown press conference in his office at 2:00 P.M.

Buckley and Musgrove left through a side door. The jurors were locked in the jury room to await the last bus ride to the motel. Barry Acker asked to speak to the sheriff. Ozzie met him in the hallway, listened intently, and promised to escort him home and provide protection around the clock.

The reporters assaulted Carl Lee. 'I just wanna go home,' he said over and over. 'I just wanna go home.'

The celebration kicked into high gear on the front lawn. There was singing, dancing, crying, back-slapping, hugging, thanks-giving, congratulating, outright laughing, cheering, chanting, high fives, low fives, and soul brother shakes. The heavens were praised in one glorious, tumultuous, irreverent jubilee. They packed closer together in front of the courthouse and waited impatiently for their hero to emerge and bask in his much deserved adulation.

Their patience grew thin. After thirty minutes of screaming 'We Want Carl Lee! We Want Carl Lee!' their man appeared at the door. An ear-splitting, earth-shaking roar greeted him. He inched forward through the mass with his lawyer and family, and stopped on the top step under the pillars where the plywood platform held a thousand microphones. The whooping and yelling of twenty thousand voices was deafening. He hugged his lawyer, and they waved to the sea of screaming faces.

The shouting from the army of reporters was completely inaudible. Occasionally, Jake would stop waving and yell something about a press conference in his office at two.

Carl Lee hugged his wife and children, and they waved. The crowd roared its approval. Jake slid away and into the courthouse, where he found Lucien and Harry Rex waiting in a corner, away from the mad rush of spectators. 'Let's get out of here,' Jake yelled. They pushed through the mob, down the hall and out the rear door. Jake spotted a swarm of reporters on the sidewalk outside his office.

'Where are you parked?' he asked Lucien. He pointed to a side street, and they disappeared behind the Coffee Shop.

Sallie fried pork chops and green tomatoes, and served them on the porch. Lucien produced a bottle of expensive champagne, and swore he had saved it just for the occasion. Harry Rex ate with his fingers, gnawing on the bones as if he hadn't seen food in a month. Jake played with his food and worked on the ice-cold champagne. After two glasses, he smiled into the distance. He savored the moment.

'You look silly as hell,' Harry Rex said with a mouthful of pork.

'Shut up, Harry Rex,' Lucien said. 'Let him enjoy his finest hour.'

'He's enjoying it. Look at that smirk.'

'What should I tell the press?' Jake asked.

'Tell them you need some clients,' Harry Rex said.

'Clients will be no problem,' Lucien said. 'They'll line the sidewalks waiting for appointments.'

'Why didn't you talk to the reporters in the courthouse? They had their cameras running and everything. I started to say something for them,' Harry Rex said.

'I'm sure it would've been a gem,' Lucien said.

'I've got them at my fingertips,' Jake said. 'They're not going anywhere. We could sell tickets to the press conference and make a fortune.'

'Can I sit and watch, please, Jake, please,' Harry Rex said.

CHAPTER FORTY-FOUR

They argued over whether they should take the antique Bronco or the nasty little Porsche. Jake said he was not driving. Harry Rex cursed the loudest, and they loaded into the Bronco. Lucien found a spot in the rear seat. Jake rode shotgun and gave instructions. They hit the back streets, and missed most of the traffic from the square. The highway was crowded, and Jake directed his driver through a myriad of gravel roads. They found blacktop, and Harry Rex raced away in the direction of the lake.

'I have one question, Lucien,' Jake said.

'What?'

'And I want a straight answer.'

'What?'

'Did you cut a deal with Sisco?'

'No, my boy, you won it on your own.'

'Do you swear?'

'I swear to God. On a stack of Bibles.'

Jake wanted to believe him, so he dropped it. They rode in silence, in the sweltering heat, and listened as Harry Rex sang along with the stereo. Suddenly, Jake pointed and yelled. Harry Rex slammed on the brakes, made a wild left turn, and sped down another gravel road.

'Where are we going?' Lucien demanded.

'Just hang on,' Jake said as he looked at a row of houses approaching on the right. He pointed to the second one, and Harry Rex pulled into the driveway and parked under a shade tree. Jake got out, looked around the front yard, and walked onto the porch. He knocked on the screen door.

A man appeared. A stranger. 'Yeah, whatta you want?'

'I'm Jake Brigance, and –'

The door flew open, and the man rushed onto the porch and grabbed Jake's hand. 'Nice to meet you, Jake. I'm Mack Loyd Crowell. I was on the grand jury that almost didn't indict. You done a real good job. I'm proud of you.'

Jake shook his hand and repeated his name. Then he remembered. Mack Loyd Crowell, the man who told Buckley to shut up and sit down in the grand jury. 'Yeah, Mack Loyd, now I remember. Thanks.'

Jake looked awkwardly through the door.

'You lookin' for Wanda?' Crowell asked.

'Well, yes. I was just passing by, and remembered her address from the jury research.'

'You've come to the right place. She lives here, and I do too most of the time. We ain't married or nothing, but we go together. She's layin' down takin' a nap. She's pretty wore out.'

'Don't wake her,' Jake said.

'She told me what happened. She won it for you.'

'How? What happened?'

'She made them all close their eyes and listen to her. She told them to pretend that the little girl had blonde hair and blue eyes, that the two rapists were black, that they tied her right foot to a tree and her left foot to a fence post, that they raped her repeatedly and cussed her because she was white. She told them to picture the little girl layin' there beggin' for her daddy while they kicked her in the mouth and knocked out her teeth, broke both jaws, broke her nose. She said to imagine two drunk blacks pouring beer on her and pissing in her face, and laughing like idiots. And then she told them to imagine that the little girl belonged to them – their daughter. She told them to be honest with themselves and to write on a piece of paper whether or not they would kill those black bastards if they got the chance. And they voted, by secret ballot. All twelve said they would do the killing. The foreman counted the votes. Twelve to zero. Wanda said she'd sit in that jury room until Christmas before she'd vote to convict, and if they were honest with themselves, then they ought to feel the same way. Ten of them agreed with her, and one lady held out. They all started cryin' and cussin' her so bad, she finally caved in. It was rough in there, Jake.'

Jake listened to every word without breathing. He heard a noise. Wanda Womack walked to the screen door. She smiled at him and began crying. He stared at her through the screen, but could not talk. He bit his lip and nodded. 'Thanks,' he managed weakly. She wiped her eyes and nodded.

On Craft Road, a hundred cars lined both shoulders east and west of the Hailey driveway. The long front yard was packed with vehicles, children playing, and parents sitting under shade trees and on car hoods. Harry Rex parked in a ditch by the mailbox. A crowd rushed to greet Carl Lee's lawyer. Lester grabbed him and said, 'You done it again, you done it again.'

They shook hands and slapped backs across the yard and up to the porch. Agee hugged him and praised God. Carl Lee left the swing and walked down the steps, followed by his family and admirers. They gathered around Jake as the two great men came face to face. They clutched hands and smiled at each other, both searching for words. They embraced. The crowd clapped and shouted.

'Thank you, Jake,' Carl Lee said softly.

The lawyer and client sat in the swing and answered questions about the trial. Lucien and Harry Rex joined Lester and some of his friends under a shade tree for a little drink. Tonya ran and jumped around the yard with a hundred other kids.

At two-thirty, Jake sat at his desk and talked to Carla. Harry Rex and Lucien drank the last of the margaritas, and quickly got drunk. Jake drank coffee and told his wife he would leave Memphis in three hours and be in North Carolina by ten. Yes, he was fine, he said. Everything was okay, and everything was over. There were dozens of reporters packed into his conference room, so be sure and watch the evening news. He would meet with them briefly, then drive to Memphis. He said he loved her, missed her body, and would be there soon. He hung up.

Tomorrow, he'd call Ellen.

'Why are you leaving today!' Lucien demanded.

'You're stupid, Jake, just stupid. You've got a thousand reporters in the palm of your hand, and you're leaving town. Stupid, just stupid,' Harry Rex shouted.

Jake stood. 'How do I look, fellas?'

'Like a dumbass if you leave town,' Harry Rex said.

'Hang around for a couple of days,' Lucien pleaded. 'This is an opportunity you'll never have again. Please, Jake.'

'Relax, fellas. I'm going to meet with them now, let them take my picture, answer a few of their stupid questions, then I'm leaving town.'

'You're crazy, Jake,' Harry Rex said.

'I agree,' said Lucien.

Jake checked the mirror, adjusted Stan's tie, and smiled at his friends. 'I appreciate you guys. I really do. I got paid nine hundred dollars for this trial, and I plan to share it with y'all.'

They poured the last of the margaritas, gulped it down, and followed Jake Brigance down the stairs to face the reporters.